# STORM OF SECRETS AND SORROW

### THE LEGACY SERIES
BOOK TWO

## MELISSA K. ROEHRICH

# ALSO BY MELISSA K. ROEHRICH

## LADY OF DARKNESS SERIES (COMPLETE)

*Lady of Darkness*

*Lady of Shadows*

*Lady of Ashes*

*Lady of Embers*

*The Reaper* (A Lady of Darkness Novella)

*Lady of Starfire*

*Unrelenting Winds* (A Lady of Darkness Novella)

*Treasures of Darkness* (A Lady of Darkness Compilation)

## THE LEGACY SERIES

*Rain of Shadows and Endings*

*Storm of Secrets and Sorrow*

*Tempest of Wrath and Vengeance*

*Book Four (Final Book)*- coming 2025

Editing Services: Megan Visger

Cover Design: Covers by Jules (www.coversbyjules.crd.co)

Rights and Representation by Katie Shea Boutillier: ksboutillier@maassagency.com at Donald Maass Literary Agency.

ISBN:

978-1-960923-07-3 (*Hardcover*)

978-1-960923-08-0 (*Paperback*)

❀ Created with Vellum

# A COUPLE THINGS & CONTENT INFORMATION

Welcome back to Devram! If you're here, I'm assuming you already know this world is a dark little realm of depravity and wickedness. The tropes, tags, and trigger warnings have been updated on my website. You can click here to see those, or go to www.melissakroehrich.com and click on Book Extras. Your mental health matters, and they are there if you need them. Don't go in blind if that's not for you.

I know we covered this at the beginning of *Rain of Shadows and Endings*, but it's worth repeating now, especially if you haven't read the Darkness series. The Legacy Series takes place in the same universe as the *Lady of Darkness* series, but this is an entirely new world with brand new characters. You do NOT need to read the Darkness series to understand The Legacy Series. This series can be read separately. Theon and Tessa's story will have its own conclusion by the end; however, you WILL come across spoilers for the Darkness series and some dragon eggs along the way, even if you don't recognize them as spoilers at the time.

Finally, guys, I know there were big feelings after the last book. I can promise you another book full of the same— emotional whiplash and morally gray characters that will make you question yourself and them around every corner. Remember this is a series. Some characters need room to grow, and sometimes survival in a realm full of villains requires sacrifice. Trust the process.

Now settle in, grab your wine and maybe something to throw, so it's not this book or your e-reader, and enter the chaos.

*XO- Melissa*

PLAYLIST

I adore when books come with playlists that follow along with the story. You feel everything more. It immerses you more. It brings everything to life. If you find this to be true for you too, here you go! Enjoy!

If you don't have Spotify, the full playlist can also be found on my website: https://www.melissakroehrich.com under Book Extras!

*For those who have shoved down their light so others could shine,*
*it's time to fight for you.*

# LEGACY SERIES REFERENCE GUIDE

I know. There's a lot to remember and keep straight as you dive into Devram. So here's a little reference guide to help you out!

## OUR MAIN PLAYERS

**Tessalyn Ausra:**
Tes-uh-lin Ah-sruh
~~Fae~~. Legacy... Maybe
Source of the Arius Heir,
A little (or a lot) wild and impulsive

**Theon St. Orcas:**
Thee-on Sānt Or-kus
Legacy, Heir to the Arius Kingdom,
A morally grey, walking, talking red flag

**Luka Mors:**
Loo-kuh Morz
Sargon Legacy, Theon's Guardian
and advisor

**Axel St. Orcas:**
Ax-ul Sānt Or-kus
Legacy, Second-in-Line for the Arius
Kingdom, Theon's brother

## OTHERS OF NOTE

**Dex:** Dex
Wind Fae, Tessa's best friend,
claimed by Achaz Kingdom

**Oralia:** Or-āl-eeuh
Water Fae, Tessa's Friend

**Corbin:** Kor-bin
Water Fae, Tessa's friend, involved
with Lange

**Lange:** Lāng
Wind Fae, Tessa's friend, involved with
Corbin

**Brecken:** Brek-in
Wind Fae, Tessa's friend

**Katya:** Kat-ya
Fire Fae, Tessa's friend, claimed by
Arius Kingdom

**Tristyn Blackheart:**
Tris-tin Blak-hārt
~~Mortal,~~ Legacy, owns Lilura Inquest

**Penelope:** Pen-el-ō-pee
Fae, personal servant of Theon & Axel

**Cressida St. Orcas:**
Cres-ee-duh Sānt Or-kus
Legacy, Theon & Axel's mother

**Eviana:** Eve-ee-on-uh
Earth Fae, Source of the Arius Lord

# LEGACY SERIES REFERENCE GUIDE

## OTHERS OF NOTE

**Felicity Davers:** Fel-i-sit-ee Dav-ers
Gracil Legacy, Theon's prospective
Match

**Cienna:** Cee-en-uh
Banished to the Underground

**Auryon:** O-ry-un
Listen, we don't know what she is

**Ford:** Fōrd
Fae, Pen's replacement

**Pavil:** Pah-vil
Sleazy Legacy that works for Valter

**Metias:** Meh-tī-us
Sleazy Legacy that works for Valter

# LEGACY SERIES REFERENCE GUIDE

## THE GODS

### THE FIRSTS

**Achaz** (Ā-kaz)
God of light and beginnings

**Serafina** (Sār-uh-fee-nuh)
Goddess of dreams and stars

**Anala** (Uh-nall-uh)
Goddess of sun, day, and fire

**Arius** (Ar-ee-us)
God of death and endings

**Falein** (Fā-leen)
Goddess of wisdom/cleverness

**Celeste** (Sel-est)
Goddess of moon and sky

### THE LESSERS

**Zinta** (Zēn-tuh)
Goddess of magic and sorcery

**Sirana** (Seer-an-uh)
Goddess of love and fertility

**Sargon** (Sar-gon)
God of war and courage

**Pax** (Pax)
God of peace and serenity

**Silas** (Sī-lus)
God of earth and land

**Rai** (Rā)
God of seasons

**Nith** (Neeth)
God of creativity

**Anahita** (On-uh-hee-tuh)
God of sea, water, and ice

**Reselda** (Rez-el-duh)
Goddess of healing

**Sefarina** (Sef-uh-ree-nuh)
Goddess of winds and air

**Gracil** (Grah-sil)
God of empathy

# LEGACY SERIES REFERENCE GUIDE

## THE KINGDOMS

### ACHAZ KINGDOM

- Ruling Lord: Rordan Jove (Ror-dan Jō-vā)
- Heir: Dagian Jove (Dāj-ee-un Jō-vā)
- Heir's Source: Sasha (Sah-shuh)
- Responsibilities: upholding Devram's laws and accords, ruling the realm
- Loyal Lesser Bloodlines: Zinta and Sirana

### ARIUS KINGDOM

- Ruling Lord: Valter St. Orcas (Vall-tār Sānt Or-kus)
- Heir: Theon St. Orcas. (Thee-on Sānt Or-kus)
- Heir's Source: Tessa (Tes-uh)
- Responsibilities: Underground
- Loyal Lesser Bloodlines: None

### SERAFINA KINGDOM

- Ruling Lady: Maya Isleen (My-uh Iz-lēn)
- Heir:  Lealla Isleen (Lee-all-uh Iz-lēn)
- Heir's Source: Maxson (Max-sun)
- Responsibilities: artists and architects
- Loyal Lesser Bloodlines: Anahita and Nith

### FALEIN KINGDOM

- Ruling Lady: Raye Farhan (Rā Far-han)
- Heir: Prudence Farhan (Prū-dens Far-han)
- Heir's Source: Dade (Dād)
- Responsibilities: scholars and healers
- Loyal Lesser Bloodlines: Reselda and Pax

### ANALA KINGDOM

- Ruling Lady: Kyra Aithne (Kī-ruh Āth-nee)
- Heir: Tana Aithne (Tan-uh Āth-nee)
- Heir's Source: Gatlan (Gat-lan)
- Responsibilities: food and agriculture
- Loyal Lesser Bloodlines: Silas and Rai

### CELESTE KINGDOM

- Ruling Lady: Luna Candra (Lū-nuh Can-druh)
- Heir: Mahina Candra (Muh-he-nuh Can-druh)
- Heir's Source: Jasper (Jas-per)
- Responsibilities: running the Selection
- Loyal Lesser Bloodlines: Sefarina and Gracil

# DEVRAM

EKAYAN
ISLAND

ORINTHIA

FAE ESTATE

RAGHNALL
MOUNTAINS

FAE ESTATE

ANALA
KINGDOM

FALEIN
KINGDOM

CAELAN RIVER

DOLION
WOODS

ACROPOLIS

TERRARUN RIVER

CELESTE
KINGDOM

NISHA
FOREST

ACHAZ
KINGDOM

LAKE
MOONMIST

FAE ESTATE

AROBELL

UNDERGROUND
ENTRANCE

OZUL
MOUNTAINS

ARIUS
HOUSE

CASTLE PINES

ROCKMOOR

SINVONS
LAKE

DARK
HAVEN

ARIUS
KINGDOM

HADE PLAINS

FRACTURED NIGHT WATERS
SPRINGS

RAVEN HARBO

RIVER OF ENDINGS

VER

SERAFINA
KINGDOM

DREAMLOCK
WOODS

FAE ESTATE

SANAL

ASNING
SEA

# RAIN OF SHADOWS AND ENDINGS QUICK RECAP
## AS TOLD BY CYRUS

Hi, Darling! I'm Cyrus. You might not know me, which is fine… I guess. (*Side-eye.*) But I'm here to give a quick recap of the fuckery happening in Devram. So let's get right to it because I have a card game to win.

Devram has this thing called a Selection every five years, and this is a Selection Year. Not only that, but for the first time in centuries, heirs from all six kingdoms Selected Fae in the realm who will serve as their Source of power. Tessalyn Ausra was unexpectedly Selected by Theon St. Orcas, Heir of Death and Endings. (*Pauses and looks up from his notes.*) What the fuck does that mean?

**Cassius**: Just keep going, Cyrus.

Right, right. So after receiving the first Source Mark, they return to the Arius Kingdom, where she gets to know Theon and his closest confidants better— his advisor-to-be, Luka Mors, and his younger brother, Axel. But she doesn't want this bond thing, so Tessa tries to run, and, honestly, who can blame her at this point? This guy sounds like a complete ass.

**Cassius**: Cyrus…

*(Eye roll.)* Theon and Luka hunt her down in the woods. They return to Arius House where stricter expectations are put in place with harsher consequences. Despite all of this, she still feels drawn to him, even though she hates it. Tessa tries to rein her impulsive self in to meet said expectations, but only ends up getting shoved under a table, no desserts — What. The. Fuck?

**Cassius**, *sighing*: By the gods, Cyrus...

Sorry, Cass, but no desserts? Can you imagine withholding sweets from Scarlett? Or chocolate cake from Eliza? *(Shudders.)* We'd all be dead. Anyway, two assholes show up on behalf of the even bigger asshole Arius Lord and chase her through a garden when some creepy guys crawl up out of the ground. Everyone freaks the fuck out because no one understands her power that she shouldn't be able to access yet. She has to undergo a traumatic assessment where it comes out she'll be the most powerful Fae in Devram, no matter what element she ends up with. She sees some pretty strange things in her dreams, and afterwards, she has to go out with Theon and his...Match? Don't know what that is. Moving on.

Tessa meets a random mortal named Tristyn, and they drink, smoke lull-leaf, and eat pizza. Now, I don't know what lull-leaf or pizza are, but that sounds like a pretty good time, and we should maybe try to figure that out. Theon finds her and gets all moody and possessive. This just makes Tessa more angry, and for some unknown reason, she makes a bargain with the guy. They head back to the Acropolis for the Emerging Ceremony. Along the way, we learn that Luka is a dragon shifter and Theon's Guardian. *(Pauses.)* Now that's a fun twist, huh, Cass?

**Cassius**, *muttering*: For fuck's sake.

They go to some social events, learn this Tristyn guy isn't actually a mortal, and finally give in to some building tension. But good for them. They probably needed that after all this shit. I would.

After that good time, they go to dinner with the...Achaz Heir? That's interesting. Some things are said, and the Arius Lord shows up and kills Pen. Or Axel kills her. Which...is terrible. Theon blames Tessa because, let's face it, she *is* impulsive and reckless and maybe doesn't think things all the way through. So then Theon...locks her in a wine cellar... That *cannot* be a good move.

At the Emerging Ceremony later the next day, Axel randomly selects a fire Fae that no one realized would have fire because the Anala Kingdom keeps them all. Obviously. Because fire is the best element. A mysterious Keeper guy shows up with some wolves to awaken Tessa's power, but the Mark he gives her sounds awfully familiar. Everyone is shocked when she doesn't have elemental magic. Axel tries to get her out safely, but the Achaz Lord shows up and snatches her up.

Theon makes a bargain with his dick-of-a-father to get her back. Tessa has another strange dream with— Hey, wait a minute...

**Cassius**: No, Cyrus.

**Cyrus**: But—

**Cassius**: Keep going.

**Cyrus**: Why am I the one doing this again?

**Scarlett**: You volunteered.

**Cyrus**: I believe I volunteered for an adventure, Darling. Not this.

**Scarlett**, *shrugging*: Same thing.

*(With a glare.)* Anyway, Tessa has this dream, wakes up and decides she's going to learn all of Devram's secrets. We see a glimpse of Temural, god of the wild and untamed, asking... *(Smirks at Scarlett.)* Saylah for help getting someone named Auryon into Devram. The end. *(Tosses notes aside and shuffles cards.)* Whose deal?

# AS HAPPY AS WE CAN BE

**Two and a Half Years Ago**

"W̶ho's that?" Lange asked, jerking his chin toward the estate buildings.

"I don't know," Tessa said, following his gaze. Her fingers were curled around the edge of the bench they sat on. Her shoes were off to the side, her bare feet toeing at the grass. Then she sat up straighter. "Why doesn't Dex have the food?"

The bench was in a secluded area on the estate grounds. It ran right along the estate border. Dex had moved the bench to this exact spot so she would know where the wards were since she couldn't feel them. He'd done this in multiple areas around the estate for her. At least now when she crossed the wards, it was on purpose.

Now Dex was headed their way with another Fae male. Dex's dark eyes found her immediately, and she glared at him. He'd promised her food. The male with him had brown hair that was kind of shaggy, curling around his ears. He was lean, yet somehow muscled, and his hazel eyes were taking in his surroundings.

He didn't have any food either.

When the pair reached the table, Dex dropped onto the bench beside her. "What's with the sour face, Tessie?"

"You said you were bringing food," she grumbled, digging her toe further into the dirt.

"Oralia is bringing it," he said with a knowing smile.

Oralia. Another Fae Dex had brought into their little circle. Or rather, he'd brought Tessa into *his* circle. Dex knew them from the Serafina Estate where he'd lived before moving here. He'd just missed the cutoff for the previous Selection Year and had been sent to the Celeste Estate to wait for the next Selection. Days later, Oralia and Brecken, another Fae male, had been dumped here too. Apparently everyone who was a hassle was just dumped here.

She'd been hesitant. Tessa had wanted nothing to do with any of them. She trusted no one, and she especially didn't trust strangers who randomly showed up. Dex seemed to understand this, and he never appeared offended when she told him to fuck off. He had, however, started leaving extra food around, especially when she would disappear for a day or two. He couldn't possibly know that Mother Cordelia, the Legacy who oversaw the Celeste Estate, would lock her in cellars or small cupboards and withhold food as punishment, could he?

She hadn't really cared in the end. Dex would leave the food, and she would devour it the moment she knew there wouldn't be a cost. That was what had broken her down in the end. Dex would do things for her and expect nothing in return. No affection. No sex. No favors. No cost. He just…did them. It was the first time she'd experienced such a thing. She hadn't known people actually did things for one another without expecting something in return.

It had still taken months before she had spoken with him longer than a few minutes, and never when he was with anyone else. It was over a year later before she'd finally let him introduce her to Oralia and Brecken. Tessa certainly didn't trust them, but Dex did and she trusted Dex.

Oralia was loud and seemed to have an opinion about anything and everything. Brecken was kind of funny, she supposed, but he was also an incessant flirt. He was also part of a select group of Fae who traveled to the other estates every once in a while. She'd always wanted to be chosen for those trips, but she was too *undisciplined* to be chosen to go.

In fact, Brecken was gone on one of those trips now. But last year when he'd returned, Lange had come back with him. Another Fae sent to the Celeste Estate to await the Selection Year, Lange had come from the Falein

Estate. Tessa had warmed to him more than she had to Oralia and Brecken. Lange teased her constantly, and when she would snap at him, it only made him tease her more. Dex was always gentle and soft with her. Lange didn't appear to give a shit—about anything—and Tessa admired that about him. Not caring what others thought or worrying about what was to come.

Tessa huffed loudly again, leaning back against the bench. The new male gave her a side-long look, and she quickly looked away. She hadn't told Dex yet, but she'd spent all night in the cellar. She hadn't eaten since lunch the day before, and the sun was currently setting.

"This is Corbin," Dex said slowly, finally picking up on something being amiss with her. "He just arrived from the Anala Estate."

"Anala?" Lange repeated, leaning forward to peer around them. Corbin had taken a seat down the bench on Dex's other side. "Surely you're not a fire Fae?"

Tessa clicked her tongue in annoyance. Of course he wasn't a fire Fae.

"No," Corbin answered, staring out across the grounds and kicking at a rock. "I'm predicted to emerge with water. You?"

"Air," Lange answered, leaning over a little more and forcing Tessa to lean into Dex.

She supposed there was one thing Lange cared about, and that was pretty males, especially shiny new ones. Not that Tessa could talk. She just preferred her males mortal and not located someplace she'd constantly run into them afterwards.

"That is Lange," Dex cut in. "And this is Tessa."

"Nice to meet you both," Corbin said.

Tessa didn't answer, staring straight ahead. The sun would be down soon. They would head inside, and she wouldn't get any food.

"You're being rude, Tess," Lange chided. She lifted her middle finger in his direction. "Corbin is going to think you're mean." He leaned around her again to speak to Corbin. "She's really not. She just gets like this when she's hungry."

"Can't blame her there," Corbin said.

But she could feel Dex studying her. Knew he was piecing together what had likely happened last night.

"Tessa—" he started, his voice low.

"Where were you?" she hissed.

He hadn't been there. He was always there to help her, to make sure she didn't end up alone in the dark. But not last night. He hadn't been there. For the first time since he'd shown up at the estate, he hadn't been there.

"I was assigned to help with the newly arrived Fae," Dex answered.

She said nothing, her stomach grumbling with hunger. Dex clearly heard, his eyes darting to her abdomen then back to her face.

"You couldn't control yourself for one night?" he asked with a sigh, rubbing at his brow with his thumb and forefinger.

"I didn't do anything," she gritted out.

That wasn't entirely true, but it wasn't something that warranted being locked away without food in the dark.

"Tessa, I couldn't simply leave an assignment. I can't be there to fix things for you all the time," he said, his hand falling to curl along the edge of the bench.

Fix things for her. Right.

"Understood," she replied tightly.

"Tessie," he sighed again, his arm coming around her shoulders and pulling her into his side. "I didn't mean it like that."

"I'm not sure you could mean it any other way."

"I just need you to be more careful when I'm not around. Be what they want you to be now, so you can be who you were meant to be later."

"I'm not meant to be anything," she sighed, resting her head on his shoulder.

"You're wrong, Tessie, and I'll be there when it's time, making sure nothing goes wrong."

She understood the meaning of that statement. Making sure *she* didn't cause everything to go wrong, and if she did, he'd be there to fix it all. That was what they'd become. She got herself into a mess, and Dex cleaned it up.

"That's enough talk about the future," Lange cut in, stretching his legs out before him and crossing them at the ankles. "What are we doing tonight? The Estate Mother left this afternoon, right?"

"She did," Dex confirmed. "Brecken went with her."

"How long is she gone?" Tessa asked, perking up.

Dex shrugged. "I don't know. A few days, for sure."

"So…what are we doing tonight?" Lange repeated.

"Going off the estate, of course," Tessa said with a grin.

"Don't we need a pass to go off the estate?" Corbin interrupted, his brow furrowing. "I'm pretty sure that was stated at the orientation I went through this morning."

Tessa shot another glare at Dex. Had he really brought someone here who was going to report back that they were breaking rules?

Dex ignored her, instead saying, "We're supposed to have passes for advanced tech too, but…"

"Point taken," Corbin said, looking away from them.

Tessa didn't know what that was about, but Dex apparently had a way to keep Corbin quiet.

"So again," Lange said, clapping his hands together and rubbing them in anticipation. "Where are we going tonight?"

"Obviously somewhere with food," Tessa huffed, getting to her feet and grabbing her sneakers.

Dex let out another long-suffering sigh. "Oralia is bringing food, Tessa."

"Good. We'll have a snack for the walk to Arobell," she said, shoving her foot into a sock.

"We're *walking* to Arobell?" Corbin repeated.

"Unless you have a way to travel us to Arobell in the blink of an eye, yeah, we're walking," Lange quipped.

"You're an ass," Corbin noted.

Lange shrugged. "I read that Legacy used to be able to do that. It was an ability taken away when Devram was created."

"Why would they take it away?" Tessa asked.

Lange shrugged again. "The book didn't say. I didn't get to visit that set of archives very often. They are on Ekayan Island."

"You're from the Falein Kingdom?" Corbin asked, a brow arching.

"Until a year ago," Lange said. "I guess that makes me a smart ass."

"Oh my gods," Tessa grumbled, grabbing his hand to tug him to his feet. "Let's go."

"Oralia's not even here yet," he laughed as she tugged on his hand again. She obviously wasn't going to move him.

"Sorry, sorry! I'm here," came Oralia's shrill voice as she came rushing from another direction, a brown paper bag clutched in her hand.

Her white-blonde hair was pulled back into a sleek ponytail, and the standard-issue clothing they were given clung to her lithe body as though they were painted onto her. How did she manage to still look like ethereal perfection?

"This is yours, Tessa," Oralia said, holding out a doughnut with chocolate frosting.

"Aren't they all the same?" Lange asked, snatching the bag from her hand and peering inside.

"Of course," Oralia said with a laugh. "I just know how Tessa can get when she's hungry. No one wants to deal with that."

Tessa gave her a weak smile as Dex grabbed the doughnut and passed it over.

"Why are you so late?" Dex asked, taking the bag and passing it to Corbin.

"Oh, that," Oralia said, her features going taut. "They just announced they're moving up the next assessment. To next week."

Tessa's stomach dropped. It wasn't supposed to be for another month. She'd had a whole month to prepare, to try to get in the right headspace. They hadn't even planned what they were going to do after the assessment yet, and last time, it had been bad. So bad.

*Trapped. She was trapped underground in what seemed to be a network of caves and tunnels, and she couldn't find her way out. There were others here, leading her through the maze of narrow caverns. They were people she didn't recognize, and they were moving too fast for her to properly see their features. That or she was too panicked to care. One almost appeared to have wings. Which was madness. They pulled her along, whispered pretty words, and coaxed her to put one foot in front of the other. And she didn't want to be there, so far from the sky and fresh air and light, but they wouldn't let her go.*

*They wouldn't let her go.*

*They wouldn't let her go.*

*Not as figures stepped from the shadows, fangs glinting in the low light of sconces along the cave walls. Not as fighting broke out, and for some reason, she cared if the strangers survived. Not as black flames and darker shadows swirled around them. Not as pain flared deep in her belly and fangs pierced her throat, and gods, she couldn't scream. Couldn't breathe. And it was dark and she was alone and—*

*"Not yet."*

*That was what the female said who appeared at her side, crouching down to peer at her. Her violet eyes were hard and narrowed. Her shiny mahogany hair was braided down her back, and she wore close-fitting black clothing.*

*"Lost for so long, but not much longer. Fate changes, moment-by-moment, and I can't keep up. But it is not time for this, for chaos and death. Much can change. Much will change. That war will come." She reached out and placed a*

*hand over Tessa's heart, and faint light flared as she murmured, "It slumbers still. Now is not the time for this. Not yet."*

And Tessa had gasped awake, still strapped to the chair for the assessment, blood dripping from her nose. She had tasted it on her tongue as she'd gulped down air. Another fucking vision they'd designed to drive her mad, to force her magic to surface and reveal itself.

"Next week?" Corbin was saying. "I just did an assessment two weeks ago at the Anala Estate. I won't have to do another one so soon, right?"

It was Lange who spoke after a moment of long silence. "I had to," he said quietly, the usual glimmer in his eyes gone. "I was moved here days after an assessment in Falein Kingdom, and a week later, I had one here."

"That doesn't make any sense," Corbin said, his brow furrowing. "All the Estates share records. They would be able to see assessment results."

"It always seems to happen," Tessa said thoughtfully, taking a bite of her doughnut. "Anytime new Fae arrive, we have an assessment within a week."

"Don't be silly," Oralia scoffed. "We didn't have an assessment for almost three months when I came here."

"I guess that's true," Tessa replied.

She suddenly felt restless, shifting on her feet as something felt like it was pressing against her skin, clawing at something deep in her soul trying to stir it awake.

"Finish your doughnut, Tessie," Dex said, nudging her with his elbow, but his focus was fixed on Oralia, the two of them exchanging a dark look.

"Come on, sweetheart," Lange said, looping his arm through Tessa's and tugging her from Dex's side. "Let's get out of here and pretend like none of this matters tonight."

"Doughnuts always matter," Tessa said, popping the last bite into her mouth and sucking the frosting from her fingers.

"As much as good dick?" Lange challenged with a wink.

Tessa laughed, a real one she felt in the dark places of her being. "I know you're an ass, but you're my favorite ass."

Lange bent down, pressing a kiss to her cheek as he whispered, "Think you can help me get Corbin to say the same thing?"

She huffed another laugh as Dex fell into step on her other side, a wary look still lingering in his eyes. She ignored it as she said to Lange, "If that's what will make you happy."

"As happy as we can be anyway," Lange muttered, his smile faltering a little.

"As happy as we can be," she agreed, making sure the five of them were all connected before she stepped across the point where Dex told her the wards were.

But she'd stopped dreaming of happiness a long time ago.

# PART ONE
# CONTROL THE UNCONTROLLABLE

# 1

## TESSA

Tessalyn Ausra rolled over in bed, reaching across the mattress only to find the other side cold. She cracked her eyes open, her vision blurry for a few seconds while she adjusted to the soft morning light spilling into the room. One curtain had been pulled aside. The rest remained tightly shut, keeping the top floor of the townhouse in the dark.

The dark.

So much darkness. No room for light. No room to breathe. No room to—

The rustling of pages drew her from her thoughts, and her attention fixed on the Legacy seated on the sofa across the room. Theon St. Orcas, Heir to the Arius Kingdom and her Master, had already showered and dressed for the day. Or he'd started to dress anyway. He wore his suit pants, but his black shirt wasn't buttoned, untucked and hanging open to leave his chest on full display. A chest she'd watched heaving as he bound her with his shadows. A torso she'd watched the muscles of flex as he'd sank into her—

*Godsdammit.*

The one and only time they'd fucked plagued her memory in both the best and worst ways possible. Because that sex had been... Well, he'd been right. It was different than sex with a mortal. Different and a thousand times better, and he swore it wouldn't happen again until she said she was his. He didn't even care if she lied about it, as long as she said it.

She was an excellent liar, but this? She just couldn't bring herself to say the words, and she couldn't figure out why. One would think the bond would make it easier, but the bond only made her life more chaotic.

Tessa studied him, his ebony hair falling across his brow as he looked between two books open on the small coffee table and his laptop balanced on the arm of the sofa. Probably researching her. Again. He was obsessed with figuring out her lineage ever since the Emerging Ceremony a week ago. Ever since it had been revealed she wasn't Fae like all the other Sources. Ever since it had been revealed the Source of the Arius Heir had magic of Achaz. No one understood how someone with magic of the god of light and beginnings had gone undetected for her nearly twenty-four years, but the fact that she was the Source of power for a descendant of the god of death and endings was irony at its finest.

She lightly cleared her throat as she pushed into a sitting position, reaching for Theon's thermal shirt he still left out for her every night. As she finished pulling the shirt on over her sleep tank, it caught on the dark bands on her wrists that kept her magic from manifesting. She could take them off, but Theon and the others didn't seem to know that. The bands were becoming increasingly annoying, though. Her magic buzzed beneath her skin, constantly searching for a way out and driving her a little mad. A necessary nuisance until she learned to control her magic, but who knew when that would be. The Fae were already learning to control their elements, but mastering an element differed from a Legacy power.

Or so she'd been told as she'd watched from a balcony overlooking the arenas where the power training took place. Twice this week they'd been there because Theon had wanted to observe the newly awakened Fae, and she'd wished she were down in the arenas with her friends as they learned to control water and air, earth and fire.

But she wasn't one of them anymore.

No one seemed to know what she was, although plenty of people had ideas. Theon. Rordan. Valter. She'd heard the whispers in passing of Fae and Legacy when they entered a room.

She supposed that was why Theon was suddenly so obsessed with her lineage. But the truth of it all was she didn't belong anywhere. She'd always felt alone in the world; now she truly was.

A swirl of dark shadows appeared, carrying a mug of coffee over to her. Theon didn't even look up when she wrapped her fingers around the warm cup, clutching it close to her chest. She sat for a few minutes, waiting to see if he was going to say anything. The fact that he'd let her sleep in told her there was something important happening this morning. It was a break from their routine these past few days. Normally, Theon had been waking her up to go running as the sun rose before he dropped her off for training with Luka, Theon's Guardian, advisor-to-be, and best friend. Then Axel, Theon's younger brother, had been picking her up and bringing her back here so she could shower and dress for whatever she'd be doing the rest of the day. Next week, she'd start private lessons with Mother Cordelia. At least, she assumed that was still the plan. The other Sources already attended their own private element training while she stayed with Theon, which is where she preferred to be anyway. Sitting through endless meetings. Observing the Lords, Ladies, and Heirs.

Watching.

Listening.

Learning everything she could about the countless people who wanted something from her. Who'd lied to her. Who had secrets she coveted.

When Theon still didn't acknowledge her, she let out a sigh before climbing out of bed and moving to the balcony, slipping through the curtains and door. It was cool outside, the autumn temperatures helped along by the constantly cloudy sky. The floor of the balcony was cold on her bare feet, but it was better than shoes or socks.

Sipping at her coffee, she watched the Acropolis come to life below. She may loathe running with Theon, but at least it got her outside. She probably wouldn't get much time outdoors today. The one and only other time she hadn't gone running this last week was when they'd had to attend a breakfast with all the Lords and Ladies two days after the Emerging Ceremony. She'd been present physically, but mentally she'd still been in the wine cellar, clawing at the walls, trying to find a way out.

And since that time, Theon had been…different. Still demanding. Still controlling. Still all the things she hated, but also different, especially when they were alone. He gave her space, gave her choices on things that didn't matter, and, probably the most suspicious, he'd let her have pizza two nights ago.

Which made her trust him even less.

It was as if he was trying to lure her into a false sense of security, and if she wasn't careful, she had no doubt she'd find herself shoved into the dark once more.

*If only I'd known this is all I needed to do from the beginning.*

That was what he'd said to her. Even now, standing outside where the sun was trying to find its way through the clouds, she could see his hard emerald eyes staring at her. Feel his fingers brushing the hair back from her brow. Feel his shadows peeling her off him while she begged him not to leave her in the dark.

"We can walk today if you'd like."

Tessa jolted, spinning around to find Theon leaning in the doorway. He held his own coffee mug, his shirt still unbuttoned, all the grooves and indents of his abdomen taunting her. Because the dark still plagued her, and time spent in pleasure at his hands still managed to drive it away, and fuck him for being both her destruction and salvation.

Her fingers tightened around her mug, and her eyes dropped to the ground, finding his black shoes. He never went barefoot. Even half dressed he had shoes on his feet. How ridiculous was that?

"Tessa? Are you—"

But she was crossing the small distance between them. She reached up, wrapping her hand around his neck, and pushed up onto her toes, pressing her lips to his as he bent to meet her. The bond made things too unbearable ever since that night, and she was done fighting it when giving in didn't mean anything but a momentary reprieve from this life she'd been fated with. For weeks she'd resisted his advances after the initial Source Mark had been given, and for what? She thought she'd lose herself completely, but nothing had changed when she'd finally given in, even though at that point, losing herself was exactly what she'd wanted. No, the only thing that had changed was the intensity of the physical need for him, and if he was going to use her for her power, she was going to use him right back. She was done denying herself one of the few things that quieted the chaos. This was nothing but physical needs being satisfied so the bond would ease up and let her breathe for a godsdamn minute.

An arm wrapped around her waist, and her feet were moving, the warmth of their room wrapping around her as he tugged her back inside. At some point he'd set his mug down and had taken hers from her hand. Her hands slipped beneath that unbuttoned shirt, fingers sliding over muscle as they moved lower, his stomach caving beneath her touch. How had she not realized how much control she had in this?

Even when his hand came up to grip her throat so he could take control of the kiss, the groan that came from him when she licked into his mouth told her she still held more control than he did.

She let him nudge her backwards. Let him lay her down on the bed. Let her knees fall apart so he could step between them, his hard length pressing against her aching center. Her hips rose to meet his when he rolled against her. His hand slid beneath her shirt, finding his way to her breast, and she pushed at his shirt, wanting bare skin.

"Say it," he growled against her lips. "Say it, and I'll give you what I know you want from me. The only thing you want from me."

"No," she gasped as he rocked against her again, her nails raking down his back.

"Tessa, just—"

But he broke off into another groan when she brought her mouth back to his. Anything to keep him from asking for more of her. Always more. Never enough.

"Godsdammit, Tessa," he cursed, his lips sliding along her jaw before they stopped completely, his brow falling against hers.

She could feel his heart beating as fast as her own. More than that, her magic was thrashing, trying to get to his darkness that had appeared, hovering around him like a mist of midnight. They reached for her before they were yanked back. She was so close to begging. So close to asking him to use those shadows like he'd done before. But she knew he wouldn't. She knew he'd torment her even in this until he got what he wanted.

Instead, her eyes fell closed as she tried to regulate her breathing. The bond was sated for now, and while she wanted more, this was enough.

It had to be enough.

He wanted everything from her, and she had nothing left to give.

Theon rolled off her, lying on his back beside her. She fisted her hands in the comforter, inhaling another deep breath and going through song lyrics in her head.

She felt the bed shift after a minute or two, then his hand cupped her cheek, gently turning her face towards him.

"Look at me, little storm," he murmured.

His thumb swept across her cheekbone, and it took everything in her not to lean into the touch.

With one last ragged breath, she pushed down the want. She shoved every bit of self back down, becoming nothing once more. Then she opened her eyes and met his.

Nothing was said for a long moment until Theon finally spoke again. "Are you all right?"

She almost let out the broken laugh that formed in her throat, but instead she said, "I'm fine."

His lips pursed in obvious frustration. It was the same answer she always gave whenever he asked that question. She slowly unclenched her fists, hissing as the bands clamped down on her surging power. Theon's eyes darted to her wrists.

"How bad is it?"

"How bad is what?" she sighed, pushing up and off the bed to retrieve her coffee mug. Which was now cold. Great.

Theon was there, taking the mug from her hand and setting it aside before pouring her a fresh cup from the heated pot. Ford must have brought up breakfast while she still slept.

Ford was the Fae male who had replaced Pen. Everyone was on edge with the new Fae in the townhouse. Theon, Axel, and Luka clearly didn't trust him, not that Tessa could blame them. Theon's father, Valter, had chosen the male himself after he'd murdered Pen in front of all of them to prove a point. Then again, Axel had done the actual murdering. His father had just pushed him to a breaking point.

Axel had been different since that night. In fact, Tessa rarely saw him. He would bring her back to the townhouse after her training with Luka every day, and then she'd only see him if his presence was required for something or other.

Or if Katya was around. But even that wasn't very often. The female was staying at the townhouse, but Tessa still scarcely saw her too.

Katya was still going through all the trainings with the other Fae, despite already having been claimed and assigned to the Arius Kingdom. Axel had claimed her himself, and Tessa still hadn't figured out why. She didn't know Katya well. Kat had come to the Celeste Estate only a few months before they'd all been herded to the Acropolis for the Selection. It had been odd that she'd been moved at all. It had seemed pointless, but Tessa's friend Brecken had been smitten with her from the moment she'd arrived at the estate. Now Kat was here, nearly as trapped as Tessa was. Kat may not have been a Source to a Legacy, but she did have the fire element. The Anala Kingdom never let any other kingdom have fire

Fae, so the fact that Kat could control flames was nearly as big of a scandal as Tessa not being Fae.

Theon's fingers brushed along one of the bands, and Tessa sucked in another sharp hiss. It wasn't that they hurt her physically, but her magic writhed as if it were dying.

"Why didn't you tell me it was getting this bad?" he asked.

She shrugged, sipping on her coffee before she said, "I didn't think you'd care."

"Of course I care."

"Because I'm your Source," she retorted. "My discomfort has never bothered you as long as I am obedient and my power is secure."

Theon raked a hand through his hair, a harsh breath escaping him. "Tessa, you need to tell me when your power is growing restless."

"It's always restless."

"I know, but when it's becoming unbearable, you need to tell me."

She didn't bother swallowing down the humorless laugh this time. "Everything is unbearable, Theon. All the time. My entire life. You think this is something new? Me enduring something painful?"

"I'm not trying to start a fight with you, Tessa."

"You never are," she retorted. Then she added tightly, "My point is, I can handle a little discomfort."

"But I can help you," he argued, his tone growing harsher as he became more agitated. She opened her mouth to argue again, but he spoke over her. "I know that is not some slight discomfort, Tessa. I know the agony of having your magic trapped inside you."

"I'm sure you do," she muttered, sipping on her coffee as she moved to step around him and go shower. But his hand was on her elbow, spinning her back to face him.

"Aside from the fact that Legacy wear those bands to help them control their magic when it first emerges, my father prefers to use them to get a point across," he snarled into her face. "I know what it feels like to have your power trapped inside you, trying to force its way out. I know how mad it can drive a person, and I know what can happen when those bands are in place for too long. I assure you, all three of us know the discomfort of those bands and how bad it can get."

She blinked up at him, his fingers still wrapped around her arm. She'd always known the Arius Kingdom and its Lord were to be feared, but she'd learned that even his own sons were not free of his wrath and cruelty. Theon had consistently tried to shield her from his father, keeping her sequestered to his rooms at Arius House and making sure they spent as little time as possible with his parents. But after the events of the Emerging Ceremony, not to mention the night before the ceremony, Valter was coming around more and more, and Theon could no longer keep her hidden and protected. It was a miracle she was even here. The Achaz Lord had pushed for her to be housed at the Pantheon until her lineage was figured out, but Theon had fought for her.

Well, maybe not *for* her, but to keep her at the very least.

Theon suddenly released his hold on her, his hand dropping to his side. "I should have made sure we were removing those bands every other day at the very least. Things have been chaotic, and—" He sighed, his hand going through his hair once more. When he spoke again, the agitation was gone, replaced by something that sounded almost defeated. "I'll make some time today to take you to the training arenas so they can come off for a bit."

Tessa looked down at the bands, as black as the Mark on her right hand. "But I can't control the magic," she said, suddenly wary of the gesture. He never did anything for her just because. There was always some ulterior motive, something he could gain from her or his actions.

"The power training arenas are enchanted for working with magic," he replied.

"For the Fae," she deadpanned. "I do not have elemental magic, Theon."

"I am well aware of that, Tessa," he retorted. "The training arenas are warded and enchanted with old magic from when Devram was created. The Keeper maintains them. They can withstand Fae and Legacy power."

"Oh," was all she said.

"Go get ready. I'll have clothes out for you."

She rolled her eyes. He hadn't picked out her clothing since they'd made their pointless bargain about her being free of him when he ruled Arius Kingdom. Why he suddenly felt the need to start doing so again she didn't know, but she was also already too exhausted to care. Without another word, she slipped around him and went to the bathroom, brushing her teeth and taking a shower.

When she emerged and made her way to the large walk-in closet and dressing room, she found rather formal clothing waiting for her. A tight fitting black skirt with a white blouse. Black heels, of course. It was never flats, always heels.

"Hair up and light makeup. Nothing drastic today," came Theon's voice, and she turned, finding him fully dressed now. He was even wearing a tie. He didn't usually wear one for their day-to-day activities, and it only furthered her suspicion of something bigger happening today. His body was tense and coiled. She could tell he'd restyled his hair, but he'd also already run his hand through it again.

Worried.

He was worried about something today.

She didn't ask questions. He had made it perfectly clear it wasn't her place to know anything. Just to do as she was told.

So, she watched and listened and learned all she could.

Thirty minutes later, Theon was leading her out of their room. "Luka is waiting for us downstairs. Do you want to walk?"

"Walk where?" she muttered. If she was walking anywhere in heels, it needed to be a short distance.

"To the Tribunal."

She tripped on the stairs, Theon catching her arm to keep her from tumbling down. Turning to face him, she said, "The Tribunal? Why do we have to go there?"

His features hardened, that muscle feathering in his jaw. "I will explain on the way."

The Tribunal was where hearings and trials were held in the Acropolis. Most were held in Faven, the capital of the Achaz Kingdom, since the Achaz Lord, Rordan Jove, and his kingdom were responsible for upholding the laws and accords of Devram. But the Tribunal? That was where the laws and accords were made. That was where all six of the kingdoms came together to discuss matters.

Theon didn't ask if she wanted to walk again. Instead, she found herself being ushered into their usual vehicle, Luka sliding into the driver's seat. Axel was meeting them there after he dropped Kat off at the Pantheon for her daily trainings.

Theon had scarcely shut the back door when she asked, "Why do we all have to go to the Tribunal this morning?"

"There is a hearing being held," he answered, eyes fixed straight ahead.

"A hearing? At the Tribunal? Is that normal?"

"No. A hearing with all the ruling Lords and Ladies is rare. It only happens in…atypical circumstances."

"Is it normal for you to be present during these hearings?"

"The last one that was held like this was when Prudence was born. I was only two years. And that wasn't so much a hearing as it was an agreement being made regarding all six heirs coming of age to Select Sources during the same Selection year."

"And now?"

Theon finally turned to meet her gaze. "And now they are having a hearing because of you."

"Me?" she balked, lurching back from him.

"Yes."

"But what about me specifically?"

That muscle ticked again, and she started to lift a hand. To do what? She didn't know. The bond always pushed her to try and soothe him when he was upset. She dropped her hand back to her lap, annoyed with herself.

Finally, he said, "The hearing is to determine whether you can remain my Source. We are to present our arguments today, and the final decision will be given this afternoon."

To determine whether she could remain his Source? That made little sense because—

"I thought the only way to end a Source bond is by death?" she said.

"It is."

That probably should have caused her to panic. A normal person probably would have felt something. Fear. Dread. Some form of hysteria.

She felt nothing.

"It's not going to happen, Tessa," Theon said when she didn't speak.

She only shrugged, turning to look out the window.

A Source was Fae. That was what they'd been taught. That was their purpose. To serve the Legacy in whatever way they demanded.

But she wasn't Fae. Not even demi-Fae. That was what Lord Jove had told her, not that she was entirely sure she believed him. She didn't really trust anyone at this point, and she'd only had a brief time with Rordan before Theon and Valter had come to claim her once more. But the things he'd said…

"Do you think any part of me is Fae?" she asked suddenly, watching the people wander along the streets to wherever they were going.

There was a long pause before Theon said, "I don't know the answer to that, Tessa."

"I didn't ask for a definitive answer," she replied, her head tilting as she caught sight of her reflection in the window. Her finger came up to the glass, tracing around the violet rings that now lined the outer edges of her grey eyes. "I am told you are academically inclined. I asked if you *think* any part of me is Fae."

"I…" When he trailed off, Tessa finally turned to look at him. "No, Tessa, I don't think any part of you is Fae."

"So I am a Legacy then?"

"Perhaps."

She hummed, her knee beginning to bounce. Then she was leaning between the seats to speak to Luka. "What do you think I am?"

Luka shot her a quick glance before focusing on the road once more. "Vexing."

"Funny," she groused, reaching to mess with the music. Luka slapped her hand away and she frowned. "Why can't Axel and Kat ride with us? His music choices are better than yours."

She saw his gaze flash to the rearview mirror, presumably connecting with Theon's.

"We don't know Katya well enough to trust her yet," Luka answered, sighing when she reached for the music again and letting her change the song.

"Where were you last night?"

"What?" Luka asked, glancing at her side-long again.

"You weren't at the townhouse all night," she answered, finally settling on a song.

"How can you possibly know that?"

Tessa shrugged, drawing patterns on the leather console with her finger.

"Tessa," Luka growled. "How do you know I wasn't there?"

She sighed in resignation. "I came to talk to you in the middle of the night. You weren't in your room."

"When was this?" Theon demanded.

She looked back at him over her shoulder. "In the middle of the night. I just said that."

"Where was I?"

"Sleeping."

His eyes narrowed. "Why didn't you wake me up?"

"Because I don't like you."

That muscle ticked yet again. "What were you going to talk to him about?"

Tessa bit her lip, already knowing how he was going to react to this. "To see about taking these bands off for a while because my power is unbearable right now."

Theon's eyes widened briefly in disbelief before the expected anger took over. "We just talked about this," he gritted out.

"*This morning*," she retorted, sitting back in her seat and crossing her arms. "This was *last night*."

Theon took a deep breath, visibly calming himself as he swiped his hand down his face. "As soon as this hearing is over, I will take you to the magic training arenas."

"What if they decide I can no longer be your Source?" she asked curiously.

"They won't."

"But what if they do?" she pushed.

Theon straightened as they pulled up to the Tribunal. Tucking his phone into an inside suit pocket, he answered, "No one is taking you from me. Ever."

# 2

## THEON

Theon sat at a table staring coolly back at the ruling Lords and Ladies who sat along the raised dais above him. The Achaz Lord sat at one end, Theon's father at the other. The Ladies sat between them. All their Sources stood within reach behind their bonded, males with hands clasped behind their backs and females with hands folded in front of them, all their eyes downcast. Exactly the way he'd always seen a Source act amongst Legacy. The other heirs were here too, their Sources seated with them off to the side with the Matches of the Lords and Ladies and some of the more prominent Legacy.

Axel sat at Theon's side while Tessa sat on a bench behind them with Luka. They'd planned that so he could keep her calm should things get heated during the hearing, but she'd scarcely reacted when Theon had told her what would be decided today. She'd merely shrugged as if her life wasn't in the hands of the six Legacy looking down on them as though they were kings and queens. In a way, they were, he supposed. They were about to decide his fate, Tessa's fate, the fate of all his carefully laid plans. Their decision this day would surely alter history in one way or another.

"Should we get started?" asked Rordan Jove, looking at the other rulers. "I have a feeling this could be quite the drawn-out affair."

"I don't know why it would be," said Luna Candra, the Celeste Lady.

"His Source isn't Fae, therefore, she cannot be a Source. It's as simple as that."

"It's not that simple," Theon's father cut in, his finger tapping on the arm of his chair. "A Source bond has been initiated. Forcing him to take another now puts him at a disadvantage with the other heirs."

"It is no different from when we have had to take new Sources," the Serafina Lady, Maya Isleen, cut in with a shrug of her slender shoulder.

"The difference," Valter bit out, "is that his Source still lives."

"That is a valid point," interjected Raye Farhan, the Falein Lady, her hazel eyes looking past Theon and studying Tessa. It took all of him not to look over his shoulder to check on her.

"It is a point that can easily be rectified," the Celeste Lady said with a curl of her lip.

"To make sure I am understanding your argument correctly, my Lady," Theon said, cutting off whatever was about to be said next. "You are proposing taking the life of my Source?"

"She cannot be your Source," Lady Candra replied.

"Because she is not Fae," Theon clarified.

"Correct."

"So your solution is to kill a Legacy?"

"That is not—" Lady Candra snapped her mouth shut, glaring at Theon.

"Do you have proof she is a Legacy?" asked Lady Isleen.

"No," Theon admitted, his gaze falling to his laptop open before him with all the information he'd been able to gather this last week. But the truth was he'd found nothing concrete, only theories to explore and trails of information that led nowhere.

"You understand the predicament here, do you not?" asked Lord Jove, his elbow propped on the arm of his chair and his finger steepled along his temple as he met Theon's gaze. "If she is a Legacy, she cannot remain your Source. It would put you at an unfair advantage. Not only that, what is to stop any of us, of our heirs, from Selecting a Legacy as a Source?"

Theon saw all the other Sources shift uncomfortably on their feet, a few of them exchanging quick glances. It was a valid argument. None of the Lords and Ladies would hesitate to end their own bonds to take a more powerful Source.

"I understand the predicament, but I think we can all agree it is not as simple as Lady Candra seems to believe it is," Theon answered.

"That is fair," Lord Jove conceded. "But it does not change the fact of the matter that she cannot remain your Source."

"The only way to sever a Source bond is death of either party," Theon argued. "Unless the plan is to kill one of us, I do not see a way around letting it remain."

Lord Jove's brow arched. "Are you offering yourself in her place?"

"No," Valter interrupted with a growl. "That is not an option."

Lord Jove's attention shifted to the Arius Lord. "And what do you propose, Lord St. Orcas? One would think you, of all people, would detest your offspring having an advantage you yourself are not afforded. Or is it simply because it is your son that you find this acceptable?"

"Careful, Rordan," Valter said softly, his darkness appearing and coiling around the tips of his fingers.

"We are simply gathering all the facts," Lord Jove replied. The male still hadn't moved from his casual position, but Theon could swear he was fighting a smirk. "Is that not what we are here to do? And one cannot deny you have a bias in this matter."

"And you do not?" Valter retorted. "She possesses magic from your bloodline."

The Lord's bright blue eyes turned to Tessa now, and Theon didn't need to turn around to know she was staring back at him. He knew it from the shuffle of Luka's feet, knew he was likely nudging her with his knee. But Tessa had spent time with Rordan after the Emerging Ceremony and had said little about it. Theon needed to discuss it with her, needed to discuss so many things, but if he wasn't allowed to keep her at his side, he wouldn't have that time. So preparing for today had become his main focus to the point of obsession. Once this was over, he'd fix everything else, get everything back on track.

Rordan was still studying her when he spoke again. "While she does have some power from the Achaz line—"

"Some power?" Lady Candra interrupted. "That was not *some* power, Rordan. She is strong."

"I am not denying that, Luna," Rordan replied, his attention still fixed beyond Theon and on the female in question.

"But not all of her power is of the Achaz line."

Every head turned to Kyra Aithne, the Anala Lady. Her bright copper hair tumbled over her shoulders in waves. She tilted her head, and as she did, the lighting made the golden undertones stand out, as if her hair was flames itself.

"You are exactly right, Kyra," Rordan replied, finally sitting up straighter. His shoulder-length golden hair was pulled back, and he lifted a hand, light glowing in his palm. "We may have light and can use it as we see fit, but we cannot summon a storm indoors."

"Then what line is she crossed with?" Lady Candra demanded.

"Isn't that the question of the day?" Rordan replied, turning to look down at them once more.

"Can she do more than summon storms?" the Falein Lady asked, genuine curiosity in her tone.

Everyone's attention settled on Theon. His hands were curled around the arms of his chair, just like his father's were. "We do not know the full extent of her gifts," he answered. "Her assessments always predicted the air element, but that clearly is not the case. Her Emerging happened a week ago, and there has been little time to explore her gifts in the last few days."

"So you do not know?" Lady Farhan clarified.

He felt the muscle tick in his jaw as he ground his teeth. "She clearly has Achaz gifts, but I believe she can do more than simply summon a rainstorm indoors."

"Clearly," the Serafina Lady scoffed. "We all saw the damage done to the Pantheon that night."

"That was not entirely her fault," Axel chimed in. "There was more than Tessa's magic being flung around the Pantheon. Legacy and Fae alike panicked. *Everyone* lost control. All of your kingdoms sent sentinels after her. Do not place the blame for that destruction at her feet. None of the events of the past few weeks have been entirely her fault."

He turned then, and Theon turned with him, watching his brother's gaze connect with Tessa's. "The blame in all of this does not lie with you."

The room was silent for a heartbeat, and Tessa held Axel's gaze, her features expressionless as she listened to everyone debate what she was. Something flickered in her violet-grey stare. Theon saw her throat bob, and then she dropped her gaze to her lap, her fingers gripping the edge of the bench. Theon glanced at Luka, where his elbows were braced on his knees, his fingers loosely clasped.

"Be that as it may," the Serafina Lady said, bringing everyone back to the debate at hand. "That kind of power cannot simply remain unchecked."

"Bullshit," Valter scoffed. "Every Kingdom has an advantage against the other kingdoms. Every Kingdom but Arius. This levels out more than one playing field."

"This is not a game, Valter," Lady Candra snapped.

"If this were any other kingdom, this would not even be a debate," Valter retorted, and Theon thought for sure his father was going to get to his feet, but he managed to stay seated, the shadows thickening around him.

"That isn't true," Lord Jove said calmly.

"No?" Valter sneered. "If she were part of your kingdom, you would still be open to this debate?"

"If she were part of *my* kingdom, she would be where she belongs," the Achaz Lord replied, his voice low and cold, and all the Legacy shifted, power flickering at their fingertips as their Sources tensed.

"Are you proposing that you take possession of her and leave my heir without a Source?" Valter replied, his tone as cold as Rordan's.

"I am proposing the same thing I proposed the night you showed up on my doorstep," Lord Jove replied, settling back in his chair once more. "Tessalyn should be housed at the Pantheon until her lineage and power can be determined. Once that is taken care of, then we decide the next steps."

"That leaves my son without a Source bond to cultivate in the meantime," Valter snapped. "Not an option."

"Is there anything else you can tell us about her lineage? Anything else that might help us make the most logical decision in this matter?" the Falein Lady asked, directing her questions back to Theon.

"Due to her parentage being altered, we must assume everything in her documents has been altered," Theon answered. "I need more than a few days to sort through all of that and find answers. I am respectfully asking for the time to do that, and if it is granted, it will be far easier to have her with me for such a task rather than having to track her down at the Pantheon every time I need to ask her a question or test a theory."

"And in the meantime, you continue to foster a Source bond with a being that is clearly not Fae? Absurd," scoffed Lady Candra.

"Is a Source bond being fostered? Is it even possible?" asked Lady Farhan, her attention flitting between Theon and over his shoulder to Tessa.

This was the question he'd been dreading because he didn't know. He didn't fucking know if the Source bond was doing what it was supposed to do. When he looked at the Sources of the Lords and Ladies standing obediently at their backs or to the Sources of the heirs, that was not Tessa. But she could pretend and act with the best of them, and what if that's what all the Sources were doing? Despite what the Celeste Lady had said, this was a game of kingdom politics and power grabs. But every single one of them? Did every Source fake that adoring look in their eye when they looked at their Legacy? Did they loathe the role they'd been Selected to serve? Behind closed doors, were they scheming with their Masters and Mistresses, or were they compliant because it was simply easier to be miserable at this point? How had Tessa managed to turn everything he knew upside down in the span of a few godsdamn weeks?

His fingers flexed where his hand rested on the table, his darkness pushing to be let out at the thought. He'd lost so much control over this entire situation. His father had made that perfectly clear over the last few days full of verbal onslaughts and threats of consequences should this hearing not go in their favor. This wasn't just his own well-being at stake. It was Axel and Luka and Tessa and so many innocent lives who had nothing to do with any of this. Payment for failure might lie with him, but everyone else would be the ones to suffer, just as it had always been.

The Tribunal room was quiet as everyone waited for his answer, and Theon could feel his father's gaze burning into him. Finally, Theon answered, "There is a bond. Having never experienced another Source bond, I have nothing to compare it to. I cannot say if it is the same or different, but there is something there, yes."

The Lords and Ladies all began speaking at once, trying to be heard over one another as arguments broke out between them. Theon couldn't follow all the conversations, and he turned to look at Axel, the brothers sharing a grim look.

"It's not looking good, Theon," Axel muttered low under his breath.

"We will not lose. We *cannot* lose," Theon returned, a hand falling to his lap so he could let some of his power pool and relieve some tension. Except he immediately had to clamp down on that power as the shadows reached behind him, trying to find their way to Tessa. It'd been this way ever since her power was released. His magic had always seemed curious about her, but now it was as obsessed with her as he was.

"I know we have a plan in place should they vote against you, but that plan involves us getting her out of here. I don't know how we're going to do that with all the power in this room," Axel said, his gaze fixed on the Lords and Ladies. "What if she doesn't respond like you anticipate?"

Then they were all fucked.

It was as simple as that.

Their entire plan hinged on Tessa standing with him, fighting beside the three of them. She was as strong as any of the Lords and Ladies, possibly stronger. That power alongside his own and Axel's and Luka's? The four of them together would be a force, even if she was untrained, and it would be their only chance of getting out of here.

But Tessa's reaction on the ride over here had him worried. Or rather, her complete lack of reaction when the possibility of her death was mentioned had him worried. He'd ignored her statements of wishing for death these past weeks. He'd chalked them up to her being difficult and fighting this bond in any way she could, but after what he'd done to her in that wine cellar…

He couldn't help himself then. Casting a look over his shoulder, he found her gaze already fixed on him. Her expression gave nothing away. It rarely did. She'd been right all along. She had more self-control than he gave her credit for.

Tessa didn't move, her hands still curled around the edge of the bench she sat on, her knuckles white from her grip. That was the only sign of her nerves, and gods, he wanted to reach for her. Let whatever this bond was between them soothe her, even if only for a moment.

Luka leaned over then, speaking low into her ear. She nodded slowly, the tension in her shoulders easing a fraction, and Theon found himself suddenly jealous that Luka got to be that comfort in this moment. Just as he'd been jealous when he'd learned she had sought Luka out about the bands at her wrists instead of coming to him.

The bark of curses had Theon turning back to the Lords and Ladies, flames winking out at the feet of each of them, save for the Anala Lady.

"Was that really necessary, Kyra?" Valter sighed, probing at the scorch mark at his feet with the toe of his black shoe.

"Yes," the Anala Lady said simply.

"You have our attention," Lord Jove said. He still appeared casual, but his tone betrayed his annoyance at being silenced in such a manner.

"We all agree the female is not Fae, yes?" Lady Aithne asked. There were murmurings of agreement from the others before she went on. "Then perhaps we should not be treating her as such."

The room went still, and the Lady's amber gaze was fixed on Tessa as a small smile played on her lips.

"What are you saying, Kyra?" Lady Isleen asked, her nails clicking as she drummed her fingers along the arm of her chair.

"I am saying that perhaps Tessalyn has some insight into this matter. I am saying perhaps she has an opinion on how this should be handled, and if she is indeed a Legacy, her opinion should be considered," Lady Aithne said.

Valter looked livid as he glared at the Anala Lady, and this... This was something Theon hadn't expected.

Theon moved his attention back to Lady Aithne just as her amber gaze flicked up, and he twisted to find the Keeper leaning along the railing of the upper deck. His cloak shrouded him from view as it always did. Theon only assumed he was a male based on Tessa's testimony of him. No one truly knew, but what was he doing here? And what did he have vested in Tessa because he clearly had some interest in this.

"Tessalyn Ausra."

Lord Jove's deep voice pulled Theon's attention back to the front of the room, but only for a second before he was turning back to look at Tessa. She was rigid, any tension Luka had eased back tenfold. Her knee was beginning to bounce, and her hands had left the bench as she began wringing her fingers together.

"Speak, Tessa," Theon said, but it wasn't the commanding order he'd intended. It came out soft and low, something he was sure only the four of them could hear.

"Yes, my Lord," she answered, her gaze dropping to the ground. Her knee ceased its movement, her hands clasped tightly in her lap.

"Come stand before us," the Achaz Lord said, and there was a softness to his voice, as though he was coaxing a spooked animal.

She peered up at Theon from beneath her lashes, and he nodded at the question in her eyes, telling her to follow the Lord's instruction. Something in his chest loosened the smallest amount at that, at the fact that she was still seeking his permission above others. That she was still following the Source bond commands, even if their bond was anything but conventional.

"Go, little one," he heard Luka murmur, a hand falling to her back and urging her to her feet.

Theon moved to stand with her, but Lord Jove spoke before he'd even lifted his ass from his chair. "Not necessary, Theon. Stay seated."

He bit the inside of his cheek, tasting blood as Tessa took a few steps past the table he sat at. She started to drop to a knee, but Lady Aithne said, "That is not necessary, my dear. A simple bow shall do."

"We allow such disrespect now?" Valter demanded.

"The Fae kneel. We have all agreed she is not that. Why should she be forced to kneel?" Kyra argued.

His father pressed his lips into a thin line but did not argue further, and Tessa bowed at the waist before straightening and clasping her hands before her once more.

"How are you, Tessalyn?" Lord Jove asked, and her head snapped up.

"Excuse me, my Lord?"

"How are you?" he repeated. "It has been a few days since we spoke, and you have had much to process. I simply inquire as to how you are faring?"

"Fine, my Lord."

At least that was the answer she gave to everyone and not just him.

"And your power? How have the first few days of mastering that gone?"

Tessa was silent for a long moment before she said, "I have not been able to access my power since that night." As if in emphasis, she lifted her hands to show the black bands on her wrists.

The Achaz Lord's gaze snapped to Theon. "You have not taken the bands off once since that night?"

The accusation was heavy, and the anger was clear in the question. Theon opened his mouth to reply, but Lord Jove spoke again before he could.

"Do you not know what happens if you contain power like hers for too long?"

"Yes, I know quite well," Theon replied tightly. "I will admit that removing the bands escaped me, but—"

"Escaped you?" Lord Jove said incredulously. "You simply *forgot* to take care of your Source's needs?"

"Do not speak to my son like that," Valter snarled.

"If he cannot tend to her basic needs, it does not make me inclined to leave her in his care while this is figured out," Lord Jove replied.

"The matter has already been discussed," Theon cut in. "This morning. We already have plans to go to a training arena as soon as this hearing has concluded."

"A week is too long," the Achaz Lord said.

"I understand. I know it is. That failure is mine. It will not happen again."

"Tessalyn, is it?" the Anala Lady interrupted.

"Yes, my Lady," she replied, her voice stronger now than it had been before.

"They call you Tessa."

"That is my preferred name, my Lady."

"May I use it?"

"I— Of course, my Lady," Tessa replied, trepidation creeping into her voice.

"Is there indeed a bond between you and the Arius Heir?" Lady Aithne asked.

"As he said, I do not know if it is a true Source bond, but there is… something, yes."

"You have lived your entire life believing yourself to be Fae?"

"Yes, my Lady."

The Lady's head tilted, red hair spilling over her shoulder. "And what are your desires in this matter?"

Theon's stomach went to his throat at the question.

"I…" Tessa shifted, her hands dropping to her sides and fingers curling inward. "I do not understand what you are asking me, my Lady."

The Anala Lady gave her a small, sympathetic smile. "Do you wish to stay with the Arius Heir, Tessa?"

Tessa lifted her chin. "I trust you will make the best decision for us all as the rulers of the realm."

That sympathetic smile turned into an amused one, and the Lady gave a soft huff of laughter. "While that was indeed the correct answer to bolster our over-inflated sense of self-importance, now I wish for your true answer, Tessa."

Theon wasn't sure he could draw in air. He had no idea how Tessa was going to answer this question, but he needed her answer more than he needed to breathe at the moment. He knew if she said she wanted out, this would be it. The Achaz Lord was waiting for any reason to take her from him.

A hand landed on his shoulder, but Theon couldn't look at his brother. His entire focus was on the golden-haired female facing the rulers of the realm.

"I wish to stay with him," Tessa finally answered, and Theon sucked in a breath at the words.

"Why?" asked the Falein Lady.

"Because many things are changing," Tessa said. "It is overwhelming at times. I know there are only more changes coming, and having something constant, at least for the time being, would be...comforting."

"You understand that if we decide to let this remain for the time being, you will still be considered a Source," Lord Jove cut in, his entire being fixed on Tessa. "Even though you are not Fae, you will still receive the next Source Mark on the fall equinox. You understand this is beneath you now?"

She didn't tremble, falter, or stutter when she answered, "I understand where my choices will lead."

She was *choosing* this. Theon couldn't believe what he was hearing. She was *choosing* the bond. She was *choosing* this life.

She was *choosing* to stay with him.

"Is there anything else we should consider in this matter?" the Serafina Lady asked.

Theon was still so shocked at what Tessa had said that it wasn't until Axel kicked him under the table that he answered, "No, my Lady. I believe all the facts of this matter have been stated."

Lady Isleen nodded, and the Lords and Ladies all stood, filing from the room and leaving them to sit and wait. The moment the door closed behind them, Theon was on his feet, closing the distance between him and Tessa. He turned her to face him, gently taking her face in his hands.

"I'm sorry I didn't prepare you for that. I didn't think they would..." he trailed off, faltering at the blank expression on her face.

"You didn't think they would deign to ask what *I* wanted, despite the fact I am not Fae?" she asked flatly.

He supposed that was exactly what he'd thought.

When she only continued to stare back at him, he murmured, "You did beautifully, Tessa."

"I'm glad I finally managed to meet your expectations," she retorted before stepping from his hold and moving back to the bench where she took her seat next to Luka.

Theon sighed internally before moving back to his own seat, spinning his chair as Axel had done to face Luka and Tessa. But as he did, his gaze snagged on the upper balcony again, where the Keeper was still leaning on the railing. Even with the hood, Theon could tell his attention was on Tessa.

And it was just another thing in all of this chaos Theon was determined to figure out.

# 3
## TESSA

"Do you want me to go grab some food while we wait?" Axel asked, swiping at his phone screen.

"No," Tessa murmured, staring at nothing as they waited for the Lords and Ladies to return. How long had it been? Minutes? Hours? She didn't know. The thing beneath her skin was pacing, wanting out, out, out, and she wanted out. What was with all the buildings in the Acropolis not having windows? Why did they all have this strange aversion to the sky and sunlight and nature as if they were the vampyres that were not as mythical as she'd once believed?

"Tessa?"

"What?" she answered absent-mindedly, not even sure who had said her name. Her knee was bouncing as she clutched at the bench edge. She wasn't paying attention to what they were discussing. She really didn't care. Not as her power thrashed again. Not as it seemed to scream inside her to the point that Tessa wanted to slam her hands over her ears as if that would silence it.

"Tessa," Theon said again.

"What?" she gritted out.

"Look at me, Tessa."

Her eyes snapped to his, finding his brow creased as he studied her. "We are prepared if they vote against us."

"Against us," she repeated.

"Yes. If they say you cannot remain with me, we are prepared to fight our way out."

"Right," she murmured, breaking his stare.

"You choosing this should help matters."

*Choosing this.*

She lurched to her feet, her stomach churning. "I need a restroom."

Theon was on his feet too, that concern deepening. "Are you all right?"

Clamping a hand over her mouth, she shook her head, and Theon finally understood, stepping aside to let her pass. She moved as quickly as she could through the room and out into the hall before shoving through the door to the female bathroom, dropping to her knees and heaving into the bowl.

*I wish to stay with him.*

The words had been as bitter as the bile on her tongue when she'd said them.

*I wish to stay with him.*

She knew the Achaz Lord would wonder, especially after the things he'd said to her at his estate home.

*I wish to stay with him.*

But it hadn't been a lie. Even if saying those words had tested her very being, staying with Theon was going to give her the best opportunities at uncovering secrets and figuring out who was lying to her, who was trying to use her. If she was bound to the Pantheon, she wouldn't be at his side for meetings. More than that, being separated would almost certainly be miserable. Whatever bond they shared would be unbearable, and the bands on her wrists were already that.

She heard the door open to the single restroom as her brow dropped to her forearm that was draped along the bowl. There was the rustling of paper, and then shiny black shoes came to a stop beside her. Turning her head, she looked up and met sapphire eyes. Luka extended some paper towels to her, and Tessa reached to grab them before wiping at her mouth.

He crouched beside her, sliding her ponytail over her shoulder. "Tell me what you need right now, Tessa."

His words brought her back to the first time she'd entered Theon's suite at Arius House. Luka had said those same words then, crouched before her just like this. There had been so much uncertainty then too.

Shifting so she wasn't sitting on her heels but rather against the wall, she asked, "Where's Theon?"

"It would be...problematic if the Lords and Ladies returned and Theon wasn't present. Particularly with Valter," Luka answered, maneuvering so that he was sitting on the floor as well. He leaned back on one hand while his other arm rested on a bent knee.

"We're sitting on a bathroom floor," Tessa muttered. "Theon would have a fit."

Luka shrugged. "Sometimes sitting on a bathroom floor is necessary. And Theon has had to take a moment for himself in far less appealing places. He'd understand the need."

Tessa glanced at him. "Theon doesn't understand anything about what I need."

"He's trying."

She huffed a humorless laugh. "He is not, and if he is, he's failing."

"I would agree with that," Luka conceded.

"Why didn't he tell me? If he'd just explained so many things to me..."

So much could have been avoided if he'd simply told her about his father, more about his plans, the politics. Instead, he was only focused on her accepting the Source bond. A bond she wasn't even sure she *could* accept seeing as she wasn't Fae.

"He's not trying, Luka," she sighed.

"He had his reasons. He wanted to protect you. Ease you into things. He does not trust easily. Surely you understand that at least," he replied pointedly. "But that aside, I agree things would have gone...smoother if he'd been more upfront with you about many things."

"You could have told me," she retorted.

"My loyalty is—"

"To Theon, not me," she interrupted bitterly. "You've made that clear on more than one occasion."

"Do you wish my loyalty was to you?"

She lifted her head, and the crease between his brows told Tessa he was as perplexed by his question as she was.

"Why would you be loyal to me?"

"I don't know," he murmured, more to himself than her.

They fell silent, but his words repeated in her mind over and over. And the truth was she just wanted *someone* to be loyal to her. Not Luka. It would never be him. He would always choose Theon. So would Axel. Theon would always choose whatever furthered his goals, and he'd choose it without remorse. Not even Dex truly chose her. He still put his assignments above her, along with the laws and the decorum of this realm.

But it would be nice, just once, to know what it was like to be so important to someone that they chose her above all else.

In the end, though, she supposed dreams were like hope.

Completely pointless.

Tessa set the paper towels aside and adjusted the bands on her wrists. "What do you think they'll decide?"

"I think they'll grant your request."

"Theon's request," she corrected.

"Was it not your request as well? Did you not state you would prefer to stay with him?"

Her stomach churned again at the words. "Why do you think they'll grant it?"

"Valter will vote to keep you. You seem to have some sort of sway over the Anala Lady, and the Falein Lady is intrigued by you," Luka answered, listing off reasons as if reporting the weather.

"That's only three votes."

Luka nodded. "Lady Candra will vote against it, and the Serafina Lady will vote however Lord Jove votes."

"And if there is a tie?" Tessa asked.

"In a matter like this, I don't know," he said. "Lord Jove usually decides matters pertaining to the Accords, but this is not that. I can only assume when they return, if there was a tie, it will already be sorted out."

Tessa nodded, her eyes dropping back to the black bands. After a few minutes, Luka stood and silently held out a hand to her. She studied it for a moment, this time remembering a grand hall where she'd stood in shock after being Selected, where this same hand had been extended to her, had fallen to her back to guide her up to a stage.

Had guided her into an entirely new fate.

"Come on, little one," Luka said, his voice low as he waited. There was no impatient gesturing like Theon always did when she didn't respond immediately. There was no quick grip latching onto her when she slid her fingers into his waiting palm. There was just the slow curl of his fingers, his large hand engulfing hers.

She let him pull her to her feet, and he immediately released her hand once she was standing and steady. Moving to the sink, she rinsed her mouth and washed her hands before they made their way back to the hearing room.

The Lords and Ladies hadn't returned yet, and Theon cupped her face in his hands the moment she was within arms' reach, searching for damage as he always did.

"Are you all right?" he murmured, brushing a stray hair from her brow. The concern in his emerald eyes was almost enough to convince her he truly cared.

"I'm fine," she replied.

Theon sighed, his hands dropping to her upper arms as though he was going to pull her into him, but then he seemed to think better of it. After all, that would be inappropriate in front of all these prominent Legacy, even if she was more than a Fae, more than a Source, now.

Instead, he was guiding her back to the bench, and, to her surprise, taking a seat beside her. Her hands fell to the edge, fingers once again curling around it, but only for a moment. Theon's hand was curling around hers, prying her fingers right back off and intertwining them with his own.

"I can still help," he murmured, leaning in to speak into her ear. "Even in a room like this, I can still be the comfort that you need right now."

"The bond is comforting, Theon. Not you," she replied tightly, resisting the urge to lean into him, to take more from him as she felt the bond already loosening the tightness in her chest, calming her anxious thoughts, soothing her soul. But sitting beside him was enough.

It had to be enough.

"Of course," he replied just as tersely, rigid beside her.

There was nothing but the murmurs of quiet conversation around them. Axel was thumbing through something on his phone again. Luka was being his usual stoic self. So she and Theon sat, side-by-side, not speaking. It was becoming so familiar to her now, it was a comfort in and of itself.

Theon didn't release her hand until some time later when the doors opened and the Lords and Ladies were striding back into the room. Then he was standing, buttoning his suit coat, and stepping forward while she remained seated, focusing on the sudden lack of warmth around her hand.

Axel took Theon's place beside her while Luka remained standing a few feet away, his arms crossed, and they all waited for someone to speak. The room was quiet, everyone seeming to hold their breath.

"While there are several valid concerns, we have come to a compromise of sorts," Lord Jove finally said, settled casually in his chair as he had been for much of the earlier proceedings.

"A compromise," Theon repeated.

Lord Jove nodded. "Tessalyn, come forward."

She looked up then, meeting bright blue eyes ringed with gold. There was none of the gentleness with which he'd spoken to her the night at his home after the Emerging Ceremony. This was the Achaz Lord, the silently agreed upon ruler of Devram. If he'd wanted this to play out some other way, it would have. Tessa could see that truth staring back at her.

Lord Jove gave a sharp jerk of his chin, and Tessa was standing and moving to Theon's side.

"We have agreed to let Tessalyn remain with you for the time being," Lord Jove finally said, and Tessa could feel the relief rolling off Theon. He opened his mouth to speak, but Lord Jove held up a hand to stay him. "You have until the winter solstice to uncover her lineage, Heir St. Orcas. If, at that time, you have not been successful, alternative arrangements will be made."

"What kind of alternative arrangements?" Theon demanded.

Lord Jove's smile was tight and laced with an arrogance that said he knew exactly how much power he held here. "None that involve *you*."

"That's impossible," Theon returned. "How will you sever a Source bond?"

"Which brings us to our next contingency," Lord Jove went on. "Should you be successful in discovering her lineage, it will be reported to us immediately, and the next courses of action will be determined. In the meantime, you are permitted to continue with the Source Marks as Tessalyn has stated she is willing."

From the corner of her eye, Tessa saw the muscle in Theon's jaw tick. She knew he was likely biting his cheek to keep from speaking, and not once had he looked at his father.

"After the Samhain Feast, she will spend a week in Faven—"

"Absolutely not," Theon said at the mention of the Achaz Kingdom capital.

"Hold your tongue, Theon," Valter growled, and finally Tessa glanced at the Arius Lord. He was as tense as his son, that same muscle ticking in his jaw. He didn't like this either, but had clearly lost any arguments against it.

"She will spend a week in Faven with some of our most skilled priestesses for testing," Lord Jove went on as if neither of the Arius Legacy had spoken. "This is a *gift* from us to aid you, Heir St. Orcas."

Testing?

It took everything in her not to take a step back because testing meant assessments. They already knew her gifts. Why would assessments be necessary?

"Testing for what?" Theon gritted out.

"Several things. To see if we can assist in discovering her lineage. To determine the strength of her gifts," Lord Jove replied casually.

"Anything else?" Theon asked.

"Yes," the Achaz Lord answered, and Tessa could practically hear the curse words Theon was swallowing down. "She needs to work at mastering her gifts."

"She will."

A fair brow arched as Lord Jove said, "And who will be teaching her?"

"We are still working that out," Theon said.

"Consider the matter handled. We will provide an Achaz Legacy to train her on the basics in Faven. Should it be needed, that instruction can continue upon her return to the Acropolis as well."

"No," Theon replied, shaking his head in emphasis. "I will draw a line there."

And then Rordan Jove was standing and taking long, purposeful steps towards Theon. The Lord may have been an inch or two shorter than Theon, but that didn't keep him from looking down his nose at the Arius Heir as the gold in his eyes fractured like lightning across his irises. "Let me be very clear: you are not in a position to be drawing lines anywhere. You are not yet a Lord in this realm, and even if you were, you do not have a fully intact Source bond. The fact that we are allowing this is a kindness in and of itself, and you will adhere to our contingencies, or you will find us not so gracious. Is that understood?" Theon stared back at him, and when he didn't answer, Lord Jove said, "An audible answer is expected from an heir to a Lord."

Tessa blinked as she looked between the Achaz Lord and her Master. It was probably not what she was supposed to be doing. Her gaze should probably be fixed on the ground, but she couldn't help herself. Not as she watched Theon fight against his nature to be in control.

Not as something inside of her smiled at Theon being forced to bow to another.

"Understood," Theon ground out from between his teeth, and when Lord Jove only stared at him expectantly, he added, "My Lord."

Lord Jove's eyes stayed fixed on Theon's as he held out a hand to Tessa. "You understand you are only prolonging the inevitable, do you not?"

Knowing that if Theon couldn't defy the Achaz Lord, she certainly couldn't either, she hesitantly placed her hand in his. Her fair skin was stark against the golden tan of his, and his other hand came up and grasped the band around her wrist. She gasped at the sting against her skin, and then she was nearly dropping to her knees in relief as he slid the band free.

Light flared at her fingertips, all of her magic rushing to the point of freedom.

"What are you—" Theon started, reaching as if to pull her away from the Achaz Lord, but the Lord's power was flaring too. His power worked to counteract the bit of a reprieve he was granting her. Her power still thrashed, unable to fully be free with the other band in place. But this… This was more than enough to ease all the maddening feelings that had been building.

She stumbled forward as her power turned from a flare to a crackle she could feel in her bones, and Lord Jove moved a steadying hand to her elbow, finally meeting her gaze. "You are only prolonging the inevitable," he repeated to Theon. "She is not meant to be with you."

"You may be a Lord of this realm, but even you cannot dictate fate," Theon retorted, and Tessa watched him curl his hands into fists while shadows danced along his knuckles. Luka was at his side in the next breath, a hand on his shoulder, attempting to quell the darkness stirring in his Ward's soul.

But Lord Jove's lips twitched at the words. "Wise words," he replied. "Words I hope you find solace in when Fate takes what is hers." His eyes never left Tessa's while he slid the band back into place, trapping her power once more. He released her hand, finally returning his attention to Theon. "But for the sake of clarity, should you learn she is indeed a Legacy and the Source bond cannot be severed another way, it is not an

Achaz Legacy whose life will pay that price. That is the cost of this kindness we've extended to you."

# 4
## TESSA

Tessa stood near a window, staring at the greying edge of the Shade Plains in the distance as she tugged the sides of Theon's suit jacket tighter around herself. They were at the Arius manor house just outside the Acropolis. She had come to realize that the manor estates were situated in their kingdoms surrounding the central sacred city. It was why the Lords and Ladies preferred the manors instead of the townhouses minutes from the Pantheon.

As soon as the decision had been announced, the ruling families had dispersed, and Valter had made it clear he expected them to meet him here to discuss the matter further. Axel had separated from them to pick up Kat from the Pantheon and would meet up with them later tonight, and Luka and Theon had gone back and forth the entire drive about what this meant for the coming months. Or rather, Theon had ranted, and Luka had listened, making a few statements here and there.

When they'd reached the manor house, Theon had helped her from the backseat and said, "As soon as this is dealt with, we'll go to the training arenas."

She had only nodded.

"I need you to say something, beautiful," he'd said, a hand cupping her cheek.

She supposed his concern was valid. She hadn't spoken much since returning from vomiting.

"I'm cold," was all she'd said, wrapping her arms tightly around herself, and that was how she'd ended up with his suit coat draped around her shoulders.

"Here."

Tessa turned to find Theon extending a glass of water to her. She nodded as she took the glass, swallowing a small sip before letting the glass dangle from her fingertips.

"This is good, Tessa," Theon said. "It gives us time. Not as much time as I would have liked, but time to figure out a plan."

She nodded again.

Time.

Theon had been given a deadline, but so had she.

The doors banging open made them all spin to the entry where Valter was striding into the study, Eviana a step behind him as always. Her red-brown hair hung loosely around her shoulders in waves, and her turquoise eyes slid over all of them. They lingered on Tessa for a moment, and Theon clearly noticed since he slid a step closer as though to block Tessa from view.

No one spoke while Valter settled into a wingback chair near the unlit hearth, taking a tumbler of liquor from Eviana when she brought it to him. Then the Fae retreated to a plush chair nearby, waiting until her Master needed her again.

"Would you consider today a success, Theon?" Valter asked after taking a deep drink, then proceeding to study the liquid in his glass.

"It was not ideal," Theon answered, edging further in front of Tessa until he was standing completely in front of her.

"Not ideal?" Valter repeated.

"You were in the room for the conversation about the final decision, not me," Theon answered mildly. "You had more say in this outcome than I did."

Valter slowly lifted his gaze to Theon, and Tessa found herself reaching up and curling her fingers into the back of Theon's shirt. She had no idea why. Maybe it was the bond, something instinctual. Theon didn't react; she could only assume that was to keep his father from suspecting anything.

"I meant no disrespect," Theon continued. "But what was said to make these contingencies agreeable to you?"

"Agreeable to me?" Valter sneered, sucking down the rest of his drink. "You know damn well I did not find these terms agreeable."

"The others posed valid arguments," Luka cut in, and Tessa tilted her head as she watched him several feet away.

His feet were planted in the same defensive stance he constantly made her stand in at training. His arms hung loose at his sides, and he'd loosened his tie. He was ready to defend Theon at a moment's notice, and why wouldn't he be? He was Theon's Guardian, a bond that would drive him to protect Theon at all costs. A bond that was somehow worked into the Source Marks and would eventually require her to do the same.

"What is to stop future heirs from forcing Legacy to be their Sources if this is allowed to stand?" Luka continued.

"I am not discounting the concerns," Valter snapped. "I simply wished for them to allow this to remain until we found a way to sever the Source bond that didn't require death in some manner."

"Lord Jove made it perfectly clear whose death would be required in this matter," Theon said.

"If Rordan tries to end your life, Devram will no longer know the fragile peace it currently possesses," Valter said.

The room fell silent, and all Tessa could think was that the male before them wouldn't really start a war over this? Over Theon?

No. Ultimately, the war would be over *her*.

And it wouldn't be the Legacy in this room who would pay the ultimate price. It would be the Fae forced to fight in their kingdom's legions. It would be the lower Legacy shoved into sacrifice. It would be the mortals who simply existed in this godforsaken realm.

All those innocent lives lost would be because of her.

Just like Pen had been.

And suddenly, for the very first time in all of this, she found herself on the same side as Theon. Not because she was forced to be, but because their desired outcomes aligned in some twisted way.

Finally, Theon broke the silence as Eviana rose to refill Valter's glass. "We will not need to worry about that. We were given time. Not as much as I would have liked, but time nonetheless. We will figure out Tessa's lineage. We will figure out how to navigate this Source bond. No one's death will be required."

"And she will stay bound to our kingdom," Valter added, and Tessa couldn't help the wince, glad Theon's frame was still hiding her from the Lord's view. She reached behind her, setting her water glass on the windowsill.

"Yes, of course, Father," Theon answered.

"You will not only figure out what her bloodline is, but you will report it to me first."

"You want me to go against the entirety of the ruling families?"

"*This* is where your loyalty lies, Theon. *This* is your kingdom."

"I am not denying that."

"And if you learn she is, in fact, a Legacy," Valter continued, "you will discreetly figure out a way to end the Source bond in a way that does not require death."

"If we are not tied together by a bond, it will only give Lord Jove more grounds to have her removed to Achaz Kingdom, especially if she is found to be an Achaz Legacy," Theon argued.

There would clearly be no asking her what she wanted in this room like there had been at the Tribunal hearing.

"I am aware, Theon," his father replied in annoyance. "Which is why the moment the Source bond is severed, she will be bound in a Match union."

"Match ceremonies cannot be performed during Selection years," Theon shot back, clearly working to control his temper, and clearly failing as Tessa watched darkness dance along his skin and curl around his arched ears.

"I'm sure you can find a way around that. You are, after all, adept at finding loopholes," Valter answered coldly, and Tessa could only assume he was referencing the Guardian bond between Luka and Theon that was supposed to have been between Luka and Valter.

"Fine. Done," Theon retorted. "The Source bond will be severed, and a Match ceremony performed—"

"Between her and Luka," Valter interrupted.

"What?"

It wasn't Theon who spluttered the response, but Luka. Tessa looked over to find clear shock on the dragon's face as he stared back at the Arius Lord. Before her, Theon was rigid, and that darkness was swirling, tendrils reaching for her. Her hand was still curled into the back of his shirt, and she released it, running her fingertips along his spine before dragging them through the darkness as though it was a fine mist. The shadows shuddered around her before crawling along her fingers and up her hand to her wrist, and then recoiling from the band they encountered.

She couldn't blame them for that.

"Whatever power she possesses, it is clearly strong," Valter was saying. "I cannot risk it overcoming the Arius power in our own blood-line by Matching her with Axel."

*Axel?*

Tessa's nose scrunched at the mere idea of such a thing.

"So you wish to overcome *Sargon* power?" Theon demanded. "When Luka is the only Sargon Legacy in the realm? Shouldn't we be keeping his power prominent?"

Valter crossed one leg over the other, sipping at his drink again, visibly calmer than he'd been before. "That's exactly what I am doing. The female may be powerful, but Luka is a closer descendant of Sargon than we are of Arius, certainly more than she is from whatever god or goddess she descends from, including Achaz. Her power will only serve to strengthen the Sargon gifts of the offspring they would produce."

Tessa could swear Theon stumbled a bit at the mention of children.

"Unless you would prefer me to hand her over to someone else?" Valter added, a brow arching in a knowing look. "The two of you share everything else. Certainly this wouldn't have to be any different as long as the babes produced are Luka's."

*Share everything else?*

Tessa's fingers paused their twirling of the shadows as she glanced at Luka. She'd certainly had her own experiences with *sharing*, but consider her interest suddenly peaked. Not that she wanted to share *them*. If it were up to her, she wouldn't have any of them, but—

The Lord's next words pulled her from all thoughts she was currently entertaining.

"It isn't as if we can Match her with you anyway. You already have a Match contract signed in blood."

"What?"

This time it was her spluttering and peering incredulously around Theon.

"Hush, Tessa," Theon hissed, not even bothering to glance back at her with the order.

But she saw Valter's face. Saw the look of satisfaction at being the one to reveal this to her. Saw the cruel smile, the glint in his hateful eyes. Saw the way he was controlling everyone in this room with moves and countermoves.

Saw exactly where Theon had learned it from.

"Get this Source bond severed, and we'll get a new bond sorted with the fire Fae," Valter continued. "I suggest you begin spending time with her so the bond has something to build on to avoid the complications experienced this time."

"You are going to take Katya as a Source?" Tessa blurted.

When had all of this been planned and decided? Theon now had a Match and a new Source all lined up? And she was just to be...passed around to wherever it was most convenient to have her?

To *share* her?

To produce children?

How was this any different from being sent to serve the Sirana bloodline in the Achaz Kingdom?

"Tessa," Theon hissed in warning again.

There was a hand at her elbow, and she was jerking away from Luka's touch because it wasn't Theon, and the bond was having a fit at all the new information, and these fucking bands were driving her half-mad, and—

There were hands on her face, tilting it up to look into emerald irises. "I need you to breathe, Tessa. Take a breath. Now."

The command settled in her soul, and she sucked in a sharp breath.

"I'm sorry," she whispered, because surely this display would have consequences with his father. "I didn't mean—"

"Another breath," Theon demanded.

She nodded, taking in two more to calm whatever this was. Although, the calming was likely due more to his touch than the actual act of breathing.

Theon held her gaze a moment longer before releasing her and turning back to his father. "Is there anything else we need to discuss at the moment?"

"Do not fuck this up, Theon," Valter warned, pushing to his feet and stalking over to them. "I've spent too many decades preparing for this to let your female fuck it all up."

Luka shifted, coming to stand beside Theon and adding an extra body between her and the Arius Lord.

"I understand," Theon said gruffly.

"To make sure you do, it is not death that will be a consequence for failure. I can, after all, give her to others, even if she is Matched with Luka."

"I said I understand," Theon snapped, and then he was kneeling with a grunt and darkness was engulfing them. Luka was shoving Tessa back before black flames were flaring as vines worked to ensnare him.

When the shadows had receded, she found Luka had subdued Eviana, but Theon had…a dagger sticking out of his side.

Tessa was blinking hard, trying to process what she was seeing, and she stumbled back farther as Theon struggled to his feet, pulling out the dagger with another sharp hiss between his teeth. The blade disappeared in a swirl of shadows. He pressed a hand to his side, but it didn't keep the blood from seeping between his fingers.

"Anything else, Father?" Theon bit out.

"That reminder of expectations should be sufficient for now," Valter answered, turning his back on them and moving to the desk across the room.

Eviana followed, and Luka was at Theon's side, trying to inspect the wound.

"It's fine," Theon muttered. "We'll take care of it at the training arena. Tessa needs those bands off for a while."

The male had just been stabbed, and he was thinking of her?

"You will not be going to the training arenas," Valter called out, his back still turned to them.

Theon's jaw visibly clenched, and Tessa, once again, didn't know what the fuck to do.

It took several seconds before Theon managed to ground out, "Is there a reason why?"

"I don't want the full extent of her gifts known until it can no longer be avoided. A training arena is too public of a place. Anyone can see too many things," Valter answered, finally turning back to them. "Is that going to be a problem?"

Tessa could see it. The desire to argue with his father. The fury he was biting back. The helplessness he was pushing down. She could see it because she knew the feelings so godsdamn well.

She could see it because she was feeling them all now. The desire to argue about Kat becoming Theon's Source. The fury at the idea of being passed around to be used. The helplessness of these fucking bands having to stay in place for only-the-gods-knew how long.

"Of course not," Theon finally said with a bow of his head.

He turned, striding from the room.

"Come, Tessa," Luka said, jerking his chin to the door.

She said nothing as she moved to Luka's side, following him from the room as her magic screamed as loudly as her soul.

# 5

## AXEL

"Thank Arius," Axel muttered, swiping one of the chilled bottles of blood from the counter.

Most Legacy preferred to sip it from a glass like a fine wine. His mother certainly did. But he was desperate enough to drink several swallows directly from the bottle.

Most Legacy were also able to make their weekly ration of Fae blood last the entire week. He would be lucky if this bottle lasted three days.

Eyeing the other two bottles that had just been delivered, he took another drink of his own, sighing as he felt his power reserves swell. He knew Theon and Luka would ration theirs meticulously for the week. Partly because it was the responsible thing to do, but also because if Axel needed more, they would give him some of theirs without a second thought.

He'd been pacing near the front door waiting for the delivery. The day had been exhausting. He'd already been fighting off the feelings of need for two days, and there was a Fae in his room one floor up that was far too tempting. It was why he'd been sleeping in Luka's room, if he slept at all. Mostly, he was keeping busy in the shadows of the Acropolis well into the night.

Sighing, he grabbed the other bottles and took them to the pantry. Pressing a palm to the wall near the wine cellar door, wards hummed as a secret panel disappeared, revealing a spelled compartment designed to keep the Fae blood at the perfect temperature. He slid the bottles in, the compartment sealing itself again as he heard the front door open.

He glanced at his watch. It was too early for the others to be back. There was no way they'd had a meeting with their father and taken Tessa to the training arenas already, but those were soft, feminine footfalls, and that was Luka's low rumble of a voice.

Axel stepped from the pantry as Tessa came into the kitchen, her heels dangling from her fingers and Theon's suit coat wrapped around her shoulders. Her lips were set in a thin line, and she looked as tired as he felt.

"Hey, baby doll. How are you?" he greeted, watching her carefully. He hadn't had a chance to talk with her much after the hearing. His father had demanded a meeting immediately, and Axel had needed to go collect Katya from the Pantheon.

"Your father stabbed your brother," she said simply, dropping the shoes with a soft clunk onto the floor near the kitchen island.

"For fuck's sake," Axel cursed, straightening as Luka and Theon entered the kitchen.

His brother was indeed clutching his side, dried blood all along his fingers and hand. He gritted his teeth as he sank onto one of the island stools, his gaze forever fixed on Tessa, who was now standing at the window with her back to them. There had been a steady drizzle of light rain since they left the Tribunal, and to be honest, that alone should have told Axel how Tessa was feeling about all of this.

In the days following the Emerging Ceremony, Theon had told him and Luka of his theory that Tessa somehow had influence over the weather. Axel had told him it was just another one of his unconventional theories, but not after Theon had laid out all the facts. How every time she raged, it stormed. How it had rained incessantly at Arius House where it rarely rained in the spring, let alone late summer. How the sun had shown itself when the four of them had played a makeshift game of Chaosphere one afternoon and Tessa had actually laughed. By the end, Theon had managed to convince him except for one thing: there was no known being that could control the weather. There was Rai, the god of the seasons, but not even their Legacy could control the day-to-day weather, and not with their emotions.

The kitchen was silent as Luka poured four shots of liquor before going to retrieve a bottle of blood Axel had just put away. Theon downed the shot before taking a drink from the blood bottle, then let out a groan of discomfort as he shifted on the stool.

"Is anyone going to tell me what the fuck happened?" Axel finally asked, unable to take the ringing silence any longer.

"I already did," Tessa said, still staring out the window.

"While my father is certainly a bastard, he usually has some convoluted reason for stabbing us," Axel said.

That had Tessa turning to face him. "He does it often?"

Axel shrugged, reaching for his own shot of liquor. "Often enough." His gaze slid to his brother. "Nightstone dagger?"

Theon gave a sharp nod.

"You keep it?" Axel asked before knocking back his shot.

"Added it to the collection," Theon replied grimly.

Axel nodded again.

"Did you know Theon signed a Match contract?" Tessa suddenly asked.

"You told her?" Axel asked incredulously, wide eyes on Theon.

Tessa scoffed. "Of course he didn't tell me. Theon never tells me anything. No one does."

Theon sighed audibly. "Tessa, I—"

"But it's fine," Tessa interrupted casually, "because I'm going to be Luka's Match."

"What the actual fuck?" Axel asked, turning to Luka.

The male was leaning back against the counter, and he dragged a hand down his face. "That is, indeed, Valter's plan."

"But… How? When?… What?" Axel sputtered, trying to wrap his mind around…any of what was just said.

"Theon's Source. Not Theon's Source. Luka's Match. Fae. Not Fae," Tessa started muttering, the suit coat slipping from her shoulders as she began pacing in front of the window. "Beginnings and Endings. Light and Dark. Fire and Shadows."

The males all exchanged looks as Tessa reached up and pulled her fingers through her hair, tugging lightly on the ends.

"She comes. He comes. Who will be left standing when Chaos comes to call?" she continued to murmur as she twisted her hair in her hands.

"She needs those bands off her wrists for a while," Luka said in a low voice. "All that power being trapped now that it's been set free with a Mark? It's going to drive her mad."

"*Going to?*" Axel said with another pointed look at the female whose mutterings were indecipherable now. He could only catch small phrases.

"*...flames in her eyes...more than...she'll come...too late...*"

"I thought you were going to take her to the training arenas," Axel said tightly.

"Father forbade it," Theon said, shifting gingerly again. A wound made with nightstone would take longer to heal, even with additional Fae blood. Theon had only taken one drink; Axel had guiltily taken another as well.

"Is that how you got stabbed?" Axel asked.

"No. I got stabbed after Father informed us of his plans to Match her and Luka and force me to take Katya as a new Source," Theon bit back, motioning to Luka to pour him another shot. "Tessa, do you want something to drink?"

"No," she replied, not pausing in her pacing and immediately returning to her muttering. "It will all be over soon he says, but he's a liar just like the rest of them." Then she stopped and turned to face them. "You're all liars," she said louder.

"According to you, you're an excellent liar, so I guess you fit right in," Theon retorted, sounding exhausted as he got to his feet. "Come, Tessa. Let's go for a walk."

"You can hardly stand," she said, eyes dropping to his wound. "And you need a new shirt. May I go and change?"

Axel could hardly concentrate on what was being said around him. Theon's words kept ringing in his ears.

Katya was going to replace Tessa as his Source?

That wasn't possible, but even if it was, he wouldn't take a new Source, right? Theon was obsessed with Tessa. Match contract or no, there was no doubt which female actually mattered to him. And even if he found a way to sever the Source bond with Tessa, he wouldn't add yet another person to this mess, let alone create a new bond, would he?

"You done with this?" Luka asked, startling Axel from his thoughts.

He was holding the bottle of Fae blood in his hand.

"Uh, yeah," Axel said, rubbing at the back of his neck. "Where'd they go?" he asked, realizing Tessa and Theon were gone.

"Upstairs," Luka said, heading for the pantry.

"Anything else I need to know about the meeting?"

"I think they covered it."

Axel waited until he returned before he said, "Theon has a plan, though, right? He's not going to… You and Tessa won't be—"

"Of course not," Luka cut in, pulling a hair band from his pocket and gathering his hair into a small ponytail.

"You going flying?" Axel asked.

"Yeah," he answered, already working the buttons on his shirt. Now that his lineage had been discovered, Luka had a little more freedom, but he was still cautious when it came to being seen flying. He usually waited until dark to stretch his wings. "But I need my room tonight," Luka added.

"For what?"

"Tessa came looking for me last night."

Axel's brows rose. "For you?"

"The bands are becoming an issue."

"And she came looking for you?"

Luka shrugged his shirt off, tossing it over the back of a chair with his tie. "I guess."

"Shouldn't you be encouraging her to go to Theon for this kind of stuff?" Axel ventured.

"I think we need her to talk to one of us, and if we try to force her back to Theon right now, she'll shut us all out more than she already does," Luka answered. "Too much depends on her. It always has."

"Right," Axel said, his eyes narrowing.

Luka had been different with Tessa from the very beginning. He'd avoided Theon's rooms as much as possible, trying to give them space and encouraging Tessa to bond with Theon. But there were other things Axel had noticed and brushed off. There were the perplexed looks when Luka thought no one was looking, like he was trying to work something out, but they were all trying to work out Tessa and the Source bond. There was the way his eyes lingered when Tessa wore tight dresses, but that was because… Well, he was a male attracted to females, and Tessa was a female.

"Quit looking at me like that," Luka said, bending down to grab the shoes he'd slipped off.

"All I'm saying is—"

"What are you going to do about Katya?" Luka interrupted.

Axel blinked. "What do you mean?"

"She's been staying in your room. You've been staying in mine. Are you going to keep her in there with you tonight?"

"I'll just…sleep in the lounge."

"The fuck you will. Not with Ford lurking around and reporting everything back to your father. If he finds out you slept in the lounge so a Fae could have your bed, you'll be snapping her neck next."

Something inside Axel recoiled at the thought. At the memory of doing that to Pen. At the idea of doing that to *her*.

"I'll figure it out. You can have your room back. Although I'm sure I messed up your nest of blankets and pillows," Axel said, pouring himself another shot.

"Ford does that every fucking day when he goes in there and *cleans*," Luka grumbled. "Pen knew to leave it alone."

"Where do you even go to nest here? Did you find a secret cave in the nonexistent mountains surrounding the Acropolis?"

"Fuck off," Luka growled.

"Or do you just perch on the roof? Do you have a nest up there?"

Luka said nothing else, just held up his middle finger over his shoulder as he left the kitchen.

Axel huffed a laugh, but it died in his throat as he knocked back the shot of alcohol. What was he going to do with Katya tonight? He'd been avoiding her ever since he'd gone back to get her after the Emerging Ceremony. Limping and bloody, he'd returned to that warded room he'd left Kat in before going to help Tessa. She'd been standing in almost the same spot he'd left her, but he'd been so injured and so weak. It had taken every ounce of self-control not to take from her because her blood could have fixed everything.

Instead, he'd roughly told her to come with him, hadn't said a word the entire way to the townhouse, and had dumped her in his room before going to the Arius manor house where Luka had helped him clean up. They'd all had fresh Fae blood waiting for them, and Axel knew the cost of that favor was still yet to be paid.

And other than escorting Katya to and from the townhouse each day, Axel hadn't spoken to her. He'd seen her, of course. He'd watched some of her training and taken longer paths to his destinations to catch glimpses of her. He always knew when she was nearby, that damn scent of hers calling to him—jasmine and citrus and something smoky with underlying spices—but being around her made him feel… He didn't know how to describe it, but there was too much at stake and too much other shit to figure out right now. This odd feeling was at the bottom of a very long list.

Taking the stairs two at a time, Axel shoved through his door when he reached the second floor. Kicking it closed behind him, he yanked his unknotted tie from his neck, tossing it off to the side. Then he went still at what stood before him.

Katya was motionless, clearly surprised at him being here. Her amber eyes were wide. Her black, curly hair looked like it had been braided back in a haste, several curls falling free around her face. She was wearing the same pants and long-sleeve shirt they wore for their element training. Close fitting yet still loose enough to move, the outfit hugged all those curves that taunted him every time he looked at her.

In one hand, she held an open book. Her other hand was wrapped around the handle of…a spoon? A spoon that was still between her lips. There was classical music playing softly. She must have figured out his music system.

She still hadn't moved, and Axel supposed he couldn't blame her. He was never here at night, and she had clearly become somewhat comfortable in the space.

Something warmed in his chest at the thought of her feeling safe enough to relax in *his* room, and it had the corner of his mouth tilting up as he started to unbutton the cuffs of his shirt sleeves. His eyes stayed fixed on hers when he said, "Hello, kitten."

The sound of his voice seemed to snap her out of her shock. She pulled the spoon from her mouth, the book snapping closed, and, gods, she looked like she was about to kneel.

"Don't do that," he said in a rush, stepping further into the room. Then his gaze landed on an open jar on the side table near the sofa. "Are you…eating peanut butter with a spoon?"

Katya slowly set the book and spoon on the same end table, her eyes downcast, but Axel could see the faint blush even on her dark skin when she said, "Yes, my Lord."

"Out of the jar?"

"I apologize—"

"Don't apologize," he said.

Her mouth snapped shut, and she clasped her hands in front of her, waiting.

Axel inexplicably wanted to throw something.

"I have to stay in here tonight," he said, toeing off his shoes and kicking one off to the left and the other across the room. That Ford fucker could clean up the mess he left behind.

Her head tilted curiously to the side. "I thought this was your room?"

"It is." She only nodded, but Axel could practically see her biting her tongue on her questions. "You can speak freely here, Kat."

Still she didn't speak again, and Axel held in his sigh. Tessa couldn't control her mouth, and he couldn't get Katya to speak.

"Enjoy your peanut butter," he murmured, moving past her to finish undressing in the bathroom. He needed to shower, and admittedly, he was looking forward to sleeping in his own room for the first time in days.

"Wait," she called as he started to shut the bathroom door.

"Yes?" He paused at the button he was working through the hole.

"What am I…" She cleared her throat, shifting on her feet. She was still wearing the training boots too. "What do you want me to do?"

"Whatever you were doing before I came in here," he answered. Then glancing at the boots again, he added, "Although if you want to get more comfortable, you can."

She nodded, something flickering across her features. But Axel was more than ready for his shower, so he said nothing else, closing the door with a click.

He lingered in the shower, letting the hot water soothe tense muscles and relishing in the buzz of full power reserves. This would all work out. Theon would figure out Tessa's lineage. Surely Cienna would have ideas as long as she was in a helpful mood when they went to visit in a week's time.

Axel was feeling far more relaxed when he stepped from the bathroom, a towel wrapped around his narrow hips and steam billowing out around him. He was starting to mentally go through his agenda for tomorrow as he made his way to the walk-in closet, and then his bare feet stilled against the carpet.

Katya was standing there wearing nothing. Her head was bowed, hands clasped, and his mouth completely dried out because those were full breasts and hips perfect for digging fingers into. Those were soft curves, and suddenly it was visions of those lips being wrapped around something other than a spoonful of peanut butter and *fuck*.

"What are you doing, Katya?" His voice was low and strained even to his own ears, and he was painfully aware of his cock thickening beneath only a godsdamn towel.

She looked up, confusion evident in her eyes. "You aren't going to… This isn't what you wanted?"

"Why would you think I asked this of you?"

"You told me to get comfortable."

"And you thought this was what I meant?"

"It's not?"

"No, Katya, and I'm not sure why—"

Except he did know why. He knew exactly why, and the fury that surged through his blood had him clamping down on power and any arousal immediately disappearing.

Without another word, he crossed the room to the sofa and grabbed a throw blanket, wrapping it around her shoulders. She gripped it between her fingers, covering her nakedness and watching him with wary eyes.

"Stay here. Let me get dressed. I'll be right back," Axel said, and she nodded.

He quickly slipped on a pair of loose pants. Normally he'd lounge around shirtless, but he slipped on a short-sleeved shirt. He went to grab something for Kat to wear, but he didn't know where she kept her clothing. There was nothing in the closet that he could see.

Going back to the bedroom, he asked, "Where are your clothes? I'll grab them, and you can get dressed."

"That's all right," she said, moving to retrieve a pile of folded clothing from a chair. It was the same training clothes she'd been wearing when he came into the room.

"Don't you want something else? That's what I meant by 'more comfortable' clothing…"

"My other set is being laundered."

"Your other… Katya, do you have other clothing besides these two sets of training clothes?"

"The dress I wore for the Emerging Ceremony," she answered. "Would you like me to wear that?"

He really was a rude fuck, just like he'd told her while he drew the markings on her wrist that night.

Axel swiped a hand down his face. "Do you have clothing and other personal items at the Fae dorms?"

"Yes."

"I will have those items delivered here tomorrow."

"All right."

"Do you want something to eat? You know, other than peanut butter. Have you been eating?"

She shifted again, adjusting her hold on the blanket. "I eat at the Pantheon."

"Ford doesn't give you dinner here?" Axel demanded.

Katya was quiet for a moment, clearly debating what to say. Finally, she said, "I'm sorry. I do not understand why you are upset."

*She didn't understand why he was upset?*

"I'm upset because you don't have clothing here," he said.

"But I *do* have clothing here."

"Two sets of training clothes hardly counts as clothing," Axel scoffed.

Her brows creased. "So you are upset about the amount of clothing I have here? That doesn't make sense."

"By the gods," he muttered, stalking back into the walk-in closet and grabbing the same kind of long-sleeve shirt Theon always gave to Tessa and the smallest pair of pants he could find. He'd considered going to get some of Tessa's clothing, but Kat had those delightful soft curves that Tessa didn't. His own clothing would have to do until hers were delivered tomorrow.

He took the items back to Kat, sending her into the bathroom to get dressed, and while she was in there, he called Ford and got his ass out of bed, ordering him to prepare a variety of food and bring it to his room.

When he hung up the phone, he turned to find Katya standing in the same spot, hands clasped and waiting, and Axel pushed out a heavy breath. "We need to discuss some things."

Still she stood and waited.

"Sit down, Kat."

She moved immediately, lowering primly onto the edge of the sofa, and Axel fisted his hand at his side.

"Tell me about the Falein Estate."

Her head snapped in his direction. "What?"

"I want to know about it."

"Why?"

"Call it curiosity," Axel said, dropping onto the other end of the sofa.

"It doesn't make sense."

"Then let me ask you questions about it."

She nodded slowly, stray curls falling forward.

"I understand you were taught to behave a certain way in the presence of Legacy." She nodded. "Like not speaking unless asked a direct question." She remained silent. "And being instructed to…service Legacy."

Katya shifted. It was a small movement, but it was there. A mere motion of repositioning herself; nothing that told him she was uncomfortable with what he was saying. And gods, he hated that this was so *normal* for her. He hated that she simply accepted this was her role in life. Speak when spoken to. Eat when given food. Drop to your knees when commanded. Spread your legs when told.

"Did you ever leave the Falein Estate? Before you went to the Celeste Estate, I mean," he clarified.

"At times, yes."

"Where did you go?"

"Where I was told to go."

He choked down his frustration. This was like talking in circles. After the Emerging Ceremony, she'd been more vocal, asked more questions. Maybe she'd just been shocked at being claimed so early.

Or maybe he'd just irritated her enough.

There was a knock on the door, and Katya moved to rise, but Axel said, "No. I'll get it."

Her brow creased at the command, but Axel was already striding for the door, pulling it open to find Ford with a tray of food.

"The coffee table," was all Axel said, turning his back on him and going back to the sofa. And as Ford was leaving the room after depositing the tray, Axel added, "So we are clear, I expect food prepared for Katya in the evenings from now on. And not shit food like sandwiches. Proper food. If we are here, she will dine with us."

The Fae gave a curt nod, and Axel knew he was already making a note to mention this to his father.

"Eat," Axel said when the door clicked shut.

Kat looked at the food, then back at him. "You're not eating?"

"I had dinner. You've had peanut butter."

"I *like* peanut butter," she admonished, and there it was. Annoyance creeping into her tone.

Axel hummed, propping his head back on his hand so he could hide his smirk behind his thumb. "Is it your favorite food?"

"You have an obsession with food," she muttered, tentatively reaching for a carrot stick.

"If you mean I have an obsession with making sure a person who is spending hours a day training with their magic element is eating enough to properly refuel their power reserves, then yes, I have an obsession with that," he retorted.

Katya paused, the carrot halfway to her mouth. "That makes sense."

"I'm a sensible person," he said with a wink.

She hummed something that was almost a laugh, but then she took a bite of the carrot instead.

"All this food and you choose carrots," Axel said, reaching for a small plate of raw fish wrapped in rice. He held it out to her. "Eat something with protein."

She stared at it a moment before dragging incredulous eyes back to him. "Is this what you were talking about at the Emerging Ceremony?"

"Yep," he answered, swiping up a roll and popping it in his mouth.

Katya shook her head, the disgust clear on her face. "Eggs have protein," she said, reaching for one of the already peeled hard-boiled eggs on the tray.

"You're not even going to try it?" he pressed once he'd swallowed his bite.

"I'll stick with my peanut butter, thanks," she volleyed back.

"Someday I'm going to get you to try it, kitten," he sighed, reaching for another roll.

"Only if you order me to," she scoffed.

Instead of snatching up the roll, Axel leaned over, taking her chin between his thumb and forefinger. Startled eyes peered up at him from beneath thick lashes. "I'm never going to *force* you to try it."

Their eyes held for a long moment before she whispered, "Okay."

Axel released her chin, grabbing another roll off the plate before he placed it back on the coffee table. Katya finished her egg, then went back to her carrots.

"Classical music, huh?" Axel finally said to break the awkward silence that had settled between them.

"You don't like it?"

Axel shrugged. "It's fine enough, I suppose."

"It was always played in the libraries and archives back home. Or what was… The Falein Kingdom," she finally finished.

"In the libraries? I thought those were supposed to be all quiet and shit."

"The music drowned out the sounds of the 'other shit' happening, so it is comforting in its own way," she said shortly, reaching for another carrot.

Axel was quiet for a long moment before he said, "The classical music is lovely, Kat."

She nodded, and they sat in silence a little longer before Katya said, "Can I ask you something?"

"Of course."

"So you will not make me... I mean, I'm not resisting. If you told me to, I would, and I would be fine with it. And I know what is expected of me, and I'm just trying to make sense of it all because—"

"Katya."

It was just her name, but it silenced her fumbling of words, and she met his gaze, worrying her bottom lip.

And the thing was, he couldn't promise her it wouldn't happen here, in this house or in the Arius Kingdom. Axel couldn't promise her his father wouldn't demand she do the very thing she was asking him about, especially when he was planning to force Theon to take her as his replacement Source. He couldn't promise her she wouldn't be forced to suck a cock or let herself be fucked because he wasn't in any position to challenge his father and win. He wasn't the one who would bring some sense of twisted dignity back to their kingdom. That was Theon's fate. Always had been. That was what they'd been working so tirelessly toward for years now. It was why Theon was the way he was, single-mindedly focused on their goals. So much depended on Theon, but not so much on Axel. He was just the spare. His father's back-up plan and the one who did the behind the scenes dirty work.

So he couldn't promise her that none of that would happen here, but he could promise her something else.

"In this space, between you and me, that will never be demanded of you. Only a few select people can demand such a thing from you right now, and I will never be one of them," Axel said.

Katya was quiet, and he watched her throat bob once. Twice. Before she said, "Thank you, my Lord."

"You can call me Axel, Katya. You're smart enough to know when it would be ill-advised to do so."

"It's still inappropriate, my Lord."

He arched a brow, wanting more than anything to reach over and touch her, but he didn't think she'd appreciate being touched in this moment. "More inappropriate than eating directly from a peanut butter jar?"

Kat laughed. A genuine laugh that was better than any music he'd ever listened to.

"Fair enough...Axel."

Finally.

Finally, she'd said his name, and it was better than he'd imagined it would be coming from her lips. But why? Why did he care so godsdamn much?

They sat there sharing idle chitchat for another hour, Kat eating and relaxing more and more with each passing minute as she found he hadn't been lying. That he was perfectly content to sit here and visit while she ate food.

She'd shifted, now sitting cross-legged on the sofa so she was facing him. His body was angled towards hers when he asked, "What were you reading when I walked in here?"

Her eyes brightened. "A book your brother gave me."

Axel's jaw nearly dropped. "Theon gave you a book?"

"You didn't know?"

Axel shook his head. "What is it about?"

"Mostly history," she answered. "He said you told him I'd been raised in the Falein Kingdom. He knew that learning the Lost Language is required by all who live there."

"Even the Fae?"

"It was part of our studies at the Estate."

Now that she mentioned it, Theon was partial to the Fae from that kingdom when they were narrowing down choices. This made sense with his never-ending theories, but when had Theon spoken to Kat without him knowing?

Axel cleared his throat, rubbing his chest at the feeling settling there. "We should probably get some rest. Especially you, with all that training you've been doing. Leave the food," he added when Kat reached for the various plates spread across the coffee table. "It'll give Ford something to do tomorrow."

He got up, pushing the table back to make more room. "I just need a pillow off the bed."

"I thought you said you needed to sleep in here tonight," Kat said, looking up at him from where she still sat on the sofa.

"I am. I'll sleep here; you'll sleep in the bed."

Her eyes went wide for what seemed like the hundredth time tonight. "I can't do that."

"You can't?"

"It's your bed."

Axel chuckled, sliding his hands into the pockets of his pants to keep himself from reaching out and sliding his fingers along her jaw. "Have you not been sleeping in it these past few days?"

"No," she answered, her curls bouncing as she shook her head.

It was his turn for his eyes to go wide. "Where have you been sleeping?"

"Right here. On the sofa."

"Why?"

"Because it's your bed," she repeated.

Axel didn't know what to say to that. "Just get in the bed, Katya."

"But you're a Legacy. I'm just a Fae."

"You aren't *just* anything," he snapped in annoyance, not sure where that had come from. He took a breath as she slipped back into the role he'd spent the last hour coaxing her out of. "I'm just saying you need a good night's rest more than I do. You're the one training with your power. Just like with needing to eat, you need the bed more."

She wouldn't look at him, but she shook her head in refusal.

"Fine. Sleep on the sofa. I'll sleep on the floor."

That had her head snapping up. "You can't sleep on the floor."

He shrugged, moving to the bed to grab a pillow. "I'm a Legacy and an heir. I can do almost anything I want."

"My Lord—"

"Axel," he interjected.

She sent him an unimpressed glare. "*Axel*, it does not make sense for you to sleep on the floor."

"What doesn't make sense is you sleeping on the sofa the past few days when there's been a perfectly fine bed right here. It isn't *logical*."

"You're...frustrating," she sputtered.

"But my arguments are more logical than yours," he said with a knowing smile.

"Fine. I'll sleep in the bed if you'll sleep on the sofa and not the floor," she snapped, and Axel had a feeling that if she didn't have the shirastone bands on her wrists keeping her power under control, flames would have flickered in her eyes.

"Deal, kitten," he said, retrieving the pillow he'd tossed to the floor.

And Axel knew without a doubt he'd be sleeping in his room every night from now on.

# 6

## THEON

"Where are we going?" Tessa asked with so much resignation in her voice that Theon immediately questioned whether they should even do this.

"Just put this on," he answered instead, handing a jacket to her. She was dressed in jeans and riding boots. It was the best he could do with the last minute decision to do this.

He'd mentioned the idea to Luka this afternoon. To his surprise, Luka had immediately agreed and said he'd take care of everything.

When Tessa had zipped the jacket, he held out a stocking hat too, and she narrowed her eyes at him.

"It's not that cold out, Theon."

"It is after sunset," he countered. When she just gave him a frank look, he added, "Put it on, or we're not going."

"You haven't even told me where we're going," she snapped.

"We're going," Luka said, striding into the foyer and moving straight to the door. "Don't make her wear it. If she wants to be difficult, she can be cold."

"I'm not being difficult," she spat. "And you're not even wearing a jacket."

He stopped beside her, giving her a mocking smile as he lifted a hand and black flames flared to life. Tessa rolled her eyes with a huff.

Reaching for the door handle, Luka said, "Bring the hat, Theon.

When she gets cold, be sure and make her say please before you give it to her."

"Why do you have to be such an ass all the godsdamn time?" Tessa grumbled, stomping after him.

"Why do you have to be so bratty all the godsdamn time?" Luka retorted.

"*You* told me to fight back," she bit back, following him out the door.

He did? When had Luka told her that? And why hadn't he told Theon about this conversation?

"And yet you're still not fighting back," Luka called over his shoulder, moving around the vehicle as Tessa wrenched open the back door. "You're still just whining."

"I am not whining," she groused.

"And I'm not an ass," he drawled sarcastically.

"I liked you better when you barely spoke to me," she grumbled under her breath as she crawled into the backseat.

But Luka heard her and said, "I liked it better when I didn't have to constantly deal with your attitude, but here we are. At least I can deal with you in a training room now."

"*Deal with me,*" Tessa scoffed under her breath.

Theon's phone pinged with a notification, and when he pulled it from his jacket pocket, he sighed at the email he'd just received. Tessa was already in some kind of mood tonight. He didn't particularly want to bring this up now and make it worse, but he was trying to be more open with her, not withhold as much information. He still didn't know just how much he could trust her, but she'd proven some loyalty yesterday at the hearing when she chose him. The least he could do was try to trust her more. Wasn't that their original bargain to begin with? Give and take?

Shoving a hand through his hair, he braced himself for the coming conversation. Luka was already sending him a look in the rearview mirror. It came with being inseparable their entire lives. They could pick up on the smallest shifts in moods and knew each other's tells.

Lightly clearing his throat, Theon said, "Tomorrow afternoon is your class with the other Sources, Tessa."

She'd been looking out the window, but her back straightened, shoulders tensing. It was a few seconds before she said, "All right."

"As for the other lessons, I'm working on finding someone else, but until then…"

"It's fine," she said tightly.

"If I had the time—"

"I said it's fine," she interrupted.

"Can you at least look at me while we discuss this?"

After another few seconds, she slowly turned to face him, those violet-grey eyes hard, betraying nothing of what she was thinking or feeling.

One more week.

That's all he could think as she stared back at him. One more week and she'd have the next Mark. It wouldn't be such a godsdamn guessing game as to what she was feeling. He'd be able to feel her emotions. He wanted to believe that would make this whole bond easier, but he was realizing nothing with Tessa would ever be easy.

Without thinking, he reached across the space between them. The tips of his fingers brushed along her jaw, and her eyes fluttered closed for the briefest of moments as she leaned into the touch.

"I promise I will find someone else. Just give me a little more time," he said softly.

Her eyes snapped back open, and she pulled away from him, turning back to the window. "Don't bother, Theon. I survived nearly two decades with her. I can survive this."

"Tessa—"

"Where are we going?" she interrupted. "Why are we leaving the Acropolis?"

"You need to take those bands off, little storm," Theon said gently.

She spun back to face him once more. "What?"

"I know those bands are making things difficult, Tessa. I know what happens when your power is trapped. I know that agony. They need to come off. Your power needs a chance to breathe," he answered.

"But your father said..." She trailed off, shaking her head. "No, Theon. No. I can't be responsible for another... We cannot make him angry again. *I* can't make him angry again."

"Luka and I have this all planned out, Tessa. He will not find out, and if he does—"

"Someone else will suffer to punish you!" she cried.

Clever. She'd pieced together how his father worked.

"And it will be because of *me*. Again. No. I don't want to do this," she went on.

She swallowed thickly, clear panic settling over her. He hadn't expected her to have this kind of reaction.

"I'm doing fine. I'll be fine," she went on, sounding like she was trying to convince herself just as much as she was trying to convince him.

"You're not fine, Tessa," Theon said, trying to sound soothing, but even he could hear the bite of frustration.

He was exhausted. He'd hardly slept since the Emerging Ceremony. Dealing with the fallout of his own failures, preparing for the Tribunal hearing, along with all his daily responsibilities, he was managing an hour or two a night, if that. Legacy didn't need sleep like a mortal did. They didn't even need it like the Fae did for refilling power reserves. That was what Legacy drank Fae blood for. Legacy could go a few days without sleep, but he was pushing the limit, especially after having to heal from a fucking nightstone stab wound.

He'd known what his actions would cost him yesterday. He'd known that showing weakness in front of his father would result in more pain, but he hadn't cared. When he'd heard the slight panic in Tessa's voice at the idea of him taking another Source, he hadn't cared. His father would view it as weak and pathetic and would attack that weakness immediately, and he did.

"My father said we couldn't take those bands off in the training arenas, where others could observe the extent of your gifts. We're going somewhere secluded," Theon said.

"You think you can outmaneuver your father?" Tessa demanded. "He *killed* someone, Theon. Someone you actually cared about—"

"No, Tessa. *Axel* killed someone. *I've* killed people. Luka has. My father rarely does the actual taking of life. He finds the message gets across clearer when the blood is on our hands," Theon cut in. She fell quiet, fiddling with the hem of her jacket. Theon took another breath before saying tightly, "I have been outmaneuvering my father for years now. He will not learn of this. We made sure of it."

She nodded mutely, looking back out the window, and Theon let her be, tipping his head back against the seat and letting his eyes fall closed for a few minutes.

"This needs to happen, Tessa," Luka said into the quiet vehicle. "You can't tell me those bands aren't driving you half-mad."

"I can handle it," she retorted.

"But you don't need to, little one. Not when we can help. We can help with this."

And the tone of his voice had Theon cracking his eyes open to peer at his best friend. He'd kept his distance from Tessa from the very beginning, constantly telling Theon that she wasn't the one for this and that he'd made the wrong choice. But ever since they'd started their training sessions, things had been changing. He pushed Tessa more. Theon knew he'd do that during training, but the taunting on the way to the vehicle was new. And so was the somewhat soft assurance he was giving her now. That same assurance Theon suspected he'd whispered to her during the hearing to help her keep control of her emotions. Assurance that obviously worked since she was seeking him out for help in the middle of the godsdamn night.

"He's right, Tessa," Theon said. "It'll be better to release some of that power before the next Mark is given. That will be unpleasant enough without the additional strain of your power being trapped."

"That Mark is a week away."

"We will do this every other day."

She nodded once, pressing her lips together. "Well, thank you, then."

"You don't have to thank me for taking care of you."

"I suppose not. I've already paid the cost for such basic decency many times over," she retorted.

"Did you not choose this just yesterday?" Theon demanded.

She clicked her tongue. "Don't kid yourself, Theon. Neither option was desirable."

"Then why choose this over the alternative?" he challenged, leaning towards her.

"It'll be easier to get what I want."

"And what is it you want, Tessa?"

Her hand landed on the seat between them, her fingertips brushing his outer thigh, and Theon ground his teeth at the small touch she granted him. She leaned forward, closing the distance between them so her breath danced across his lips when she answered, "Your salvation and destruction."

"You're already both, little storm," he said, his voice gravel and his gaze darting to her mouth when her tongue flicked along her lower lip.

Her other hand came up, a single nail tracing his jaw, and he could swear those violet rings around her eyes flared like lightning when she whispered, "Not yet, but I will be."

Then she was pulling away, back to staring out the window. Nothing else was said, which was fine, because Theon wasn't entirely sure how to feel about that entire exchange. He was sure that the lust that was flooding through him at her viciousness certainly *wasn't* what he should be feeling, but fuck. She'd left his balls aching since the one and only time they'd fucked. It was part of the reason he kept himself so gods-damn busy. He stayed up late to research, sure, but it also kept him out of their bed. Tessa had suddenly stopped caring if they fucked, and it clearly had done nothing to solidify this bond.

The vehicle slowed twenty minutes later, and they stepped out into the cool night air. Tessa immediately wrapped her arms around herself, and Theon stepped forward, pulling the stocking hat from his coat pocket, holding it out to her. She sighed, snatching it from his hand before tugging it down over her ears.

"The river?" she said dubiously, adjusting her hair beneath the hat. "This is where we won't be seen?"

"The opposite side of the Wynfell," Luka clarified, coming up beside them. "We're in Arius Kingdom."

"Arius Kingdom?" she repeated, spinning slowly to look around. The clouds were fewer tonight, the moonlight glinting off her golden strands that flowed out from beneath the hat.

Luka nodded. "As you know, the Wynfell runs through the Acropolis. It emerges on the other side where the Arius, Serafina, and Achaz King-doms meet. The bank we're on is in Arius Kingdom."

Tessa bit her lower lip. "And how do you two plan to contain my gifts?"

"We don't want it contained," Theon said. "It needs to be let out."

"Then how do you plan to protect yourselves from it?" she asked.

"My gifts rival my father's, and we have yet to find something that can withstand dragon fire."

"Then wouldn't that make Luka stronger than you?" Tessa asked.

"Arius is a First God. Sargon is a Lesser," Theon answered.

Tessa only hummed in response.

"But I am here to protect Theon," Luka cut in.

The corner of her lips tipped up. "Of course you are. You're his Guardian. You have to protect him."

"We've discussed this before, Tessa," Luka said tightly.

"Yes, yes. You *chose* your bond. The lesser of two evils. Just like me," she retorted mockingly, taking a few steps closer to the river.

Theon threw a questioning glance at Luka, but his friend just waved him off, muttering, "Let's do this."

Tessa must have heard him, because she turned back to them, holding up her wrists. Theon stepped forward, gently pushing the sleeves of her jacket back and trying not to move the bands any more than they had to.

"Your magic will flare when the bands come off," Theon explained. "We're going to do one at a time to hopefully lessen the strain a bit. Don't fight it. Let your magic do what it's meant to do. Once both bands are off, I'll use my power to help guide yours until you learn to do so yourself."

"How can your power guide mine? They're different," Tessa said, her feet already planted in a stance Theon knew Luka made her stand in for hours during training.

"You'll see," Theon said. "You just have to—"

"Trust you?" she finished for him when he stopped speaking.

"Yes," he answered tightly.

"I don't," she said simply.

"Then this won't work."

"I don't trust you," she repeated. "But I trust your motivations. You need me to learn to control my gifts. This benefits you as much as it does me."

"This isn't about any of that," he argued.

"No?"

"No," he replied, growing more frustrated by the second. "I've already told you: both of us know what it is like to have our power trapped by bands like that. I'm trying to help you, Tessa. That's all we're trying to do."

"It's all right to be nervous," Luka cut in.

"We'll be right here, beautiful," Theon said softly, reaching for the band on her left wrist. "Let us help."

"It's better us than some random sentinels, right?" Luka said with a smirk.

"That's debatable," Tessa muttered, taking a deep breath.

Her hand trembled beneath his fingers as he pulled the band over it. He hadn't even slipped it into his pocket before light was flaring from her palm so forcefully, he stumbled back a step. Luka was already stepping between them, his eyes shifted to vertical slits and black flames hovering.

"I'm fine," Theon gritted out, letting his darkness free to coat him like a shield.

"I can't help it," Luka bit back, shoving him back farther when Theon tried to step around him. "Give me a second, and we can take the other band off."

"She's holding back. She's fighting her power," Theon replied, watching as the light continued to flare. There were sparks of energy appearing at her fingertips, but it should be more. Even yesterday at the hearing when Lord Jove had guided her power it had been so much more.

"When the other band is off, she won't be able to," Luka said, a tremor going through his entire body. Theon could only assume he could feel the weight of her power as he stood between them. That power was enough to call to any Legacy.

"Let me talk to her. Prepare her," Theon said.

Luka nodded, the motion stiff and jerky as he stepped aside, going against every instinct of the Guardian Bond. He didn't go far, circling around Tessa, and Theon stepped in front of her.

"You need to let go, little storm," he coaxed, reaching to cup her face with a shadow-coated hand.

"I don't know what that means," she gasped, her hand closing into a fist as another wave of light flared.

"It's going to feel like you have no control, and it's going to be terrifying. Let it happen. We'll be here." She shook her head, and he could swear there were pools of silver lining her eyes. "You don't have a choice, beautiful. This has to happen."

"No choice," she whispered, her eyes falling closed and a single tear sliding down her cheek.

"Tessa—" he started, but she just held up her other wrist.

He didn't ask if she was ready. He didn't bother with some sort of pointless countdown. He just slid the band over her hand and braced himself for the storm that erupted.

Her knees buckled as her power spilled out of her, and Theon caught her, lowering her to the riverbank. Icy rain pelted at his skin, and streaks of fractured light came from Tessa, skittering along the ground and illuminating the dark night. Theon could feel it all, every bit of her extraordinary power slamming against his shield of shadows and darkness, and fuck. No wonder she was terrified. This was…

There weren't words for it as lightning flashed in the night sky, striking straight down nearby. Luka was already there, his dragon fire eliminating any damage she might cause.

There weren't words for it as winds howled around them, her hair whipping so violently it felt like glass shards against his face where she was huddled into his neck.

There weren't words for it as she slowly lifted her head, bright violet-gray eyes connecting with his, light swirling the way shadows would in his own when he lost control.

"Breathe, little storm," he murmured. "Let your power breathe."

"It's so much," she gasped, her entire body trembling violently as another wave of magic radiated out from her, slamming into a wall of dragon fire Luka had positioned around them, trying to contain something never meant to be contained. "I'll never be able to control this."

"You will. It takes time, but you will, Tessa. I promise."

"Your promises mean nothing to me," she hissed, her hand dropping to the ground and more light crackling out from her fingertips.

Theon said nothing to that, letting her power rage. After several minutes, he sent his darkness slowly winding into her light. To wrap around it. To lead it and guide it. And he sucked in his own sharp breath as their power fully merged for the first time.

"Theon," she breathed. It was more of a moan, and she'd *never* said his name like that. Not when his lips had been on hers. Not when his cock had been deep inside her. Not when he'd watched her come undone beneath him.

His magic strained, pulling at the tight leash he held on it. His darkness wanted more of her light, and he wanted more of her.

Then he felt her power tentatively reach back.

"Good girl," he groaned, his brow falling to hers.

It was all there was to say.

It was all there was to feel.

Wisps of light reached for the darkest parts of his shadows, curiously searching, seeking, and he let her play. Let her lift a hand and watch the light dance along her fingertips, chasing the shadows he let drift around her. He let her find a shred of control in a world where she had none. Where even if she was indeed Legacy, she still wouldn't have much control in a realm ruled by villains.

Dark and light tangled. Pushing and pulling. Giving and taking.

Gods, he wanted to get her back to the townhouse right fucking now.

No, he wanted to let her have this reprieve as long as he could because those bands would have to go back on before they got back into the vehicle, and he knew the torture of the things. So when he reached into his coat pocket some time later and pulled the bands out, he expected the way her face fell. The momentary panic that filled her eyes before she tucked away her emotions once more.

"Two days," he said into the night, slipping the first one over her hand. "We will bring you back here in two days."

She nodded, letting him slide the other band into place, before she untangled herself from where she'd somehow ended up straddling his lap on the ground. Without a word, she turned away from him, wandering a little ways down the river.

Theon stood, brushing off the back of his pants, before shoving his hands deep in the pockets of his coat. Luka came to his side, his eyes still shifted, the blue as bright as the stars above them.

Stars they could actually see.

The rain had receded as Tessa's power had been allowed to flare, and now the sky was clear. The first truly clear sky Theon could remember since he'd Selected Tessa as his Source. He didn't count the sun briefly peeking out of the clouds when they'd played Chaosphere on the way to the Acropolis.

"She did better than I expected," Luka said.

"Yeah."

It was all Theon could think to say.

"Did doing this give you any insights into her heritage?"

Theon sighed, knowing Luka had waited to ask this until she was out of hearing range. The last thing he needed was Tessa thinking they'd done this solely for their own benefit, but she'd been right before. He needed her to learn to control her gifts, and to do that, she needed to feel them so she wouldn't fear them.

"No," he answered. "The closest I can come is Rai, but there is nothing to suggest the god of the seasons could control the weather. In theory, if she can truly control the weather, once she masters her gifts, she should have some sort of control over the wind and water too."

"Her lightning could start fires if she can control where it strikes. I had to put out more than one," Luka said.

Theon hadn't noticed. He'd been too focused on the female in his lap and their powers coming together.

"Are we…" He trailed off because it couldn't truly be possible, but the evidence was all right there. "Are we saying she will essentially be able to somewhat control all the elements the Fae can?"

"I don't know that it will be exactly like Fae magic, but if she truly created those crevices in the gardens at Arius House—"

Theon saw them at the same time Luka abruptly stopped talking.

And then they were both running.

And Tessa was screaming.

Theon's power was racing for her, but Luka was faster. His wings had already appeared, and he was in the sky, dragon fire erupting around Tessa.

"Let me through!" he yelled to Luka when he was a few feet away, a break appearing in the flames so Theon could move past the burning shield. "Release her. Now," he snarled to the figure who held Tessa.

The figure wore a black cloak, their face obscured by a hood. It was so similar to the Keeper's attire that if it weren't for the pearly-white mask obscuring the face, Theon would think it *was* the Keeper. That and the fact there were at least twenty more of these fuckers outside the shield.

Tessa's back was pressed to the figure's front, and based on height alone, Theon guessed it was a male. The dagger pressing against her throat, however, made sure Theon didn't give a fuck if they were male or female. Either way, he would deliver death tonight.

When the figure only backed up another step, dragging Tessa with him, Theon bared his teeth, pulling a dagger of his own from a swirl of shadows. "I will not say it again."

"You do not know what you harbor, young heir," the figure said, confirming Theon's suspicion he was indeed male.

"I have a pretty good idea," Theon retorted, twirling the dagger in his hand. "You, however, do not appear to know when you are moments away from a very painful death."

"As long as we accomplish our goal, my death will serve its purpose."

"The only purpose your death will serve is my need to avenge what is mine," Theon returned, slowly moving forward.

"Theon—" Tessa started.

But she was cut off as the figure yanked her back, lifting her off her feet.

"This is your fault," the figure continued, even as Theon continued his advance. "She cannot remain your Source. If you had simply agreed at the hearing yesterday, this could all have been avoided."

"Who sent you?" Theon asked, pausing at his words. How did he know about the hearing and what was said there?

"No one sent me. We serve only to keep Devram what it is supposed to be."

"So you serve the Keeper?" Theon asked sharply.

"No," the figure shook his head. "The Keeper keeps many things, but not this."

"Riddles only make me want to make your death more agonizing." A roar pierced the air, and Theon smiled, his darkness swelling like the death it came from. "Too late."

"It is true then," the figure said, his face tipping to the sky. "The Everlasting War has found its way here at last." The masked face focused once again on Theon. "But it only does so because of *her*."

"She has nothing to do with any war," Theon snarled, his shadows creeping forward.

The figure was still holding Tessa off the ground, but she wasn't struggling. Her eyes were darting from Theon to the sky and back. She had to be exhausted after expending all that power only minutes ago. She didn't know how to manage it yet, and her power wouldn't have let her siphon slowly right now anyway.

"She has everything to do with the war," the figure answered. He moved the dagger down from her throat until it stopped over her heart. "It has to be this way, or this world will fall like all the others."

The male brought his hand back, preparing to plunge the dagger into her heart, and that was the opening Theon had been waiting for. His shadows wrapped around the male's wrist, halting the killing blow.

"You don't understand!" the male cried in a panic as the darkness wrapped around Tessa and yanked her hard from his grip. "You sentence an entire realm to death!"

Theon had stopped listening. He'd heard enough, and his shadows devoured the male, seeping through his cloak and clothing and sinking deep into his being. His darkness flooded his veins, moving throughout his body, destroying and killing, until the only sound Theon could hear was the male's anguished screams. He'd threatened her, had come so close to killing her. His. She was his to protect, his to avenge, and this male had almost taken her from him. He'd almost lost her again.

"Theon."

Soft hands were on his face.

"Theon, stop!"

He could feel her trying to turn his attention to her, but not until this male had suffered and paid the cost for trying to take something from him.

"Theon, I need you!"

Those words pulled him from the vengeance-induced haze he was in. He blinked, finally meeting Tessa's gaze, and there was the fear he had been expecting to see in her eyes while the male had held a dagger to her throat.

"Theon," she whispered, her gaze darting around, and he finally turned to find Luka's black flames were gone.

Instead, the two of them were standing in the center of a circle of people. All of them wore black robes and the pearly-white masks. All of them held the same black dagger.

"Where is Luka?" Tessa whispered.

"He'll be here," Theon said, slipping an arm around her and tucking her into his side.

"But *where* is he? We can't— I can't do anything to help you fight them," she said, his darkness coating her skin the same way it was coating his own.

Thunder rumbled in the distance, the clouds already filling the sky that had been clear only moments ago. She shouldn't be able to do any of that right now.

"I know who you are," Theon said, addressing the masked group around them. "I know what you seek to protect. She is not the enemy."

"But she is," spoke a figure to his right, a female. "Allowing her to remain your Source will upset the balance. It will upset everything. This realm will fall."

"One female will not be the downfall of an entire realm," Theon snapped.

The masked face tilted to the side. "No, but the two of you together will be."

"You're wrong," Theon gritted out, his arm tightening around Tessa. Another roar sounded, closer than before, and Theon smirked. "You're also dead."

Because that wasn't a cloud blotting out the moon now.

It was wings and scales and claws.

That was Luka in his full dragon form.

It was black flames raining from his mouth as he roared into the night again, diving swiftly for them.

The masked figures scattered, racing for cover, but Luka's fire didn't miss. His black flames chased them down, incinerating all those in their path, leaving not even ashes behind.

The ground shook as he landed, his large body curling around them and a growl rumbling from deep in his chest.

"He's a dragon," Tessa whispered in awe. She reached out a hand and ran her fingers along scales so dark they appeared black in the night, but the moonlight glinting off them gave away shades of blue darker than his glowing sapphire eyes.

"We told you this," Theon answered, easing his arm from around her.

"It's different seeing it," she replied, wonder in her voice despite the danger Luka was currently protecting them from.

Theon moved, trying to see around Luka's massive form to see how many of the cloaked figures they had to deal with yet, but a large snout was there, shoving him in the chest and smoke furling from nostrils directly into Theon's face.

"Fuck off," Theon snarled, shoving at the dragon's face. "I'll be fine."

Another rumbled growl had Tessa asking, "You can't understand that, can you?"

"No," Theon answered. "We've just known each other long enough that I know what he's doing." Looking into a sapphire eye, he added, "And it's unnecessary. Are there any left?"

The dragon's long neck twisted, a diamond-shaped head taking in their surroundings. Another huff told Theon the threat had passed, but Luka wouldn't shift back. Not yet. He was too lost to the Guardian bond, and the need to protect would keep him in this form a little longer.

Especially when a howl sounded.

Then Luka was herding him back to Tessa, curling around them again.

"He's very…protective," Tessa muttered, studying a wing that was folded against Luka's side.

"It's the Guardian Bond," Theon answered. "He'll settle down in a minute. How are you feeling?"

"I'm fine."

"Tessa, you can't be fine. You got to truly feel the full effects of your power for the first time. Then you were attacked minutes later."

She shrugged, idly stroking her hand down Luka's scales again.

Another soft huff from Luka had Theon turning his attention back to his friend, where he'd moved enough for Theon to see the source of the howling.

Two wolves were standing along the riverbank. One was dark charcoal grey. The other was such a light grey, it was silver in the moonlight. They had to be the same two wolves that had been with the Keeper at the Emerging Ceremony. There was no such thing as coincidences when it came to Tessa.

Tessa noticed them a second later, her hand dropping to her side. She took a step forward, but Luka was already there, nudging her back with his head.

"They won't hurt me," she said, her voice holding that eerie ring it sometimes held these days. "They're making sure I'm all right."

"How can you know that?" Theon demanded.

She shrugged again. "I just do."

The wolves stared back at the three of them a moment longer before they turned and disappeared into the surrounding trees.

"Shift back, Luka," Theon said into the silent night.

"He can just…shift back?" Tessa asked, her hand smoothing down his scales once more.

There was a soft flash of blue light, and Luka stood there, Tessa's hand now pressed to the naked skin of his muscled abdomen. She snatched it back as if he'd burned her.

"That was rude," she muttered.

"You're the definition of rude," Luka said, eyes still scanning their surroundings.

"How do you have pants?" Tessa asked.

Luka arched a brow. "Are you wishing I didn't?"

"Gods, no," she scoffed with a curl of her lip.

"We should get out of here," Luka said, already striding for the vehicle.

It wasn't until they were crossing the boundaries back into the Acropolis that Luka said, "Any ideas who they were, Theon?"

"I know exactly who they were," Theon answered, glancing at Tessa who was back to staring out the window. Her bouncing knee was the only tell he needed to know she was worked up about everything that had happened tonight. The only tell he needed to know that she was listening to every word. "They were the Augury."

# 7

## TESSA

"For fuck's sake," Luka muttered, turning onto a street Tessa recognized. "The Augury. That's what you're going with?"

"I don't hear you offering any ideas," Theon said, his defensive tone making Tessa glance at him sidelong.

She'd been quiet on the drive back to the Acropolis. They all had been. Each of them processing the events of the last hour in their own way.

She'd felt her power, and Theon had been right. It had been terrifying. And Luka had been right. She'd been nervous. But the relief when Theon had taken the second band off? When her power had taken control?

*That* was freedom.

Not having to think.

Not having to feel.

Her power— wild and untamed and fierce—had let her simply be. Had let her simply exist.

Until Theon had started using his power with hers. Then she'd felt *everything*.

She was still feeling it. The way her magic had been drawn to his. Was that what Theon had felt all this time? When he would talk about his power seeking her out?

The want.

The need.

Was *that* what was making this bond so godsdamn unbearable? Their power? Maybe it wasn't a bond at all. Maybe it had been their power this whole time.

She knew she should focus on the conversation happening between Theon and Luka, but it was hard when her power was once again trapped. Not only that, but it seemed to know Theon was nearby, and with him, his magic that called to it.

Which was just great because all she could think about was his fingers skimming down her body, his shadows toying with her, his heated gaze—

No.

Tonight was enough.

It had to be enough.

"Axel is going to give you so much shit about this," Luka was saying when Tessa forced herself to tune back into the conversation.

"What's the Augury?" she asked, trying to distract herself from the ache between her legs.

"It's a group of people who believe the Revelation Decree is not a law to govern Devram, but rather that it's a prophecy or an omen," Theon explained.

"It is a *theory* that this group even exists. There has never been any proof of its existence," Luka said.

Tessa frowned. "So it's like the female in the mirror?"

Luka snickered as he got out of the vehicle and moved to open her door for her.

"It is not like— The female was there," Theon snapped before getting out on the other side of the vehicle.

Tessa looked up at Luka as he pushed the vehicle door shut behind her.

"You look tired," he said with a frown.

"Thanks," Tessa grumbled.

"You should eat after expending all that power."

Tessa hummed an acknowledgment, trailing the two as they made their way into the townhouse. "Why do you think this Augury group attacked me?"

Theon reached over to grab the hat she'd pulled off her head. Setting it off to the side, he unzipped her jacket as he answered, "Like I said, they believe the Decree is an omen. They believe that if the prophecy comes to pass, Devram will be destroyed, and they consider themselves some kind of divine protectors of the realm."

"Isn't that what the Keeper is supposed to be?" Tessa asked, turning so Theon could help her out of the jacket.

"Do you remember what I told you about the Keeper?"

"You believe he does more than keep the Decree. You believe he guards something inside the Pantheon."

"Theon believes the Keeper has nothing to do with the Decree at all," Luka said, appearing from the kitchen and holding an orange out to her, already peeled.

"What are you doing?" she asked, glancing at the fruit.

"Handing you an orange."

"Why?"

"I told you, you need to eat after using so much power."

"Do I?" Tessa countered. "If I'm a Legacy, wouldn't I need blood?"

She watched Luka's gaze move to Theon, and Tessa turned to look at him too.

Theon was hanging up his jacket, and he started rolling up the sleeves of his button-down shirt as he turned back to them. "That is something we will need to test."

"Test," Tessa repeated doubtfully.

"I think we forgo the blood for now and see how much of your reserves have refilled when we do this again."

"The bands might keep her power from refilling naturally," Luka said, trying to hand Tessa the orange again.

"Stop trying to feed me," she snapped.

Luka arched a brow. "You always want to eat."

"I want doughnuts or pizza or fries, not an orange."

She could swear Luka's lips twitched as if he was trying not to smirk.

"Anyway," Theon cut in, "we were given a deadline to figure out your heritage. Knowing if your power wells will refill on their own will narrow things down."

Her eyes narrowed. "So now I am some grand experiment for you?"

"That's not what I said," Theon answered. "But the sooner we figure out your heritage, the better. We can move forward with other plans, get the other Kingdoms off our backs, and keep the Augury at bay."

"For fuck's sake," Luka muttered. "I'm not talking about this with you again until Axel is with us."

"That's fine," Theon said, moving deeper into the foyer. He grabbed

Tessa's hand and swiped the orange from Luka with a nod. "We'll see you in the morning."

Tessa followed because she had questions, like why the fuck Theon thought these Augury people were after her.

"What did they mean when they said 'the Everlasting War has finally found its way here?'" she asked.

"I don't know. I don't know what any of that means," Theon replied, and she could hear how much that annoyed him.

"Why do they think I have something to do with it?" she pressed.

"I don't know."

"You said you know what they seek. You said—"

Theon whirled on her as they reached the third floor landing. "I know what I said, Tessa. I was there." She blinked up at him, inwardly wincing at the darkness drifting across his eyes. "Eat this," was the only other thing he said before forcing the orange into her hand and pushing through the door into their room.

She followed, pausing to slip the riding boots off. Why did he even have riding boots for her here? There weren't any horses here.

He'd already moved into the walk-in closet, and Tessa sighed, plopping down on the sofa and peeling off a wedge of the orange.

All the books Theon was looking through were stacked on the coffee table. He never left his notes out. She could only assume that was so Ford didn't snoop through them. She'd tried to talk to the Fae once, but he'd ignored her entirely. She hadn't bothered trying again.

Grabbing the book off the top of the stack, Tessa idly flipped through the pages. It was some sort of history book detailing the various gods, but she paused when a page mentioned the Chaos they came from. The way it was worded made it sound like more than just the Firsts had emerged from the Chaos. She'd never given much thought to it all, but she supposed it would stand to reason that more than the gods emerged. So what happened to the other beings?

She was still studying the pages, the orange now gone, when she heard Theon come back into the room a few minutes later. She didn't bother looking at him. He came to a stop beside her, and from her periphery, she saw him slip his hands into the pockets of the loose pants he'd changed into.

Lightly clearing his throat, he asked, "How are you feeling? And I swear to Arius, if you say *fine*—"

"You'll what?" Tessa muttered, turning the page. "Lock me in a wine cellar?"

He was silent for a moment before he said, "We should discuss everything that happened tonight."

"No."

"No?"

She turned another page, not even reading at this point. "I needed to talk to you earlier. You, once again, made it clear it is not my place to know things. So, no, Theon, I do not want to talk about what happened with you."

"With me," he repeated tightly. "But you would discuss it with someone else?"

There was an edge to his tone that had her lifting her head. "It doesn't really matter, does it?" she sneered with a mocking tilt of her lips. "Soon enough you'll have a Match and a new Source, and I'll be with Luka, right? I'll no longer be yours to talk to."

"Do you really think being Luka's Match would change anything between us, beautiful?" Theon asked, taking another step closer. Her mocking grin faltered, and she tried to look away, but he caught her chin in his hand. "It will not matter if you have a union Mark on your skin and a ring on your finger. It will not matter if I have the same with someone else. If I am forced into a new bond, it will not erase this one. Haven't you figured it out yet?"

His hand slid up her jaw and into her unbound hair, wrapping the golden strands around his fist. Her breathing was uneven, and her gaze was darting between his eyes and his mouth as he leaned over her.

He tugged at her hair, forcing her to tip her head back farther, and his breath danced across her lips as he said, "You'll still be mine, Tessa."

"I hate you too much to ever be yours," she whispered bitterly.

He shrugged, his shadows appearing and winding along her throat. "I said I wanted everything you have to give. That includes your hate. It's all mine."

Tendrils of darkness caressed her cheek and slid along her jaw as if it were his own hand. Just like that, all the want from earlier tonight when their magic had merged was back. She was leaning into his power, finding everything she could need in that darkness— pleasure and comfort, relief and freedom.

"Did you ever think that maybe I hate this just as much?"

His voice was a whisper in her ear, and she opened her eyes, unsure of when they had fallen closed.

"Not possible," she rasped.

"No?"

She shook her head, his shadows continuing to skate along her skin, making it hard to think about anything other than the heat flaring in her belly and the feeling of utter rapture when her light had met his dark.

"You think I enjoy being obsessed with someone that clearly doesn't feel the same way? You think I like that my power fights me? That it constantly tries to get to you? You think I appreciate how much my plans have changed since you came into my life?" he continued.

Fighting against the cloud of lust, Tessa pushed back against him. He released her hair, but his shadows continued to drift around her, as if he truly couldn't control them. She clambered up, standing on the sofa. Her bare feet sank into the cushions, but from here at least she wasn't looking up at him.

"That is not you hating me, Theon," she retorted. "That is you hating your situation, the circumstances around it. That is you hating that you realize just how little control you truly have."

He leaned forward, crowding into her, and she stumbled back, her ass landing on the back of the sofa. His hands landed on either side of her hips, caging her between his arms. "And that's different from you? Do you not hate your situation? The circumstances around it? Do you not hate just how little control you have?"

"I have more control than you," she snapped.

His head tilted to the side. "Do you?"

"I've proved that once."

He hummed in thought, his shadows no longer drifting around her, but pressing along her ribs, her hips, her torso. They skimmed along the top of her jeans, and—

"You know," she blurted.

Because gods, he *knew*. He knew exactly what she was desperate for.

"Know what, little storm?" he replied

"You know that— You know what…"

"What you're needing right now?" he finished for her, his magic almost frenzied as it touched her. As if it were indeed obsessed with her, just as he'd said. "I always know what you need, Tessa."

"You don't," she said, shoving at his chest as she pushed to her feet.

She didn't acknowledge the fact that he let her push him aside. "I'm going to take a shower."

"It won't be enough," he called after her.

"I don't know what you're talking about."

"Your fingers," he added. "They won't be enough, just like my hand hasn't been enough for me for weeks."

She didn't reply, slamming the bathroom door shut behind her.

But later, when she was sitting on the bench, the steam of the shower around her and her hair dripping, she admitted to herself that he was right. As her fingers worked her clit and she found release, even as she remembered the time she'd walked in on Theon pleasuring himself in the shower, it did nothing. She was still an aching mess of need and want.

Tessa tipped her head back against the wall, and memories of their power connecting enveloped her.

It wasn't enough.

# 8

## TESSA

She couldn't breathe.

Not as Theon stood over her, a black dagger in his hand.

She couldn't get air down to even speak.

"Breathe, little one," Luka soothed. "It will all be over soon."

The dragon was near her head, his hands resting gently on her shoulders. Axel was at her side, his shadows twining around her legs and keeping them still.

She choked down a sob, gasping as tears slid down her face. "Please, Luka. Don't let him do this."

Luka's brow pinched, his gaze darting to Theon. "Maybe we should wait. She said the same thing to me before you gave her the first Mark, and look how this has turned out."

"We don't have a choice," Theon said, still standing over her, his hair stirring in the breeze.

A light rain was falling, thunder rumbling in the distance.

"I still think there is another way to interpret this."

Tessa's head snapped to the side to find a tall male. He looked familiar somehow, but Tessa was sure she'd never met him. He had a sword strapped down his back, as did the female standing next to him. Her red-gold hair was braided over her shoulder, and flames flickered in her eyes. Standing next to them was...

Tristyn?

"Life must give, and death must take," Theon said. "There is no other way to interpret that. Not if we wish to save our world."

For so long, Tessa had wished for death, and now, in this moment, she didn't want it. She'd finally found something to fight for, and she would be robbed of that too.

"You're wrong," Tristyn said, his features taut and his hands clenching and unclenching at his sides. "Have you learned nothing over these past months? You yourself have questioned things from the very beginning, even before you knew Tessa."

"And all that questioning has led me here. To understanding why we were drawn to each other," Theon said, his grip on the dagger tightening.

"Theon, don't!" Tessa cried. "It's more than a bond! I know that now."

Emerald eyes cut to her. "You're right, and now that I understand what that means, I'm the only one who can do this."

She was writhing on the ground, trying to free herself of Luka and Axel. They were too strong though, and even if she could free herself, she'd never win. Not with the ring on her finger keeping her separated from her gifts.

One of Luka's hands moved to her brow, smoothing hair back.

"Luka," she sobbed, the sound defeated and broken.

"I know, Tessa," he whispered. "I know."

"This is wrong," the female with fire was saying to the other male. "This will alter everything."

"We cannot interfere," the male replied, reaching for her when she took a step towards Tessa. "It will upset the—"

"Fuck the balance," the female seethed, shoving his hands away.

Axel was refusing to look at Theon, but that was regret shining in his eyes when they connected with Tessa's.

"I'm sorry, baby doll," he murmured before turning away from her.

"Theon, we should wait," Luka said, his glowing eyes never leaving her face.

"She can get here," the female was saying, panic in her voice. "She can stop this."

"Not even she will be fast enough," Theon answered.

"She is a World Walker and a—"

"And even she has been ordered not to interfere with this," Theon cut in, dropping to Tessa's side.

"She will not care."

"She will be too late," Theon said again, his fingers sliding along Tessa's jaw. "You will forever be mine, Tessa. Whether in this life or in the After."

*"Please don't send me to the dark alone," she whispered. She'd stopped fighting now, but her body was trembling.*

*The male and female were arguing with Tristyn, but Tessa couldn't hear them. Not as she got lost in dark emerald eyes and black hair. In a small dimple, and lips she'd kissed more times than she could count.*

*"I'm sorry I failed you, little storm," Theon said, sorrow flashing in his eyes.*

*"I'm sorry I loved you too late. But I'm yours. Every piece of me."*

*Theon didn't say another word.*

*Only lifted the dagger above her chest and sank it into her heart.*

She couldn't breathe. There wasn't enough air. Her lungs were on fire as she gasped, but her chest wouldn't expand around the searing pain. She could feel the blade, smell the blood that was spilling from her body.

Sapphire eyes were suddenly in her vision, chin-length brown hair hanging in his face.

"Calm down. You just got the air knocked out of you," Luka said.

He was crouched beside her, his forearms on his knees and his hands hanging loosely before him.

She sucked in a shuddering breath, the ache in her chest sharp.

"What the fuck was that, Luka?" Tessa gasped out, still not able to take a full breath.

"That was you not focusing," he retorted, his eyes narrowing when she sucked in another gasp. "You're not dying. Take a full breath."

"Easy for you to say," she grumbled, pushing onto her elbows and forcing her lungs to fully expand.

"Better," he said, pushing back to his feet, his arms folded across his chest.

"You're a bigger ass today than normal," she replied, finally feeling her racing heart slowing. The ache in her chest lingered though, and she absentmindedly rubbed at it. The dream had been different from the vision the priestess had forced on her. That had never happened before.

"Are you ready to talk about last night?" Luka asked, pulling her from her thoughts.

She went still. "What?"

"Last night. Your power. The attack."

"I'm sure Theon told you everything there is to know," she said, getting up and moving to grab her water bottle.

"I do not need a replay of your bickering and refusal to let him help you. I witness that every day," he replied dryly.

"I do not refuse to—"

"You didn't fight back, Tessa," he interrupted, suddenly in her face.

Her water was halfway to her lips. "What?"

"You didn't fight back. Didn't even try," he repeated.

"He had a dagger at my throat," Tessa said. "What was I supposed to do?"

"Before he even touched you, you didn't fight back," Luka growled, and Tessa slowly lowered the water bottle. He smirked at her. "You think I didn't know? I was in the air, Tessa. Before I fully shifted, before I made a path for Theon through my flames, I could see you. You didn't fight back. But you could have. I've taught you enough in the short time we've been doing this. If you had fought, even a little bit, that dagger would have never touched your throat because Theon would have been there in time."

Tessa was silent as she held the dragon's stare.

"Which leads me to believe one of two things," Luka continued, taking the water bottle from her hand and replacing the cap before tossing it aside. "Either you knew the person somehow—"

"What? Why would I know him?" Tessa interrupted at the accusation.

"You spent time with Lord Jove by yourself at his residence," he replied matter-of-factly.

"I was attacked and unconscious when I was brought there. Are you going to reprimand me for not 'fighting back' then too?" she demanded, her hands going to her hips.

"Of course not. Axel told us what happened up until the moment you were taken," Luka said, his annoyance heavy. "What none of us know is what happened at Lord Jove's residence from the time you were taken until we showed up. That's a good chunk of unaccounted time, Tessa. You could have discussed any manner of things."

"I was unconscious for most of it," she replied. "But what does any of this have to do with last night?"

Luka shrugged casually. "Maybe you struck some kind of deal with Lord Jove. Maybe it was staged somehow."

Her mouth fell open, her head shaking in disbelief. "You've lost your mind."

"Have I? How would we know?" he countered. "You want to know why Theon waited to tell you things? You want to know why we didn't just tell you all our secrets and plans? It's this, right here. You've given us no reason to trust you."

She threw her hands in the air. "Now you sound like Theon. I keep forgetting I'm supposed to simply blindly trust the three of you while I have to *earn* your trust in return."

Luka's large hands were suddenly gripping her shoulders. "When will you understand this is bigger than you? Bigger than us? There are *millions* of people whose safety and survival depends on those secrets, Tessa. We cannot just give them away. When we do, innocent people suffer for it. For a minute there, you made an effort. For a split second, you asked questions and seemed as though you were trying to understand; that's when Theon started giving you more information. You're smarter than this, Tessa. Surely you see the connection. You simply choose not to."

"Apparently, I'm so godsdamn clever I've conspired with the Achaz Lord against the Kingdom I'm forced to be loyal to," she sneered.

Luka bared his teeth in a sardonic smile as his hands slipped from her shoulders, his fingertips dragging down her arms. "That's the thing, Tessa. I don't think that at all."

"Then why are we having this conversation?"

"To prove a point. But I said there were *two* possible reasons you didn't fight back last night."

"I cannot wait to hear this," she said dryly.

"You truly don't have any regard for your life and didn't care if that dagger at your throat ended it."

Tessa unwittingly took a step back from him. "It takes more than a blade to kill a Fae, let alone a Legacy," she replied, but her voice wavered.

"That wasn't an ordinary dagger, and you know it."

Luka watched her, and gods, she felt like he could see right through her. Because he was right. She hadn't fought back. She hadn't struggled. She hadn't cared.

The silence in the training room was loud. Too loud. She wanted to run her hands through her hair, tug at the ends just to ground herself, but she also didn't want to give Luka the satisfaction. Didn't want him to know just how right he was.

Instead, she said, "Does Theon know?"

His head tilted the smallest amount, and it was so animalistic, she could see the dragon that lurked beneath his skin. "Know what? That you didn't fight back? Or that you don't *want* to fight back?"

"I've told him before that I've thought death to be a kinder option more than once," she answered.

"Theon *is* death, Tessa."

She blinked at his words.

"But that aside, I haven't said anything to Theon about last night."

"Why?"

"Because you get to feel this way, Tessa. Anyone who's lived the life you have, who's learned new truths about who they are, who's been forced into something they don't want would feel the same. We *have* felt the same. But like I told you before, only you get to decide what to do with those feelings. Only you get to decide how long you're going to feel sorry for yourself before you decide to do something about it. Until then, this training time is pointless and not worth my time if you're not ready to fight back."

"Not worth your time?" she repeated, the words slicing deep.

*Too much of a hassle.*

"Don't twist my words around, Tessa," he growled, a thumb and forefinger gripping her chin. "I did not say *you* were not worth my time. I said *training* is pointless if you're not even going to try." She nodded once, but he held firm when she tried to look away. "I'm saying *you* need to decide you're worth it. Even on the hard days. Even on the days you feel like giving up. Even on the days where it feels pointless. You need to decide *you* are worth it."

"What is the point?" Tessa retorted. "You want me to try? For what? So everyone can take what they want from me? Pass me around as they see fit? Use me?"

Luka straightened, releasing her chin. "You have this self-centered idea that you are the only one who's ever been in the position of being wanted for what they can give. Why do you think Valter *wanted* me, Tessa? Because of what I would be to him when I was of age. Because I was the only one in Devram. Because of what he could use me for."

Tessa blinked at him. She'd never really thought of it that way before.

"And while we're talking about it, what are his children to him? Does he not *use* them to further his own goals? I told you once before you have far more in common with the three of us than you realize. You're not so different."

"I don't want to be one of you," she snarled, her power stirring beneath her skin at her irritation.

Luka gave her a cruel smile. "I don't think you know what you want, Tessa. I think you're so used to letting someone else take care of you, dictate your every move, and make decisions for you, that when you're given control, it terrifies you because you have no idea what to do with it. So you let people take care of you. You let others dictate your every move and decide for you."

"Fuck you, Luka Mors."

"Until you start fighting for yourself, we're done here."

"Fine."

"Fine," he retorted. "Grab your shit. I'll take you to Theon. He can decide where you park your ass until it's time for your afternoon lessons."

"I hate all of you," she spat, grabbing the small bag that held her phone and a few other items.

"Right now, the feeling is pretty fucking mutual."

# 9
## THEON

Theon stepped into the warm foyer, Luka shutting the door behind them. Quickly removing his coat, he hung it on a hook before following the bond that told him Tessa was nearby. Today had been her first afternoon of lessons with Cordelia and the other Sources. He'd wanted to be there when she got done, but he'd been in meetings with his father. Axel had escorted her home with Katya, as he did every night.

He followed the bond down the hall, voices carrying from the dining room a moment later. When he rounded the corner, he found the three of them placing serving dishes on the table. Ford wasn't much of a cook —nothing like Pen had been anyway—so they'd resorted to hiring a chef to prepare meals. To see them setting the table themselves, however, was uncommon.

"I sent Ford out for the night," Axel said before Theon could ask.

"And he left?" Theon replied, his eyes on Tessa where she was straightening from placing a bowl of salad on the table. Her gaze connected with his for a brief moment before she sent a glare over his shoulder. Sure enough, Luka came up beside him. Theon didn't know what had happened between the two. Luka wouldn't tell him, claiming what happened during their training sessions stayed between them, but those training sessions hadn't happened for the last five days. Luka suddenly didn't have time, and Tessa hadn't spoken a single word to him.

Axel shrugged. "Not willingly, but he'll be down in his quarters for the rest of the night."

"Where does Ford sleep?" Tessa asked, plopping into her dining chair.

"There are quarters in the basement with a separate outside entrance," Theon answered, taking the seat next to her. "How are you?"

"Fine."

Of course she was.

Luka sat across from her, where she dutifully refused to look at him, and Axel was lowering to his own seat when he paused. "You can sit, Kat."

Theon looked up, finding the Fae standing near the wall. This was the first time they'd all had dinner together in a week, and Katya had never joined them since she started staying here. In fact, he'd hardly seen the female.

"I can wait," she said primly, her hands clasped in front of her.

Theon glanced at Axel, whose mouth was pressed into a thin line. He said nothing further, taking his seat and reaching for the basket of garlic bread.

Tessa had already snagged a piece of bread, tearing off a piece as Theon took the bowl of noodles from Luka that he handed across the table.

"You can sit, Kat," Tessa said, popping the bread into her mouth. "It isn't a test. There will not be consequences."

Theon paused, the spoonful of noodles he was dishing onto a plate for Tessa frozen halfway there. He glanced at Axel, whose brow was furrowed. Luka was still dishing up his dinner, but Theon knew he was listening.

"I would rather not," Kat said, tucking some of her curls behind her ear.

"I'm sitting and eating," Tessa offered.

"But you are not Fae."

Tessa seemed to contemplate this for a moment before she said, "That's fair, but even before that discovery was made, I ate at this table."

"You are a Source," Katya said.

Tessa sighed, setting her bread down, but before she could speak again, Axel said, "What, exactly, do you think is going on here, Kat? You heard me tell Ford you'd be eating with us if we were all here." His eyes narrowed. "He has been making you dinner each night, right?"

"Yes, my—" She glanced around at the rest of them before all but whispering, "Yes, Axel."

Axel turned to Tessa. "What is she worried about?"

Tessa reached for her wineglass. Theon hadn't given her that. She must have gotten it before dinner. "We were sometimes tested at the estates. Even if given permission, we were still never to break decorum in front of Legacy. There were consequences if we did."

She brought the glass to her lips, taking a drink.

"Are you saying they would trick you into thinking you could..." Axel trailed off, his attention going back to Kat.

Tessa set her glass down. Theon had spooned cream sauce and chicken over her noodles, and she began twirling the pasta on her fork. "One only made the mistake once." She glanced at Kat. "I swear there will not be consequences from anyone at this table if you eat with us."

"And those not at this table?" Kat asked, her amber eyes holding Tessa's.

"No," Axel said sharply. "Nothing is going to happen if you sit and eat. Sit down, Katya."

She hesitated a moment longer before taking the seat next to Tessa. Tessa passed her the bread basket before grabbing her plate and passing it over to Axel, who heaped food onto it.

The room was full of tense silence as everyone started digging into their meals, and Tessa nudged Kat's fork towards her before she took a bite of her own food. She leaned over, whispering something low into Kat's ear that Theon couldn't hear, even with their enhanced senses. Kat nodded at whatever she'd said and picked up her fork. Axel shot her a grateful look, but Tessa didn't acknowledge it, digging into her own meal.

"What's the plan for tomorrow?" Axel asked after a few minutes. He was never one to let silence linger.

"Normal day until the evening," Theon answered, watching Tessa from the corner of his eye. She was quiet, and her body language was relaxed. His father had kept him busy this week in constant meetings with various council members. He'd hardly had time to do his research at night, and a part of him wondered if his father even wanted him to figure this out.

Of course he did. This was just another one of his impossible tasks he expected Theon to complete. Failure anywhere along the line would be his own fault, and excuses would not be tolerated.

But with all the business, he hadn't had much time to talk with Tessa either. They were still taking her to the river in Arius Kingdom every other day to let her power breathe. Her power never lessened, and he didn't know if that meant it was replenishing itself or if her well of power was just that deep. There had been no other attacks, and on the drives to and from, he answered emails while Tessa stared out the window. With her first lesson with Cordelia looming over her, he hadn't wanted to add to everything she was feeling by discussing this too.

And now he'd run out of time.

"We won't have to stay at the Pantheon after this Mark like we did for the first one. We'll come back here right away."

"When do you plan to leave for Arius House?" Axel asked between bites.

That had Tessa going rigid. He couldn't really blame her, but Theon was curious about Arius House making her react that way and not the next Mark.

"First thing the next morning, if we're all feeling all right."

They all knew he meant if Tessa was feeling all right.

Tessa took a long drink of her wine before saying, "We're going back to Arius House?"

Theon nodded, reaching under the table and placing a hand on her knee. She might hate it, but he felt her immediately relax some at the touch as the bond eased some tension. "My father will go back tomorrow. They give us seven days to adjust to the newest Mark. The other Fae will continue their lessons. It's another reason the Sources have a separate instructor."

"Seven days," Tessa murmured.

"Where will I stay while you are away?" Katya asked curiously, Theon noting she was also relaxing the more time passed.

"You'll be coming with us," Axel said, scooping more salad into his bowl.

"She will?" Theon asked. "What of her lessons?"

"She'll be fine missing a week," Axel replied. "I'm not going to leave her here alone with Ford, and Father demanded it anyway."

Theon huffed in annoyance. Their father would never want her left alone when the fire Fae wasn't even supposed to be claimed by a Kingdom other than Anala. But the words that came from Luka's mouth next had Theon's fingers tightening around Tessa's knee.

"He strongly suggested that Kat should spend some time with you, Theon," Luka added pointedly.

Tessa had stopped eating, her palms flat on the table, and he saw her fingers curl slightly.

"Of course she'll spend time with him. We'll all be together," Axel said tersely.

"Is she to stay in Theon's rooms?" Tessa asked just as tightly.

"No," Axel said quickly. "She'll stay in mine."

Tessa sat back in her chair, studying Axel as Theon said, "Don't be stupid. You really think it's the best idea that she stay in the private wing of Arius House?"

"She can stay with us," Tessa said with a too casual shrug. "There's plenty of room."

"There is not," Axel said. "The bed in that small space is terrible."

"I'm aware," Tessa said dryly.

"I'll stay with Theon and Tessa. You and Katya can stay in my rooms," Luka said, standing and taking his dishes with him.

"No," Tessa said flatly at the same time Axel said, "Really?"

Luka arched a brow. "No? Are you going to *fight* me on it, little one?" When Tessa only glared at him, he smirked. "That's what I thought."

"Eat, Tessa," Theon said after Luka left and she hadn't picked up her fork again.

"I'm not hungry."

"*You're* not hungry?" Axel mused.

"You should eat. You'll need your strength for tomorrow," Theon insisted, ignoring Axel.

"I'm not hungry," she repeated. "I just want to go to bed."

Theon frowned. "It's early yet."

Tessa swiped up her wineglass, draining the last of it. "Yep. And going off experience, I'm going to need the rest for tomorrow more than the food."

With that, she pushed away from the table, her bare feet padding across the hardwood floor and out of the dining room.

"Should we be worried about that?" Axel asked, drinking from his own glass that Theon was certain wasn't wine.

"I'm constantly worried about her," Theon muttered, glancing at her plate that was hardly touched.

"I only knew her a short time before coming here, but she is...different. Very different from the female I met at the Celeste Estate," Katya said, placing her fork down beside her clean plate.

"How so?" Theon asked, wondering why he hadn't thought to ask her about Tessa before. It was so obvious now.

"For starters, she left food behind."

"She does love to eat," Axel said. "Do you want more, Kat?"

Katya shook her head. "No, thank you, but you misunderstand. She left food behind. She never did that at the estate."

"What do you mean?" Theon asked.

"She didn't tell you?"

"We…"

But how was he supposed to tell this Fae that his Source bond was faulty because Tessa wasn't Fae? How was he supposed to admit he didn't have control over this situation despite doing everything in his power to have just that?

Katya's head tilted, and it took everything in him not to shift under her amber gaze. It was as unnerving as Tessa's stare, but in an entirely different way. This felt like Katya could see through every mask and persona he portrayed.

"You never tried to figure out why she is the way she is?" Katya asked.

"She is not very trusting," Theon said tightly.

Something akin to pity crossed the female's face. "Of course she isn't. Not when—"

"Not when what?" Theon pressed when Katya cut herself off.

"If she hasn't told you about her past, I do not think I should be the one to do so," she said. "Please do not ask it of me."

Theon looked across the table at Axel, his brother giving a slight shake of his head.

Fine. He wouldn't press it any more tonight, but once Tessa had the next Mark and he could feel her emotions?

Everything would change.

# 10

## THEON

"Why do we have to be in the same room?" Tessa groused, moving around the perimeter of the Pantheon room. She'd already slipped off her socks and her shoes, and Theon watched her drag her fingertips along the wall as she moved.

"This is the dedicated Arius Marking room," Theon answered.

"Every Kingdom has a dedicated room for this?"

"Yes."

She hummed as she moved, her hair braided into a plait that hung over her shoulder. She had already changed into loose pants and a low-cut shirt, nothing form-fitting after the last Mark. He'd also changed, though not nearly as comfortable or casual. He'd lost the suit, but still wore black pants and a button-down shirt, the sleeves rolled back to his elbows.

"After this, we go back to the townhouse?" Tessa asked, having made her way to the opposite wall.

"Yes. As soon as you're ready."

She hummed again in acknowledgment as Luka emerged from the back room where he'd just finished changing. He set the bag containing their clothing near the door, then crossed his arms as his gaze followed Tessa making another round.

"You ready for this?" he asked quietly. If Tessa heard, she didn't acknowledge it.

Theon nodded, his hands sliding into his pockets. "It shouldn't be as bad as last time…right? Her power isn't locked down now. The bands sure, but not like before."

"I don't know," Luka said. "Everything we've read says each Mark gets easier for both of you, but that's with a Fae. The other Sources will already have at least a little control over their gifts, but those gifts are nothing like hers."

"We've been preparing for this," Theon said, his voice still low.

"I still think Axel should be here instead of me," Luka said.

"You know why we can't do that. We don't need Axel using any more of his power than necessary. He's going through his weekly ration in three days."

"I noticed."

"So you thought it'd be a good idea to give him your rooms with a Fae for the week?" Theon asked sharply, causing Tessa to momentarily pause her movements and glance over at them.

"He's staying in rooms with her now. What's the difference?"

"It's a big godsdamn difference, Luka. You have a room directly across from him, and I'm directly above him here. At Arius House, your rooms are farther away."

Theon raked a hand through his hair. It wasn't his brother's fault he was so addicted to Fae blood. They could thank their father for that, just as they could thank him for nearly every other shitty thing in their life.

"Axel isn't going to hurt Kat," Tessa suddenly said, her voice taking on that eerie tone.

"Not intentionally," Theon said. "You don't know everything about his situation though."

"Of course I don't," she replied with a mocking smile. Then she added, "But neither do you."

Before Theon could ask what she meant by that, there was a soft knock on the door. Luka went to let the priestess in, while Theon crossed the room to Tessa. He cupped her face, tilting her head up. The violet rings seemed more vibrant today.

"I know it means nothing to you, but I'll be here. The entire time. Take what you need. Let the bond do what it's meant to do," he said softly, but even though her eyes were locked on his, he got the sense she was looking right through him.

"Theon, the priestess is waiting," Luka said, and Theon found himself wishing he had just a few more seconds, another minute. He was constantly wishing for a little more time these days, which was ironic considering he was essentially immortal.

He wanted to pull Tessa into him, hold her for a minute and press a kiss to her brow, but he wasn't entirely a fool. That would be a comfort to him, something to ease the guilt churning in his stomach.

Guilt.

It had taken him a while to work out that was what he was feeling.

Instead, he released her face, but took her hand in his, leading her over to the sofa.

"Lie down on your back," the priestess instructed.

"No drink this time?" Tessa asked, doing as she'd been told. The portrait of obedience.

"That was because your power had not emerged yet," Theon answered. "With it awake, it is not necessary."

"And later?" she asked, referencing the additional injection of tonic she'd had with the first Mark.

"No. That shouldn't need to happen either."

She nodded, her hands folded on her stomach, and he reached to push her braid off her shoulder. The low-cut top gave them perfect access to the place over her heart where the next Mark would go. Luka had already moved to a spot near her head, and she glanced up at him.

"You always stand there," she murmured. "Even in my dreams."

The priestess stepped forward, the ceremonial dagger in hand. "When you draw blood, I will draw the Mark. As before, your power will need to overtake hers, but be aware, as the Mark settles into place, you will experience a flood of her emotions," she explained.

"I understand," Theon said. Then, turning to Luka, he added, "Once the Mark is drawn, remove one of the bands."

Tessa shot up, and she moved so godsdamn fast, Theon stumbled back. The only other time he'd seen her move that fast was in the wine cellar the morning after he'd locked her down there.

"Tessa," Theon said in disbelief because he didn't know what else to say.

She was already across the room, pressing herself to the wall.

"You can't take these off in here," she said, lifting her wrists.

"We're prepared for this, Tessa," Theon said. "We've been preparing for this every time we've gone to the river."

Her head tilted. "What?"

"Every time we've gone to the river, my magic has studied yours, and

Luka has always been nearby gauging threats and the best way to miti-gate them," Theon explained.

"So it wasn't…" Her eyes flashed with sparks of light, and he heard the priestess suck in a sharp breath. "Of course you weren't *taking care* of me. That was all for *you*."

Fuck.

That wasn't true, but that was exactly how it sounded.

Because yes, they'd been taking Tessa to the river bank in Arius Kingdom to give her a reprieve from her power, but they'd also been taking her there for this. In order to receive the next Mark, at least one of those bands would need to be off so he could access her magic.

"No, Tessa," Theon said, taking a step toward her, and he couldn't help but remember the first time they'd been in this same position. Her across the room, pressed to the wall while he tried to get near. "That was for you. For *us*."

"You chose this, Tessa. Remember?" Luka chimed in, still standing near the sofa.

Her gaze slid to him, offering the same glare she'd given him all week, but her hand fell to her side, right atop the space where Theon knew a bargain Mark was on her skin. He assumed it was tingling, reminding her of their deal. The same deal that required her to make others believe they were so connected they were a threat, and with the priestess here to observe, she was dangerously close to breaking that bargain.

"Come on, beautiful," Theon said carefully, taking another step and holding out his hand to her. "Let's get this over with, and then we'll go home."

"Home," she repeated, studying the Mark on the back of her hand. "Will it look the same?"

Theon blinked at her sudden change of subject, but relaxed some as she placed her hand in his outstretched one.

"Different," Theon answered. "The Marks all look different. You've seen Eviana's."

"True," she murmured, settling back onto the sofa as if nothing had happened.

Theon exchanged a confused look with Luka, but his friend was studying Tessa, reaching out to move her braid out of the way.

"It will be like before," Luka said, meeting her stare.

Tessa's lips pursed, but she didn't answer, and Theon turned back to the priestess. Normally, the priestesses would retreat to the hall after drawing the Mark. It was for their own safety since a Fae's power was awakened and uncontrolled, but he'd already been informed that she had been instructed to remain in the room the entire time to observe. It had been a unanimous decision by the ruling Lords and Ladies.

"We're ready," Theon said tightly.

The priestess only nodded, extending the dagger to him again. Ready to get this over with, he sliced his palm before kneeling beside the sofa.

"Ready?" he asked.

"How nice of you to ask this time," she drawled. "But yes, Theon. I am prepared for this. I know what to expect this time."

"I'll draw blood, let the priestess draw the Mark, and then Luka will remove the band. Only one. It will be fine."

"No need to explain things to me. You never have before."

He bit down on his retort. She was nervous and upset. Lashing out at him is what she did. Lifting the blade, he sliced a gash along her chest, blood immediately welling and flowing along her skin. He moved to the side, letting the priestess near to draw the Mark, and as soon as she was done, Luka pulled the band from her wrist.

At first, her power crackled faintly at her fingertips, just as it did the few times they'd done this before, and Theon felt a small sense of relief that at least that had gone right. Taking a deep breath, he lifted his bleeding palm, looking into violet-grey eyes as his blood met hers.

Any ounce of relief he'd momentarily felt was gone as her light wrapped tightly around his darkness. Energy crackled out of her, lightning skittering along the floor, and Theon heard the priestess let out a small scream. This is exactly why she shouldn't be in this room. Luka already had a shield of black flames surrounding her though. The gods help them if a priestess was killed during this.

Gritting his teeth, he pressed his palm more firmly to Tessa's chest, pouring more of his darkness into her. Her back was arched, her breath coming in gasps as her fingers latched onto his wrist, holding him there. Luka's hands were on her shoulders, and Theon leaned over her, smoothing his other hand over her brow.

"You're okay, little storm. You need to let this happen," he rasped, pushing more power into her. "Just like when we're by the river. Let me help. Don't try to control your magic right now. Let me show it what to do."

Tessa nodded, her eyes squeezed shut as a tear escaped, sliding down her temple. Her nails were digging into his flesh, drawing blood, but if that's what she needed to endure this, then so be it. She didn't realize just how much he was willing to bleed for her.

Inhaling another deep breath and giving himself a second to regain control, he sent another wave of power through their connection, and Tessa's magic seemed to pause. His shadows moved slowly, tentatively, and he could swear her light was watching, studying.

Waiting.

For what, he didn't know, but his darkness was straining now. It was reaching for her magic as it always reached for her. He forced it to wind slowly around her power, rather than force it into submission. His shadows coaxed and teased, and a tendril of light sparking with energy started to reach back. He could feel the small shocks in his bones, feel the warmth of her light in the darkest places of his shadows.

More.

He'd always want more of this, of her.

Even if she willingly gave him everything as he'd demanded, it wouldn't be enough.

"That's it, Tessa," he murmured, his thumb swiping at another tear. "We're almost there."

They had to be, right? But he wasn't feeling anything. He wasn't feeling emotion like he thought he would. This just felt like he was torturing her for no godsdamn reason.

Wanting this to be over with, he summoned another wave of shadows, letting it pool and swell, before sending it into her.

Tessa screamed.

But so did he, a sound of agony ripping through him.

Because her power hadn't been content teasing and playing and watching. It had been waiting, luring him into a sense of security.

Light sank into his darkness as if it were the fangs and claws of a wild animal, and it didn't let go. What had been little shocks before were streaks of energy jolting his entire body. Instinctively, he tried to yank his hand away, but her nails digging in further had him stilling, keeping the connection. Fuck, if they had to do this again—

But then he felt it. A flicker of emotion. Agony that wasn't his own.

Then he barked out a curse as her power wrapped around his, and suddenly, it wasn't his shadows forcing her light into submission. It was her light taking what it wanted. Her light caressing his darkness, and his power going willingly, as though it couldn't resist the call of what she was.

He gasped, not able to take in a full breath as emotion barreled into him.

Agony and fear and helplessness.

Loneliness and despair.

Longing and desperation.

But beneath it all was determination.

And anger.

So much fury.

He grunted again as her power yanked on his, and with a start, he realized he would not be strong enough.

They'd known she was likely just as powerful as they were, but they'd never voiced the idea that she might be *more* powerful than them. He knew Luka had thought it though, just as he had. If he were being completely honest, it just hadn't seemed plausible. How could a being more powerful than a ruling family member be hidden in the realm for decades?

But there was no denying that her power was taking what it wanted.

"Luka," he rasped out.

He was still holding Tessa by the shoulders, keeping her anchored on the sofa while maintaining a shield around the priestess.

"She won't let me—" He grunted again at another vicious yank from her magic. "I won't overpower her."

"What do you mean you won't overpower her?" Luka snapped in a low whisper. "She has a band on."

Theon shook his head. "You need to help."

"I can't help."

"Our magic. Together," Theon gasped, feeling his magic weaken as hers only seemed to strengthen.

"Theon, that's not how this works," Luka argued, still keeping his voice low so the priestess wouldn't overhear.

"None of this is how it was supposed to work," Theon snapped. "Not a fucking thing has gone the way we'd planned. Why would this be any different? *Fuck.*"

The curse came as Tessa screamed again, Theon having to fight back with everything he had at this point.

"Luka!" Theon snapped. "Now!"

Then Luka's hand was beside his own. When and how he'd sliced his palm, Theon didn't know, but he could feel the heat of his black flames. Tessa's power seemed to stutter. It wasn't much, but it was enough for Theon to wrench his shadows from the grip her magic had on them. Completely in sync, darkness and black flames merged, bearing down on her power, forcing it to submit.

Finally, that cord of obsidian black and gold appeared, a silvery-blue faintly interwoven among it. It hovered above their hands, over Tessa's heart before sinking back into them. Theon knew there'd be consequences for what they'd done, but they'd deal with that later.

He sat back on his heels, utterly drained, but more than that, he could feel everything Tessa was feeling. Her emotions were so volatile, he couldn't entirely discern which were his and which were hers. He was too exhausted to try. Or maybe that was her exhaustion.

Coughing and spluttering, Tessa rolled off the sofa. Luka caught her before she fell flat on her face. He immediately passed her over to Theon, and he pulled her into his chest. The bond was frantic, vibrating wildly, and Tessa curled into him. This was nothing like the last Mark where she'd fought against him.

"I need to see her Mark," came the priestess's voice.

Theon had forgotten she was here.

He tried to ease Tessa back, but her fingers were curled into his shirt and her face was pressed to his chest.

"Come on, beautiful," he murmured. "Just for a minute."

She shook her head. He could feel her tears soaking through the fabric of his shirt, but more than that, he could feel her weariness.

"Tessa, we show her the Mark, and then we can get out of here," he coaxed.

With a shaky exhale, she lifted her head and pushed away from him. The bond immediately panicked, and he saw her flinch.

No.

He *felt* her flinch.

His gaze dropped to her chest as Luka appeared with a warm, damp cloth. Theon took it, gently wiping at the Mark, his brow furrowing. The Mark looked perfect, but there was an additional swirl that hadn't been there before.

"This isn't right," the priestess said, reaching towards Tessa as if to trace the Mark, but a low rumble from Luka had her stilling. "This isn't right," she repeated.

"Is there anything we can do about it?" Theon asked.

After a moment of thought, she answered, "I have never seen a Mark like that. I do not know, but I am required to report this to—"

"The ruling Lords and Ladies," Theon interrupted. "If there is nothing to be done, your services are no longer required this evening."

The dismissal was clear, and the priestess bowed her head before leaving, Luka shutting the door behind her.

Both of their attention settled on Tessa, who had curled back into Theon.

"What the fuck was that?" Luka demanded.

"I didn't have a choice," Theon answered.

"You didn't have a choice?" Luka repeated. "We weren't fucked enough? You had to add to it?"

"No one knows why it looks like that," Theon argued. "They're all going to assume it's because she's not Fae and that's why the Mark looks different. Only the three of us know. We'll keep it that way."

Luka's brow arched. "Axel?"

Theon looked away. "I've brought enough shit into Axel's life. I don't need to put this on him too."

Silence fell for a minute before Luka said, "Think we can get her home before the vomiting starts?"

"Tessa?" Theon asked, stroking her hair. She only nodded against him.

That was good enough for him. Get her home. Get her safe. That was all he truly cared about in this moment. They'd figure the Mark out tomorrow.

He'd just add it to his never-ending list of things to figure out about her.

# 11

## TESSA

She was curled into Theon as she always managed to do in sleep. Her hand was on his chest, Theon's fingers loosely intertwined with hers, and she sighed, hating herself for taking this comfort from him.

Hating herself for being weak enough to need the comfort. She'd been just fine by herself for years.

But she'd also had the ability to drown in vices.

Maybe she'd never really been fine.

Gods, what she'd give for some time with a mortal right now. Then again, she knew it wouldn't be enough. This godsdamn bond had made her crave Theon and only Theon, especially knowing what he could do to her with his hands and his mouth and his power...

A mortal would never be enough again.

Right now, that bond was so content, it warmed her soul as much as the hand on her hip did. That hand was *hot*. So was the chest pressed to her back.

Wait. What?

With a start, her eyes flew open, and she sat up abruptly.

The males in the bed with her also woke, and godsdamn weapons appeared in their hands along with traces of their magic.

"Why are you holding a dagger?" Tessa asked, her voice raspy, likely from vomiting.

"Why are you flying out of bed like you're being attacked?" Luka retorted, tossing the dagger aside and flopping down onto his back when he realized there was no danger.

"Why are you in this bed?" Tessa demanded. Then she realized where they were.

A large bedroom with double doors leading to a balcony overlooking gardens at the base of mountains. A doorway that would lead to an extravagant bathroom. Another doorway that would lead to a small room with a single bed and desk. The portrait of four black horses above the bed.

They were at Arius House.

"How did we get here?" Tessa asked.

"You're full of questions for someone who just woke up after sleeping for nearly two days," Theon muttered, his dagger disappearing in a swirl of dark mist. He dragged a hand down his face, his ebony hair mussed and disheveled.

"Two days?" she repeated.

"How are you feeling?" Theon asked, now appearing fully awake. He was watching her wearily, and she could feel apprehension that wasn't hers.

Oh gods.

She was feeling what he was feeling. She could scarcely handle her own emotions, let alone his.

"Tessa…" Theon said, trailing off as he clearly felt her sudden inner turmoil. "This is fine. We'll figure it all out. We just need to adjust a little."

"Right. Adjust," she murmured, watching Luka slide from the bed.

Naked.

She looked down as if she might find herself naked as well. But no, she was in the loose pants and Theon's shirt she vaguely remembered changing into at the townhouse. Looking back up, she found Luka sliding on a pair of pants, which was kind of disappointing.

"Why are you naked?" she blurted.

"I'm not," was his answer, and Tessa rolled her eyes.

"Why were you naked?"

"I sleep naked."

Her head tilted, watching as he buttoned his pants. "All the time?"

"Obviously," he answered dryly. His gaze flicked to Theon. "You good?"

Theon nodded. Luka stalked to the balcony door, and Tessa watched the muscles in his back ripple as wings appeared when he stepped outside. Then he was launching into the sky, and something in her was upset to see him go.

Which was stupid.

She was still furious with him.

"You feel…a lot of things very quickly all the time," Theon said, drawing her attention back to him.

Tessa was fiddling with the bands on her wrists. If she'd been sleeping for two days, no wonder she was restless and feeling out of sorts. It certainly had nothing to do with waking up between two males, one of them very naked.

The thought alone made her hot.

She glanced at Theon. At least he had pants on.

Except she was irritated by that rather than relieved.

*Godsdammit.*

"Why was he in bed with us?" Tessa asked.

Watching her carefully, Theon said, "Axel and Katya are in his rooms. You knew he was staying with us."

"This house is huge. There's no other rooms he could stay in?"

"Not without attracting unwanted attention."

"Because your father won't find it suspicious that Axel is sleeping in this wing when his rooms aren't here?"

"We are dealing with it."

"But in this bed?"

"It's designed for three people, Tessa."

"There's a bed in that room designed for *one*. Or a sofa. Or the floor."

Theon sighed, slipping from the bed. "I don't understand why you're upset, other than that you two seem to be in the middle of some kind of stand-off. He wasn't going to leave us alone with you basically unconscious and me drained from the last Mark."

"I'm not upset. I just…wasn't expecting it," she retorted. "What are you doing?"

"Coffee," was his only answer before he left the room.

With a huff, she shoved her hair back from her face as she crawled out of the massive bed. She could smell herself, and whatever was coating her tongue was like sandpaper. After brushing her teeth twice, she stepped into the large shower. She'd been hoping the warm water would wash away everything she was feeling, but it was doing the opposite. Her magic buzzed, trapped beneath her flesh, and she was turning the water to cold. The bond was pushing for her to go find Theon, and she sank down onto the bench, forcing herself to take a deep breath. There were ways to block the bond. Theon had done so, and she'd found ways to take subtle control of the thing, but she couldn't block it like he could.

And gods, she wanted to block it. She didn't want him knowing that she was wanting and hating every second of it. She didn't want him knowing that even the cold water was doing nothing to ease it. She didn't want him knowing that even as she found release again with her own fingers, it did godsdamn nothing. Only made the want increase rather than give her any sort of relief. There was no distraction in this. It did nothing to keep her thoughts and feelings from becoming too much.

With a frustrated sigh, she finished her shower. After drying off, she grabbed a silk robe that hung nearby, and gritted her teeth at the smooth fabric against her still oversensitive skin. She almost wished for the agony she'd experienced with the first Mark when she couldn't handle fabric against her skin because it *hurt*. This was arguably worse.

Tessa fiddled with one of the bands, contemplating taking it off, even if just for a minute. She could control it for a minute, right?

Of course she couldn't control it. Taking it off would just create another mess she wouldn't be able to clean up herself. She didn't have Dex here, and she didn't want Theon knowing she could remove the bands herself.

Dex.

She missed him, despite her suspicions that had surfaced finding him with Lord Jove. It wasn't just Dex she missed, but Corbin and Lange. Brecken and even Oralia. Kat being around helped some, but she hardly saw the female. Dex always found a way to get her off the estate, found a way to let her forget about her life for just a little bit.

It was too much. All of this was too much.

"Tessa?"

She had her hands braced on the vanity, her head hanging as she tried to get control over just one godsdamn thing, but she couldn't even manage that.

She sucked in a sharp breath when she felt his touch. Just a single finger. That was all it was that dragged down her spine. That was all it was, but it pushed her over an edge of desperation, and when she lifted her head, those were two tears slipping down her cheeks as she met Theon's gaze in the mirror.

"Let me give you what you need, Tessa," he murmured, his voice rough in a way that made her squeeze her thighs together even more.

"And what is it you think I need?"

That finger was trailing back up her spine now, and when it reached her nape, his hand slid around her throat. The grip was loose, a thumb running along the underside of her jaw.

"Something only I can give you."

"Or you could let me get it from someone else," she retorted.

His eyes flared, the dark in them intensifying. "You and I both know it wouldn't be the same, and it certainly wouldn't be enough. Just like your fingers weren't enough earlier. Again."

"You don't know that."

His lips twitched. "Lies," he whispered into her ear, before he slowly lowered his lips to her neck. He held her eyes in the mirror the entire time. Until he started mixing the soft kisses with sharp nips and bruising sucks. Then her head fell back against his shoulder, her eyes fluttering closed.

He was trailing the fingertips of his other hand up and down her side, along her ribs to her hip and back up. The robe tugged a little looser with every pass he made. His lips moved from her neck along her bare skin, the silk fabric slipping down her shoulder.

"Tell me," he murmured.

She shook her head, and he nipped at her shoulder, making her gasp. "I told you I would never say it."

"You also said there would never be a next time," he replied, his fingers dragging along her torso again, but this time his hand slid around her hip and tugged her back into him.

"This means nothing," she said on a breathy moan as she felt him pressing against her. The bond was frantic and so was her magic, and she wasn't strong enough to resist any of it. Giving in was easier than fighting the inevitable anyway.

Twisting in his hold, his brows raised in surprise. He was still shirtless. One of her hands slid up his chest, while the other dropped to the band of his loose pants. She dragged a nail along it, his stomach tensing at her touch.

"This means nothing," she repeated. "It's a distraction."

"A distraction. Of course. Nothing more."

"Don't do that. Don't placate me."

Another gasp slipped from her as his hands landed on her hips, lifting her onto the vanity.

"Wouldn't dream of it, beautiful," he replied, tugging on the sash of the robe.

"Tell me," she demanded.

He smirked, pulling the tie free. The robe remained in place without it, but barely. "Now who is making demands?"

"You want me to lie to you," she scoffed. "I want you to tell me you understand exactly what you are to me."

A hand slid into her wet hair, tipping her head back as he leaned into her. "I am your distraction from a life you never wanted." A kiss to the corner of her mouth. "I am everything you hate about this world." A kiss to the other corner. "I am your villain that has taken everything from you." A nip to her jaw. "So take from me, Tessa. Take what you need. That's what you want, right? That's all you want from me, so take it."

He pulled back, once again holding her stare as he released her hair and slowly slid the robe down one arm, then the other. Somehow, his eyes darkened even more, full of carnal lust at her bare breasts and naked flesh.

Was she doing this again? She'd told him it wouldn't happen, but fuck, the distraction was already working. Her only thoughts had been on him and his touch and his lips since he'd walked into the bathroom. A reprieve from her life, exactly what she wanted him to be.

Not giving herself another second to think about it, she surged forward, fingers curling into ebony strands as her mouth crashed into his. His answering rumbled groan told her he'd been using every shred of control he had, and this was her permission to let it go.

The kiss was hot and searing and full of the need they'd denied each other for days. The licks of tongues and nips of teeth spoke to every time they'd teased and edged each other since their first time, of all the ways they'd tried to satisfy the need themselves and failed.

Because only this, only them, would ever be enough.

Fury burned through her at the thought, and she yanked on his hair, eliciting a grunt from him.

"Tell me, little storm," he murmured against her skin, "what did you think about when you were touching yourself minutes ago?"

"Not you," she spat.

"More lies," he hummed as he made his way down her chest. "I'm beginning to crave your lies as much as I crave your mouth."

"I'm not lying," she gasped, his mouth closing around a nipple and his tongue flicking against the hard tip.

"I'm told you're an excellent liar," he said, moving to her other breast while his fingertips skated up her leg, starting at her calf and gliding to her inner thigh. Her legs fell wider by themselves, and his thumb slid against her center. It was the barest of touches, but it had her jolting, and a dark chuckle came from him. That thumb came to his mouth, his tongue darting out to lick the pad. "I suppose next you're going to tell me I'm not the reason you're dripping?"

Sitting up straighter, she leaned towards him, a sneer on her lips as she taunted, "Maybe I'm thinking about Luka since he's to be my Match and all."

"Careful, Tessa," Theon said sharply.

A satisfied smirk formed. "Maybe I was thinking about how much I'm going to enjoy having him naked in a bed with me while we're here. Maybe I was thinking about what it would be like to feel his hot skin against mine, his tongue between my legs—"

"If that's what you want, beautiful, you only need to ask," Theon interrupted, and her mouth fell open as he dropped to his knees.

A squeak of surprise came from her as he gripped her thighs and yanked her to the edge of the vanity. He didn't give her any time before his tongue was hot and wet against her center. Her knees tried to snap closed at the sudden sensation, but he'd already braced them with his shoulders, keeping her open.

"Theon," she gasped. She'd expected him to make her beg. That was what he liked. He liked hearing her ask for him, the words from her lips making him feel like he had that control he valued so highly, knowing he could deny her if he wished.

He didn't acknowledge her though. All of his attention focused on where his tongue was driving her to an edge she'd been chasing for days. It flicked against her clit before there was another long, hard lick that had her grinding against his mouth. She felt him smile against her, and she cursed as he lifted his mouth from her, his lips glistening. His eyes met hers, a wicked gleam of triumph in them.

There was a nip to her inner thigh that had a whimper coming from her as he asked, "Tell me again, Tessa. What were you thinking about when you were touching yourself in the shower?"

"You," she gasped. "It's always you, and I hate it."

Then she was moaning as his power snaked up her body, coils of

shadows skittering along bare flesh in a way that had her magic struggling beneath her skin. It wanted out.

"Theon," she gasped again.

"Tell me what you want, little storm."

But she wasn't telling him shit. Her hand went back to his hair, and
she yanked his mouth back to her aching center. He didn't fight her, but
she felt the shiver roll through him down the bond. Her grip never loosened, holding him to her, and her head fell back as he did exactly what
he'd promised and gave her what she needed to forget. He alternated
between kissing and sucking her clit and taking the time to swirl his
tongue in the deepest parts of her. He didn't seem to mind that she was
holding him there, forcing him to do this to her. Something inside of her
recognized it was a sense of control he was giving her. Another thing he
knew she was needing right now, but she wouldn't let herself dwell
on it.

She might hate that her feet had found their way to his shoulders,
bracing herself against him, but she didn't care. Not as he acted like a
starving male. In a way, he probably was. He had to be as crazed with
want as she was. He was right. This was all she wanted from him, and as
long as he didn't make her say those words, she would take what she
needed.

He hit a particularly sweet spot, and she bucked against him. His
groan reverberated through her. She was panting, her vision shimmering as she came so close to bliss. He gave her no reprieve. There was
no teasing or demanding from him this time. If she was going to take,
apparently so was he.

Every swirl, flick, and lick coaxed her closer to that edge, the tension
building in her lower belly, her thighs, her entire body, and with a sharp
nip to her clit, he forced her over it. He took her pleasure, just like he
said he would. She was a quivering mess as she came on his tongue, and
he didn't stop. Not until she was all trembling limbs and sweat-glis-
tening skin did his tongue stop moving. He dropped an open-mouthed
kiss to her inner thigh. Then another.

He climbed to his feet, his heated gaze taking her in, before he was
gathering her up. For once, she didn't care as he carried her back out to
the bedroom. She was fairly certain her legs would have given out if
she'd tried to stand.

Theon set her on the bed before grabbing a glass of water and
handing it to her. She took a long drink. The moment she was done, he

was taking the glass from her and setting it aside. He took her chin in his hand before his mouth was back on hers, forcing her to taste herself on his lips. He pulled back enough to look into her eyes.

"Tell me what other things you think about someone else doing to you when you're touching yourself," he demanded, something frenzied filling his eyes that had a shiver of excitement rolling through her.

"Why?"

"Because I want to make sure that I'm the only one you're thinking about doing anything to you."

She smirked. "I think I'll keep my fantasies to myself."

His features darkened. "Then I'll be forced to replace them."

"Good luck with that," she taunted, because she knew exactly what it would get her.

And she wasn't disappointed as a low growl rumbled from him, and he was pushing her down onto the bed while shoving off his pants.

She wasn't disappointed at all as she took what she wanted from him for the rest of the morning.

Because that's all this was.

A distraction.

"Luka will be back soon," Theon said, sliding into the seat beside her at the table.

There was a spread of roasted chicken, salad, fruit, bread, cheese, and some kind of soup full of vegetables. Theon had filled a bowl for her, but she'd pushed it aside, loading her plate up with chicken, fruit, and bread instead.

"Where did he go?" Tessa asked.

"Flying."

"Yeah, but *where*?"

"I'm sure he went to his place for a bit."

Her brow furrowed. She remembered them saying he had a place nearby. "His estate?"

"Something like that."

"Where is it?"

"In the mountains."

Tessa sat back. "His estate is in the mountains? So it's like a cabin or something?"

Theon lifted his glass to his mouth as he answered, "Or something." Before she could ask more, he added, "Eat. It's been days."

"Yes, that's why I'm famished," she drawled. "It has nothing to do with the last few hours of fucking."

"I should have let you eat before we did that."

She could feel his inner conflict down the bond. Did he actually feel guilty about something?

No. He didn't know how to feel guilty. Theon had said it himself. He does what needs to be done without remorse. He didn't care about her. He just did what needed to be done to keep her together. That was why he'd taken care of her in other ways before taking care of the physical need to eat. He'd felt what a fucking mess she was, that she was on the brink of shutting down, and he'd taken care of her. That was it.

Clearing her throat, she said, "Have you figured anything out in all your reading?"

"Not really," Theon answered. "But now that the hearing has been held and the newest Mark is in place, I will be able to focus more on it."

Tessa nodded, tearing off a piece of bread.

"But I will need your help."

"You seem to need that a lot," she quipped.

"I need you to tell me about your past."

"There's nothing to tell. It's all in your file you have on me."

"But I have to assume those are all falsified. They clearly aren't all factual," Theon said.

She hummed, spearing a piece of melon with her fork.

"Were you always at the Celeste Estate?"

"As far back as I can remember, yes."

Theon nodded, reaching for the chicken. This felt weird. A civil meal with just the two of them. She'd just been in a bed with him for hours, and yet this was the awkward part of her day.

"Is there anything else you can think of that might be helpful?"

"I don't know what exactly you're looking for, Theon," she answered, moving fruit around her plate with her fork.

"Anything really. Even if it seems mundane, it could be important."

"There's nothing."

"Can you at least try— Fuck."

He'd clearly felt her tense at the word.

"I didn't mean to imply you're not trying," he said quickly. "But the other night at dinner suggested there are things we don't know."

"Like what?" she muttered, ready to be done with this conversation. She'd just had the best sex of her life to distract her from all of this, and now he was bringing it all back up.

He hesitated, causing her to glance over at him. He was studying her, clearly debating what to say next. Letting her fork drop to her plate with a clatter, she sat back in her chair, rubbing at the area around the bands. "Stop doing that."

"Doing what?"

"Trying to figure out what I'm feeling."

"You feel a lot. All the time."

"Where are Axel and Kat?" she asked, changing the subject and reaching for her water.

"I haven't told anyone else you're awake."

"Why?"

"You'll have to forgive my negligence. I've been a little busy with your needy cunt, beautiful."

Tessa choked on her water as Theon continued to casually eat his meal, but she felt his amusement trickle down their bond. Sliding her bowl of soup back towards her, she picked up her spoon solely to have something to do with her hands, but of course, now she was remembering all those things he did between her thighs. She was deliciously sore in a way she hadn't been in ages.

"We will be some place where you can take the bands off tomorrow," Theon said after a moment. "It is a place similar to the training quarters, so you'll be able to do more than merely siphon it off." When she only nodded, he added, "We're planning to be there a few days, so it will give you plenty of time without them."

"We're leaving Arius House?" she asked, her spoon halfway to her mouth.

He nodded. "Tomorrow morning. We're going to the Underground."

Tessa dropped her spoon, hot soup splashing, but she didn't notice. "The Underground?" she repeated.

Theon was frowning slightly as he used a napkin to clean up the soup. "Yes. We have an opportunity to meet with Cienna."

"But it's not actually underground, right?"

"I guess not," he answered, and all the tension in her muscles eased until he said, "But it's a system of caves and tunnels in the Ozul Mountains, so I suppose technically it is underground." His head snapped up, taking her in. "Tessa, what's wrong?"

"Nothing," she rasped, but she was already on her feet. Already moving through the room, through the bedroom. She only wore loose pants and Theon's shirt. She'd pulled her hair up into a loose knot on her head after rinsing off again before their food arrived. Now she wrenched open the double balcony doors, stumbling outside and gulping down fresh air.

A hand gripped her elbow, tugging her to a stop at the same time a figure was dropping from the sky.

"What is going on?" Luka demanded, his wings disappearing as he took them in.

But Tessa couldn't focus on what they were saying. They were going to the Underground. For multiple days. And it was *under* the ground. Let alone the *people* that were there. The Arius Kingdom may oversee them, but from what she knew and what Theon had said, the Underground was a kingdom in and of itself.

"Tessa? Tessa, look at me."

There were hands on her face, trying to force her to look at him, but her eyes were shut tight. She shoved his hands away. Curling her bare toes against the marble floor, relishing in the freezing bite as it grounded her. Inhaling deeply, she could smell the autumn air and feel the cool breeze on her face.

"Open your eyes, Tessa." That was Luka. "Now."

"I'm not in a training room," she rasped.

Another hand cupping her face, this one hot. "Tessa, open your eyes."

She blinked, the bond doing something weird in her chest as she focused on sapphire eyes. He didn't say anything, just stood there. Giving her something else to ground herself in.

Footfalls sounded, and a moment later, Theon was back. "Here," he said gruffly, a blanket wrapping around her shoulders. "We can sit outside for a while."

She let him lead her to the patio sofa, Luka's fingers trailing along her jaw before he dropped his hand. Theon lowered to a seat beside her, while Luka took a chair across from them. She liked that. She could still see him there while Theon's touch soothed the bond, and in turn, her.

"We're going to the Underground tomorrow," she finally said, barely audible.

"We are," Luka agreed.

"There's no light there."

"They have light."

She shook her head, clutching the blanket tighter around herself. "No light. No air. Only darkness and stars going out."

"What are we going to do about this?" Theon asked, tucking her closer into his side.

"We have to go. Who knows when Cienna will see us again," Luka said, pulling the tie from his hair. The brown strands fell around his face. "You know she's going to have answers for us."

"And those answers will require payment," Theon sighed.

"She'll be interested in her," Luka agreed.

"Wait, I'm the payment?" Tessa asked, looking up at Theon.

"No, beautiful, but she'll want to meet you before she answers questions about you," he said, tucking hair behind her ear. "But we'll be there with you. All of us. It doesn't feel like you're underground once we get to the main districts."

She broke his stare, looking out at the view over the balcony railing. "Can you see the sky?"

He was quiet for a long moment before he answered. "No, Tessa. You cannot see the sky."

"And we will be staying there?"

"For a few days," he confirmed.

"But you won't leave me there?"

His answer was filled with some sort of fierce determination when Theon said, "No, Tessa. I won't leave you there."

Her eyes flicked to him before they settled back on Luka. "I wasn't asking you. You leave me in the dark all the time."

Luka's gaze never left hers when he said, "I won't leave you there, Tessa."

She didn't know why she sought his confirmation. She didn't believe him, but something in her settled at his vow.

She stayed on the balcony for the rest of the day.

# 12

## AXEL

"It's only a little farther," Axel called over his shoulder.

"You keep saying that," Tessa growled back. "Yet we're still in these tunnels."

He did keep saying that, but he didn't know how else to contribute to keeping her calm. Theon and Luka had filled him in on her reaction to coming here, but even if they hadn't, the storm that had been gathering as they'd coaxed her through the Underground gate said enough about how she felt about it.

Theon kept her hand firmly in his, and Luka was behind them, keeping close. The passage they were currently navigating was scarcely wide enough for two people to walk side-by-side, let alone three. The only light was the glow from Luka's black flames. It wasn't much, but they all had enhanced eyesight, so it was enough.

"You doing all right?" he asked, casting a glance at Katya.

She walked beside him dressed in her training attire. He'd offered to get her other clothes, but she'd insisted that wasn't necessary.

He was going to do it anyway. She needed more than training clothes. He'd never really paid attention to the attire of the Fae who were assigned to Arius Kingdom, but being in the Acropolis and seeing so many others had him realizing just how differently the Kingdoms controlled their Fae. Not only that, but how different the Fae were in general before they were assigned to their Kingdoms and positions.

"I'm fine," Kat replied.

"Being here doesn't bother you?"

"Not at all."

She kept her focus straight ahead, and Axel clamped down on the irritation that prickled. She was slowly becoming comfortable around him when they were alone, but with the others, she was overcautious, despite his assurances.

Silence had fallen, the only sound their footfalls against the rocky ground. They were going straight to Cienna. Or that was the plan. They wouldn't see Cienna until she decided she was ready, and they'd know that when a messenger appeared to take them to her. So, for now, they simply kept following the passages.

"I spent time in the catacombs of the archives," Katya said.

Axel glanced at her again. "What?"

"There are catacombs beneath the archives. I spent time there. It is why it does not bother me to be below ground," she explained.

"That makes sense."

"I know."

The corner of his lips twitched. "So modest, kitten."

"It is not modest to state facts."

Her arm brushed against his as they moved, and she snatched it back. But not before his magic practically jumped from his skin at the contact. He gritted his teeth, forcing the shadows to stay put. They might control the Underground, but he'd use the word 'control' loosely. He still would never come here without full reserves, and letting his power out to satisfy its curiosity wasn't an option right now.

Or ever, really.

"Sorry," Kat muttered.

Axel silently cursed himself because of course she thought he was reacting to her touch, and he was but— Fuck. Why did any of this matter? Why did he even *care*?

This was ridiculous.

A moment later, the passageway emptied into a decent-sized cavern. There were several passages branching off of it, but there was no need for Luka's flames here. Large braziers lined the perimeter every few feet, and there were a few market stalls selling essentials.

Food.

Elixirs.

Weapons.

Maps.

Everything one would need to survive the Underground.

"This is it?" Tessa asked.

Axel glanced back at her. "What do you mean?"

"I expected the Underground to be...not this," she said, her gaze taking in the cavern.

"This is one small outpost," Theon explained, releasing her hand when she tugged it from his grip.

"There is no one here," Kat said, following Tessa deeper into the cavern.

Axel slipped his hands into his pockets, rocking back on his heels as he watched the females take everything in. He could only imagine what they were going to think when they saw the central districts.

"There are a few here," Axel replied. "They are staying hidden, but they are watching."

"Why?" Tessa asked.

Axel shrugged. "Some have been following us since we arrived. They will report back to whomever they are indebted to. Others are waiting to see weaknesses they can exploit. Most likely assume you two are prisoners with the bands on your wrists, and they do not want to be associated with you until they know why you are here."

"You personally escort prisoners through the Underground?" Tessa asked, both females subconsciously rubbing at their wrists.

"Sometimes," Axel agreed.

"They never go outside?"

"Some cannot leave. Most find it safer not to."

Tessa nodded. She wandered closer to one of the stalls, but Luka was there, pulling her to a stop.

"I just want to look," Tessa groused.

"No," Luka said. "We are not in the market for anything."

"Let her look," came a voice from the shadows.

*Brave soul,* Axel thought, his eyes narrowing in the direction the voice came from.

"We have no needs at the moment," Luka answered, pulling Tessa back to the center of the cavern.

The voice tutted at him. "Everyone has needs, and here, any need can be met."

"Any need?" Tessa said, her brows knitting together.

*Shit.*

The question had the figure appearing from the shadows. Tall and lithe, the female had dark hair that hung loose and limp around her shoulders. Her lips were curved into a cunning smile, and her gaze slid over them all.

Axel had already stepped in front of Kat, but she was peering curiously around him.

"Don't ask her questions," Axel whispered, and he saw her nod in his periphery.

"Anything you need can be found in the Underground," the female answered. "Spells. Glamours. Weapons. Secrets. Revenge."

Tessa rubbed at her wrists, the flesh red and raw from the bands keeping her magic subdued.

"Do not speak to her, Tessa," Theon said sharply.

He had stepped in front of Tessa, and Luka had moved beside her. Theon's darkness was drifting along the ground. Some were making their way towards the female, some were winding around Tessa's legs, snaking up her torso. Luka bent and murmured into her ear. Tessa's eyes went wide, and she nodded in understanding. Axel assumed he had filled her in on the fact that currency here wasn't coin but favors, and simply having a question answered was enough to have you indebted to another.

The female tilted her head. "She is a prisoner."

Clever with her non-question.

"She is mine," Theon replied. "And you'd do well to remember such a thing, Witch."

"Of course, my Lord." Her tone held a hint of mocking. "But her question was answered."

A swirl of darkness before Theon was tossing a knife at her feet. "I trust this to be sufficient payment."

"It is, my Lord," she answered, snatching the knife from the ground. "Safe travels."

Then she disappeared into the shadows once more.

"I didn't know," Tessa whispered.

"It's fine," Theon said tightly.

None of them had expected to be approached, but they should have. The Underground was growing restless, and Axel hadn't been able to make appearances as often as he had before. Another reason they were here on this small holiday from the Selection Year.

"Let's keep moving," Luka said. "News of this will have already spread."

"I didn't know," Tessa repeated.

Axel offered her an understanding smile as he ushered Katya towards a passageway.

They'd been walking for another few minutes when he said to Kat, "Your training is going well?"

"Yes."

"The first round of testing is after the Samhain celebrations."

"I know."

"According to reports, your instructors believe you will be able to have your bands removed," he continued. "That's impressive. Few have them removed at the first testing."

"Being away for these days might alter those results," she replied.

"You are worried about it?"

"No, but it stands to reason that practice is required. Is that not how you mastered your gifts?"

"I can take you to train while we're here," he offered.

"Really?"

He huffed a laugh. "You only need to ask, Kat."

"That is not as simple as you make it out to be."

Then she was letting out a gasp as he tugged her into him, his shadows creating a shield as a figure stepped in front of them.

"Where did he come from?" Kat whispered.

But Axel was pulling the small mirror from his pocket, finding Cienna's message. Looking over at Theon, he said, "It's time."

They'd followed the messenger for another hour. He took them through winding passages, many of them forcing their group to go single file. Axel stayed at the front, directly behind the messenger, but he could hear the constant coaxing from Theon and Luka. The first tight passage they'd had to force her to go through. The messenger wouldn't wait for them. If they lost him, they were fucked. Cienna had wards that purposefully misdirected those who didn't already know how to find her.

Finally, there was a faint light that only grew as they made their way towards it, and when they finally stepped into the open cavern, Axel let out a breath of relief.

This cavern was bigger than the others they'd encountered. There were shelves fashioned to one wall, various bottles and tins of the gods only knew what was in them. Dug into the stone wall was a hearth where there was a make-shift stove with various pots bubbling and steaming. Several tables littered the space, and there were four other passageways leading off the room.

"Chaos follows you everywhere now?"

They all turned at the sharp voice, finding a tall female standing before them. Her mahogany hair was braided down her back, and her black clothing hugged her figure. Her violet gaze was fixed on Theon where Tessa was peering around him.

"Cienna," Axel said, stepping forward. "Thank you for seeing us."

"*You* are Cienna?" came Tessa's shocked voice.

Cienna said nothing. Only continued to watch her.

It was Theon who said, "Do you know each other?"

"No," Tessa muttered, breaking Cienna's stare and looking around the space. "I am just surprised."

"Cienna?" Theon asked, clearly not believing Tessa.

"Speak carefully," the Witch retorted sharply. "There are five of you. I will answer five questions. One from each."

"Five questions is not nearly enough," Theon argued.

"Perhaps not, but it is far more than you deserve."

A huff of laughter had them all turning to Tessa.

"What?" she asked. "I like her." Turning to Theon, she asked, "Did you lock her in a wine cellar too?"

But it was the Witch who replied coolly, "I suppose a network of caves is slightly more comfortable."

"I didn't—" Theon started, but then snapped his mouth shut at Cienna's arched brow.

"Okay. Five questions," Axel said, stepping forward. "We will be grateful for whatever information you can give us. Right?" He sent a pointed look at Theon. He was tired of being the middle person, but Cienna refused to work directly with Theon and Luka after she'd been forced into hiding for bestowing their Guardian bond behind their father's back.

The muscle feathered in Theon's jaw, but he gave a sharp nod of his head. "Of course, Cienna. Whatever you can provide will be invaluable."

"And you, descendant of Sargon?" Her attention switched to Luka, and then her eyes seemed to widen before they narrowed. "What did you do?"

"As usual, I don't know what you're talking about, Cienna," Luka said, folding his arms across his chest.

She hummed in disapproval before her attention shifted once more, this time to Katya. "You are unexpected to see down here."

Axel stopped himself from asking if she knew her. Barely. But he managed to hold his tongue.

Turning her back on them, Cienna moved to a table that had multiple books laid open atop it. "Ask your questions."

"We need a few minutes if you're only allowing us one each," Theon retorted.

She waved a hand in an impatient motion to get on with it, and Axel hid his smirk as his brother bristled. Tessa was watching them curiously as she made her way to the shelves of ingredients.

"The Witches are said to be wicked," she commented, reaching for a tin.

"We are," Cienna replied, not bothering to look up from her book but rather flipping a page. "Put that back."

Tessa shrugged. Replacing the tin, she ran her finger along a leaf on a plant. "Plants don't seem all that wicked."

"Tell that to the priestesses who perform your assessments," Cienna retorted.

"The priestesses aren't Witches."

Cienna lifted her head. "Aren't they? They might call themselves something different, but make no mistake about what they are."

Tessa's eyes widened, but before she could speak again, Theon said, "No questions, Tessa."

She glared at him, moving to another table.

"I do not have all day, Theon," Cienna said irritably. "Ask me what you seek to know."

"As I said, it is more than five questions, and I have no doubt your answers will only create more questions," Theon replied, having made his way to the same table Cienna was at.

"Ask the right questions, and that won't be the case."

"Speak what you know, and none of this would be necessary."

Cienna slammed her book shut. "If you do not wish for my help, simply say so."

Tessa had joined them now, and Axel watched her eyes bounce back and forth between Cienna and Theon, an intrigued expression on her face.

"I have my question," Tessa suddenly announced to the room.

Theon's head whipped to her. "No, Tessa. We need to discuss which questions we will ask."

"She said we each get one. Not that you get to assign us each a question to ask."

"Tessalyn, *do not speak*," Theon ordered, the entrancing stilling Tessa's tongue.

And Axel watched as the violet in Tessa's eyes flared bright with rage. Her fingers curled in, but he could swear light had crackled there. She had her bands on though…

"So foolish to play with things you do not understand," Cienna said cryptically.

"Then help me understand," Theon said in frustration.

"I am waiting for your questions."

Theon's darkness made an appearance, telling Axel just how irritated his brother was getting, and Cienna gave him an unimpressed stare. Then her head tilted to the side as she watched his magic drift towards Tessa.

"By the gods," Luka muttered. "I'll ask a fucking question. What is the Everlasting War?"

Cienna straightened, her palms flat on the tabletop. "That is not a question I anticipated."

"It appears to be something we need to be concerned with," Luka replied.

"Is this the Augury thing?" Axel asked, watching Katya tentatively pull a book towards herself.

Cienna noticed as well, taking the book from her, but also sliding another towards her.

"The 'Augury thing' is apparently very real considering they tried to kill Tessa," Theon retorted.

They'd filled Axel in on that night, though no one had come after Tessa since. Still, it wasn't nearly enough proof to convince him. A secret society who thought their purpose was to keep a prophecy from coming true was too much for him. But it still begged the question of who had attacked them and what this war was. Because yeah, if a war was coming, they should probably be prepared for that.

He unwittingly moved closer to Kat, and now he peered over her shoulder at the book she was looking through. He couldn't read it though. From what he could tell, it was written in the Lost Language.

"So this war…" Axel urged when Cienna remained silent.

"The Everlasting War began long before Devram was created," Cienna said. "It is why it is called everlasting. It was believed to have been won for a period of time, but choices were made that altered Fate, and the war continues across the realms."

"But what—" Tessa rolled her eyes when Theon sent her a look telling her not to ask a question.

"I can research that more on my own," Theon said. "We need to be careful with our questions unless Cienna suddenly finds herself in a more generous mood."

"Has your father rescinded his order for my death?" Cienna asked sharply.

"No," Theon answered.

"Then be grateful I am seeing you at all, Theon St. Orcas."

Theon inhaled deeply, clearly calming himself, before he said, "Tessa has the ability to create storms of some kind. She can manipulate the weather. I know of no god or goddess that can do that, which leads me to believe she is not a Legacy."

"What?" Tessa demanded. "You've said nothing of this to me."

Axel slid his hands into his pockets. Theon liked to have everything figured out before sharing his thoughts and plans with everyone else. He and Luka were used to it, but Tessa…was not.

Theon didn't look at her, keeping his attention on Cienna when he asked, "If she is not a Legacy and she is not Fae, what other options are there?"

Tessa scoffed, pushing off the table and wandering around the space again. "Other options. As if I am one of his prized hounds," she muttered to herself, but they all heard her. Luka threw an exasperated glare at Theon.

"How else am I supposed to word that? Is that not what we are trying to figure out?" Theon asked, his thumb and forefinger rubbing at his brow.

Cienna fell silent, appearing to debate her answer. Or maybe she simply didn't know how to answer it. Axel wasn't sure. She had always been somehow vague yet helpful.

Finally, she said, "I do not have all the answers you seek."

"But you have information that will help," Theon countered. "That is my question. She's not Fae. She's possibly not Legacy. So what else could she descend from?"

"There are countless realms and countless bloodlines," Cienna said, reaching for another book. "Some still thrive. Some long gone. Some have been reborn."

"That is not an answer, and you know it," Theon argued.

Her violet eyes flashed with anger when they snapped back to Theon. "You may wish to tempt fate, Theon, but I do not. I will tell you what I can. If that is not sufficient, our business here is done."

"But I still have a question," Tessa suddenly chimed in. "Don't fuck me out of my question, Theon."

"I'm not—" Theon started, but Axel cut in.

"You said his name."

Tessa didn't acknowledge him, peering into one of the bubbling pots, but Theon spun towards her. "I feel your frustration at having revealed that. You can overcome the demands of the Source bond?"

"I don't understand," Katya said, looking up from her book.

"She isn't supposed to be able to say my name in the presence of those outside of the four of us," Theon explained, his gaze never leaving Tessa.

She finally turned to him, power flickering in her eyes that shouldn't be there with those bands on her wrists. Axel found himself sliding closer to Kat, partially blocking her from Tessa.

The corner of Tessa's mouth tipped up in a mocking smirk. "You insisted I had secrets when I didn't, so I found some to keep."

"You realize this information could help us figure all this out, right? Why would you keep this from me?" Theon demanded.

Her head canted to the side. "Why did you keep your suspicions of me not being a Legacy from me? Why did you keep information from me? Why do you continue to do so?"

"Enough of this," Cienna cut in. "You asked me what other beings she could be descended from, I answered. I may not be able to give you the definitive answers you seek, but trust I have given you enough to find the answers on your own."

Theon ran both his hands through his hair in frustration, and Axel watched his brother. Always in control. Always making sure he was the smartest and most informed in the room. That was why he pushed himself so hard on his studies. It was why his nose was always in a book while he and Luka were playing Chaosphere. It was why Theon had researched bizarre theories on the off chance he might find the smallest bit of truth to give him an advantage. They might give him a hard time about it, but the truth was, Axel knew everything he'd ever done was to prepare for this. Their father wanted to rule Devram. Theon had only ever wanted to prevent that and to keep the people of the Arius Kingdom safe from any retribution from the other Kingdoms. They had been a shunned Kingdom for centuries, and they were fine being so.

It was during his unending research that he'd unearthed truths about the Underground. Then all their plans had changed. Then it wasn't just Arius Kingdom.

Then it became about Devram.

"You have three questions remaining," Cienna said into the silence that had descended.

"Give us a minute," Theon snapped. He'd started pacing, and Luka was monitoring Tessa, who was continuing to explore everything in the space.

"Here's my question," Axel said, holding up his hand when Theon started to argue. Because fuck him dictating all this. There was more that needed to be learned. "How did no one know she wasn't Fae for over two decades? How is that possible?"

"Who says no one knew?" Cienna countered.

"Even if they did, how was it kept a secret?" Axel said.

"Your power is released upon birth," Cienna said. She nodded to the faint silvery Mark visible on Axel's forearm due to his sleeves being rolled back. "She was obviously not given that Mark until the Emerging Ceremony."

"But her power would have broken through that at some point," Axel argued.

"It did," Theon said. "From the day I Selected her."

"But never before then? It doesn't make sense," Axel said.

"As I said, do not mistake what the priestesses are," Cienna cut in, snapping her book shut. "They can create the same potions and elixirs I can. Some are just as skilled at Marks and glamours and all manner of spells."

Theon drew up short. "Glamours? Like the ones Lilura Inquest is renowned for?"

"Yes," Cienna answered. "That counts as one of your questions."

"Cienna," Theon said in disbelief. "You cannot be serious."

"Yet I am. One question left. Perhaps let the females ask, since you refuse to let them speak," she said sharply.

Yeah, that wasn't smart. Axel knew the Witches were not particularly fond of males to begin with. Then they'd come in here with Kat, who he had to drag words out of the way it was, and Tessa, who Theon kept telling to hush.

"Do you have a question, Kat?" Tessa asked, and Axel's eyes widened in surprise. All Tessa had spoken about was her question, yet she offered it to Katya.

"I always have questions," Katya replied. "But you may ask yours."

Tessa nodded, beginning to draw a random design atop a table with her finger. "The night of my Emerging Ceremony, I spoke with Rordan."

The males in the room all went still, but Axel heard Theon's low growl at her using the Achaz Lord's first name. In true fashion, Tessa ignored him.

"He said something to me about questioning why I was in Devram at all," Tessa continued. "With Theon's revelation that he believes I am neither Fae nor Legacy, it all furthers the theory that I was not born of Devram."

"No," Theon interrupted. "The gods left this world and promised never to interfere. We are locked away and forgotten. You know this, Tessa. It was part of your studies."

"It was also part of my studies that Sources must obey their Masters no matter what, and we have all learned that is not true, *Theon*," Tessa said.

Axel turned to Cienna just in time to see the female's lips twitch. "Speak your question."

"If I am not from here, it stands to reason that others in Devram could... Are there others? Like me?"

Axel could swear her voice cracked at the end, and Theon was looking at her in a way that told Axel he could feel everything she was.

"While I doubt there are any like you... Yes, Tessa, there are others," Cienna said, the Witch's tone holding a touch of pity. "I cannot say more, or I will be tempting fate, but know this: just as you seek to find those others, they seek to find you. Lost for so long, but no longer. Tread carefully."

Tessa's brow furrowed, and she raked her teeth over her bottom lip.

"Why do you feel...apprehensive?" Theon asked.

Said apprehension instantly vanished as she glared at Theon, and

Axel had to choke back his huff of laughter when she retorted, "I'm not. I'm annoyed. With you. Again."

"You were very not annoyed with me yesterday. Multiple times," he replied with a casual shrug, and Axel did laugh this time as Tessa's eyes widened in disbelief. But before she could toss back whatever she was about to say, Cienna spoke.

"Leave. I will send for you again in three days' time," she said, already having moved to one of the pots and beginning to sprinkle whatever witchy things into it.

Theon was about to argue, but the pointed look Luka sent him saved them all from that. Thank the gods. The fact that Cienna was telling them to return in the same week should be a victory to Theon.

"Thank you for your time, Cienna," Theon gritted out before making his way to the same passage they'd entered from. The messenger was waiting there to guide them back.

Luka herded Tessa towards the passageway, her face already pale at having to go back into such tight quarters. He fell into step beside Kat, but then Cienna called out, "Axel. A moment."

Kat paused, looking up at him in question, and he gave her a quick grin. "Go with Luka. I'll only be a minute."

"You won't get lost?" she asked uncertainly.

"Nah. I won't be long."

She nodded, hurrying her steps to catch up to Luka, who had stopped to wait for her. With a quick nod, they left the cavern, and Axel turned to the Witch. "Theon is anxious. Thank you for dealing with him today."

Cienna waved her hand in annoyance. "Your brother has many trials coming. He will need to learn to let people in before he has all the pieces. And so will she."

"Tessa?"

"Her as well," Cienna answered, stirring the pot three times before setting the wooden spoon aside.

That was…an interesting answer.

"But I wanted to discuss the question you did not ask," Cienna said, turning to face him. "Or rather, one of the questions you did not ask."

"You will need to be more specific," Axel said with a wink, crossing his arms and leaning a hip against the table.

Cienna did not return his light-heartedness. Instead, she said, "You worry if you are close to crossing a line, and the answer is yes."

Axel straightened, swallowing hard. "You can...tell that just by looking at me?"

"No, I can tell that because of my gifts," she retorted.

"The healing?"

"That's not the question you wish to ask," Cienna said. "You wish to know if you *do* cross that line, if it can be undone."

Axel's gaze darted away from her. Because yeah, that question had been plaguing him. His weekly rations weren't enough. He was needing more and more. A path that only led to a Legacy triggering the curse of Arius to be forever controlled by the bloodlust. To correct the balance, those who overstepped were stripped of their gifts and cursed to weaken in the sunlight, forever bound to the dark and the cravings.

It didn't matter that his father was the one who'd forced him to this place. That was how his father controlled him. His father would find a way to force him to expel all his magic and then leave him in that state for days with chains on his wrists made of the same material as the bands on Tessa's that wouldn't allow his power to refill. His father would leave him in that place until he was nearly mad from the lack of power and feral with the need to fill the emptiness.

"Can it?" Axel asked around the lump in his throat. "Can the curse be undone?"

"Is it a curse?" Cienna countered.

His gaze snapped back to hers. "How can it be considered anything else?"

"For some, it is a curse. For others, it was a blessing."

"I do not know how any Legacy could consider losing their gifts to be a blessing."

"How incredibly conceited to assume only the Legacy were affected by such a thing," she chided, moving to a nook that was carved into the wall. She reached inside, withdrawing a small flask. When she handed it to Axel, he was surprised to find it cool to the touch.

"It is spelled to stay cool," she explained.

"Don't tell Luka you can do that. He'll be wanting you to visit his cave," Axel joked, spinning the top off the flask.

Cienna clicked her tongue. "I do not think I would be counted among the few he would let near his treasure hoards."

"That's fair," he conceded, bringing the flask to his nose and sniffing. Then his head snapped up. "This is blood."

"It is."

"Fae blood."

Cienna nodded. "You will need it."

"That's…great," Axel muttered, twisting the lid back on before sliding it into an inside pocket of his jacket.

"Your path is not yet decided," Cienna said. "Fate waits to make her final choice for you. Choose wisely."

"Helpful as always, Cienna," Axel said with another wink. "Anything else?"

"Not now, but thank you. For not revealing you know your way here."

"Of course." Sliding the mirror from his pocket, he flipped it over in his hand. "I'll see you around?"

She waved him off, as much of a goodbye as he was going to get. To be honest, the thank you itself was a shock. But he'd never risk the fragile trust he'd worked so hard to build with the Witch. He knew Theon and Luka felt immense guilt over the death order their father had issued when he found out Cienna had bestowed the Guardian bond. They'd expected retribution, sure, but not that. Cienna had been on the Arius Council long before any of them had come into this world.

So Axel had done what he did best— damage control. Theon might know how to make the hard decisions and do what needs to be done, but Axel was the one who cleaned up afterwards. He was the one who knew how to talk to people. He was the one who knew how to mitigate and talk people down. He was the one who could spin something so all appeared to benefit, but those relationships had come with keeping secrets of his own.

Like the fact that he really didn't need to wait for Cienna to make contact through the mirror. He'd known for over a year now how to find her when he came to the Underground. Which is also why he wasn't worried about getting lost when he went to catch up with the others.

He jerked his chin at Kat when he strode past her, making his way back to the front of the group. Theon and Luka wouldn't ask him questions with Cienna's messenger still leading them out. More than that, they were too focused on Tessa and coaxing her through these passages once more.

Once back to the same spot he'd found them, the messenger bowed before disappearing back into the dark, and Axel took the lead again.

"What was your question?" he asked Kat after they'd started moving again.

She tilted her face up to peer at him, a few curls falling into her eyes. "What?"

"You didn't get to ask Cienna a question. If you would have gotten your chance, what would you have asked her?"

Her eyes darted away, and she tucked those stray coils of dark hair behind her ear. "I…"

Without conscious thought, he reached out as if to take her hand before realizing what he was doing at the last second. She seemed almost embarrassed. He could practically feel the discomfort as if it were his own.

"Kat?" he pressed, his voice low to keep the others from overhearing.

"It's nothing," she said in a hurry. "I am sure the answer will reveal itself at some point."

"Wouldn't it make more sense to share what you are hoping to discover? Maybe I know something? Or Luka or Theon?"

"You don't."

"You can't know that."

"I *can* know that," she retorted with a huff, those same curls freeing themselves and falling across her brow once more. Sighing, she added, "I would have asked her how my gifts could have been hidden."

"That…is a damn good question," he said, and it was one he should have thought to ask himself.

"My assessments never once indicated a fire element. Certainly not outside the Anala Kingdom. I was expecting to emerge with water," she went on as the passageway they were in emptied into another crossroad cavern. "So I would have asked how they could have been hidden so I could figure out…"

"Where you came from," Axel finished for her in realization. She was just like Tessa with an unexpected power that had changed everything she'd known about herself.

Taking a few seconds to figure out how to respond, Axel said, "Well, you were right."

"About what?"

"I don't know the answer to that. Neither do Luka nor Theon." She gave a soft laugh, and when she looked up at him with a small smile playing on her lips, he added, "But I will help you figure it all out."

# 13
## THEON

Theon stood a few feet away as he watched Tessa. She sat cross-legged on the ground of the training pit. They'd come here as soon as they'd left Cienna. He'd felt all of Tessa's panic in the passageways, felt her moments of relief when they came to crossroad caverns. They could have gone straight to the central districts, but he was hoping if she got to release some of her magic, it would ease a bit of her tension.

And he'd been right.

Now he felt her marvel as she slowly commanded the light pooling in her palms. When they'd first removed the bands, it had exploded out of her as it always did. He'd used his power to help her guide it and calm it, and after a while, he'd slowly pulled back. He wasn't even sure if she had realized he wasn't helping her control it anymore. But there was no rumbling of thunder, no flashes of energy, no hints at a storm. There was just her and her fascination with her magic.

He vaguely recalled when his gifts had first manifested. There had been a moment of that same wonder before it had quickly become a determination to master it. He'd never spent time just *enjoying* his magic. It had always been about controlling it so he could move on to the next goal.

"How are Axel and Kat?" Theon asked when Luka came to a stop beside him. His brother and the female were in a smaller training pit next to this one.

"Katya is quite proficient with her fire already," Luka replied. His shirt was off, tucked into the band of his pants so his wings could be out. "She will easily pass her exam when we return, and her bands will be removed."

"Father will be thrilled," Theon muttered, but he couldn't hold on to the foul mood for longer than a second as a soft laugh came from Tessa at the tendrils of light coiling around her arms. There was a soft golden mist drifting around her as well, and Theon, tired of fighting his darkness, let his shadows back out. They immediately reached for her, snaking across the ground. He felt her sharp inhale and the spike of want the moment their powers met.

"You couldn't just let her be?" Luka said, shifting beside him and his wings rustling in irritation.

"I'm not trying to do anything, but my magic seeks her out. It's exhausting to constantly hold it back."

Luka made a sound of acknowledgment, then said, "I think once her lessons start, she will find her control rather quickly."

"As long as she can control her emotions," Theon agreed. "But now that I feel them... She somehow has no control and complete control all at once."

"Her instructor will help her."

"An instructor from the Achaz Kingdom," he said bitterly.

"It makes sense," Luka said. "We don't have her gifts."

"You mastered your gifts just fine without a Sargon instructor."

"I didn't have a choice. I am the only one."

"And she is the only—"

Theon broke off, already striding towards Tessa while Luka called after him. He reached her in a few quick strides, dropping to a crouch beside her and turning her face to his with the tip of his finger. She looked up at him in surprise, her irises bright and flashing with streaks of violet.

"You believe Luka might not be of this world just as you might not be," he said, focusing on her emotions.

He felt a flicker of surprise and then that same frustration at being discovered. The same irritation she'd felt when she'd revealed she could overcome the orders of the Source bond.

When he remained silent, waiting for her answer, that feeling shifted to determination. "I never said that," she answered.

He couldn't help the dark smile that formed, because she was...

"You beautiful, clever tempest," he murmured, his hand sliding along her jaw and into her hair. "What other secrets are you keeping?"

A smile as dark as his own filled her lips as she twisted, rising onto her knees so she was eye level with him. He held still as her power slowly wound around his arm, golden strands moving up to his neck, then sliding through his hair as if it were her own fingers. He suppressed the shudder that wanted to roll down his spine as her power flared. His darkness, however, didn't hold back, tangling with her light.

"You've taught me everything I need to know about secret keeping," Tessa crooned, leaning in even closer.

"And what is that?"

"Secrets are currency," she replied, her hands landing on his chest as her magic wound around him, sparking with energy and making him jolt. "Secrets are leverage." Her lips brushed along his in the barest of touches. "Secrets are how you get what you want."

She pushed off of him, gracefully rising to her feet. Small sparks of energy appeared with each step she took. Of course she'd removed her shoes as soon as they'd entered the arena, her bare feet leaving tracks on the dirt-covered floor.

Luka stepped in front of her, and she held up her wrists before he'd even pulled the bands from his pocket. She held his gaze the entire time he slid them on, and Theon could feel...uncertainty? Curiosity? That didn't seem right, but he wasn't sure how to define what she was feeling. She felt so much all the damn time.

But by the gods. He'd been underestimating her all this time. He'd known she was smart. He'd seen her marks on her lessons, but her cleverness had been revealed little by little, and he'd missed all the signs. He'd been too focused on trying to get her to submit to this bond. Too focused on his own means to an end. Too worried about having her completely bound to him before he let her in. It was the only way he knew how to protect all his carefully built plans and, more importantly, the people those plans were meant to protect. But if she had theories about Luka, she had theories about other things, and they could work through all those theories together.

The problem was he needed her to trust him, but any hope of that had been shattered alongside wine bottles and her spirit in the dark of a cellar.

He got to his feet, following her as Luka bent to murmur something in her ear. She nodded at whatever it was, and Theon felt a prickle of irritation. They'd been doing this more lately. Luka speaking words clearly only meant for her. He'd been refusing to tell him about their training sessions, but that would not be an option anymore. Not if she was revealing things to him that she was keeping from Theon.

"Glad to see the two of you are getting along again," Theon said casually.

But Tessa ignored him, instead saying, "Can we go find Axel and Kat?"

Theon nodded, and she didn't wait for them. As they followed her, he said to Luka, "She thinks you are not of this world. Did you know that?"

His brow furrowed. "Why would I know that?"

"Maybe she said something during training."

"Why would you think that?"

"Perhaps because you don't tell me what happens in those training sessions. You won't even let me in the room."

Luka sent him a dry look. "You know why you can't be in there. Your need to protect her would prevent me from properly training her. As for her training, I keep you apprised of her progress."

"Then what caused the days' long stand-off between you two?"

"That is between me and her."

"Except it can't be. Not anymore," Theon said. "She has ideas. Her past holds secrets, whether or not she knows it."

"She hasn't told me anything about her past, Theon."

"Maybe nothing that seems obvious. But the question she asked Cienna? That seemed innocent enough too, and it wasn't."

"You're becoming paranoid," Luka muttered.

"I am not paranoid, you ass. I recognize we have a deadline, and I'll admit that I've been underestimating Tessa."

Luka snickered. "You think?"

"We ready to go?" Axel called, meeting them at the entrance of the smaller training pit.

Kat and Tessa had their heads together, murmuring to each other. Theon should really speak to the Fae more too, but a stubborn part of him was refusing to spend any more time with her than he needed to. His father wanted him to take her as a new Source, and that was never going to happen.

And then there was Felicity.

He felt Tessa's eyes dart to him when his thoughts went to the female he was bound to with a Match contract. That was the deal he made with his father in exchange for his help in retrieving Tessa from Lord Jove. It had been impulsive, something he never was, but when it came to Tessa, he'd panicked. And his father had taken advantage, striking this gods-damn bargain. His Match union would occur within a month of the Selection Year ending, but with the contract signed, it was as good as solidified.

It hadn't escaped him that Tessa had not asked who the Match contract was with. In fact, she'd hardly mentioned it again since learning of it in his father's study, and truth be told, he hadn't wanted to bring it up either. Would she be upset? Or worse, would she suddenly not care?

"It's not too far to the central districts now," Axel was saying.

"But there are more tunnels?" Tessa said, already dragging her hands through her hair and tugging at the ends.

"Yeah," Axel answered. "Sorry, baby doll."

"Can't we just come back in three days or tomorrow or—"

"Come on, Tessa," Theon said, stepping forward and gently taking her wrists. "We've gone over this."

She whirled to Luka, gesturing to his wings. "How can you like it down here?"

"It's not ideal, but I can still fly in the caverns and in the central districts," Luka said, his tone low and coaxing. "It's open there. It doesn't feel like you're underground."

"But you can't see the sky," she said. Then to herself, she muttered, "No fresh air. No way out. Trapped because they won't let me go."

"Let's get to where we're staying tonight. We'll eat. You can rest…" Theon trailed off, threading his fingers with hers and tugging her along. Luka fell into step beside them. He'd drop back when the passages got narrow.

"What did you think of Cienna?" Theon asked when Tessa began muttering to herself again.

"What?" she asked.

"Cienna. What did you think of her?"

"She doesn't like you."

"She…does in her own way."

"Why wouldn't she answer more questions?"

"We will have to pay in some way for more answers," Theon answered, feeling her entire body tense as they neared the first tunnel. "You'll be fine, little storm."

"Can Luka go in front of us?"

"We have this formation for a reason," Theon said, feeling her begin to dig in her heels. He could feel his own frustration growing, and he worked hard to keep his emotions from filtering down the bond to her. "You've done great today, Tessa. We're almost done."

"One step in front of the other, little one," Luka said. "Just focus on the next step."

"One step," she murmured to herself, moving forward. "One step."

Theon didn't care if she had to say it for every step she took, as long as they got through this.

"One step. One step. They won't let me go. One step. Trapped. No sky. One step. One step. No air."

They were nearing the end of the passageway when her head snapped up and panic flooded down the bond.

"Stop!" she cried, yanking her hand from Theon's. She stumbled back, Luka catching her in his arms.

"Tessa? What is wrong with you?" Theon demanded. Axel and Katya had both paused, turning back to see what the commotion was.

"We have to go back," Tessa said, clawing at Luka's arms, but he held her firmly.

"Go back?" Theon repeated. "We're almost through the passage, Tessa. You'll be fine in a minute."

"No," she said, shaking her head. "No, no, no. I've been here— We can't. You were here," she twisted, looking up at Luka. "And you. And— She knows. She knows too. Oh, gods."

Theon reached for her as she continued to struggle in Luka's hold. "One step in front of the other, beautiful. Just like you've been doing."

"They're waiting for us," she whispered.

"Who is waiting for us?" Luka asked.

"I don't know," she said, her voice full of foreboding.

"Everything will be fine, Tessa," Theon said again, taking her trembling hand in his. "One step. Good girl," he coaxed as she took a shaky step forward. "We're almost out."

"So much blood," she muttered. "There's going to be so much blood. Kat wasn't here, but you were. And Luka. And Axel." Her other hand drifted to her chest, and he felt the dread coiling there.

Looking back at Luka, his friend shrugged, but his eyes kept darting around, searching for whatever had spooked her.

The moment they stepped into the crossroads cavern, though, he knew.

He released her hand, letting Luka tug her into him. Then he was stepping to Axel's side, shielding Katya.

"Hello, Jagger," Axel said. "Something we can help you with?"

"Hoping you can clear something up for us," the Night Child said. He wore loose pants and a shirt that hugged his muscled torso.

He'd once been a Celeste Legacy, but had fallen to the curse decades ago. The last Theon had heard, he was under a clan run by a Night Child named Cade. There were four main ones in the Underground. Axel had told Theon a few smaller ones had formed, but they still seemed to fall under one of the main four. And all of them answered to the Arius Lord. Or their heirs, as it so happened.

"If I can't, I'm sure I can find someone who can," Axel replied, toying with the shadows at his fingertips.

"Word is spreading that you brought a Fae to the Underground," Jagger said.

"She is not for any of you," Axel said darkly, and Theon side-eyed his brother. There was an edge to his tone that he rarely heard from him.

"There is also a rumor you brought an Achaz Legacy," Jagger continued.

"She is also not for you," Theon said, his darkness spreading at his feet.

"So it's true?" Jagger said. "You brought a fucking *Achaz* Legacy to the Underground. Achaz. The Kingdom who forced us here. The Kingdom that keeps us here. The Kingdom that represses us. Represses *you*?"

"Calm down, Jagger," Axel said.

"Calm down?" the Night Child repeated. "Are you allying with them now? With that fucking light lord?"

"No—"

"Then what other explanation is there?"

Axel's shadows struck, but they didn't wind around the throat like Theon would have done. No, because Axel didn't calculate his attacks. His moves were all feeling and in-the-moment. His power went straight down the Night Child's throat, Jagger gagging around the shadows. "Interrupt me again, and you will never learn the answer to that question. Are we clear?"

Jagger nodded frantically, and Theon saw specks of black appear in his pale skin. Bits of shadows allowed to drift into the male's blood.

Theon might be the heir of the Arius Kingdom, but this was Axel's domain. He knew that, and he let his brother take the lead here.

Axel finally withdrew his magic when he asked, "Did Cade send you?"

Jagger, gasping for air, shook his head.

"Then who?"

"I came myself. I split from Cade weeks ago," Jagger spat, his dark eyes drifting to Theon. "When word came what you'd Selected as a Source."

"Weeks ago?" Theon repeated. "We only learned of her gifts recently. Weeks ago she was just another Fae."

The spike of emotion down the bond had him glancing back at Tessa, still being shielded by Luka.

"There were rumors already circulating that she was more. But even when she was revealed, you fought to keep her," Jagger said, more Night Children drifting from the dark passages that converged here. "For years, you've preached to us. Told us you were the answer. You were going to free us of the confines of these fucking tunnels and caverns. Now you ally with the enemy?"

"We have not allied with them," Axel snarled. "But if you're telling me you have formed your own clan outside of the main four, you do not have the protection of the accords I have with them. Think very carefully about your next actions, Jagger. For you and those under your command."

"Under my command?" Jagger scoffed. "That's the thing. We don't want to be under anyone's fucking command."

Without warning, the Night Children descended. Three lunged for Theon, while another group went for Axel. Theon couldn't focus on his brother as he pulled two daggers from his shadows. Weapons stored in a pocket realm for easy access.

Weapons he'd collected over the years.

Weapons designed to end various beings, including Night Children.

Three wasn't a big deal. His darkness converged on them, holding them in place for his blades to slice along throats. Theon didn't even move, his shadows shoving those same blades deep into hearts.

But more and more Night Children appeared. This was clearly a planned attack. How had they not known this much unrest was happening in the Underground?

Then Luka was there, black flames taking out two more while Theon actually had to work. His darkness coated him like armor as he pulled a sword from the same shadowy depths. The mortals had silly weapons that did nothing against the magic beings of the realm. A blade made of shirastone or nightstone or worse? Those were the real weapons in Devram.

"Where is Tessa?" Theon demanded as the two parried attacks in tandem.

"She is nearby. I have a shield around her," Luka called back, black flames engulfing a Night Child as his sword went into another.

Theon sent a female Night Child to the ground, a hiss coming from her when his foot landed on her chest to keep her down. Blood sprayed when his sword slid into her heart.

"You were supposed to stay with her," Theon snapped.

"Guardian bond, you prick," Luka shot back, snagging a male Night Child by the throat as he rushed him. "Did you really think I was going to stand by while these fuckers attacked you?" Said fucker let out a strangled scream as black flames flared around the same hand wrapped around his throat.

Theon snarled as he felt fangs sink into his torso, directly over the bargain Mark with his father. These fucking vampyres.

But then there were more flames, and these weren't black. These were orange and red and had the Night Children hissing as they backed up from the flames.

Theon spun, finding Katya standing next to Axel, her hands raised. There was a circle of flames surrounding them, Axel's shadows snaking among the fire. He must have removed her bands to let her defend herself, something they couldn't risk with Tessa's out-of-control chaos, but where was she?

He heard Luka suck in a sharp breath before he felt a jumble of fear and...pride? Theon couldn't focus on the emotions right now as his power took one more vampyre to the ground while he kicked out at yet another, sending it backward onto Luka's waiting blade.

But then he glimpsed her. A Night Child had her, and she was struggling against his hold.

"We're coming, Tessa!" Luka yelled to her. "Keep fighting!"

A wave of darkness poured out of Theon, blanketing the entire cavern. He heard Axel curse, yelling at Katya to get down, seconds before black flames rained down. This was exhausting their power, but the Night Children sealed their fate the moment they touched Tessa. This was the Underground. They'd find blood somewhere to replenish their reserves.

Except when the darkness and flames cleared, that was Tessa on her knees. Her hands were wrapped around a dagger in her sternum, directly below her heart. The same place she'd held in the passageway when she'd told them not to come in here. She'd known.

She'd somehow *known* what was waiting for them.

And that was Jagger at her throat, fangs in deep.

That was more vampyres flooding into the cavern.

He was drained. Too drained to end this many at one time, even with Luka and the others.

But he could end one.

His shadows moved ahead, trembling with his fury as the Night Child took another pull from Tessa. She didn't scream, but Theon felt every bit of agony down their bond. Jagger was so lost to his blood lust and the taste of Tessa's blood, he didn't even notice Theon when he crouched beside him.

He noticed when his midnight-coated hand gripped his jaw, though.

With every ounce of control he had, Theon gently removed the vampyre's fangs from Tessa's throat.

Then he squeezed, hearing bones crunch and feeling Jagger's jaw crush beneath his fingers. When the vampyre opened his mouth to scream, tendrils of darkness reached up, yanking his fangs from his mouth before shoving them down his throat, the pointed tips tearing a path all the way down. Then his shadows began working on ribs, cracking them one by one. With his throat shredded, Jagger couldn't scream, but Theon could see the anguish in his eyes. Watch it on his face.

Feel it coming from Tessa.

That pain jolted him out of his vengeance, and with another thought, his darkness wrapped around the vampyre's heart, squeezing until it burst.

Tessa was still on her knees, her hands wrapped around the handle of the knife.

"Let go, Tessa," Theon said, trying to move her hands away, but she shook her head.

"You need…to fight," she gasped out. "Or this…is pointless."

There was blood streaming down her neck. More seeping out around the dagger.

Luka appeared, a wall of black flames cutting them off from the fight. When his eyes landed on Tessa, his face paled.

"I…fought," Tessa gasped out, two tears tracking down her cheeks as she looked up at Luka.

He immediately dropped to a knee, wiping a tear with his thumb. "I saw, little one."

"Looks like…the training—" She sucked in a shaky breath. "Was still pointless."

Something feral filled Luka's face, and he turned to Theon. "Get her in the air. I'll take care of the rest."

Theon didn't need to be told twice. Dragging up what remained of his gifts, his shadow wings formed. He scooped Tessa into his arms, trying not to react to her grimace or the pain that screamed down the bond. Then he launched into the air, keeping them far above the fighting below.

Keeping them out of range as Axel did the same, grabbing Kat and launching into the air.

Keeping them out of range as Luka shifted fully, taking up half of the cavern with his size. The Night Children tried to scatter, but just like by the river, it was no use. Not as Luka let loose a roar before breathing those black flames and incinerating everything, leaving not even ashes.

"He said something to me," Tessa murmured, her eyes half-closed.

"Hey, beautiful," Theon said, panic bubbling up. "I need you to look at me."

"Eyes on you," she mumbled.

"Yes. Exactly. Eyes on me."

They needed to get that dagger out right fucking now.

Luka looked up at him, huffing out a plume of smoke telling Theon the coast was clear. When his feet touched the ground, the dragon's large snout was looking over his shoulder as he laid Tessa on the ground. Luka would stay in that form until they were ready to move on, just in case.

"He said something to me," Tessa said again as Axel and Katya appeared.

Axel passed a flask to Theon, and he gave his brother a quizzical look.

"Cienna gave it to me. Said we'd need it soon," Axel said grimly.

Theon knocked back a swallow. Fae blood. Of course she'd known.

But so had Tessa.

He'd have to think about that later.

"What did he say to you, little storm?" Theon asked, nodding subtly to Axel, who had casually folded a hand around her arm, pinning it to the ground.

"That he had to kill me. They told him if I lived, Devram would fall," she rasped, lifting her other hand into the air. "They look like feathers," she murmured.

"What do?"

But then he felt her fingers drift through his shadow wings, and holy fuck. He lurched back as pure lust bolted through him, despite Tessa bleeding out on the ground.

"Not the time, Tessa," he gritted out, shaking out his arms and hands to get some control back.

She shrugged weakly. "Don't really have much time left, do I?" A low growl came from Luka, and Tessa shifted her focus. Her fingers traced down the side of his jaw, and Luka huffed into her palm. "Stay where I can see you, okay?"

Katya had lowered down beside Axel and ripped a piece of fabric from her shirt, pressing it to Tessa's throat.

"You're not going to die, Tessa," Theon said.

Her gaze darted to him. "If not now, you'll just kill me later."

"What? No. I'm not going to—"

"She's rambling, Theon," Axel cut in. "She doesn't know what she's saying. Get the dagger out, and we'll take her—"

"Katya is never there, but you are," Tessa said, meeting Axel's gaze. "You hold me down. Just like now."

"Get it out. Between the two of us, we can pool our magic to keep the wound closed until we find a Witch in the central districts," Axel said.

"Deep breath, beautiful. Can you do that for me?" Theon asked, smoothing her hair back from her brow.

Her eyes fluttered closed, and when they remained so for a few seconds, Luka nudged her with his snout. They didn't open, and Theon wasted no more time. Gripping the dagger, he pulled it straight up, cursing when he found it to be one that could end a Legacy. Where had Jagger gotten this from? They were highly regulated. It would have cost a fortune, even here.

But more concerning, Tessa hadn't moved when he'd pulled the dagger out.

He felt nothing down the bond.

He felt nothing at all.

# 14
## AXEL

"I still can't feel her," Theon said as they burst into the penthouse suite they always stayed in when they came to the Underground.

It was more Axel's place than anything. Theon rarely spent more than a night at a time here, and their father only came to the Underground a few times a year for appearances. Valter didn't care about the people here. Only that everyone understood who controlled their fate.

Thankfully the Charter District had been the closest district to the attack, so they hadn't had to maneuver through the other four districts. Although it would have been nice to go through the Apothecary District to order a Healer to follow them. Now one of them would need to go find one. Phone reception was shit down here, and the people were too paranoid to use them anyway. Signals and messages could easily be intercepted, and soon enough, the wrong person was at a pick up or they found a blade at their throat.

Axel knew he would be the one to go find the Healer. Theon wouldn't leave Tessa's side, and Luka hadn't spoken a single word since shifting back from his dragon form.

Theon and Axel had pooled their power together to hold the wound in Tessa's sternum closed, but they were both drained. The sweat on Axel's brow wasn't just from racing here. He was down to the last dregs of power. It was flickering, and when he was out completely...

Well, Tessa wasn't his only worry.

"I should be able to feel her, right?" Theon said, laying the unconscious female onto the sofa. The wound at her throat was bleeding through the fabric Katya had tied around her neck.

Shit, Katya. Where was she?

Spinning to the right, he found the Fae was emerging from the hall that led to the kitchen. Axel wasn't sure how she'd known exactly where to go, but she held a bowl and cloth.

"To clean the blood so you know how bad everything is," Kat explained, faltering when Axel's gaze locked on her.

He nodded, his entire body too tense to do much more. Taking the bowl, he found warm water inside. He came to Theon's side, dropping the cloth into the bowl.

"Throat or chest first?" Axel asked.

"I've got it," Theon snapped, scarcely bothering to wring the cloth out before he was lifting Tessa's top and wiping away blood. "Her heart still beats. I can feel it," he muttered, his other hand pressing atop her chest, just above where she'd been stabbed.

If that dagger had hit her heart, she would have been dead. There was no doubt about it. That dagger was made from material that could kill Legacy. Only the ruling families had such weapons.

Or so they'd been led to believe.

But Axel supposed what they said was true: A person could find anything in the Underground if they were willing and able to pay the right price.

"If her heart still beats, I should be able to fucking feel her," Theon said, the words more of a growl. "How is she always so godsdamn difficult without even trying?"

Axel couldn't focus much on his brother's words though. No, his attention was fixed on the blood that was still seeping from her wounds. Theon had told them it had tasted more divine than Fae blood. Legacy blood didn't do anything for other Legacy, but somehow Tessa's had restored his reserves. And all that blood dripping to the floor, soaking into the cloth…

What a waste.

He lurched back a step, snapping himself out of the daze he'd been in. He needed to find blood now. Before things got worse. The three of them had split the flask Cienna had given him, but that hadn't been nearly enough for any of them to fully replenish their reserves. It certainly hadn't been enough for Axel. The entire flask wouldn't have been enough.

"I'm, uh, going to find a Healer," Axel said, raking a trembling hand through his hair.

"Do you want me to go with you?" Kat asked, and her voice startled him. She was so close.

"No!" he barked, taking two more steps back to put space between them.

Kat's eyes widened, an emotion Axel couldn't read flashing in her eyes, before it was gone and replaced with her submissive demureness.

"I just mean— Stay here. With Luka. I'll be back soon," he said, stumbling over his words because shit. There was a Fae. Right here in the room with them. Blood so close he could smell it. And she was powerful. He'd watched her wield her fire in the training room, and then again when they'd fought the Night Children. His shadows had fought alongside those flames, and that had been nearly as intense as the fight itself.

But the sound of the lift had him pausing, momentarily distracting him from his desperation. Luka had heard it too, moving to stand in front of Theon and Tessa, taking a protective stance. Katya hadn't moved, and Axel found himself wanting to pull her into him and wanting to push her away at the same time. How could he keep her safe when he was the biggest threat to her in this room?

A minute later, the lift doors opened, a female with dark auburn hair striding through. Her hair reached just past her chin, framing her sharp features in loose waves. Violet-blue eyes scanned over all of them, her tight black pants and long-sleeve suit clinging to her as she moved deeper into the room, a leather bag slung over her shoulder.

Axel released a breath of relief, but Luka did not, a faint trace of smoke drifting from his nostrils.

"Relax," Axel said. "She's a Healer."

"How did she get up here without an escort?" Luka demanded, his voice dark.

"I'm assuming Cienna sent her," Axel answered, looking back at the female.

"She did," she answered, dropping her bag onto the coffee table and beginning to dig through it.

"You're a Healer?" Theon demanded. "Who trained you?"

"Cienna did," Axel answered for the Witch, who was completely ignoring Theon. "Since Cienna obviously cannot come here herself, she sent Gia."

"And this Gia has the skill for this type of wound?" Theon retorted, still kneeling beside Tessa, the bowl of water now red with the blood he'd wiped from her skin.

"More skilled than anyone here," Gia replied, her arrogant tone making Theon straighten.

"If Cienna cannot be here, I will only accept the next best Healer," Theon said.

"And you have her. Move," Gia retorted.

Theon slid murderous eyes to Axel. "For the love of Arius, please tell me she knows who we are."

"I know exactly who you are," Gia said, her hands full of vials as she approached the sofa. "You can either let me work, or wait at least an hour while Axel tracks down another Healer. Of far less skill, I might add."

"She knows who we are," Axel said. "And I would advise not pissing her off any more than you already have, or you might find Cienna even less willing to help us than she was today. They are lovers."

Theon looked back at Gia, who was giving him an unimpressed glare that Axel swore only the Witches could manage. With a glare of his own, Theon pushed to his feet, stepping back just enough to let Gia slip between him and the sofa.

"Give her room, Theon," Axel said. "Let her work. We can trust her."

"How long have you known her?" Theon asked through gritted teeth, moving a little farther away and beginning to pace.

"A few years," Axel answered.

"A few years?" he repeated. "And you've never thought to mention her?"

"It didn't seem relevant at the time."

"It didn't seem relevant?"

"By the gods, are you going to repeat everything I say?"

"Everything is relevant, Axel," Theon seethed. "Even if we don't see the relevance right away."

"Now you know."

"What if I'd needed this information sooner? What if it could have somehow helped us figure something else out?"

Axel sighed, shoving his hands deep in his pockets, trying to find some shred of patience to deal with his brother. "What could you have possibly learned by knowing about Cienna's lover, Theon?"

Theon rounded on him. "What other information have you withheld?"

"Excuse me?" Axel asked, his mouth dropping open.

"You heard me. Did you know of Jagger forming his own clan?"

"No," Axel snapped. "I would have told you."

"Would you have?"

Axel took a step forward, painfully aware of his empty magic reserves as the remnants of his gifts stirred uselessly beneath his skin. "I know you're worried about Tessa, but you need to take a breath and back the fuck off."

"This was your one job, Axel," Theon snapped, his hand cutting through the air as he continued pacing. "I asked you to monitor the Underground because I couldn't be everywhere at once."

"What the fuck do you think I have been doing these past few years?" Axel demanded.

"How the fuck could you not know of the unrest among the Night Children?" Theon countered. "We walked into a godsdamn trap tonight. We shouldn't have been surprised like that. You should have known it was coming. It's your only fucking job."

Axel stared at Theon, completely at a loss for words. The only thing he could muster was, "Fuck you, Theon," before he was striding for the lift.

"Cienna said to tell you to take the Fae with you," Gia called over her shoulder.

"That's a bad idea right now," he called back, repeatedly pressing the button for the lift until the doors opened.

"Do with the information what you will," Gia replied. She sounded so unbothered, as though she truly didn't care what Axel decided to do.

He looked back over his shoulder. The Witch held her hand over Tessa's wound on her chest, a faint glow emanating from her palm. Her eyes were closed as she concentrated on her work. Luka was back to saying nothing, and Theon was still pacing, refusing to look at Axel like the utter prick he was.

Already regretting his decision, he looked at Katya. She was standing off to the side, her hands clasped in front of her. There were smudges of soot on her brown skin from the fight, and her shirt was torn where she'd ripped the strip of fabric from it.

"Come on," Axel said, jerking his chin to the open lift, but Kat hesitated. He couldn't really blame her. With another heavy sigh, he said, "Kat, come with me. We'll go get…supplies."

She nodded, tucking curls behind her ear as she moved, stepping into the lift behind him. No one said anything else to them as the lift doors slid shut, but when Theon met his gaze at the last moment, Axel lifted his middle finger in goodbye.

The two story suite spanned the entirety of the tower that stretched high into the cavern. The ride down the several levels was silent and filled with tension. Kat's scent assaulted him. Jasmine and citrus, something smoky. He was leaning against the back wall, his fingers curled tightly around the railing that ran the perimeter, breathing through his godsdamn teeth as desire warred inside of him.

Desire for blood.

Desire to punch something.

Desire to fuck.

Desire for her.

Fuck, fuck, fuck.

He practically burst out of the lift, the doors not even fully open when he pushed through them. He could hear Kat's hurried footsteps to keep up with his long strides. It wasn't until they were outside the tower that he took a full breath. It wasn't quite fresh air being inside the mountains and all that, but at least it felt open and spacious. The sounds of the Charter District assaulted him, grounded him. People yelled to each other across the make-shift roads. Passersby ducked their heads, pulling hoods down over their faces to avoid being recognized. There weren't vehicles down here, but there were animals. Horses. Dogs. Griffins and even some birds of prey. And, of course, the Shifters. But they ran the Leisure District and tended to stay there.

Right now, though, he needed to get to the Dispensary District, not only for the blood, but to talk to the four people who ran the District—the leaders of the main four Night Children clans.

Because while Theon had been an absolute dick about it, he'd been right. Guilt churned in his stomach. This was his territory. This was his only job. The spare heir whose only purpose was to secure their foothold in this domain.

And he'd failed at it.

The sound of Katya softly clearing her throat had him turning towards her. He'd just been standing there, staring at nothing. She peered at him from beneath her thick lashes, clearly uncertain of what she was supposed to do, if she should say anything. All that time drawing her out of her shell, and he'd scared her right back into it.

He wanted to touch her, reassure her, but he didn't trust himself to do either of those things right now. The problem was, he also couldn't risk having her trail behind him. Not here.

Gritting his teeth, he grabbed her hand, his grip tight. "Keep up," was all he could muster as he towed her along behind him.

"Slow down," she hissed in return.

But he didn't. He didn't acknowledge her again as he led her through the Charter District. Main roadways connected all five central districts, but the Dispensary District was on the opposite side from the Charter District. They'd have to pass through the Leisure, Apparel, and Apothecary Districts on their way. It would take more than an hour to move from one end to the other on foot, and he could only assume there would be hold ups along the way.

In short, he would never make it to the Dispensary District without needing at least *some* blood to hold him over.

It didn't take them long to cross out of the Charter District; it was the smallest of the five. The main road divided the next two districts— Leisure to the north and Apparel to the south. He could likely find a dealer in the Leisure District, but he was leery of trusting anyone at the moment. Not until he spoke with the clan leaders to find out exactly what the fuck was going on down here. The Shifter Alpha and Beta that ran the Leisure District were fickle. They'd side with whoever would give them the best deal.

The Fae ran the Apparel District, and while that seemed fundamentally wrong compared to how the rest of Devram was run, these were Fae that had been sent to the Underground for some heinous crime or another. They were Fae the ruling families had decided were not worth their time to correct and tossed to the Arius Kingdom to deal with. There was a male and female who ran the District that specialized in apparel— not just clothing, but the weapons that a person could adorn themselves with as well.

With a frustrated sigh, he turned south. He'd have better luck in the Apparel District, especially with—

He sighed again. Especially with a Fae at his side.

Godsdamn Cienna and her Seer abilities.

At least they could find Katya some new clothing while they were here.

They turned off the main road, ducking into a small shop a few minutes later. It was tucked into a back alleyway, but Axel knew the owner. Ringing the small bell on the counter, he waited. His fingers flexing around Kat's hand still tucked into his own. A moment later, a Fae appeared. He was shorter and more than a little stocky, but he bowed when he saw Axel.

"My Lord," he said.

Axel didn't miss the mocking jeer in his words. "Samson," he greeted. "Any way I could learn where Turner is?"

Samson stood upright, his fingers tapping on the counter he stood behind. "Always for the right price."

"Name it."

Axel heard the small gasp that came from Kat when Samson named a sum that was far too high for the information, but he was too desperate to care. He sealed the deal with a Bargain Mark he'd make good on as soon as he could transfer the funds, and they were back out on the side roads again in minutes.

"Axel," Katya said, already sounding breathless. "You need to slow down."

"Just keep up," he said again. He still didn't trust himself enough to look at her.

"I know you didn't want me to come with you," she insisted, tugging at his hand. "But I used a lot of power in that training pit and then in the fight."

"You think I don't know that?" he said, rounding another corner.

"I don't think you do," she spat, the fire in her veins ringing in her voice and pulling Axel to a sudden stop.

He finally turned to look at her, a little shocked at the way she'd spoken to him. Then his eyes went wide. Her warm skin had paled, making the flush on her cheeks stand out vividly. There was a sheen of sweat on her brow, and she looked utterly exhausted.

He took a step towards her as he asked, "Are you all right?"

"Am I all right?" she repeated, that flush flaring for a different reason now. She was angry. Axel could almost feel the anger radiating off of her. "No, I am not 'all right,' Axel. That was the most I have used my power at one time. I have had no time to rest afterwards, let alone let any of the magic even begin to replenish. Then you make me all but run to keep up with your long strides. In case you are unaware, Fae need food and rest to replenish their reserves, not blood like the Legacy. By Anala, you truly are a rude fuck, you know that?"

He was staring at her as she finished her little tirade, her hand still clutched in his own. As if suddenly realizing what she'd done, she looked at the ground, digging the toe of her boot into the dust covered road. But she didn't apologize, didn't even attempt it, and for a reason he would never be able to explain, he had her pressed against the side of a building in his next breath. Because now he wasn't thinking about where he was going to find blood, although the thought of taking it directly from her crossed his mind as his lips hovered above hers.

"I'm going to kiss you," he said, his voice so low and rough he didn't recognize it.

Her eyes widened again. "Why would you do that?"

"Because you yelled at me."

"So that means you need to kiss me? That makes no sense," she said, shaking her head slightly.

"I know," he answered. His other hand was on her hip and his hold tightened. "So many things don't make sense. Too many things. It's utter madness. May as well fall into it."

"You're…" she trailed off, the look on her face telling him just how mad she thought he was.

But he was mad. Distraught with the need for blood. For the taste of her lips. For both. He didn't know, and it was all so godsdamn confusing. There was absolutely no logical reason for him to have her pressed up against a wall on a side street in the Underground. Fuck, she shouldn't even *be* in the Underground. This place was far too dark and depraved for someone like her.

*He* was far too dark and depraved for someone like her.

And yet the depravity made him not give a single fuck.

"Please let me kiss you," he murmured, his focus entirely on her mouth as her tongue darted over her bottom lip in her nervousness.

"I can't stop you."

"Of course you can, kitten. Say the word."

"That doesn't do anything."

His gaze snapped to hers. "Did I not tell you I would never be one to demand such a thing from you?"

"Yes, but—"

"But nothing. My word is everything. Tell me no, and we go find Turner."

But she didn't say no. She studied him, her free hand on his chest where it had landed when he'd pushed her here. Her fingers flexed against his shirt.

"It's my choice?"

It was a question, as if she didn't understand being given such a thing. Why would she? Tessa didn't understand it either. None of the Fae understood control when it was being freely given to them. They were so used to being told where to go, how to behave, who to fuck, and what to be, that when given choices, they couldn't even recognize them for what they were.

"Okay," she finally whispered.

"Okay what?" Axel questioned, not sure he'd heard her correctly.

"Kiss me."

"Why?"

Her brow furrowed. "You asked to kiss me."

"And you said yes."

"I did."

"Why did you say yes?"

"I… I don't know," she admitted. Then she added, "Should I say no?"

"Gods, no."

"You're confusing," she said, that irritation that Axel loved to pull from her creeping into her voice.

But he was just as confused as she was.

Fuck it.

His mouth landed on hers, and he felt the surprised gasp she made. She didn't move for the longest time, so frozen, Axel almost pulled back.

But then she tentatively kissed him back.

It took all of him, but he let her lead it. Let her slowly move her lips against him. Let her explore with each press of their lips. Let her slide her tongue along the seam of his mouth, which he greedily parted to let her have access.

When he did finally pull back, his hand was somehow tangled in silky black curls. His other hand still clutched hers, and she was staring up at him with curious eyes. He didn't know what she was thinking or feeling, and he didn't know what he was thinking or feeling either.

"We need to find Turner," he said gruffly.

Her cheeks flushed. "That's what you're thinking about after a kiss?"

"After a kiss with you? No," he answered, tilting her chin back up with his finger when she looked away from him at her question. "I need to find Turner because I am either going to fuck you or draw blood from you, kitten, and I'm assuming neither of those options are desirable at the moment."

"I mean…not on a public road," she answered.

Axel choked on a laugh, stepping back from her. "But if we weren't on a public road?"

"It doesn't matter. We *are* on a public road."

"Oh, it matters, kitten," he replied. Squeezing her fingers, he added, "Turner should be at a shop a few blocks away. Can you manage that far?"

"As long as I'm not running to keep up with you," she retorted.

"Point taken," he said, beginning to meander down the road at a much slower pace. "I was…upset, and like you, my power is drained."

"You can have blood," she said.

And she said it so simply, nonchalantly, that Axel was tugging her to a stop. "I can't just take blood from you."

"Of course you can."

"No, I can't."

"Why not?"

"Because we are only given a weekly ration. Taking more than that—"

"Can send you to the Underground?" Katya interrupted, looking around at the obviousness of where they stood.

"Well…yeah. It's a grave offense in Devram to need more than what you are allotted," Axel said, suddenly feeling very foolish at trying to convince her of this when he was one of the worst offenders of them all.

"Most aren't caught," she said with a shrug, beginning to walk down the road again.

"How do you— Wait a minute," Axel said, finding himself rushing to catch up to her now. "How long have you known Legacy need blood? You aren't told that until your Selection."

She huffed a laugh under her breath. "I was raised in a kingdom that values knowledge above all else," Kat replied. "I know a great deal of things that other Fae do not, even once they have been Selected."

Axel wasn't sure how to respond to that, so instead, he took her hand once more, leading her through the Apparel District until they came to a shop that specialized in garments the hired mercenaries favored. A bell rang above the door when they stepped in, and a tall Fae looked up from what he was doing at the shop counter. Then he straightened.

"Axel St. Orcas," the Fae said, eyeing him before his pale green eyes drifted to Katya. "You brought a friend."

"Turner," Axel said with a nod. "Samson told me where to find you."

"Did he now?"

"I need some blood."

"Go to the Dispensary District," Turner said.

"No time. I'll pay whatever you want," Axel said, the desperation suddenly back in full force. Katya had been a distraction for a moment, but not anymore. Certainly not after she'd offered him *her* blood. Now that was all he could think about.

"She a prisoner you're transporting?" Turner asked instead, his gaze flicking back to Kat.

"No."

"She the fire Fae everyone has been whispering about, then?"

"What have they been saying?" Axel asked.

Turner shrugged. "Just that the Anala Lady is upset that she was taken from her kingdom."

"Oh?" Axel said. "What else have you heard?"

Turner smirked. "The blood or the information. Your choice."

"The blood," Axel answered immediately. He could get the information from someone else.

Turner wandered through a door to some back room, returning a minute later with a bottle twice the size of the flask.

Fuck. Yes.

He'd have to find more for Theon and Luka, but he'd worry about that after he could think clearly and not around a haze of need.

"The cost?" Axel asked, reaching for the bottle.

"I need something from the clan leaders," Turner said, pulling the bottle back.

"What do I have to do with that?"

"You can convince them to give it to me."

Axel's eyes narrowed. "What is it?"

"They stole a weapon from one of my establishments. I want it back," Turner answered.

"What kind of weapon?" Axel asked, unease coiling in his gut.

"A rare and very expensive kind."

"Let me guess: the kind that can kill a Legacy?"

Turner arched a brow. "You know of it?"

"You know having such a thing is cause for immediate death?"

"Without it, death is imminent anyway. If the rumors are true, that is," Turner answered, stretching a hand towards him. "Do we have a deal or not?"

The blood was right there. Axel could practically taste it, and he knew, deep down, that if he didn't take it, he'd be taking some from Kat. Something in him was both horrified and intrigued by the idea, and that scared him more than this godsdamn deal. He'd figure something out.

"It's a Bargain," Axel said, slapping his hand into Turner's and feeling yet another Bargain Mark prickle along his flesh.

It was seconds from the time his fingers closed around the bottle to the liquid sliding down his throat as he drank. Katya was staring at him with wide eyes, but Turner was chuckling. Axel ignored him, pulling Kat out of the shop.

"Axel—"

But he cut her off. "Let's get you some fresh clothes, then we'll go back to the penthouse."

"You said we needed supplies," she argued.

He took a few more swallows, already feeling his empty reserves start to well, relief flooding through him as he sank into the comfort of having his power back. No craving controlling him anymore. No withdrawal driving his actions.

"Looks like we need to pay a visit to the clan leaders," Axel said, nudging her towards a shop across the road. "And I think Theon will want to be a part of that."

"And if Tessa isn't awake?" Kat asked.

"We're all making sacrifices here," Axel said darkly. "If he doesn't trust me to find out the reasons for the unrest among the Night Children, he can come with and get the answers himself."

# 15
## THEON

"We're making this fast," Theon said, striding across the bridge.

It spanned a wide cavern, and it separated the House of Four from the rest of the Dispensary District. Of course, once they got across the bridge, they'd have to climb a steep staircase because the House of Four overlooked everything below, much like the penthouse they stayed in did in the Charter District.

The same penthouse he'd left Tessa in.

She still hadn't woken. Theon had managed to hold Axel off for the rest of the day, but this morning, his brother had insisted on having this meeting. Gia had told him Tessa would make a full recovery, and that said recovery would come faster if she was allowed to rest properly. He'd begrudgingly thanked the Witch. She was skilled, he'd give her that.

They'd hired a thief in the Charter District to discreetly get them more Fae blood, and he and Luka had refilled their reserves. Then he'd left Luka to stay with Tessa while he'd traipsed across the Districts to meet with the clan leaders. He'd tried telling Axel to handle it himself, but Axel had insisted. And yeah, Theon couldn't blame him. He'd been a dick to his brother yesterday, even if the words rang somewhat true. He wouldn't apologize. Axel should have known, but they could have had the conversation differently.

The stone walls of the House of Four branched off into four distinct wings, each painted with a symbol of the four clans. Before they reached the House though, they came to a single story structure, the stone sanded so smooth, it looked like marble. This was their meeting house. Their own version of the tribunal building in the Acropolis. Theon had sent word ahead to have all the clan leaders in attendance, and if they weren't all here, he was more than prepared to remind them who ruled the Underground.

The Night Child at the door said nothing as he and Axel strolled into the building. Katya had stayed behind with Luka as well. Axel didn't want her near the Night Children, and Theon agreed. He wouldn't put it past the clan leaders to try to barter for her.

Theon led the way, striding straight into the circular meeting chamber and coming to a stop in the very center. The clan leaders were all here, each staring back at him with varying degrees of interest. Henry had short brown hair, his nearly black eyes narrowed in annoyance. Rayell had blonde hair, cut short and dyed with streaks of pink. Her bright green eyes danced with mischief. Cade had blonde hair too, but his hair hung to his shoulders. Numerous tattoos marred his flesh, reminiscent of the Marks that had once adorned his skin as a Legacy. Then there was Bree. The female lounged in her seat, long legs crossed and twirling her shiny onyx hair around her finger as her honey-colored eyes regarded them both. From his studies, he knew she had been in power the longest. The other three had taken the places of previous clan leaders, but Bree was an original.

"The Arius Heirs," Cade drawled, resting his chin on his fist. "To what do we owe the summons?"

"A rude summons," Bree added with a slight pout on her red painted lips.

"Rude or not, we summon, you answer," Theon retorted, letting his shadows drift along the floor like a fine mist.

"Well?" Cade repeated, sounding utterly bored. "Let's hear it then. What can we do for you?"

"Funny," Axel replied, his hands in his pockets as he rocked back on his heels. "I asked Jagger the same thing yesterday."

Cade straightened. "And?"

Axel shrugged. "He attacked us. Him and a whole host of other vampyres. I'm assuming that was on your orders?"

"I would never tell them to attack the Arius Heirs," Cade seethed.

"He was part of your clan, no?" Axel asked. "Are you telling me you don't have control over your clan, Cade?"

Cade's jaw visibly clenched, and Theon had to admit, Axel knew how to handle the clan leaders perfectly.

"Why don't you simply ask Jagger yourself?" Henry cut in.

Axel regarded him with the briefest of glances before looking away dismissively. Henry bristled. The youngest of the clan leaders, Theon knew he hated being seen as less than. Which meant Axel's next words had the young vampyre seething even more.

"I'm talking to the elder leaders, Henry. I don't believe that involves you."

Bree huffed a soft laugh, her keen gaze still fixed on Theon.

"If they're such great leaders, why did Jagger defect from Cade's leadership?" Henry spat, leaning forward in his chair.

"Did he now?" Axel asked as if this news was a surprise to him. "Why would he do that?"

Henry fell quiet, suddenly realizing he'd said too much as Cade glared at him.

"How many more have defected from your clans?" Theon asked, his tone far too calm. All the leaders noticed, each of them straightening.

"Better question," Axel said. "Which clan has the most leaving?"

Bree tsked lightly, getting to her feet. She wore heels that clicked against the stone as she moved, her dress as red as her lips. "Don't try to pit us against each other, young heir," she said with a mock simper.

"Then answer our questions without omitting important details," Axel replied as she came to a stop in front of them.

"You forget your manners, Axel darling," she cooed, dragging a nail lightly along his jaw.

"You forget your place," Theon sneered, his darkness latching onto that finger and wrenching it away from his brother.

Her lips formed that pout again. "Always so protective," she chided. Then she waved a dismissive hand, moving back to her chair. "There are always those who think they do not need the clans. Young and old who believe they can survive better without us." She smiled widely, her fangs on full display. "They learn soon enough they are wrong, as I'm sure Jagger already has."

"Still skirting the truth, Bree," Axel tsked in the same simpering tone. "Jagger spilled some secrets, and I suggest you do the same. They attacked us, and Theon's Source was severely injured. You know how... vengeful us Legacy can get for such an act."

Bree's playful demeanor dropped in an instant. "Do not threaten me, Axel St. Orcas."

"And do not test me, Bree DelaCrux," Axel retorted. "Jagger said someone came to him and told him if Tessa was allowed to live, it meant the end of Devram. I want names."

"I don't have any to give you," she spat.

"Are you saying you were not approached with the same information?" Theon demanded.

"Of course we were approached," she retorted. "When we declined aid, they went to others in the clans and tried to convince them. Obviously they succeeded with some."

"Who? Who went to them?" Theon said.

"I already told you I do not know. They wore dark robes with hoods and pearlescent masks."

"How many were there?" Axel asked.

"When they stood in the same spot you stand now, there were nine."

"And none of you offered aid?" Theon asked, glancing among the four clan leaders.

"Is that not what I said?" Bree sneered.

"You said it, yes," Axel said. "But none of the others offered their answers."

"You grow too clever, young heir," Bree gritted out.

"Or you are simply not as cunning as you gain more years."

"Speak wisely," Bree warned softly.

Axel gave her a smirk that Theon had to commend. Turning to Cade, he said, "I can assume you said no, and that is why Jagger defected."

Cade gave a sharp nod but didn't speak.

Rayell spoke before Axel could question her, her green eyes twinkling. "They made a very convincing argument. I'll admit I was nearly swayed."

"What stopped you?" Theon asked.

"Nothing really," she admitted. "I simply do not care if Devram survives or not."

Theon blinked at the vampyre's frankness.

"Henry?" Axel said.

The young Night Child glared back at them. "I was outvoted, three-to-one."

"Rayell said she didn't vote."

"Which also means she did not side with me."

"And what was so convincing that you would side with complete strangers who have not proven themselves to you and your kind?" Axel asked.

"Everything," Henry sneered. "Everything they claimed would come to pass has. One can only assume that trend will continue, and then you bring an *Achaz* descendant here."

"There is no proof that is what she is," Theon cut in.

"I do not care. We have been waiting to be free of these dark caverns, and still we sit in the dark."

Axel clicked his tongue. "The sunlight weakens you anyway, Henry."

"What else did they tell you?" Theon asked before Henry could reply to Axel's taunt.

The vampyre stood, taking a single step towards them. "They said that if she is not killed, the Arius line would be wiped from this realm."

"That's impossible," Axel said, all the mirth gone from his tone.

Henry smirked. "Is it? You brought a *suspected* Achaz descendant into these caverns. Directly into the heart of your greatest weapon. She is a poison that will spread." He paused, looking Theon up and down once. "Then again, there's really no hope when she's already so deeply rooted in Arius blood."

Theon moved as fast as any Night Child, the dagger in his hand appearing a moment before it sank into Henry's chest. The vampyre's eyes went wide in shock, blood dribbling from the corner of his mouth.

"Don't want the vitriol you're spewing spreading throughout the Underground now, do I?" Theon said casually.

He pulled the dagger out before his darkness converged around the wound. The same dagger that had been used to stab Tessa. Henry's veins turned black as his power moved, dark streaks webbing across his skin, until Theon pulled the magic back. When he did, a heart sat in the midst of the shadows, the organ just as black. Letting the body slump to the floor, the heart fell atop it. There was a sickening smack as it rolled off the lifeless body to the pristine floor, black blood splattering.

"Be sure and let the new clan leader know what happens should they try to rise against us," Theon said, stepping back to avoid getting the pooling blood on his shoes.

"Dangerous games, my Lord," Bree said with a soft venom.

"Just a reminder of who will always win those games," Axel replied darkly before they both turned on their heels and left.

Theon slammed his laptop shut. Connections were dreadful in the Underground. The only place with decent technology service was the main gate. That was where Bohden, his father's Commander-of-Forces, resided, but the male had eyes and ears everywhere. He knew just as much as Axel did when it came to the inner workings of the Underground. Which begged the question had he known of the unrest among the Night Children? Had his father and he'd just conveniently not mentioned it?

Sighing in frustration, he raked his hand through his hair, glancing over at the bed. They'd moved Tessa to his room after Gia had finished…whatever the fuck she'd done. Not enough, obviously. Tessa still slept. He still couldn't feel her. Every once in a while, he was sure he felt a flicker of emotion, but it didn't seem quite right. The emotions were a mixture of guilt and regret and longing. But the fact remained, she hadn't so much as shifted in her sleep. She remained exactly as they'd placed her.

When he'd returned from the meeting with the clan leaders, he'd found her in fresh clothing, courtesy of Katya and Gia. He hadn't seen the Witch since. She hadn't checked in or even bothered to send a messenger to do so. If she were with Cienna when he saw her later today, they'd certainly be exchanging words about it.

It was day three. The day that Cienna had said to return to her. Theon had no choice but to go. If he refused, the-gods-only-knew when she would deign to invite him back. It was infuriating, but he more than deserved it.

The sound of footsteps had him lifting his head. He watched Luka enter the room and go straight to the armchair by the bed. He'd dragged it over there the moment they'd laid Tessa in the bed, and if he wasn't in the bathroom, he was in that chair. At least this morning he had a mug of coffee in his hand as he took a seat.

"You need to take a break," Theon said. "Go out. Stretch your wings."

"I'm fine," Luka said, taking a drink.

"At least you're saying more than one word at a time now," Theon scoffed, which earned him a middle finger from his friend. The seconds ticked by before Theon said, "We need to go back to Arius House."

"I know."

"She's still unconscious."

"I know."

"My father will learn of the attack."

"I know."

"For fuck's sake, stop," Theon snapped, getting to his feet and moving to stand beside the bed. "I don't know how to play this. Either he knew of the unrest and sent us in to be blindsided, or he didn't know, and he will be livid when he learns of it."

"You already took care of it. A dead clan leader should be more than enough to assuage his fury," Luka said, settling back in the chair and bringing his ankle to rest on his knee.

"Who knows," Theon muttered. "He's on edge with this whole Source thing. We all are."

Luka said nothing, taking another drink of coffee, but Theon knew he had something to say on the subject.

"Just say it," Theon sighed, already knowing he wasn't going to like it.

"Maybe it's time to appease Valter a little, just to get him off your back for a bit," Luka said.

"And how do you suggest I do that?"

"Spend time with Felicity."

"Fuck off," Theon said. "I already signed the Match contract. That's enough for now."

"And Katya?" Luka pressed.

"I am *not* taking another Source."

"That's fine, but we're already keeping a lot of information from your father. Doing these small things to keep him somewhat content wouldn't be a bad idea. He doesn't need to know it's just an act," Luka said. "At least *acknowledge* Felicity when you see her at the Acropolis."

Theon's gaze drifted back to Tessa. Katya had braided the golden strands into a plait that lay over her shoulder, her features softened in sleep.

"She doesn't know," Theon said quietly.

Luka's brow arched. "You haven't told her who your Match is?" When Theon shook his head, Luka added, "And she hasn't asked?"

"No," Theon said, reaching out to run his knuckles along her cheek.

"The only time she brings it up is to taunt me about how she is to be Matched to you."

Luka scoffed. "We all know that's not going to happen."

Theon hummed an acknowledgment, but something in his gut twisted. Being seen with Felicity, even acknowledging her presence at the Acropolis in passing made it all seem more real. As if this were a fate he couldn't escape despite all his carefully laid plans.

A knock had them both looking to the doorway, where Axel leaned against the doorjamb. "Still nothing?" he asked, eyes lingering on Tessa.

"No," Theon said, scrubbing a hand down his face. "Do you need something, or just checking in?"

"Cienna's messenger is here," Axel answered. "We can't keep her waiting."

Theon nodded, turning back to Luka.

"Go," Luka said. "I'll stay with her. We'll figure this all out later."

"Yeah, all right," Theon said, crossing the room to grab his suit jacket.

He followed Axel down the stairs to the first floor of the penthouse, the same messenger from the passageways standing next to the lift doors. Kat was waiting for them too, dressed in clothing befitting of the hired mercenaries. Apparently it was all Axel could find in the short time he'd had to shop.

When they were ready, they silently rode the lift down to the streets and followed the messenger through the districts and back into the tunnels. They moved quickly, much faster than they had with Tessa since they didn't have to coax her through every narrow passage. Soon enough, they were stepping into the same spacious cavern as before.

Cienna didn't bother to look up from whatever she was doing. Gia was next to her, their heads bent as they murmured softly between themselves. It took Theon sighing in frustration for Cienna to finally deign to speak.

"So impatient," she chided as Gia gathered all the papers they'd been studying and tucked them away into a drawer.

"My time is limited. I have to return to Arius House today," Theon said tightly. "But I'm sure you already knew that."

"I did," Cienna agreed, coming to a stop before them.

When Gia appeared at her side, Theon couldn't help but say, "She still sleeps, not that you've bothered to come check on her."

"Why would I do that?" Gia asked.

"To see if everything is progressing as it should," Theon answered incredulously.

"No need. My abilities are unmatched. She will wake when her body is ready," Gia replied, clearly unbothered.

"I sent you the best," Cienna said before Theon could argue further. "Gia speaks the truth. She will wake when it is time."

"When it is time," Theon repeated, resisting the urge to pace. "And when is that going to be, Cienna?"

"Careful, Theon," Cienna warned, Gia going deathly still beside her.

"I will not be careful," Theon snapped. "I do not have time for your games. Not anymore."

"Theon," Axel hissed, a hand gripping his elbow in warning, but Theon was over it.

He had a kingdom that wanted his Source, a father that wanted the realm, a secret organization that wanted his Source dead, an entire underground city of people who wanted revenge and were tired of waiting for it, and Tessa wouldn't wake the fuck up. He did not have time to spend weeks figuring out Cienna's riddles and hints at the future.

"Answers. That is what I need, Cienna," Theon said, pulling his arm from Axel's grip.

"Then speak your questions," the Witch said tightly, straightening as her violet eyes narrowed on him. "I would hate to be an inconvenience to you. Perhaps if I were not stuck down here, I could be of more assistance."

Theon ignored her sarcasm, his hands clenching into fists at his sides. "Tessa seems to know things."

"Explain," Cienna said.

"The attack where she was wounded. She knew it was going to happen." Then he added, "Apparently, so did you."

"I did not know how it would play out," Cienna said. "Had you made the choice to listen to her, fate would have shifted."

"Do not give me that fate bullshit. She could have been killed," Theon snarled, taking a step closer to her.

Gia moved to step in between them, but Cienna raised a hand, effectively stilling her. Cienna's head canted to the side, a dark smile tilting on her lips. "Had she been killed, entire destinies would have been changed," Cienna replied. "Yours included. Perhaps you should put a little more stock in this 'fate bullshit.'"

Theon wanted to pull his fucking hair out. "I need direct answers. Do you know her parents?"

"No."

"Was she born in this realm?"

"No."

"Is she a Legacy?"

"No."

"Godsdammit, Cienna," Theon seethed, using every bit of his self-control to not begin throwing things. "I need more than that."

"You asked for direct answers. That is what I am giving you," Cienna replied, and she was far too calm in her answer as that smile turned positively wicked, just like the Witch she was.

Inhaling deeply to calm his rising anger, Theon gritted out, "If you do not know her parents, how can you know she is not a Legacy?"

"You asked if I *know* them. I do not. I have never met them," Cienna said, turning her back on him and walking to a shelf lined with books. "Ask proper questions, and you will receive proper answers."

Reining in his rising temper once more, he said tightly, "Do you know *of* her parents? Her lineage?"

"I know pieces of it."

"And those pieces are?"

Cienna returned to stand in front of them once more. She had a book in her hand that she passed off to Katya, but Theon was too close to answers to worry about that at the moment.

"Her father is a god. Her mother may as well be one. She is as powerful as a Lesser," Cienna said simply. "That is all I can tell you. Any more and I will be tempting fate. I already am."

"I swear to Arius, Cienna—" Theon started, but then he was cursing.

Cienna had moved. Theon didn't know where she'd gotten the two long knives from, but he did know one was at his throat while the other pressed to his side. Her eyes flared, and she bared her teeth as she spoke low and vicious. "You speak of not having time for my games, Theon St. Orcas? I do not have time for yours. I am down here because of *you*. Do you know how much more I could do if I could leave the Underground? Do you know how many more answers I could find for you? I have limited resources and no freedom. Do not ask me to test fate when I have already done so and lost *everything* because of it."

Theon swallowed, feeling the blade at his throat when he did so.

"I can't fix any of this without answers, Cienna," he said carefully.

The Witch couldn't kill him with those blades, but she could certainly incapacitate him for an extended period of time. "I can't change this; I can't rectify the failures without answers."

"I have given you answers, Theon. I have given you as much as I can, and what I cannot give to you, I've given you the means to find the answers yourself," she replied, lowering her weapons and stepping back.

He knew it was foolish and only asking for more trouble. He knew she wouldn't be able to give him a definitive answer, but he asked her anyway. "Have you seen how this turns out?"

"You still ask the wrong questions," she answered, the long knives sliding into hidden sheaths on the suit she always wore.

"Then what should I be asking?"

Violet eyes met his when she said, "You should be asking what you can do to control that fate."

"We can't control fate," Theon replied.

"We can change it, though," Cienna replied. "Every action, every word, every breath. The simplest of things can change fate." She smiled again, a knowing thing that had Theon suppressing a shudder. "I think you will learn soon enough that wrestling with fate leaves scars. Only you can decide if they're worth it."

# 16

## TESSA

Her bare feet padded softly on the cool, white marble steps as she descended them, her fingers dragging along the wall made of the same. There were sconces every few feet. Orbs of golden light filled them. The same golden light that crackled at her fingertips as she reached the bottom of the stairs.

Her breath hitched. Even with the ceiling so high above her and the space vast and open, she was still underground. Even with her light, even with her power, the remnants of shackles long since shed still clung to her. She took a moment, willing her racing heart to calm. It wasn't that she couldn't be down here. She could go anywhere in this place she chose. There were no rules. No orders. No demands made of her. Not here.

Yet still...

A cold nose nudged her hand, and she peered down at the wolf beside her. It was massive, its head reaching above her waist. As large as *his* hounds were. Her fingers glided through silky fur such a light shade of grey it appeared silver in the lighting. The wolf nudged her hand again, a low whine coming from him.

Taking another deep breath, she moved forward, following a wide hall. Thick panes of glass lined the passageway, allowing her to see into the rooms on either side. A few were occupied; most were vacant. Cells to hold any manner of being.

She sang softly to herself as she moved. Lines from a decree that wasn't a decree at all.

"In all things, there must be balance. Beginnings and Endings. Light and

*Dark. Fire and Shadows. The sky, the sea, the realms. But when the scales tip, and Chaos rains, who will fight? And who will fall?"*

*Her long gown swished as she moved, the silky fabric cool against her skin. The white dress dipped low between her breasts, reaching nearly to her navel and revealing just as much skin down her back. The material tied at her shoulders, and a deep slit up the side let her move freely. Threads of black and gold and pale blue were woven into the garment.*

*The colors both grounded her and drove her mad.*

*"Life must give, and Death must take. But Fate requires more." She came to a stop before one of the glass cells. "Destiny beckons, and sacrifice demands." The glass sparked, imbued with the same magic in her veins to contain the being within.*

*A male sat on the floor. His brown hair was long, reaching well past his shoulders. It was a tangled mess of knots and needed to be washed and trimmed. She'd expected the scruff on his face to be longer. The facial hair was trimmed close, as if it had been recently tended to. A large onyx ring that matched his sat on his finger, but she was more interested in the manacle at his throat. A thick band of pure white stone, it contained flecks of gold.*

*Flecks of light and energy.*

*A chain attached to the manacle was anchored to the wall, allowing for such little movement, she was unsure how the male could even eat or take care of his needs. He wore loose linen pants, but his torso was bare, allowing her the perfect view of the Marks that ran the length of his left arm.*

*The wolf beside her whined, lowering to his belly as Tessa stepped forward, resting a hand on the glass. The Mark on the back of it caught her eye. A Mark she'd put there. Energy crackled where her palm met the glass, but she absorbed it. This power wasn't meant to keep her out.*

*It was meant to keep him in.*

*The male lifted his head, bright sapphire eyes connecting with hers.*

*And she smiled as she sang, "Who will be left standing when Chaos comes to reign?"*

# 17

## TESSA

The bond in her chest was conflicted. Theon wasn't near. She could tell that, and it didn't like that. But somehow she was also content. It didn't make any sense.

Then again, it didn't make any sense that she was alive either. Not when she'd been stabbed.

Maybe she was dead.

Death seemed peaceful. Comfortable. Freeing. Something she'd craved for so damn long.

*Theon* is *death*.

The words came from nowhere, clanging against the walls of her mind.

Her limbs felt heavy, her mouth dry. She inhaled, fresh air filling her senses, and that had her forcing her eyes open.

Arius House.

She was back in Theon's rooms at Arius House. No more Underground. No more being trapped in narrow passages. No more darkness and stale air.

Good.

She didn't want to die in a place where she couldn't even see the sky.

She'd decided she couldn't actually be dead. Surely the After didn't resemble Arius House.

Unless she went to the Pits of Torment?

Then it made perfect sense.

With another deep breath, she prepared to push into a sitting position, but she'd scarcely shifted an arm when a voice said.

"Don't try to move just yet."

Her heart was in her throat as Luka appeared in her line of vision, leaning over her.

"By the gods," she muttered. "Warn a person next time. Or, at the very least, wear a bell."

His lips twitched, but of course the smile never fully formed. She suddenly found herself wondering if she'd ever seen him truly smile.

"Just take it easy for a minute," he said when she tried to move again.

"I can't just lie here," she argued.

"It's all you've been doing for days. I'm sure you can manage another minute or two."

She sent him a glare. "Excuse me for almost dying."

But instead of a jaded response, Luka looked away from her.

"Can I sit up now?" she asked after another minute.

"Go slow," he said, reaching to help her. "How do you feel?"

"Like I was stabbed in the chest," she grumbled. Her body still ached, and yeah, sitting up somehow made it harder to breathe.

"The Healer said you would be fine if you gave your body the rest it needed to heal."

"Great," she mumbled, her gaze landing on the nearby armchair. "Have you just been sitting there?"

"I was sleeping."

"You're not naked."

Luka's head snapped up. "Why would I be naked?"

"You said you always sleep naked."

He huffed, and Tessa couldn't decide if it was in annoyance or if it was actually almost a laugh. "I'm going to get you some water. Do not try to get out of that bed."

Tessa scowled at him, and the moment he left the room, she did just that.

Or she tried to.

She scooted to the edge, flinging the blankets back, but each movement pulled at her chest. Lifting her shirt, she tried to see where the wound was, but that pulled at something in her neck. She needed a mirror.

Sliding her legs over the edge of the bed, she gingerly placed her bare feet on the floor. The enchantments on the room kept the floors nice and warm, and she slowly started to rise unsteadily to her feet.

"Sit your ass back down," came a growled command.

It wasn't an entrancing, but Tessa found herself obeying as she immediately plopped back onto the mattress.

Luka rounded the bed, two bottles of water in hand. "You couldn't listen for two godsdamn minutes?" he demanded, twisting off the cap of one of the bottles and handing it to her. She didn't answer, taking a big drink of water. "I just wanted to be there. So you didn't hurt yourself further," he said, his tone softening.

Tessa shrugged, the motion pulling at her aching neck. "Where's Theon?"

"Handling some things for his father," Luka answered.

She hummed an acknowledgment, taking another drink of water. "When did we get back to Arius House?"

"Yesterday."

"It's been that long? What about Cienna?"

"Theon and Axel went to see her."

She eyed him as she twisted the cap back on the water bottle. "And you just sat around?"

"Did you think we'd leave you unattended? What if you woke up and we were all gone?" Luka asked, watching her just as carefully.

Tessa shrugged again. "I mean, I'm sure you had better things to be doing with your time."

"I didn't."

She shifted awkwardly at those words, clearing her throat. "Are you going to let me use the bathroom? Just so we're clear, that will involve me standing from this bed."

"Do you always need to be such a brat?" Luka asked, reaching to help her to her feet.

She was about to spout something back, but the moment his hand connected with her arm, the bond did something...weird. She stumbled, and then his hands were on her waist, steadying her. And gods, he was warm. Which had her remembering waking to him wrapped around her while she was curled into Theon. Then *she* was hot.

"You good?" Luka asked, clearly not as affected as she was.

She nodded, not trusting herself to speak, and he stepped to the side. His hand fell to her lower back, guiding her to the bathroom. Thankfully, once inside the spacious room, he let her go to the private toilet area without fuss.

When she emerged, he wasn't in the bathroom any longer, but the faucet was running, filling the oversized bathtub. A bath sounded divine.

She moved to the vanity and brushed her teeth. Inspecting her neck as she did so, she brushed her fingers along her throat. That vampyre had bitten her. What was his name? Jagger? She was certain his fangs had been deep in her throat. That hadn't been a dream.

Or maybe it had.

Her dreams and reality were beginning to merge, and it was unsettling. She'd been so sure that attack was going to happen, as if she'd lived it before. She hadn't been able to figure out where she'd recognized Cienna from. It had seemed impossible, considering she had been sequestered to the Underground for over a decade. Where would she have possibly seen the Witch before?

Apparently in her dreams.

Setting her toothbrush aside, she lifted her shirt to just below her breasts. The place the knife had been was completely healed, not even a scar. But then why was each breath she took so godsdamn painful?

Noise behind her startled her, and she jumped, gasping at the sharp stabbing pain that ran through her.

"Sorry," Luka said gruffly. He had some packages of various food items in his hands—crackers, an orange, a doughnut—and he set them on Theon's side of the vanity. "The last we checked, the wounds had healed nicely. Is that still the case?"

Tessa turned back to the mirror, lifting her shirt again. She ran her fingers lightly over where a scar definitely should have marred her skin. Instead, the only visible mark was the Bargain Mark along her ribs.

"It still hurts," she said, meeting Luka's eyes in the mirror.

He nodded, crossing his arms and leaning back against the counter. "Gia said the internal pain would be the last to fade. It's because of the type of blade you were stabbed with. It's meant to end a Legacy."

"But it didn't."

"Jagger missed your heart," Luka said. "Legacy or not, it would not have been fatal."

"Oh," was all she could think to say.

"The bath is about ready. I can help you in."

Her eyes went wide. "You're going to… I'll be naked," she blurted.

His godsdamn lips twitched, and she wanted to punch him right in the face. "Most are, in fact, naked when bathing. That is kind of the point."

"Won't Theon be upset?"

Luka shrugged. "Perhaps."

"And you don't care?"

"I am not going to delay your comfort for him. If you, however, are uncomfortable with being naked around me, you can wait for Theon."

Her brow furrowed. "I don't care if you see me naked."

"Then I suppose it is settled," he answered.

Right. Nudity didn't bother her. She usually enjoyed getting naked with men. Or males. Or whatever.

But now her mouth was dry, and her palms were sweaty, and—

This was stupid.

Moving to the side of the tub, she didn't let herself think about it anymore. She pushed the loose pants over her hips, letting them fall to the floor, her undergarments with them. Then she pulled the shirt over her head, Theon's scent filling her nose as she did so. The bond was even more confused and so was she, because she was pretty sure the bond should be having a fit about another male seeing her without clothing.

Without a word, Luka stepped forward. He held out his hand, and she took it, allowing him to steady her as she climbed over the high lip of the tub. The water was perfect, and she held in her moan as she sank into the hot water, going completely under. When she came back to the surface, she pushed her wet hair from her face, finding Luka had moved to the seat at the cosmetic table.

"Are you just going to sit there?" she asked.

"Can't have you drowning now, can I?"

"Maybe I'm a brat all the time because you're constantly an ass," she retorted, settling against the back of the tub and running her fingers through the bubbles.

"Doubtful."

She clicked her tongue, rolling her eyes. A comfortable silence fell between them, and that was even more weird. Why was she comfortable with Theon so far away? Yes, a part of her was longing for him, but she was also content in the moment.

"You fought," Luka said into the quiet.

She glanced at him briefly before focusing on the bubbles again. "I did."

"Why?"

"I…" She swallowed thickly. "I didn't want to die where I couldn't see the sky."

"Is that the only reason?"

"I mean, I guess it was the stuff you said too," she admitted. "I don't know that I'm necessarily worth it, but I'd like to think I am."

"You are, Tessa."

She shrugged again, sinking into the water up to her chin. "I don't…" She sighed. "I don't want to feel that defenseless ever again, Luka."

"Then we make sure you aren't," he said, and there was a fierceness in his voice that had her turning to look at him. And gods, the look on his face said he believed that. He truly believed she was worth his time. That he could teach her to not only defend herself but actually fight back.

She cleared her throat again. "You brought snacks?"

"Those are for me."

She couldn't stop the bark of laughter. It hurt her chest, but it also felt good to laugh. "The doughnut too?"

"Especially that. You can have the crackers," Luka said, and the corner of his mouth tipped up in a smile so small it could barely be called one, but it was there.

"Ass," she muttered.

She heard his huff of laughter as she slid beneath the water again.

After she'd bathed and was dressed in fresh clothing, the two of them went out to sit with Katya. She was reading a book on the sofa, but Tessa went straight to the bay window she'd spent so much time in weeks ago. Luka indeed let her have the doughnut, and she was just finishing it off when Theon and Axel came through the door.

She'd felt him approaching, the bond buzzing with excitement. Theon must have felt it too, because he came rushing through the door, tossing his suit jacket over a chair. He was across the room in a few long strides and taking her face in his hands.

"You're awake," he breathed, his thumb sweeping along her jaw.

"Awake, bathed, and fed," she retorted. "Your babysitter did well. Better tip him extra." Theon's eyes fell closed as though he were thanking Arius himself. "What is wrong with you? Luka told me the Healer said I would be fine."

His eyes opened, emerald irises bright with emotions she could feel down their bond.

Emotions she didn't like one bit.

"I haven't been able to feel you, Tessa. Nothing. Not a single thing."

"I'm fine. Just a little sore still," she said, pulling back from his touch.

He turned to Luka. "Is that true?"

Luka nodded, his legs stretched before him where he sat on the sofa. "You've seen the wounds. They're healed. She said it still hurts, but Gia said that would linger."

"Who is Gia?" Tessa asked. "Luka mentioned that name earlier."

"The Healer who fixed you up," Axel said, sitting on the arm of the chair where Kat sat. She didn't acknowledge him, and Tessa found herself a little jealous that she seemed to be more comfortable around them than she was. How had the female become that comfortable in such a short period of time? She had to be convinced to sit and eat with them, but here she was fine.

Axel leaned over, pointing to something in the book. Tessa couldn't hear his question, but Kat shook her head, turning a page and pointing at something else. She wasn't even listening to what Luka and Theon were discussing now, too intrigued by what she was watching. Those two seemed like the ones who had a bond, not her and Theon.

"Dinner will be brought up in an hour," Theon was saying, pulling her from her thoughts. "Tomorrow we go back to the Acropolis."

Tessa nodded, turning back to the window. The gardens below were becoming barren, leaves beginning to fall and littering the ground. Rain would become snow soon, the rivers turning to ice. She suspected a layer of frost would blanket everything in the morning being this high in the mountains.

"Do you think I can make it snow?" she wondered aloud.

Whatever small chatter had been happening went quiet, and she tilted her head to look up at Theon. "Why would you think that?" he asked cautiously.

"You told Cienna you believed I could control the weather."

"You made it rain *inside* the Pantheon," Axel said from across the room.

"Not on purpose," she argued, immediately going on the defensive.

"No one is blaming you. Just saying if you can make it rain indoors, one could logically assume you've been responsible for the odd weather lately," Axel continued.

"That seems a little far-fetched. Who can control the *weather*?" she argued.

"And yet you ask if you can make it snow," Theon countered.

"Achaz can't control the weather, can he?" she asked.

"No, he cannot."

Tessa nodded, turning back to the window. "I have to go there. To the Achaz Kingdom. When we return."

"Not right away," Theon said tightly. When she didn't respond, he added, "The Samhain Feast is the day after we return. We have time to try to get you out of this. It's not like you will leave the moment the feast ends."

"There will be an assessment," she murmured.

"I know, beautiful."

"But I suppose there will be light there," she mused, trying to comfort herself.

"Tessa."

It was just her name, but she could hear the note of agony ringing in it. She turned to look at him once more. "None of you will be there. I'll be alone."

His eyes momentarily fell closed, and she could feel his helplessness down the bond. It was interesting, watching him experience something she'd felt so often because of him. She half expected him to reach for her, bring her into his arms. Not to comfort her, but because he wanted the bond to comfort him. Instead, he said, "I'm going to shower before dinner."

"We're not eating with Valter?" Luka asked, watching Theon head to the bedroom.

Theon paused. "My meeting placated him, so he didn't demand it of us this evening."

Luka nodded, and Theon left. Tessa stared after him.

She knew she should ask what that had meant, but something told her she wouldn't like the answer. Call it a feeling, instinct, intuition.

She didn't know why it mattered. She didn't understand why she'd been waiting for him to pull her into his arms. She didn't understand why she'd *wanted* him to. It had to be the bond, but that had been different for a while now too.

She didn't understand any of it.

Or she was too afraid to because there was no way that taking what she wanted from him was leading her to *depend* on him for anything. She knew better than to expect explanations or apologies. She knew she was on her own when it came to figuring things out, which meant she should ask Luka what that meant, but…

Tessa turned back to the window, watching dead leaves blow across the garden paths.

She'd woken up.

That seemed like enough bravery for one day.

# 18

## TESSA

Eating with a mask on was nearly impossible. Yet here she was, dressed in a stunning midnight blue gown that showed off the Source Mark over her heart. The blue and gold mask covered the upper half of her face, but it kept slipping down her nose with every bite she took. She sat at a table with the other Sources, including those of the heirs and the Lords and Ladies. Theon sat with Axel and his parents at one of the two long tables on the dais. The same dais she'd sat on a few months ago when she'd been Selected. Now she sat at one of the circular tables just before the thing. Below the ruling families, but also between them and the rest of the Legacy. The other Fae weren't even given tables. They milled about in a sectioned off area across the grand hall, a buffet of much less ornate food spread out for them.

Tessa wished she was with them.

Glancing up at Theon again, she found him and Axel in a conversation with Tana Aithne, heir to the Anala Kingdom, and her younger sister. Down the table, the Falein family sat.

"Do they always sit together?" Tessa asked, moving roasted vegetables around her plate with her fork. When would they get dessert?

"Yes," Eviana answered from her left. "For the same reason we will always be seated like this."

Tessa glanced to her right where Gatlan, Tana's Source, sat, and next to him was Hollis, the Anala Lady's Source. Gatlan raised his glass of liquor to her in a cheers motion with a wink. His plate was empty, and

Hollis was finishing the fresh fish they'd been served. They both wore red and grey masks that only covered their eyes. Those were practical masks. Why couldn't she wear one like that?

"The Northern Kingdoms sit together and the Southern Kingdoms sit together," Gatlan explained.

"Why?" Tessa asked, glancing back at the dais where the Serafina, Achaz, and Celeste families were indeed seated at the other table.

"No idea," he answered. "It's how it's always been done from my understanding."

"That seems…counterproductive to building relations among the Kingdoms."

"One would think," Gatlan said. "Any other observations to make?" Tessa glared at him, and he laughed lightly. "It wasn't meant to be a jab at you. I know you were not as prepared for this role as the rest of us were, and now you are…"

"Not Fae?" Tessa finished for him. "I am aware, thank you. As for my 'observations,' I won't be giving you any information to take back to the others tonight."

"Not Fae, yet still shoved off to the side, huh? That's rough," Gatlan said, swirling his glass of liquor.

Tessa bristled, and she saw Theon glance over at her at the sudden burst of emotion. Scowling, she stabbed a carrot with a little too much force. "Stop baiting me, Gatlan."

"Where's the snappy little thing from before the Emerging Ceremony?" Gatlan asked. "Watching you put Maxson in his place was the best thing I'd seen in a long time. Shut him up for at least an hour. I've been meaning to thank you."

"Thank me," she repeated doubtfully.

"He is being genuine," Eviana cut in. "He is not trying to rile you."

Tessa turned to her. The female never spoke to her. Not unless instructed by Valter. "Forgive me for not trusting you."

Eviana only shrugged a slender shoulder, returning to her nearly clean plate. She didn't appear to have any issue eating with her glittering black mask in place. Then again, she'd been doing this for… How long had she been Valter's Source?

"Jasper and Maxson are asses to everyone. Don't feel bad," Gatlan continued, as if Tessa hadn't been questioning his motives. "Dade is quiet and observant like his Mistress. Sasha tries to keep the peace."

Tessa sat back in her chair, placing her fork on her plate. "Not that I asked for a rundown of the other Sources, but how do you fit into the mix then?"

"I don't," he said with another wink before knocking back the last of his drink. Within seconds, a server was there replacing it with a fresh, full glass. Gatlan clearly noticed her slightly shocked stare because he asked, "Need a taste?"

"No," she said quickly, her gaze going to the half-empty water glass before her. But why couldn't she have some alcohol? She wasn't Fae. Theon didn't even think she was Legacy. Sure, she was still a Source, but—

But nothing.

She was still a Source. If she fucked up, everything could change. The ruling Lords and Ladies could move up their timeline. They could change the terms, and she wasn't ready. She needed more time.

Pushing out a harsh breath, Tessa forced a tight smile to her face when she met Gatlan's gaze once more. "No, thank you. I'm fine."

He had a small smirk on his lips as he watched her. "Figured I'd offer before you helped yourself this time."

Tessa felt her cheeks grow hot at the memory. That had been incredibly impulsive of her that night.

"It's fine, Tess," he said, and her eyes narrowed.

Only one other person called her that. "Do you know Lange?" she asked.

The small smirk increased. "By association."

"You know Corbin," she said, realization dawning. Corbin had come from the Anala Kingdom.

Gatlan nodded, his eyes dancing with what Tessa could only call mischief as he took another sip of his liquor.

"How well do you know him?"

"We were quite close," Gatlan said, that delight in his eyes dimming a little. "Not in the way he and Lange are, but we were very good friends. Grew up together."

"Were?"

"Still are, I suppose."

He set his glass down, his finger tapping on the table. He didn't have bands on his wrists. The Sources had been allowed to take their assessments earlier in the day. Of course, they'd all passed and were free of the restraints. Only Tessa still had to wear them, which Jasper and Maxson had been sure to discuss loudly upon seeing her.

"Do you get to see him often?" Tessa asked.

Gatlan shrugged, shifting in his chair. "We saw each other every day before he was moved to the Celeste Estate," he answered bitterly. "We both have other responsibilities now, and he has Lange."

"Corbin isn't the kind of person to toss aside a friend simply because he's involved with someone romantically," Tessa cut in.

Gatlan eyed her, his finger tapping again. "He said you were friends."

"We are. One of the few I had at the Estate."

His brow arched. "You only met him a short time ago."

"Yes, well, this might come as a shock to you." She leaned in as if she were going to tell him some great secret, lowering her voice, and Gatlan leaned closer too. "But I tend to be rather impulsive so people like Jasper have something to talk about."

Gatlan snickered, swiping up his drink again. "Things are certainly more interesting when you're around. I'll give you that much. Being seated next to you at these events won't be so bad, even if only for a time."

Tessa frowned. That was a weird caveat, but before she could ask about it, servers appeared, removing plates and cleaning the table. Were they seriously not getting dessert?

She turned to Eviana to find the female already standing, her hands clasped loosely in front of her. How did she get her mask to stay in place? It hadn't moved once, and Tessa was constantly readjusting hers. Or maybe that was just because she was constantly fiddling with the thing.

Tessa stood, standing beside her. "What are we doing?"

"They will move tables to make the space bigger for the Legacy and to set up an array of snacks for them to enjoy throughout the night," Eviana explained, moving towards one side of the room.

"And what will we do?"

Eviana looked over at her, turquoise eyes emotionless as always. "We stay with the other Sources, within reach of our Masters."

It was a pointed statement, and Tessa could hear the underlying warning. Eviana said nothing else as she veered left to where Hollis and the other Lords' and Ladies' Sources gathered. Which meant she was spending the evening with the heirs' Sources.

Which was just fucking great.

With a harsh sigh, she made her way over to what was apparently her group of people. Her heels clicked with each step. She'd started counting the minutes until she could take them off the moment she'd slipped them on. Katya had helped her with her hair, the female wearing a dark orange dress and mask that were stunning against her complexion. Tessa could tell she'd felt flustered, the dress far more extravagant than anything she'd likely worn. But she hadn't complained once, making quiet small talk as she'd helped Tessa curl and pin her hair.

It had been…nice.

Tessa slipped in between Sasha and Gatlan. Without a word, Gatlan offered her his drink again. It was nearly gone now, but Tessa didn't care, taking the glass and swallowing the last of it.

"We were just talking about you," Maxson said with a smirk.

She was going to need another drink for this.

"I know you have a little crush on me, Max, but you're starting to sound a little desperate. It's sad really," she simpered, handing the empty glass off to a passing server.

Maxson scoffed, lifting a hand where a small funnel of wind swirled at his fingertips. "The only thing I'm desperate for when it comes to you is for them to figure out what to do with you. I'm sure your *Master* is eager for that too. Then he can Select a real Source and everyone can move on."

Tessa nodded mockingly. "I know you were at that hearing, but I see Lealla didn't explain it clearly enough for you to understand. I'll see if I can simplify it."

"We were not talking about Tessa," Sasha cut in before things could escalate. "We were discussing the next Selection and how Axel will be the only one of age to Select a Source."

"An Arius Heir. An Arius Source. Both from the same rejected kingdom, so semantics," Maxson said with a shrug.

"It should be a less eventful Selection Year then," Gatlan said.

"Assuming no replacements need to be made," Dade replied.

"Anyway, we were just discussing whether or not the other Arius Heir knew of a hidden being he's planning to Select," Maxson went on. "Arius Kingdom is so…secretive. I guess now we know why."

The pointed sweep of his eyes over her made Tessa's skin crawl, but she sighed dramatically. "I'd be disappointed in my Mistress too."

Maxson stilled. "What's that supposed to mean?"

"Oh, I thought you were lamenting my Master being more clever than yours. My mistake."

Maxson's smirk grew. "How much longer will you be able to call him that? I suppose we can assume he'll have a new Source by the next Selection as well, hmm?"

"How will that work?" Jasper mused, cutting into the conversation. "Will those Marks still work? Will you feel him...*bonding* with another? Hear his thoughts when he's with her?"

It was Tessa's turn to still, something inside her balking at the mere idea of Theon with someone else. The bond. It had to be the bond.

But the flash of lightning outside the window, followed by the rumble of thunder, had more than their little group turning to the sudden change in weather. Jasper and Maxson slowly turned back, and when she met their gazes, she knew her smile was anything but sweet. She slowly lifted her hands, showing them her bands still in place as she said, "Interesting weather lately, wouldn't you say?"

For once, neither of them had anything to say. Their group was still. Except for Gatlan. He was sipping at his fresh drink, one hand in his pocket as he hid his smile.

"Excuse me?"

Tessa turned at the voice to find a server standing there. He held a tray with a single shot glass on it.

"I was told to bring this to you, along with this."

His hand trembled a little when he extended a note to her.

"To me?" she asked, taking the note from him. Unfolding the paper, she read the one line of simple, elegant handwriting:

*Should you find it conducive to your agenda tonight, I have an entire bottle, fury.*

She couldn't help the smile as she swiped up the shot of *agaveheart*, relishing the burn as it slid down her throat and warmth pooled in her belly.

"As fun as this has been, I have better company to keep," Tessa said, dropping the glass back onto the tray with a nod to the server, who scurried away.

"We can't go anywhere," Maxson blurted.

She gathered her dress into her hand so she wouldn't trip on it. "Apparently you're free of your bands, but not your leash," she said with a wink before she sauntered away.

She wasn't entirely sure how she was going to find Tristyn Blackheart in the vast space of the grand hall. On top of that, everyone was wearing masks. Then again, he tended to find her. She'd just have to wait him out, but it didn't keep her from scanning faces. Theon's dismay trickled down the bond, and with a single thought, she blocked it. She hadn't wanted him to know she'd figured out how to do that yet, but she'd already let it slip she could overcome the demands of the Source bond. She'd sacrifice this secret to keep others close.

Tessa was so busy scanning the room, she didn't see the female until it was too late. With an *oomph* she ran right into her, stumbling in her heels as she tried to catch her balance.

"I apolo—" Tessa started, but a shrill voice cut her off.

"Oh my gods! Tessa?"

Tessa looked up into dark eyes behind a black mask, her pale blonde hair loose around her shoulders. "Oralia?" she said in disbelief.

"Oh my gods!" she cried again. "I didn't think we'd get to see you tonight. The others will be thrilled."

"But I—" Tessa tried again as Oralia grabbed her wrist, making her wince as the band dug into her skin. Oralia started tugging her through the crowd of mingling Fae and Legacy. She was unsure when she'd crossed the invisible line that separated the commoners from the elite, but everything was more relaxed on this side of the room. The air wasn't as stifling.

She could *breathe*.

But she also wanted to find Tristyn.

"Dex!" Oralia was calling to be heard over the crowd. "Dex, look!"

Seconds later, large hands were pulling her into a hug. "Tessie. Thank the gods," Dex murmured, but then he was pushing her back, gripping her shoulders. "What's wrong?"

"Why do you think something is wrong?" Tessa asked.

"You're stiff as a board. Are you not supposed to be here? Tessa," he sighed, already sounding resigned at having to deal with this. "This is not the time to cause a scene."

"I'm not—"

She took a deep breath, feeling her power stretch beneath her skin as another bolt of lightning flashed outside. She hadn't used her power since the training pit in the Underground. That was…too long ago. It was getting restless, which only meant *she* was going to start getting restless and more impulsive. She'd figured that much out at least. When

Theon was religiously taking her to the river to let her siphon off her gifts, she felt more in control of... Well, everything.

"I'm fine," she replied. "I'm probably not supposed to be here, but it will not cause a scene."

"And later?"

Later it would probably cause a scene that would end with having an incredible orgasm if she were being honest, so...

The crease at Dex's brow increased as he studied her. "You seem different. Are you sure you're all right?"

But before she could answer, another male voice had her spinning around.

"Tessalyn Ausra." The male was a little shorter than Dex, and he'd pushed his mask up onto his forehead so he could see her properly. His brownish-blonde hair was neatly trimmed and combed, and he had his signature flirty smile in place.

"Brecken," she greeted with a small smile of her own, embracing him when he pulled her into a hug. "It's been a while."

"I always seem to miss you lately," he agreed. "I was hoping I'd get to see you tonight, though. Is Kat with you?"

He'd always had a thing for the female, and Tessa shook her head. "I haven't seen her, but Axel keeps a close eye on her. I'd be careful."

Somehow his eyes went darker. "Has he claimed her then?"

Tessa blinked in surprise. "Arius Kingdom claimed her before her power even emerged."

Brecken rolled his eyes, and Tessa was even more taken aback.

"Everyone knows that," he said. "They don't usually put them on the same leash the Sources are put on though," he said, before he grimaced a little. "Sorry. I didn't mean..."

Tessa stared at him for a long moment before saying tightly, "Clearly my leash is quite long."

"He didn't mean it that way, Tessie," Dex said. "No need to be over-dramatic."

He was probably right. She was being overdramatic. Her trapped magic was making her oversensitive, and she *did* need to be careful. She was already pushing the limits tonight.

"Where are Corbin and Lange?" she asked, glancing at the three who were crowding around her.

"You know those two," Oralia said, reaching over and adjusting Tessa's mask. "How do you always look such a mess?"

"I don't know," she murmured, still trying to look for Tristyn, but it was impossible to see around Dex and Brecken.

"So talk to us, Tessa," Dex was saying. "How are you? I'm sure we don't have much time."

"I'm fine," she replied automatically.

"Don't give me that bullshit. You are not fine." He took her chin, trying to force her face up, and she jerked back from him. His brows shot up in surprise. "Tessa? I didn't mean to… It's just me."

*It's just me.*

But her eyes fell to his wrist where the Achaz Mark stood next to the Celeste Estate and wind element markings. He'd been there when she'd woken in Lord Jove's manor house. He'd said things she hadn't forgotten, even if none of it made sense.

Dex noticed her stare and lowered his arm, hands sliding into his pockets. "I'm still on your side, Tessa. You know that, right?"

But she couldn't answer him. She didn't know *how* to answer him.

"Don't be silly," Oralia scoffed. "We've known her for years. Of course she knows we're on her side. We've always been there for her." She turned her attention to Tessa, flicking her long hair over her shoulder. "Dex has more than proven he's on your side, Tessa."

Oralia had a point. From the moment she'd met him beneath a set of stairs, he'd done nothing but help her. He got her food, helped her avoid Mother Cordelia's wrath whenever he could, and had accepted her when no one else did. He'd never asked for or expected anything in return.

"Sorry," Tessa finally muttered, rubbing at her arms. "I'm just in a mood tonight."

"It's all right," Dex said, his entire demeanor shifting. "Is he still not letting you expel power regularly?" At her furrowed brow, he added, "Lord Jove informed me of how things went at the Tribunal Hearing."

"Why?"

"Because I serve in his house, Tessa," Dex said, his eyes narrowing. "We can talk about this later, when you're not so defensive."

"I'm not being defensive," she snapped. "It is just odd that a Lord— the *Achaz* Lord at that—is confiding in a Fae he only chose weeks ago."

"Does the Arius Heir not confide in you?" Brecken asked, leaning against the wall to her right.

"No. I mean, yes," she quickly corrected at Brecken's arched brow. "But that's different. I'm his Source."

"And yet he only chose you weeks ago," he countered with a shrug.

"That's…" She huffed. Fine, it was a somewhat valid point.

"She's already said she's feeling off and in a mood right now because of her power. Leave her alone, Breck," Dex cut in. Looking down at her, he added, "Are you hungry?"

"No."

"No? You hardly ate your dinner."

"You were watching?"

"Of course I was watching. I rarely get to see you. He keeps you hidden away. No training. Private lessons," Dex replied in frustration. At her perplexed expression, he added, "I worry about you, Tessie. We all do."

She hummed an acknowledgment, her attention turning to the makeshift dance floor at the end of the room, as far away from the ruling families as it could be. There were several Fae dancing, even some Legacy. Males and females in stunning dresses and masks. One female with silver hair tipped her head back, a laugh falling from her lips as her partner spun her around. His black clothing was elegant, threads of red and gold along the lapels of his jacket. His gold and silver mask matched hers, and Tessa frowned. She was clearly Legacy, but was he? They both had rings on their fingers, but those were not Union Marks on the back of their left hands. The only Marks that went there were Source Marks. She had other Marks on her bare arms. Some black. Some a faded silver.

The male spun her again, and Tessa could swear there were wisps of shadows and white flames that echoed her footsteps. Silver eyes connected with hers for the briefest of moments, and Tessa could only describe the smile that filled her face as darkness itself. Then the male was pulling her back into him, bending to speak into her ear, and her eyes were back on him as he held her close.

Tessa's power strained, thrashing against the bands. Another crack of thunder sounded, and she didn't understand. It had never been like this. Before it had been a slowly building ache in her bones, but this was different. This was her magic wanting something, demanding she take it. She didn't understand why it was suddenly so restless, so uncontrollable. It was as if it was being drawn to something, and Tessa didn't know what. But it was demanding something from her she couldn't give it. Not in a crowd full of people, and not without risking revealing things she wasn't ready to share.

"Tessa? Did you hear me?" Dex was saying, stepping into her line of vision and blocking her view of the dance floor.

"What? No, I'm sorry. What were you saying?" she asked, shaking her head a little as her power flared again.

"I was saying I will be there when you come to the Achaz Kingdom for your week in Faven," Dex said.

Her gaze snapped back to him. "What? Why?"

"Because Lord Jove thought it would make you more comfortable to have a familiar face while there," he answered, reaching to fix her mask yet again.

"But your lessons?"

"Kat was just gone for an extended period of time from her lessons. Rules are bent a little when a Fae has already been claimed by a Kingdom."

"But—"

She turned as something caught her eye. Light glimmering off of a pearlescent mask. A mask that completely covered the wearer's face. They weren't in black robes but in a suit, blending in with the crowd. No one else seemed to notice anything amiss, but the figure was moving through the crowd, making their way to an exit.

"Tessa," Dex said, his irritation heavy. "Can you focus for one minute?"

But the person with the mask was almost out of the room, and if this Augury society was real, they would have answers. Answers she needed.

"I need to go," Tessa muttered, shoving past Dex.

"Go? Go where?" he asked in disbelief. "Is this because of Theon?"

"No," she said quickly, although she probably should go find Theon. But that just gave the masked person more time to get away. "I need to use the bathroom."

"I'll go with you," Oralia immediately cut in.

"No," Tessa replied, already walking away and slipping between a group of people.

"Tessa!" Dex called after her, but she knew he'd let her go. He wouldn't want to—What had he said? Make a scene as she so often did.

It took her a few minutes to make her way through the crowds of Fae and Legacy, but she finally pushed through the same doors the masked person had been headed towards. Of course, she found the space completely empty, but she recognized the hallway. It was the same one

Theon had found her with a bar of chocolate in, which meant there were a few alcoves here.

Getting Theon or Luka would be a really good idea right now. She knew that. But it was also quiet out here. She could breathe.

Her power stirred again, once more restless and demanding, and gods, she just wanted to scream. This entire night had been one big, uncomfortable mess. Maybe she could find her way back to that balcony Luka had found her on when she'd crawled out a bathroom window.

A flicker of concern down the bond reminded her she should go find Theon. She just needed another minute before she went back into the crowded great room. She focused on keeping their connection blocked just a little longer. He'd come find her soon enough. Maybe she'd just wait for him here. She'd already made a mess of the evening. She shouldn't have even come down here, but she'd been looking for—

"You look like you need some air, fury."

She spun, finding Tristyn standing there in a navy suit. A plain navy mask covered his eyes, and his brown hair was styled as immaculately as Theon's. And why wouldn't it be? He was an elite Legacy that seemed to hold nearly as much power and sway in matters as the ruling families.

But where had he come from?

"Were you following me?" she demanded.

His lips tilted into that playful grin she knew a little too well as he held up an *agaveheart* bottle. "Not at all. Just waiting for you."

Her eyes narrowed, very aware of how he'd conveniently shown up at this exact moment. "How long have you been out here?"

That grin faltered, concern taking its place. "Are you all right, Tessa?"

"Have you been out here a while? Did you see someone else…"

He studied her for a moment before saying, "I saw you come out here from across the room. It took me a few minutes to extract myself from the festivities inside."

She nodded mutely, her power flaring once again. As if he sensed it, his gaze dropped to her hands that were curled into fists at her sides. His mouth pressed into a thin line, clear disapproval lining his features.

"You need some air," he said again.

"I was just going to find Theon."

"Probably not a good idea to go back in there quite yet," Tristyn said.

He had a point, and Theon was already going to be in a mood now anyway.

She shrugged. "I could use some air. And a drink of that."

That grin returned, but the concern lingered as he passed the bottle to her. "This way, fury."

She followed him around a corner, and he pushed open a door. The double doors across the room led to a balcony, and she was striding through them before Tris had even finished closing the door behind them. The night air was cool against her face, and she tipped her head back, taking in a deep breath. Her power rattled her soul again, and for the life of her, she couldn't figure out why. Lightning flashed. Thunder rumbled in the distance. She wasn't angry or sad or feeling anything really. Frustrated with everything, sure, but this was restlessness. Her power surged again, wild and out of control, and light flared at her fingertips. Glancing up quickly, she was grateful to find Tristyn staring out over the balcony, a roll of lull-leaf between his lips. He clearly hadn't noticed her power breaking through the bands.

Slipping her shoes off, Tessa sank to the ground against the railing. She pulled the mask off, setting it aside and taking a pull from the liquor bottle before handing it back to Tristyn.

"Need to talk about it?" he asked.

Russet-colored eyes met hers, and why did he always *care*? From the moment she'd met him in a hotel lobby, she'd felt relaxed around him. Calm and composed, as if she could simply exist without the anxiety and expectations that constantly plagued her.

"You're a Pax Legacy," she said in realization.

He smiled softly. "Not quite, but close enough."

"Pax is the god of peace and serenity," she said warily. "That's why I always feel that way around you."

"I'm flattered, fury."

"Don't be," she muttered, taking the bottle he extended to her once more.

"Can I sit?"

"I need to go back in there. Theon will be upset. His father—" Her eyes went wide. "Oh, gods. His father will be livid." She scrambled to her feet, grabbing her mask and shoes. What the fuck had she been thinking?

Once again, she hadn't been. She hadn't been careful enough, no matter how justifiable her actions had been.

*Reckless. Impulsive. Too wild.*

Dex had tried to tell her; she hadn't listened, and now she'd created yet another mess.

"Tessa," Tristyn said, his hand resting on her elbow. Her anxiety bled out of her, but her power bit back too.

Tristyn yanked his hand back. "Should have seen that coming," he muttered, shaking his hand out. "Those bands won't contain you much longer."

"How do you know that?" she asked, all her previous suspicion coming back in full force.

He bent to retrieve the mask she'd dropped at some point. Handing it back to her, he said, "Because chaos can't be contained."

Tessa took the mask from him just as the doors banged open behind them. She didn't even flinch. She'd felt him coming.

"Of course it's you," Theon sneered, striding onto the balcony with Luka at his side. Both of them looked pissed.

Tessa didn't have it in her to care.

"At least there's no pizza this time, right?" Tristyn said with a wink as he tipped the *agaveheart* bottle in greeting before taking a drink.

Theon's gaze slid to her, and before he could say whatever he was opening his mouth to chide at her, she said, "I know, I know. Discussions will be had. Expectations and consequences."

But Tristyn was stepping in front of her. Startled, she stumbled back.

"Is there a reason you are standing between me and my Source?" Theon demanded.

"Is there a reason she hasn't expended her power in, what I can only assume, is days?" Tristyn retorted.

"That is none of your concern."

"It is when it's consuming her to the point of near madness. It is when I had to intervene and get her outside before we experienced a repeat of her emerging in there," Tristyn said, and by the gods, he sounded…terrifying.

Lethal.

Wicked.

"It's fine, Tris," Tessa mumbled. She reached out to touch him, but then remembered the shock thing from earlier and thought better of it.

"It's not fine, Tessa," he seethed, still holding Theon's stare. "He's supposed to be training you, not stifling you."

"And what would you know of it?" Theon asked.

Tristyn reached into his pocket, and Tessa choked down her huff of laughter when he pulled out another lull-leaf roll and lit it up. "More than you, apparently. I was the one who got her out of there. I believe the words you're looking for are 'thank you.'"

"You seem to know an awful lot about her, Blackheart," Theon said, his eyes narrowing. "And yet I can't get you to return any of my calls at Lilura Inquest."

"Probably because I don't want to talk to you," he answered with a shrug.

"No, you only wish to speak with my Source."

"Can you blame me?" Tristyn asked, taking another toke off the lull-leaf.

"We need to get back in there, Theon," Luka cut in. "Are we done here?"

"I don't know," Theon said, his glare cutting to Tessa. "Are you done here?"

"Judging by that look on your face, I could probably use a few more shots of *agaveheart* and my own roll of lull-leaf," she grumbled, rubbing at her wrists as her power pressed against her skin. It was out of control. The bond was reaching for Theon. She could feel Luka's gaze on her but couldn't meet his stare. Whatever the fuck Tristyn could do was pressing at her, trying to do the gods-knew-what, and her magic just wanted out, out, out, desperate to find whatever had riled it up.

"Alcohol is the last thing you need," Theon said tightly, jerking his chin at Luka to go get her, but Luka seemed to hesitate.

"Something's wrong," Luka said.

"Obviously," Theon snapped. "That's why we came to find her."

"No, she's… Tessa, look at me," Luka said in that same coaxing voice he'd used in the Underground.

"Look at you," she muttered. "Look at you. Eyes on him. Don't focus on the bands that keep you locked away below the ground, below the sea. Always in the dark. Always, always, always."

The sky flashed with a bright bolt of lightning, and thunder cracked so loud she felt it in her bones.

And she knew her power was about to take what it demanded.

Freedom.

# 19
## THEON

"I think we need to go," Tessa rasped, her voice ringing with that eerie tone that it sometimes took on.

"Fuck," Tristyn cursed. "You two need to get her out of here."

"I don't think anyone should touch her right now," Luka said cautiously, but his eyes had shifted, as if already preparing for a fight.

"You're the only ones who *can* touch her right now. You've altered everything," Tristyn said. "If you don't want the terms of your agreement with the Lords and Ladies to change, you need to go."

"I don't know that we have the option to take her anywhere at the moment," Theon said. "Even if we could get near her, what are we supposed to do? Escort her through the Pantheon and down to the parking valet?"

"Wherever you take her, those bands need to come off and stay off," Tristyn said. "I thought it was made clear that her power needed to be expelled regularly."

"I know what needs to happen. I do not need you coming in and telling me how to handle this," Theon snapped.

"Obviously you do," Tristyn retorted, stepping closer. "Because it never should have gotten to this point. I felt her power the moment you stepped into the Pantheon tonight, and I've felt it steadily growing all evening. Everyone in there felt it. They just didn't realize where it was coming from."

Theon watched for it. For some flicker of magic. Any hint of his lineage. The elusive Tristyn Blackheart was as hard to find information on as Tessa. He'd been around for decades, long before Theon had been born, but the little bit of information available about him was all the same. He'd founded Lilura Inquest, the company that was responsible for numerous advancements in Devram, from elixirs to technology to translating lost languages and everything in between. But actual information about *him*? That was virtually nonexistent. Then again, with his company, he could effectively bury any information he wanted.

He would also have the resources to alter documents.

Keep someone hidden.

Show up when it was convenient for him to do so.

Theon had been trying to gain a meeting with the male since the Emerging Ceremony. He'd called Lilura Inquest every day since, but he could never get past Blackheart's godsdamn assistant. But the moment Tessa is at a public event and accessible again, he shows up?

"Theon."

His name was a harsh whisper from her, and he turned, finding Tessa sinking to her knees. He could see her entire body trembling. It shouldn't surprise him. He'd held her by the river bank several times now when the bands would come off and her power would erupt. Light was flickering and sparking at her fingertips. Winds were whipping around them as the incoming storm increased, wild and unrelenting. A few big raindrops splattered to the ground, icy water droplets sliding down his neck. There was howling, and with the winds, he couldn't tell how far away it was.

"Where are we supposed to take her?" Luka was demanding again.

"I cannot believe you have not figured out how to— What are you doing?" Tristyn asked.

But Theon was done with this. His darkness was coating his skin, and his shadow wings had formed. They needed to get out of here. They couldn't go through the halls of the Pantheon, but they didn't need to.

"We'll go to the training arenas. They're only a few blocks away," Theon answered, crouching down next to Tessa. Glowing violet eyes met his, a mixture of desperation and malice radiating down the bond. He could feel everything she was feeling. The clever thing had figured out a way to block their bond for short periods of time, but it seemed she had lost that control when her power suddenly decided it wanted out. He could feel her panic and her helplessness, her fear and her agony.

The desire to simply give in.

"I can't control it," she rasped. "I don't... I didn't mean... Your father—"

"Let me worry about my father," he answered, reaching out and letting his fingertips brush along her jaw. "Control it a little longer, then I can help. Just like we've done before."

But she shook her head. "I... I don't think I want to."

"The training arenas won't contain her fully," Luka argued as Theon scooped her into his arms.

"Unless you have a better idea, it's our only choice," Theon replied, tightening his grip on Tessa as she somehow managed to curl into him and push him away at the same time.

He could tell Luka wanted to argue more, but he said tightly, "I don't have any better ideas. Do you want me to get Axel?"

Theon shook his head. "I think it's better if he stays. Father will already be livid we left the way we did."

"Fair point," Luka agreed.

Theon turned back to Tristyn. "The next time I call on you, I expect to speak to you directly."

The male smirked at him. "Arius Heir or not, unless Tessa is the one contacting me, you'll continue to speak to Maggie."

Another flash of lightning and Theon was turning his back on the male. He'd deal with that later.

With a smooth leap, he was dropping over the balcony railing, Tessa tensing in his arms as he glided them swiftly to the ground. Her light crawled along the darkness coating his skin as if it were looking for weakness, seeking a way in.

His feet hit the ground as he said, "I know it's calling to you, Tessa. Don't let your magic take control. I'm going to help. Just a little longer."

The small smile on her face was terrifying as she whispered, "Too late." She lifted a hand, her fingers combing through his hair. "Don't you see? It wants out, and I can't stop it. No one can stop it. No one can stop chaos when it comes to reign."

He nodded slowly. "Can you walk?"

In answer, she shifted, and he lowered her to her bare feet. He didn't bother asking if she wanted shoes. Her steps were surer now, her trembling having ceased, and all Theon could feel from her now was an unnatural peace as she let her power have control.

Luka landed beside him, and the only thing Theon could say was, "She's lost to it."

"No she's not," Luka argued.

"She is. I can feel it. She finds it safer there." He turned to look at his closest friend. "She finds it safer to let her power have control than to learn to harness it. We failed her."

"Then let's fucking fix it," Luka retorted, stalking forward.

Theon watched as he summoned his black flames, Tessa's head snapping in his direction at the display of power. If her magic was in control, it would seek out other power.

Strong power.

"You want to play?" Luka asked her. She'd gone still, her head tilting in a predatory manner as she watched him walk backwards down the path.

Then she lifted a hand and slid off one of the bands.

Fuck.

"Not here, clever tempest," Theon said, following Luka's lead and letting his darkness trail him as he moved past Tessa. "We'll take you somewhere."

Her eyes narrowed, but when he sent a tendril of dark mist to her and let it slide along her throat and under her jaw, that wicked smile returned, and she started to follow.

Neither of them dared say anything as they led her as quickly as they could to the training arenas. Using the side roads and sticking to the shadows meant it took longer than he would have liked, but they couldn't risk being seen.

Or rather, they couldn't risk Tessa seeing someone else and suddenly finding another power more interesting.

Luka led them past all the smaller training rooms to the largest of the arenas. It was a risk. Anyone could enter and anyone would be able to observe, but it would be a bigger risk trying to contain whatever Tessa was feeling in a small room.

The doors had scarcely closed behind them when he heard the growling.

Two wolves came prowling from the dark corners of the arena, hackles raised and teeth bared. One was dark grey, the other light.

"We're helping her," he found himself saying to them as they began to circle.

Luka was beside him, flames crackling and hissing in his hand. The wolves growled again, one snapping its jaws.

"We're trying to help her," Theon said again, questioning his sanity at trying to explain himself to wolves.

Tessa had moved deeper into the arena. Her hands were in her hair as she pulled pins from it, her light winding around her arms and lightning skittering across the floor with each step she took. She was pacing, muttering words Theon only caught bits and pieces of as the wolves kept themselves planted between them and her.

"Control the uncontrollable…too wild…the balance…it tips…"

"She needs the other band off," Luka said, tracking her with vertical pupils. "And Blackheart is right. We can't put them back on her."

"She can't control it. It will take both of us to manage that power," Theon replied.

"Yes, but that leaves us both defenseless," Luka said. "Not an option."

Tessa stopped then. She was in the center of the arena, and she turned to face them. Energy flickered in violet glowing irises. Lifting a hand, Theon could only watch as she showed them the other band.

"These trap us," she said, and her voice wasn't hers. It was otherworldly, somehow dark and light. Wild. Chaotic.

"How long has she been able to take those off herself?" Luka asked, his voice low.

"I don't know," Theon answered. "But she is very angry. Or her magic is."

"Probably both," Luka finished. "Fuck."

Fuck indeed.

Because Tessa's magic would consume her. It would take and take until there was nothing left. That was why learning to control it was so vital. It was why they used the bands—both Legacy and Fae alike—until they had mastered their gifts enough. But they hadn't been able to give this the attention it needed. Between the hearing and his father's demands, the newest Mark and the trip to the Underground, there simply hadn't been enough time. But it still shouldn't have come to this. Not this quickly.

"It came out of nowhere," Theon said. "I know it's been a few days since we've taken the bands off, but this is like a switch flipped. There was no slow build up."

"We'll have to dissect the matter later," Luka said. "Right now, we need to handle this."

Tessa was reaching for the band, sliding it down her wrist, over her hand. Luka had already had a shield in place, ready to try to deflect the eruption of power that was sure to come from her, and Theon was dragging up as much of his own magic as he could to at least attempt to overcome hers.

And it did just that. Blinding bright light flared as the band slipped free. Even with the shield in place, Theon felt the tremors of energy skitter across the stone floor. There was no way they'd be able to control this.

He braced himself for the collision of power, praying to the gods, the Fates, *anyone* who would listen.

Her light collided with power, and the force of it sent him flying into the arena wall. He felt the agony in his side that was likely ribs cracking, but he scarcely registered the pain. Because her power hadn't crashed into his darkness or Luka's black flames.

It had collided with flames of pure white, shadows and something *other* dancing among the fire.

Two figures had appeared out of the very air.

One in black clothing that was…not modern, but somehow elegant and fitting for the male. Fine gold and red thread ran along the edges, and he wore boots that Theon was certain had a knife slid down the side. His gold and silver mask hid half of his features. But the other figure?

She had silver hair.

Her black dress had deep slits up the side, and when she moved, Theon could see the daggers strapped to her thighs.

She had panthers of pure shadow prowling around her as white flames poured from her, going head-to-head with Tessa's golden light.

Theon was scrambling to his feet, and so was Luka, but as they moved towards the female, the male stepped in front of them. The small smirk on his lips was all threat as he shook his head in warning and lifted a hand, fire appearing—flames of gold and red and the hottest blues.

"She won't hurt her, but if you distract her, I will be forced to intervene," the male said, a slight accent to his voice that Theon couldn't place.

"She's attacking my Source. I'm going to fucking distract her," Theon snarled.

The male's brows rose. "She's *your* Source?"

Who the fuck was this male? How did he not know the Sources of the realm?

Glancing back at the females, two very different kinds of light were winding and dancing. Tessa didn't seem to be panicking or in pain. In fact, down the bond all he could feel was a twisted sort of curiosity mixed with the fury.

It didn't matter. He'd never seen these people before, which could only mean they were here for Tessa.

"Yes, she's my Source, so if you value the life of the female, you'd better do the godsdamn distracting," Theon retorted, stepping forward again, but one of those shadow panthers turned. Bright eyes of the same white flame locked on him, and the thing *snarled* at him. When he looked back at the male, flames flickered in his amber irises and—

And he was holding a sword with flames igniting down the dark blade. "She gets excessively violent," the male sighed. Glancing over his shoulder, he added, "I'm assuming it runs in the family. I swear she's helping, not hurting."

"If you don't put that sword away, I'm going to get excessively violent," Luka growled, smoke flowing when he breathed out.

"Just give her a moment, and then she'll explain as much as she can, but—"

A loud growl interrupted the male. They both spun just in time to see the light grey wolf lunging at a cloaked figure with a pearlescent mask on.

The fucking Augury was here.

The wolf sank its teeth into the figure's neck, the person letting out a garbled scream as the animal shook its head viciously.

"I am going to assume he is not on our side?" the male asked.

"*Our* side?" Theon repeated. "I don't even know who the fuck you are."

"Valid point," he conceded.

An arrow suddenly whizzed by, embedding in the figure's chest, effectively silencing them. Luka stalked forward, yanking the arrow from the chest. "Where the fuck…"

But he trailed off as more masked figures began emerging from the shadows. Theon looked up, finding more lining the upper decks overlooking the arena.

They were so incredibly fucked.

The silver-haired female was suddenly there, snatching the arrow from Luka's hand.

"Do you not know what to do with this?" she drawled, a bow appearing from a swirl of shadows. The tip of the arrow burst into white flames, and she had it nocked and sailing through the air at one of the cloaked figures before Theon could blink.

In the next moment, the bow was gone, and she was holding an elegant sword. Looking between Theon and Luka, she said, "I cannot tell which one of you belongs to her."

*Belonged* to who? To Tessa?

He didn't know what to say. Clearly, neither did Luka, because he was staring at the female as if she were half-mad.

The female's gaze slid to the other male. "Do they not speak?"

He sighed. "They speak, Love."

"A different language?"

"For fuck's sake, no," Luka cut in.

"Thank fuck," she said. Gesturing to the Augury members who were all still silent on the edges of the arena, she added, "Just to be clear, we do not like them, yes?"

"Considering they are attempting to kill my Source, no, we do not... like them," Theon replied, beyond perplexed at this point.

Her nose wrinkled. "She's *your* Source?"

Why did they keep questioning this?

When Theon just stared at her, she shrugged. Then she flipped her sword in her hand before pointing it at Theon. "You go bring your... Source back from the thrall of her magic," she ordered. The sword slid in Luka's direction. "Do you know how to fight?"

"Do I what?" he demanded, traces of smoke appearing on his exhale.

She smirked. "That's what I thought. You do your war god thing." The sword slid to the other male, and her smirk turned wicked. "You, come and play with me."

Then she was running at the Augury members, her shadow panthers at her sides. At her advance, the cloaked members all produced their own weapons.

Swords and bows, daggers and...spears?

What in the actual fuck was happening here?

"Theon, get to Tessa," Luka ordered, his wings appearing before he was in the air, flying up to meet the members on the upper decks.

"You cannot possibly take on all of them..." Theon said, but then he was trailing off as the female plunged her flaming sword into the gut of an Augury member, her panthers ripping apart two more. She let go of her sword as the figure sank to the ground, pulling a dagger from her thigh and throwing it. It hit her target, but she had already retrieved her sword and engaged her next victim.

"Do you have weapons?" the male asked.

"Of course I have weapons," Theon retorted, pulling two short swords from his darkness.

The male nodded in approval. "Go to her," he said before he was striding forward, his sword raised as he entered the fray.

Theon turned, finding the two wolves sticking close to Tessa. Her violet stare was fixed on him, and when he met her gaze, her eyes narrowed. Lifting her hands, light crackled, golden mist swirling around her. She was lost to her power, and there was chaos all around them. He'd brought Tessa here to help her, protect her, and he'd once again taken her right into peril.

Again.

Luka was on the upper decks, taking on at least a dozen on his own. The two strangers were taking on even more around them. She was nothing but a blur of white flames, darkness, and blades, while the male took care of the ones she left behind.

He may not have liked that the silver-haired female had given him a task, but she wasn't wrong either. Tessa needed to be brought back.

"*Tessalyn*," he started, preparing to entrance her, but her lips tilted up, and she slowly shook her head.

He should have known. The moment she'd revealed she could defy the Source bond commands, he should have known. He should have known the moment Cienna had told him she wasn't Fae or Legacy.

Her eyes dipped to the short swords he still held before flicking back up to him in question.

"They're just in case," he explained, sending one away.

"Who are they?" Tessa asked, her voice still holding that eerie ring.

"I don't know," he admitted, unsure if she was asking about the Augury or the strangers. The sound of the fighting rang out around them, and her attention darted up to where black flames were flaring once more. "But I need you to keep your eyes right here, little storm."

"Little storm," she scoffed. She lowered to a crouch, one of the wolves coming to her side. She ran her fingers through its fur. "What do you think?" The wolf let out a growl, baring his teeth.

"Tessa," Theon said, hearing the unease enter his voice. "I need you to take control—"

"Take control?" she interrupted. She rose gracefully back to her feet. "What do you think I have done?"

"Letting your magic have control isn't taking control, Tessa," he countered.

"So I let *you* control me instead?"

The warning bark and growl of a wolf had him spinning, his short sword raised on instinct. A handful of Augury members had broken from the melee and had made it to them. Whips of darkness ensnared two, yanking them to the ground, ropes of shadow keeping them there. Another met his sword across the throat. Two more rushed past him, and in a panic, he turned. The wolves were already there, tearing into them. Blood sprayed, and Tessa was standing in the middle of it all, splatters of red marring her face, her arms, her hair.

She lifted a hand, sparks of light erupting as a streak of lightning bounced along the ground. It speared for one of the figures still tied on the ground with his shadows. The figure screamed, a sound of pure torment as his back arched and his limbs went rigid. Theon whipped his gaze back to Tessa, a faint smile on her lips as she slowly lowered her hand.

When he turned back, the figure was still, and Theon knew in his gut whatever she had done had killed him, Legacy or not.

He went to the other, using his short sword to flick the mask off, revealing a female. Her face was pale, dull brown eyes wide. Strands of blonde hair were matted to her sweaty face as she writhed within the confines of his dark magic.

"This is how it starts," the female gasped, and he felt her power try to fight against his own. His darkness easily clamped down on her gifts, holding them hostage just as he was holding her physical body hostage.

"You have seconds to explain yourself," Theon replied, the point of his sword at her heart.

"You cannot control the uncontrollable," she insisted.

"She can learn to control it."

"And who will control *her*?"

That was enough for him. His sword sank into flesh, and his power followed, snaking through veins and melding with blood.

This was enough. The Augury needed proof Tessa could be controlled? He could do that.

Tossing his sword aside, he turned, prowling towards her. Surprise filled her features, and she took a step back, uncertainty flickering down the bond. The wolves seemed to sense what he was coming for, slowly backing away and widening the area they were protecting. Theon had a feeling no one would get past them.

"Theon..." Tessa started, but she trailed off when he slowly shook his head the same way she had minutes ago.

He sent his power to her, shadows twining up her legs, wrapping around her arms. Her magic answered in kind, immediately sinking claws and teeth into darkness, and he let her. He held his darkness back, and he let her take, wrapping her gifts up in his so tightly, he couldn't tell where his power ended and hers began.

When he reached her, he took her face in his hands, and only then did he finally let his power fight back. She gasped, eyes flaring with surprise and anger as she tried to pull from his hold, but he wouldn't let her go. His shadows only yanked her into him even more.

"I know you think it feels freeing to let your power have you, Tessa, but what have I told you from the very beginning? I want everything you have to give. Your power does not get to have you. I do," Theon said.

She glared at him, her power straining under his. Whatever that other female had done had weakened her gifts enough to let him do exactly this. The male hadn't been lying. She'd been helping.

"Fight it all you want, little storm, but you are going to belong to me. Every piece of you," he said, echoing words he'd said to her once before. He'd meant it then, and he meant it now. "I will never stop fighting for you."

"You mean fighting to control me. Fighting to trap me and keep me," she retorted, but her voice wavered, and he was feeling more than blatant fury down the bond. There was desperation and fear trickling in.

"I'll forever fight to keep you, Tessa," he agreed.

"I can't breathe in the dark. I need the light," she whispered in agony as she leaned into him even more, her power struggling and thrashing.

"But too much light can blind you," he countered. "You still need the dark to find the balance."

"In all things, there must be balance," she murmured.

"Beginnings and endings. Light and dark. Fire and shadows," he recited in kind.

She went still, and for the first time, he felt like she truly looked at him. Not through him. Not seeing him as her master or her villain, but as if she was seeing some part of him she'd never realized was there.

Probably because he'd never let her see it before.

But her magic suddenly quieted, letting his darkness wrap around it. She took a shuddering breath, her brow falling to his chest, and his hand came to her hair, stroking it softly as he dropped a kiss to the top of her head.

He hadn't realized the commotion had died down. He hadn't noticed the wolves had lowered to their bellies, heads raised and keen eyes still watching. But Luka was suddenly dropping down beside him, and she turned her head to look at him. Something else in her seemed to settle in his presence.

"Are you back, little one?" Luka asked, and she nodded. "Good," was all he said before his eyes flicked to Theon. "We need to deal with these two."

"Who are they?" Tessa asked again, twisting in Theon's hold to peer around him.

"We don't know," Luka answered tightly.

But he was wrong.

Theon knew exactly who they were. Or at least, who *she* was.

"Call Axel," Theon said, eyeing the two across the arena. Standing among blood and bodies, the female tipped her head back and laughed, the male shaking his head, flaming sword still in hand. "Tell him the female from the mirror is here."

# 20

## TESSA

"How was your class with Cordelia?" Theon asked.

"Fine," Tessa mumbled from where she stood at the window in the large kitchen of the townhouse.

"I'm hoping to have a new instructor lined up for you soon."

"Great," she answered, watching the sun sink lower and taking the light with it.

"I'm still not understanding this," Axel cut in. "How and when is the female from the mirror going to find her way here?"

"Everyone knows where the family townhouses are," Theon replied.

"Yeah, but if she really is the female from the mirror—"

"She is," Theon interrupted.

"All I'm saying is it doesn't add up."

Tessa was grateful for the interruption. The class with the other Sources was always dull, but Mother Cordelia had insisted her bands be put back in place as she "didn't feel comfortable otherwise." That was probably a fair statement. The problem was the bands had disappeared. They couldn't find them at the training arena, and Theon had been forced to put different bands on her. Her magic hated these even more, immediately thrashing and pushing against the restraints, making it impossible to focus. They were like the ones Lord Jove had put on her. She was still no closer to controlling her power, and to be honest, she was almost looking forward to her time in Faven. At least there someone should know how to help her control it.

Then she'd had to endure an hour of her private lessons. Every time she would fidget because of the damn bands, Tessa would find it hard to breathe courtesy of the Estate Mother's air magic. Mother Cordelia had proceeded to lecture her on her behavior at the Samhain Feast and how much she had disrespected the family she served with her behavior. Tessa already knew all that.

After the Augury attack, they'd returned to the Samhain Feast for appearance's sake. She'd taken one look at the Arius Lord and known he was not happy, but Theon had handed her off to Luka. She didn't know what Theon had said to his father to placate him, but he'd obviously known the right thing to say. Part of dealing with him for years, she supposed.

But now they were waiting for the mysterious couple that had appeared and fought alongside Theon and Luka. Theon swore it was the same female from the mirror, but they hadn't had a chance to speak to them. The couple had only said they would find them when it was safe to do so before disappearing as if they'd stepped through a rip in the air. Seconds later, sentinels were swarming the training arena, and they had gone back to the Pantheon to deal with Valter.

"I don't know, Theon," Axel was saying from where he sat at the kitchen island. "I'm starting to doubt you really saw her. Again."

"Shut up, Axel. It wasn't only me this time," Theon retorted, brushing against Tessa's arm as he passed her something. She looked down, finding him holding out a glass of wine.

"Am I to hold that for you?" she asked tonelessly, gaze flicking up to his.

That muscle in his jaw ticked before he said tightly, "I thought you might want a glass."

Wordlessly, she took the wine before folding her arms, the stem of the glass at her fingertips. A message had been delivered a few hours ago that the couple would stop by tonight.

She was opening her mouth to ask Theon if they could go for a short walk when Luka walked in. His sapphire eyes swept over her in the briefest of glances before he was walking through to the wine cellar. He emerged moments later with a bottle, drinking directly from it.

"Where's Kat?" Luka asked.

"In the lounge," Axel answered, eyeing the bottle.

"Do you need some?" Luka asked, Tessa watching the exchange curiously. Axel seemed to debate his answer, his fingers drumming on the counter, before Luka made it for him, sliding the bottle across the surface. "Take what you need."

Something akin to shame filled Axel's features as he stared at the bottle. "You're the ones who just fought. You need your ration."

"We will get more in two days. I'll be fine," Luka replied.

After a long pause, Axel shook his head, sliding the bottle back towards Luka. "If these two mystery people show up, you need full reserves. I'm good."

Tessa finally realized they were discussing Fae blood, but why would Axel need some when he hadn't fought at all last night? His reserves should be plenty full.

But her magic suddenly jolted, and Tessa nearly dropped her wineglass.

Theon's attention whipped to her. "What's wrong?"

But she'd felt this before. An intense curiosity. A craving for more. A recognition of something she knew intimately.

"She's here," Tessa said simply.

"Who's here?" Theon asked.

"The female from last night."

Luka was immediately on alert, and Axel was on his feet and out of the kitchen in the next breath. Tessa assumed he was going to Katya.

"Why do you think that?" Theon asked cautiously.

Tessa shrugged. "My magic senses her."

"That's not—" Theon started, but then he turned to Luka. "Did you feel them at the wards?"

Luka shook his head, already striding to the foyer. Theon followed, Tessa trailing after them. After being stuck inside all day, a quick walk would have been nice, but that wouldn't be happening now. Seconds later there was a knock, and Luka was pulling open the door.

"See!" the silver-haired female exclaimed. "He looks just like him."

The same male from the night before was rubbing at his brow. "Not the time, Scarlett."

"But you see it, right?"

The male sighed, an apologetic smile filling his face as he looked between Luka and Theon. "Is this an all right time? We haven't seen anyone else come or go in a few hours."

"How can you possibly know that?" Theon demanded. "And how did you get past our wards?"

A sly smirk curled on the female's lips that clearly set Luka even more on edge as he slid in front of Theon.

The female only laughed.

"This is the part where you invite us in," she said, gesturing beyond them into the townhouse. Silver eyes met Tessa's where she was peering around Theon as the female added, "This is a family matter."

After a tension-filled moment, Theon said, "Let them in, Luka. This has been a long time coming."

Theon turned, his hand falling to Tessa's lower back as he ushered her to the lounge, but when she glanced back over her shoulder, the female winked at her.

Kat immediately got to her feet when they entered, and Tessa couldn't blame her. Old habits died hard, and when those habits could save you from any manner of correction, you never let them die. But Axel slid casually in front of her, the same way Theon and Luka did to her.

"Right then," the female started, her gaze moving around the room as if she were marking every possible exit. "Do we need to worry about being overheard here?"

"Normally I would say no, but considering you just entered our wards without fuss, I can't be so sure," Theon said dryly.

She waved a hand dismissively. "No one else can do that."

"Forgive me for not believing you after you attacked my Source last night."

She glanced up at the male. "I thought you told him I wasn't hurting her."

He sighed. "I did, Love."

She turned back to Theon, looking at him expectantly. As though she was waiting for some sort of explanation. As though he *owed* her an explanation.

As if he answered to her.

Tessa swallowed down her huff of laughter. She had no idea who this female was, but the way she was getting under Theon's skin made her somewhat amused.

"Perhaps introductions would ease some tension," the male cut in. "I'm Sorin Aditya. This is my wife, Scarlett Sutara Aditya."

Scarlett had started wandering around the room, looking at various items. Luka seemed to have decided she was the bigger threat, keeping himself between her and them while Theon kept his focus on Sorin.

Luka wasn't wrong. Tessa could sense both their magic, and while Sorin was indeed powerful, Scarlett was more so.

"And what kingdom are you from?" Theon demanded.

Scarlett glanced over her shoulder with a slight frown. "Rude not to introduce yourself. Aren't you a prince or something?"

Tessa could feel Theon's indignation down the bond, and she settled back in her chair, sipping on her wine.

"I am Theon St. Orcas," he bit out through gritted teeth. "The Arius Heir."

Scarlett only hummed an acknowledgment, studying a lamp.

"Axel St. Orcas, my brother," Theon went on, and Tessa could hear the dismay in his voice. Gesturing at Luka, he said, "Luka Mors."

"Mors?" Scarlett repeated, finally looking up from the lamp that seemed to fascinate her. "Interesting."

"Why would that be interesting?" Axel asked.

She shrugged. "I was expecting a different surname. He's a Guardian?"

"Yes, he's my Guardian," Theon answered.

"He's your…" She trailed off, her nose scrunching for a brief moment. "Interesting."

"How did you know he was my Guardian?"

"I didn't know he was *your* Guardian," she replied, picking up a remote for the television above the fireplace. "But I assumed he was one based on the annoying overprotectiveness. I have one of those too."

Tessa couldn't stop her huff of laughter this time, and Theon and Luka both turned to her, glaring. She shrugged, taking another sip of wine.

"If you have a Guardian, where is he?" Axel asked. "These two can scarcely stand to go to the bathroom without each other."

"For fuck's sake, Axel," Theon groused.

"My Guardian stayed behind. Threw a fit about it too. But if I'd brought him, then Cyrus would have needed to come. It would have been a mess. Cyrus threw an even bigger fit about having to stay behind," Scarlett answered.

"Cyrus is your Guardian?" Theon asked.

"No. Cassius is my Guardian. Cyrus is his…mate? Husband? I don't know what you call them here," she replied. "Can we finish the intro-ductions?"

"We did," Theon answered, but judging by Scarlett's face, that was the wrong thing to say.

The pleasantness quickly disappeared, morphing into something wraith-like. "I see. And you are the Arius Prince or whatever?" Scarlett asked, her tone making all the males tense. Even Tessa sat up a little straighter.

"The Arius Heir," Theon gritted out. "I will be the Arius Lord."

A smirk tilted on the corner of Scarlett's lips. "Did you hear, Sorin? He's going to be the Arius *Lord*."

"I heard, Scarlett," Sorin replied, golden eyes watching them all warily. "The arrogance certainly tracks for an Arius descendant."

Scarlett turned to her husband with an unimpressed glare, and Sorin huffed a laugh, as if she'd said something only he could hear.

"You never said which kingdom you're from?" Luka cut in.

Scarlett completely ignored him and made a big show of peering around him, meeting Tessa's gaze. "At first, I assumed they were simply protecting the females in the room, but apparently the males here are just assholes. I'm Scarlett. Sorry we met yesterday under unfortunate circumstances. I trust you are feeling a little more grounded?"

Glancing at Theon, Tessa bit her lip, unsure if she was supposed to answer or stay silent. Her tone was icy once more, and Tessa could swear the temperature in the room had dropped when Scarlett said, "She is your Source?"

"Yes, and you speaking to her without permission is grounds for immediate detaining," Theon replied tightly.

Scarlett gave him a simpering smile before turning her attention to Axel and Kat. "And she is your..." Her head tilted, a silver braid falling over her shoulder. "Sorin?"

"I know, Scarlett," her husband answered. "Remember what Juliette said."

Scarlett rolled her eyes as she muttered, "Yes, yes. Fate and all that nonsense."

"This is Katya," Axel supplied from where he still stood, blocking the Fae from view. "She serves the Arius Kingdom."

"Is she your Source?" Scarlett asked.

"I'm not of age to have a Source yet," Axel explained.

"How do you not know any of this?" Theon interrupted. "I am answering no more questions until you answer some of mine."

Scarlett's brows rose. "By all means, ask away, Arius Lordling."

It was Axel who choked on a laugh this time, but Tessa was utterly fascinated with the female.

"For the third time, which kingdom are you from?" Theon asked.

"There's so many ways to answer that," she replied, tapping her chin in mock thought. "But all you really need to know is a kingdom not of this realm."

The entire room went still.

Except for Axel, who blurted, "Bullshit."

"Shocking, I know," she replied, picking up Theon's phone that he'd set on the side table when they'd come in here. "I see people with these all the time. What are they?"

"What is... It's a phone," Theon said, clearly perplexed.

"What do you use it for?"

"To call each other. Or send messages."

"Seems a little complicated."

"It's really not," Theon replied.

"Why don't you just send messages with your magic?" Scarlett asked, turning the phone over in her hand and studying it.

"What do you mean?" Axel asked.

"Like a fire message or a water message." Scarlett flicked her wrist and a burst of white flames appeared beside Tessa's head. "Reach up and grab the paper out of it."

"Just...reach into the fire?" Tessa asked tentatively.

"It won't burn you. Not unless I want it to." She flashed her a grin, and Tessa wasn't entirely sure how a smile could be that unnerving.

"No," Theon ordered, but Tessa was already lifting her hand and dipping her fingers into the flames. She couldn't help the small gasp that escaped her as she plucked a small piece of paper from them. She unfolded it and barked a laugh.

*Is the Lordling always so petulant?*

She handed the paper to Theon, who read it quickly, then glared at Scarlett.

"Right then," Scarlett announced, dropping the phone back to the side table with a loud clatter.

"Those are expensive," Theon snarled, swiping it up and examining it, presumably looking for damage.

"I thought you were a lordling or whatever?" Scarlett said.

"I am the Heir of the Arius Kingdom," Theon snapped.

"Well, then, *Heir of the Arius Kingdom*," she drawled. "Buy a new one. Or better yet, learn to use your magic properly."

"I know how to use my magic properly."

"Clearly," Scarlett deadpanned.

And Tessa could only look back and forth between the two.

"Love, perhaps you can stop antagonizing him?" Sorin said, his mouth twitching when she sent him an irritated look. "I know it goes against your nature." She slowly lifted her middle finger. "Always so queenly."

"Gods, Sorin," she said with an exaggerated sigh. "You've been especially annoying today with the constant fate reminders. I know it goes against *your* nature, but could you please stop being such a mother hen?"

"I have a question," Axel announced, all attention landing on him. "Did Theon really save you from death in a mirror?"

"That's absurd," Scarlett scoffed. "He definitely did not save me."

"It happened," Theon snarled. "A female attacked you."

"You're going to have to be more specific. That used to happen quite frequently."

Theon raked a hand through his hair, and Tessa could feel his agitation down the bond. To be honest, she was surprised he hadn't lost it completely when Scarlett had called him 'lordling.'

"It was a stone chamber. You were dressed like that," he said, gesturing to her attire of a black suit of some sort. It reminded Tessa of the way Cienna dressed. "A female wearing a black cloak or hood or something was sneaking up behind you with some sort of curved blade, and I warned you."

"I think I would remember you saving me," Scarlett said.

"I saw you in a mirror," Theon insisted.

"Oh, that?" Scarlett said with a laugh. "That was my sister. You definitely did not save me."

"Your sister," Theon repeated.

"Mhmm."

"Your sister tried to kill you?" Luka asked dubiously.

"Yes and no. It's a long story, and one my other sister would be upset if I told you," Scarlett answered. "But moving on, I did not come here to discuss any of that with you. Tell me, just how far down the Arius line are you?"

"No," Theon cut in, and Tessa could tell by his tone he'd reached his breaking point. Well, that and the darkness that had suddenly appeared. "Somehow you manage to keep evading our questions, but no more. We ask the questions, and you answer them."

Darkness crept forward, and Sorin moved as if to step in front of Scarlett, but she held up a hand. "No need, Prince," was all she said before her own shadows were swirling, those shadow panthers forming and snarling a warning. She took a single step forward, white flames appearing in her hand. "I have information for you, but if you threaten me again, you're going to learn it in a very unpleasant way."

"Threaten *him* again, and he won't be your only problem," Luka cut in, his eyes having shifted.

Scarlett bared her teeth at him. "I promise, dragon, my bite hurts more."

Sorin stepped between his wife and Theon, his tone somehow placating and commanding when he said, "I know there are a lot of things at play here. Bonds and magic. Bloodlines and…aggressive personalities." He glanced at Scarlett, who was still eyeing Luka as if she would *enjoy* showing him just how much she meant her threat. "We already told you we came from another realm. That is a lot to take in. It is only natural that you have questions."

"And yet she won't answer them," Theon said, and Tessa huffed another derisive laugh into her wineglass as she drained the last of it.

Theon turned, a brow arching in question. She'd like to say it was the wine that made her say what she did, but that would be a lie. She was already in a foul mood after the afternoon with Mother Cordelia, and she tended to be even more impulsive when she was in that state.

"It's annoying, isn't it?" Tessa mused, studying her empty wineglass.

"What is?" Theon asked.

"Asking questions and not getting answers."

His eyes narrowed, but it was Axel who said, "He's just annoyed he doesn't have all the facts. He's used to knowing everything all the time."

"No, that's not it," Tessa said, her head tilting to the side as she held Theon's stare. "He doesn't like that he's not the most powerful in the room."

"I am the Arius Heir. I am one of the strongest in this realm," Theon snapped, but Tessa's smile only grew.

"And she just told you she is not from this realm." She set her empty glass down on the end table before propping her chin in her hand. "Did you not notice she has the same magic you do? It appears you are not the only Arius Legacy in the room, *Master*."

The dismayed scoff that came from Scarlett had them both turning to her, the female's features twisted into clear disgust. "I'm sorry. Master?"

"She is my Source," Theon gritted out. "That is the proper way to address the one you serve."

There was an extended second of silence before Scarlett burst out laughing as she turned to Sorin, but he was already pinching the bridge of his nose. "I am not calling you Master or Mistress or anything of the kind."

"Hold on," Axel cut in. "Am I understanding that he is your Source?"

"Among other things," Scarlett agreed.

"How?" Tessa asked, leaning forward to peer around Theon. "Where are his Source Marks?"

"On his forearm."

"All of them?"

"All of…" Scarlett's brow furrowed. "There is only one Source Mark." When the room stayed silent, she asked, "How many do you believe there are?"

Still silence lingered until finally Theon said, "Four. There are four Source Marks."

"I assure you, there are not," Scarlett said, shaking her head.

Tessa was too… She didn't know what she was feeling as she pushed to her feet, stepping around Theon. He reached for her, his fingers closing around her arm to keep her from moving any closer.

"How can there only be one?" Tessa asked, a tremor to her voice she wasn't sure what to do with.

Something dark was filling the female's features as she said, "How many do you have that you believe are Source Marks?"

"Two," Tessa answered. "I am still to receive the final two."

"I do not understand why you think there are four Source Marks," Scarlett said, shaking her head. "Can I see them?"

"No," Theon said as Tessa started to lift her hand. He tugged her back, pushing her behind him yet again. "Not until you've given us some semblance of a reason to trust you. You show up here, tell us you're from another world, ask questions and give us no answers in return. I can only assume you are here for her."

"I am here for her," Scarlett said simply.

Theon went preternaturally still.

So did Luka and Axel.

Tessa could feel violence and anger and a strange fierceness down the bond. But before she could attempt to work all that out, Scarlett spoke again, driving all other thoughts from her mind.

Silver eyes settled on Tessa where she was peering around Theon once more as she said, "Your father sent me."

"My father?" Tessa breathed, not sure what to do with all the emotions slamming into her.

Disbelief at the possibility.

Anger at being abandoned here.

Betrayal at her father not bothering to come for her himself.

Denial at the very idea this random female knew her father.

And beneath all that, a seed of hope that it was all true. That she was finally finding answers to questions that had plagued her for years.

"You expect us to believe that?" Theon demanded. He took a single step forward, his darkness thickening around him. "How could you, a Legacy from an entire other realm, know who her father is?"

"Because he's my uncle," Scarlett replied. Then she added, "He's also the son of Arius."

"Oh, fuck off," Axel scoffed. "You expect us to believe— That would make Tessa the granddaughter of Arius himself."

"Which is why I asked just how far down the Arius line you are," Scarlett replied.

"Hundreds of generations," Tessa murmured, remembering what Theon had once told her. "Tristyn said the St. Orcas family is so far removed from Arius it is laughable to call them such a thing."

"Well, that is a relief on many levels," Scarlett said as she toyed with white flames at her fingertips.

Tessa had to agree with her. She didn't even want to think about... *that*.

"No," Theon said, shaking his head in disbelief. "It's not possible."

"Why not?" Scarlett asked, her head tilting in curiosity.

"She doesn't have any Arius gifts for starters," Theon snapped.

That was a good point, but Tessa was still stuck on the idea of being Arius's *granddaughter*.

"That you know of," the female countered. "Admittedly, I do not know my uncle well as he stays in another realm."

"No, he is right," Tessa cut in, trying to focus on the conversation.

She could sort through all of this information later when she was by herself. "My magic is not Arius magic."

Scarlett gave her a soft smile. "Arius magic is not just shadows and darkness, Cousin."

*Cousin.*

She swallowed thickly at the idea of blooded family, that fragile seed of hope that this was somehow true growing a little bigger.

"Shadows and darkness are the same thing," Axel said.

Scarlett shook her head again. "Similar, yes, but vastly different at the same time. My brother has darkness. It is chaotic, constantly trying to take control. He uses it differently than I do, and he can sense other's power levels. My shadows, on the other hand…" She trailed off as her power appeared, winding around her, caressing her, *loving* her.

"And the white flames?" Luka asked, and Tessa felt Theon's irritation that his Guardian appeared to be encouraging this.

"From my mother. Or rather, my grandmother, Serafina," Scarlett answered.

"Now I know you are lying," Theon cut in impatiently. "Serafina was to be Matched with Achaz."

"I don't know what that means," Scarlett said. "But I do know Arius and Serafina started a war because of their love. Or rather, they caused the continuation of one."

"You speak of the Everlasting War," Katya said, speaking for the first time. A faint flush filled her cheeks when all eyes landed on her. "I apologize," she said softly. "I should not have spoken."

"Why not?" Scarlett asked.

"She is Fae," Tessa supplied when no one answered. "She is to be silent in a room full of Legacy."

That dark and terrifying look filled Scarlett's features again, and Tessa found herself leaning into Theon a little more.

"Is this why I have seen the Fae treated so…differently here?" Scarlett asked in a too calm voice.

"Different from what?" Axel asked.

"Scarlett," Sorin warned again. "Remember the agreement with Juliette."

"Who is Juliette?' Theon asked.

"My sister," Scarlett muttered, beginning to pace. Tessa could swear the temperature in the room dropped again.

"The sister that didn't try to kill you?" Theon said dubiously.

"No, the other one."

"Two sisters. A brother. How many siblings do you have?" Luka asked.

Scarlett stopped her pacing, meeting his stare. "How many do *you* have?"

"The point is," Sorin cut in again, bringing a hand to Scarlett's back. She appeared to visibly calm at his touch, rolling her shoulders a little. "We can only say so much. We made a deal with Juliette because revealing too much can alter fate, and Witches are very cautious when it comes to fate."

"A deal," Theon repeated. "Like a Bargain?"

"Yes," Scarlett sighed, tugging at the collar of her suit to reveal a Bargain Mark along her collarbone.

"Your sister is a Witch? Doesn't that make you one?" Axel asked.

"That wouldn't make sense if she has Arius magic," Theon argued.

"But she also has gifts of Serafina," Axel countered.

"Which shouldn't be possible. Legacy only get gifts from one blood-line," Theon said, raking a hand through his hair.

Tessa almost felt bad for him.

Almost.

He was experiencing everything she'd been through these last few months. Everything he'd thought to be true getting flipped around? It was enough to drive a person mad. Then again, Scarlett was probably driving him mad simply in the way she was delivering the information. She always answered Tessa's questions without fuss, but she was vague and snarky when answering Theon.

"I am not a Witch," Scarlett said, as if indeed annoyed by their constant questions. "And if I were full Legacy, I would probably only have one set of gifts. My father was an Anahita Legacy, but my mother is a goddess, which alters a few things."

"Your mother is a goddess? As in a daughter of Arius and Serafina?" Theon asked.

"Yes. Saylah is the goddess of shadows and night," Scarlett said, sounding exasperated, as if he were dense for not understanding all the realm-altering information she was sharing in a very short period of time.

Tessa liked her more and more.

"Which would make my father a god?" Tessa said, suddenly doubtful. Her father couldn't be a *god*.

A god wouldn't leave his daughter in a forgotten realm. A god wouldn't let her be treated like someone who was a nuisance simply for existing. A god wouldn't just *abandon* her.

"Your father is Temural, god of the wild and untamed," Scarlett said, her tone softening. "I know it is a lot to take in because I didn't learn of my heritage until I was twenty years. Everything you are feeling? It is all valid, Tessa. Anyone who tells you it isn't is wrong."

Tessa said nothing, hugging herself. Theon's hold on her tightened, but not even the bond could give her any comfort right now. She didn't know what to believe, and she couldn't think in here.

"From what we've been told, Arius and Serafina violated some sort of accord when they chose to be together," Sorin said. "If what you said is true, and Serafina was at one point supposed to be with Achaz, that would fit. Temural and Saylah were kept a secret from the other gods for centuries. When they were discovered, it only escalated an already tense situation."

"All of this must have happened after Devram was created," Theon said. Tessa was certain he was recounting every history text he'd ever read. "The gods agreed to never interfere here, so we wouldn't have known."

"The gods also agreed not to have more demigod children which would lead to more Legacy being born," Luka said dryly. "Clearly they didn't keep those accords either."

"You will find the gods keep more secrets than the Fates," Scarlett said darkly. "They play games, and if you let them, they will use you to further their own position and achieve their own goals."

Tessa held back her huff of amusement. She was already being used to further someone else's position and achieve their own goals. How would this be any different? Her father had already abandoned her. A god wanting to use her was fitting for the life fate had dealt her.

"You do not like the gods?" Axel asked. "Despite your mother being one?"

"Saylah and I have an…agreement of sorts," Scarlett said, keen silver eyes watching Tessa. "But having experienced the same array of emotions Tessa is currently feeling, she deserved to know. She deserves to know that the gods are not above using their own blood as a means to an end. I refused to aid Temural unless he agreed to let me come and meet her."

"Why would a god need *your* aid?" Theon asked.

That wicked smile returned, the one that had him tucking Tessa in closer and Luka tensing even more. "I am many things, one of them being a World Walker."

"They are myths," Katya blurted, once again blushing at her outburst, but Tessa recognized the excited glint in her amber eyes. It was the same mannerism she'd observed in her mornings watching Theon. A frenetic energy that hummed around him when he stumbled upon something interesting or promising in his studies or research.

"I assure you they are not," Scarlett said. "Rare, but not myths, and I am the only one who can ferry people across the stars to other realms."

"If this Temural is my father, then where is he?" Tessa asked, unable to move past this.

A sad, knowing look filled Scarlett's features. "He is a god. It is my understanding that the gods cannot enter Devram."

"Then what is the point of telling me any of this? Can you take me to him?"

She shook her head. "It would endanger more than you."

"Then what is the point?" Tessa repeated.

"You misunderstand," Scarlett said. "The gods cannot come here, but they have found ways to influence events here."

"They cannot interfere with Devram," Theon argued.

"But there are always loopholes," Scarlett said. "I suggest you start finding your own if you plan to play their games."

"If the gods can't come here, I don't think I need to worry about their games," Theon replied dryly.

"Silly, little Lordling," Scarlett said with a bitter laugh. "Haven't you figured it out yet? You're already in the middle of them."

# 21

## AXEL

Axel could see his brother's mind working, mulling over everything Scarlett and Sorin were telling him. He knew Theon would obsess over this for days. To be fair, anyone would, but not like Theon. He'd be going over all possibilities, different ways to use the information to his advantage, and how all of it worked with everything else he knew. He'd suddenly have some new insane theory. Although some of those theories didn't seem so insane anymore. The silver-haired female sitting across from him was the prime example. The Augury was the second.

After yet another tense standoff between Scarlett and Theon, Sorin had suggested everyone take a moment to breathe. Axel had offered drinks. Now the couple sat across from him and Katya on the other sofa. Tessa had taken a seat in the armchair she'd originally occupied. Theon was in the other armchair, sitting stiffly. Luka, of course, was still standing.

"And my mother?" Tessa asked, sounding tired. "What do you know of her?"

"I tried, but Temural refused to speak of her," Scarlett said, setting her glass of wine aside. "I know nothing of your maternal line."

"Convenient," Theon said, his knuckles white around his liquor glass. He was lucky he wasn't shattering the thing.

"I may be powerful, but even I must still play the games strategically," Scarlett retorted. "Temural is more unpredictable than my mother.

A little…mercurial. That whole wild and untamed thing, if I had to guess. I do not know him well enough yet to properly negotiate with him."

Silence settled in the room once more, those of Devram lost in their own thoughts. Scarlett's head tilted to the side. She did that often, as though she could hear something the rest of them couldn't. It was interesting to observe. Axel assumed it was their Source bond, but that brought him back to—

"So he is your Source?" Axel asked with a nod at Sorin.

"I am," Sorin agreed.

"You have both gone through your Staying?"

Scarlett snorted a laugh, jerking her thumb at Sorin. "This one is older than a sage."

"That delightful tongue of yours," Sorin quipped, flicking her nose before she batted his hand away.

"And you?" Tessa asked, watching her cousin.

"I went through my Staying a few years ago. It was an interesting ordeal," Scarlett answered.

"A few years ago?" Axel asked. "How old are you?"

"How old are *you?*" she countered.

"Twenty-four years. Your turn," he shot back.

"Twenty-six years."

"When did Sorin become your Source?"

"On my twentieth birthday."

"Twenty years?" Axel said. "How?"

Scarlett's nose scrunched in confusion. "What do you mean 'how?' I gave him the Source Mark."

She gestured to her husband, who pulled up the sleeve of his tunic revealing a Mark Axel had never seen before on his forearm. Then again, that wasn't entirely true. It looked similar to one of their own Source Marks, but there were differences.

"Only one Mark?" Tessa asked.

"I feel as though we've already covered this, and with my limited time, it is foolish to revisit it," Scarlett said. "But I am curious about these four Source Marks. Why four?"

"One for physical connection, one for emotional connection, one for mental connection, and the final to share power," Tessa said as though reciting a lesson.

"Among other things," Theon tacked on.

"Oh, yes," Tessa said, the sarcasm thick. "I forgot about the whole forcing me to give my life for yours thing."

Scarlett and Sorin were both staring at them as if they weren't sure what to say. Scarlett slowly set her wineglass down, faint traces of shadows appearing and hovering. "May I see the Marks you *do* possess?"

Her tone was tight and even, and Theon was on his feet in the next blink. "Why?"

"Call it curiosity." When Theon still didn't move out of her way, Scarlett rolled her eyes. "I'm not going to hurt her. She's family."

"You've told us repeatedly you do not get along with your mother."

Scarlett clicked her tongue. "That's different."

"She won't hurt her," Sorin said, pushing to his feet. "Scarlett is well-versed in Marks. The idea of there being more than one Source Mark is intriguing to her."

"If you attempt anything," Theon warned, his darkness making an appearance.

"That's cute," Scarlett said, patting his arm patronizingly as she stepped past him. White flames at her fingertips left faint singe marks on his shirt.

Axel bit down on his bark of laughter, but Tessa didn't.

Coming to a stop a few feet in front of her, Scarlett said, "Show me."

Lifting her right hand, Tessa showed her the first Mark, three inverted triangles.

Scarlett's brows rose. "That is the Arius symbol. Not a Mark."

"It must be more than a symbol," Tessa groused. "The moment it was given, I could feel his presence, and he could feel mine."

At that, Scarlett's brow furrowed as she reached for Tessa's hand. "May I?" Scarlett studied it for a long moment before turning her hand over and running a finger over the Marks on her inner wrist. "And these?"

"Identification marks," Tessa answered before giving a simple explanation of each.

"You said you have two of these so-called Source Marks?" Scarlett asked, her tone even tighter now.

Tessa reached up, pulling down the collar of her shirt to reveal the swirling Mark atop her heart.

"What does it do?" Scarlett asked.

"We can feel each other's emotions," Tessa said flatly.

Turning to Theon, she said, "Show me the last two Marks."

Theon's eyes narrowed. "Why?"

"We cannot interfere with this, Scarlett," came Sorin's low voice. He'd moved to stand beside her as she'd approached Tessa, and Axel could swear there was a hint of sadness in his voice.

"Not interfere? You cannot be serious," Scarlett argued, rounding on her husband. "Do you not see what I see? What they've done?" She punctuated this by holding up her left hand, where a Mark of her own matched the one on the back of her husband's hand.

"I see it, Love," Sorin said softly. "This could change…too many things."

"When have I ever cared?"

"And what prices have you paid by not carefully considering the costs?"

The female's lips pursed. Finally, she said, "I can't do nothing, Sorin."

"Someone needs to explain. Right fucking now," Luka snapped. "For fuck's sake, it's like being in a room with Cienna."

Scarlett and Sorin again seemed to have some sort of argument only the two of them could hear, but Kat's arm brushing against his startled Axel from whatever he was observing. The rush of warmth along his skin had him unwittingly leaning towards her, but she was entirely focused on the couple.

She'd been so quiet this entire time, other than a couple questions for which she'd quietly apologized to him for, not that she'd needed to. But she was absorbing all this the same way Theon was. Kat was completely enthralled by the idea of beings from another realm coming here.

After a long, tense moment, Scarlett sighed, her hands going to her hips. "Fine," she snapped at her husband. Turning to the rest of them, she asked tightly, "Who bestows the Marks here?"

Theon and Luka exchanged a look before Theon said, "The Priestesses do most of them."

"And the Source Marks?"

"Certain Priestesses are trained specifically for that purpose."

Scarlett's eyes narrowed. "Who trains them?"

"They are Zinta Legacy so—"

"Zinta Legacy?" Scarlett interrupted. "And the Taika Legacy?"

"Who are the Taika Legacy?" Tessa asked. When Scarlett appeared to be debating what to say, Tessa's gaze went to her bonded. "Theon?"

Theon rubbed at his brow with this thumb and forefinger. This was information not taught to the Fae. "There are two goddesses of witch-craft and sorcery," he said. "They are sisters. Zinta and Taika."

"Sister goddesses?" Tessa repeated. "Are there Taika Legacy here?"

"Yes, but a small number of them. Many were killed off when the few Sargon Legacy were killed," Theon said.

Tessa turned to Luka. "Your parents?"

Luka shrugged. "From my understanding, this happened long before I was born. My parents were somehow an exception to the slaughter."

Tessa swallowed thickly, turning back to Scarlett. "Why does it matter if both are here?"

"Because one goddess is loyal to Achaz, and the other is loyal to Arius," Scarlett replied. "Balance is required in all things, and Devram seems to have…tipped the scales," she said, silver eyes dropping to the Mark on Tessa's hand.

Suddenly, there was a burst of fine grey and blue mist. Scarlett reached inside her suit, pulling out a chain with a pendant where the mist was coming from.

"What is that?" Theon asked, eyeing the thing.

Scarlett frowned, tucking the pendant away once more. "A reminder that my time here is almost up."

"You're leaving?" Tessa asked, lurching forward in her chair.

Scarlett looked sincerely apologetic when she said, "I have to, Tessa."

"So you're just going to show up here, tell me I am the daughter of a god, the granddaughter of a First, and then, what? Leave me to do with the information what I will?" Tessa demanded.

"I can't do any more," Scarlett said. "I am bound by a blood oath that was sealed in a Bargain Mark. All I *can* do is give you information."

"Then why even come here? If you can't help—"

"I never said I can't help," Scarlett cut in sharply. "Just not in the way you want me to."

Tessa went silent, and Axel wondered how Scarlett knew what Tessa wanted of her.

"We will be late if we do not leave soon," Sorin said gently.

"Yes, yes," she sighed, waving him off. "The Crown Prince will be most upset if we are late to his birthday party."

Sorin smirked. "Prince Finn is turning three years. I do not think he will remember nor care. I think you will be more upset to miss Callan and Tava announcing their second pregnancy. You told Callan you'd be there, and you promised Tula we wouldn't be late."

"I know," she sighed again. "The Fates forbid I have to deal with the Ash Rider for breaking a promise to Tula."

"How will you leave the realm?" Katya asked. "I understand you are a World Walker," she amended quickly. "But…how does that work?"

Scarlett smiled softly at her, but Axel still tensed, prepared for anything.

"You are quiet and observant," Scarlett said. "I would be willing to bet you are quite clever as well."

Axel expected Katya to bow her head, but she held Scarlett's gaze, despite the flush filling her warm skin once more.

"I can walk among the realms by simply willing it." Scarlett said. "But to bring others with me, it is easier to use the mirror gates. It is less draining on my reserves."

"Mirror *gates*?" Axel said. "You mean figuratively, right?"

Scarlett's smile morphed into a sly grin as she lifted a hand. White flames and shadows swirled with what looked like flecks of bright white embers, but they were something *more*.

"It is Chaos," Scarlett said simply. "I possess more than the standard Legacy."

"She is being uncharacteristically modest," Sorin said flatly. "She is as powerful as any First god or goddess."

"Impossible," Theon scoffed.

"Yet here I stand, Lordling," Scarlett drawled. "Chaos at my fingertips, gifts from *four* gods and goddesses, and two Fae elements."

"You are telling me the mirror in the Underground is a gateway to other worlds?" Axel cut in before Theon and Scarlett could start bickering again.

"Obviously they are mirrors to other realms," Scarlett replied. "Your brother saw me in one years ago. Why not gateways?"

"But…how?" Axel repeated.

"Now I control them with Chaos," she answered, that power flaring in her palm again. "Before I took that control, though, I cannot say."

"Before… Are you saying someone else could have used the mirror?" Theon cut in.

Scarlett gestured to Tessa. "How do you think she got here? The gateways were…broken, I guess one could say, before I obtained the means to control them. But that doesn't mean others weren't using them in the meantime. Anyone willing to pay the cost could find a way."

"The cost?" Tessa asked.

"All power comes with a cost. The greater the power, the higher the price," she answered grimly.

"And what was the cost of *that* power?" Theon sneered, jerking his chin at the Chaos swirling in Scarlett's palm.

"More than you could ever imagine. But if you think I took this power because I *wanted* it, you are mistaken," Scarlett answered. "The realms require balance, and when the demand for it comes, you have little time to decide how to correct it before fate intervenes. Sometimes it requires choosing between two unwanted outcomes, but in the end, I think you will find your own costs just as steep."

"I need to show you something."

"Fucking Fates," Axel muttered, his hand going to his hammering heart as Katya all but ran across the room to where she had a couple books and some papers spread across the coffee table.

He'd taken a quick shower after the events of the day, and he'd just opened the bathroom door to find her standing there. She'd scared the shit out of him. Or, at the very least, his shadows, which now hovered around him. He let them linger as he made his way over to Kat, and his heart rate slowly went back to normal.

She was kneeling on the floor, looking back and forth between two books and something she'd drawn on a piece of paper. She'd changed too, wearing soft pants that clung to her and a loose top that rode up as she reached for another book. Her curls had clearly been piled hastily atop her head, several falling free.

Scarlett and Sorin had left, Scarlett pulling Tessa into an embrace and whispering something into her ear no one else heard. Then Scarlett and Sorin had disappeared into the air, leaving them with a few answers, sure, but really only more chaos to wade through.

Traveling is what Scarlett had called it. The ability to step from one space to another within the same realm. An ability that Theon had mentioned in passing many times. It was supposedly taken from the Legacy when Devram was created, or at least from the ones who'd been sequestered here. How Scarlett could Travel *within* Devram though was something Theon would surely obsess over along with all the other information he'd learned.

But Theon wasn't the only one obsessing.

"What's all this, kitten?" Axel asked, plopping onto the sofa. He was exhausted. His next round of rations wouldn't be here for another day, and he was on edge. He should have taken Luka up on his offer.

Peering over her shoulder, he studied what she'd drawn a little closer. It was a Mark of some kind, and that had him sitting up a little straighter. Marks weren't something to mess around with. One minor imperfection could change the entire meaning and purpose. When she reached for her pencil again, Axel's hand snapped out, grasping her wrist.

Startled amber eyes met his. "What are you doing?"

"What am *I* doing?" Axel said. "What are *you* doing? Surely you know you should not be experimenting with Marks."

"I'm not *using* them," Kat remarked. "It is simply a reference."

"For what?"

"Scarlett was very adamant that there was only one Source Mark," Katya said, tapping the sketch. "This is a rough drawing of what Sorin's Source Mark looked like."

"Sorin's Source Mark? We hardly saw it," Axel said, his brow furrowing.

She waved him off. "That's not the point. *This* is the point," she said, dragging a book forward. Axel immediately recognized it as a basic academic book, the four Source Marks on the page. Pointing to the fourth and final Mark, she said, "Look how similar they are."

He leaned forward more, his bare chest pressing to her shoulder as he did. The contact did something to him. Something he'd been trying to forget since kissing her in the Underground.

Axel lightly cleared his throat. "Again, we didn't get a good look at Sorin's Mark, but I would imagine they would be somewhat similar if they're doing the same thing."

Some sort of exasperated huff came from her.

He fought the small smile trying to form and said, "What am I missing here, kitten?"

She turned to look up at him again. "They must not do the same thing, or what would be the point in altering it? If only one Mark is needed to draw power, why require the other three?"

Axel swiped a hand down his face. This was like listening to Theon when he got going on one of his theories.

"I don't know, Kat," he sighed. "She did mention our world is more advanced. We probably found a way to make the Marks more streamlined."

"More streamlined?" she said, blinking in disbelief. "How is *four* Marks more streamlined than one?"

He frowned. "That's a good point."

"I know."

"Has anyone ever told you that you're incredibly humble?" he teased.

"It is not conceited to acknowledge I was right about something," she tsked.

"Of course not."

She twisted around to glare at him. "You have no desire to know *why* the Marks are different here?"

"Who says they are different here?" Axel countered. "Maybe they're different in whatever world Scarlett is from, and our Marks are the same as every other world."

"That doesn't make sense."

"Why not?"

"One would think Scarlett would be more knowledgeable on the matter. She is a World Walker. A *real* World Walker," Kat said.

"As opposed to a fake World Walker?" That glare deepened, a spark flickering in her irises, and Axel chuckled. "She did seem rather upset by the Marks when we were talking about them."

"She did," Kat agreed.

"But one could assume, given what the other Marks do, they are given to strengthen the bond between the Master and Source," Axel went on.

"I suppose," Kat muttered. "But how?"

By the gods. Back to how again? She thought in circles like Theon did too.

"I don't know, kitten," he sighed, settling back into the sofa and tipping his head back. He let his eyes fall closed as he felt her lean forward and pick up another book.

"There are Marks in this book I've never come across before," Kat said.

Axel cracked his eyes open, watching her flip through the pages. "What book is that?"

"The one Cienna gave me."

"The one we can hardly translate?" he asked doubtfully.

"It's just slow-going is all," she replied, climbing onto the sofa beside him.

Too engrossed in the book, he was certain she hadn't even realized she'd settled against his side, but he sure as fuck had. Every part of his being was aware from the places where their bodies touched to the sparks of pleasure shooting through his veins to his shadows momentarily stilling and now curiously drifting closer. He swore he could feel her fascination with all of this, but more than that, he could smell the power in her veins.

The power in her blood.

He forced himself to focus on the book she was flipping through, having no idea how to read it, but when she turned another page, he stopped her.

Leaning over and pointing at one of the Marks, he said, "This is the Guardian Mark."

"Really?" She moved the book between them, smoothing her hand over the page.

"Mhmm," he murmured. "Theon and Luka researched it for months. Years, really."

"That is why Cienna is in the Underground?"

"My father was very displeased," Axel said. "There are some Marks only Legacy can see. This is one of them."

"I know that," she retorted. "I've found such Marks in other books, but this one has more."

"And you can really translate all of this?"

"It'd be easier with some reference books, but yes, I can," she answered, turning to look at him. They were so close now, her breath coasted over his lips as she spoke.

Amber eyes went wide, and she made to lurch back, but he found his arm around her, keeping her in place.

"Axel?"

His name was breathy on her tongue, and he swallowed the groan at the sound of it. His shadows crept closer, and he could tell the moment she noticed them because she sucked in a sharp breath. They curled around her ear, winding among her dark strands of hair. He leaned in more, inhaling deeply. Gods, she smelled so good. That jasmine and citrus scent that wouldn't leave him alone, and the power humming in her veins.

He was the one lurching back now. Shooting to his feet, the books fell to the floor.

"Fuck," Axel muttered, dropping to a knee to gather them at the same time she slipped to the floor to do the same.

"Sorry," she murmured.

"Don't be."

They were both too careful not to touch each other again, and she stood, stacking her books and straightening the papers. Axel dragged a hand through his hair, unsure how he both wanted to pull her back to him and push her away to keep her safe from him.

"Can I ask you something?" she said, moving to a bookshelf where she'd created space to hold some of her things.

"Of course."

"After the Selection Year, where do you think I will be assigned?"

His hand dropped back to his side. "What do you mean? You're assigned to Arius Kingdom."

"Yes, but what will I be doing?"

"I guess I don't know," Axel admitted.

She nodded, turning to him and clasping her hands in front of her.

"Is there a reason you're asking?"

Katya reached up, tucking a stray curl behind her ear. "No, I merely thought you might have an idea as to if I would be at Arius House or somewhere else."

"Arius House?" he repeated in confusion.

"It's nothing," she said in a rush. "We should get some sleep."

She made her way over to the bed, and Axel found himself following. "Do you *want* to stay at Arius House?"

"Why does that sound so crazy to you?" she countered, pulling back the blankets.

"Because nobody *wants* to stay at Arius House."

"But that's where you will be?"

"Me?"

"And Tessa. Theon. Luka," she added.

He slipped his hands into the pockets of his loose pants. "If my father gets his way, you will be at Arius House, yes."

She paused. "You sound upset by that."

"If they can find a way to sever the Source bond, my father wants Theon to take you as his replacement Source."

"Theon?" she said, whirling to face him.

"Yes."

"Not…" She trailed off, pressing her lips together.

"You are a powerful fire Fae, Katya," Axel said. "Of course he'd want you as a Source."

"It's a waste of a resource, really," she scoffed.

His head tilted. "Why do you say that?"

"He's going to tie the only fire Fae in the kingdom to someone who will drain that power? It's foolish."

"I guess that's logical," Axel conceded.

"Thank you, by the way."

His brow furrowed. "For what?"

"You are always straightforward with me. You don't try to make it sound less than what it is," she answered.

"You deserve the truth, even if it's unfavorable."

She turned, sitting on the edge of the bed. "There are ancient texts in the catacombs on Ekayan Island. If Theon could secure a trip there, we might find more answers on these Marks. Perhaps more answers he is seeking."

"Theon would do a number of questionable things to go to Ekayan Island," Axel said, and Kat barked a laugh. "Can I ask you a question?" Kat nodded. "Where do you *want* to serve in the Arius Kingdom? Why the Arius House?"

"When I was claimed at the Emerging Ceremony, I didn't expect to be staying in your personal room," she answered.

"Okay…" he said, waiting for her to continue.

"I guess I like it here more than I thought I would. Or rather, I like the company more than I thought I would," she finished.

"It's understandable to want to stay near those you are comfortable with," Axel said.

"It's logical," she agreed.

"It is."

They stared at each other a moment longer before she lightly cleared her throat. "Anyway, good night, Axel."

"Kat?"

"Yes?"

"I'll do whatever I can to keep you with me," Axel said. "It might not be much, but I'll try."

She smiled softly. "You don't give yourself enough credit."

"Why do you say that?"

She shrugged before snuggling down into the blankets. "Can you put on music to fall asleep to?"

"Classical?" he asked, already pulling his phone from his pocket.

"Whatever you choose. I don't need classical music here."

He didn't know why her words mattered, but they did something to him. She felt safe with him when she should feel anything but. He couldn't keep her safe from whatever fate his father decided for her. He couldn't keep her safe from the horrors of the Arius Kingdom. He couldn't keep her safe from him because his blood lust would only get worse. More than that, she wasn't his to protect.

His magic bristled at the thought, but it didn't matter. Attachments were dangerous. Look at Caris. Look at Pen. Fuck, look at Theon and Tessa.

No, Katya wasn't safe with him at all.

# 22

## THEON

"I hear a Match Contract was signed. The first one of the Selection Year."

Theon looked up from his phone to see Dagian Jove, Heir of the Achaz Kingdom. Dagian was scrolling on his own phone, one hand in his pocket. A seemingly civil conversation between two of the realm's heirs.

"What does it matter?" Theon asked, returning to his own scrolling.

"The Match of an heir is always a big deal, and yet there has been no formal announcement made," Dagian noted.

"Again, what does it matter?"

"It doesn't look good, does it?"

That had Theon looking up again to find Dagian's golden eyes on him. "How does my having a Match Contract look bad?"

Dagian shrugged, slipping his phone into his other pocket. "Arius Kingdom has so many secrets coming to light lately. Keeping a Match Contract quiet only adds more suspicion."

"And when has Arius Kingdom ever given a fuck?"

A small smirk curled on the corner of Dagian's mouth. "I am only suggesting that perhaps Arius Kingdom should be trying to build a better rapport rather than further distancing itself from the rest of the realm. Relations, after all, are rather important, especially when we'll be housing your assets in the near future," he said, waving in greeting to Lealla and Mahina, who had just entered the room.

Theon's phone buzzed with a message at that moment. His fingers tightened around the device as he read it. He looked back up, ready to snap a retort to Dagian, but he was already walking away.

Which was fine. He didn't have time for Dagian's games.

*Haven't you figured it out yet? You're already in the middle of them.*

Scarlett's cryptic words rang through his mind as he left the room, and he'd come to the conclusion he hated the silver-haired female.

He hated her for showing up here and being so fucking vague.

He hated her for her arrogance and constant dismissal of him.

He hated her because he knew she was right, that this was bigger than Devram. He knew the pieces were all there. He just couldn't seem to put them all together to see the bigger picture.

But more than any of that, he hated her for giving Tessa a false sense of hope that didn't matter in the end.

Theon headed across the street to collect Tessa from her last lesson. She was supposed to have her time with Cordelia again, but after the message he'd just received, that wouldn't be happening.

He ducked inside the building, striding quickly through the halls. He didn't bother knocking as he opened the door, finding the six Sources in chairs with their laptops balanced on their laps.

"Arius Heir," Cordelia said, bowing her head while the Sources immediately stood and dropped to a knee.

Everyone except Tessa, who was staring at him with wide eyes, clearly confused.

"Tessalyn," Cordelia snapped a moment before Tessa was scrambling to her feet, hissing in discomfort at the bands on her wrists. She dropped to her knee, one hand going to her throat, and Theon felt the momentary panic before she sucked in a sharp breath.

His eyes narrowed as he turned back to Cordelia, finding her tight-lipped and staring at Tessa with displeasure. It was all he needed to see to confirm his suspicion she'd used her magic on Tessa.

"I apologize for her disrespect," Cordelia said. "I know this is the type of behavior you have asked me to rectify."

Theon said nothing, darkness filling the edges of his vision. Instead, he moved further into the room, stopping in front of Tessa and holding out his hand. "Come. We have somewhere to be." The minute her fingers touched his palm, he closed his hand around hers, pulling her to her feet. "Gather your things," he said tightly.

She did as she was told, quickly packing up her laptop.

"We have a lesson after this, my Lord," Cordelia cut in.

"The lesson has been cancelled," he replied, not bothering to look at the Estate Mother.

"As you can see, her education is still lacking. I do not recommend missing such instruction," Cordelia argued.

"And I do not recommend taking it upon yourself to discipline my Source when I am standing in the same room," Theon retorted, his darkness appearing and snaking out. The other Sources all fidgeted where they remained on a knee. He let them stay there as the darkness found its way to Cordelia, pausing, coiled to strike. "Do we have an understanding?"

"Of course, my Lord," she said, bowing her head.

Without another word, he led Tessa from the room. It wasn't until they were stepping outside and she'd inhaled a breath of fresh air that she said, "You didn't need to do that."

"It's not her place to discipline you, just as it isn't your place to question me," he retorted, dropping her hand and removing the bands, slipping them into his pocket.

"Of course," she sneered under her breath.

He waited, watching her power flare with the bands off. Once he was sure she had it under control, he turned and headed down the walkway, Tessa trailing after him.

Neither of them said another word on the walk back to the townhouse, and when they were inside, she went straight to the kitchen, grabbed a bottle of water, and disappeared up the stairs. She didn't even acknowledge Luka, who watched her the entire time.

Theon went straight to the liquor, pouring himself a drink before sliding his phone to Luka with the screen open to the message he'd received. The dragon's face went dark, faint traces of smoke appearing on his exhale.

"I take it this is why her emotions are so conflicted at the moment," Luka said, passing the phone back to Theon.

"I haven't told her yet," Theon said. "But why do you think her emotions are conflicted?"

"I've just learned to read her, I guess," he replied.

Theon's eyes narrowed. "And what do you think she is conflicted about?"

"I have no idea. What happened before you got home?"

"I picked her up early from her lessons. Cordelia *corrected* her behavior in front of me, and I made it clear that was not acceptable," Theon answered.

Luka gave him a frank look. "And?"

Theon swirled his drink with a sigh. "And when Tessa told me I didn't need to do that after the fact, I said things I shouldn't have."

"That certainly explains the conflicting emotions," Luka muttered, moving to the pastry tray on the back counter. He returned with two sugar cookies on a napkin. "She needs to eat something. She's hardly touched food all day."

Theon glared at the sweets. "You're encouraging poor nutrition habits."

"By all means, take her a salad and see how that goes," Luka drawled.

With another curse, Theon snatched the outstretched cookies and stalked from the kitchen, taking the stairs two at a time. When he entered their room, he found Tessa on the sofa. Her head was tipped back, eyes closed. She held her phone in her hand, and earbuds were in her ears. She was likely listening to one of the playlists Axel had set up for her.

He'd like to think she hadn't heard him enter, but he knew it was far more likely she was ignoring him. And now that he could think around his anger at the Estate Mother making Tessa uncomfortable, he could feel exactly what Luka had said. Gratitude and satisfaction mixed with trepidation and annoyance flickered down the bond.

Placing the napkin with the cookies down by her bottle of water, he took off his suit jacket and loosened his tie before rolling his sleeves up his forearms. Dinner was in a few hours, so he didn't bother changing completely, but as he finished rolling back his second sleeve, he plucked an earbud from her ear.

"Hey!" Tessa cried, sitting up straight and reaching for the earpiece. Sure enough, a song Axel played frequently was blaring out of the tiny speaker.

"I didn't mean to snap at you on the walk home," Theon said, setting the earbud aside.

Tessa blinked up at him. Once. Twice.

"I'm sorry," she finally said, pulling the other earbud from her ear. "Are you *apologizing* to me?"

"No," Theon said quickly.

"My mistake," Tessa said, rolling her eyes and moving to replace her earbud, but Theon snatched it from her hand, setting it aside with the other one. "Theon!"

"We need to talk about a few things," he said.

"I don't want to talk to you."

"Too bad," he said, taking her phone from her hands too. "We haven't discussed anything Scarlett and Sorin told us. You have to have thoughts and questions. Maybe some insights to share?"

"What's there to discuss?" she countered. "Nothing she told us changes anything."

"How do you figure that?" Theon asked, utterly baffled at the statement.

But Tessa pursed her lips, turning away from him. "There's nothing to talk about."

He reached out, taking her chin and turning her face back to him. "What did you want her to do, Tessa?"

"I don't know. Everything. Nothing. It doesn't matter in the end."

"There must be something."

She was silent, her gaze fixed out the window.

"You clearly had some idea. You've been quiet since she left, and I could feel everything you were feeling while they were here. What expectations did you have of her?"

"I said I don't know," she snapped.

Theon tsked. "I don't believe that."

"Believe what you want."

"By the gods, you're infuriating," Theon said, releasing her chin and driving a hand through his hair. "Even being able to feel your emotions, I can't—"

"Can't what?" she retorted, pushing to her feet. "Can't figure out how to manipulate me? Figure out how to word something just right to give me the illusion of control? You're already getting everything you want from me. What more do you need?"

On instinct, his hand snapped out, his grip loose around her throat, but he could feel her pulse hammering away beneath the tips of his fingers. "You think I am getting everything I want, clever tempest?"

"Aren't you?" she countered. "You have a powerful Source, a Bargain with me to overtake your father, a Guardian, and a Match. Soon enough you will rule this Kingdom and likely the realm. Tell me what I'm missing."

"You," he snarled.

"You get me in your bed. You get my power. You get unfettered access to everything I am. I don't know what else you can possibly take from me, Theon." Her smirk was cold and harsh, but the crack in her voice was anything but. The agony screaming down the bond was desperate and furious. "There's nothing left to take. I have nothing else to give. How can I when I don't know who I am? When I'm something to be used by even my own blood? I always knew I was unwanted, but to be tossed away in a forgotten realm? I wasn't unwanted, Theon. I was truly *nothing.*"

"Tessa," he breathed, not knowing what else to say as he felt the rawness in those words down their bond.

This place was where they were the most real with each other. In the middle of the hate and the tension, the arguing and the passion. This was when they both spoke without trying to get the upper hand. It was all naked truth and bleeding desires. This was when she let him take what he wanted, and he took because it was what she needed— to get lost in pleasure and away from her thoughts. But this time, there was more to it for both of them.

It was evident in the way she surged forward, her lips landing on his in a violent kiss. It was the only way they knew how to be with each other. Teeth clashing and tongues battling. It was in the moan as his hands fell to her ass, lifting her off the ground. It was in the way she wrapped her legs around his waist, as if she needed him near, but the sharp nip at his lip told him she hated it. Her arms looped around his neck, keeping him close as he dragged his lips along her jaw, down her throat, across her collarbone.

Then she was leaning back, pulling at his tie, clawing at buttons. Her hands slid beneath his dress shirt, and the sigh that came from her at the skin-to-skin contact broke any restraint he was trying to keep in this moment. Because she was trusting him with something in her own broken way, the only way she knew how to trust him, and tomorrow he had to let her go for a week. He should tell her before they did this, but he was a selfish prick. He'd admit that. She was going to be gone for a week, and he wanted her to remember who she belonged to. He wanted his scent so entwined with hers, others in Faven would know too.

He shoved her legs down, despite her protests, before reaching for the hem of her dress and dragging it over her head. Then he was gathering her back to him, legs back around his waist, and lips back on his as he walked them to the bed. He lowered her down, tongue lapping at her neck, his mouth sucking, leaving marks as he made his way to her breasts. Her head tipped back, a hand sinking into his hair as he tossed her bra aside and took a nipple into his mouth. His darkness rose up, flitting along bare flesh and pushing her back down onto the bed, and he followed, dropping open-mouthed kisses along her torso as he finished the buttons she'd neglected. He made quick work of shucking off his shirt and pants, sliding her undergarments off too.

Violet-grey eyes full of heated want watched him, and for once, there was nothing smart coming from her mouth. This time was different. He could tell she knew it too, even if she wouldn't admit it. She'd already slid up the bed, and he climbed on, coming over her. He reached to smooth her hair back, but she turned her head to the side.

"Don't," she snapped.

"Why?"

"Because this isn't that. It's nothing different from what we've been doing," she rasped.

"Is that what you need to believe, little storm?"

"Yes."

"Fine, but I still need your eyes," he replied, pushing himself up. He had a hand on each of her knees, and he waited until she did what he'd ordered before he pushed her legs wide, kneeling over her.

Lifting a foot, he kissed her ankle before draping her leg over his shoulder and opening her even wider. He gripped his cock, dragging the tip through her wetness, finding her more than ready for him. She hissed, her hips jolting, seeking more.

"You know what I need to hear, Tessa," he said, his hand coming to her hip, holding her in place when he did it again.

"I won't say it," she gritted out, her fists clenched in the bedding. "So either fuck me, or let me do it myself."

Theon clicked his tongue. "We both know that won't leave you even close to satisfied. The bond requires more. *We* require more."

"I don't care what—"

But her words dissolved in a cursing moan as he sank into her to the hilt without warning. Fuck, it never got old. The heat. The rightness. Her writhing beneath him, already wanting more. Her hands were at his shoulders, nails digging in as she panted through clenched teeth.

"Tell me, Tessa," he said again, pulling out the smallest amount before sinking back in. But she shook her head, golden strands stark against the dark bedding.

"This isn't that," she repeated. "It will never be that."

"We'll see," he said, circling his hips one way and then the other, drawing another ragged moan from her. "Fuck, the sounds you make," he groaned. "It's enough to make me come right now."

"Don't you fucking dare," she snarled, her eyes going wide.

Theon chuckled softly. "Maybe I should," he mused, his hand sliding to her belly when she tried to buck against him again. "Keep you on an edge until you're so desperate you finally admit it."

"It will be a lie. Pretty words to get what I want," she gritted out, a whimper following when Theon pulled out a small amount and didn't push back in.

"Your lies are the sweetest sound, little storm."

"Theon, please!" It was a cry of frustration and need.

The begging.

It always did him in.

He spread his knees, pushing her legs wider still before he pulled all the way out and slowly sank back in a few times to loosen up the muscles that had tensed in her frustration. Then it was all hard thrusts and thick pumps that had her nails sinking in deeper and more of those fucking sounds that drove him mad. It was rushed kisses and nipped skin, hands roaming, and feeling around every inch of his cock. It was throwing her other leg over his shoulder at some point so he could sink in even deeper.

He knew she was close, those cries desperate and her hips grinding mindlessly against him as he drove into her again and again. That was when he let his darkness loose. It had been hovering and waiting, but now it wound around her throat and tightened. Forced her hands above her head. Held her in place as her climax shuddered around him. With the next thrust, he held himself deep, hitting that perfect spot. But it was her light flaring and raking down his darkness that had his cock jerking deep inside her, his own release barreling up his spine and making his eyes roll back with a growled, "*Fuck.*"

Later, after he'd slowly lowered her legs, kissing her calves along the way, and after she'd crawled back into bed from cleaning up, she was lying with her head on his chest. Her soft breathing told him she was close to sleep. He'd already sent a text to Luka telling him they wouldn't be at dinner.

"I need to tell you something," Theon said softly, his fingers drifting through her hair.

"Is it going to ruin this?" she asked, nestling in deeper to his side.

He swallowed thickly, feeling a contentment he'd never felt from her before.

"Then tell me tomorrow," she murmured, taking his silence as his answer.

"I can't," he finally answered.

She let out a sigh, pushing up and off of him, wrapping the comforter around her bare body. "What is it?"

The question was filled with resignation and acceptance.

"I received word you are to go to Faven tomorrow," he said, his hand clenching beside him. "Someone will come to collect you first thing in the morning."

Tessa stared at him for a long moment before she nodded once, eyes darting to the balcony windows. "So I should pack or something?"

"Ford can do that," he answered quickly, not wanting her to get out of the bed.

"That's stupid. I can do it myself."

"In the morning then." When she still hesitated, he added, "Take what you need from the bond tonight."

Her eyes snapped to his. "Is that why we did this? Wait. Is that why you picked me up from lessons early?"

"Yes."

"And it's why you were so testy with Mother Cordelia?"

"I was ill-tempered with Cordelia because she punished you for no reason," he retorted.

She huffed a humorless laugh. "That is nothing new, Theon. You should have left it alone."

"Absolutely not. There was no reason to punish you when I was standing right there. That is not her place," he argued.

She pursed her lips, tugging the bedding tighter around herself. Her emotions shifted from irritation to unease.

"Tell me what's wrong," he said, leaning forward to tug her lip from where she was worrying it between her teeth.

She sent him a fake smile. "I'm fine. Is Luka here?"

Theon stiffened. "He's downstairs. Tell me what's wrong."

"Can he come up here?"

"Why?"

She fidgeted, looking out the window again. "Can he sleep with us? Like he did at Arius House?"

He couldn't believe what he was hearing. "You threw a fit when you woke up next to him in bed."

"I did not."

"You did," Theon said. "In fact, you said he could sleep on the floor before sharing a bed."

"And you didn't care. So why does it matter now?" she countered.

Theon studied her, feeling her anxiety increase. "Tell me why, and I'll get him right now."

But before she could say anything else, there was a knock on the door, and the dragon himself entered the room, two covered plates stacked on top of each other in his hand.

"Food," he said by way of explanation. "I figured you needed to eat since you couldn't bother coming to dinner." His gaze skipped from Theon to Tessa. "What's wrong?"

"Nothing," she said, but Theon could feel the utter relief down the bond.

Holding her stare, Theon said, "Tessa wants you to *sleep* with us."

"That is *not*—" Her eyes went wide before she was throwing Theon a dark glare. "Don't say it like that."

"You want me to sleep up here?" Luka asked. "Why?"

"In the same bed," Theon clarified.

"Shut up," Tessa snapped.

"Why, Tessa?" Luka repeated, the command ringing in his tone.

"Because Theon said I go to Faven tomorrow, and there will be tests. I don't want to feel alone tonight when I'll be alone for a week. I know it's just the two of you, but—"

"Okay," Luka cut in with a shrug. Uncovering a plate of food, he handed it to Tessa, who snaked a hand out from the blankets cocooned around her to take it from him.

Just like that.

Luka had asked what was wrong, and she'd told him. No arguing. No prying an answer from her. No pushing her until she became so furious the answer slipped free.

"I just need to grab a few things," Luka said before he left the room.

Tessa wouldn't look at him as Theon slipped from the bed. In the closet, he pulled on loose pants before grabbing a shirt and sleep shorts for her. When he returned, she reached for them, but he held them out of reach.

"You feel alone without him?"

"I feel alone all the time, Theon," she said, her tone hard. "I can at least pretend I'm not when there's two of you."

"You couldn't have told me that?"

"No, because you get like this," she retorted, holding out her hand in demand for the clothing.

He studied her a moment longer before leaning over and taking her chin between his thumb and forefinger. "You told me not to do this tonight, but after that, I don't care what you said. You clearly need to hear it."

Her eyes went wide, panic skittering down the bond. "Don't you dare say it, Theon."

"You are not nothing to me, Tessa."

"Stop. Now."

"You're not nothing because you're—"

"You don't get to do this," she interjected, lightning cracking in her eyes. "You don't get to lock me in the dark, tell me you'd do it again, and then tell me I matter to you. You don't get to whisper lies disguised as sweet words in a bid to win me over and get me to play nice. You don't get to play on my emotions because you feel them now when you were too inept to understand them before. And you certainly don't get to ask for my affection because you are jealous of Luka."

"I have nothing to be jealous of," Theon retorted.

"You're right. You don't. If I had the choice, I'd be rid of both of you, but I don't have choices, do I?" she said, snatching the clothing from his hand and nearly upending her plate of food. "So quit acting like I've done something wrong. You don't get to make me feel guilty about how I choose to survive any of this."

With a huff, she climbed out of the bed, quickly shimmying on the clothing before taking her dinner into the bathroom and slamming the door behind her. At the same moment, Luka came back, looking between the door and Theon and shaking his head.

"Something you need to explain to me?" Theon demanded.

"Nope," Luka said.

"What the fuck was all that?"

"Did you ever think that maybe that is the problem here?"

"Don't act superior right now," Theon retorted.

"She told you what it was. You clearly weren't listening," Luka said, sitting on the sofa and stretching his legs out before him. "She tells you things all the time. You just choose not to hear her."

"I want full access to her while she is gone," Theon said, standing in front of Tessa and facing off with Dagian Jove.

"My father agreed to one phone call a day. Considering she may be… indisposed at times, the time of those phone calls may vary," Dagian replied, not even looking up from his phone.

Theon felt Tessa's dread down the bond. From his periphery, he also saw Luka bend down to speak into her ear. She shook her head slightly, but the anxiety didn't ease much.

"I also want daily reports on what is learned," Theon said, returning his attention to Dagian.

The Achaz Heir smiled at him as if he were a child asking for a toy. Sliding his phone into his pocket, he said, "I'm sure you do, but we both know you have no negotiation power here. If you refuse to let me take her, your agreement with the Lords and Ladies is broken."

Basically, he was fucked, and Dagian knew it.

Turning to Tessa, he took her face in his hands. "You have your phone?"

She nodded, but Dagian interrupted again.

"Her phone stays here."

"Are you fucking mad?" Theon demanded, rounding on him.

"No. We're just not stupid. Who knows what kind of spy programs you have on her phone. You think we're letting her bring that into our capital city? Our *home*?" Dagian replied, his tone riddled with superiority. "All of her tech stays. In fact, all of her possessions stay. She'll have clothing provided."

"She can't even bring her own clothing?" Theon objected.

"Calm down," Tessa muttered behind him. "It's not like I got to bring my own clothing to Arius House. It's fine. I'm used to it."

Turning his back on Dagian again, he met her stare. "It's one week, and you'll be back."

She nodded, Luka having already taken her messenger bag and setting it aside.

Her eyes darted to Dagian before coming back to Theon. "You

don't… You'd tell me if there was something you'd learned, right? I know everything you know?"

"In regards to what?"

Her brow furrowed. "Me, Theon. My heritage. My mother. My bloodline. Anything."

*Her father is a god, and her mother may as well be one.*

Cienna often spoke in riddles, not wanting to tempt fate. He rarely took what she said at face-value, but apparently with this, he should have. Scarlett certainly hadn't been vague when it came to her father, but he hadn't told Tessa he'd already known her father was a god, even if he didn't know which one at the time. And he hadn't told her what he knew of her mother either. He hadn't told her she was essentially the daughter of two gods. He knew the power of keeping information close, and he didn't want this one getting back to the Achaz Lord in any of these testings and assessments.

"Of course, beautiful," he said, bending to press a kiss to her brow.

"One week," she whispered.

"One week," he agreed.

He stepped to the side at the same moment Sasha, Dagian's Source, opened the back door of the vehicle and a Fae stepped out.

"Dex?" Tessa said, and Theon felt her shock but also hesitation. "What are you doing here?"

Dex smiled softly at her before glancing quickly at Theon and Luka. "Lord Jove knew this would likely be a stressful situation for you. He was hoping my presence would make you a little more comfortable. A show of good faith, if you will."

Tessa nodded slowly, taking a step forward, but she stilled when Theon reached for her arm. Violet-grey eyes blinked up at him in question.

"Do not trust them, Tessa," he murmured. "Remember where your loyalties lie."

"I trust no one, Theon," she replied. "And I know exactly where my loyalties lie."

With that, she tugged her arm from his grip and descended the steps. She returned the hug Dex pulled her into, albeit stiffly, and then she was climbing into the backseat.

A moment later, she was gone. He had no way to contact her. No way to see her. No way to protect her.

*One week*, he repeated himself.

But he knew all too well how much could change in one week.

# PART TWO
# OR TO FURY THEY BOTH LOSE

# 23

## AXEL

"Congratulations," Luka said as Axel climbed into the vehicle behind Katya.

It was weird to be in the backseat, but with Tessa gone, Theon was in the passenger seat and pissy as fuck. He'd hardly spoken all day, and when he did, it was mostly growled demands.

"Thank you," Kat replied, settling into her seat with her hands in her lap.

"One of only twenty Fae to pass initial exams is impressive," Luka said as he pulled the vehicle into traffic. "Especially for someone as powerful as you are."

Her bands were in Axel's pocket, and they quietly clinked together while he bounced his knee in anticipation. Rations should have been delivered by now.

"I've always been a quick study," Kat said. "But we were also taught young that emotions have no place in academics, and since our powers are tied to our emotions, it makes sense that I excelled."

"Were all the Fae who passed today from the Falein Estate?" Luka asked.

"Most of them," she answered. "A couple were not. Corbin was originally from the Anala Estate."

"What?" Theon asked, turning to look at her.

"He speaks," Luka said dryly.

Ignoring him, Theon said, "Corbin? As in the Fae Tessa was friends with?"

"That Tessa *is* friends with, yes," Kat answered.

"He was raised at the Anala Estate?"

"Yes. He was transferred to the Celeste Estate a year or so before I was."

"But he didn't emerge with fire," Theon said.

"For someone who is exceptionally educated, you state very obvious things much of the time. It is rather interesting to observe," Katya replied.

"He just chooses which parts to acknowledge, then acts surprised when the things he ignored come back and blow up in his face," Luka said.

Theon glared. "You're being a bigger ass than usual today."

"You're both being broody jackasses with Tessa gone," Axel muttered. *Could Luka drive any slower today? Fuck.*

"Your mood isn't much better," Theon shot back.

Axel said nothing, only lifting his middle finger.

Katya was studying the three of them as if they were some fascinating experiment.

"What did Corbin emerge with?" Theon asked after a tense moment of silence.

"Water," Kat answered.

"And the other one?"

"What other one?"

"The one Corbin is involved with," Theon said impatiently.

"Lange emerged with air," Kat answered tightly.

"And he came from another estate as well?"

"Falein."

Axel glanced at her, her answers getting shorter and more curt. She was definitely more than irritated.

"Get to the fucking point, Theon," Axel grumbled, kicking the back of Theon's seat.

"Godsdammit, Axel," he snarled, darkness coiling in warning.

Axel smirked, his shadows stretching and taunting Theon's magic.

"Not in the vehicle, you idiots," Luka groused.

"Then fucking drive faster," Axel snapped. "I could walk home faster than this."

"Unlikely. Pretty sure I'd run you over for a few hours of quiet."

"Nice, fucker," Axel retorted, his shadows snapping out and biting at Luka's arm, a line of red appearing.

"The fuck, Axel!" Luka yelled, the vehicle swerving as Luka jerked the wheel, spinning to glare at him with vertical pupils.

"Eyes on the road," Axel said, settling back in his seat once more with a satisfied smirk.

Katya was staring at him, and yeah, he knew he was acting like an asshole. But godsdammit, she was sitting right there. Without the bands on subduing her magic, he could practically taste it. So much power in her blood. He didn't even need it for that. His reserves were fine. There was absolutely no reason for him to be this frenzied, yet here he sat. Controlled by a craving with the cure for it sitting a few feet away. He needed the fucking distraction.

She lightly cleared her throat, smoothing her hands over her loose training pants. "Is there a reason you were asking about Corbin and Lange, Theon?"

"Did Lange pass his exam today as well?" Theon asked.

"He did."

"Did anyone claim them?"

Katya blinked in surprise. "Not that I am aware. Are Fae normally claimed so early?"

"If they show exemplary skills, some are. You were," Theon answered before going quiet again.

"Are you going to share your thoughts with the rest of us for once?" Luka drawled.

"Are *you*?" Theon snarked in return.

That had the dragon pressing his lips together.

"If you're trying to figure out what connects us all, I haven't been able to come up with anything logical," Kat offered after a few more minutes of tense silence.

Theon glanced over his shoulder. "There has to be something."

"I agree," she said simply, turning to look out the window as Luka pulled into the garage.

Thank the gods and the Fates and whatever other beings got them here before the next Selection Year.

Axel was out of the vehicle and inside before the others had even opened their doors. He didn't bother taking his coat off as he made his way straight to the kitchen and into the pantry, opening the glamoured icebox. His hand was trembling when he reached inside.

Only to find it empty.

*What the fuck?*

He pressed onto toes, peering inside. There was nothing in there.

Axel spun on his heel, striding to the fridge and yanking the door open, condiments rattling with the force. He shoved aside juice cartons and a container of yogurt. A few eggs fell out, cracking and creating a mess when they hit the floor.

"Axel?"

Her voice had him cursing, and he went utterly still. "Get her out of here. Now," he gritted out.

He knew.

He knew if he looked at her, it would be over. His canines would be in her throat, and then it would truly be over. That would be the final tipping point. He'd no longer control shadows but would be a slave to the same bloodlust he was experiencing now.

"Theon took her to the lounge," Luka said grimly, a hand landing on his shoulder. "You good?"

"No. I am not fucking good," Axel snapped, slamming the fridge door shut. "Godsdammit!" he cursed again when he stepped in the broken eggs. Inhaling sharply through his nose, he said, "Ask Ford where in the realm our rations are."

As though he'd heard his name, the Fae himself appeared, frowning at the egg mess. Moving to grab paper towels, he said, "Can I help you find something, my Lord?"

"Where are our rations?" Axel snapped.

Ford was unfazed as he lowered to clean up the eggs. "Lord St. Orcas sent word he would bring the rations later tonight when he visits."

"Why?"

"To save the carrier a trip, I suppose. Since he was stopping by anyway," the Fae answered. "Remove your shoes."

Axel quickly slipped them off, Ford grabbing them and leaving the kitchen, presumably to clean them off before he came back to finish cleaning the kitchen floor. It took everything in him not to drop more eggs just because.

"It's a power move. You know that," Luka said, leaning against the counter, his arms folded.

"Of course I know that," Axel growled, both of his hands going into his hair and yanking at the roots.

"If I'd known, I'd have saved the last of mine. I drank it this morning."

"If any of us had known, then Father wouldn't be the bastard he is," Axel snapped, beginning to pace.

"Do you need me to go hunt some down?" Luka asked grimly.

Both of his hands went through his hair again. He'd have to fix it before his father got here, or the prick would likely withhold the ration because he wasn't *presentable enough.*

"Axel?" Luka pushed.

"No," he ground out. "We don't know when he's coming. The last thing we need is for you to not be here when he shows up."

"Okay," Luka said, pushing off the counter. "We'll help keep things under control until you get your ration."

"I don't..." Axel trailed off. "I'm going to shower. Keep Katya down here."

Luka nodded as Axel left the kitchen and went upstairs. He pulled out his phone, turning on one of his favorite playlists before pouring himself a large glass of liquor and swallowing half of it in one go. He could do this. It was only, what? Another few hours at most? He'd stay up here until his father arrived, and all would be well.

Until next week at this same time.

He knocked back the rest of the liquor, pushing aside those thoughts and refilling his glass before starting to wander around his room. It smelled like her. Hints of jasmine and citrus, something smokey with underlying spices. All of her clothing was neatly folded and tucked away in a corner in the closet. Her lesson books, reading books, and notes were organized on a shelf. He should get her a phone. She was an Arius Kingdom Fae now. She could have a phone.

Axel took another sip of whiskey as he reached for a notebook on the top of the stack. Flipping it open, he laughed out loud. Of course she wrote notes in another language. Putting the notebook back, he grabbed a book stacked beside them, taking it to the sofa. He was pretty sure it was the same one she'd said Theon had given to her.

Setting his glass aside, he flipped through the pages. The thing was entirely about the gods and their bloodlines, how their powers manifested, known allies and disagreements among them before Devram was created. Naturally, the history was thousands of years ago, given they would have no idea what was going on outside the realm now. Apparently, young females were securing godlike powers and controlling mirror gates.

Fucking mirror gates.

He still couldn't believe those were a real thing or that the silver-haired female had actually been real.

Setting the book aside, he tugged his shirt from his pants before unbuttoning it and tossing it aside. Leaving a mess for Ford to clean up later had become his favorite pastime.

He took his time in the shower, letting the hot water and the alcohol in his system calm his anxious nerves. He was toweling off his hair when he heard movement in the other room, and he immediately tensed. How hard was it to keep her downstairs?

With a frustrated sigh, he wrapped his towel around his waist and stalked to the doorway. He'd left it open, assuming Theon and Luka could handle this one simple task.

"You shouldn't be—"

The words stalled in his throat when he found his father standing in the middle of the room, Eviana at his side.

"Axel," Valter greeted, flipping through the same book Axel had been looking through earlier. He also held Axel's glass of liquor in his hand. He made a point of taking a long drink before saying, "Perhaps some pants before we speak?"

"Of course," Axel said, moving quickly to his closet and pulling on navy suit pants and a white button down. He didn't bother with a tie, knowing his father was already impatient.

He was buttoning his shirt cuffs when he came back out to the room. "Ford said you'd be stopping by."

"And yet you chose to make me wait when I arrived," Valter said tightly, snapping the book closed. He handed it off to Eviana without even looking at her, the Fae taking the book and quietly setting it aside.

"My apologies," Axel said, slipping his hands into his pockets and clenching them into fists. "I erroneously thought I had more time."

His father made a displeased noise, and Axel waited for the slice of pain as penance, but it never came.

Instead, his father said, "I am told the fire Fae passed her exams today and is now free of her shirastone bands."

"She did, yes. She is very skilled," Axel said carefully.

"It appears your brash decision at the Emerging Ceremony continues to pay off."

Axel forced himself not to shift under his father's shrewd gaze, the calming effects of the shower and alcohol now long gone. "I am happy to know you are pleased."

Valter hummed again, taking another drink of the liquor as he slid his other hand into his pocket. "She and Theon seem to be getting along well."

"What?" Axel blurted before quickly evening out his tone. "I mean, I haven't seen them spend much time together. She is busy with her lessons and training, and he is busy with Tessa."

Valter studied him for a moment before saying, "They appeared quite close in the lounge when I arrived."

"That is good to hear then," Axel said, the words like acid on his tongue.

"I suppose, but with the female having passed her exam, it gives us a little time," Valter went on, swirling the drink. Now his eyes never left Axel, as though he was watching for something.

His palms were sweaty, and he wasn't entirely sure if it was from the increasing withdrawal or from the way this conversation seemed to be heading. Forcing himself to remain loose, he said, "A little time for what?"

"A powerful fire Fae is quite coveted," Valter went on. "We would be fools not to use the asset to secure some deals before she is bonded to Theon. Once that happens… Well, you've seen how he is with the other one," Valter said, his lip curling. "I hope that when your time comes, you don't act so foolishly when you Select a Source."

"Tessa is obviously a unique case, considering her unknown heritage," Axel replied. "But Katya still has her other lessons, despite passing her element exams. She'll go straight into advanced element training. I think that would be rather important for her to master."

"You just told me she is very skilled," Valter said.

"She is."

"Then she should be able to keep up and still begin fulfilling her duties to the kingdom. She has a small window of time before Theon can Select her. We need to be strategic with that time," Valter went on.

Axel tried to swallow, but his mouth was too dry. "And why aren't we including Theon in this discussion since he is the heir?"

"Because I have been informed you may be becoming…attached to the female," his father said, swirling his drink once more. "I wanted to visit with you personally to see if you were going to cause any issues. The gods know you enjoy your dramatics."

That godsdamn Ford fucker. They knew he was reporting everything back to their father, but he clearly hadn't been careful enough.

"I see," Valter said when Axel didn't answer soon enough.

"You see what?" Axel asked.

"That the information is correct."

"It isn't."

His father arched a brow. "No? I do not need to worry about you interfering with matters?"

"Like you said, she is strong and a rare asset," Axel said. "Why do you think I make her sleep in my rooms?"

Valter tsked, rolling his eyes. "Of course I know why you keep the female in your rooms."

"Aside from that," Axel said, his stomach roiling at the implication. "I keep her under close watch. I escort her to and from the Pantheon. She eats with us not because I am attached to her, but because I know the value she holds for our kingdom."

His father's hazel eyes continued to study him, and for the life of him, Axel couldn't figure out if he found what he was looking for or not. He didn't know if he'd been convincing enough, but the implications of his father's next words were perfectly clear.

"Your weekly rations are in the kitchen," Valter said, draining the last of the liquor from the glass and passing it off to Eviana. "Should you suddenly find a need for your theatrics, I trust you recognize I could have waited until tomorrow to deliver them. Or another few days. Weeks."

"That won't be necessary," Axel said tightly.

His father's smile was all teeth when he said, "I suppose that's up to you."

Drinking Fae blood made him feel better than any alcohol or roll of lull-leaf ever could. He could taste the power in it, something earthy and bold in this bottle. A bottle he was drinking far too much of, he realized when he held it up to the light and found it over half gone.

Shit.

He replaced the cork, his fingers still trembling slightly. He was sitting on the pantry floor.

The godsdamn floor.

He'd pulled the bottle from the icebox and slid right down the wall as he drank. Not daring to rush to the kitchen until after his father had left. Valter hadn't said a word about his plans for Katya when they'd gone downstairs to join the others. Instead, he'd spent a casual fifteen minutes interrogating Theon on his progress in figuring out Tessa's lineage and severing the Source bond with her.

Footsteps sounded. Axel didn't bother looking when Theon's shoes stopped in the doorway.

"I'll save you some of mine this week," his brother said.

Axel only nodded, wiping at his brow where sweat still dampened his hairline. He should probably shower again.

"This was about more than Tessa," Theon said.

"Clever as always," Axel muttered sarcastically, his head falling into his hands.

"Tell me so I can help."

"Where is Kat?"

There was shuffling, and then Theon was sinking down beside him. "She went up to your room."

Axel lifted his head, only to let it fall back against the wall. With his eyes closed, he relayed the conversation he'd had with their father.

When he was finished, Theon was quiet for a long moment before saying, "You can't have feelings for a Fae, Axel."

"You think I don't know that? In five years, I'll be Selecting my own Source. I'll likely be chained to my own Match contract."

"Are you fucking her?"

His eyes snapped open, and his head jerked up. "No, I'm not fucking her."

"Really? I assumed you were."

"She was claimed unexpectedly, brought here instead of the dorms, and was forced to do all manner of things at her—" He stopped speaking at the look Theon was giving him. "I know I'm the asshole we were raised to be, but I'm not *that* kind of asshole. Thanks for thinking the absolute worst of me."

"I didn't mean it like that," Theon said. "She's obviously comfortable with you. I assumed it was a mutually beneficial exchange for the time being."

"Yeah, well, you assumed wrong," Axel grumbled.

"But you do care for her."

It was a statement, not a question.

"I spend a lot of time with her."

"It endangers her. Think of Caris. Think of Pen—"

"*I know*, Theon. Why do you think I've never gone any further? We don't even sleep in the same bed," Axel said.

He conveniently left out the part about kissing her in the Underground.

Neither of them said anything for several minutes until Theon broke the silence with a sigh. "I'll do what I can to prevent it from happening, but be careful, Axel. If Father realizes what she means to you…"

Theon didn't have to finish the thought. Axel knew it ended with snapping Katya's neck the same way he'd snapped Pen's. He was her biggest threat in more ways than one, but it didn't stop him from getting to his feet and putting the bottle of blood away before climbing the stairs to his room. It didn't stop the way he could already feel her before he'd even opened the door, and it didn't stop the way he could breathe a little easier when he found her with a spoonful of peanut butter and a book in her hand.

She said nothing as he pushed the door shut, leaning against it and holding her amber gaze.

"Are you all right?" she finally asked, lowering the now empty spoon.

And because she'd thanked him only a few days ago for always being honest with her, he said, "No."

Kat nodded, setting the spoon and book aside. "Do you need to talk about it?"

"No."

"Do you need me to help with something?"

"No."

"Do you want some peanut butter?"

A laugh fell from his lips. "Why would I want peanut butter?"

"One, because peanut butter always makes me feel better, and two, I figured it would get you to say something other than 'no.' Or, at the very least, smile."

He *was* smiling, but it quickly faded. Of course, she noticed. Clasping her hands in front of her, she said, "I am assuming you acquired blood?"

He was too ashamed to say anything about it, so he just gave a curt nod.

"I would have given you some, you know."

"I would never ask that of you," Axel said sharply, still leaning against the door.

"Yet I will still offer it if you need," she countered, lifting her chin in a way that made him want to kiss her all over again.

Instead, he said, "You shouldn't," before finally pushing off the door and stalking to the closet, where he changed clothes for what felt like the tenth time that day. He slid on loose pants, again not bothering with a shirt.

When he emerged, she once again startled him by being right in his face.

"For the love of the gods, stop doing that," he griped, stepping around her and heading to the bathroom to brush his teeth.

But, of course, she followed him. "It's not like you have to drink it *from* me," she was saying as he started cleaning his teeth. "I can fill a glass or something."

*Fuck me.*

Because now he was thinking about taking blood directly from her. Again. And instead of making him sick at the thought, it was doing other things.

He spit toothpaste into the sink, trying to ignore her and her words and those fucking curves and the way she'd tasted when he'd kissed her—

"I did it before for Legacy at my estate," she was saying.

Before he knew what he was doing, he turned on her. "Never again," he snarled.

Her eyes were wide, and she took an unsteady step back from him. "Never again what?"

"Never give your blood to another Legacy again."

The room was so silent, he could hear every drip of the faucet.

"I have to give my weekly donation, Axel," she said slowly. Carefully. Clearly trying to avoid whatever had come over him happening again.

He knew it was an irrational demand. No, it was an *impossible* demand in Devram. Fae were required to donate blood weekly to supply the rations. The only way around it was if the Fae was a Source.

"I don't understand it either," she said quietly, moving to put away his toothbrush he must have thrown in his absurd outburst.

"Don't understand what?" Axel ground out, exhaling sharply when her arm brushed against him.

"Why I'm drawn to you and you to me."

"You shouldn't be. I'm not a good person, least of all for you," Axel returned, stalking past her once more.

She scoffed.

Fucking *scoffed*.

That had him rounding on her again. "You disagree?"

"I do," she said, lifting her chin in challenge once more.

"I'm an Arius Legacy."

"And?"

"And…we're not good people," he spluttered.

"Because you make sure I get enough food?"

"What?"

"Or are you not a good person because you let me listen to classical music even though you don't really like it?"

Axel clenched his fists at his sides. "I kill people, Katya, and people—good people—have died because of me," he said, trying to drive the point home.

"If you think I have not witnessed death, you are wrong," she said, and he couldn't believe she wasn't backing down.

He prowled forward. For each step he took, she took one back until he had her caged against the wall. Still she held his gaze, small flames igniting in her eyes.

Winding one of her curls around his finger, he said, "I didn't say I witness death, kitten. I said I *do* the killing."

"Do you enjoy it?" she shot back.

"Sometimes."

That answer had her faltering, and a satisfied smirk curled on his lips until she said, "Someone who wasn't a good person would have lied about that."

He couldn't stop the frustrated growl that crawled up his throat.

"And if you weren't a good person, you wouldn't sleep on the sofa and give me the bed," she went on.

"Maybe I'll sleep in the bed tonight," he retorted.

"That's fine."

"Fine."

"I'm not three, Axel," she said, irritation creeping into her tone now.

"I'm not going to sit here and repeat the same word over and over in some ridiculous bid to have the last word."

Cursing under his breath, he shoved off the wall, and all but stomped to the bed, feeling exactly like the three-year-old she'd just chided him about. He yanked the covers back and slid beneath them before pulling them over himself. A moment later, the rustling of blankets on the other side of the bed had him flipping over.

"What are you doing?" he demanded as she slipped beneath the bedding.

"Going to bed."

"I said I was sleeping in the bed tonight."

"You did, but I never said I wasn't," she replied. "Turn the light off."

Not knowing what to say to her, he clicked the bedside lamp off, plunging the room into darkness.

"You did this on purpose," he said after several minutes, thinking about how thoroughly she'd goaded him into this.

"You were in a foul mood," she replied. "Sleeping on the sofa would have only made it worse."

"How do you figure that?"

"No one likes sleeping on a sofa, Axel," she muttered.

He shifted onto his back, a hand sliding behind his head. Gods, he *had* missed an actual bed. Even at Arius House he had slept on the sofa so she could have the bed.

More minutes had passed when he whispered, "Thank you."

"Only someone attempting to be a good person says 'thank you,'" she murmured.

"Maybe those attempts are futile in the end," he replied.

"Or maybe those attempts are the very thing that make you different from what you believe yourself to be."

# 24

## TESSA

For nearly an hour, Tessa had been debating what she was going to do when Lord Jove got here. Drop to a knee like it was required of the Fae? But she wasn't Fae. Bow at the waist like the Legacy did to the ruling families? But she wasn't a Legacy, even if her mother was one, because her father was a god. So what did that make her? A godling?

Her face scrunched in distaste. If anyone ever called her a godling, she hoped she'd learned to use her magic enough to make sure they never dared say that again. If not, Luka had taught her how to throw a basic punch. That should do.

The thought of Luka had her rubbing at her chest. There hadn't been any time for training since returning from the Underground, and now she was here. She had no real way of defending herself. Although Dagian never made her put bands on. She had expected it when she'd climbed into the vehicle, but she supposed if anyone could counter her power, it would be the Achaz Heir.

The trip to Faven had taken nearly as long as the drive from Dark Haven to Arius House, although the drive hadn't been nearly as scenic. There were no mountains that took her breath away, but the road did keep them near the Wynfell River so that was something, she supposed. The house itself sat on the banks of the Wynfell, just like Rordan's manor outside the Acropolis did. Faven also sat along the northern edge of the Dreamlock Woods, and from the window, Tessa could just make out the eerie silver mist that surrounded the forest. If one managed to make it all the way through the woods, they'd find Sanal, the Serafina Kingdom capital, on the south side of the trees.

They'd only arrived at Achaz House an hour or so ago, and she'd been brought directly to this room to meet with Lord Jove. Low lighting attempted to cast a glow around the room, but no amount of light could make this place warm and homey. The pristine marble walls were as white as the halls in Arius House were black. Everything in this room was white, from the sofa she was perched on to the fireplace to the white rugs. Anything that was accented was done so with gold. Picture frames. Vases of white flowers. The sconces where orbs of light were flickering.

Cautiously, she lifted a hand, that same light flaring at her fingertips so brightly she turned away before clasping her hand closed, trying to snuff it out. Within seconds, it had quieted. Her magic seemed calmer here, easier to manage, but maybe that was simply because it was finally being allowed to exist freely.

The sound of footsteps had her lurching to her feet seconds before Lord Jove entered. Instinctively, she started to lower to a knee, but a chuckle from him had her pausing.

"Lady Aithne was correct at the hearing, my dear," he said, shrugging off his suit jacket and tossing it over the back of a chair. "There is no need to kneel. You are not Fae."

"My apologies," she murmured, her face heating as she straightened and bowed her head instead.

"No need for that either. I am sure adjusting to such a thing is quite the process. It will take a while to form new habits," he said, crossing to a cart across the room. "Would you like some tea?"

"Um, sure. I mean, yes, thank you," she quickly corrected, clasping her hands in front of her.

"I do apologize for keeping you waiting," he went on, the sound of delicate glass gently clinking filled the room. "I was held up in a meeting."

The door opened again, and Tessa spun to find a female entering. Her dark hair was half up with some kind of gold comb. Warm brown eyes swept over Tessa before landing on her Master. In one hand, she held a plate of small sandwiches. In the other was a small box she held out to the Lord.

"I found some in the kitchens," she said.

"Thank you, Dysani," Rordan said, taking the box. Glancing at Tessa, he added, "It's my favorite tea, and my staff cannot keep enough stocked in the various rooms of the house, it would seem."

Not sure what to say, Tessa only gave him a weak smile. Dagian hadn't said much on the drive here. Dex had tried to draw her into conversations here and there, but after the first hour, he stopped when he found her lost in her own thoughts. Dex had brought her here, but couldn't stay, saying he had some things to complete for his lessons the next day.

At first she had been fine by herself. Then her nerves started getting the best of her, thoughts wandering to worst case possibilities, but there was a part of her that was also excited. Someone here had to have answers, or, at the very least, insights. More than that, they could help her control this power.

"Here you are," Rordan said, bringing her a cup of tea himself before motioning for her to sit. Dysani followed, handing him his cup once his hands were free.

"Dagian said your travels here were uneventful?" Rordan said, settling back into an armchair.

Tessa cleared her throat. "Yes. Nothing exciting."

"Dagian also said he did not have to remove your bands?"

"No, but I was surprised he didn't have me wear some for the drive," she admitted.

Rordan smiled. "I assumed your power would need to breathe, but don't worry. He was prepared should your magic have been uncontrollable."

She didn't want to know what that meant.

"How have things been at the Acropolis? Your lessons are going well?"

Tessa was becoming more anxious by the minute. "Yes."

Rordan took a sip of his tea. "And your magic training?"

She hesitated.

"I see," Rordan said. "Not to worry. We will take care of that this week."

"And the testing?" Tessa blurted. She immediately pressed her lips together, inwardly wincing at the impulsive outburst.

"No need to worry about that until later this week," he said with a smile.

Easy for him to say. He wouldn't be the one enduring it.

"But back to your lessons," he continued. "I am assuming you are not being provided any additional instruction?"

"I spend extra hours with Mother Cordelia, but—"

When she hesitated again, Rordan said, "You can speak freely, Tessa."

"I do not find the additional instruction helpful," she finally said.

"And you've told the Arius Heir?"

"He is working on finding a replacement, but he's...busy," Tessa answered.

"I see." He set his tea aside, lifting a hand. There was a swirl of golden mist, and when it dissipated, he held a book. An old book, from what Tessa could tell. When he held it out to her, she blinked at him. "Take it," he said.

Setting her own tea aside, she took it from him. The cover was leather, smooth and worn. She ran her fingers over it before pulling at the leather strap that held it shut. When she flipped open the first page and found another language, she said, "I can't read this."

"You'll learn in time."

Leafing through a few more pages, she paused again, her gaze snapping back to his. "These are Marks."

"Among other things."

"I am not a priestess. I can't..."

"The most powerful can perform the Marks, whether they are a priestess or not," Rordan said. "That now includes you. But that is beside the point. Theon should have given you something similar. All the Legacy are taught such basics."

"They are?" She turned another page, studying the Marks scattered among words she couldn't decipher.

Lord Jove hummed a response. "You can take that one with you for the time being."

"Oh, that's not necessary," she said hastily, closing the book and trying to hand it back to him.

"Of course it is. Wherever you end up in Devram, you will need to know such basics."

"What do you mean 'wherever I end up?'"

"Exactly what I said. It seems your future is yet to be determined."

"And how, exactly, will it be determined?" Tessa asked, unease creeping in.

Lord Jove smiled again as he picked up his tea once more. "That choice, my dear, is up to you."

"You're quiet," Dex said.

They were sitting on the floor at the foot of the bed in the room Tessa had been given for the week. It was just as white and pristine as the rest of the palace. That was what she was calling it now. If Arius House was a castle, Achaz House was a sprawling palace.

"I've never been much of a talker," Tessa said, relishing the cool breeze that was blowing in from the open window.

"That's true, but you never leave a doughnut sitting this long, let alone reduce it to crumbs," he countered with a pointed look.

She only shrugged, picking off another piece of the pastry and rolling it between her fingers.

"It's not the same here, you know," Dex said.

She looked up into his dark eyes. "What do you mean?"

"I mean, I know things are bad in Arius Kingdom, but you can breathe here, Tessie."

"Things aren't— Things don't seem all that different here," she amended.

"Was your time with Lord Jove unpleasant?"

"Not exactly. It was more nerve-racking than anything."

"That's understandable, but he's made several shows of good faith," Dex said. "Me sitting here with you is one of them."

"I guess," she murmured, picking off another piece of doughnut.

"Gods, I hate what he's managed to do to you in a few short months," he spat, his hands clenching where they rested atop his bent knees.

She stiffened. "What do you mean 'do to me?'"

Dex gestured to her, clearly irritated. "You used to talk to me, for starters."

"I am talking to you."

"You're talking to me like you did when we first met."

"When we first met, I was under a set of stairs and told you to fuck off," she said blandly.

Dex shifted, another sign of his growing frustration. "Exactly. How long did it take for you to trust me? And in a few short months, he's undone all of that."

"All of that," she repeated dryly.

"You know what I mean." When she only hummed in answer, he said, "I'm doing the best I can, Tessa."

"What is that supposed to mean?"

"It means while I'm trying to fix this, you seem upset that you're even here. We've hardly spoken since the Selection," he said, his tone hardening with every word.

"How is that my fault?" Tessa demanded.

"That part isn't your fault. There was nothing you could do once you were Selected."

For a few seconds, she could only gape at him. Finding her voice again, she said, "I'm sorry, but are you implying that Theon Selecting me is my fault?"

"You were the one who left the hall. He would have never found you in that alcove if you'd just stayed put."

"He would have... He was already looking for me," she said, trying to comprehend how they were having this conversation.

"And you wandering away made it easier for him to find you," Dex snapped. "You can never just—"

He snapped his mouth shut, but Tessa knew where that was going. Mother's Cordelia's voice rang in her head.

"I can never just *do as I'm told*, right?" she said bitterly.

"That's not what I meant."

"But it's what you were going to say."

"It came out wrong."

"I'm sure it did," she murmured.

Several minutes of silence passed, Tessa continuing to pick at the doughnut. It wasn't even chocolate. It was just a plain doughnut with a sprinkling of sugar that only made her fingers sticky. At least she'd eaten a few of the small sandwiches while she'd been with Lord Jove. While her time with him had indeed been nerve-racking like she'd told Dex, it had also been...interesting. She'd expected him to at least ask *something* about Arius Kingdom, but every question had been about her, her studies, how she was feeling. He never asked if they figured out anything new about her heritage. He never asked how Theon was faring in his tasks. It had been like having tea with... Well, she imagined it was what having tea with an old mentor would be like if she'd ever had such a thing.

"How is Katya?" Dex asked.

"What?" she asked, pulled from her inner contemplation.

"Katya," Dex repeated dryly. "How is she?"

"Fine, I guess," Tessa answered with a shrug. "I don't see her much."

"How do you not see her? Doesn't she stay at the townhouse?"

"Yes, but we're never together during the day. And other than a dinner here and there, we don't see much of each other in the evenings either. But she seems fine," she added with another shrug. "Axel takes care of her."

"I'm sure he does," Dex said with a curl to his lip.

Tessa leveled him with a glare. "Would you rather she not be taken care of? He makes sure she has food and is protected."

"I'm sure that's all he does," he retorted with a pointed look.

"Axel isn't like that," she snapped, and Dex's brows rose.

"Now you're defending them? Next you're going to tell me the dragon cares about you too, when everyone knows everything he does is to make sure Arius Legacy maintain their power," he said with a roll of his eyes.

Tessa bristled, attempting to brush the sugar off her hands a little aggressively. Of course she knew that. Luka's loyalty was to Theon not just because of the Guardian bond, but because he was an Arius descendant. The Sargon line had long been loyal to Arius; it only made sense.

She stilled suddenly.

But *she* was Arius blood too.

More so than Theon and Axel and Valter.

She was Arius's granddaughter if Scarlett was to be believed.

Tessa sank back against the bed, letting that revelation sink in. She didn't know what it meant. Maybe it didn't mean anything at all.

"She passed her exams today, if you wanted to know," Dex said, his tone clipped now.

"Who did?"

"Katya," he answered, not bothering to hide his annoyance now.

"That's great," Tessa said, genuinely happy for her. "But how do you know that?"

"I saw the report while you were with Lord Jove."

She hummed an acknowledgment. It still made absolutely no sense to her that he was given such a high station in the Achaz Lord's home. He'd only been Selected weeks ago, and he moved around this palace as if he had the freedom to do as he wished. And the information he was given access to? None of it seemed right.

"Corbin and Lange?" she asked.

"They also passed."

"That's good."

When she didn't speak for another few seconds, Dex said, "You're not going to bother asking about Oralia and Brecken?"

"You told me about Kat. I assumed you'd tell me about them as well if they passed," she shot back.

"By the gods, you're in a mood tonight."

Her gaze swung to his. "You would be in a mood too if you'd been brought to yet *another* unfamiliar place. And let's not forget the testing I'll be facing while I'm here."

"We're trying to make you more comfortable. It's why I'm here," he argued.

"I don't know what you want me to say, Dex," she said, twisting her fingers together. "I'm bound to be restless and unsure in new surroundings."

"Surely it's better than where you were," he said dismissively. But when she didn't immediately agree, he said, "Right?"

She hesitated, trying to find the words to accurately describe how she was feeling. "I know what to expect there," she finally said.

"You mean you know your place there," he sneered.

"No, I mean I know the control I have there," she bit back.

Dex clicked his tongue, rolling his eyes. "You have no control, Tessa."

She was on her feet in the next breath, fists clamped tightly around the power surging beneath her skin. "You can leave now."

"I didn't mean that," Dex said. He was also on his feet, watching her carefully.

The faint howl of a wolf sounded, and Dex seemed to tense even more.

"I didn't know there were wolves in the Dreamlock Woods," Tessa said, glancing at the open window.

"I guess there are," he said tightly.

The two stared at each other for a long moment before Dex's shoulders sagged, a look of utter defeat coming over his face. "I can't believe he did this in such a short period of time."

"Did what?" she asked, trying to tamp down on her growing irritation.

Dex gestured to the space between them. "Put this distance between us. I've been nothing but there for you since I first saw you at the

Celeste Estate, and yet you spend a few months in Arius Kingdom and we're this."

Guilt surged up, and she looked away, wrapping her arms around herself. "I'm sorry," she murmured. "There's just so much I don't understand. So much I'm trying to figure out. It's overwhelming, and I…" She could feel the tears welling, and she blinked them back.

Dex was pulling her into a hug, a hand smoothing down her hair just like he'd done so many other times. But this hug wasn't comforting like those had been. She wanted it to be. Gods, did she wish this would soothe her the way it always had before. But it did nothing.

Because it wasn't Theon.

And she knew this wasn't the bond because she also knew a hug from Luka or even Axel would be more comforting.

Despite all of that, Dex still knew her. Their years of friendship hadn't been erased, and that had to mean something, right? In the midst of all the change and uncertainty, Dex was right. He was here. He didn't have to be, but here he was, letting her cry into his shirt.

When her soft cries had subsided, Dex leaned back, cupping her chin in his hand and tipping her face up. "You know I only want what's meant for you, right? All I've ever wanted was for you to find your place in this world? To be who you were meant to be?"

"I know," she sniffled. "I'm sorry."

"You're my best friend, Tessa. Do you have any idea what it's been like not being able to talk to you for weeks? Only catching glimpses of you here and there? And when I do get to talk to you, you're short and defensive. I don't know what to do. I'm trying to fix it, but I can only do so much," he said.

"I know," she whispered again. "I can talk to Theon. Try to get more phone calls with you. I bargained for one before; I can do it again."

Dex scoffed. "He doesn't bargain, Tessa. He lies and manipulates to get what he wants."

"You think I don't know that?"

"Do you? Because the way this night has gone?" He gave a dejected sigh. "Maybe it's not my place to meddle any more because I don't know where we stand—"

"We're the same as we've always been," Tessa cut in. The words were spoken out of desperation because so much was changing, and she might not completely trust him, but she wasn't sure she could handle acknowledging he might be right. Not right now. Not in this place without—

"I know you think you've found control there. That he's giving you some semblance of freedom with his deals and promises, but you're smarter than this, Tessa. The Arius Kingdom is ruthless. You truly think he's any different? That any of them are different? You can't tell me he hasn't hurt you, tried to break you."

*I told you there would be harsher consequences. If only I'd known this was all I had to do from the beginning.*

The words echoed in her mind as she remembered clinging to his arm, begging him not to leave her in a dark cellar.

"He's not going to change, Tessa," Dex said softly.

"I'm not trying to change him," she said quickly.

A sad smile lifted on his lips.

"I'm not," she insisted. "He's not mine to change. I'm just trying to survive, and if that means making a bargain with a villain, then so be it."

Dex only shook his head. "Villains don't bargain, Tessie. They take what they want and refuse to settle for anything less."

She looked away from him, worrying her bottom lip as she tried to collect her thoughts.

"I'm fixing this," Dex said. "I promise. I'll fix it like I always do."

"Right," she murmured.

But long after he'd left and she was nestled beneath a soft comforter, her mind was still screaming. She'd never sleep like this. Not with Lord Jove's words and Dex's words replaying in her mind. Not when she was still trying to process the information Scarlett and Sorin had shared. Not when she felt so alone in this giant bed. Not when the quiet was so damn loud.

# 25
## THEON

"This is seriously what we're doing tonight? Again?" Axel groused from the chair.

"I have weeks to figure this all out," Theon retorted. "Instead of being closer, we just have more questions. You could help instead of just sitting there"

He reached for his phone, flipping it over to see the screen.

"Checking it every two minutes won't make it ring," his brother said, reaching to grab a book off the stacks on the low table.

Kat's hand shot out, landing on top of the book he was reaching for. She didn't even look up as she murmured, "Not that one," before sliding another book to him.

Axel shrugged, taking the other book and settling back into his chair. He wouldn't look at Theon as he opened the cover. He hadn't said much to him since their father's visit and that had been two days ago. Yesterday, he'd talked to Tessa for a few minutes in the morning. There had been no report sent as requested, and now it was well into the evening. He could feel her, but her emotions were muted by the distance. There was restlessness and agitation, but also trepidation and intrigue. He couldn't figure out her emotions when she was near, let alone hundreds of miles away.

What wasn't muted was the bond's franticness over being so far away from her. He'd hardly slept more than an hour at a time since she'd left. Legacy didn't need a lot of sleep, but only an hour here and there was going to wear him out sooner rather than later.

"I don't understand why we're looking for something about her mother," Axel said after only a few minutes of leafing through the book. "If her father is a god born after Devram was created, couldn't her mother be the same?"

"Of course she could," Katya said.

"Except Cienna said her mother *may as well* be a goddess. Not that she actually was one," Theon said.

"But the Achaz power has to come from somewhere," Kat replied, finally looking up from her book.

"And the Witch traits need to be taken into account," Theon agreed. "There has to be at least one in her lineage. Her eyes. The way she knows things are going to happen. I don't think she even realizes she can do that yet."

"So she's Arius, Achaz, and Witch?" Axel said doubtfully. "And you expect to find the answers in a book in Devram?"

"Where else do you suggest we look?" Theon asked, rubbing at his brow. "The smallest clue could lead us to the answer."

Axel gave a half shrug, shutting the book and setting it aside. "There's nothing in her file of information? Wouldn't we be more likely to find a clue there?"

"We've read through it multiple times," Theon sighed. "Luka was going through it again last night, but I'm sure he didn't find anything. And if her files were altered, it's pointless anyway."

"We could go talk to the Estate Mother," Axel suggested.

A soft sound came from Katya that had both the males turning to her. When she didn't continue, Axel pressed, "Kat?"

"Sorry," she murmured. "That was inappropriate and disrespectful."

"You think speaking with Cordelia is a bad idea?" Theon asked. "Why? She's known Tessa her whole life. She has to know *something*."

"I shouldn't say anything," Kat replied. "The Falein Estate Mother wasn't someone I would call maternal by any means. None of the other Estate Mothers are either from what I've been told, but Mother Cordelia…"

"You can speak plainly, Kat. You know that," Axel said.

Her hands fell to her lap, where she began wringing them together. "Mother Cordelia was strict and demanding when it came to interacting with the Fae."

"Estate Mothers are not there to coddle the Fae," Theon said. "They are there to make sure they are properly prepared for the Selection and their subsequent assignments."

"Yes, but—" Kat stopped speaking abruptly.

"But what?"

"Nothing. Your statements are correct."

"The Celeste Estate has consistently produced the most powerful Fae, even over the Anala Estate," Theon continued.

Kat nodded, resuming the turning of her pages. "For over two decades."

"Exactly, for the last twenty-three—" Theon sat forward, placing his hand on her book to stop her movements. Axel shifted forward too, his body tensing, but Theon ignored him. "You think it's related to Tessa."

Katya lifted her head, amber eyes meeting his. "I don't believe in coincidences."

"Neither do I." After a few seconds of silence, he said, "Tell me your theories."

"Oh, gods," Axel grumbled. "I need a drink for this."

While Axel left the room to get his alcohol, Theon checked his phone again, cursing at the blank screen.

"I don't have much in terms of theories about that," Kat said, idly turning pages in her book as she spoke. "I was not raised there. I only experienced her for three months of my twenty-two years."

"And you have no ideas as to why you were moved there?"

"*Now* I do," she answered, as if it were obvious. "My power."

"I've seen your file. There was nothing in there about fire or even estimated power levels," Theon countered. "How would she have known?"

"Exactly. How is she consistently producing the most powerful Fae? Sure, the other estates have a few every Selection Year, but to always have the most?"

"It's not coincidence," Theon said.

"It's not."

"Who was moved there before you?"

"Corbin. Before him, it was Lange. Brecken. Oralia. Dex. Before Dex, it was harder to track. Tessa told me those. I don't know that she really paid attention or cared before that. But there were a few Fae taken *from* the estate. Dade, for example, when he was tagged to be Prudence's Source. Then he was moved to the Falein Estate."

"In the hopes that he was one of the more powerful?" Theon mused.

"That was my assumption. I know he endured intense testing," Katya answered.

That wasn't surprising. All the potential Sources did.

"How was Cordelia different from the Falein Estate Mother?"

"The Celeste Estate was just…harsher, maybe? I don't know how to explain it. Mother Cordelia had her favorites, and the restrictions were stricter for some more than others. It took a few weeks to figure out where I stood."

"And Tessa?"

"Was not a favorite."

Theon hadn't realized his darkness had appeared until Kat edged away from him a little. "What did she do to her?" he asked tightly.

"It's really not my place."

"It's not a request at this point, Katya."

Her eyes darted to the door. "Understood, but I would like to wait for Axel, please."

It annoyed him, but Theon nodded, checking his phone again. He'd already tried calling the number she'd called from yesterday.

He'd tried twice.

The door opened, and Axel walked in. Luka was behind him, each with two drinks in hand. Luka handed one to Theon, while Axel passed one to Kat.

"When did you get back?" Theon asked Luka.

"A bit ago," he answered, grabbing a book before taking the chair opposite Axel.

The bond shifted, guilt but also satisfaction drifting down it, and again Theon flipped his phone over.

"He's here, Katya. Tell me about Cordelia," he said.

"Tessa can be…impulsive, especially when she's upset or— Well, you know," Kat said, fiddling with the hem of her shirt.

"What is this about, Theon?" Axel asked, his voice hard as he watched Katya.

"We were discussing the powerful Fae coming from the Celeste Estate, and she mentioned Cordelia had favorites. Tessa was the opposite," Theon replied.

"What did she do to her?" Luka asked, his tone tinged with a growl.

A growl Theon felt down the bond that had his head snapping to Luka, sapphire eyes already fixed on him.

Luka gave him a pointed look before he turned back to Katya. "What did Cordelia do to Tessa?"

"This should really come from Tessa herself," she said, worrying her bottom lip.

"She's not here, so it looks like you're going to have to tell me," Theon replied.

"Don't be a dick," Axel snapped.

"What didn't she do? She found any reason to reprimand Tessa," Katya finally said. "And if there wasn't a reason, she created one. She knew how to manipulate her, make her frustrated so she'd lose that control. Then she'd punish her for being reckless. Told her it was training because she wouldn't be able to lose control when she was assigned to a kingdom. Why do you think she eats like she does? The Estate Mother would withhold food, sometimes for days at a time. Other times she gave her just stale bread and broth."

"Other times? How often did this happen?" Theon asked.

Kat shrugged. "I don't know. I was only there three months, but in those months, at least four times."

"She's twenty-four years," Axel said. "Even when she aged out of adolescence?"

"She was raised there," Luka said, his features hard. "Tessa didn't know any different, and on top of that, she was probably at a point where fighting back wasn't worth it."

"When she argued, she would disappear for days at a time. Brecken told me there was a cupboard in her office," Katya said quietly, twisting fabric around her fingers.

"A cupboard," Luka repeated. Vertical pupils snapped back to Theon. "Did you know?"

"No," Theon said, shaking his head.

"Do not fuck with me right now, Theon. Did you know?"

"No," Theon bit back. "I didn't know about the cupboard until after. I wouldn't have—"

"Yes, you would have," Luka cut in.

Katya cleared her throat. "There are rumors she lost control once, and some Fae died. I've tried to find incident reports, but never found anything."

"That can't be true," Axel said. "That kind of news would have traveled, even to Arius Kingdom."

Katya met Theon's gaze again when she said, "Not if she knew what

Tessa was this whole time."

"You think Cordelia is the one who altered her files?" Theon asked. "She could lose everything. That is a death sentence."

"And if Cordelia knew, she would have known it would be revealed at the Emerging Ceremony," Axel said.

"That's true," Kat sighed, pushing hair back from her face. "I don't—"

But the phone ringing cut her off as Theon snatched it off the arm of the sofa.

"Tessa?"

"Hi," came her tired voice.

"Are you all right? Is everything okay?"

"I'm fine, Theon. Just tired."

He'd pushed to his feet, beginning to pace around the room. "What did you do today?"

"Nothing much. Some instruction with my power. I was shown around Faven."

"That's it?" Theon asked. Why in the realms did Lord Jove want her to come to Faven just to show her around the capital city?

"Mhmm," she hummed, a rustling sound coming down the line.

"What are you doing?"

"Sitting outside."

"So there were no assessments today?" Theon asked.

"No. Just a dinner with Rordan this evening," she said with a yawn.

*Rordan.*

Theon's lip curled at the casual use of the name.

"Why are you so tired?"

"I don't sleep well here," she answered quietly.

"That makes two of us," Theon muttered.

There was silence for a long moment, and he wandered out to the balcony, pulling the doors closed behind him.

"Tessa?"

"Hmm?" she murmured, sounding like she was half-asleep already.

"Did Cordelia routinely withhold food from you?"

He could feel the tense silence through the phone before she said, "Who told you that?"

"Is it true?" When the seconds ticked by and she didn't answer, he pressed, "Tessa?"

"Is Luka there? I want to talk to him again."

"Again?"

"I mean I want to talk to him."

"I'm assuming we don't have much time. I think it'd be better for both of us to talk to each other," he said evenly.

"You mean better for the bond," she countered.

"No, I mean for you. Maybe it would help you sleep better."

"Everything is so white here," she murmured. "There's no room for darkness."

"Tessa."

"I know, I know. The balance," she muttered.

"I wasn't…going to say anything about that."

"Oh."

"Have you had any dreams lately?"

"What kind of dreams?"

"Any odd ones?"

"Only the same one of you killing me," she said around another yawn.

"What?"

"I have to go."

"Tessa—"

"I'll talk to you tomorrow sometime."

The line went dead, and he was left staring at the blank phone screen yet again.

Theon turned, going back into the room. Katya and Axel were gone, but Luka was still sitting there, sipping on his drink and looking through a book.

"Want to tell me why I can feel your anger down this godsdamn bond?" Theon asked, the balcony door snicking shut behind him.

"Want to tell me why you thought there weren't any repercussions for bringing me in on her last Source Mark?" he shot back casually, flipping a page.

"How long?"

"Since that night."

"You can feel her too," Theon said, not asking.

"Yes."

"And the reason you didn't say anything is because…?"

Luka finally met his gaze. "I didn't know if you two were feeling it as well or if it was just me."

"Does it matter?"

"Tessa is already struggling. I didn't want to add to it," Luka answered.

Theon nodded, tapping his fingers against his thigh. "And you can feel my emotions?"

"Sometimes. When they're strong enough. But mainly hers."

"What are we going to do?"

Luka sent him a dry look. "What do you mean, 'what are we going to do?' We can't even figure out how to *end* the Source bond, let alone what to do when another is involved. We have enough shit to figure out. This can wait."

Theon shoved a hand through his hair. He didn't *want* to end the Source bond. His entire goal was to *keep* Tessa, not sever his bond. If the only repercussion was Luka being able to feel their emotions, that wasn't the be-all end-all.

"I found something earlier tonight," Luka said, pulling Theon back to the discussion at hand.

"What?" Theon asked distractedly.

"In Tessa's files."

That had his full attention.

Reaching for Theon's tablet on the table, Luka pulled up her files in the database before coming to stand beside him. He pointed to the bottom of the screen where the Lilura Inquest logo was at the bottom. It was on every screen because they were the tech company that stored all the data.

"Son of a bitch," Theon cursed, taking the tablet and enlarging the logo. "That fucking son of a bitch."

Standing outside the towering building, Theon held Tessa's phone to his ear, exchanging a dark look with Luka. After the third ring, a male voice answered.

"Hey, Fury."

"How do you know her number?" Theon demanded.

There was an extended silence, and Theon smirked to himself for finally getting the upper hand on Tristyn Blackheart.

Until he answered in the same arrogant voice he always used.

"My company controls the cellular data. Of course, I know her number."

"But it's listed under my name," Theon countered.

"A line that was set up days after the Selection?"

The muscle in Theon's jaw ticked in frustration. His hand tightening around the phone, he said, "I'm outside. Tell your people to let me up."

"You don't make demands here, Arius Heir," Tristyn replied, sounding utterly bored.

"You will let me up, or I'm prepared to drag your company into this conspiracy surrounding Tessa."

"What the fuck are you talking about?"

"Not only does your company control cellular data, it houses all of Devram's most important information. Tessa's files were clearly tampered with, and you've suddenly become fine with being recognized in public after decades of reclusiveness," Theon said.

"That is ridiculous," Tristyn scoffed in annoyance. "No one is going to believe you. My company's reputation speaks louder than the accusations of a desperate heir."

"This isn't for me, you arrogant ass," Theon hissed into the phone. "It's for her."

"She's in Faven. Is everything all right?"

Of course he knew she was in Faven. Everyone knew his Source was gone for a week.

"Let me up, Blackheart."

There was a heavy sigh on the other end. "Fine. You have thirty minutes."

Theon nodded to Luka, and the two of them entered the building. They were met by a sentinel who escorted them to a side room, where they were both required to sign in with their magical signatures to prove there were no glamours being used. Then they were taken to an elevator where two other sentinels rode the lift with them to the top floor.

When they stepped off the elevator, they were met by a female Legacy. She was taller with sharp features, and there was no smile to greet them, let alone a bow for an heir. Her dark hair was cut to her chin, and her steel-blue eyes looked them over heavily before she said, "This way."

They followed her down a hall before she pushed open a door to a corner office where Tristyn Blackheart sat behind his desk, three computer monitors along one wall. He closed his laptop as they entered, nodding at the female, who closed the door behind her as she left.

"Your thirty minutes started the second you stepped off that elevator," Tristyn said, getting to his feet and rounding the desk. He leaned against it, crossing his arms, waiting.

"You honestly expect me to believe you had nothing to do with altering her files?" Theon demanded, getting straight to the point.

"No," Tristyn said simply.

"So you did alter them?"

"I didn't say that. I said I don't expect you to believe me."

"How else would they have been altered?" Luka asked.

"That's a good question. One I haven't been able to find an answer to," he replied.

"Convenient," Theon said dryly.

"Not particularly," Tristyn replied with a shrug.

"And yet you don't seem too concerned."

"I am more than concerned, but if you think I have access to all the files, you're delusional. The company was hired to create a program that no one could access. I had to prove that *I* couldn't even access it before they were satisfied," Tristyn said.

"So who can access them?" Luka asked.

"Each Lord and Lady has a network, and there is one shared network among them. So I guess the answer is *you*," he replied with a pointed look at Theon.

"I've never heard of these networks," Theon replied tightly.

"You honestly expect me to believe that?" Tristyn parroted.

With a frustrated huff, Theon slid his hands in his pockets, taking in the office. A conference table off to the side with seating for eight. His desk with two chairs before it. Floor-to-ceiling windows on two sides overlooking the Acropolis.

Finally, Theon asked, "Do you have access to information on the Estate Mothers?"

"I do."

"I want everything you have on Cordelia."

Tristyn clicked his tongue. "That's not how this works, Arius Heir. I'll need something in exchange."

"Like what?" Theon bit out.

"A trip to the Underground."

Theon blinked in shock. "For what?"

"That's my business. Everything I can find on Cordelia, the Celeste Estate Mother, in exchange for a one-day unaccompanied trip to the Underground. Do we have a bargain?" Tristyn asked, holding out his hand.

"It's an accord," Theon replied, slapping his hand into his. The prickling sensation above the crook of his elbow told him he'd find the Bargain Mark there when he changed tonight.

Rounding his desk, Tristyn opened his laptop once more, the three monitors coming to life. Theon couldn't keep up with the male as he entered codes and passwords in various programs. Theon and Luka said nothing as he worked, though Theon checked his phone again, not knowing when Tessa would call today.

The knock on the door had the two of them turning, but Tristyn never looked away from his screen.

"Yes, Maggie?"

The female who'd met them at the elevator pushed the door open. She glanced at Theon and Luka before she said, "There are reports of wolves in the Dreamlock Woods."

Tristyn's only response was a hummed acknowledgment before she shut the door once more.

"Is there significance to that?" Theon asked when he continued to do whatever it was he was doing.

"There is."

"And what will the cost be for that information?" Theon asked darkly.

"Nothing," Tristyn said with a shrug. "They're not mine."

"Then why are they important?"

"They're hers," he said simply before shutting his laptop once more. "I sent everything over to you. It's encrypted and coded to your magical signature in the system. Only you will be able to open the files."

"And the wolves?" Theon asked.

"What about them?"

"Their significance?"

"The Dreamlock Woods is not known for its wildlife," Tristyn said.

"Because of the magic that inhabits it," Luka cut in.

"Exactly," Tristyn said, coming around his desk once more. "Since you're here, I've heard you're looking for a new private instructor for Tessa."

"It will not be you," Theon said sharply.

"We'd never get anything done with all that drinking and pizza-eating," Tristyn said with a smirk. "But I do have a suggestion. I will send her to you for an interview."

"Fine," Theon said tightly, not that he'd hire anyone recommended by Tristyn Blackheart at this point.

The door opened, the female somehow knowing they were done here. Theon turned to follow Luka out.

"St. Orcas," Tristyn called, making Theon pause and look back over his shoulder.

Something about him had shifted. His entire demeanor seemed darker, more menacing.

Wicked.

"Threaten me again like you did today, and your brother will be the new Arius Heir," he went on with a smile that was anything but pleasant.

"You think you can kill me?" Theon asked with a sneer, his darkness pooling at his feet.

Tristyn only turned around and went back to his computer, opening the laptop back up. "Destruction or salvation. The choice is yours," he answered. "Get out."

His phone rang, pulling his attention away, and when he found the number Tessa had been calling from flashing on the screen, he walked away from Tristyn.

"Tessa?"

"Hi."

"I'm about to go into an elevator. The connection might be bad for a second."

"Where are you?"

"Lilura Inquest."

There was a small gasp. "You went to see Tristyn? Why?"

He waited to answer until he was off the elevator. "How do you know I went to see him?" he asked, stepping back outside.

"Why else would you go there?"

"It's a huge tech company," he answered.

She hummed a reply.

"You're calling early today."

"Yep."

"Everything going all right?"

"I guess."

"Tomorrow is the halfway point."

"Great," she muttered.

"Are you getting enough to eat and everything?"

She sighed. "Yes, Theon. They're feeding me and bathing me and everything. Taking good care of your pet."

"That's not what I—"

"Is Luka nearby?"

Theon glanced at his friend, who was watching him with his arms crossed. He arched a brow.

"He's here," Theon answered.

"Can I talk to him?"

Without a word, he held the phone out to Luka. He took it stiffly, bringing it to his ear.

"Hello?"

There was a pause while she spoke. A long pause that had Theon bristling at the fact she could hardly muster two words for him, yet could apparently give a small speech to Luka.

"I think that's a reasonable assumption," Luka said before pausing again. "No, don't do that—" Another pause. "Tessa—" A pause, followed by a long sigh. "Can you not wait until you're back for that?" Another pause. "Yes, I will... No... For fuck's sake, Tessa. I already said yes."

There was another pause, and then, with an irritated huff, he handed the phone back to Theon.

"Tessa—" he started.

"I had a dream last night," she announced.

"...what kind of dream?"

"Yesterday you asked if I'd had any dreams. I did."

"What was it about?" he asked, trailing Luka to their vehicle.

"Felicity."

Theon tripped on nothing, stumbling a bit. "Why would you dream about Felicity?"

"I don't know. You were..."

"I was what?"

"Nothing. It's nothing."

"Tessa—"

"I have to go."

The line went dead, and Theon lowered his phone to his lap. He didn't know when he'd climbed into the vehicle.

"What happened?" Luka asked, waiting to back out of their parking spot.

"I should ask you the same thing. What the fuck was that about?"

"Her training," Luka answered simply, putting the vehicle in reverse.

"It sounded like it was more than that."

His phone rang again, and when his eyes dropped to the screen, he thought he might lose his lunch.

*Felicity.*

*Tessa knows*, he realized.

Or at the very least, she suspected.

It was why she'd never asked about his Match contract.

Godsdammit.

# 26

## TESSA

Taking a deep breath, Tessa focused on her light, pulling it back into herself. Energy still crackled. She could feel it at her fingertips, still straining.

"No," the instructor said. "Let that go. Focus on the light for now."

That was easy for her to say. She was an Achaz Legacy. Some cousin or something of Rordan who had trained Dagian in his magic. But an Achaz Legacy didn't have all her abilities.

They couldn't make it rain indoors.

Or summon a storm.

She winced as her power flared, then her eyes flew open at the sound of Dagian cursing.

"It's going well, I see," the heir said tightly, his arms crossed while he toed at a small crack that had appeared in the stone floor of the training chamber.

"I lost my focus," Tessa muttered, flexing her fingers where her palms still glowed faintly. Her gaze darted to Dex, who was keeping watch near the door, instructed to only let certain people into the space.

"Clearly," Dagian deadpanned.

"We all know playing with our magic is different from *using* it," Rordan said, all of them turning as the Lord strode through the heavy stone door, Dysani behind him. After her first day here, she only saw the Lord at dinners. Never during her training or the tours of Faven.

The instructor bowed at the waist, and Tessa immediately lowered her gaze, clasping her hands tightly in front of her.

"She needs a reason to use it. Control it," Rordan continued, coming to a stop beside his son.

Tessa frowned a little. "I have a reason to control it. I don't want to hurt anyone with it."

"And that's admirable," Rordan said with a smile. "But Legacy power is power of the gods. It needs to be used. It demands it. Surely you feel that?"

"Yes, but…" She trailed off, feeling her magic beneath her skin.

Restless.

Excited.

Seeking.

"What do you think our power is?" Rordan asked, his light flaring, slithering out from him the same way Theon's darkness did. It coiled, snaking up the walls of the chamber as though it were golden vines. Bright white flowers of pure light bloomed, glowing like the orbs in all the sconces in the palace.

It was beautiful.

"I don't know," Tessa answered.

"All the power of the gods comes from Chaos," Rordan said.

"The gods came from the Chaos," Tessa said.

"Ah, they came from it, yes. But so did their gifts. And the Firsts? They are Chaos themselves," Rordan said. "That same power trickles down in their offspring. Diluted, of course, especially in the case of the Legacy. The mortal blood weakens the Chaos. It is why we are so particular about our Matches."

Tessa frowned. She knew why the Legacy, especially the ruling families, were so strategic with Matches. They wanted to erase the mortal blood from their lineage as much as possible.

"But even with all our plans, the mortal lineage remains, and thus, Legacy will forever be at a disadvantage," Rordan went on.

*At a disadvantage?*

It took everything in her not to laugh at such an absurd statement.

But he sent her another knowing smile. "You think I am delusional saying such a thing, but think of this, Child. The gods designed the Fae. They are magical beings. All magical beings, including the Fae, have Chaos. It is where power comes from, but the Fae?" He gestured to where Dysani and Sasha stood to the side of their Masters. "If no mortal blood enters their line, they do not have a weakness, do they?"

"They are still not descendants of the gods," Tessa argued. "Even the original demigods the Legacy descended from had to be more powerful than the Fae. They were direct descendants of a god or goddess."

"That is correct," Rordan conceded. "But, if the Legacy continue to reproduce with mortals, the Fae continue to reproduce with other Fae, who will eventually become more powerful? And if two powerful Fae have children? It is the Chaos in your blood that determines how strong your gifts are."

"Forgive me, but I don't understand where this lesson is going," Tessa said, working to tamp down on her frustration. She was here to learn how to control this power, not receive a history lesson on the Legacy. At least not *now*. Couldn't this be the dinner conversation tonight?

"It matters because Chaos is drawn to power itself. The more powerful one is, the more they crave it. Chaos always wants more, and you are powerful, my dear," Rordan said, his light reaching for her and causing her own power to tremble in anticipation.

It was too much. She couldn't stop it as it responded, spilling out of her and racing to the power that was calling. But where she had no control, Rordan had complete control. In a blink, all traces of his power vanished, leaving only her light, crackling with flashes of energy and sparks of power in the chamber.

"Tell me a time you've had the most control over your gifts," Rordan said, eyeing her lingering magic. He wasn't wary of it. There was no concern or tension, but fascination and satisfaction as he walked among her light.

"I've never had control over it," she answered, trying to pull her magic back.

"I don't think that's true," Rordan said knowingly. "The night of the Emerging Ceremony?"

"That was not control," Tessa said.

"And yet you used it to protect an Arius Heir," he countered.

"I didn't—"

But she had.

Sentinels had been coming for her. For Axel. She'd thrown them backwards. Just like she'd done to Theon and Axel in a parking lot.

She'd had control over it by the river too. The first time the Augury had attacked. Sure, the bands had been on, but she also hadn't *wanted* to fight back that night. Luka had been right. She hadn't cared if she lived or met her end, and her power had followed suit.

And when the Augury had attacked last time in the training arenas? She'd *used* it that night. She'd known exactly what to do, exactly how to wield it. But she'd also given herself over to her magic, completely lost to it. She'd let her magic have control, and that was not what she wanted.

"You use it when you need to protect yourself," Rordan said, somehow closer to her. "Whether that threat is physical or emotional. It is why when you are angry, it appears. Our power is connected to our emotions. It feels what we feel, and it will do whatever it must to protect you both. It is why our Chaos is drawn to more like it. Because the more power one has, the better one can protect themselves."

"So I will only be able to control it when I'm threatened?" she asked, not liking the sound of that.

"No, but I think that will be the best way for you to learn."

Her eyes went wide as she took a step back from him, remembering exactly what his power felt like coursing through her body. Then she downright panicked when Lord Jove said, "Dagian?"

The heir stepped forward, a smirk on his face, and all Tessa could think about was the assessment where he'd attacked her, berated her, and kept her on her knees in pain.

"No," she said, shaking her head, her magic already swelling in response to her sudden trepidation.

"Would you rather it be a Fae?" Rordan asked. "Start with less power? Dex?"

"No!" Tessa gasped, her gaze darting to where he was standing stoically off to the side. He sent her a grim look.

"Proceed then," Rordan said, gesturing to Dagian, who already had power pooling in his palm.

"Just wait!" Tessa cried. "Wait! Please!"

But there was no waiting.

Power slammed into her, sending her flying. She landed on her back with the air forced from her lungs the same way she always ended up when training with Luka. She coughed, trying to catch her breath.

Dex's voice carried over to her. "Let your power protect you, Tessa."

But she didn't want to give her power control. Theon wasn't here to bring her back from that place, and the longer she stayed there, the more she'd lose of herself.

More pain hit her, vibrating through her veins, her bones, her soul.

"Stop!" she gasped. "I'll try harder."

"It's never enough though, is it?" Dagian asked, appearing in her line of vision as he stood over her. His head cocked to the side. "You can try and try, but you'll never be enough. Maybe it's best you remain a Source. Then at least *someone* can control that power in your blood."

"I just need more time," she gasped again, pushing onto her hands and knees.

Dagian lowered to a crouch beside her, his voice going low. "You know when you become the most desperate? When I attack those you think care about you."

"They do care about me," she hissed, light flickering in her hands.

"Some do. Some don't. How can you tell the difference? How can you tell who is using you and who is trying to save you?"

"Save me? From what?"

The smile Dagian gave her was chilling when he leaned in closer to whisper in her ear, "Yourself."

Then she was screaming as his power coiled around her, biting into her skin, clawing at her.

"I need to see your power, Tessalyn," Dagian was saying, more of his magic flooding through her.

"Stop!" she cried. "Please!"

There was no one here to save her. No one was coming. Dex wouldn't do anything. Theon *couldn't* do anything. Rordan wanted this. It was why she was here. To see the extent of her abilities.

"Tessa! Let your power fight back! You can't do it yourself!" Dex was yelling at her, but it was Luka's voice echoing in her mind.

*Start fighting for yourself.*

*Fight back.*

But she didn't know how.

No one had taught her how to fight back. She'd only been taught to submit. To be less than she was. To shove all that she was down—all of her light into the dark—so that someone else could shine.

She'd only been told she wasn't enough.

Too wild.

Too impulsive.

Too much of a hassle.

Uncontrollable.

So she became what was expected of her, and she let her power out. All of it.

And this wasn't like in the training chambers when she'd submitted to her power, letting it take what it wanted. This was her calling on her magic, dragging it up from the depths of her being. Every wild and untamed piece of her.

This was *her* whispering to her power and telling it to take what she was owed.

She felt Dagian's magic strike out at her again, but it slammed into a wall of her own power. Lifting her head, Dagian's face paled as she smiled at him. She was still on her knees, and she lifted a hand before slamming it to the ground. Lightning skittered out from her palm, bouncing along the floor, a fissure appearing. Light flared before golden mist started floating up.

"Father?" Dagian called, unease in his voice as he took a step back from her, then another.

She pushed to her feet, that crack widening as she kicked off the shoes she'd been wearing, the stone floor cool beneath her bare feet. With another thought, light was arching from her palm. It didn't slam into Dagian though. It wound around him before dragging him forward, his feet scrambling for purchase while he cried out in dismay.

When he was directly in front of her, she tilted her head, studying him. Her voice held that eerie ring to it when she said, "Is this what you wanted to see, Dagian?"

"Yes," he said, straining against the hold of her power.

She could feel his magic struggling too, pushing against her light, and a moment later, he was bellowing a curse as she sent lightning into her power coiled around him.

"Enough!" he snarled. "Father!"

But she put a hand over his mouth, his golden eyes widening in shock. "No one answers my calls for help," she said simply. "You don't get to scream for aid."

"I think that is enough for today, Tessa," came Rordan's voice. It was calm, but full of demand and order, and she turned to him, her eyes narrowing.

Dex was at his side, a small smile on his lips. "You did well, Tessie."

"No thanks to you," she retorted.

"This was for you," he replied, studying her magic still wrapped around Dagian.

"What does that mean?"

"It means you needed to know what you are capable of," Rordan said, his own power appearing and slowly snaking forward once more. "You needed to understand the full depth of your gifts. I suspect there is more to them," he added, his gaze dropping to the fissure in the ground, "But this will do for now. You can release him."

"Release him?" she repeated, her power only tightening around Dagian, making him grunt in pain.

"Tessie," Dex coaxed, reaching a hand out to her. "Let him go. You did beautifully. I'm so proud of you."

She stared at him for a long moment, not sure what to do with his words. The entire chamber was tense. Dysani was circling, preparing to protect her Master. Sasha was fretting, not yet forced to fight for Dagian, but feeling her bonded in trouble. The instructor was standing off to the side, something Tessa couldn't make out clenched in her hand.

"You are powerful, Tessa, but I am still more so," Rordan said, his power slowly flowing over hers like a blanket. It wrapped around her magic, gently prying it back from his son. "We still have a few days left together. You can decide if they will be beneficial to you or uncomfortable."

She pushed out a long breath, letting him guide her power back. It felt wrong. Nothing like when Theon would guide her magic. The bond thrashed at the thought. She'd been able to keep it subdued while here, the daily phone calls doing little to abate the discomfort of being so far from him. But in the end, Rordan was right. He was still more powerful than she was.

But as her power sank back into her, she could feel something else. Something that seemed to be waiting for her to call. Something more than her magic settling, content to let everyone believe it had been contained.

So for now, she'd let them tell her pretty words. For now, she'd let them believe her to be compliant.

Because she was learning secrets here, and there was more to discover.

"Breathe, Tessie," Dex said, slinging an arm around her shoulders and giving her a squeeze.

"Right. Breathe," she repeated, trying to suck in a breath. She felt like Mother Cordelia was here withholding her air. Each inhale was too short.

Dex looked down at her with a frown. "You're going to hyper-ventilate."

"You know what these are like," she said, feeling the sweat break out at her brow and the nape of her neck.

She'd worked more with her magic that morning. It'd been a little easier after that time in the training chamber two days ago. Releasing her power on Dagian had taught her how to summon it. It had shown her where to go to find it. Now she just needed to learn how to release it in small amounts. Right now, it was like plunging a bucket into a well when all she wanted was a few drops.

"This will be different. I'll be here the whole time," Dex said.

Tessa didn't answer, scratching at the skin where the IV was in her hand. It wasn't even hooked up to anything. It was there just *in case*. This did seem different, but he wasn't the one undergoing it. Normally they gave her something to make her less *resistant*, but her power was flickering. It was feeling the same apprehension she was and preparing to protect her, just like Rordan had said it would.

"Can I have some water or something?" she rasped, attempting to force her lungs to expand more.

"Of course," Dex said, motioning to a Fae to fetch some.

"You give other Fae orders now?" she asked, moving to the window and pushing it open.

"I don't want to leave you alone right now."

She didn't say anything else as small raindrops fell, and she stuck her hand out the window, hoping the cool water would ground her some.

It didn't.

Two more days.

That's what she found herself thinking.

Two more days, and she could go—

Tessa sucked in a sharp breath. That wasn't home.

*He* wasn't home.

She jolted at the sound of the door, spinning around to find Lord Jove and a female striding in, Dysani a step behind.

The new female was hauntingly beautiful. Tall and willowy, she had pale skin and raven hair that was braided into a simple plait over her shoulder, strands of something gold woven into it. Her gold gown swished on the floor as she moved, and the gold bangles on her wrists clinked lightly with every step. Bright violet eyes landed on her, and a smile curled on her lips.

A priestess.

Instinctively, Tessa shrank back as they came to a stop in front of them. Dex bowed deeply, which she probably should have done too, but it was suddenly far too difficult to breathe again.

"Good morning, Tessa," Rordan said warmly, extending a glass of water to her. "I was told you requested something to drink."

She swallowed thickly, her throat too dry, taking the glass from him with a trembling hand.

"Thank you, my Lord," she whispered, her power flickering again as if in warning.

Rordan only smiled.

"Let me introduce you to Elowyn," he said, gesturing to the priestess.

"The Source who is not Fae," Elowyn said, her voice as melodic as any other priestess. "I've heard much about you."

Tessa smiled weakly.

Elowyn's lips turned down in a small frown. "You are anxious. That is understandable."

She said nothing, and Dex reached to take the glass of water from her. She hadn't taken a single sip.

"Elowyn is the Head Priestess here in Faven," Rordan said. "While she works mainly for the Achaz Kingdom, she is the most powerful of the Zinta line and is often consulted by all the kingdoms on matters that pertain to the entire realm."

"Like me," Tessa said warily.

"This is nothing to be concerned with, my dear," he went on, reaching around Dex to take her hand and tug her forward.

"With all due respect, my Lord, you are wrong."

He chuckled softly. "I understand the trepidation. Past assessments were undoubtedly uncomfortable."

"And this will not be?" she asked as he led her to a sofa.

"Not as it was before," he replied, guiding her to take a seat.

What did that mean?

"Your previous assessments were attempts to assess what element you would emerge with," Elowyn said. "Knowing what we know now, we can adjust our methods to make this more comfortable for you."

"You'll be fine, Tessie," Dex said, a hint of irritation in his tone. "It's not like you're by yourself like we were for the assessments at the estate."

"Right," she murmured, her knee beginning to bounce. She glanced up at Rordan. "Will I be able to speak with Theon afterwards?"

"Of course, my dear," he answered. "I know the bond will be a comfort for you."

"Hopefully soon that will no longer be an issue," Dex added, his mouth pressed into a thin line.

Elowyn reappeared. Tessa wasn't even sure where she'd gone and what she'd been doing, but she held a cup of tea in her hand. Extending it to her, she said, "All you need to do is drink, Tessalyn."

Tessa took the cup, wrapping her hands around it. The cup itself was hot, but her magic flared, providing a barrier.

"That's it?" she asked, looking down at the liquid. Scents of orange and cinnamon and an underlying sweetness. Her gaze snapped to the Achaz Lord. "This is the same tea you gave me when I arrived here. The tea I've been drinking every night."

"So it is," he agreed.

"What's in it? And what is the purpose of this?" she asked, lifting her hand with the capped IV catheter.

"Only a precaution. Drink, Tessie," Dex interrupted, looking pointedly at the cup. It was more than a hint of irritation. Now it was flat out annoyance, and something inside her snapped at the utter dismissiveness of his words.

The teacup in her hand shattered, shards flying. Energy crackled before a stream of light crashed into Dex's chest, shoving him back. His eyes went wide before they flashed to something *angry*. But that was fine. She was just as furious.

"I get to ask questions, Dexter," she seethed, pushing to her feet and stalking towards him. She didn't even know what she was doing. Only that energy was coiling in her hand before it was unfurling into a whip of raw lightning. Light pooled in her other hand, white embers dancing among it. She could feel the frenzy of her magic pushing her to take more.

"She's right," Rordan said calmly, and Tessa's gaze whipped to him. Dysani was before him, a dagger of ice in her hand, prepared to protect her Master. Elowyn was at his side, but she didn't seem fazed in the slightest. "What have I said from the beginning? This is for you more than it is for us. You deserve to know what you are capable of. Where you come from. Who you are meant to be."

Her eyes narrowed, her power creeping towards him now. Dysani tensed, another ice dagger appearing in her other hand.

"I've been waiting for this moment," Rordan continued. "I was beginning to fear it wouldn't come."

"What moment?" Tessa asked, her voice hard and ringing with the power she could feel still building.

"The moment when you realized you were meant to *take*," Rordan said. "You want answers? The tea you've been drinking is more than tea. There is an elixir in it. One that was preparing you to find those answers you seek."

Tessa looked at the floor, at the pieces of shattered glass she hadn't even realized she was stepping on with her bare feet.

Just like in a wine cellar when she hadn't realized there was glass in her skin.

"Fetch more, will you, Elowyn?"

The priestess moved to a table filled with items Tessa hadn't noticed before.

"I do not wish to drink it," Tessa said.

"Tessa, it will—" Dex started, but Rordan lifted a hand to silence him.

"You do not have to, Tessa," the Achaz Lord said.

"I...don't?" she asked, her magic faltering in confusion.

"Of course not," he answered. "If you do not wish to face those answers just yet, that is perfectly understandable. Truth is tricky business."

Her brow furrowed. "There should be nothing tricky about truth. It is facts."

"Ah, but facing truths? That is where the difficulty lies. And deciding what to do with those truths? That is the greatest burden of all, isn't it?" the Lord said, his power slowly surrounding hers once more. "That is what keeps so many from seeking truth. There are choices that come with learning it."

"Choices?" Tessa repeated.

"What will you do with the information you learn?" Rordan asked. "Will you embrace it? Or fight it? And at what cost?"

"I don't…"

She didn't get choices. She didn't even know how to make them. Someone had always made them for her. Mother Cordelia. A priestess. Dex. Theon.

"Are you saying you are going to let me decide?" Tessa finally asked.

"But, of course," he answered as his power placated her own.

"And if I don't believe you?" she asked, lifting her chin.

"That is also your choice."

The magic disappeared, the light and energy dissipating into nothing as she held the Lord's golden gaze. "The tea. What will it do?"

"Let your magic do what it is meant to do. Be what it was meant to be."

"Will it burn? Like the tonic for the Marks?"

"No, Child," Elowyn answered, approaching with a fresh cup. "But I think you will find it will help make your choices easier."

The Priestess extended the cup to her, and once more Tessa tentatively took it from her. "It will be my choice?" she repeated.

"Would you like me to make a Blood Vow with you?" Rordan asked.

Shock rippled through her. "You can't be serious," she blurted.

"But I am," he replied, taking one of the ice daggers from Dysani. "Whatever you learn in your time here this week, I vow to leave the choices of what to do with that information completely in your very capable hands."

He sliced his palm before offering her the dagger. Dex took her tea while she did the same, placing her bleeding palm against the Lord's. A flare of white light emitted from their palms, and Tessa felt the vow settle in the depths of her being. She had vowed nothing, while the Achaz Lord had made a vow that would result in something truly unfavorable if he broke it.

And he had made that vow to *her*.

"Now that such a thing is settled," Rordan said, handing the dagger back to Dysani. "What is your choice with the tea this day?"

Glancing at the cup Dex held, she looked at her still bleeding palm once more. Whatever happened, she could do with it as she pleased. A choice. That was what he had offered her.

A show of good faith.

A freedom.

"I'll drink it," she said, reaching for the cup.

"Excellent," Rordan said. "I suggest you sit, my dear."

Taking his advice, she settled back onto the sofa, taking a deep breath.

"Just drink," Elowyn said. "And let your body naturally respond."

The same words the priestesses always said at assessments.

She tried not to think about that as she brought the cup to her lips and drank.

# 27

## AXEL

"What do you mean she's not here?" Axel snarled, his shadows shoving the sentinel against the wall and holding him there.

The male's eyes were wide, his magic attempting to shield him, but Axel's shadows shoved it aside.

"The Arius Heir picked her up," the sentinel said gruffly.

"*Theon* picked her up? When?" Axel demanded.

"I don't know. An hour ago?"

"You don't know?" Axel repeated. "Isn't it your job to know where the Fae are? Especially a powerful fire Fae that a kingdom has already claimed?"

"Yes, but—"

Axel was already shoving him aside and walking away. He didn't need to hear his excuses. Pulling out his phone and powering it back on, he found the text message confirming what the sentinel had said. Theon had picked up Katya a little over an hour ago, and they'd gone to the public archives in the Pantheon. Of course, he'd missed the message because he'd been in the back alleys of the Acropolis trying to secure more blood since rations were still a few days away. He always shut his phone off there so the patrons didn't think he was some undercover sentinel or something. It'd been a waste of time anyway. He hadn't been able to track anyone down.

Muttering curses under his breath, he made his way to the Pantheon, not even bothering to stop at the security check-in. His shadows trailing in his wake said enough about who he was. He stalked through the halls, taking the stairs to the lower levels. He knew where he was going, but even if he hadn't, Kat's scent would have found him and led him to her.

The scholars who maintained the Pantheon archives gave him dirty looks as he barged into the main atrium, and he silently chided himself. It wasn't as if someone random had retrieved Kat. It was Theon for gods' sake, and yet he could still feel the absolute panic when the sentinel had said Katya wasn't there.

He found them seated at a long table in the back, side-by-side with books spread out between the two. Kat immediately looked up at his approach, her smile faltering as he prowled forward.

Without a word, Axel dropped into the chair on the other side of her. Theon still hadn't bothered to acknowledge his presence, absorbed in whatever he was reading. Reaching across Kat, Axel flipped his book shut. Theon's head snapped up.

"What are you doing down here?" Axel hissed, not wanting to draw attention from the scholars again.

Theon sent him a sarcastic glare. "Research. Obviously."

"And you needed to take Kat from her studies for this?"

"She's very knowledgeable," Theon answered, forcefully reopening his book.

"It could have waited an hour."

"My time is limited," Theon replied, already checked out of the conversation, but Axel wasn't done.

He reached across Kat, again flipping the book closed.

"The fuck, Axel?" Theon snapped, darkness swirling in his irises.

"Axel, stop," Kat said in a low voice. "I don't mind. I've never been to the Pantheon archives before."

"That's not the point," Axel retorted.

"Then what is the point?" she tossed back.

"The point is, I came to pick you up, and you weren't there."

"I sent you a message," Theon bit out, again forcefully reopening his book. "It is not my fault you didn't check your phone. What were you doing anyway?"

"I was…out," Axel said, looking around at the shelves of books. "Where's Luka?"

"Also out," Theon replied curtly.

"So flying?"

"Yes."

Axel drummed his fingers on the table.

"Be useful if you're staying," Katya said, sliding a book towards him. Her tone was clipped, and her annoyance only made him more irritated.

With a huff, he opened the book, not even looking at the pages as he flipped them. "Did you talk to Tessa yet today?"

"No," Theon answered.

That explained his brother's mood, he supposed. Around mid-morning yesterday, Theon had abruptly excused himself from a gathering they'd been attending. Luka had followed, once again leaving Axel to deal with the questions. The same thing they'd done to him at the Samhain Feast. He'd later learned Theon had felt a sudden flood of emotion down the bond. They could only assume she was undergoing an assessment. He'd received a message from Lord Jove last night that Tessa was too exhausted from her day to call yesterday. Theon had tried calling him several times before finally giving up. Now to have not heard from her yet today?

Fine. He understood. Theon was stressed and didn't like the fact he didn't have control here, so he was trying to keep himself busy. He'd done this their entire lives. When he craved control, he buried himself in books and research, but that didn't mean he could just take his—

Axel pushed to his feet, shutting the book. "I'll be back," he muttered, not really sure where he was going. He moved among the bookshelves, letting his fingers drift along spines.

The sound of footsteps had him pausing, waiting for a scholar to round the corner, but it wasn't a scholar he came upon in the next row. It was a female with midnight hair that flowed down around her shoulders. It moved as if there were phantom winds stirring it, or maybe that was the…ashes? Her black pants and shirt were fitted with what appeared to be leather strapped atop them. Her head tilted with interest, and Axel felt like she was sizing up her prey. Swirling grey eyes met his, and he took a step back out of instinct. He was an Arius Legacy, but she was…something other. He could feel it in his bones.

"I'm, uh…just going to…" Axel backed away slowly. His shadows appeared like a thin fog, providing a barrier just in case.

The female smiled, but it was too sharp to be pleasant.

It was terrifying.

Without another word, Axel turned the corner, his heart beating way faster than it should. He was one of the most powerful Legacy in Devram. There was no reason he should have reacted like that.

Pausing, he turned and peered back around the stack of books, but she was gone. There was no trace of her. Only a set of ashy footprints on the ground.

Quickly making his way back to the table, Katya looked up as soon as he appeared. "What's wrong?"

"Why would anything be wrong?" he asked, lowering back into the chair and pulling a book towards him.

"I don't know," she replied. "That's why I asked the question."

Theon snickered, and Axel glared at his brother, opening the book. "What am I looking for?"

Not looking up from her own book, Kat slid a piece of paper to him.

*Tessa's Bloodline*
*Witches*
*Achaz*
*Temural, Arius, Serafina*
*Everlasting War*
*Weather/Storm Magic*
*The Augury*
*Revelation Decree*
*Source Marks*

"You have an entire list?" Axel muttered, reading through the items.

"Anything could help," Theon answered.

"It is simply to keep us organized," Katya offered.

"Shouldn't you have severing the Source bond on here then?" Axel asked.

"I don't want the Source bond severed," Theon said tightly. "Once I figure out her lineage, I can come up with a plan."

"Right, and if you don't figure it out in time?"

"Not an option," Theon replied. "So be useful and start looking."

"I mean, what aren't you looking for at this point?"

"Axel, shut up," Theon snapped.

Begrudgingly, he flipped through more pages, reading about the history of Devram for what felt like the millionth time in his life. He could practically write these books by now.

Shoving that one aside, he grabbed another, this one discussing the

Beginning and how the Firsts emerged from the Chaos. They, in turn, created the Lessers. The gods then joined others to create the various realms and beings. Again, all standard history he knew.

"How do you think Arius and Serafina came to have children if she was to be Matched to Achaz?" he wondered aloud, turning another page.

"We don't know. That's why it's on the list," Theon muttered.

"According to Scarlett, it perpetuated a war that was about to end."

"With the World Walkers," Kat murmured, going back and forth between two books.

"What?" Theon asked.

"I read somewhere that some think there was a war between the World Walkers and the gods," Kat said.

"And what? The World Walkers just disappeared?" Axel asked.

"That's why it was so interesting," she answered, finally looking up. "The World Walkers were said to be myths. This was a theory they were real and attempted to explain their disappearance. Some believe the remaining went into hiding. Clearly, there is some truth to it if Scarlett is one."

"But she acquired the power," Axel argued.

"She had to get it from somewhere," Kat pointed out.

"The World Walkers have nothing to do with Tessa," Theon cut in.

"What happened to 'anything could help?'" Axel drawled. "Especially if it's what truly started the Everlasting War. Isn't that what you said the Augury person told you? That the Everlasting War has found its way here?"

"That has to refer to Tessa though," Katya cut in. "If Arius and Serafina crossed Achaz, it would stand to reason that Arius and Achaz are the ones with the feud."

"And if Tessa is the granddaughter of Arius…" Theon mused, sitting back in his chair and drumming his fingers on the table.

"Then how does she have Achaz power?" Axel asked. "And some type of Witch gifts?"

"I don't know," Theon said, clearly frustrated as he dragged a hand through his hair. "If I knew that, I'd have moved on to other things by now."

"This is interesting," Katya said, sliding it over so Theon could look with her. He leaned forward, their heads together, and Axel bit down on his annoyance.

"What is it?" Axel gritted out.

"The Sister Goddesses," Theon murmured. "They were part of creating new bloodlines, particularly the Fae."

"As a gift to the Legacy," Axel said, rubbing at his temples. "We already know that."

"No," Theon said, that excited note entering his voice. The one that told Axel he'd be hearing about whatever this was for the next few hours. "This contends that the Fae were created to keep the balance."

"Then the Fates would have been involved," Axel said.

"Or the Fates required something be done, and this was the answer," Katya suggested.

"Time to go."

The three of them turned to find a scholar standing behind them, his long brown robes dusting the floor.

"We aren't done yet," Theon said, straightening in his seat.

"Yes, you are," the scholar asserted, taking a step closer. "The archives close to the public at sundown."

"I am not the public," Theon countered.

The scholar shuffled his feet, but held his ground when he said, "I respectfully request you follow the decrees of Devram that state the Pantheon is sacred ground entrusted to those of us who reside here."

Getting to his feet, Theon buttoned his suit coat. "Do not put these books away. I will return tomorrow. Understood?"

"Yes, my Lord," the scholar said with a bow of his head.

Turning, Theon grabbed his bag that contained his laptop, scooping up various notes and things from the table.

Axel stood as well, stepping aside to make room for Kat. Theon brushed by the scholar, leaving them to follow, and even Axel had trouble keeping up with his brother's hurried strides.

"Where's the fire?" Axel called to him as they moved among the rows of books.

But, of course, Theon didn't answer.

They made their way down a few more aisles. Axel hadn't realized how deep in the archives they'd actually been.

"Are the archives on Ekayan Island this big?" he asked Kat, who was keeping pace beside him.

"Larger," she answered. "Although there are four separate sections of them."

"How do they decide what gets kept there and what is housed here?"

"I honestly don't know."

They turned down the next aisle and nearly ran into Theon, who'd come to a sudden halt. His darkness was hovering, and he'd pulled one of his favored short swords from his magic. Blocking the other end of the aisle were two figures with pearlescent masks.

"Holy fuck, they're real," Axel breathed.

"Of course they are real," Theon hissed. "Did you think we've been fighting phantoms?"

"No, I've just never been around for the encounters," he answered. "But Tessa isn't here, so what do they want?"

"To speak with you," came a female voice that had them all spinning. Two more figures stood at the other end, trapping them in the aisle. Axel grabbed Kat, shoving her behind him as he pulled his own weapon from his shadows. Katya wouldn't be able to use her fire in here. The archives were warded against certain magic that could harm the volumes and texts housed in the passageways.

"Your organization has tried to kill my Source twice now," Theon said. "I have nothing to say to you."

"She brings only death here," the female voice replied.

"I am death," Theon said darkly, his power seeping forward.

Kat pressed into Axel, and he felt her gasp.

"Good," the female said, taking a step forward. The figure beside her moved too. Simultaneously, as if they were one. "That is what you need to be."

"Haven't you people learned that the riddles only make me want to kill you faster?" Theon said casually, taking a step towards her.

"Theon," Axel warned, nodding to the other end of the aisle, where the other two figures were making their way closer.

"No riddles, Heir of Arius," the female said. "Only knowledge. You know who we are."

"I know what you *think* you are," Theon countered. "Self-proclaimed protectors of Devram."

"It is our destiny," she countered. "Devram was created to keep the balance, and now that balance is threatened. She brings the war here."

"She has nothing to do with the fucking war," Theon snarled.

"How can she not when her existence upsets the balance? You cannot control the uncontrollable. Life must give, and death must take," the figure said, stepping closer yet again.

Katya tensed, pressing further into Axel, and the motion had him lifting his blade. The figure froze, but she continued speaking.

"She will bring about the downfall of the realm. Destiny beckons and sacrifice demands. Will you not sacrifice one to save us all?"

"The only sacrifices that will be made will be for her," Theon retorted.

"The rivers will run red," the female said, desperation creeping into her tone. "The realm will split, and all will fall. None will be left standing when Chaos comes to reign. It does not favor, only wants for more."

"He is not listening," came a frustrated male voice from the other side.

Axel turned to find the other two figures closer still.

"He will only hinder us," the male continued, pulling a crooked dagger from his cloak.

The same type of dagger that Tessa had been stabbed with. The kind that could kill a Legacy if it hit the heart. A Fae, however, could die from the blade within minutes.

"He will see reason," the female insisted.

"We don't have the luxury of time to see if that is true," the male replied, and then he lunged forward.

Theon's darkness slammed into him, forcing him to the ground where his magic sank into his being, black lines forming as his blood became the same darkness Theon commanded. The male cried out, but Theon was already swiping the dagger from the male's hand and plunging it into his chest.

A web of thick vines appeared, woven together to block the ends of the aisle, telling Axel a Silas Legacy was here. He didn't know which one of the remaining three it was, but he knew all three of them would die here tonight.

He went for the female, his shadows winding around her and dragging her forward as she cried out, continuing to try to persuade them of her cause. She was still a few feet away when he felt the sharp slice of pain down his arm. The gasp had him turning away to find Kat with her hand clasped over her arm, blood seeping between her fingers.

And then red was all Axel saw.

With a dark growl, his shadows poured out of him. They no longer dragged the female to him, but yanked her violently. Pulling the mask from her face, he paid no attention to the startled pale blue eyes that stared back at him, or the plea that had scarcely formed on her lips before his shadows were silencing her. He saw her attempt to strike him with the dagger she held, but he only smiled a dark thing as his magic caught her wrist.

Then forced her to shove the blade into her own heart.

He left her dying on the floor, ready to find the one who had hurt what was his, only to find another already there.

The same female he'd run into in the archive stacks was here. Not only was she here, she had a bow and was firing three arrows at once directly at him. His shadows swelled, but not fast enough. It didn't matter anyway. The arrows whizzed by him so close he felt the air stir in front of his face. The sound of a pained grunt had him turning to find one of the masked figures almost upon him, his dagger raised. He sank to his knees, the weapon clattering to the floor.

She'd saved him.

He whirled back, but she was gone. Only a smattering of ashes drifting to the ground remained.

"Who the fuck was that?" Theon snapped, and Axel found his brother taking care of the last Augury member. The figure was writhing on the ground, strangled moans of agony coming from behind the mask. Theon was letting his power feast before he took life.

*Good,* was all Axel could think as he stalked towards Katya.

She had pressed herself against the wall of books, trying to make herself as small as possible. Without access to her fire down here, there was little she could do against them. She still clutched at her arm, and when he drew nearer, he could see the thin pools of silver in her golden eyes. The dagger that had caused the wound was wedged in the book behind her, a blade of gold he'd never seen before.

"Let me see," he said gruffly.

But she didn't move her hand.

Holding her gaze, he slowly reached for her wrist, gently pulling her hand from her arm. Red streamed down, the cut deeper than he'd originally thought, and there were already faint lines of black appearing around the wound. He should be concerned about that, but all he could focus on was the blood sliding down her skin. He could smell it and her power and *her.*

Without conscious thought, he brought her hand up, taking two fingers in his mouth and sucking. The blood *tasted* like her—citrus and fiery, a hint of smoke and spices—and gods, her *power.* Heavy-lidded eyes dropped to her arm, and every part of him went alive with excitement. Fresh blood. Right there for the taking.

A hand on his shoulder was jerking him back, and he turned with a snarl, teeth bared at whoever was trying to come between him and—

"Get a grip, Axel," Theon growled, shoving him back even more as he stepped between him and Katya.

But he couldn't because he'd already been craving more, and that small taste had been everything. He'd never tasted blood like that. It called to him, called to his magic, called to his very soul.

"He can have some," Katya said softly, her hand clamped over the wound again.

"No. He can't," Theon said firmly, sliding an arm around her shoulders and guiding her forward. "Let's get you out of here, and we'll find a Reselda Legacy to look at that arm." With a hard look at Axel, he said, "Go cut a path through the vines."

But he barely heard him. Still focused on the blood dripping to the floor.

"Axel!" Theon barked.

He jerked, as if coming out of a trance. His gaze snapped to Katya, whose wide eyes were watching him, and he could swear there was something he'd never seen there before.

A hint of fear.

He was *scaring* her.

Shame flooded through him, so bitter he couldn't have swallowed it down if he'd wanted to. But he didn't want to. He deserved to feel the shame and guilt of this moment. If Theon hadn't been there, he would have taken from her. There would have been no stopping him, and from the look on her face, she realized that too.

Axel bent and retrieved a blade, moving silently to the end of the aisle and making quick work of the vines blocking their path. The scholars said nothing. They wouldn't have acknowledged them if they had. Fae bowed their heads as they passed, likely having been summoned to clean up the aftermath of whatever the fuck that had been in the aisles.

It wasn't until they were outside the Pantheon that Theon finally spoke again.

"Are you good, Axel?"

"Fine," he replied curtly. He couldn't bring himself to look at Katya.

"Fine enough to stay with her while I call Prudence to get a Reselda Healer to meet us at the townhouse?"

"The Falein Heir? She will do that?" Katya asked.

Theon's lips thinned. "She will for a price. We are on amicable terms. Fragile, but amicable."

Axel blinked. He hadn't realized just how much progress Theon had made in that regard. He knew he'd been in endless meetings, countless socials, and various engagements these past weeks. On top of all that, he'd been dealing with Tessa and trying to find answers.

"But a Reselda Legacy will be the best option, seeing as they are descendants of the goddess of healing," Theon went on. "I'd prefer to take you to Cienna, but we all know that is not an option right now. Even if it were, we'd never get to the Underground in time."

"In time?" Katya asked.

"That dagger is not an ordinary dagger," Theon answered, pulling his phone from his pocket.

"No, it is not."

They all whirled to find the female from the archives standing there. Theon immediately pulled a short sword from his darkness again, stepping in front of Axel and Kat.

"Who are you?" he demanded.

She tilted her head, amusement dancing on her lips as she studied them. "I am the one who will save her life. Or rather, I can tell you *how* to save her life. Where is the one of Sargon?"

"Luka? What is he needed for?"

"He will need to burn the poison from her veins," she answered simply, looping her bow over her back.

"I have fire magic," Katya said, and Axel looked down at her, finding a faint sheen of sweat on her brow.

"Anala's fire will do nothing," the female answered, moving forward and leaving ashy footprints in her wake. Swirling grey eyes swept over all of them before settling on Axel. "You need the fire of a dragon."

"That sounds painful," Axel said, having just listened to Auryon explain what needed to happen.

Auryon.

That was her name, and she'd artfully avoided any questions about where she came from. Convenient. He knew a silver-haired female who'd been the same. But while that was certainly a concern, it wasn't his greatest concern at the moment. His greatest concern was the fact that she had just said Luka needed to send his dragon fire into Katya to burn out whatever poison was on that gold blade.

"It is excruciating," Auryon agreed. "But it is better than death, I suppose."

"I agree," Katya said from the sofa in Theon's room at the townhouse. It was the only place warded well enough to keep godsdamn Ford from knowing what they were doing.

"Death?" Axel demanded, whirling to Auryon. "I thought you said the poison would paralyze her?"

"It will, which in time, will probably lead to death."

"Probably?"

Auryon shrugged. "I am not an Oracle, so I cannot say for sure, but death has followed in the past."

"What if I kill her?" Luka asked, looking more apprehensive than Axel had ever seen him.

"That is a possibility," Auryon answered, not straying far from the fireplace.

Theon, of all people, had cleaned Kat's wound. The blood might be gone, but the wound was far from healed. Axel still kept his distance, though, not trusting himself to be near her after what he'd nearly done in the archives.

Luka moved forward, dropping down beside Katya. "Are you sure about this, Kat? We can find a Reselda Legacy, a Healer who might—"

"I think she's right," Kat rasped, her speech already sluggish. Every blink was slow, as if it was too much work to reopen her eyelids.

"Just do it," Axel said, panic starting to bubble up.

Luka glanced at him, nodding once before doing just that.

Black flames flared, casting dim shadows all around them, before he wrapped that same fire around Katya.

And she screamed.

It was a scream Axel felt in his soul, and it had him lunging forward. Theon was there though, wrapping his arms around him from behind. One was wound tightly around his waist, the other banded across his chest. Axel knew he was saying something, but he couldn't hear him. He may as well have been speaking in a different language because all he could hear was Katya's screams. All he could feel was agony and *burning*.

Gods. He *was* fire. That was all he could think. He was on fire, and she was screaming, and he couldn't get to her.

His shadows appeared, trying to pry Theon off of him, and Theon was forced to battle back. Shadows and darkness fighting, both desperate, but in the end, Theon was still stronger. He always would be.

It could have been minutes, but it felt like hours that dragged on and on. Katya's screams would haunt him for the rest of his days. At some point, he'd sank to the floor, Theon going with him, his hold never lessening. Axel clawed at the floor, trying to crawl to her, until finally Theon released him.

In the next blink, Axel was shoving Luka aside with a snarl and scooping Kat into his arms. She was naturally warm with fire in her veins, but now she was *hot*. Her clothing stuck to her, but golden eyes blinked up at him.

"Are you all right?" she whispered, her fingers drifting up and brushing across his lips.

All he could do was huff a laugh of disbelief, tucking her in closer and resting his chin atop her head.

It wasn't until that moment that he processed what he was doing. That he realized he was holding her tightly to him. That he realized Luka and Theon were staring at him. Luka was looking back and forth between Kat and him, and Theon had a look of knowing disapproval on his face.

Theon could go fuck himself.

"Is there anything else?" Axel bit out tightly, directing his question to Auryon.

"She will be tired, but recover fine. The wound will scar," the female added.

With a look at the others, he said, "I'll leave you two to deal with her," before he rose in a fluid movement, bringing Kat up with him.

"Axel—" Theon started.

"Don't," was all he said to his brother as he started for the door.

"You need blood," Theon called after him. "After all of that, you need it. To keep her safe."

"I won't hurt her," Axel ground out, pausing in the doorway.

"Are you sure about that?"

Gritting his teeth, he hated that he wasn't sure at all. "I'll get some. I'll get her settled and—"

"I'll leave some outside the door," Theon cut in. "Luka, stay with Auryon."

The brothers didn't speak as they descended the stairs, and when they came to the second floor, Axel silently turned into his room, kicking the door shut behind him.

With a heavy sigh, he went to the bed, lowering onto it. He didn't let her go, but continued to hold her tightly to him. Kat shifted, a soft moan coming from her.

"Hey, kitten," he whispered, leaning back and tipping her face up to his. "How are you feeling?"

"Tired. Sore," she admitted. "I'm sorry."

His mouth dropped open. "What could you possibly be apologizing for?"

She blinked at him several times, as though it took her a minute to process his question. "For getting hurt."

"For getting... Gods, Kat," Axel sighed, pulling her back into him again. "I knew I wasn't good for you to be around, but I never imagined — I should be apologizing to you."

"You are a Legacy," she whispered.

"What's that supposed to mean?" he asked, pushing matted hair back from her brow.

"You don't apologize."

Something twisted in his chest at her words, but he shoved it aside. "Do you want to clean up some?"

"Yes, please."

He nodded, helping her to her feet before guiding her to the bathroom. Leaving her to it, he left the bathroom door open when he went to the bedroom door. Sure enough, Theon had left a bottle of blood. It was over half gone, likely the rest of his weekly ration. Theon probably needed it after fighting the Augury and then battling him again upstairs, and Axel recognized it for what it was.

A peace offering.

He drained the bottle, setting it aside before he went back to the bathroom. He found Kat still fully dressed, struggling with her shirt, as if she was too tired to even properly lift her arms. Stepping forward, Axel gently brushed her hands aside. When she lifted her face to his, he said, "I'm only going to help, nothing more."

She nodded, letting her hands fall to her side. Once he had her sweat-laden clothes peeled off of her, he led her into the shower, keeping the water lukewarm. Then he quickly stripped off his shoes, socks, and shirt before stepping in beside her. She leaned against him the entire time he washed her hair, whispering instructions about what hair products to use and how.

After he'd helped her dry off, he put her in one of his shirts, simply for the ease of being able to button it quickly. Leaving her in the bathroom, he went to the closet and quickly shucked off his soaked pants. He changed, grabbing a pair of sleep shorts for her as well, but when he came back out, she had already made her way to the bed and was nestled into the blankets.

Axel didn't even debate the decision. He couldn't have slept away from her tonight if he'd tried. Something in him demanded he stay near, watch over her, protect her.

So he slipped beneath the covers, settling in beside her, and when she turned into him, her soft breaths drifting across his bare skin, he curled his arm around her, keeping her close. He savored every rise and fall of her chest, running his fingers over the wound on her arm. Sleep wouldn't find him tonight. Not until she woke, and he was sure she was fine would he even attempt to rest.

As the night hours slipped by, he found himself thinking back to their time in the archives.

*"This contends that the Fae were created to keep the balance."*

*"Then the Fates would have been involved."*

*"Or the Fates required something be done, and this was the answer."*

What if the Fae were the answer to something that needed to be corrected?

What if the Fae were never meant to serve the Legacy at all?

What if, in the end, the Fae had saved them?

# 28

## THEON

"I'm just going to assume you are not of this realm at this point," Theon said, rubbing at his temples. He was hoping to get at least an hour of sleep tonight. That clearly would not be happening.

"Why do you assume that?" Auryon asked, those strange eyes of hers constantly swirling.

"I've never seen you before, and your power would have been noticed."

"Do you regularly peruse the archives beneath the Pantheon?"

"No."

"Then perhaps I have simply been there this entire time."

Theon stared back at her, not sure how to respond to such a thing.

"You are obviously not a scholar," Luka cut in.

He'd been a bundle of broodiness since he learned there had been a fight and he hadn't been present for it. Now he was in full Guardian mode, hovering between him and Auryon. His pupils were vertical slits, glowing bright blue, and smoke lingered every time he exhaled.

"You are clearly observant," she replied.

Theon was surprised the glare Luka gave the female wasn't laced with fire.

"There have been a lot of people suddenly making appearances these last weeks," Theon cut in. "All of them are tied to Tessa, so I can only assume that is why you are here."

"And if it is?"

"While your actions tonight proved you are not on the side of the Augury, and we are grateful for your aid in saving Katya, your motives are still in question," he replied.

"That is wise of you," she said.

Theon arched a brow. "That is brave of you to say and imply your intentions may be anything but favorable."

"No more brave than you threatening me with depleted power reserves," she said, that manic grin widening.

"My reserves are just fine," Luka cut in, baring his teeth.

Auryon looked him up and down. "Until he starts drawing from you."

"The fact remains that your magic is rare and would have been noticed long before now," Theon said.

"Are there not beings hidden in your own kingdom beneath your mountains?" Auryon countered. "How naïve of you to believe the other kingdoms do not have secret beings of their own."

Theon didn't have it in him to contemplate that right now. There were too many other things he needed to focus on. Too many other things he couldn't stop thinking about. He didn't have it in him to add that to his already too long list of things to figure out. The fact was everything he thought he'd known about their realm had been twisted around since he Selected Tessa, and every day he felt a little more control slip away.

"Get on with it then," Theon said, ready for her to get to the point. "What is it you want? She's not here if you are hoping to speak with her."

"I wasn't looking for her. I was looking for you," Auryon replied.

Theon's brows rose. "For me?"

"Is it not appropriate to go through you to get to her?"

That was one way to try to gain his trust, he supposed.

"There is a rumor that you are seeking a new instructor for her," Auryon went on. "I wished to inquire about the position."

He let out a bark of incredulous laughter. "You cannot be serious."

"I am always serious."

"What makes you believe you are qualified to be her private instructor?"

"That depends on what you need her to be instructed in," the female answered, and she stood so still. The only thing that moved was her raven-black hair as smoke from the fire drifted through it.

And her eyes.

Those never stopped swirling.

"She needs to know everything about Devram, including the history and teachings not taught to the Fae," Theon answered.

Auryon tsked. "She needs to know how to play the underhanded games of kings and queens."

"She does," Theon agreed. "But she needs to learn how Devram truly works first. Not the pretty picture painted for the mortals, Fae, and common Legacy."

"From what I've gathered, she already knows that."

"She needs to be taught control. That knowledge will mean nothing if she can't wield it at the proper time," Theon went on.

"Agreed."

His brow arched. "And you believe you can teach her such a thing?"

Auryon smiled again. This time it was all predatory and made the hair on the back of his neck stand up and his darkness tense.

"I believe she needs not only an instructor, but someone who can protect her as well. I've already proven I can do one of those things," she answered, ashes swirling as she lifted her hand and an arrow appeared between her fingers.

"But you are not a Legacy," Theon said.

"Not in the same way you are, I suppose," she agreed, twirling that arrow between her fingers.

"And your gifts?" Luka demanded.

"I can move among smoke and ashes, among other things."

"Other things," he repeated flatly.

"Killing types of things."

Theon had already seen that, and as much as he hated it, he'd done a shit job of protecting Tessa. How many times had she been attacked since he'd claimed her?

"Fine," Theon said before Luka could voice another question. "A trial run."

"What?" Luka demanded, rounding on him. "You, who won't leave her with anyone, are going to let a random stranger become her tutor? We don't even know what she can do."

"I saw plenty of what she can do," Theon said. "And she won't be alone. You'll be there with them."

"Repeat that," Luka said, his tone low and cold.

"You're right," Theon said. "I won't leave Tessa alone with someone we just met, especially *knowing* what she can do. So you will be with them." Turning back to Auryon, he said, "She returns in two days. Leave your contact information, and we'll be in touch."

"I'll be around," the female said with that dark curl of her lips.

"But be aware," Theon added as she took a step towards the door. "If Tessa expresses any concerns about you... Well, let's just say it is not only my trust you need to earn."

Auryon said nothing else, her bare feet leaving ashy footprints behind as she left the room. Luka followed her out, making sure she truly left, and Theon sank onto the sofa. His head fell into his hands, and he let out a frustrated sigh.

Pulling his phone from his pocket, he flipped it over. He'd missed her call tonight. He'd felt his phone vibrating while he'd been guiding Katya out of the Pantheon and keeping her away from Axel, but he hadn't wanted to risk answering it. Axel would never forgive himself if he hurt Katya. Despite knowing it was a terrible idea, his brother had developed feelings for the female, and that was now yet another thing they'd need to navigate.

But Theon knew there would not be another call tonight.

"What the fuck are you thinking?" Luka demanded, kicking the door shut behind him as he stalked back into the room.

"I was thinking neither of us want her near Cordelia right now," Theon answered, his voice monotone as he stared at his phone.

He hadn't felt her since yesterday.

Yesterday, when he'd felt her terror and panic. He had no doubt she'd undergone an assessment. Luka had felt it too. Theon hadn't talked to her afterwards, being told she was too tired, and now he'd missed her godsdamn call.

"So you think some random female is the answer?" Luka continued. "What is wrong with you?"

"You'll be with her, Luka," Theon said flatly. "You'll be there to hear everything she's being told and monitor how she's being treated."

"I don't understand how you are okay with all this."

Theon shot to his feet. "Okay with all this? I'm okay with *none* of this, Luka," he said, his voice rising. "I am not okay with Tessa being in Faven. I am not okay with speaking to her once a day, if that. I am not okay with my time running out. I am not okay with not being able to feel her, see her, touch her. I am not okay with the fact my father wants to see me first thing in the morning. I am not fucking okay, so I'm entrusting her to you during those times. Because at least in this, in this one fucking thing, I have some godsdamn control."

"It is not my place. *You* are hers, not me. You need to be there—"

"I'm done debating this. It's final," Theon snapped.

Luka went silent, his mouth pressing into a thin line. After several seconds, he said, "This meeting with your father—"

"I'll attend it alone."

"Theon."

"Good night, Luka."

His friend studied him a minute longer before he made his way to the door. He paused at the threshold, not looking at him when he said, "I talked to her tonight."

Theon's head snapped up. "When?"

"When you didn't answer, she called me," Luka said. "It needs to be you there."

"How is she?"

There was an extended silence before he finally looked over his shoulder, meeting Theon's gaze. "She's starting to trust you, Theon, which is why it needs to be you there."

"She doesn't trust me," he retorted, reaching for his bag that held his laptop.

"It's fragile, but it's there," Luka replied before he left the room, pulling the door shut behind him.

Theon pulled a book from his bag, along with a stack of notes. Separating the notes into piles, he opened the book, flipping to the page that had made him risk taking the book from the archives. He'd return it tomorrow, but if someone learned he took it…

He'd deal with that if it happened.

This book was the one Kat had found with dozens of pages devoted to the Sister Goddesses of Witchcraft and Sorcery. It was in an old language, one of the ancient ones that would take him ages to translate. Katya would be helpful. She was more proficient, but he wasn't going near Axel's room any more tonight. No, translating it would be long and tedious, especially with most of his resource books back at Arius House.

He'd shed his suit coat long ago. Now he finally took the time to remove his tie. He unbuttoned his top few buttons before rolling his sleeves up to his elbows. Slipping off his shoes, he set them aside, along with his socks, before padding barefoot back to the sofa. They were still within reach though. He almost always wore shoes, always ready for his father to show up and demand something of him. Never wanting to be caught unprepared.

Powering on his laptop, the next hours were spent slowly translating the text and typing it up in an encrypted document. His eyes ached by the end, but he wouldn't have been able to sleep anyway. Tessa was clearly tied to the Witch history in some way, and the Witches all descended from Taika and Zinta. But even if her mother was a Witch, where did the Achaz power come from? And the ability to summon a storm? None of that was Achaz or Arius. And what gifts did she get from her father? A god of the wild and untamed?

It explained her recklessness, he supposed. That wildness and that inability to control herself at times, but there had to be more. To be a direct descendant of a god, let alone a First? There was more.

The first peeks of sunlight were filtering into the room when he finally sat back, shoving his hands into his disheveled hair. There were a few words he'd had to guess at, but he understood the general idea of the pages.

Taika and Zinta were two Lesser goddesses, but they'd been created with a purpose far greater than the other Lessers. They were the first two Lessers brought into existence by the Firsts, and their purpose was to provide a balance. They could create new forms of life, but their gifts had to be combined with another's. They worked closely with the other gods and goddesses to do just that, and eventually, one became loyal to Achaz and one to Arius, just as Scarlett had said. New beings were created in addition to those that emerged from the Chaos, and when the gods needed to provide for their Legacy, they came together to create the Fae.

Theon had skipped the next section that spoke of the various Fae created, leaving that for another time. He didn't need to read about that when the Fae lived among them. He knew of their magic, but the next passage? That was of interest. Because that passage seemed to speak of history that had taken place *after* the creation of Devram.

Achaz approached them both at separate times. He wanted a child with both his gifts and their gifts. Both Zinta and Taika refused him. With good reason. A child of Achaz and one of the Sister Goddesses, theoretically, wouldn't need to combine gifts with another. They could, essentially, create new life just by willing it. Achaz became enraged and cursed the goddesses as punishment. The passage didn't go into detail about the curse, but it did say it plagued their descendants forevermore, even when Achaz achieved what he desired with one of Zinta's daughters.

A quick knock had him locking the document in a hurry, but he breathed a sigh of relief when Luka came through the door. He had two mugs of coffee in his hand, and he held one out to Theon. He drank half of it in one go.

"When was the last time you slept?" Luka asked.

"Truly slept? The night before Tessa left," Theon answered.

"For fuck's sake, Theon—"

"Thanks for the coffee," he murmured, moving into the bathroom and shutting the door behind him.

One look in the mirror told him why Luka was concerned. In addition to depleted reserves from yesterday, he had dark circles under his eyes. That never happened to Legacy. His hair was a mess from running his hands through it all night, and he hadn't shaved in a few days. In other words, his outward appearance matched the utter mess of his mental state. He took a cold shower, hoping it would help wake him up.

It didn't.

But he dressed in a black suit and tie, slid on his shoes, and slipped into the person he was required to be for a meeting with his father.

One more day.

She'd be home tomorrow.

The clicking of computer keys was the only sound in the dining room, making Theon's grip tighten on his fork. He sat across the breakfast table from his father at the Arius manor outside the Acropolis. Eviana was beside him, typing on a laptop. Whatever she was typing his father was relaying through their bond while he cut into his steak and eggs.

Most of his mornings had been spent this way growing up. Silently eating his breakfast, waiting for the sounds of the keyboard to cease. When Eviana stopped typing, his father's attention would shift to him. Although his mother had often been there, filling the silence with her endless chatter of kingdom gossip and upcoming engagements. Axel and Luka had been there too, silently eating their own breakfasts, wondering the same thing he was: would today be a normal day of studies with their private instructors or a day of father's *lessons*?

And even though Theon was twenty-eight years now, he had the same apprehension rolling through him. His reserves were depleted. He'd used a good portion of his power yesterday and had given the last of his rations to Axel. It wasn't a big deal. Rations were due to be delivered later today, but it meant he needed to be extra careful with this conversation. Even with full reserves, his father's Source sat beside him, while Theon sat here low on reserves and Sourceless. Not that Tessa's presence would have made a difference. He couldn't draw from her, and he wasn't sure she'd readily come to his aid at this point.

No, she would. She'd chosen to stay with him. That meant something. It had to.

*She's starting to trust you, Theon.*

Maybe Luka was right. Maybe those nights spent tangled together really were something more, despite her insisting they meant nothing. She was turning to him more when her power felt out of control. She was helping him search for answers, asking him questions…

That he'd flat-out lied to her about, even if it was to protect her.

After feeling her emotions a few days ago though, he didn't regret that choice. Who knew what they were putting her through, and the last thing he needed was for them to figure out what she was before he did. Had she told them she was the granddaughter of Arius? Had they pieced together there was Witch blood in her somewhere along the line? Did they know how she had Achaz gifts?

Would she remember any of it if they did?

He motioned to the Fae standing by the wall to bring him another cup of coffee. He'd lost track of how many he'd had this morning. When he saw Tessa tomorrow, he was hauling her straight to bed. Oddly enough, not to get lost between her thighs as decadent as that sounded, but to get some godsdamn sleep.

The sudden silence in the room had Theon glancing up, finding Eviana setting the computer aside and a plate of food being placed before her. She was never allowed to eat until after his father had finished his morning ritual of reviewing his calendar, planning his day, and responding to any urgent matters.

Eviana murmured a soft "thank you" to Valter before picking up her fork and slicing off a small piece of the omelet she'd been served.

But Eviana being given food now meant that—

"How is your task coming along, Theon?" Valter asked, his tone feeling obnoxiously loud after the endless silence they'd been sitting in.

Swallowing his bite of steak, Theon washed it down with a quick drink of juice before clearing his throat. "You've given me many tasks, Father. Which do you wish to discuss?"

Irritation immediately filled his father's face, shadows drifting across his hazel eyes. "Your Source. Have you learned what she is? How to sever this bond?"

"I have made progress on lineage, but nothing concrete," Theon ventured carefully. "As for severing the bond, there is nothing. Source bonds were created that way. Only death can sever a Source bond."

"Surely you will find a workaround," his father replied casually, reaching for his toast.

"You are asking an impossible task of me," Theon argued.

His father paused, toast in mid-air. "I am telling you to find a solution to a problem you created. Just because you find the task unpleasant does not make it impossible."

"But it *is* impossible. How am I to undo something the gods designed not to be undone?"

His father shrugged a shoulder. "I trust you will find an alternative solution."

"And if I don't?"

"Failure is never an option, Son," he replied darkly, his power thickening around him and Eviana tensing as he presumably drew from her reserves. "But I suppose if you do not find a suitable alternative, her death will have to do."

Theon went rigid, his darkness bursting forth at the mere idea of Tessa being threatened.

His father's lips lifted in the smallest of smirks before his power was slithering across the table and winding around Theon's throat. He could do nothing, not with Eviana's power fueling his father's. So he sat there and took it like he had for years. Unable to breathe, but forced to keep calm and collected. Forced to not show any type of reaction or his father would drag this out even longer. There were plenty of times he'd slipped into unconsciousness only to come to on the floor.

Finally, his father withdrew his magic, Theon's own darkness dissipating to prove submission. Something he'd learned long ago appeased the bastard. Some days he fought more, but this meeting needed to end favorably, so today he'd play by his father's rules.

Valter was already back to cutting the last of his steak as if nothing had happened. "Your Source problem is not the reason for this morning's meeting."

*Source problem.*

"How is our other agreement coming along?"

Theon's brow furrowed. "What other agreement?"

"The one that mars your skin."

"Our Bargain?" Theon asked in surprise. "A Match contract is signed. You know this already. You witnessed it."

"And the rest of that agreement?" Valter asked before taking a drink of his juice, unblinking gaze fixed on Theon.

"The rest of that..." Theon lurched back in his chair. "The *heir*? We can't have our Match Ceremony until the Selection Year is completed. It is in the accords."

"There is no law stating an heir cannot be conceived before a Match Ceremony has taken place," his father replied, placing his silverware on his empty plate. A Fae immediately appeared, clearing the dirty dishes while another refilled his coffee cup. "As long as the child is produced with your Match, there will not be any issues. The problems come if a child is conceived with...another."

The last word was said pointedly, and Theon bristled at the implication. "I think I am dealing with more than enough at the moment. Producing an heir is not high on that list," he bit out, his patience thinning.

"I do not give a fuck about your priorities, Theon," Valter returned, his voice turning low and deadly. "The only priority here is securing our position in Devram. An heir is necessary."

"Not for decades," Theon argued.

Valter scoffed. "If you think I am waiting decades to make sure our bloodline is secure, you are mistaken."

"Surely it can wait until after the Selection Year. Until after everything with Tessa—"

The growl that came from his father at her name had Theon tensing and using all his control to keep his darkness from making another appearance.

"She was never supposed to end up as yours," Valter snapped.

"What the fuck does that mean?" Theon demanded.

His father inhaled deeply, his calm, collected mask visibly slipping back into place. "It means you were supposed to Select a Fae, not some mixed lineage mutt that is delaying everything. Somehow you managed to fail at something that was seemingly impossible to fail at."

He didn't flinch at the words. His father had slung enough insults at him throughout his life. He'd been hearing how much of a failure he was for as long as he could remember. So he said nothing, his palms flat on the table as he worked to control the only thing he could in this room: his power.

His father stood, Eviana doing the same despite her breakfast being only half finished. "You will do this, Theon. It was part of our agreement."

"There was never a timeline stated," Theon spat.

A dark, amused look formed on his father's features. "You think you are clever enough to outmaneuver me on this? If you think you can find a loophole in a Bargain, surely you are capable of finding one in regards to your Source." Theon opened his mouth to say something in response, but his father raised a hand, effectively silencing him. "But since you are determined to defy me on this, apparently you need to be reminded of the hand that feeds you, so-to-speak. Your rations will be withheld this week."

"What?" Theon said, the word falling from his lips before he could stop it. He needed that ration. His reserves were depleted, and he'd given the last of his previous week's supply to Axel last night.

"Maybe this will teach you to stop pandering to your brother's short-comings," Valter sneered, buttoning his suit jacket as Eviana appeared with his long-coat and a pair of leather gloves. "But more than that, should I not see effort put forth on your part, I'll make sure *his* rations are withheld as well."

"You fucking bastard," Theon hissed, shoving to his feet only to have his father's power force him back to his chair before snaking around his throat once more, robbing him of the ability to speak.

"I do not know what you thought was going to happen here, Theon," his father continued casually. "Did you truly think you would gain a Source and suddenly overpower me? Did you think you would be more powerful? Suddenly able to take the kingdom from me? Did you think I have not spent years—decades before you even entered this realm—preparing for every possibility?"

He glared back at his father, his lungs beginning to burn.

"You will do this, Theon. While your weaknesses continue to disap-point me, I suppose they continue to provide me with a means to make sure we understand each other." Valter slipped his gloves on. "I expect a report on what your Source learned in Faven within a day of her return."

With that, he turned, leaving the dining room. Eviana's heels echoed as she followed, and it wasn't until he heard the front door slam shut that he could finally draw in a gasping breath.

*You think you have control because your father gives you the illusion that you do.*

Tessa's words filled his head as he worked to even out his breathing.

*Who in their right mind wants to be chained to someone who craves control because he doesn't have any?*

She was right. She'd been right from the very beginning. He had control over nothing.

That's all he could think as he pulled his phone from his pocket and called Felicity.

# 29
## TESSA

S he couldn't breathe.

Not as Theon stood over her, a black dagger in his hand.

She couldn't get air down to even speak.

"Breathe, little one," Luka soothed. "It will all be over soon."

The dragon was near her head, a large palm cupping her cheek, keeping her gaze fixed on him. Axel was at her side, his shadows twining around her legs and keeping them still.

She choked down a sob, gasping as tears slid down her face. "Please, Luka. It doesn't have to be like this."

Luka's brow pinched, his gaze darting to Theon. "What if she's right, Theon? What if there's another way?"

"We don't have a choice," Theon said, still standing over her, his hair stirring in the breeze.

A light rain was falling, thunder rumbling in the distance.

"I still think there is another way to interpret this."

Tessa's head snapped to the side to find a tall male. He looked familiar somehow, but Tessa was sure she'd never met him. He had a sword strapped down his back, as did the female standing next to him. Her red-gold hair was braided over her shoulder, and flames flickered in her eyes. Standing next to them was Tristyn and Katya, a strange Mark stark against the back of the Fae's hand.

"Life must give, and death must take," Theon said flatly. "There is no other way to interpret that. Not if we wish to save our world."

For so long, Tessa had wished for death, and now, in this moment, she didn't want it. She'd finally found something to fight for, and she would be robbed of that too.

"You're wrong," Tristyn said, his features taut and his hands clenching and unclenching at his sides. "Have you learned nothing over these past months? Everything you thought you knew has been wrong. This is no different."

"It is all different. All that questioning has led me here. To understanding why we were drawn to each other," Theon said, his grip on the dagger tightening.

"Theon, don't!" Tessa cried. "It's more than a bond! I know that now."

Emerald eyes cut to her. "You're right, and now that I understand what that means, I'm the only one who can do this."

She was writhing on the ground, trying to free herself of Axel's shadows. They were too strong though, and even if she could free herself, she'd never win. Not with the ring on her finger keeping her separated from her gifts.

Luka pulled her into him, his hand smoothing down her hair.

"Luka," she sobbed, the sound defeated and broken.

"He won't do it, Tessa," he whispered. "He can't harm you. The bond—"

"This is wrong," the female with fire was saying to the other male. "This will alter everything."

"It will correct the balance," Theon said.

"It will tip it beyond repair!" Katya cried. "Theon, there's another way. We've spent hours together researching. We can find another way."

"We're out of time," Theon said. Then, in a barely audible murmur, he added, "Once again, I'm out of time."

"We cannot interfere," the familiar-looking male said, reaching for the female with fire when she took a step towards Tessa. "It will upset the—"

"Fuck the balance," the female seethed, shoving his hands away. "She sent us to help. This is the exact opposite of that!"

Axel was refusing to look at Theon, but that was regret shining in his eyes when they connected with Tessa's.

"I'm sorry, baby doll," he murmured before turning away from her.

"Theon, stop," Luka said, his hand never ceasing its movement along her hair as he clutched her tightly to him. "We will find another way."

"She can get here," the female was saying, panic in her voice. "She can stop this."

"Not even she will be fast enough," Theon answered.

"She is a World Walker and a queen among the realms. She—"

*"And even she has been ordered not to interfere with this," Theon cut in, dropping to Tessa's side.*

*"She will not care."*

*"She will be too late," Theon said again, his fingers sliding along Tessa's jaw. "You will forever be mine, Tessa. Whether in this life or in the After."*

*"Please don't send me to the dark alone," she whispered, her body trembling in Luka's arms.*

*The male and female were arguing with Tristyn, but Tessa couldn't hear them. Not as she got lost in dark emerald eyes and black hair. In a small dimple and lips she'd kissed more times than she could count.*

*"I'm sorry I failed you, little storm," Theon said, sorrow flashing in his eyes.*

*"I'm sorry I loved you too late. But I'm yours. Every piece of me."*

*Theon didn't say another word.*

*In a sudden burst of power, his darkness yanked her from Luka's arms. She screamed, and Luka bellowed a roar that she felt in her soul. Black flames flared, but it was a female who appeared, blocking Theon's dagger with one of her own as two wolves prowled around them, brushing up against Tessa's legs. Midnight hair flowed around the female, her bare feet planted as she stared up at Theon, a dark grin on her face.*

*Her voice was a predatory purr as she said, "You may have stolen her Guardian from her, but that only means you must now deal with me."*

She jolted awake, her hands flying to her chest where the dagger always sank into her heart.

Except this time.

This time it didn't.

"Easy, Tessie," Dex said from where he sat beside her in the car. "You're all right."

She nodded, willing her heart rate to slow as she recognized the outskirts of the Acropolis. Her brow fell back against the cool window. She was returning a day early. Granted, the sun was setting, so it wasn't much earlier, but she'd been surprised when Rordan had greeted her that morning dressed for travel. He'd had something urgent come up and was satisfied with her time spent there, so he'd instructed Dagian to escort her back today rather than tomorrow. He'd already spoken with the St. Orcas family, and they would be expecting her early arrival.

Anticipation hummed through her, and she hated to admit it wasn't just the bond. She'd been…*worried* yesterday when Theon hadn't answered her phone call. He always answered. Not just with her being gone this week, but anytime she'd needed to call him, he'd answered without fail. Granted, she only called when she truly *needed* something, but there was a comfort in knowing he would answer.

She'd called Luka, who'd assured her he was fine, but his voice had been tight as he'd talked her through her panic. While he'd made her feel a little better, she'd hardly slept, and she'd been exhausted after another day of working extensively with her power. When she did sleep, her dreams were more vivid, everything feeling more real.

As though they weren't dreams at all.

According to Elowyn, that was the case, and true to his word, Rordan had given her the time and space to do with that knowledge what she would. He'd never once asked her what her plans were. Even when he'd said goodbye this morning, he'd handed her a card containing a number to reach him directly and said he would see her soon back at the Acropolis.

That had been it.

And she didn't know what to make of it, which seemed to be the story of her life these days. It was strange he'd asked *nothing* of her.

Even knowing how powerful she was.

Even knowing she wasn't Fae, wasn't even Legacy.

Even knowing… Well, more than she did.

She didn't trust any of it, but she was preparing herself for all of Theon's questions. More than that, she found herself *wanting* to talk this through with him. He'd have ideas and theories with these dreams or whatever they were. She knew he would. He'd specifically asked her about her dreams on a phone call, which meant he'd discovered things of his own while she'd been gone.

"Are you worried about going back?" Dex asked, glancing at her bouncing knee.

"No," she answered absent-mindedly. "Why would I be worried?"

"It is the Arius Kingdom," Dagian drawled from the bench seat across from her, the two seats facing each other in the back of the vehicle. "Everything about the kingdom is worrisome."

"Why do you say that?" Tessa asked.

"Surely you know why they were banished in the first place," he answered.

"I know the history that was taught, but I've learned that history is not quite accurate."

"Don't you have a private tutor for these matters?"

Tessa shifted, fiddling with the hem of the sweater dress she was wearing. The Acropolis was a little cooler than Faven had been, and she had a jacket draped across her knees. Overall though, the clothing she'd been provided had been quite comfortable and not nearly as formal as she was usually required to wear.

"I do," she answered. "But I believe there is much she still keeps from me."

Dagian huffed a derisive laugh. "I am not surprised in the slightest he hired someone ill-suited for the job."

"Why?"

"Because Theon St. Orcas delights in controlling knowledge. I am sure she keeps much from you on his orders," Dagian replied, sliding an arm along the back of the seat. Sasha leaned into him as she continued reading her book, and for all the world, they looked like a couple truly content with each other. They portrayed the exact portrait Theon wanted the world to believe about their own bond.

"That is an accurate statement, I suppose," Tessa conceded. "So will you tell me?"

Dagian studied her, some kind of approval flickering in his golden eyes. "The Arius Kingdom was sequestered to their corner of the realm because they refused to acknowledge the Revelation Decree, specifically the part about 'life needing to rule.' They were given many warnings and chances, but in the end, they still chose to ignore the decree. When it was discovered they were building an army and planned to start a war with the other kingdoms, something had to be done."

Tessa's brow furrowed. A war? She'd heard nothing of that.

"The other kingdoms came together and agreed to banish them to their mountains and the Shade Plains. They refused to trade with them, and anything they imported was heavily taxed," Dagian continued, reciting the history in a bored tone.

"And these armies?" Tessa asked.

"Were dealt with. Many were sentenced to the Underground where they rotted away in the kingdom they made the poor decision to serve."

"But the Arius Kingdom hasn't suffered. They are prosperous," Tessa said, her confusion growing.

"*Now* they are," Dagian replied. "It took centuries to get back to that state. For many of those centuries, their kingdom was a desolate place full of starving, desperate people. It's why the kingdom is so dark and depraved."

Tessa couldn't exactly blame them. Outside of the elite, the common Legacy, Fae, and mortals were simply trying to survive. Desperation would make people do unspeakable things. If survival had depended on thieving, killing, and treachery, it was no wonder the kingdom had become what it was.

"The point is the kingdom cannot be trusted," Dex said, interrupting her thoughts.

"Funny," Tessa replied, turning back to the window. "Theon said the same thing to me about Achaz Kingdom before I left."

"Of course he did," Dex scoffed in annoyance.

Tessa bit the inside of her cheek to keep from saying something snarky in return. Every time she tried to talk to him about anything in the Arius Kingdom, he found a reason to insult them. Eventually, she'd stopped speaking about it at all. She didn't want him to fix this, and she didn't want his opinion. She'd simply wanted to talk through everything that had happened so she could process it, and he refused to let her do so.

Her heart rate picked up as they turned down the street with the ruling family townhouses. She half-expected Theon to be waiting on the side of the street for her, pacing like the annoying thing he was. But as the vehicle came to a stop, there was no one waiting for her. No one on the front step, not even a Fae.

That was fine. They probably had some engagement or other that they couldn't change without angering Valter. She didn't *need* someone to greet her. Now that she thought about it, it would be rather nice to get back and settled. She could have a little alone time before Theon's incessant hovering became the norm once more.

Dex, however, was sure to comment on their lack of presence as he escorted her up the walk. When they came to the front gate, he stopped, turning to face her. "I'd make sure you get inside safe, but I cannot cross their wards unless you let me cross with you?"

"It's fine," Tessa replied, brushing a strand of hair from her face. "It's not like I have luggage to carry in."

"It's fine until something happens to you, and then they try to blame us," he retorted bitterly.

"Us?" Tessa repeated.

"The Achaz Lord. You know what I mean," he replied dismissively. Then, taking her shoulders in his hands, he said, "You did amazing this week, Tessie. Don't hesitate to reach out to Lord Jove if you need anything."

"Right," she answered, worrying her bottom lip as she glanced at the townhouse. The lights on the top floor were on, so *someone* was here. "I should go."

Dex pulled her into a hug, and she returned it half-heartedly. "Be who you need to be now, so you can be who you were meant to be soon, Tessie," he said softly, pressing a soft kiss to her cheek. "We'll talk soon."

She said nothing else, going through the gate and feeling the wards glide across her skin. Climbing the front steps, she pushed through the front door, flipping on the switch for the foyer. Warm light flooded the space, and she quietly unzipped her jacket, hanging it on the hook and then removing her heels.

She scooped them up as she padded barefoot through the main floor. Theon wasn't here. The bond would know, and the disappointment flooding through her was as much her own as it was the bond's. She'd been more than ready for some normalcy, even if that normalcy included Theon.

Although, if she were being honest with herself, she was looking forward to seeing Theon for more than that. Numerous times on the drive here she'd found her mind wandering back to being in bed with him. Letting him distract her from all her thoughts and choices that needed to be made. Letting him give her what she craved and needed, because as much as she hated it, he always knew. Gods, she'd let him do anything he wanted with her tonight if it meant ending the night so well-fucked she couldn't think and didn't dream.

The mere thought had her climbing the stairs a little faster. She paused on the second floor landing. Axel's door was open, his room empty. Luka's door was closed as always. She turned the knob, feeling the wards unlock around her. Peeking her head in, she found it dark as well, his bed a mess of blankets and pillows. Closing it once more, she started up the stairs to her room. Theon must have simply left a light on for when he came home.

This was fine. It would give her time to change and—

Walking into their room, the heels slipped from her fingers, landing with a loud thud on the hardwood floor as she came to an abrupt halt.

A female with glossy chestnut hair lurched to her feet from the sofa. Her golden-tan skin glowed softly in the low light of the room, and her brown eyes were wide as she whirled to the doorway, a glass of red wine in her hand.

Felicity Davers.

Theon's Match.

"My goodness," she said breathily. "You startled me. We weren't expecting you for a few more hours."

"We?" Tessa asked, her voice eerily devoid of any emotion.

"Theon will be back in a bit," Felicity said, setting her wineglass aside. "He was called to tend to a matter."

Tessa just stared at her, unable to think of anything to say.

She was *here*.

In their rooms when she'd been gone an entire week.

When she—

*"Less than a month," Cressida chattered excitedly from down the table.*

*"It will be an exciting month indeed," Valter said with a wide smile at the head of the table, tipping his liquor glass in Theon's direction.*

*Theon's smile was tight, and his emerald eyes were streaked with black when they flashed to Tessa across the table where she sat next to Luka. She held his stare until he looked away before she picked up her fork and began eating her salad. The marks on the backs of her hands seemed to glitter faintly in the low candlelight of the dining room at Arius House.*

*Directly across from her sat Felicity in a pale blue gown, and she leaned back in her chair, her hand coming to rest on her very round stomach. A Union Mark stood out on her skin that had paled some since she'd moved to Arius House, a ring on her finger catching the light.*

"Tessalyn?"

Tessa blinked from the memory of the dream that hadn't been a dream at all. Felicity was standing right in front of her. If there had been any doubt about what Rordan and Elowyn had told her about her "dreams," it was gone now. Because here was Felicity, casually sitting in her— No, in *Theon's* room. Shoes off, wine in hand, and clearly comfortable. Fuck. How long had he been bringing her here? Often enough he was comfortable leaving her upstairs, inside his wards.

"Tessalyn?" Felicity said again. "Are you all right? I know you were traveling all day. That can be so exhausting, and I'm sure your time in Faven was very trying."

"My time... How do you know about any of that?" Tessa asked, her gaze darting to the perfectly made bed.

"Theon told me, of course," Felicity said, a slight frown pulling at her full lips. She reached out, placing a hand on Tessa's arm. "Perhaps you should sit down. You don't look well."

She didn't look well?

Tessa looked down at herself. The cream sweater dress stopping mid-thigh. Her bare toes curling against the floor. Her palms glowing at her sides.

She slowly lifted her head, and Felicity's eyes widened as she yanked her hand back.

"You are upset, but Theon will be back—" Felicity started, but Tessa was already turning away from her. She clumsily made her way back down the stairs, catching herself with the railing more than once. Frantically, she tried to shove it all down. Everything she was feeling, because none of it mattered.

None of this should surprise her. Of course Felicity would have his child. She was to be his Match. The bed was made for *three* for fuck's sake. The ruling families must have heirs, and what did it matter to her?

*Because you will never be mine!*

Those were the words she'd all but screamed at Theon that night. It was a truth she'd never been able to admit to herself. Never wanted to admit because it was something she didn't want to want.

But gods, she did want it.

She wanted one godsdamn person to care enough to choose *her*. Just one. And she'd stupidly thought maybe it would be him. Even if it was just the bond making him so infatuated, these last few weeks had been nice in a way. Waking up next to someone. Rarely being alone. Someone who always made sure she had warm coffee and left his shirt out for her and had told her when her birthday was.

She recognized that those were common decencies, that those minor things weren't any sort of standard she should be measuring against, but no one had ever given those common decencies to *her*. And she wasn't naïve enough to think that she meant any more to him than her power, but some part of her had wanted to. Some part of her had thought maybe he hadn't just been whispering pretty words in her ear to get what he wanted.

Because he always answered her calls until last night, and oh gods. He was probably with her and that was why he didn't answer.

*Ah, but facing truths? That is where the difficulty lies.*

An arm wrapped around her waist, and suddenly she was in the sky. She screamed, but it was lost in the howling winds. Rain pelted her face, but she was trying to figure out when she'd gone outside. She didn't remember walking through the townhouse or going out the back door to the gardens. She hadn't heard the thunder cracking or felt the cold water trickling down her back.

The sun hadn't quite set yet, but it might as well have with the dark clouds blotting out the light. She instinctively knew the touch of the dragon who was flying through the dimming sky, and she turned into him, feeling him cradle the back of her head as she buried her face into his bare chest.

It felt like seconds, but it must have been minutes when they were dropping to the ground. She didn't know. Her stomach hurt, and she was too busy trying not to vomit to care. Her bare feet touched the cold earth, and then warm hands were on her face, trying to force her eyes up.

"Tessa, look at me," Luka said, his voice hard and laced with the order, and she found herself looking into glowing sapphire eyes. There was pity and fury and something else in them, but seeing him had something settling her soul. It was minor, but it was there. "That's my girl," he murmured. "Breathe, little one."

Lightning flashed, illuminating their surroundings. The river. The same place they always took her when she needed to expend her power. A familiar space.

"How long has he been bringing her there?" Tessa demanded in a hoarse whisper.

"Tonight was the first night," Luka answered.

"You're lying," she spat, jerking from his hold and beginning to pace. Her bare feet sank into mud with every step.

"I'm not, Tessa. He didn't want to bring her there. He didn't have a—"

She whirled, pointing a finger at him. "Do not tell me he didn't have a choice. He could have taken her anywhere else."

"I know you are upset, Tessa, but it's his Match—"

"I'm not upset," she snarled, fingers dragging through her hair as she tugged at the strands.

"A rain storm certainly wasn't forecasted in the beginning of winter," he drawled, and Tessa found herself with light pooling in her palm.

"Is that what you need right now, Tessa?" Luka said with a sneer at her power, black flames appearing and hovering at his shoulders. "Because I can fight with you. That's fine. We both know I'll have you knocked on your ass within seconds."

His flames barely formed the shield in time as she sent her power racing towards him. She still forced him to stumble back a few steps.

And the storm raged around them. *Her* storm. Violent winds and rain that burned as it splattered against flesh. Thunder that shook the ground, and lightning that struck nearby, forcing Luka to split his focus and put out fires while countering her magic.

Light welled at her feet, and energy crackled at her fingertips. Luka took everything she threw at him until finally he had enough. Black flames banded around her wrists and legs, throwing her off balance, and she dropped to her knees with a frustrated scream.

"I'm sorry, Tessa," he said, and gods, he sounded like he truly meant it as he pulled two black bands from his pocket.

She didn't fight him as he slipped the bands onto her wrists, her power instantly vanishing. Instead, it just thrashed inside of her now. She scarcely felt it.

The storm lessened, but rain continued to fall and lightning still streaked across the sky.

A finger pressed beneath her chin, tipping her head back once more. He said nothing, only held her gaze.

There was too much happening, and she couldn't deal with all of it. The pain and the betrayal and the—

"Fuck me," she blurted, the words desperate and pleading.

Luka's eyes went wide. "What?"

"Please, Luka," she begged. "It's too much. I can't handle it. I just want to— No, I *need* to drown in something that isn't this. Something that doesn't feel like *this*."

"Tessa," he started, her name sounding like an agonized plea.

"*Please*, Luka," she said, the words a broken sob. "I've never asked anything of you. Never. Please do this for me."

"If I thought that's what you needed right now, I'd fuck you until the only thing you could say was my name," Luka said, taking her face in his hands.

And she let out something that could only be described as a wail. "That *is* what I need!"

"No, little one," he said, shaking his head. "You need to feel."

"Feeling hurts," she said on a gasp as she sobbed harder. "Everything I do is so that I *don't* feel, and this is why."

"Feeling is what keeps us from becoming the monsters, Tessa."

"Maybe I want to be the monster!" she cried.

Luka didn't say anything to that. He only pulled her into his chest, but she was starting to get her emotions shoved down, locking them away tightly one-by-one. Slowly, the rain turned to a steady drizzle that indeed froze as the temperature steadily dropped, and by the time Luka was landing back in the gardens at the townhouse, a light layer of snow covered the ground. And her?

She was feeling nothing at all.

She felt nothing as he guided her into the house and led her to his room.

She felt nothing as he peeled her wet clothing from her body and wiped dried mud from her skin.

She felt nothing as he slid one of his shirts over her head.

She felt nothing as he squeezed water from her hair with a towel before sitting her in front of the warm fire.

"I got to you first," he said gruffly, shuffling about behind her and presumably shedding his own wet clothes. She was staring at the flickering flames trapped behind the glass, remembering months ago when she'd done the same at Arius House. "We were both racing back to you when we felt your emotions. I was faster, but he'll be back soon. He took care of— He's coming back to you. As fast as he can."

"I don't want to see him," she said flatly.

"You need to, Tessa. The bond needs it. You both need it. It will help."

"Fine. After I'm asleep. Then I don't have to see him."

"All right," Luka agreed after a moment of silence.

"And I don't want to sleep up there."

"Okay."

She twisted to look at him, finding him leaning against the doorway of his closet, arms folded across his chest and wings still out.

"I mean it, Luka. I do not want to wake up in that bed in the morning."

"I swear it, Tessa."

She nodded, turning back to the fire. She wished she had some alcohol. If Luka wouldn't help her get lost in pleasure, she could at least drown in a bottle.

Instead, she was stuck with her feelings, trying to shove their way out of the pit of her soul where she had them locked away.

And that was where they'd stay because the only thing feeling did was give her hope.

Foolish girl.

She wouldn't make that mistake again.

# 30
## THEON

Theon burst through the door from the garage, not bothering to remove his coat and shoes as he ran through the main floor and up the stairs. Luka met him on the second floor landing, holding his door open.

"She's sleeping," Luka said. "Do not wake her. It would be bad for all of us right now."

Theon's breath caught as he finally laid eyes on her. The room was dark, only lit by Luka's black flames around the room, but Theon could see her. She was curled up in the middle of Luka's nest of pillows and blankets. Her hair still looked damp, and her bare legs were tucked into her chest, Luka's shirt not covering much. There were traces of mud along her legs and arms, as if she'd tried to clean up but stopped caring. One hand was tucked under her cheek, the other splayed on the pillow. She looked utterly spent.

"You had to put the bands on," Theon noted, swallowing thickly.

"I did," Luka said, shutting the door quietly.

Theon plunged his hands through his hair, blowing out a harsh breath. "What did she say?"

"She asked how often you've been bringing Felicity here."

"Never," Theon said vehemently. "I never bring her here."

"I told her that. She said I was lying," Luka replied. Theon started to say something else, but Luka cut him off. "She wasn't going to listen to anything I had to say. Not tonight. What did Felicity say?"

"She said Tessa startled her when she got here, that she told her I'd be back shortly, but Tessa turned and left," Theon answered, quickly removing his jacket and suit coat.

"I caught up to Tessa in the gardens," Luka said. "I managed to get her to the river before she lost complete control. I questioned being in the air with that storm she summoned, but I held off on the bands as long as I could. I didn't want to do that to her, especially not knowing what she went through in Faven. But Theon, she's…" Luka sighed, running a hand through his hair that hung loosely around his face.

"I felt her, Luka," Theon said, toeing off his shoes. "I know what she was feeling."

Hurt.

Betrayal.

Anger.

So much fury.

"It's all too coincidental, right?" Theon said, untucking his shirt before quickly unbuttoning it and slipping it off. "My father calling in the bargain. Tessa coming home early. Us being called away when she arrives."

Luka rubbed a hand along his jaw. "Dozens of people were killed. You think it was all a set-up? For what purpose?"

"I don't think it was a set-up. I *know* it was," Theon replied, lowering himself to Luka's bed. The male slept on a mattress on the floor, for fuck's sake. Theon hated it.

"What are you doing?" Luka said, watching him warily. "I'm telling you, do not wake her up, Theon."

"I'm not going to wake her."

"I promised her she'd wake up here. She didn't want to wake up upstairs."

"I'm not moving her," Theon replied, settling down beside her.

She immediately turned to him, seeking him out in her sleep like she always did. He wasn't fooling himself. He was well-aware this was the bond, but he also knew what he felt from her tonight. If the bond would comfort her enough to let her sleep soundly, then he'd let her take what she needed. She'd endured enough this past week, let alone whatever had happened tonight.

"Felicity was in our room," Theon said.

"What?" Luka asked, lowering to the other side of the mattress.

"I felt her enter the wards," he went on. "Tessa found her up there."

"Fuck," Luka muttered, shifting onto his back.

"It was her suggestion to drop her off here when I got the call. In my hurry and the chaos, I just agreed. I wanted her out of my hair so I could focus on Tessa, and…" He smoothed a hand down Tessa's hair.

"You think Felicity is in on whatever this is," Luka finished for him.

"I haven't figured it all out yet, but it won't matter in the end," Theon said as Tessa shifted, her brow pinching.

"What do you mean?" Luka asked, extinguishing his dark flames.

"She won't believe anything I have to say. I've never given her a reason to."

He slept. He shouldn't have been able to knowing what this morning would bring, but he'd been so exhausted, and Tessa had been back. He woke with her head nestled on his shoulder, and her hand on his chest. And he savored it, not opening his eyes until he heard movement; then he found Luka on the sofa.

"That bed is not made for three," Luka grumbled, noticing him awake. He was already partially dressed for the day.

"If you didn't have so many godsdamn pillows and blankets everywhere, there'd be more room," Theon retorted in a whisper, pulling one of the blankets up over Tessa's shoulder as she shivered against him.

Luka muttered something under his breath, propping a foot on the coffee table. "Ford is bringing coffee up."

"That will be good," Theon said, gently brushing his fingers up and down Tessa's arm.

The quiet lingered between them until Luka said, "She's going to say some things, Theon. You can't get frustrated with her. She's… In all the shit we've put her through, I've never seen her like that."

Silence fell again, and it wasn't until the knock sounded from Ford with the coffee that Tessa stirred. Not knowing what to expect from her, Theon gently worked his arm out from under her. From what he could gather, she would not be pleased if she woke up nestled into him. He slid from the bed, feeling rested for the first time in a week. His reserves were still low, painfully so, and he knew he'd be drawing from Luka if he used any more of his magic.

He swiped up his phone, scrolling through emails and messages as he sipped on a mug of coffee, but he sensed the moment she fully woke. The bond seemed to sit up straighter, as if waiting for her to acknowledge it.

She didn't.

He quickly clicked his phone off, setting it aside, and turned back to the bed. She had curled back into herself, a blanket wrapped tightly around her. Violet-grey eyes were fixed on him, but she didn't see him. It was as if she was looking right through him.

This was the wine cellar all over again.

Filling another mug of coffee, he approached her, setting it down on the nightstand before stepping back.

"Tessa?" he said carefully.

She didn't answer him. Only stayed curled in a ball, her knees to her chest.

Theon glanced at Luka, who was watching her with a tight expression. He leaned forward, his elbows resting on his knees and hands loosely clasping in front of him.

"There's a lot to talk about this morning, Tessa," Luka said. "And I can't take those bands off until you're at least acknowledging us."

Her eyes flicked to him for the briefest of moments before they were back on Theon.

"That's fine, beautiful," Theon said quickly. "You don't need to speak. I just need you to listen." She didn't give any other sign of acknowledgment, and he didn't expect her to. "I wasn't told you were returning early until late afternoon, and I was told you wouldn't be home until well into the night."

Her eyes narrowed slightly at that, and he was cataloging every single mannerism because right now he felt nothing from her. Not a single flicker of emotion to clue him in on what she was thinking and nothing to help him navigate this.

"I had dinner plans to appease my father. We were on our way to our dinner reservation when I received a call that there had been an attack by the Augury at the same spot where I was supposed to pick you up later that night. Naturally, I assumed they were waiting for you," he went on. "I called Luka. He'd already received word of the attack and was on his way there. Axel was also already there because it was outside the arenas where he was with Katya. She's fine," he added hastily when Tessa's eyes widened some. "They both are, but others... There were a lot of casualties from the attack. Both Fae and Legacy." He saw the bob of her throat as she swallowed. "I haven't seen the list of the Fae lost. I only received the list of Legacy lost this morning."

The truth was they wouldn't bother naming the Fae. They'd receive a brief report of the powers that were lost and no longer available to be claimed, but he'd already told Axel to find out if any of Tessa's friends were among the casualties.

"I didn't want to have to...split my focus while I was there," he went on. "You were the only thing that mattered. We were near the town-houses, and she suggested dropping her off here. In my hurry, I agreed. It was close and a quick solution to the problem. Admittedly, I didn't think about it. She wasn't my focus. You were. But I know she went in our room, Tessa. I felt her enter the wards. I was furious and planned to confront her when we got back, but I was in the middle of chaos. There was still fighting going on when I got there. I wouldn't leave until I had you back, but I know that's where you found her. And gods, Tessa, for that I am sorry."

But she was back to seeing through him. He wondered if she was even hearing him at this point. But he pushed ahead, hoping she was, despite some part of him knowing this was pointless.

He cleared his throat, swallowing down something he hadn't experienced in years as his eyes burned. "I was with Luka when we felt you. I was repeatedly calling Dagian, even Dex, trying to find out where you were. But then every bit of what you were feeling slammed into me, and I have never..." She was expressionless, and something in his soul was cracking as he watched her. Because he wasn't blocking a godsdamn thing. He knew she could feel every bit of what he was experiencing in this moment.

And she didn't care.

"I knew Luka would be faster. We were both racing for you, but I knew he'd reach you first. When I got back to the townhouse, he was already gone with you. My father was here, speaking with...*her*. Axel and Kat were back, and my father had already threatened Axel earlier in the day. Katya was the easiest target. So I had to... I took *her* home. Or to the place she is staying at in the Acropolis. My father rode with us, so I couldn't question her like I wanted to. But I came back as soon as I could, Tessa. Every action was to get back to you as soon as I could."

His words seemed to echo in the silence of the room. He didn't know what to do. He'd long since set his coffee mug aside. His hands were trembling slightly with the need to reach for her, and he shoved them into his pockets. When she did finally speak, he nearly fell to his knees at the sound of her voice.

"So they were waiting for me?" she asked, her voice void of inflection. "I am the reason people are dead. Again. This is my fault."

"Gods, no, Tessa," Theon said, lurching forward a step and making himself still once more. She still didn't move, didn't react. "This is *not* your fault. Do you hear me?

"No?" she asked, blinking once. It was like something cleared with that one action, and she was looking at him. Really seeing him.

And she cut him down once more with her next words.

"Is the attack near the arenas not directly correlated to me? The same way Pen's death was?"

"This was a set-up, Tessa," he said, lowering to sit on the edge of the mattress. "It was a set-up to get to *me*, not you. I haven't figured it all out yet, but some things happened this past week, particularly yesterday. When you're feeling…better I will tell you everything. But this was not your fault, Tessa. Please know that. You were used to draw me out."

"So she could get to her," Luka said grimly.

Theon looked back over his shoulder. "What?"

"I think you're right. This was all a set-up, but it wasn't just about you. It was about both of you. You were drawn away from here so Felicity could get to her."

He turned back to find Tessa's eyes squeezed tightly shut, her breathing a little too fast, but it evened out again within seconds.

"But then she would have known Tessa would be back earlier than I was told. But why? What could she have to gain from it?" Theon said.

"The same thing anyone has to gain in a realm of villains and monsters," Tessa said, her voice flat as she opened her eyes.

"She already has a Match contract," Theon said, shaking his head. "There is no greater status for her to attain."

She fell quiet again, and he wished she had the third Mark. He'd thought things would be better with the second, when he could feel her emotions, but no. The third Mark would let him hear her thoughts, and he would have given just about anything to know what was going through her head in that moment.

Finally, Tessa moved. She pushed to a sitting position, shoving hair back from her face. "It doesn't much matter in the end."

"Of course it matters, Tessa. If she is going to interfere with us, I'll—"

"You'll what?" she cut in, unwrapping the blanket from around herself. Her voice had shifted. Smooth and even, yet eerie with a hint of madness. "You already signed the contract at your father's demand. Everything you do is because of him. And yes, I understand you do so to keep others safe. Axel. Kat. Me. But it doesn't change the fact that his demands and threats control you. It doesn't change the fact that, in the end, you will still bow to him and his wishes." She pitched forward, running her fingertip atop the Bargain Mark along his ribs. An inverted triangle with three horizontal lines running through it. "It does not matter. In the end, you are still hers, and she is still yours."

"No!" Theon snarled, snatching her wrist in his hand. "No. I do not want her."

"It doesn't matter," she repeated. "You are hers. I've seen it."

"It fucking matters, Tessa," he said, lurching forward and clasping her face between his hands. "She isn't who I— Wait. What do you mean, 'you've seen it?'"

Violet-grey eyes lifted to his, and the violet was deeper. Darker. Specks of her light magic now swirled within their depths. She reached up, her fingers closing around his forearms as she pulled his hands from her face. "She is to be your Match. Yes?"

"Yes, but—"

"And an heir is required of her per the Match contract. Yes?"

"Yes, but—"

"And you have been with her. Yes?"

"With her?" he repeated in confusion. Then his eyes went wide. "Tessa, no. I have not fucked her. Nothing even close. We've gone to dinner and had a few lunch engagements. That's it. There has been no one since you."

Her head tilted. "But you will."

"No," he said, shaking his head in denial.

"I understand why you will."

"You... What?"

He could not believe what he was hearing. Not after what he'd felt from her last night. Not after what he'd been feeling from her these last weeks. Not as she spoke to him too calmly now.

"And if it's not her, it will be another," she replied, gracefully rising to her feet. Theon looked up at her standing over him, Luka's shirt not even reaching mid-thigh. Her face was expressionless. If anything, there was a morbid acceptance there. "You will forever be someone else's."

"If I am forever someone else's, what does that make you, little storm?"

"The same thing I've always been. Nothing."

She stepped from the bed, picking up her coffee cup as she did, and Theon scrambled to his feet. "That's cold," he said, reaching to take it from her and get her a fresh cup.

But she pulled it from his reach, tucking it against her chest as she said, "It's fine."

"I can get you warm coffee, Tessa."

"I'm fine," she repeated.

"You're fine," he deadpanned.

"Mhmm," she hummed, turning to Luka. "Can I use your shower?"

"Yeah," he said carefully, studying her as she crossed the room and closed the door to the bathroom behind her.

Theon immediately turned to Luka. "You felt nothing from her, right?"

Luka nodded, getting to his feet. "That's going to be a problem."

"You couldn't feel her before the second Mark and seemed to understand her just fine," Theon said.

"That's the problem," Luka replied. "She's not blocking the bond. She's feeling nothing. Eventually, she's going to break, and when she does, I don't know if we'll be able to bring her back. Not again."

The two of them stood there, side-by-side, staring at the closed bathroom door. What was there to say at this point?

"She learned about her visions," Theon said.

"That's what it sounds like."

"My father wants a report of her time in Faven by the end of the day."

Luka made a sound of acknowledgment.

"It doesn't feel right to ask her about it with everything else going on."

"What are you going to do?"

"I don't know."

He didn't know what he was going to do about any of it. Once again, he'd lost control over everything.

"I should go get her clothing," Theon said after another silent minute of staring at the bathroom door.

"Probably," Luka agreed.

Theon left the room, climbing the stairs slowly to the third floor. The message of her using Luka's shower had been more than clear. Just as her demand to sleep in his room had been. She didn't want to go into their room right now, and it again left Theon wondering what exactly she'd walked in on when she got home.

He hadn't been up here at all, but the room was exactly as he'd left it. The bed was perfectly made. He hadn't slept in it in two days. He'd packed up his books and papers as always, not trusting Ford not to go snooping. Nothing looked amiss, but he knew that didn't mean anything. If Felicity was in on something with his father, Ford would have made sure her tracks were covered.

He brushed his teeth and took the fastest shower of his life before grabbing a few necessities for her, along with a pair of leggings and a sweater. When he'd learned she would be back early, he had already cleared his day, but that didn't mean his father wouldn't drop in unexpectedly as he'd been doing more and more lately. He would have loved to just let Tessa wear something relaxed and comfortable, but they had to be ready for anything.

When he returned to Luka's room, she hadn't emerged yet. Luka had finished dressing, wearing a button down with his black jeans. He'd pulled his hair back, tying it on top of his head, and he was writing something on his tablet. He glanced up briefly when he heard Theon before going back to whatever it was he was doing.

"Have the plans for today changed at all?" Luka asked.

"No. We'll let her set the pace for the day. I want to go through that information on Cordelia if I can," Theon answered, setting Tessa's items aside. "I heard movement across the hall. Axel and Kat must be awake too."

Luka nodded. "I already told Ford we'd be down in the next hour for breakfast. Here."

He held the tablet out to Theon, and when he looked at the screen, he found several names written on it in Luka's quick scrawl. Some were circled, others had question marks beside them.

"Felicity is obviously involved in whatever this is," Luka said. "But I don't know that she's cunning enough to pull something like this off by herself."

"She's smart, but she'd need help with this. My bet is on my father," Theon replied, noting the question mark beside Valter's name.

"You need to be sure, Theon."

"I am. I told you what he said to me yesterday. He knows we've been plotting against him this entire time. Of course he was going to come for me. He's always used my weaknesses against me," Theon said. "He wants this bond severed. What better way than to cause a rift between me and Tessa?"

"He's not the only one who wants it severed," Luka said, taking the tablet back. "All the Lords and Ladies do."

"You think there's more involved? That *this* is what has somehow brought the kingdoms together?"

"I don't know what to think right now," Luka answered, glancing at the bathroom door. "But she was dropped off here, which leads me to believe Achaz Kingdom is also involved."

"That's plausible," Theon agreed, mulling the idea over. "It would—"

But he forgot what he was going to say as the bathroom door opened, and Tessa emerged wearing absolutely nothing. She was all bare skin and naked breasts and fuck, fuck, fuck.

She had Luka's brush in her hand, pulling it through her hair as if she didn't even realize she was out here completely nude. "I didn't know what I was supposed to wear."

His mouth too dry to speak, Theon only pointed at the pile of clothing. She nodded as she finished brushing out her wet hair before slipping into the clothing.

Theon cleared his throat as she worked her hair into a braid, Luka already handing her one of his hair ties when she turned to look for one.

"Are you hungry?" Theon asked.

"Not particularly," she replied, reaching for the tablet Luka still held. "What is this?"

"We're trying to work out who is involved in all of this," Luka answered.

She hummed in response, handing the tablet back to him before making her way to the door. Exchanging quick glances, they followed her. Dragging her fingers along the wall, she made her way downstairs and into the dining room.

"Morning, baby doll," Axel said, a forced cheerfulness to his voice.

"I'm glad you're not dead," Tessa answered, taking her usual seat.

Katya choked on the drink of juice she'd just taken. Axel seemed startled for a minute, but then the corner of his lips tilted in a small smirk. "I'm rather delighted by that fact as well."

Her gaze flicked to Katya. "You are truly all right?"

"I'm well, Tessa," she answered softly.

Tessa nodded, reaching for the yogurt and scooping some into a bowl. They all watched her add fruit and granola.

"There are doughnuts," Axel said carefully.

"I'm fine," she replied, taking a bite of her yogurt.

Axel's gaze shot to Theon, his brother's eyes narrowing into a glare.

"You can have what you like, Tessa," Theon said.

"Can you teach me to read the Lost Language?" she asked instead.

Perplexed, his answer was more of a question when he said, "I can?"

She nodded, and her eyes flicked up to Luka. "And training? You told me you would."

"We can continue training, Tessa," Luka agreed, taking a bite of his toast.

Theon reached for the platter of pancakes, suddenly realizing he was the only one who hadn't dished up food yet. "I found a replacement tutor while you were away."

"It's a trial run," Luka cut in, clearly still unhappy about the idea.

"Right. It's a trial run. Luka will stay at your lessons with you until we are sure she is an adequate replacement," Theon said.

"And she will teach me the Lost Language?" Tessa asked.

"I can do that," Theon answered.

She only shrugged, scooping up another bite of her yogurt.

They ate in silence for the rest of breakfast, Axel mentioning he was sending a new playlist to Tessa before he left to take Katya to her daily lessons and training. It wasn't until later that Theon was alone with her for the first time since she'd come back. They were in the lounge, and Tessa was standing in front of the window, watching snow flurries drift to the ground. He'd been reading through the information Blackheart had sent over on Cordelia, but he hadn't been focused on the task. She hadn't said much, providing only short answers if asked a question, and not once had he felt a single flicker of emotion down the bond.

"I need to know where we stand, Tessa," he said, setting his computer aside and getting to his feet.

She glanced over her shoulder briefly before returning her attention out the window.

"I need to know so I can prepare for tomorrow and the next day, the next week," he went on.

"We will be as we've always been, Theon," she answered.

"I don't want to be like we've always been," he countered, coming to stand beside her.

"It does not matter what we want."

"You truly believe that?"

"I've seen it."

"Visions are just that, Tessa. They can change. They are merely glimpses of what could be," Theon said.

"What if they aren't?" she murmured, rubbing at her wrists.

Theon reached over, gently brushing her hands aside. Her eyes fluttered shut for the briefest of moments, almost as if she was blinking. The bond in his chest calmed at the touch. It had been straining all day, and he hadn't touched her once since he'd woken next to her that morning. But now he slipped one of the bands from her wrist, then the other, sliding them into his pocket. Tessa visibly relaxed, tension leaving her shoulders as she lifted a hand, letting light pool there. She'd learned some control in Faven.

"We can go talk to Cienna," Theon finally answered. "She also has Seer gifts."

"She does?" Tessa asked, studying her light as bolts of violet energy flickered through it.

"Yes, and honestly, it'd be a good idea. She'll be the first to tell you the smallest thing can alter fate, changing an entire vision," he replied. "I will see if Axel can make contact with her."

"When did you know?"

"When did I know what?" Theon asked, watching her play with her power.

"That I was having visions."

"I… The Underground. When you tried to go back in the tunnels and then we were attacked. I recognized the power then and asked Cienna about it when I went back to see her," he answered.

And he waited.

He waited for her to demand why he hadn't told her. He waited for her to snap at him for keeping yet another secret from her. He waited for her fury.

He wanted it.

He wanted *something*.

But she only nodded.

Slowly, he reached out, and when she didn't react, he took the lock of hair that had come free of her braid, twirling it between his fingers. "Where do we stand, little storm?"

"Where we always have. On the precipice of destruction or salvation," she murmured.

"What does that mean?"

"We have an agreement. I can't back out of it, just like you can't back out of the agreement with your father."

He froze for a moment before tucking the lock of hair behind her ear. "Do you know why I made that bargain?"

"It is not my place to know."

He felt the blow whether or not she meant it to be one.

His hand slid to her cheek, cradling it as he swiped his thumb along her cheekbone. "The night of your Emerging. Lord Jove had taken you, and my father would not help me get you back unless that deal was made. All of it was so I could get to you. To make sure you were safe."

"The purpose behind the choice doesn't change the outcome, Theon. No matter how noble you thought it to be."

"It was a sacrifice I was willing to make," he countered.

"And now? What sacrifices will you make, Theon?"

"Any that are required," he answered immediately.

"And if fulfilling your bargain is the required sacrifice?"

"Tessa," he pleaded. "Give me time."

"You ask where we stand? Our roles haven't changed. Source. Master. Our responsibilities haven't changed. Nothing has changed."

"Bullshit. Everything has changed," he retorted, his voice rising.

"Refusing to accept something doesn't make it false," she replied. "You taught me that. Our bargain remains. I will fulfill my end of it."

"You will?"

Tessa nodded, turning back to the window.

Some sort of relief flooded through him because that meant he had time.

Time to figure out a solution.

Time to fix this.

Time with her.

"What else did you learn while you were gone?" Theon asked, daring to take a step closer to her.

Her gaze once more fixed out the window, she said, "That facing truths is difficult, but deciding what to do with those truths is the greatest burden of all."

# 31

## TESSA

"Goddammit," Tessa cursed as she was knocked down onto her hands and knees from behind yet again.

"You did better this time," Luka said, extending a hand to her, but she batted it away, getting back to her feet on her own.

"Again," she demanded, setting her feet in the ready stance he'd made her stand in for hours when they'd first started these training sessions.

"I think that's enough for today," Luka said, turning away from her and making his way to the table that held their water bottles, towels, and other things.

"I'm not ready to be done," she replied, not moving from her spot. "Again, Luka."

"We need to get ready for your afternoon lessons. You're meeting Auryon after your group instruction."

"There's time to go a few more rounds," she insisted.

"Tomorrow."

"No, Luka," she snapped. "Now."

Finally, he turned back to her, a brow arching as he leaned against the table, crossing his arms. He didn't fucking *say* anything. He just stared at her as if waiting for her to fall into compliance.

And she glared back.

"I'd consider it if you were eating properly," he finally said. "But you're not."

"I haven't been hungry," she grumbled.

It had only been one day since she'd been back in the Acropolis, and she'd been grateful Theon had given her a day at the townhouse to re-acclimate and figure everything out. She'd listened to his explanation. None of it surprised her. Felicity was a Gracil Legacy. While Gracil was the god of empathy, some of his descendants could use their gifts to manipulate feelings. Felicity, in particular, was gifted at conflict—either escalating or de-escalating it. Tessa even understood the set-up that Theon and Luka speculated had happened. It all fit. It was all plausible.

But none of it mattered.

Just like she'd told Theon. He would still be Matched, whether it be to Felicity Davers or another Legacy. And Tessa? Well...

She crossed her arms, jutting her hip out in annoyance as Luka continued to look at her like she was the stubborn brat he always claimed she was.

Valter wanted this Source bond broken so she could be assigned as Luka's Match. But if she wasn't Legacy, would that stand? Or would the other kingdoms come together once more and demand it be changed like they were doing now?

Witch blood accounted for her visions. That was what Elowyn had told her. There could be Zinta or Taika blood in her, or she could just be descended from a Witch. Some of the Witch lines were not direct descendants of the Sister Goddesses but had been gifted their magic in the way the Fae were. Descendants of the goddesses were obviously more powerful, but whether she was or wasn't, none of that accounted for her Achaz magic.

"Let's go, Tessa," Luka finally said, turning back to the table and packing up a few things.

"No," Tessa said again. "You promised to teach me how to protect myself, Luka Mors."

"I am training you," he answered, not bothering to look back at her.

"It's not enough."

"It's not something you'll suddenly become proficient at overnight."

"But if we keep training now, I'll get there faster," she insisted.

With an exasperated huff, he turned back, slinging the small bag of items over his shoulder. He stalked back to her, shoving a water bottle into her hands. "Did I not promise you I would train you?"

Tipping her head back to see his face, she held his sapphire gaze as she said, "I know you did, but it's not enough."

His head canted to the side, a lock of hair falling free from the small ponytail it was tied back in and brushing his jaw. "How is it not enough?"

"It's just not," she retorted. "This is no different from what we were doing before. I'm not a Sargon descendant, Luka. I will not pick up on everything as quickly as you did. I need more practice."

"Tessa, you successfully countered several moves today. Considering we haven't trained in a few weeks, that's saying something."

"It's saying nothing," she snapped in frustration.

"What's this really about?"

"It's about you saying we're done when we still have more time."

He was quiet for a moment, studying her, and she forced herself not to fidget.

Finally, he said, "You want to be able to defend yourself, right?"

"Yes. I want to be able to protect myself."

He nodded. "Given the past several weeks, that's understandable, but did something happen in Faven? Did something happen there to make you push so hard for this?"

Tessa pursed her lips, shuffling her feet. The truth was she didn't feel safe anywhere, but being in Faven, in an unfamiliar place...

She was just so tired of having to depend on others to be protected. It's what the Legacy wanted. For the Fae to be dependent on them. Even once they Emerged and could access their gifts, the Legacy were still stronger. A Legacy could still demand anything from a Fae, and failure to comply only made things worse. And sure, she wasn't Fae or likely even half Legacy at this point, but the fact remained she wasn't prepared.

She'd never been taught to fight back, but she'd also never had anything to fight *for*.

"A lot of things happened in Faven," she finally answered, turning away from him and heading to the exit. He easily caught up with his long strides, pulling the door open for her. "I'm surprised Theon hasn't asked me a million questions about it yet."

"He should have been asking you all those questions," Luka replied. "His father demanded a report, but he's stalling. To give you time and space. Again."

She glared up at him as they walked down the hallway, but when she did, she caught the small wince. It was so fleeting, she questioned if she'd actually seen it, but it also almost seemed like she'd *felt* it.

"What's wrong with you?" she asked, dragging her feet.

"Nothing."

"You grimaced."

"I did not."

"Yes, you did."

"After your lesson with the other Sources, I'll meet you outside the room. Theon hasn't informed Cordelia yet of the replacement instructor. He didn't want there to be any negative ramifications for you," Luka said.

Tessa rolled her eyes at the change of subject, but the mention of Mother Cordelia had her letting it go. "She's going to be upset either way."

"Let us deal with her."

"Right," she muttered. She was sure the continued lessons with the other Sources would go just swell after this. "You don't seem too thrilled about the new instructor."

"We've only met her once. I still can't believe Theon did this," Luka said, his tone hardening.

"Why don't you like her?"

"Because we know nothing about her."

"Theon didn't spend hours obsessively researching her?" Tessa asked.

"He only does that with you."

"I'm not flattered by that statement," she deadpanned.

Luka shrugged, stopping by the main entrance and passing her a sweatshirt. She tugged it on over her sweaty tank.

"Even before he Selected you, he was researching you," Luka replied, handing her a stocking hat next.

"Me and his other options," she retorted, pulling the band from her hair so she could slip the hat on.

"But mainly you," Luka said, pushing the door open.

The snow that had fallen from her storm had melted, but the temperatures were cool now. Cold air hit her face. She grimaced for a second, then inhaled deeply.

"Anyway, Theon doesn't even believe Auryon is from this realm, yet he's comfortable letting her tutor you? It doesn't make sense," Luka said as they made their way to the vehicle.

"He doesn't think she's from the *realm?*"

"With her gifts, I'm inclined to agree with him."

"What is her magic?" Tessa asked.

"Something about moving among smoke and ashes. She can summon weapons, and not like we do from a pocket realm. It's like she can *create* them," Luka explained. "But there's more. I know there is."

"You sound like you fancy her," Tessa teased as he opened the door to the passenger seat.

"Get in," was all he said, shutting the door behind her.

Luka was quiet as he started the vehicle and pulled into traffic while Tessa fiddled with the music.

"Can I ask you something?"

Luka sighed. "Yes."

"What's your earliest memory?"

"That's a bizarre question," he muttered.

She twisted in the front seat to see him better. "It's really not. You don't trust this Auryon because she has gifts not readily found in Devram, but so do you. Don't you think it's possible you weren't born here either? Don't you think it's possible you're like…"

She trailed off, and he glanced over at her. "Like you? Some lost child of a god?"

"*Unwanted* child of a god," she corrected.

"You don't know that, Tessa."

"I'm here, aren't I? In a realm forgotten by the gods."

Luka was quiet for a few seconds before saying, "I do not remember my parents. I don't really have memories of them, only what Valter has told me."

"You were five years when they passed. You should remember *something*," Tessa argued.

"I don't," he said in a tone that told Tessa to drop it.

"But there were Sargon Legacy here before?"

"Supposedly. Centuries ago, if history texts are to be believed."

"Why were they killed off?"

"According to history, Sargon and Arius were as close as brothers. Arius ruled as a First, and Sargon commanded his armies. When the Arius Kingdom tried to overtake Devram before, they failed. They were banished to the territory they now hold, and any Sargon Legacy—"

"Were dealt with," Tessa finished, remembering what Dagian had told her on their return trip to the Acropolis.

"Something like that," Luka said tightly.

They rode the rest of the way to the townhouse in silence, but as Luka turned off the vehicle, she said quietly, "It's lonely. Being the only one of your kind."

"Yeah, little one, it is," he answered before climbing out and shutting the door.

"In a few weeks, you will all be receiving your third Mark," Mother Cordelia said from the front of the room. "This Mark is often the hardest one for a new Source to adjust to. You will be able to hear your Master's thoughts and that can take some getting used to. There will be an extended time away as you adjust. You need to use that time to do two things: make sure your own thoughts are where they need to be— focused on your Master's needs and desires. The second thing, I'm sure will come easier to *most* of you," she said pointedly with a glare in Tessa's direction where she sat away from the others as usual. "You need to be sure your reactions are under control when you hear your Master's thoughts and wishes down the bond. They are trusting you to give nothing away. You keep their secrets, but your mannerisms will always speak louder than words."

An alarm going off on the Estate Mother's phone signaled the end of the lesson, and she picked it up, silencing it. "You are dismissed."

The other Sources gathered their things, but Tessa waited. Mother Cordelia still expected her to stay for her lessons. As the others started filing out, Luka stepped around them, and then Tessa was sucking in a breath because Theon was with him. She hadn't expected him to be here.

"My Lord," Cordelia said with a small bow.

"Cordelia," he answered tightly, moving to Tessa and packing her things for her.

She wasn't sure what to do. And *why* was he doing that in front of her? The disapproval on Mother Cordelia's face said she was not impressed, and when Theon slung the bag over his shoulder before helping Tessa to her feet, the Estate Mother's features went positively livid.

"My Lord, we resume her private instruction today. She has missed far too many, and I must insist—"

Theon stiffened, his darkness appearing, and again Tessa saw the flash of a wince from Luka as he turned away from her.

"You insist *nothing*, Cordelia," Theon said, his voice too calm and too low.

It had Tessa stepping closer to him as his arm slipped around her waist. Two faint red splotches appeared on the Estate Mother's cheeks, and *that* had Tessa trying to slide behind him. But Theon held her firm, his thumb brushing along her hip.

His smile was sharp as he continued. "We were finally able to find a suitable replacement for your services. We have been incredibly grateful for your willingness to give extra time to…*help* Tessa. I am sure you will be happy to have several hours of your week back."

Mother Cordelia blinked rapidly, clearly trying to come up with something to say, and Tessa knew she would pay for this moment the next time she saw her.

"I apologize if I have seemed inadequate, but she has very little *control*," Cordelia said, that one word holding a sneer. "But I assure you, my Lord, as we discussed at the beginning of the Selection Year, I am the best option for the position. I know her best, and—"

"Are you asserting that you know my Source better than I do, Cordelia?"

Her face paled a little, making those dark splotches stand out a little starker. "Of course not, my Lord."

"And is it your place to question my decisions?"

"No, my Lord," she replied, lifting her chin a little as she spoke. "But I have had an impeccable rapport with the ruling Lords and Ladies for decades, and—"

"Oh, I am quite aware of your rapport with them," Theon interrupted yet again, and Tessa glanced up at him, wondering what that meant. His face betrayed nothing, but when she looked back at the Estate Mother, her eyes were wide. A tight, dark smile lifted on Theon's lips as he said, "Should we require your services again, I will let you know, but I trust you have plenty to fill your suddenly free time with."

"I do," she replied curtly.

"Wonderful. I'm glad we could provide that for you," Theon said, continuing to hold her gaze. "One would think you'd be grateful."

It was several seconds before she said, "Thank you, my Lord."

Theon said nothing else, guiding Tessa to the door where Luka was waiting for them. Tessa waited until they'd climbed a set of stairs before she said, "You shouldn't have done that."

"She shouldn't have argued with me," Theon replied, his hand still on her lower back. "And I meant what I said, Tessa. If she gives you any push back in your sessions with the other Sources, tell me or Luka."

"And if this new instructor doesn't work out?"

They had come to a stop outside another room. Luka had already pushed through the door, but Theon had tugged Tessa to a stop. With his finger, he tilted her chin up, "I have informed Auryon that it is not only my trust she needs to earn, but yours as well. Luka will be there monitoring, but if you have concerns, I want you to tell me. Understood?"

She nodded, but she wouldn't say anything. The last thing she needed was Mother Cordelia *more* upset with her.

It likely wouldn't matter soon anyway.

Theon bent, brushing a light kiss to her temple. She'd slept beside him last night in Luka's room again. Theon hadn't even suggested they go up to his room. She'd gone to bed alone, but she knew he'd slept beside her once she was asleep. At one point, she'd woken up only to find a male on either side of her, the bond humming away contentedly. Too groggy to care, she'd simply rolled into one of them. She didn't even know which one, but she did know when she woke the next morning, she was alone in the bed again. If she was feeling *anything* right now, she might have been disappointed.

Following Theon into the room, Tessa took in the space. This was nothing like Mother Cordelia's grand room. This was a smaller office, quaint and sparsely furnished with oversized cushions on the floor rather than desks or chairs. In fact, there weren't any chairs to be found in the room. A small stack of books was beside the cushions. They looked old and well-read. With the curtains open wide and the windows cracked, there was more than enough light, but there were still a few candles lit nearby.

Luka was standing off to the side, his arms crossed and broody as usual, but where was—

Tessa went completely still when her eyes landed on who she could only assume was Auryon.

Midnight hair flowed around her.

Black pants and tunic.

Bare feet.

Her leather armor was missing, but the vambraces still adorned her forearms.

The grey eyes swirling with smoke.

And she knew when she spoke, her tone would be a dark purr.

She had been in her vision at the assessment, had protected her from Dagian.

"Tessa? Are you all right?" Theon asked, concern etched on his features.

"Yes. Fine," she said hastily, eyeing the female who was watching her with an intrigue Tessa wasn't sure what to do with.

"You seem surprised," he said.

Tessa quickly shoved down any emotion that had slipped through. "A little," she replied. "This room is nice. I like the window open."

"As you should," the female said, stepping forward.

"Tessa, this is Auryon," Theon said.

"It's a pleasure," she recited automatically.

Auryon's lips tipped up in a terrifying sort of smile. "I've been waiting to meet you properly," she replied.

"What do you mean 'properly?'" Luka asked.

She flicked those strange eyes to him momentarily. "Hearing and reading about someone can only do so much to assuage curiosity."

Theon pulled his phone from his pocket, that muscle ticking in his jaw as he glanced at the screen. "If there is nothing else you need, I have a meeting I need to get to." Looking at Tessa, he added, "With the other heirs."

As if he suddenly found the need to tell her where he was going to be and who he would be with.

When she didn't reply, he turned away from her, handing her bag off to Luka, but she could feel his frustration down their bond as he left without another word.

"Take a seat," Auryon said, motioning to the fluffy cushions on the floor.

"You don't have any chairs?" Luka muttered, looking around.

Auryon's grin grew. "I would think you'd enjoy them. Makes it feel more nest-like, don't you think?"

Luka's eyes narrowed, but she turned back to Tessa, motioning again to the cushions. Cautiously, she made her way to them, sinking down onto one. And holy gods, it was more than comfortable. She could curl up and sleep on this thing. She found herself smiling as Auryon sat on the cushion across from her. Looking over her shoulder, Tessa said, "Are you really going to stand there the entire time?"

"Yes," Luka said.

"Why?"

"Because I don't need to sit on the floor."

"But if this were a cave floor, he'd have already shifted and been sprawled out, taking up way too much space," Auryon said, picking up a book off the top of the stack.

"A cave floor?" Tessa asked in confusion.

Auryon was busy flipping pages as she muttered, "Yes, yes. Dragons and their caves. Probably full of treasure too."

Tessa whirled back to Luka. "What is she talking about?"

"Nothing," he ground out.

"Do you like caves?"

His lips pressed into a thin line, but he didn't answer.

"Oh my gods. Why?" Her face scrunched up, equally disgusted because there was no light in a cave, but also somewhat fascinated.

"It's a place to keep their treasure," Auryon answered, bringing Tessa's attention back to her.

She was holding the open book out to her, and Tessa reached for it as she asked, "How do you know all this?"

"One would assume I am to be knowledgeable if I am to teach you."

"Yes, but how do you know so much about dragons?"

"What do you know about the dragons?"

"Nothing really," she admitted. "I knew *of* them in the sense that they were a being of other worlds, but I never really gave them much thought until I learned he was one."

"Partially. More than a halfling, but not a full-fledged dragon," Auryon said.

"Again, how do you know all that?"

"I do my research to make sure I am adequately prepared for a job," she answered. Tessa started to ask another question, but Auryon pressed a finger to the book Tessa held as she said, "And my job is to adequately prepare *you* for what you will face."

"I thought your job was to tell me about Devram? The things Fae lessons leave out."

"It is. What do you see?"

Tessa focused on the book, surprise coursing through her as she found the page with various shapes. Some were spheres, while others appeared to be flat planes that simply ended. Another looked like several islands clustered together, as if they were islands in the sky.

"Are these...other worlds?" Tessa asked, somewhat in awe as she brought the book closer to her face.

"They are," Auryon agreed. "And before I can tell you about Devram, you need to know about this one."

She tapped the page atop one of the spheres. Beside it, in a neat print, was the name *Siadrin.*

"The realm of the gods?" Tessa asked.

She knew the name. It was taught in their early history. The world the gods inhabited and where Achaz ruled as the god of gods. She'd simply never given it much thought otherwise considering the gods did not interfere with Devram.

"You know it. Good," Auryon said, something pleased in her voice. "What else do you know?"

"Aren't you supposed to be teaching me?"

"Yes, but what is the point of teaching you something you already know?"

That was a good point.

"I know that at some point, the gods became bored and started having children with mortals. The descendants of those demigods are the Legacy, and they feared them someday becoming too powerful. So they created Devram," Tessa recited dutifully.

"While eloquently stated, there are some points we need to correct," Auryon said. She'd grabbed another book, holding it out to Tessa.

Setting the first aside, she took it. She scarcely glanced at the picture before saying, "This is Silas, god of the earth and land."

"It is. He was the first to fall in love with a mortal, and it was not because he was bored," she said. "He truly loved her. In fact, he has not loved another so thoroughly since."

"How can you possibly know that?" Tessa scoffed.

"The point is," Auryon continued, "some of the gods truly loved the mortals they had children with. They mourned them when they passed, some grieving for decades. Others became jealous of gods having something they didn't, and still others feared it would somehow make them less powerful if they didn't have the same. Some mortals did not have children with the gods out of love. Some were selected by a god or goddess, but none of it was done out of boredom."

"Selected," Tessa repeated, her eyes flying to her swirling ones.

The female nodded. "You heard me correctly, and now you understand why we need to discuss *Siadrin* to properly learn about Devram.

Mortals were carefully selected, many observed for years before a god or goddess decided to claim them. I believe you know the rest. They feared the Legacy would one day become too powerful and attempt to overthrow them. An agreement was made, and Devram was created."

"But the gods didn't uphold the agreement," Tessa said, thinking of Scarlett. Her father had been a Legacy.

Auryon tsked. "That is when they became bored."

"So in the end, what is the point of Devram? Why force everyone to stay here? If they broke one of the agreements, what do the rest matter?" Tessa asked.

Auryon's terrifying grin appeared again. "Clever girl. There are many who question that same thing, and I think you will find some of them are trying to do something about it."

# 32
## AXEL

"Please stop," Katya said from where she sat cross-legged on the bed, three different books spread out around her.

"I'm not doing anything," Axel argued. He was reclined against the headboard, one knee bent, his phone in his hand as he fiddled around with some new music.

"You are," she replied. "You don't leave a song on for more than a few seconds."

"I do too."

"You don't," she retorted, her hand snapping out and grabbing his phone. She swiped a few things before setting it aside, and one of his favorite playlists came through the speakers in the room. She went back to her books, and now he had nothing to occupy him.

Neither of them had spoken about the fact that they continued to sleep in this bed together since the night she'd been hurt. It was just a silent agreement they'd apparently come to. Or maybe he'd decided, and she'd just gone along with it?

Gods, was he really that much of a rude fuck?

"Axel. Stop," she sighed again, looking up from her book.

"What am I doing now? You took my phone," he said in confusion.

"You're staring at my arm. You do that a lot."

She wasn't wrong. His gaze had been fixed on her arm where the blade had sliced her perfect bronze skin. Now there was a raised ridge there, almost a faint golden sheen to it. His father had been furious that she had been *marred*. He'd apparently withheld Theon's weekly rations for the week because of it, which only made Axel feel like shit considering his brother had given him the last of his prior rations despite being drained. He was likely drawing from Luka now, putting an unnecessary strain on both of them.

"It never should have happened," he finally said, picking at a loose thread on the comforter.

"Staring at it won't change the fact that it did," she replied.

"I just don't like that you will always have this reminder."

"I have plenty of scars, Axel. To be honest, I'm glad it was a physical one this time."

Axel hated every bit of that sentence, but he remained quiet. She returned to her reading, and he leaned forward, peering over her shoulder.

"Have you found anything else about why the Fae were created?" he asked.

"As a power Source for the Legacy," she replied absent-mindedly.

"Yes, but the text from the Pantheon archives suggested there was more to it than just that."

Kat sat up straighter, a strange smile playing on her lips as she said, "Axel St. Orcas, have you been *theorizing*?"

"No," he said quickly.

"I think you have."

He shook his head, but she was already shifting to give him her full attention. "Let's hear it then."

"You read that the Fae were created to keep the balance," he said, feeling almost embarrassed that he was proposing a theory. This was Theon's area of expertise. He and Kat would go on for hours, boring Axel to near tears.

Kat waited patiently for him to go on. He cleared his throat. "Then you said something about the Fates requiring something to be done. So what if the Fae weren't designed to *serve* the Legacy?"

"Then how would the Legacy refill their power?"

"No, that's not—" He shook his head in frustration, trying to figure out how to word this so she would understand. "Yes, the Fae were created with the purpose of being a source to refill a Legacy's power reserves quickly, but what if there was more to it? What if the greater purpose was a check against the Legacy power?"

Katya seemed to mull this over as she said, "How so?"

Feeling more foolish by the minute, Axel pressed on anyway. "The gods always feared their Legacy would become too powerful one day, so the Fae would have been created as a check against that power. Right?" Kat nodded. "But what if it was necessary because if they grew too powerful, it would fuck the balance or whatever?"

"That seems very plausible," Katya mused, leaning back onto her hands. Amber eyes studied him, seeming to see through to his soul. "There's more."

"No. The rest is... There's not more."

"Tell me," she insisted.

"There's nothing to back it up. It's just an idea."

"I love ideas." When he still didn't say anything, she added, "Please tell me, Axel."

Sighing, he broke her stare, fiddling with that loose thread once more. "It was what you said about the Fae being created to keep the balance. What if the Fates found the balance tipping, so an ultimatum was made and the Fae were the answer? What if the Fae actually *saved* the Legacy?" He took another breath. It felt almost blasphemous to say the next words in Devram, and his tone was low as he said, "What if it was never supposed to be like this?"

"I guess..." Kat went quiet. They both did, until she said, "I guess we would never know because the gods agreed not to interfere here. Scarlett certainly seemed upset by the way of things here though."

"Too bad we can't communicate with her," Axel scoffed.

Katya sat up straighter. "What if there was a way to communicate with her?"

"What are you talking about?"

"Didn't Theon see her in a mirror or something?"

Axel huffed a laugh. "Do you have any idea how much shit I gave him about that only to find out it had actually happened?"

"Do you think it was really her sister that tried to kill her?" Kat asked.

"Honestly? Yeah, I think I do believe that."

Kat laughed, a real one that warmed something in his chest. "You believe her, but questioned Theon for years?"

"It's a mirror, kitten," he replied, leaning forward and tugging playfully on one of her curls. "Why would I think anything different?"

"Theon doesn't seem like the type to joke about such matters," she replied, shifting more so she was seated beside him against the headboard.

"It's rare, but he has a bit of humor that manages to sneak out from time-to-time," he answered. "He never really got to experience fun, though. I think that's why he hates Chaosphere so much."

"That's logical," Kat agreed.

"Did you play?"

"No."

"What?" Axel asked, horrified at the thought. "Why not?"

"I have always preferred reading."

"But… Do you watch it?"

"No, because I prefer reading."

Axel was quiet for several moments before he said, "Is it because you're not very good at it? Theon is terrible at Chaosphere."

Then there was a pillow smacking him in the face, and she was laughing as he yanked the thing from her hands and hit her back before tossing it aside.

"Just for that, you must now become a default Everflames fan."

Katya clicked her tongue. "That's fine. I really don't care."

"I'm getting you so much Everflames gear for Solstice. A jersey, a tee shirt, a blanket, socks—"

"Socks?" she interrupted.

"Yes, socks," he replied.

She huffed another laugh before her demeanor seemed to shift back to something more serious. "Do you think it would work? To speak with her through the mirror?" she asked.

Axel blew out a long breath, tucking a hand up behind his head. "I don't know, kitten. We'd have to get to the mirror first. It's in the Underground in my father's private study. I've only seen it twice in my life."

"Do you think he knows what it is?"

Axel started to say no, but then paused. *Did* his father know that thing was a mirror gate this entire time? Had he seen Scarlett in it before? Had he seen someone else?

"I guess I don't know," he finally answered.

"Do you think there are more of them? These mirror gates?" Kat went on. "Or is there only one entrance into the realm?"

"And that entrance is in the Underground?"

She shrugged. "Just talking out loud. There could easily be more of them."

"How would we even find them?"

"No idea," she answered around a yawn. They'd both already changed into nightclothes, and now she started gathering up her books. "Do you wish it was different? How Devram is run, I mean."

"I wish a lot of things were different," Axel answered, standing and stretching before pulling back the blankets.

"Tell me one."

He sighed, climbing back onto the bed and slipping under the covers as she did the same. "I wish you liked raw fish wrapped in rice."

"Oh my gods, Axel," she said with a groan.

"I wish we had more freedoms."

Kat was immediately serious once more. "Legacy have plenty of freedom. They run Devram."

"The ruling Lords and Ladies do."

"And you are an heir. A member of a ruling family."

"Which gives me less freedom than the common Legacy, and with my father— In many ways, Theon, Luka, and I are as chained as the—"

"As the Fae," she finished when he didn't.

"I wish that were different," he said.

"Even if you were right that the Fae were not meant to serve the Legacy, I don't think things would change here," she said softly. "The Legacy would never give up their control, and I think they still fear it. The same way the gods feared their Legacy becoming too powerful? I think the Legacy fear that about the Fae here. It's *why* we are so controlled. Every facet of our existence is controlled from our upbringing, to our power, to our kingdom assignment."

"I think it's why my father controls us so much, especially Theon. He fears the day Theon can draw from his Source."

"That makes sense."

"For what it's worth, I wish it was different, Kat."

She gave him a soft smile before reaching over to shut off the bedside lamp. As she resettled beside him, he said, "I wish I didn't feel guilty for sleeping in the same bed as you."

She went still. "Why would you feel guilty about that?"

"I never gave you the choice."

"You did," she countered. "I know I could sleep on the sofa if I wished. You are not forcing me to be in your bed."

"I guess."

"I've been meaning to apologize, by the way," she went on.

"Whatever for?" Axel asked, rolling onto his side and propping his head on his fist as he looked down at her. Her eyes almost appeared to glow like smoldering embers in the dark of the room.

"I kept offering you my blood. I didn't realize that…"

"I was addicted to it?" he finished for her. "That's probably something I'd wish to change too."

"I think that part is the same in other realms."

"And it just led to another problem in the end."

"What do you mean?"

"What are the Night Children? Legacy who couldn't control themselves so Arius cursed them to be controlled by their bloodlust. It was yet another balance that had to be corrected," Axel explained.

"And you are…?"

"Yeah, kitten," he sighed. "I am. Every week I wonder if I'll make it to my rations. Every week I wonder if this is the week I'm going to cross the line and never come back."

"I don't understand," she said, and even in the dark Axel could see her trying to work it all out. It didn't make sense unless he was being careless to begin with. Unless he'd been abusing Fae since his power first appeared. She had no idea his father often forced him to drain his power, then denied him blood to the point of madness.

He reached over, running his knuckles along her cheek. "It is not something you need to be burdened with. You only need to know I'm not good for you, Kat. You're not safe with me."

"I disagree," she said.

"That's not logical," he replied with a small smirk.

"You know where I'm not safe?" she said, ignoring his attempt at trying to lighten the mood. "Out there. Without you. Because out there, Axel? Out there I *am* forced into beds. Out there I do not have someone to make sure that I am getting enough food, or that I have clean clothing. I do not have someone who will help me in the shower and not expect me on my knees afterwards."

"I can do all those things and still not be safe for you, Katya," he replied gently. "What will you do when I lose control and take from you?"

She let out a frustrated noise, and then she was suddenly sitting up. Her hands landed on his chest, and she pushed him onto his back, slinging a leg over so she was straddling him. He was in so much shock, his hands went to her hips instinctively.

"You've had nearly two months to lose control," she said. "Never once have I thought you were even close."

"I would have in those archives, Katya," he said, begging her to understand.

"What happens?" she demanded, and this time, it wasn't smoldering embers in her eyes. There were flames because she was angry, and Axel didn't know why. "What happens if you turn? If you take too much and trigger this curse? What happens to *you*?"

"I would be banished to the Underground just like the other Night Children," he answered. "Sometimes I think that's my father's plan in the end."

"And I would go with you."

"You wouldn't, Kat. My father would never let you go to the Underground."

"I know you feel this, Axel. We don't understand it, but I know you feel it," she answered, leaning down. Ebony ringlets slid over her shoulders, and her cropped sleep shirt slid up. Axel's hands followed, fingers finding soft flesh.

"This is a terrible idea, Katya," he breathed. "If I lost control, I could kill you."

She shook her head. "You wouldn't."

"Kat—"

"You wouldn't, Axel," she insisted.

"Katya, you don't understand—"

"I *do* understand," she said, her voice hardening. "I understand because I've had blood forcibly taken from me." The growl that sounded low in his throat at her words surprised even him, but she didn't even seem fazed. "You wish the Fae had more freedoms? Then give me this one. Let me make this choice. If it's something you want—"

"If it's something I want? For fuck's sake, Kat, I've *wanted* since the moment I laid eyes on you. Before that even. If Theon feels a fraction of this draw to Tessa, I understand the obsession, because I am obsessed with you. It's why even though I know this is a terrible idea, I'm going to let you have it. I don't even know what *this* is, but I know I could never deny you a godsdamn thing."

She kissed him then, her lips soft against his, and he slid a hand up her spine into her hair, holding her in place. He hadn't kissed her since the Underground, and now he found himself trying to make up for all that lost time. His tongue slid against hers, and when she let out a soft moan, it only had him tugging her to him more. His other hand was exploring those curves that he'd dreamed about for weeks and weeks. Soft and warm and perfect. Utter perfection. That was all he could think as her mouth moved against his. Her fingers glided over his chest, down his abdomen, back up over his shoulders, and into his hair as she explored with her hands.

He made a sound of protest when she suddenly sat up, but that protest died just as quickly as she pulled her shirt over her head.

*Holy shit.*

"Kat," he said, his voice all gravel and his throat too dry. "This is—"

"I swear to Anala, Axel, if you say this is a bad idea—" Her lips pursed as she shoved hair back from her face. "You're right. This is illogical. It makes no sense, and it drives me mad that I don't understand whatever this thing is that draws us to each other. But if this is a terrible decision, I want to make it. If you do."

"You're stunning," he murmured, staring up at her. Topless, sitting atop him, hair a mess, and lips swollen. Something in her eyes flared at his words, and he was sure if he could see her a little better, there would be a flush to her cheeks. His hand drifted up, and he forced himself to pause, not wanting to take something from her that she'd been forced to give in the past. "Can I?"

"What do you think we're doing here?" she asked with a light huff of laughter.

"That's just it, kitten. I have no fucking idea," he answered, his tongue running along his bottom lip as he stared at her breasts. "But I'll do whatever you want."

She gave another soft laugh before she took his hand and placed it over her breast. He groaned, his thumb sweeping over her nipple, and her entire body shuddered at the touch.

"You can touch me, Axel. Please gods, touch me," she said.

And that plea made him forget all the reasons this was a terrible idea.

He pushed up to a sitting position, wrapping one hand around the nape of her neck and hauling her mouth back to his. His other hand alternated between squeezing her breast and rolling her nipple between his thumb and forefinger. Her whimper had him breaking the kiss, sliding his lips along her jaw before pressing small open-mouthed kisses below her ear, down her throat, along her shoulder, her collarbone.

"I get to touch you," he murmured, and he heard the awe in his voice.

"I've never *wanted* to be touched before," she replied in a breathy tone as her hands clasped onto his shoulders and back again, fingers pressing into his flesh.

"Only me?"

She nodded, her head tipping back as he lowered his mouth to her other breast.

Only him.

A primal thing inside of him liked the sound of that, and he sucked hard, pulling another cry from her. Her hips had started moving, rocking against him.

"What are you looking for, kitten?" he murmured against her skin, kissing along the valley of her breasts.

"Anything. Everything," she breathed.

He smiled as she pulled him back to her for a long, breathless kiss, her hands framing his face, while he slid his own hand down her chest, down her stomach, and beneath her pants. She went still for the briefest of moments when he cupped her, and when he pressed his thumb to her center, the sound she made had him groaning into her mouth. Or maybe that was how wet he found her.

"Fuck," he muttered, sliding his thumb up to her clit and making small circles that had her chasing his hand.

He thought she might be about to say the same thing, but all she got out was the f-sound as her head dropped forward, her nails grappling at his arms. Instead of a curse, he got a moaned, "Axel, please don't stop."

"Do you have any idea the agony I was in trying to get you to say my name, kitten?" he demanded, sinking a finger into her as he continued to move his thumb in a steady rhythm.

"Why?" she gasped.

"No fucking idea," he said. "But it was a *need*, Katya."

She cried out again when he sank a second finger in. She was grinding against his hand now, riding his fingers and chasing pleasure. His other arm was looped around her waist, holding her tight and close. And he watched.

He watched as her breaths became sharp, little inhales.

He watched as her hands moved from his arms to his shoulders, as if she didn't know what to touch or where to hold.

He watched as she tensed when he lowered his mouth to her breast, flicking his tongue over her sensitive nipple.

His eyes never left her as her knees clenched around his hips, as her mouth parted on a small cry when he thrust his fingers in again, this time curling them to hit that spot that sent her careening into ecstasy. He felt her clamp around his fingers, his thumb still moving as she rode out her high, and when her brow fell against his chest, his hand smoothed over her hair as he pressed a kiss to the top of her head.

It was a good minute before she lifted her head, her breaths still too fast as heated amber eyes met his. Then she was sliding off him, already reaching for his pants and tugging. Axel wasn't about to argue, helping her out and kicking them down his legs before flinging them out into the room. She was already clamoring back onto him. He wasn't prepared when her fingers wrapped around his cock, giving it a firm stroke from base to tip.

"Fucking Arius," he cursed, falling back onto his elbows.

She only smiled, repeating the movement before lifting her hips and lining herself up. He could feel all of her wetness and heat before she even started to sink down. He had flopped down onto his back, his hands fisting in the sheets as she moved slowly. Every part of him wanted to grab those hips and yank her down, but he was once more too enraptured by her lips parting and her eyelids already going heavy again.

One of her hands fell to his chest as she rocked down, and some unintelligible sound came from her as she finally took the last inch of him. He couldn't think around the feeling of being buried deep inside her, but his soul knew what that sound had meant because he was feeling the exact same thing.

That this was right.

That the rightness was overwhelming.

That he wanted more.

Needed it.

Unfisting his hands from the sheets, he slid them up her thighs, unable to help himself as his hips flexed up. She gave a soft moan, her other hand coming to his chest.

"This is— I can't—" Her chest was heaving again.

"Take your time," he murmured, fighting the urge to lift her and feel that slick friction.

He held still while she sucked in a deep breath, visibly getting herself under control. He bit down on a curse as she shifted, finding the position most comfortable for her, but he couldn't keep his hands from roaming. Up her ribs. To her breasts. Down her sides. Around to her ass.

Then she finally rocked into him, and he pushed out a sharp breath. "That's it, kitten."

Her rhythm was lazy and unhurried, and every once in a while she would pause and swivel her hips, grinding down against him. In the back of his mind, he wondered if she'd ever done this before. He knew she'd been fucked, didn't like to think about it really, but had she ever been on top? Ever been given the opportunity to discover what she liked and didn't?

So he let her take her time, murmuring soft praises as she did. He never stopped touching her. Brushing his fingers over her lips. Plucking at a nipple. Dipping his fingers between her legs to rub against her clit. And when she started making those desperate little noises, the ones that told him she didn't know what else to do, he pulled her to his chest. His arms wrapped around her tight as she buried her face into his neck, and his hips punched up into her. Each moan and little cry from her only made him more crazed. Where she had found a rhythm, he had no such thing. His movements were frenzied and erratic, and when he felt her start to spasm around him, he had no choice but to follow.

It wasn't until later, after they'd cleaned up and climbed back into bed that she whispered into the night, "I've never gotten to do that before."

"Do what? Be on top?" Axel asked, peppering kisses along her neck as he tugged her back against his chest.

"Finish," she answered.

Axel froze. "Are you telling me you've never had an orgasm?"

"I wasn't exactly a priority when I was there to service them," she answered sleepily, pressing her ass back even more as she wiggled to get comfortable.

He didn't know what to say. It shouldn't surprise him. It didn't when he really thought about it.

But as he felt her breathing shift and she slipped into slumber, he found himself still awake.

Because suddenly he didn't think the idea of trying to contact Scarlett through the mirror was all that crazy. Not if it meant they could somehow keep whatever it was they'd found here.

# 33
## TESSA

"This one?" Tessa asked, pointing to a word as she held the book out to Theon.

Theon looked up from his computer, leaning over to get a better look at the page. "That is a variation of the word seraph."

"Seraph," Tessa repeated, pulling the book back to her lap. "Like an angel?"

"Yes," he said. "There were different types. Some that could banish their wings and some that couldn't. Likely others we know nothing about."

Tessa hummed, mulling that over for a minute before she continued working through the book. True to his word, Theon was helping her learn the Lost Language. He'd found an easier book for her to start with. Although, "easier" was laughable. This was tedious.

Tedious but necessary.

That was what she reminded herself every time she wanted to throw the book and do literally anything else. She'd never be able to read the book Rordan had given her.

Well, not exactly *given* to her. Fearing Theon would take it from her when she returned to the Acropolis, she'd left it in Faven. Rordan had assured her it was hers, and whenever she was ready to retrieve it, it would be waiting for her. But retrieving it would be pointless if she couldn't read the damn thing.

It had been a few weeks since she'd returned. A few weeks since she'd wrestled with so many truths. A few more weeks of watching, listening, and learning everything she could.

They'd fallen into somewhat of a routine. Running with Theon in the morning, followed by training with Luka. Afternoons alternated between attending various functions with Theon, lessons with the other Sources, and private instruction with Auryon. Luka still came to all the lessons with Auryon, and Tessa would never admit it to anyone, but she liked that. There was a weird comfort in just having him where she could see him. Auryon mainly focused on Devram's history, which was exactly what she was supposed to do, but she was knowledgeable about so much more. And while most days Auryon wouldn't let Tessa stray too far off topic, every once in a while, Tessa could get her to talk about something else.

Theon's phone rang and interrupted her attempt at reading. When he looked at the screen, he immediately tensed. Setting his laptop aside, he pushed to his feet, walking over to the window in the lounge to answer it. She'd been with him long enough to know it was his father.

"Tonight? You couldn't have given me more notice?" he asked.

Tessa looked up, finding him shoving his hand through his hair. His agitation was heavy down the bond, and she closed her book with a sigh. Whatever was happening tonight, she would surely have to be with him. She'd been looking forward to a night in. She couldn't remember the last time they hadn't had some sort of function in the evening.

"I understand the Solstice is in four days. We will see her when we return to Arius House after the third Mark is given," Theon was saying. "Of course... I can let them know... *What?*"

Theon nearly yelled the last word, and Tessa jumped at the unexpected inflection. It was more than just agitation flooding down the bond now. It was anger and some dread, and it had her tilting her head as she watched him begin to pace.

"Understood," was all he ended up saying in the end before he slid his phone back into his pocket.

Pushing out a long breath, he turned back to Tessa. "My mother is here."

"I heard," she said.

"I didn't think she was coming since we will be going back to Arius Kingdom for the Winter Solstice."

Tessa nodded, waiting to hear what had caused him so much dread.

"We are to have dinner with them."

"Here?" Tessa asked.

Theon shook his head. "No. At a restaurant in the Acropolis. Luka and Axel will join us."

"I figured. Will Kat come?"

She and Axel had been inseparable, and they could all sense the shift in them. Or at least scent what was going on. Axel escorted her to and from the Pantheon and training arenas as usual, and Kat was spending more time outside the room instead of staying holed up.

"No," Theon answered. "She will not be able to sit at a table with us."

"Axel won't like that," Tessa commented, getting to her feet and stretching. "What do I need to wear?"

"Something elegant."

"Bring whatever you want me in to Luka's room. I'll start getting ready."

She hadn't stepped foot in Theon's room since that night. Theon seemed to have accepted it. He would hint at moving back up there. The room was bigger and so was the bed, but she just...couldn't. Not with everything she'd learned and what she had come to terms with.

She'd taken one step towards the door when Theon said, "There's more."

And those words had the hair on the back of her neck standing because more was never good where Valter was concerned.

"Felicity is to join us."

Tessa had gotten really good at blocking the bond. She hadn't told Theon, and she wasn't sure if Luka had clued him in or not, but it was something she'd managed to get Auryon to teach her. Not just blocking the bond for short periods of time, but mental shields. But when her feelings were strong enough or when she was caught off guard, her mental shield slipped.

And this was one of those times.

Theon's eyes went wide as she scrambled to get her shields back up, but she knew he'd just been assaulted with a barrage of emotions she didn't know what to do with. In fact, it was the most she'd let him feel of her in weeks.

"Tessa," he breathed, taking a step towards her and stilling when she took one back.

"It's fine," Tessa said, shoving those feelings back down where they belonged and becoming the nothing she'd been since Luka had held her in the middle of a storm.

"It's not fine, Tessa. None of this is fine," he said.

"And there's nothing we can do to change this. We cannot decline?"

"No, but we can talk about this."

"We should," she agreed.

He drew up short, clearly confused by her sudden agreement.

"How do you expect me to act tonight?"

"What?" he asked, more confusion drifting down the bond.

"Am I to be the submissive pet? Or are we pretending again?"

His features darkened. "I think we stopped pretending a long time ago, beautiful."

Her brow arched. "Did we?"

He moved then, in that way that was too fast. Suddenly, he was standing in front of her. He took her chin between his thumb and forefinger. "I've felt your emotions, clever tempest."

"And I've repeatedly told you I'm an exceptional liar," Tessa replied with a soft purr.

"And you promised it would always be like this. That it would always be a battle with you."

"The thing about battles, Theon, is that eventually someone has to lose," she replied, stepping into him a little more. She saw his throat bob, felt his breath hitch, as she reached up and slid her finger along his chest to his throat. "So tell me, tonight am I your pet? Or am I someone people fear as much as they fear you?"

"Our bargain stands, Tessa."

"I will not be forced beneath a table for fulfilling that role?" she asked, brushing her thumb along his bottom lip, and she didn't miss how he pitched forward the smallest amount.

"I think you have learned when and how to act with my father present."

"Yes, but that was when I was a Fae. Now I am not," she replied, faint light flaring at her fingertips.

He sucked in a sharp gasp, darkness rising up to meet her power. She wasn't prepared for it. Some part of her should have been, but other than sleeping beside her, he had kept some distance from her. They did just enough to appease the bond. Touches here and there. Quick fucks.

Just enough.

That's what they'd become.

They could never be more.

"I'll get your dress," he said, his voice gravel as his gaze dipped to her lips.

"And I'll get ready."

He left her at Luka's door, continuing upstairs while she went into the bathroom. She quickly rinsed off before wrapping a towel around her body. She took her time brushing out her hair, preparing herself for what this night would bring.

Preparing herself for what she was about to do.

A theory she needed to test.

She didn't know what dress Theon was going to bring her, so she made sure her hair and make-up would work with anything. Curling her hair into big, soft curls, she pinned them up on her head. She made her cosmetics dark with hints of gold on her eyelids.

She'd started a little stockpile of lip color in here, and she swiped up a tube of red from the antique-looking soap dish. Luka had a lot of odd little trinkets around his room. She hadn't really noticed them until she'd started coming out of her self-induced state of numbness, but there was an onyx and silver vase on his bookshelf. He kept his hair ties in a small brass tin with gems inlaid in it. He even had some sort of antique frame. It was gold and beautiful, but there was nothing in it. Just an empty frame sitting on a desk.

When she emerged from the bathroom wrapped in a silk robe, Luka was there, already dressed in a suit and tie. His hair was tied back neatly, but she knew some strands would slip free before the end of the night.

He was adjusting cufflinks, but he looked up when she emerged, bright eyes sweeping over her. She cleared her throat, pulling the sash of the robe a little tighter.

"Theon is on his way down with your dress," Luka said. "He was finishing getting ready."

"Sorry I took over your bathroom," she replied, realizing Luka likely got ready upstairs as well.

He shrugged. "I'm used to plans suddenly changing and needing to adapt."

"Yes, but this is *your* room."

"It's fine, Tessa. Are you ready for tonight?"

She looked away from him, her fingertips sliding along the wall as she moved just to have something to do. "Is there something I should be ready for?"

"I am just assuming it could be a difficult evening for you."

She paused, looking over her shoulder at him. "Why?"

"Because of Felicity."

The blunt statement had her pausing for a split second. "I think it will be fine. Theon told me what is expected of me tonight."

Luka's eyes narrowed. "And what, exactly, is that?"

"What I was meant to be." Her eyes darted to the door as the bond warmed a little in her soul. "He's coming."

Seconds later, Theon walked through the door, a black evening dress in hand. He came to a halt, looking between her and Luka before he asked, "What is happening here?"

"I should be asking you that," Luka said, reaching out to take the heels Theon held in his other hand. "I think we all need to be very careful tonight."

"Aren't we always?" Theon asked, crossing the room to Tessa.

"Some more than others," Luka said pointedly.

Tessa gave him a simpering smile before looking over the dress. "No undergarments?"

"I'm told some dresses can't be worn with undergarments. This seemed like one of those," Theon replied, a dark caress in his voice.

She almost huffed a laugh, but instead she reached for the sash of the robe, letting it slide down her body before taking the dress from Theon. The black garment dipped low enough to show the second Source Mark on her chest, and the thigh slit reached nearly to her hip. It hugged her torso, and the heels added the usual several inches. Theon pulled small emerald earrings from his pocket, and she quickly slipped them on.

Axel was waiting for them in the foyer, Kat presumably in his room. He looked annoyed, and when he didn't say anything as they approached, it only confirmed his foul mood. He didn't even turn on the music on the drive to the restaurant.

When they arrived, Theon helped her remove her long coat, handing it off to the coat check with his own. Luka and Axel did the same before they were escorted to a table near the back. The restaurant was more than fancy. Low lighting. Ornate tables and chairs. A bottle of wine probably cost more than the emerald earrings she was wearing. It was immediately clear only elite Legacy were allowed to dine here. The wait staff was even Legacy. She was sure there were Fae in the back who took care of dishes and cleaning, but out here? The only Fae in sight was Eviana as they approached the table.

Everyone else was already here, including Felicity, who immediately stood as they approached, bowing her head to the Arius Heirs.

"My darlings!" Cressida cried, clasping her hands together. Tessa could swear there were tears welling in her eyes.

"Mother," Theon greeted, moving around the table to press a kiss to her cheek. "What a pleasant surprise."

Axel did the same, and Tessa stayed close to Luka as he greeted her as well, but when Theon moved to take his seat, he noticed what Tessa already had. The table was set for eight, three on each side and two on the ends. Valter was obviously at the head of the table, his wife to his right and Source to his left. Theon always sat next to Eviana, and Tessa sat next to him, but that was where Felicity had been seated.

"I assumed you would want to sit next to your Match," Valter said pointedly. "Your mother is excited that the two of you have finally decided to make the official announcement."

"You will separate me from my Source?" Theon asked tightly and unmoving, as if he was rooted to the spot.

"She can sit across from you next to Luka," Valter replied dismissively. "Soon enough she'll be his Match anyway. Sit."

Theon looked as though he was about to argue, but then seemed to wisely decide this was not something to make a scene over.

"Go with Luka, Tessa," he said, that muscle ticking in his jaw, but she was already rounding the table. She stopped beside Theon, though, reaching up to brush back the lock of hair that always fell across his brow. She could swear he leaned into her touch.

"This is fine, Theon," she said softly. "I know what is expected of me."

She followed Luka around the table, taking the chair between him and Cressida. Theon proceeded to pull Felicity's chair out for her, but he held Tessa's gaze the entire time.

Wine was poured once everyone was settled, and the moment the wait staff had left, Cressida's attention was on Theon and Felicity.

"I already have appointments scheduled with photographers and the press when you are home for Solstice," she said.

"Come again?" Theon said, dragging his eyes from Tessa to his mother.

"For official photos to accompany the announcement," Cressida clucked, swiping up her wine and taking a drink.

Theon turned slowly to Felicity. "Are you planning to visit Arius House over the Solstice holiday?"

Her smile was tentative, and rightfully so, Tessa thought as she rested her chin in her hand, watching this all unfold. Theon's tone was too dark, too calm. She knew that voice too well.

"The Arius Lord was gracious enough to extend me an invitation," Felicity replied, her hands in her lap.

Except all Tessa could think about was her hand resting on a rounded stomach. She felt her lip curl up, and Theon's eyes snapped to her at the same moment Luka leaned over and said, "Find something you can control right now, Tessa."

It was the same thing he always murmured into her ear when everything was becoming too much. So many times she had so little control, but there was always something. Her breathing. If her legs were crossed or uncrossed. If her hands were at her sides or in her lap. What she was looking at.

But she'd learned to control so much more than that these past weeks, past few months, and now his words reminded her she had a purpose tonight. It had nothing to do with Felicity, but she supposed it could be an added bonus to the evening if she played this right.

"We don't even know what the Solstice is going to look like right now," Axel said from down the table. "I mean, there's so much unknown shit right now. Are we even going to be celebrating anything?"

"Language, Axel," Cressida chided, but Valter's glare had narrowed on his youngest.

"Care to expand on your concerns, Son?"

Gods, his tone was just like Theon's. Dark. Calm. Dangerous.

Axel apparently didn't give two fucks.

He sat back in his chair, glass of wine in hand. "The third Mark is to be given in four days. That is also Theon's deadline, is it not?"

"It is," Valter agreed.

"As far as I know, the two are still bonded, so one of them will probably be dead."

"Axel!" Cressida exclaimed.

"Theon is not dying," Valter said coldly at the same time Theon snapped, "No one is touching Tessa."

"I have been assured this problem will be solved by Solstice," Valter continued. "Is that no longer the case, Theon?"

"I will have something figured out," Theon replied, speaking through gritted teeth, and Tessa's head tilted at that information. As far as *she* knew, he was no closer to finding a solution than he'd been the day of the Tribunal Hearing.

"That is a relief," Felicity cut in. "I know this has been such a stressful time for you."

Then she put her hand on Theon's arm.

Tessa didn't move. She didn't lift her chin from where it still rested in her palm, but an arc of energy-infused light skittered across the table directly at Felicity's hand. The female yanked it back with a small cry, wide eyes staring back at her. The entire table had gone still, but the corners of Tessa's lips tipped up in a serpentine smile.

"Tessa, that was..." Theon started, but Felicity cleared her throat, smoothing her hands down the bodice of her dress.

"It is fine, Theon," she said, sitting up a little straighter. "I am sure the bond makes a Source very possessive."

Tessa felt it then. A press of power. She hadn't realized what it was until now. A coil of entitlement and pettiness, fury and indignation. Emotions that would stir up conflict.

"It can," Theon ventured, still staring at Tessa. She could feel his trepidation and confusion down the bond.

"And because I am sure you will find the solution to this, that will not be a worry much longer," Felicity continued.

Tessa clicked her tongue in mock-sympathy as Theon went too still. "I know you don't know him nearly as well as I do, in more ways than one I might add," Tessa said, her wicked smirk growing, "but he doesn't like it when people talk about us being separated, Ms. Davers."

"You can call me Felicity," she replied, a hand fluttering to her chest, but Tessa heard the hint of annoyance in her tone. "After all, I am sure we will be spending so much time together with you being promised to Luka."

Tessa's eyes flicked to Luka, who was giving her the *shut-the-fuck-up* look, then back to Felicity. With her right hand, she made sure the Arius Mark was visible as she reached for her wineglass. "Then I guess that makes them both mine," Tessa replied sweetly, lifting her glass and taking a sip while holding Felicity's gaze.

She didn't want either of them, but she sure as fuck wasn't going to let *Felicity* speak about her as if she wasn't sitting at the same godsdamn table. Tessa knew she'd been in Theon's room on purpose, had been waiting for her. She could believe Theon and his whole set-up theory. It still didn't change anything, but she'd be damned if she was going to let the female's snide comments slide. Not when her entire life she'd been forced to sit and let people talk about her as if she was a piece of property.

"Theon, how has your Source still not learned control?" Valter demanded from down the table. "She will not be allowed to speak to a Legacy in such a manner. Deal with this, or I will."

Her power flared, looping around her wrists as if it were golden bangles. "It has been proven time and again I am not Fae," Tessa said, fighting the nerves in her belly as she turned to face the Arius Lord.

"Whatever you are, it does not give you permission to speak to the Match of an heir in such a manner, let alone speak directly to me," Valter snarled.

"And what would give me that permission? Being the descendant of a god?"

"*I* am a descendant of god," Valter growled, a red flush filling his cheeks.

"Tessa, stop," Theon hissed from across the table.

Tessa only leaned forward, resting her elbow on the table and steepling a finger along her temple. The light around her other forearm began unwinding until a whip of sparking energy lay on the table at her fingertips. The flush in Valter's face faded as he paled a little, his darkness appearing as Eviana lurched to her feet, a whip of vines appearing in her hand. Cressida cried out in dismay, and Theon was pushing to his feet.

"I think a point has been made," Luka said firmly into her ear. "There will already be ramifications for this."

The Lord could try, but Tessa had seen all she needed to, had learned the secret she'd set out to uncover tonight.

She could see it in the furious set of the Lord's features as he stared at her power on the table.

She could see it in the way he didn't challenge her with his own power, but held his darkness back.

The Arius Lord had set Theon up for failure from the very beginning with this dinner, as if he was trying to learn something himself. The question was what?

That was what she pondered the rest of dinner, when Valter kept cutting glances at her. Cressida made her plans with Felicity, who wisely chose not to speak to Tessa the rest of the night. Theon rarely took his eyes off her, and when they finally got back to the townhouse, she was too exhausted to stay up and debate her actions. They trailed her upstairs, only ceasing their chastising when she shut the bathroom door in their faces. She emerged in one of Luka's shirts because it was the only thing she could find in the bathroom. The low murmurs from Luka and Theon stopped as she crawled into the piles of blankets and pillows, but she didn't find sleep.

*She was in some kind of cave or cavern, judging by the rocky floor and walls, but the windows... That was water.*

*Oh gods.*

*She was underwater.*

*Underground and underwater.*

*But before her panic could climb too high, a female voice had her turning.*

*"How unexpected. I haven't had a visitor in nearly five years."*

*There was a set of bars and behind them was a female in some kind of beige garment. Her skin was so pale, the shift looked stark against it. Her black hair was long and stringy, but her violet eyes were bright and full of interest. She stepped closer to the bars, lifting her hands as if to wrap her fingers around them, but then stopped herself.*

*"You smell of forgotten lands," she said.*

*Tessa frowned, unsure what that meant, but then the female tipped her head to the side. A smile slowly curled on her lips, and Tessa found herself taking a step back from the black bars that hummed with magic.*

*"You smell of vengeance."*

*Then she tipped her head back and laughed.*

*She had to be mad. That was the only explanation Tessa could come up with.*

*Looking to her right, she saw a staircase that led up to somewhere, but she didn't know where she was.*

*"Don't go that way, daughter of wild and fury."*

*Tessa whipped her head back to her. "What did you just say?"*

*"Beginnings and Endings. Light and Dark," she started to sing, pacing in a small circle. There was a piece of paper on the dirt floor of her cell, and she stepped on it with every pass she made. "Dark must bow, and Light must rule, but Chaos does not choose."*

*Unwittingly, Tessa took a step forward. Then another and another, until she was right next to the bars. The female's gaze snapped to hers. "Do not touch them!"*

*Tessa jerked back, unsure when she had lifted a hand to do just that.*

*"It calls to you, but then she will come," the female warned.*

"Who?"

"The deceiver who stole resurrected power. It was dead, and she brought it back."

Well, that sounded ominous.

"He will come for her in time, but you..." The female turned to face her fully once more. "We thought it would be her, but it will be you."

"What will be me?" Tessa said. "Who are you?"

But she had moved again, right along the wall of her cell now. Dragging her fingertips along the stone, she said, "You will be the beginning of endings."

# 34
## THEON

"Place your palm here and conjure some power," said the Legacy. Nodding, Theon did just that, placing his hand on the magic scanner and letting darkness pool beneath it. The male watched on a screen that Theon couldn't see, but after a few seconds, he said, "Passage for five was granted by Lady Farhan. Is that correct?"

"Yes," Theon answered impatiently.

"Documentation for the Fae?"

Luka handed over the identification documents for Tessa and Katya, and they all waited while he verified whatever he needed to verify.

Theon had only been to Ekayan Island one other time in his life. All of the heirs were brought at the same time to tour the island when they turned sixteen years. Luka had not been allowed to accompany him on that trip, and Axel had never been here. Theon had tried to get permission from the Falein Lady numerous times throughout the years, the most recent time being after the Tribunal Hearing. It wasn't until he pleaded his case to Prudence and she intervened on his behalf that he was finally granted permission to enter the Ekayan Island archives. Of course, he now owed the Falein Heir a favor of equal grandeur. It was yet another Bargain Mark inked on his skin, but he had two days until the third Mark. Two days to figure something out or face the ruling Lords and Ladies once more. He knew the outcome would not favor him a second time, even if Tessa did ask to stay with him again.

The Legacy handed Luka the documents back before handing Theon five cuffs.

"You have until sundown," the male said. "If you are not back here by that time, these cuffs will release a toxin that will render you unconscious within five seconds. You will be collected for sentencing at that time. Any questions?"

"No," Theon said, sliding a cuff on. The magic of it had the cuff sinking into his skin so it looked like a thick tattoo around his wrist, a bronze line ran through the center of it. He passed one to Luka and two to Axel before reaching for Tessa's hand.

She'd had a vision after that dinner two nights ago. He knew she had. She'd been curled up on the bed, eyes closed, but she hadn't been sleeping. He knew how her breathing shifted when she slept, the soft sigh she always let out right before she drifted off, and how she always slipped her hand under her cheek in her first few minutes of true sleep. More than that, he knew it was a vision because he watched her come out of it. Her eyes flying open, the sharp inhale, the flood of panic down the bond before she managed to get her shields back up.

Those godsdamn mental shields.

He didn't know how she'd learned to control them, but he hated it. Mental shielding was something some Fae were taught depending on what role they were assigned in their kingdom, but that was to safeguard against entrancing. Sources were taught that as well, but to completely block the entire godsdamn bond?

Tessa tapped her foot impatiently as she looked around the portal terminal. She was in a mood this morning. It didn't help that he'd had to wake her before sunrise, but they had to use a portal to travel to Orinthia. The capital city of the Falein Kingdom was the only place with a portal to Ekayan Island with some of the strictest security measures in all of Devram.

"You good, beautiful?" he asked.

"No, I'm not good. It's another band," she grumbled as he slid the cuff over her hand.

"It doesn't cut you off from your magic," he pointed out.

Power flared, cords of light winding around her forearms like golden bracelets. Just like she'd done at dinner. Each week, her control increased. She still had a ways to go to master her power, but he couldn't deny the week in Faven had propelled her forward in learning to use it.

"There will be wards around the archive buildings," Theon said. "If your power could harm the books or texts in any way, then it will be suppressed."

"In other words, everyone's power will be suppressed," she replied flatly.

"More than likely," he agreed.

Tessa nodded, slipping her hand into his. He knew it was only her seeking out the bond to ease her anxiety, but he took any excuse he could to touch her these days. While finding Felicity in their room had certainly pushed her to a tipping point, he would venture to guess there were things said in Faven that had already changed everything. They'd fucked a few times here and there, but it truly was about physical release at this point. She kept her emotions so tightly sealed off, he wouldn't have known if it was anything else. He knew it wasn't like it had been before Faven. That time they had been on the brink of something *more*. He'd felt it, and he knew she'd felt it too, despite adamantly denying it. Her words to Felicity at dinner suggested jealousy, but her exchange with his father was a power play if he'd ever seen one.

And his father had let her win.

Or perhaps thought he *wouldn't* win.

But that couldn't be. He was the Arius Lord. Tessa was powerful, yes, but their bloodline had been carefully bred for power for centuries. When he could draw from her and combine that power with his own, they would certainly be more powerful than his father. But all on her own?

*Her father is a god and her mother may as well be one.*

The Legacy sentinel let them pass, and he stepped through the portal with Tessa at his side. They emerged in the atrium of the receiving portal terminal, and he turned to Kat. She'd been here several times. As much as it went against his nature, he was letting her decide where they would spend the limited time they were granted here.

"Request the Ancient History Archives," Kat said, her fingers interlaced with Axel's.

"Ancient History?" Theon asked, unsure why they'd be looking through history when her father wasn't even in their history texts.

"Beneath that building are catacombs with texts containing theories about the historical events. It is where I once read the World Walker theory," she replied.

"Are you really going to question her at this point?" Axel asked, his tone telling Theon to get on with it.

His brother had been in a mood all week, worrying about what the outcome of all this would mean for Katya. He'd been foolish to keep going with whatever they were doing anyway. Even if his father didn't get his way and she didn't become his new Source, the odds of her being assigned somewhere that would allow her to stay with Axel were slim. More than that, Axel would be required to take a Match sooner than later, but his brother had made it more than clear he didn't want his opinion on the matter.

A scholar wearing the same sage green and bronze colors all of Falein Kingdom wore escorted them to the requested archive building, and soon enough, they were riding the lift down to the catacombs. Theon was more than a little disappointed he couldn't truly enjoy this visit. He couldn't take in any of the archives or wander the various levels. This trip was entirely business.

"Your cuffs also serve as trackers," the scholar told them when the lift doors opened. "Should you venture anywhere you shouldn't, the toxin will be released."

"I will watch over them," Katya said, her head bowed and eyes on the floor.

"See that you do," the scholar replied.

"Do you know him?" Axel asked as she began leading them down a passageway.

"I know a number of the scholars here," she answered in a hushed tone.

"One step in front of the other, Tessa," Luka said, turning Theon's attention away from his brother and back to her.

"You didn't tell me we'd be below the ground," she hissed at Theon in accusation.

"I didn't know," he answered. "I've never been in the catacombs, only the upper levels." She had paled some, her eyes a little wild as they darted around the space. "It is only until sundown, Tessa," he said, cupping her jaw and bringing her eyes back to him. "You've faced far bigger trials and survived."

"Right," she murmured. "Scarred and bruised and broken, but at least I survived."

"Everyone has battle wounds," Luka cut in. "They are proof you not only survived, but that you chose to get back up and fight again. Fighters have scars, Tessa."

She swallowed thickly before nodding. Luka stepped in front of them, and Tessa moved closer to Theon as they followed him down the passage, taking the same path Axel and Kat had.

Twenty minutes later, he was seated at the table they'd taken over. He and Katya had pulled multiple texts, and the two of them now sat here, going through them as fast as they dared. Most of the texts were written in ancient languages. The others wouldn't be much help in reading them, so they were continuing to look for books or other sources that might contain information. He and Luka had already agreed that Luka would stick with Tessa today so Theon could be focused on the information, but he still constantly found himself looking for her.

He could see her down a row of shelves now, starting to reach for a book on a top shelf, but Luka was already there, grabbing the book and handing it to her. She said something in response, and Luka gave her a flat look. But the moment she turned her back to him, Theon saw his mouth tip up in a small smile. More than that, he felt his amusement trickle down the bond. At least he was feeling *someone's* emotions.

"Look at this," Katya said, pulling him back to where his attention should be. "It talks about how Achaz and Serafina were to be Matched for the purpose of creating biological children. The Lessers were not keen on the idea, fearing they would be favored, but the Firsts argued it was necessary to secure their victory in the First War. That must have eventually become known as the Everlasting War."

"But then how did Serafina end up with Arius?" Theon mused, skimming the passage she was referring to.

"I don't know, but it explains why their children were kept a secret for so long."

"That would make sense," he murmured. "We need to find something about the creation of the Fae. I think if we find that, we have a better chance of finding something on the Source bond."

"Agreed," she said, taking the book back, "but it is hard to determine when in history that happened. Was it before or after this First War?"

"I don't know," he sighed in frustration, sitting back in his chair and running his hands through his hair. "Have you come across anything about Chaos in general?"

Katya's brow furrowed. "Not that I can recall, but I guess I'm not really looking for that. Should I be?"

"Scarlett spoke about Chaos. How she had acquired some. Perhaps that has something to do with Tessa."

"You think Tessa has extra Chaos?"

"No, I— I guess I'm desperate," he replied. "Anything will help."

"Here," Axel said, plopping a stack of books on the table before sinking into the seat next to Kat, his arm draping along the back of her chair.

"What are these?" she asked, eagerly sitting forward and taking the book from the top.

"I'm not entirely sure, but they have the Marks and words you told me to watch for. Not sure if they'll amount to anything, but..." He trailed off with a shrug.

"Anything could help," she said, beginning to page through it. "Can you go through and mark any pages with those? It might help streamline the process."

"You got it, kitten," he replied, grabbing the next book and opening the cover.

Two hours later, all five of them were gathered around the small table, books and papers scattered about.

And they'd found nothing.

Not a single fucking thing that would help.

"What is a Wind Walker?" Tessa asked into the quiet of the room.

"You mean a World Walker?" Theon asked.

"No, a Wind Walker."

"That's not a thing," he murmured.

"According to this book, it is," she tossed back.

Theon leaned over, and she pointed to a word. It was in the Lost Language, and she wasn't wrong. She'd translated it correctly. He skimmed the passage eagerly, then sat back in disappointment. There was nothing there to help.

"This contends that some descendants of Sefarina could move among the winds like she can. The winds would carry messages and secrets that only they could hear," Theon said, going back to his own book.

"So some Sefarina Legacy would be able to do this?" Tessa asked.

"In theory, I suppose."

"What about the wind Fae? Their gifts come from Sefarina too."

"I don't know, Tessa," he sighed.

"And what happens if a Fae has a child with a Legacy?"

"What?" Theon asked, his head snapping to hers.

She sent him a frank look. "It is no secret the Legacy take what they want from the Fae," she said. "Would those children not technically be more powerful with Legacy and Fae blood?"

"This is why the Fae are given the seasonal contraceptive injections," Theon answered.

"You cannot tell me it doesn't happen," she argued. "And the Fae *serving* the Sirana bloodline? If they are required to produce more Fae, they wouldn't be given the contraceptive injection."

Theon shifted, not sure how to answer her. "They are carefully controlled."

She scoffed, drumming her fingers on the tabletop.

"And any...unintended outcomes of a Legacy and Fae are taken care of."

Her fingers paused in midair.

"The Legacy will not risk such power entering the realm," Theon went on.

"What if it did?" Katya cut in, her tone telling Theon she was putting something together.

But he shook his head. "No. If the babes do somehow make it to birth, they are not allowed to live."

"Gods," Tessa breathed, and he felt a shudder of sad fury down the bond.

"Power is everything to the Legacy."

"I'm aware," she said tightly.

"Maybe the Legacy didn't allow them to live. Maybe it was desperate mothers hiding them among the Fae," Katya said.

"Then how would we ever know?" Axel asked.

"We do know," Theon said, catching on to what Katya was getting at. "Or someone figured out how to find them."

"You think— Mother Cordelia?" Tessa asked in shock.

"It all fits," Katya said excitedly.

"Not quite all of it," Theon said. "It still doesn't explain how it correlates to Tessa."

"True," Katya agreed.

"So a wind Fae *could* be a Wind Walker?" Tessa asked in confusion.

"I guess so," Theon said, trying to get his thoughts in order. "Did any of the Fae who were moved to the Celeste Estate emerge with wind and air magic?"

"Lange and Brecken," Kat supplied.

"And Dex," Tessa added.

"How about the others?" Luka asked.

"Oralia and Corbin emerged with water," Tessa said. "Do you think the Anahita Legacy have a special power that can pass down to descendants too?"

"I don't know why not," Theon said. "All the gods have some gift unique to them. The Firsts have several. It's why the Arius Legacy gifts vary. We each get one."

"Unless you can combine your power with a Source," Tessa said.

"Exactly."

"But I have several gifts."

Everyone went silent at that blunt statement of fact.

"That's why we're here, beautiful," Theon said, reaching over and smoothing a hand down her hair before brushing his lips along her temple.

"Do you think that's why I ended up at the Celeste Estate?" she asked. "Because Mother Cordelia somehow knew what I was?"

"I don't think she *knows* what you are," Theon replied. "I think she figured out a way to find powerful Fae."

"What about Kat, then?" Axel asked. "Are we saying we think she has Legacy blood in her veins?"

"I guess it's possible," Theon answered. "We haven't seen anything extra that would suggest so, but her power levels are high."

"Wait, wait, wait," Tessa cut in. "If this is happening, what do their documents say? You said they list the parents of the Fae and where they were born. How would these random babes not be discovered right away?"

"Someone is helping them. It's the only plausible answer," Luka said.

"But who?" Tessa asked.

No one said anything because no one had an answer. It had to be a Legacy. They would need connections to be able to pull something like this off. Connections to the estates and access to files. Relations with the Fae. A Legacy openly sympathizing with the Fae was unheard of.

Gods, where would they even hide a pregnant Fae? And how the fuck were they sneaking them into estates?

The whole idea was preposterous, but like Kat said, it all fit.

"Are you going to claim them?" Tessa asked.

Theon looked down at her. "Claim who?"

"The others that you think might be mixed bloodlines."

Axel leaned back in his chair, pushing it back on two legs. "It's not a terrible idea."

"How are you going to explain that to Valter without revealing everything else we've discovered?" Luka asked.

"We have four early claims left," Theon said thoughtfully. "The move would undoubtedly draw attention."

"So we don't use them all. Claim two," Axel said.

Theon glanced at Tessa. She and Katya had gone noticeably quiet. "I could justify two, beautiful, not all of them. Not yet."

She nodded, her gaze dropping to her lap. "Where will they stay?"

Theon rubbed at his brow. "We'd have to figure out logistics."

"Who do you pick?"

"The most powerful ones if I'm going to have any chance of justifying this to my father," Theon said, taking the tablet Luka had already powered up. He swiped the screen a few times. "Lange had the highest power ranking of your friends."

"Brecken was the next highest, but then it'd be two air Fae," Luka said.

"Brecken has a thing for Kat," Tessa blurted.

"Tessa," Kat said, her eyes wide with shock at the same time Axel said, "Absolutely fucking not."

"I'm sorry," Tessa said in a rush. "But Lange and Corbin— You can't split them up."

"Corbin has the water element," Luka said with a shrug. "We'd have three of the four elements covered."

"We have plenty of Fae in service to the kingdom with those elements outside of fire," Theon said.

"*Please*, Theon. Don't force them apart," Tessa said, looking up at him with those violet-grey eyes.

The godsdamn begging.

Fuck.

Fuck, fuck, fuck.

"Yeah, all right," he said with a sigh.

Axel barked a laugh. "You're serious?"

"I'm already fucked. Can't get much worse, can it?" Then, looking back at Tessa, he said, "I can't promise they'll be assigned to the same positions within the kingdom."

"I understand," she said, and he could swear there were thin pools of silver shining in her eyes. "Thank you."

"Let's get back to these books," he said. "We're wasting time."

"Of course," she replied, turning the page of the book that had started all of this chaos.

Because chaos always led back to her.

# 35
## TESSA

The female stood on a cliff, and she was tall. That was the first thing Tessa noticed as she studied her.

The second thing she noticed was that the cliff seemed to float in the sky.

The female's red-brown hair was tucked inside the cloak she was wearing. It wasn't until she turned that Tessa could see the fitted black pants, black top, and black boots. She continued to scan the surrounding area, her violet eyes pausing momentarily where Tessa was standing. If she could see her, she didn't let on, but Tessa was guessing she couldn't.

Or maybe she was just more concerned with the winged beings who were charging at her from the trees.

Tessa opened her mouth to warn the female, but she didn't need it. She was already pulling a sword from beneath her cloak, preparing to meet the five warriors head on while she backed towards the cliff edge. Moments before the winged beings caught up to her, she stepped off the side.

Tessa stood in shocked silence, her mouth agape.

What the fuck was this?

Then a dragon soared into the air, the female astride the beast.

Purplish-black scales glinted in the sunlight, and the winged males took to the sky, crying out in anger. But the dragon was circling back, flying so low Tessa ducked as it flew overhead. She felt the gust of air as large, taloned wings flapped, the force of it nearly knocking her on her ass. When she lifted her eyes back to the sky, she found the dragon already high in the sky once more. There *was a piece of faded paper floating to the ground, and she reached up to grab it. It contained only a few words she wasn't quite sure what to do with:*

*Tell him to keep fighting.*
*Tell him Lilura lives.*

These dreams were becoming too much.

It wasn't really a dream, she supposed. She'd just been sitting in a chair near the window in the lounge, watching snow gently falling outside. She had a cup of tea in her hand, and to be honest, she was surprised it hadn't spilled when the vision had assaulted her.

Dreams. Visions. It didn't matter. Whatever they were, they were becoming too much. Every time she closed her eyes, she had another one. What was she supposed to do with them? Rordan and Elowyn had encouraged her to let them come, that it was a natural progression of her power, but they made little sense. The only one she'd had where she actually *knew* anyone was the one where Theon always killed her. The rest were all people she'd never met and places she'd never been.

Theon had talked about taking her to see Cienna, but they hadn't been able to make contact with the Witch. Axel promised he'd keep trying, but now they'd run out of time. The third Mark would happen the day after tomorrow. She really didn't know how Solstice Day would play out.

"Do you want to talk about it?" Theon asked where he sat with a book and his laptop. He seemed to be attempting to translate something. She didn't care.

They'd run out of time.

Then again, maybe they'd never really had time to begin with.

"No," she said softly, looking down at her cold cup of tea.

"Do you see the same thing all the time?"

"No."

"But you've had one of me killing you."

It wasn't a question, but he knew that. She'd told him as much before she'd realized what they were.

"Yes," she answered. "It is the only one I have repeatedly."

He nodded. "But the other visions are not that?"

She shook her head, turning back to the window. "Why aren't they here yet?"

"They're on their way, Tessa. Axel was giving them their kingdom Marks himself."

"And they will stay here? So they will be safe?"

"They will stay here at least until the third Mark is in place, and we've all moved on from this."

"What if—"

"We'll deal with it, Tessa," he said sharply, and Tessa snapped her mouth shut.

Theon sighed, starting to say something, but then she heard the front door opening. She was on her feet in an instant, nearly tripping from getting tangled in the blanket she had draped over herself.

"Careful," Theon muttered, but she was already out of the room and racing down the short hall.

She skidded to a halt, Luka giving her the same once over he always did. Then he stepped to the side, and she took them in. Lange with his pale blonde hair and sky-blue eyes. Corbin with his shaggy brown hair, brown skin, and hazel eyes.

"Hiya, sweetheart," Lange said, his mischievous grin curving on his lips.

And she let out a laugh, a genuine one, as she closed the distance between them, flinging her arms around Lange's neck. He lifted her off her feet, hugging her back. As he passed her over to Corbin, he said, "We better be watching the Chaosphere game tonight."

"I didn't even know there was a game on tonight," Tessa admitted, stepping back a little from Corbin.

Lange sucked in a dramatic gasp. "But the Whirlwinds are playing."

"I've been…busy."

"We know, Tess," Corbin said. "Lange is just being an ass, as usual."

She gave him a weak smile, and Lange's entire demeanor immediately changed. "Tess, I didn't mean anything by that. I'm sorry. I know it's been a rough few months for you."

"Can we maybe move this reunion to the kitchen or something? So Kat and I can get out of the foyer?" Axel called from behind them.

"Sorry," Tessa muttered.

They all made their way to the kitchen, where she hopped onto an island stool, Kat doing the same. Axel had stayed back to talk with Theon and Luka for a moment.

"You can sit," Tessa said to Lange and Corbin, where they stood stiffly near the wall.

"We're good," Corbin said tightly, and she understood the hesitation. Katya had been the same.

"Actually, we're not good," Lange said, his voice hushed as he stepped closer. "What's going on, Tessa? Why were we claimed today?"

"You're powerful?" she suggested.

"Tess," Corbin said with a knowing look.

She swallowed, glancing at Kat, who only shrugged. The female wasn't about to spill any secrets, but Tessa didn't really have anything to lose anymore.

"We found some information that suggested you may be more than Fae," she said.

"Come again?" Lange asked, his brows shooting up.

"It's complicated, and it's a lot to take in," she said before launching into a brief explanation of why they thought this might be the case.

"He claimed Corbin because of Tessa," Kat chimed in at the end.

"What?" Corbin asked, looking at Tessa for an explanation.

"Theon mentioned possibly claiming Lange, and I…requested that he claim you as well."

"She didn't want the two of you split up," Kat added.

"It's not a big deal," Tessa said, glancing at the doorway. What was taking them so long?

"It's not a… Tessa, it's a big deal," Lange said.

"But so is this idea about Mother Cordelia and powerful Fae coming from the Celeste Estate," Corbin cut in.

"It's just a theory," Tessa said.

"I'd say it's a pretty sound one considering Brecken and Oralia were claimed by Achaz Kingdom while we were being given our kingdom markings."

The sharp look from Mother Cordelia made her stop bouncing her knee. The Estate Mother had been...tolerant of her since Auryon had taken over her private lessons. Tessa still sat by herself, but for the most part, she was ignored by everyone. More than that, the Estate Mother still insisted Tessa wear these ridiculous bands during the lessons which were the cause of her current restlessness.

Well, that and the third Mark was taking place tomorrow.

"You are being dismissed early today so you can prepare for tomorrow's Marking," Mother Cordelia was saying, and that had Tessa's attention snapping back to her. Did Luka know that? He always picked her up and stayed with her while she was with Auryon.

He took these fucking bands off her wrists.

She quickly started gathering her things like the other Sources, and then her heart sank when she heard, "Tessalyn, a word."

This was fine. She wouldn't do anything to her. Theon had made it very clear what would happen if she did. Slowly zipping up her bag before turning to face the Estate Mother, she said, "Is there something you needed?"

The Legacy's lips twisted into a sneer. "Still so disrespectful after all this time."

Tessa said nothing, pressing her lips together and waiting.

"I was assigned to keep an eye on you, but you just couldn't let matters be, could you?" she went on, taking a step towards Tessa.

"This was Theon's decision, not mine," Tessa replied. "You should speak to him if you have concerns about the arrangement."

Mother Cordelia tsked, the door to the room snicking shut with a gust of her power. "The Arius Heir has foiled many plans, but he will not take from me what I am owed."

"Again, I would discuss that with him. I don't know what you're talking about."

The Estate Mother smiled, but it wasn't pleasant. It was sinister and full of the malice Tessa had lived with nearly every day of her life. She took another step towards Tessa, but she held her ground, refusing to give in to the urge to take a step back.

"Did you know I was promised a higher station in Devram for dealing with you all these years?" Mother Cordelia demanded. "Keep you alive until they came for you. That was my entire role, and how hard could it be? I'd raised hundreds of Fae on my estate. But you were so…*wild*. From the time you could walk. Impulsive and reckless, no matter what I did."

"You… You've known what I am? All this time?"

"I do not know the specifics, but I knew you were not Fae. Then the timeline kept getting pushed out further and further, and even now, they have not acted," she spat, and Tessa suddenly felt the air in the room getting thinner.

Her gaze darted to the door. She should just go. There was nothing keeping her here. She had her phone. She could go call Luka like she'd planned to do to begin with, but before she could take a step, the door opened.

And she dropped her mental shields, letting all of her panic and terror and helplessness fly down the bond, praying to any of the gods that Theon would make it here in time.

Because those were masked and cloaked people filing through the door. One after the other until they formed a circle around her and Mother Cordelia.

"I lost faith in those I was serving," Mother Cordelia was saying, slowly backing away from her.

"So you contacted the Augury?" Tessa rasped as each of the masked figures slowly withdrew black daggers from their robes.

"They came to me with a proposition," she replied. "It would have been unwise to decline."

Tessa was frantically shoving at the bands, grimacing as they dug into her skin, but it was no use. Luka may have been training her every day, but without her power, she could do nothing against all of them. She couldn't even do enough to hold them off until Theon got here.

"He will come for you," Tessa said, abandoning her attempts to get the bands off. "He will come for you if you take me from him."

"I was sworn protection," Mother Cordelia replied, pulling up her sleeve to reveal a Bargain Mark on her forearm. "The Arius Heir does not outrank him."

Tessa opened her mouth to ask another question, anything to keep her talking just a little longer, but the air was sucked from her lungs. She couldn't speak, couldn't breathe. She could feel her power beneath her skin desperately trying to break free.

As she sank to her knees, her vision beginning to blur, the Augury began stepping closer as one, closing in. Tessa clawed at her throat, at the bands, at the floor. Then someone yanked her back by the hair, forcing her to look up at one of the masked figures as they raised a dagger.

"We must be left standing when Chaos comes to reign," said the gruff voice.

And then he was gurgling as an arrow went through his throat.

Whoever was holding her hair must have jerked around to find the source of the arrow because her head was yanked to the side. Not that she could cry out. She could feel the tears leaking from the corners of her eyes, but her body was going limp as she started to lose consciousness. She couldn't focus on what was happening. She couldn't comprehend the bursts of smoke the arrows were coming from or the glimpses of black hair that were there, then gone.

At one point, the one holding her hair released her, and Tessa collapsed, her head banging against the floor. A moment later she was gasping, sucking down air as Mother Cordelia's power released its hold on her.

Tessa blinked, her vision clearing as she gulped down air. There were dead bodies all around her, ashy footprints everywhere, and that was Auryon standing beside her. Tessa had never seen her actually move through smoke and ashes, but gods. She was fast.

Auryon looped her bow over her back, dropping to a knee. "Are you hurt?"

Tessa shook her head, then winced. "I hit my head, but I'll be fine."

"I expect to encounter more as we make our way out." Her swirling gaze dipped to Tessa's wrists. "If I remove those now, your power will overcompensate."

"Where is Theon?" Tessa asked as Auryon helped her to her feet.

"They are coming for you," she answered, grabbing her bow once more. There was a swirl of ashes, and she nocked two arrows onto the string.

"Luka says you don't keep those in a pocket realm," Tessa said, still trying to get her breathing under control.

"Does this seem like a good time to discuss that?" Auryon asked, leading her to the door.

Tessa stepped over a body, trying to avoid the pooling blood. "I do this often during inopportune times, actually."

"It is not a pocket realm. I can create them," she answered.

"How?"

But the answer would have to wait as they rounded a corner and found more masked figures. Tessa wondered just how many people were in this organization, and where the fuck did they keep coming from?

Auryon released her arrows, nocking two more before the first two found their targets, but these Augury members weren't afraid to use their power. A gust of air slammed into Tessa, and she was thrown backwards. Auryon appeared at her side a second later.

"Up," she barked. "Get up. We won't get through them. I might just have to—" The sound of howling cut her off, and Auryon smiled darkly as she said, "Finally."

Screams erupted from behind the hooded figures, and it had them splitting their focus. Auryon took advantage of the distraction, letting more arrows fly. Within a matter of minutes, they were all down, and Tessa was staring as two wolves prowled forward.

One charcoal grey and the other one nearly white.

She knew they wouldn't hurt her, just as she'd known the same that night by river. "Why do they always come when I'm in danger?"

"They are yours," Auryon answered as the wolves rubbed against Tessa.

She was short, but they were huge. Their heads easily came to her waist, and Tessa tentatively sank her fingers into dark fur.

"Why do you think they are mine?" she asked.

"Again, not a good time for questions," Auryon said. "Let's go."

They didn't encounter anyone else as they made their way to the front of the building, and Tessa was starting to breathe a sigh of relief.

Until they stepped outside.

At least fifty masked figures stared back at them.

"Fuck," Auryon muttered, adding another arrow to the two she had nocked. "Roan, stay with her. Niylah, you're with me."

The darker wolf darted forward, Auryon slipping into her smoke, but Tessa knew they would never be enough. Even with a wolf at her side, she was useless, and there were just too many of them. And gods, her power was swelling in her soul, trying to find a way out. She knew it from the thunder rumbling off in the distance. Knew it by the way Roan whined as he nudged at her hand. Knew it by the way she could hear her magic screaming in her mind, in her soul. So much anger. So much fury.

Or maybe that was just her at once again being helpless and controlled by these godsdamn bands. By yet another Legacy when she was more than that. By being abandoned in this godsdamn world in the first place.

Roan was crouched low, snarling as several Augury members drew closer. Then the animal leaped, snatching an arrow out of the air before Tessa even realized it was coming for her. The arrow snapped in half, and Tessa scrambled to pick up the half with the broadhead. It was better than no weapon, she supposed.

Where the fuck was Theon? Was he really not going to come for her?

Auryon was nothing but a blur of smoke and ashes, sets of footprints and falling bodies the only things left in her wake, but she was tiring. She had to be because more of the Augury members were getting past her defenses. Tessa couldn't see Niylah in the mass of bodies, but she heard her growls and the screams of agony from her victims.

"For Devram!" one of the masked figures cried, lunging for her while Roan was busy with his teeth in the throat of another.

On instinct, she thrust the half arrow at the being. He knocked her hand aside with ease, grabbing her around the waist and hauling her back against his chest, but she fought. Gods, did she fight. All that fury poured into her as rain began to fall.

"You bring war," the male hissed into her ear, lifting her off her feet.

She jabbed her elbow back, hearing the grunt from the male. His hold didn't release, but his mask was knocked loose, clattering to the ground. A fist connected with her ribs, and she let out a cry of pain.

Then he was bellowing a roar of agony as Roan's teeth sank into his arm. He immediately released her, her feet hitting the ground, and she spun, shoving that arrow she'd managed to hold on to straight into the male's eye. Blood sprayed, and Roan still hadn't released the male's arm, shaking it back and forth. The wolf was going to tear it right off.

Good.

She yanked the arrow out, sinking it into the other eye. Then she was blindly stabbing as rage and fury poured out of her in the only way it could. She was screaming and her face was wet. From the rain or tears or spraying blood, she didn't know. But when another arm clamped around her waist, hauling her backwards, she twisted, lashing out again.

The male tilted his head to the side, but not fast enough to avoid a graze to his cheek, a line of red appearing.

"Easy, little one. It's me," Luka said. "Take a breath."

But there was no *taking a breath*.

She was vibrating from her fury and her power being trapped and everyone thinking they could use her.

Abandon her.

Sacrifice her.

"Get her out of here, dragon," Auryon ordered, appearing at their side while simultaneously releasing another set of arrows. "And I don't mean by your wings."

"I can't—"

Grey eyes snapped to them, the ever-present swirling having slowed. "The wolves and I will make sure there are no witnesses left to tell a soul, but if you do not get her out of here, Chaos will rain."

Tessa didn't know what she was talking about, but then there was a tug at her belly. She thought she might be sick.

And then suddenly they weren't standing on a rain-drenched street, but on the bank of the Wynfell River.

The same place he'd brought her when she'd returned from Faven.

He released her, and she stumbled back, the arrow she still held falling to the ground.

"Breathe, Tessa," he said, his tone somehow gentle yet commanding all at once.

She sucked in a ragged breath, but it got stuck. Her magic was still thrashing, and she was still feeling, and—

"I'm going to take those off," Luka said, but he didn't move. He just watched her with vertical pupils. "But when I do, I have to Travel out because you are too… Your magic is angry, Tessa. *You* are angry. I won't go far, but you won't be able to see me for a bit."

"I like it when I can see you," she rasped.

"I know. I'll come back as soon as I can. I'll be in the air watching, waiting," he answered. When she didn't say anything, only stared back at him, he said, "Ready?"

She nodded once, and he stepped in front of her. Clasping both the bands at once, he slid them down her hands in perfect unison. Right before they slipped off completely, he said, "I'll come back for you."

Then he was gone, and so were the bands, and her power erupted. Light and energy crackled. Water hissed as lightning made contact. Gold mist drifted across the ground, and light coiled around her arms, legs, torso. It wove through her hair as the winds roared and dark clouds rolled in.

Untamed and free.

Wild and reckless.

Their destruction and her salvation.

The intensity lessened, but her power stayed, a faint golden glow that flowed around her, constantly moving.

Watching.

Listening.

Learning everything it could.

Luka appeared, stepping from the very air, but she didn't move. Neither did he as he stared back at her.

"Look at you," he rumbled, the growl a possessive thing she felt in her soul, and she could feel... Want? Desire?

Her head tilted in realization, another betrayal snaking through her. "I can feel you."

He nodded, slowly prowling around her, as if he wasn't sure what to expect from her.

Probably wise.

"How?" she demanded.

"The second Mark. You were too powerful. Theon couldn't do it alone. I had to help, and somehow—"

"I am bound to both of you?"

"We are unsure."

"Where is Theon?"

"Waiting for you. He couldn't come."

She scoffed. "Couldn't or wouldn't?"

That had Luka pausing. "He was with Valter. So close to the third Mark and with everything to come, we don't want to make more trouble, Tessa. He sent me."

"They'll never stop coming for me."

"No, they won't," Luka agreed. He took a step closer. "We'll figure all this out when we get home."

"What is there to figure out?" she asked. "I am forever to be hunted. By them. By him. By those who want me, and those who only want me dead. A wanted unwanted. How ironic."

"You're wanted, Tessa," he said.

"I'm wanted when it's convenient. For my power. For my blood. For leverage."

"No, little one—"

"Take me back," she demanded.

"I don't think you're ready, Tessa."

"Take me back!"

"I can't until your power is under control," he snapped. "I am still his Guardian."

And what could she say to that?

He slipped his hand into his pocket. "I can put these back on if you can't—"

"If anyone ever tries to put those on me again, I will kill them," she hissed, some of the light coiled around her arm unwinding.

Never again would she be at the mercy of those bands.

Never again would she be at the mercy of anyone.

With a shuddering breath, she closed her eyes, whispering to her power, pulling it back into herself. The only thing left when she reopened her eyes were two single cords of gold light wound around her wrists where the bands usually sat.

A warm hand slid along her jaw, tilting her face up as he stepped into her. He was so close, her front brushed against his.

"You're not one of the monsters, Tessa. Do you hear me?"

But the corner of her mouth curled up as she whispered, "You're wrong."

He said nothing else. Only pulled her into him before stepping through the air. She recognized the sensation now. He'd done this when she'd found Felicity in Theon's room. It was how he'd gotten her to the river so quickly. How many other times had he done the same thing?

In the next blink, they stood in his room at the townhouse. Before she could take a step, darkness was wrapping around her and yanking her from him. Her magic flared, already too anxious from everything else that had happened, but darkness wound around her power too, calling to something deep within her. With a shuddering gasp, she looked up at Theon. His eyes were so full of inky power, the emerald color could hardly be seen.

"Theon—" she started, but his darkness wound around her throat, effectively silencing her.

"Hush, Tessa," he snarled, his furious gaze fixed on Luka. "My Guardian has been keeping secrets."

# 36

## LUKA

He stared at the male who'd been the equivalent of a brother to him his entire life. They'd grown up together. Tessa had once asked him about his earliest memories. They all included Theon. From sneaking sweets when they were younger to sneaking alcohol long before they should have. From academic lessons to late nights spent plotting as they learned what Valter was planning. From summer seasons spent away together at combat training camps to taking the punishment together for completing the Guardian bond behind his father's back. They'd always survived together.

Now Theon was tucking Tessa behind him, refusing to turn his back on Luka. His darkness surrounded her, protecting her the only way he knew how—by controlling. It was why Theon valued control so much. When he had control, he could protect those he loved. Control meant safety, and safety meant love. It was what he'd done with her from the beginning. She didn't understand that the only way he knew *how* to love was to obsessively possess and protect. She didn't understand that growing up, his father made sure he was so deprived of safety, sanctuary, and love, that having those things—and making sure those he called his own had them too—became an obsession.

"Maybe Tessa should go find Axel and the others so we can talk," Luka said calmly, pulling off his soiled shirt.

"Is she hurt?" Theon gritted out.

"You could ask her yourself," Tessa grumbled, stepping out from behind him a little.

Luka watched as she lifted a hand, her golden light slowly twining among Theon's darkness as if studying it. That light glow still emanated around her like a golden aura. Violet-grey eyes flicked to him, and he held her stare, cataloging every mark and speck of blood on her fair skin. She'd heal, but the fact that they were there told him she'd fought. And to find her so viciously attacking when he'd arrived? With half of a fucking arrow at that?

He wasn't surprised she'd finally put it together that she could feel his emotions tonight, but the dragon under his skin had certainly noticed all the blood and violence too. Even if he hadn't been intrigued before, he sure as fuck would have been now.

"I think we should talk, and then we can get a full report from Tessa after she's had a chance to…let the adrenaline settle a bit," Luka said.

Tense silence filled the air until finally Theon said, "Your friends are worried about you. They are in the lounge."

Tessa didn't answer, but her lips pressed into a thin line, telling Luka she didn't like being sent away yet again. With a sharp nod, she turned and left the room without another word.

Theon finally turned, shutting the door behind her with a sharp snap. Luka crossed his arms and waited for him to say something. He'd let Theon choose where to start. Luka knew him well enough to know he was trying to sort through everything he'd pieced together and everything he hadn't.

When Theon lifted his head to meet his gaze again, he said, "When did you learn you could fucking Travel? That's what it is, isn't it?"

"That had always been my assumption, but seeing Scarlett and Sorin do it confirmed it," Luka answered.

"Has always been your assumption? How long?"

Luka pulled the tie from his hair, moving to the brass tin he kept them in and placing it inside. "I learned about it shortly after my gifts manifested."

"When we were *eleven years?*" Theon said, and Luka could feel his disbelief down the bond he'd been roped into. "That was… You never said a fucking thing."

"The first time it happened, I was terrified," Luka replied, running his fingers along the gems inlaid in the brass tin. "We were at that combat training camp. Your father had requested we each receive private instruction, and the instructor... We were eleven years."

Theon stared at him, and Luka could tell he was remembering the same thing Luka was. The very first time they were sent to the academy, neither of them had known what to expect. They'd assumed it was more academics, not combat training. They certainly hadn't expected to endure beatings along with having their power drained and then be chained. They surely hadn't expected to be taught how to fight with a fucking sword and dagger.

It definitely hadn't been learning how to take a life and then live with yourself afterwards.

"The trainer you..."

Luka nodded. "Apparently I'd retained just enough power to Travel. I didn't go far, but he saw me. I didn't know what had happened. I didn't know what to do. I didn't know what your father would say. I panicked. I was untrained. My magic was panicking with me, protecting me, and I killed him. When it was reported to your father, he *rewarded* me by gifting me the dagger I'd used to do it. After a few more years of training, he started sending me on his little missions."

"Does he know you can Travel?"

"No. No one knows," Luka answered. "Except Auryon. She somehow fucking knew."

"You never told me," Theon said. "Why?"

"I didn't tell anyone. It's not that I didn't trust you with the information, but..." Luka sighed, snapping the lid of the tin shut. "I'm already the only Sargon descendant. There are already expectations with that. This was just another thing that made me different from you when we were younger. There was always this need to...*prove* that I belonged here. That your family hadn't made some mistake by taking me in, and as we got older, I think it just became second nature to keep it a secret. If no one knew, it couldn't be used against us."

"Did you think this wouldn't have been useful information for... Well, fuck. *Everything?*" Theon demanded, and Luka could feel all the conflicting emotions down this fucking bond.

On some level, he knew Theon understood. He kept secrets all the damn time until he had all the pieces worked out and a plan in place. It was why Tessa drove him so mad. She messed with the plans every chance she got and didn't even realize it.

"If it somehow ever got back to your father, I think everything would be worse," Luka replied. "You can think what you want, but in the end, it was my secret to decide what to do with. Just like it's your secret to decide what to do with the information you've learned about Tessa."

Theon's eyes narrowed, and Luka sent him a smirk.

"You think I don't know you've figured some things out? Nearly three decades, Theon. We can read each other like all your godsdamn books," Luka said.

"Apparently not all of us can," Theon retorted.

"Don't act like I've done anything to jeopardize shit," he said, sliding off his shoes. "I've used the skill more times than you know to make sure our plans succeeded. I've used it when it's mattered. I've used it to get to Tessa."

Theon's eyes flashed at her name, renewed anger flooding down the bond. "Don't get me started on Tessa."

"What the fuck does that mean?"

"I should have realized this would happen when you told me the effects of helping with the second Mark," Theon said, his power flowing around him in a shimmering dark mist the same way Tessa's did.

Light and dark.

Two forces that should repel each other. Instead, they were drawn to each other.

"Or are you going to tell me that's *not* what has you looking at her like she's some shiny thing you need to take back to your cave?" Theon went on with a sneer.

"I would never take her there," Luka retorted.

"Of course you would. It's where you keep anything you find of value."

"I would never take her there because she hates the dark. But I suppose it'd be better than a godsdamn wine cellar, wouldn't it?"

Theon went still, the ripple of shock down the bond telling Luka his words had hit their mark.

"You agreed we needed to get her under control," Theon gritted out. "We all agreed she needed to accept this bond. That she would be safer and plans could move forward. That—"

"No," Luka snapped. "I told you from the very beginning she was not the one for this. I told you it wasn't in her to submit. I told you she was wild and impulsive, and would you look at that? Her *father* is the god of the fucking wild and untamed. She was never meant to be yours."

Theon's lip curled up into a sneer. "My father said the same thing to me the night before she came home from Faven. Any other secrets you need to share tonight?"

"If you think I'm plotting with your father, you can go fuck yourself," Luka retorted, smoke billowing with his exhale. "But if you think you didn't alter fate by Selecting her that night, you're wrong. All we have to do is look back at the past few months. How many of our plans have changed? How many have been altered? She's so much more than what any of us bargained for. Not only was she not supposed to be yours, she wasn't even supposed to be in Devram. Yet here we are. All of us drawn to her light like moths to a fucking flame from the very beginning."

"From the very beginning," Theon repeated, the words slow and dark. "Tell me, Luka, was she 'not the one for this' because of who she is? Or because you saw her as some valuable, shiny treasure long before that second Mark?"

"Fuck off, Theon," Luka snarled.

"It all fits," Theon said in disbelief. "Your insistence that I not choose her. The lingering looks when I did. The long period of time you stayed away. The softness. The feral protectiveness. The fucking flip-flops. You sensed what she was from the very beginning and wanted her as your own."

"And you just *wanted*," Luka retorted. "Without ever wondering *why* you were drawn to her. Then you act utterly baffled when nothing has gone to plan."

He could feel his dragon pressing at his skin, agitated and wanting out. His pupils had already shifted, and he could see the faint outline of scales on the backs of his hands. His wings were there, seconds from breaking free.

Theon wasn't entirely wrong. Luka did have a kind of sixth sense when it came to knowing something was valuable. The various collectibles around his room were evidence enough. They appeared to simply be old and rusted trinkets, but they ended up dating back to the founding of Devram. But that instinct had never happened with a *person*. Not until they started to research potential Sources for Theon.

Luka had been the first one to pull up her information. They'd made a list of possibilities, and then they'd spent countless hours debating them. It had been well into the night when they made it to the Celeste Estate Fae. They'd saved that estate for last on purpose. That estate had an impeccable record of turning out powerful Fae, and they needed a powerful one if they planned to go up against Valter. They had just finished vetoing another female when he'd pulled up Tessa's information. The moment her photo had filled the screen, his dragon had lifted its head. That same sense of *mine* had filled his soul that he always felt when stumbling upon something valuable. He hadn't understood it then, but he spent the next years trying to. He never felt it again with another person. Even when visiting the estates on Theon's behalf to watch the Fae they'd narrowed it down to. Of course, he never laid eyes on Tessa during any of those visits. That made sense now that they knew Cordelia often had her shoved into a fucking cupboard.

It was *because* he didn't understand the pull to her that he'd kept his distance. It was the same reason he'd pushed Theon to do the same. Because if they couldn't understand it, there was no way to prepare for possibilities.

And Tessa had proven his point.

Theon was pacing, his hands going through his hair and the muscle ticking in his jaw. His darkness trailed him with every step.

"What are we supposed to do about this?" Theon demanded.

"Do about what?"

"About all of it. Tessa. This bond. This—"

"You pulled me into this, Theon," Luka growled. "I was giving the two of you space. I encouraged her to accept the bond. I told her to go to you, turn to you, give you a chance. You're the one who refused to buy the godsdamn flip-flops."

"I didn't think *this* would happen," he argued.

"You didn't think at all," Luka spat. "At least not with your head."

Theon's magic flared again at that. "Did you not agree it was better I claimed her than someone else after that assessment? Do you think it would be better for her to be aligned with another kingdom? Do you think anyone would protect her, fight for her as much as we are?"

"Of course I think she is safest here with us, but she doesn't see it that way, Theon," Luka said. "How do we keep someone safe when she doesn't view us as her protectors but as her oppressors?"

"She doesn't," Theon said. "Not anymore. It's been different. It was so close to being different..." His hands went through his hair again.

"Tessa figured it out," Luka said.

"Figured what out?"

"That I'm connected to the bond. She could feel my emotions earlier today and realized what was happening."

"And what emotions were those?" Theon demanded.

"Does it matter?"

"Yes."

"No, it doesn't," Luka retorted. "What matters is she knows now, and she wasn't happy to learn about it."

"I should have realized this was happening when you were fine sharing a bed and when she was constantly asking for you. She felt the bond too and didn't realize it," Theon said. "And you encouraged it every step of the way."

"Were you not listening? I was doing everything to push her towards *you*. You are the one who pulled me into the Mark. What do you think would have happened if I'd denied her? The bond would have become more insistent, more urgent. I've seen the two of you when you go too long without speaking, touching, being in the same godsdamn room. She would have figured it out a lot sooner," Luka retorted. "And what the fuck am I supposed to do with it, Theon? Because she might not have known what was going on, but I sure as fuck did. You give in to every push from the bond and drive her to do the same. I've had to force myself to do the exact opposite."

"It shouldn't be as strong for you," Theon said. "You don't have the first Mark. You can't feel her physical presence—"

"Except I'm connected to her by a Tracking Mark," Luka cut in. "So are you and so is Axel. I can feel her presence. The only difference here is that she doesn't have a Sargon Mark on her hand. But her second Mark isn't normal, and we've just been ignoring it."

"I haven't been ignoring it," Theon shot back. "Of course I've tried to research it, but there's nothing because it's never been done before."

"Then I guess we're going to have to figure this out as we go."

"No, we need a plan," Theon snapped.

"When are you going to admit there is no plan anymore? There hasn't been a plan since the moment you Selected her," Luka snapped, heading for the door. "At this point, the best plan is to not have a plan at all."

"Where are you going?"

"To check on Tessa and see if she's ready to tell us what happened. Then we need to track down Auryon," Luka answered, heading downstairs.

He made his way to the lounge to find her sitting next to Lange, but the moment they entered, Lange and Corbin shot to their feet. Luka was surprised they'd even been sitting with Axel in the room. The two Fae were jumpy and cautious, not that he could blame them.

Tessa looked up at him from her seat on the sofa, blood still splattered across her face and clothing. Splashes of red marred her golden hair, but those bands of light were still around her wrists.

"You didn't clean up?" Luka asked, his gaze sweeping over her like it always did.

"Neither did you," she tossed back.

"I wasn't stabbing someone repeatedly with a sharp object," he deadpanned.

"Stabbing?" Axel asked, looking between the two of them. "Time to fill us in, baby doll."

They sat and listened while Tessa told them about being dismissed early, Cordelia, the Augury, and the way Auryon had fought their way out of the building.

"And the stabbing?" Axel asked, looking at Tessa.

She only shrugged.

"What does it mean, 'the wolves are yours?'" Katya asked.

Tessa shrugged again. "No idea."

"Was Cordelia killed?" Theon asked from where he stood near her.

"I didn't see her body, but I wasn't exactly looking with the whole nearly passing out thing and all," she drawled. "You'll have to ask Auryon."

"She's never given us a way to contact her," Theon replied.

"Those messages. Like Scarlett uses," Tessa said. "You send her one of those. Why do you think Devram never used them to begin with? They seem far simpler than a phone."

Theon was rubbing at his brow when he muttered, "I don't know why, Tessa."

"What if you don't have any paper?" Axel cut in. "How is that simpler? Do you just carry paper—"

But he stopped speaking when Tessa lifted a hand. With her finger, she drew a quick pattern with her light before there was a flare of that golden mist. She looked at Axel as she said, "No paper necessary."

"Where did you learn that?" Theon demanded.

"Auryon."

His gaze slid to Luka. "What other things has she taught you?"

Tessa shrugged again. "History of Devram. Like she's supposed to."

"Somehow, I doubt that is all," he replied tightly. "What did your message say just now?"

"It was a request to bring a book to the Solstice service tomorrow."

"I was unaware she would be at the service," Luka cut in.

"I don't know if she will be," Tessa answered.

She got to her feet, rubbing at her face and smearing dried blood across her cheek, Luka tamped down on the barrage of emotions that assaulted him from that one action. Anger that she was covered in blood to begin with. But by the gods, seeing her splattered in blood? Knowing it was there because she fought back? That was pride and satisfaction, but more than that, it made the dragon beneath his skin *want*. It was a feeling he'd been shoving down more and more lately, and when he couldn't, he found someone to satisfy it. Or he had until he'd been dragged into this Source Mark debacle. Since that time, the idea of being with someone else had become…unappealing.

"Can we get pizza and watch the Chaosphere game tonight?" she asked, turning to Theon.

Theon's face twisted into one of visible disgust. "Why?"

Tessa rolled her eyes. "Because out of the seven people in this room, you're the only one who doesn't like either of those things. Besides, I'm sure I'll sleep for two days straight again if I get the third Mark tomorrow, and—"

"*When*," Theon cut in. "When you get the third Mark tomorrow."

"Right. Assuming neither of us is dead and all."

There was a muffled bark of laughter, and they all turned to Lange and Corbin, who were still standing off to the side.

"I apologize," Lange said quickly. "I've just never seen…*that*," he said, gesturing between Tessa and Theon.

"Yes, well, she has a mouth on her she often forgets to control," Theon replied through gritted teeth.

"Don't let him fool you," Tessa said with a simper to her voice as she leaned towards Lange and added, "He's *obsessed* with my mouth."

"Go get cleaned up, Tessa. Now," Theon ordered, Axel bursting into laughter where he sat. Even Katya had her face turned into him to hide her amusement.

"Of course, *Master*," she replied, all but gliding from the room. "Order some pizza, Axel," she called over her shoulder.

"On it, baby doll," Axel called back, sliding his phone from his pocket.

The look Theon sent him could only be described as death.

"What?" Axel asked with mock innocence as Theon followed after Tessa. "Consider it a last meal for one of you."

"Shut up, Axel," Theon snapped, smacking him alongside the head as he stalked past. Axel's laughter covered the growled, "We have more to discuss. Now," that was directed at Luka.

By the time they were back in his bedroom, Tessa was already in the bathroom with the door closed. Luka immediately found himself wondering if she'd come out in that robe again. Or maybe wearing nothing as she was prone to doing. It'd be a terrible idea, but admittedly, he was torn about which way he wanted this to go.

"What else has Auryon been teaching her?" Theon asked.

"Exactly what she said. Devram's true history, just like you asked her to," Luka replied with a sigh, sinking down onto his sofa. He stretched his legs out, crossing them at the ankles.

"And has any of that history been new to you?"

"Some of it has been a different take, I suppose."

"A different take?" Theon nearly shouted. Luka wasn't surprised in the least when his darkness broke free again. "And you didn't think to say anything?"

"You are the one who hired her without looking into her background, Theon. Not me."

"That's why you are there."

"If you want to know what she's teaching her, then maybe you should be the one to sit through those lessons. I'm not going to sit there and take fucking notes. I did my academics. If there was something truly life-altering, I would have told you," Luka said.

"Like these messages she learned to send with her magic?" Theon demanded.

"Scarlett told us about those. It was nothing new."

Theon looked like he was going to throw something in his frustration, and a low warning rumble came from Luka's chest at the thought of him damaging any of the items in here.

"I cannot believe all the shit you've kept from me," Theon finally said after he visibly worked to get himself under control.

"None of this changes anything," Luka replied.

"Now you sound like Tessa," Theon spat.

"She's not wrong. You refuse to admit the plan is in pieces. You refuse to admit Selecting her changed everything. You refuse to see what's right in front of you. You can deny things all you want, but you can't avoid the consequences of that denial," Luka said.

The sound of the bathroom door silenced them both as Tessa emerged, fully dressed in loose pants and Theon's long-sleeve shirt. Luka ignored the disappointment as she eyed them.

Theon moved to stand in front of her, twirling a lock of her wet hair between his fingers. "How are you feeling?"

Her brow pinched. "Fine?"

"You had an eventful day, Tessa."

Her head tipped to the side. "I've become rather used to people trying to kill me."

Luka felt Theon's wince down the bond. Or maybe that was his own grimace at her words.

Then she asked, "How long have you two known about Luka's involvement with the bond?"

Theon's hand fell to his side. "Luka said he started feeling it the moment the second Mark was completed. I didn't learn about that... complication until later."

"Later when?"

"When you were in Faven."

Tessa nodded once, her eyes darting around the room, looking anywhere but at them. Luka knew she was blocking the bond. Auryon had spoken about the basics of mental shielding, but Tessa had clearly practiced it. She'd quickly become proficient at it, and while it annoyed Theon, Luka let her have that secret. He wasn't entirely sure why.

And while it would be nice in moments like these to know exactly what she was feeling, he'd learned to read her over these past months. He knew she was upset at being left in the dark with important information yet again, and he was to blame for that. He could have told her at any time, even if he was doing it because she was already overwhelmed. Was it his place to make that decision for her? Did it make him any different from Theon in the end? Probably not. Did he regret the choice? Also no. In the end, maybe he was more like Theon than he thought.

That was what he found himself thinking about later that night when the three of them were crammed onto the bed in his room. Theon had tried to convince Tessa to sleep upstairs tonight; she had refused. Begrudgingly, Theon had crawled onto the mattress beside her. He hadn't spoken to Luka much the rest of the night, but as Tessa's soft breaths became ones of deep slumber, his voice drifted over.

"We can't be on opposite sides right now, Luka."

Tessa shifted, and his entire body erupted in tingles, his teeth clenching together as she draped a leg over his.

"We're not, Theon," he replied after a moment.

He didn't need the doubt filtering down the bond from Theon to know how he was feeling. His nonresponse told him enough. But in the end, he *was* just like Theon. The only way he knew how to show he cared about someone was to protect them. Keep them safe. It was why he agreed to become Theon's Guardian in the first place.

They did what needed to be done to keep their own safe, and they showed no remorse. They didn't get the luxury of guilt, but Luka had a feeling when this was all over, they were all going to be left with just that: guilt and regrets.

# 37
## TESSA

For the first time since her return from Faven, she woke before the two of them were out of bed. Judging from the lack of light outside, it was just before dawn. She was curled into Theon as usual, his arm looped around her and his other hand threaded with hers. Luka was curled into *her*, though. She could feel the weight of his arm just below Theon's, his warm palm splayed over her belly. A thigh was wedged between hers, the coarse hairs on his leg rough against her smooth skin.

If she didn't know any better, she'd feel safe. Protected. Maybe even loved.

But she did know better.

It was why she let herself pretend.

For just a few minutes, she let herself pretend she could have this. Not one, but *two* people who chose her above all else. Two people who wanted her simply because she existed. Two people who knew she was more than a bond, more than a pawn, more than a means to an end.

She let herself pretend this was a normal morning. That this wasn't a bond drawing them all to each other. That the warmth in her chest and the heat in her veins and the desire pooling was more than just physical needs to be met, but that it was welcome and wanted. She let herself pretend she didn't feel guilty and disgusted with herself for *wanting* to begin with.

She let herself pretend that the three of them would get up and have coffee. Maybe they'd stay snuggled in bed. Maybe they'd move to the sofa. Maybe later tonight Theon would have a book, and she'd be stretched out, her feet in his lap and leaning against Luka as they watched the Chaosphere game. Theon would grumble the whole time, and Luka would—

No.

That was enough pretending.

She didn't get to have any of that.

That wasn't what she was meant for, and she'd made peace with that truth.

Still, she let herself linger in the warmth and the dark. The steady rise and fall of chests. The muscles and power that almost felt like home.

Just a few more minutes before destiny beckoned.

# 38
## AXEL

"I need to show you something," Katya said, bursting into the bathroom, and once again startling him.

"You have got to stop doing that, kitten," Axel said. He could hear his blood pounding in his ears as his heart rate slowly went back to normal. He'd just finished drying off from a shower and was wrapping a towel around his waist.

"Hurry," she chirped.

Gods, she was practically bouncing around with excitement.

"What if I had been indisposed?" he asked.

Her brow furrowed. "I heard the shower shut off moments ago."

"People do things besides shower in a bathroom, you know."

"Of course I know that."

He waited, but she just continued to stare at him as if he was the odd one for suggesting a person shouldn't barge into a bathroom.

She'd been awake before him this morning, which had been rather disappointing. Today was going to be a long day, and he had no idea what to expect. Apparently, the plan was to go about the day as normal. They'd all attend the Solstice service in a couple of hours, and then the Sources and heirs would take their leave to bestow the third Source Mark. There had been no word on Theon's deadline, and his father hadn't spoken to any of them since dinner a few nights ago. That alone had Axel on edge. Usually when his father went days without speaking to him, it meant something was coming. That something usually ended with his power drained, chains on, and days spent in a state of madness from bloodlust. Maybe this would be the time his father would force him to trigger the curse.

That was one of his greatest fears. That he would be so desperate and blinded by need that his father would shove a Fae at him, and he wouldn't care. Would he even recognize what he was doing? What if it was Kat as a way to punish him? For what, he didn't know, but his father had to know he could use her against him by this point. With all the unknown surrounding today, he once again found himself wondering why he'd ever thought this was a good idea, while knowing he wouldn't have changed his decision.

"Axel?"

Kat's voice drew him from his thoughts, and he plastered on a fake smile. Stepping forward, he brushed a kiss to the top of her head as he murmured, "Happy Solstice, Katya."

She stilled for a moment before brushing her fingers along his arm. "Are you all right?"

"Of course," he said, tugging at a curl. The warmth of her touch didn't quite sink into his soul like it usually did. "Let me get dressed, and then you can show me what you found."

A few minutes later, he had on pants and a shirt, although his shirt was unbuttoned and loose. Katya was already shoving a book under his nose.

"Look at this," she said, tapping the page.

"It's a Mark," Axel said, trying to reach around her to the coffee carafe. "It looks kind of like the last Source Mark."

"That's because it *is* the last Source Mark," Katya said. "Or at least some kind of variation of it."

"What do you mean by a variation of it?" he asked. Keeping his finger on the page, he flipped it shut, looking at the cover. "What book is this?"

"The one Cienna gave me," Kat answered. "I've looked through it numerous times, but it's incredibly complicated to translate and understand."

Axel knew that. He'd sat with her one night and watched her struggle her way through two pages.

Two pages.

In five hours.

She'd put the book away, getting lost in other books these past weeks, so what had possessed her to suddenly pull it out this morning was beyond him.

"I'm going to need you to help me out here, kitten. Why are we excited about this?" Axel asked, rubbing at his chest. He needed a drink or blood. Maybe both. Anything to keep his rising anxiety about this day down.

"I think it's *the* Source Mark," Kat said. "Scarlett was insistent there was only one. If it's this one, it's nearly identical to the final Source Mark given on the spring equinox."

"But not an exact match," Axel clarified.

Kat shook her head, black ringlets bouncing as she pulled him over to the coffee table. Grabbing another book, she said, "This is the final Source Mark."

Axel studied the two Marks. She wasn't wrong. They were very similar. With a sigh, he said, "Theon has a theory that the Guardian Mark was somehow incorporated into the final Source Mark."

"I thought only Sargon descendants could be Guardians?"

"That's correct, but Theon thinks people have tried to emulate it over the centuries. His whole theory is that advanced worlds, like Devram, figured out a way to merge Marks."

"That's dangerous," Katya said with a frown. "If Marks aren't drawn precisely, their entire purpose changes."

"I think that's kind of the point. If Theon is right, they wanted the Source Mark to be more than that. Incorporating the Guardian Mark drives the Source to protect and give their lives for their Master," Axel said.

"But then what is the purpose of the other three Marks?"

"What?" he asked in confusion.

"If the fourth Mark is the actual Source Mark somehow combined with elements of the Guardian Mark, then what is the purpose of the other three Marks?"

"You know the purpose of them. Physical presence. Emotional connection. Being able to hear each other's thoughts," Axel said, still confused.

"But if the purpose of the Source Marks is to draw power, why the other three? Why not just use this one? Why this grand spectacle of four different marks drawn out over the course of months when the desired outcome could be achieved with *one* Mark?" Kat said.

"I...don't know," he answered.

"And more than that, is a Fae even a Source without the final Mark?"

"Katya, it sounds like… Are you saying that a Source bond might not be in place until the final Mark is given? That, essentially, there is no bond for Theon to break right now?" Axel asked.

Bright amber eyes met his. "I think so? I mean, there's obviously some purpose to the other three Marks, and there is clearly a bond between him and Tessa. But an actual Source bond?"

Axel snapped the books shut. "Get dressed, kitten. We need to go find Theon."

Her hand firmly in his, Axel tried to be mindful of his long strides as he led her through the Pantheon. Luka, Theon, and Tessa had left earlier in the day. Theon had left a message about wanting to spend more time in the Pantheon archives in the final hours before facing the Lords and Ladies again.

"Axel," Kat hissed.

"I know. I'm sorry," he said. He slowed, but within moments, he was back to his original pace.

"Axel," she hissed again, tugging on his hand. "I can't move this fast in heels."

"Tessa complains about them too," he said, turning to her. "Take them off."

"What?"

"Take them off. I'll carry them. Tessa goes barefoot all the time," he said, motioning to her feet.

"Tessa is a… She's not a Fae," Kat protested.

"Just take them off so we can move faster," Axel said, gesturing at her shoes again.

With a small huff, she slipped the black heels off, bending to scoop them off the ground. Axel immediately took them from her. She had Cienna's book with her, and she tucked it under her arm as she gathered the material of the black dress in her hand so it wouldn't drag as they moved.

They started off down the hall again, heading for the stairs that would take them to the archives. Theon hadn't answered his call, but they also weren't supposed to use technology inside the Pantheon.

Entering the stairwell, Axel nearly collided with someone stepping off the stairs. Katya skidded to a halt, bumping into his back, and he instinctively reached to keep her there.

Turning back, he expected to see a scholar, or maybe even Theon. He did not expect to be face-to-face with Tristyn Blackheart.

"Heir St. Orcas," Tristyn greeted.

"Blackheart," he replied, keeping Kat tucked behind him.

"The Solstice service starts soon," Tristyn said, sliding a hand into the pocket of his pants. He was in a suit and tie like every male in attendance would be, a long black coat draped over his arm.

"It does. I was going to find Theon," Axel said. "He's down in the Pantheon archives."

"He's not," Tristyn said. "Or he's not anymore. They were down there until about a half hour ago."

"Damnit," Axel muttered.

"I don't believe I've had the pleasure of meeting the lovely Fae that has the realm in such a fuss," Tristyn said, taking a step and peering around Axel.

Axel studied him for a moment. He was always flirty and roguish with Tessa, but he also seemed to want something from her like everyone else did. He'd never seen the male interact with the Fae. Then again, the elusive Tristyn Blackheart was rarely seen by anyone until recently.

With a tight smile, Axel finally stepped aside so he could place his hand on Kat's lower back. "Katya, Tristyn Blackheart. Tristyn, this is Katya, claimed and in service to the Arius Kingdom."

The smile playing on Tristyn's lips almost seemed to be one of amusement. "It's a pleasure, Katya," he said.

"The pleasure is mine," she replied clearly with her head bowed and eyes down.

"Do you have a book tucked under your arm?"

Kat glanced at Axel, but Tristyn had already reached out, snatching the book. He seemed to still for the briefest of moments before he leafed through the pages.

"Where did you come by such a book?" Tristyn asked.

"What's it matter to you?" Axel cut in.

"These types of books are used often in my line of work."

"You work with Marks at a tech company?" Axel asked doubtfully.

Tristyn was still looking through the book as he answered, "I rarely work with the technology these days. But I know how…valuable these types of books are, so I am curious as to how a Fae came across one?"

"It was a gift," Axel said, holding out his hand.

Tristyn looked up, a brow arching. "From you to her?"

"Let's go with that."

That amusement was back, and he handed the book to Axel. "I am quite proficient with Marks like this should you ever need anything."

"I'll be sure and let Theon know that."

Tristyn huffed a laugh. "I can only interfere so much with your brother, but to clarify, I offer the aid to Katya. Although, I suppose that now includes you by default."

Reaching into the pocket of his jacket, Tristyn pulled out a business card. Then he slid it into the book Axel still held.

"I would, however, be mindful of who lays eyes on such a book," Tristyn added. "I suggest keeping it well hidden." He stepped around them, then paused. "Fire and shadows. What a perfect balance."

Then he was sauntering out of the stairwell, whistling a random song as he went.

"He is…odd," Kat remarked, staring after him.

"Every time I interact with him, I am left wondering what just happened," Axel replied, turning to her. He glanced at his watch and muttered a curse before saying, "You should put these back on."

He held the heels out to her before sending the book to a pocket realm. Maybe they could still catch Theon before the service started, assuming they were in the temple room.

Forcing himself to slow, they made their way back to the main hallways. He dropped her hand before rounding a corner. It would be unacceptable to be seen in such a way with a Fae, but the moment he was no longer touching her, all his anxiety about this day came flooding back. It was so strong, his stomach churned. He hadn't eaten much today, and he suddenly found himself grateful for that.

She stayed at his side but a step behind him, always visible. It would be expected that she'd be guarded, but he still hated all this. Still wished it could be different, just as he'd wished every day since they'd spoken about it weeks ago.

Moving into the temple anteroom, Axel spotted Theon and Luka. Thankfully, his parents weren't with them yet. Lange and Corbin stood off to the side. It would be expected they'd attend since they were claimed early.

"Theon, we need to talk," Axel said when they finally managed to make their way across the crowded foyer. "I've been trying to reach you for the last two hours."

"Is everything all right?" Theon asked.

"No. I mean, nothing is wrong, but we have information that might change—"

"Tessalyn, my dear," came a deep voice from behind them.

Turning, Axel immediately bowed, the Fae dropping to a knee, as they found Lord Jove standing there. Dagian, along with their Sources, was with him, that ever present almost sneer in place.

"My Lord," Tessa greeted. "It's nice to see you again. Happy Solstice."

"And Happy Solstice to you," he replied. "Speaking of which, I have a gift for you."

"That is not necessary," she said quickly, worrying her bottom lip.

"Of course it isn't, but nonetheless, I have brought you one," Lord Jove said with a chuckle.

There was a flare of light that had them all wincing and turning away, but when Axel turned back, he held a simply wrapped gift in his hand. He held it out to Tessa, who glanced at Theon. He gave a sharp jerk of his head. They all knew better than to refuse a Lord or Lady. Tessa stepped forward tentatively, taking it from him.

"Thank you, my Lord," she said softly.

"Open it after sundown, as is customary," Lord Jove said.

"Of course, my Lord."

He smiled at her before his golden gaze slid to Theon. "Upon further discussion with the other ruling Lord and Ladies, we have agreed none of us wish to disrupt our Solstice festivities with hearings, rulings, or other more unfavorable activities. As such, you will come before us two days from now."

"Understood, my Lord," Theon said.

"And the third Mark?" Tessa asked, her eyes widening as she realized she spoke when she shouldn't have. "I apologize."

"Now, now. We've discussed this, Tessalyn. No need for apologies. The third Mark will happen as planned. We do not wish to disrupt tradition after all," he said.

"I understand," she replied, gaze dropping. "My gratitude again for the gift."

"Enjoy the service," he said before heading into the temple along with his family.

"What is that?" Theon asked as soon as the Achaz Lord was out of sight.

Tessa sent him a frank look. "It's wrapped, Theon. How am I to know what it is?"

"You have no ideas?"

"Why don't we just wait until after sundown, and then I can open it," she replied.

"You will likely be unwell," he retorted.

"I am not going to open it now when a *Lord* specifically told me to wait," she hissed.

"He is not your—" Theon stopped, releasing a frustrated breath.

Luka stepped forward, holding out his hand. "Give it to me, Tessa. I'll store it in a pocket realm, and we can decide what to do later."

"I'm sure *we* will," Theon muttered.

Axel wasn't sure what that was about. There had been tension between Luka and Theon last night, but Axel had just assumed that was due to yet another Augury attack and Tessa being in danger again.

"There is likely a charm or enchantment on it anyway," Luka said, the gift disappearing amidst a burst of black flames. "If anyone other than Tessa opens it, Lord Jove will know."

"He can do that?" Tessa asked in shock.

"It's just an enchantment, Tessa," Theon said. "A person can do almost anything if they're willing to pay the cost."

"We need to head in there," Luka said, moving to the front of their group.

They all followed him, the four of them sliding into the Arius Kingdom's row while Kat, Lange, and Corbin were forced to stand along the wall. Legacy would take all the available seats, and there wouldn't be many other Fae here.

Tessa twisted from where she sat between Axel and Theon, peering at her friends. "I can't believe you made Kat wear heels, Axel," she whispered. "How long is this thing going to be?"

"Did you not have Solstice services at the estate?" he whispered back.

"Yes, and they were nearly two hours."

"Same here, baby doll."

"If we weren't in a temple, I would smack you," she said in a sharp whisper. "Her feet are going to be killing her by the end of tonight."

"Tessa, if my father saw her in anything other than heels, he would consider it a show of grave disrespect," Axel said.

"The priestesses don't even wear heels," she argued.

"I didn't say it would be a show of disrespect to them or to this service or even to Rai," he replied, naming the god of seasons. "He would see it as a personal affront and claim she is disrespecting the Arius Kingdom by not being properly dressed. Why do you think Theon provided you with the wardrobe he did?"

She crossed her arms, sitting back in her seat. "I know why *I* was provided the clothing I was, but she's not a Source."

"And she won't be one," Axel retorted.

Something in Tessa's demeanor shifted at his words, and she uncrossed her arms, clasping her hands in her lap. Her skin seemed paler against the black dress she wore. All the kingdoms wore their colors, and of course, Arius Kingdom was black and silver. There was also a faint glow around her wrist. Not as bright as last night, but enough that Axel knew it was there. How could she constantly use her magic like that?

He suddenly wondered exactly how she replenished her magic reserves. As far as he knew she didn't drink blood. Maybe it was rest and food like the Fae who mimicked mortals in that way.

Those thoughts were quickly scattered with the arrival of his parents, and soon the service was underway. It was nearly two hours, just as he'd said it would be. Theon and the other heirs were dismissed first so they could prepare for the ritual of the third Marking, and after they had all filed out, the ruling families followed.

At least his father waited until they were in the anteroom of the temple before he acknowledged Axel. Although when he spoke, Axel found himself wishing the service had lasted another five hours.

"Be at the manor for breakfast, Axel," Valter said. "And bring the fire Fae."

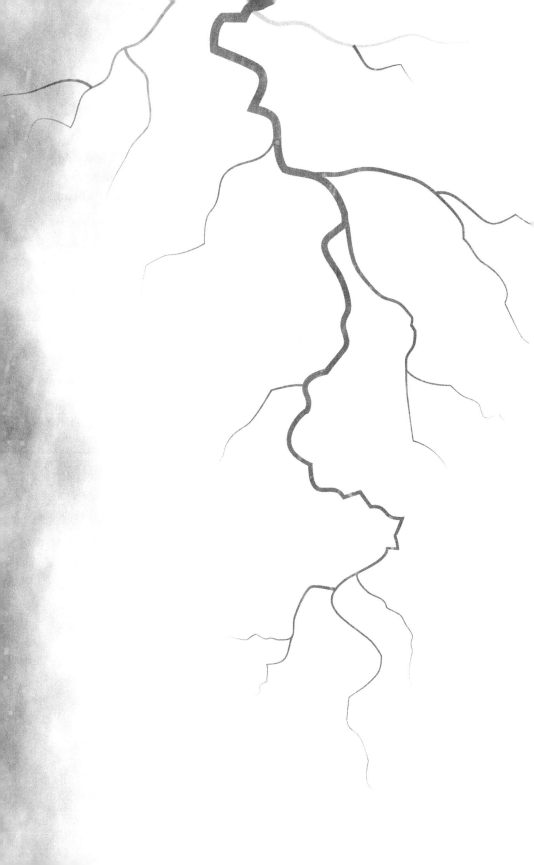

# 39
## TESSA

She'd stopped and unbuckled her glittering black heels as soon as they'd reached the second floor. Theon had taken them from her without a word, the straps of the shoes now wrapped around his fingers as he and Luka walked a few paces ahead of her. They were different. There was a crack in their unified front, and it was one a person wouldn't notice unless they spent the majority of their time with the two males. But even if she couldn't feel the tension trickling down the bond, she would have been able to tell. It was in the way they walked too stiffly beside each other. The way Theon refused to meet Luka's gaze, and the way Luka... Well, he was always broody, but he seemed more so.

Theon stopped briefly outside the same room she'd received the other two Source Marks in, pressing his palm to the door. A moment later, magic flared before the door clicked open. Theon and Luka filed through, but Tessa paused on the threshold. Her black and silver dress was suddenly too tight as she remembered the agony of the first two Marks. Her palms were sweaty, and it felt like Mother Cordelia's magic was stealing her air.

There had been no word on the Estate Mother's whereabouts, but with the increase of Augury attacks, Legacy and Fae alike were becoming concerned. There had been a notice that the Lords and Ladies would meet tomorrow to discuss a course of action, which was likely part of the reason Theon's hearing had been pushed to the day after.

"Tessa?" Theon called, reappearing in the doorway. "What are you doing?"

"Nothing," she said with a false smile, reinforcing her mental shields to make sure he couldn't feel her emotions.

Emerald eyes studied her, and she could feel everything he was feeling. Theon never shut her out. Ever since she'd returned from Faven, she could feel all of his emotions all the time. It was as if he was trying to let her in. As if he was trying to help her understand or prove something to her.

As if it wasn't too late.

As if any of it would matter in the end.

Swallowing down her nerves, Tessa stepped into the room, forcing herself not to flinch when he shut the door behind her.

"You didn't think this Mark was going to happen, did you?" Theon asked, stepping into her line of vision once more.

"Why do you say that?"

"You seemed surprised when Lord Jove said it would proceed, and now you are hesitant."

"Anyone would be hesitant about this, Theon," she retorted. "I know how this process goes. It isn't exactly pleasant."

"For a minute there, it looked like you were contemplating running," he replied, stepping into her even more and sliding a hand into her hair.

"I've tried that before," she said, her tone breathy as the bond delighted in his touch. "A couple times actually. You've always chased me."

"I've always *caught* you," he corrected. "I always will, little storm."

For a moment, she almost let herself embrace those words. For a split second, she almost let herself sink into what they could mean, but just as quickly, she sent him a dark smile. "What happens when you can no longer keep me?"

His hand tightened in her hair, and she tipped her head back even more to relieve some of the sting. His other hand drifted up, fingertips sliding along her throat. "I will always fight for you, Tessa. I will always come for you. You will forever be mine."

"Not just yours though, right?" she said with a faux innocence.

"What do you mean?"

"I am bound to you *and* Luka now. Then again, that was always the plan, wasn't it? Match me with him?" she asked, feeling Theon's fingers flex on her throat. "It seems only fair. You will never be wholly mine, so—"

"Stop, Tessa," Theon snarled.

"It's so difficult to control the uncontrollable, isn't it?" she said, reaching up and tugging on the knot of his tie.

"The priestess is going to be here any minute," Luka cut in. "Tessa, you need to change."

Neither she nor Theon moved for another few moments, and she nearly got lost in those eyes swirling with darkness. He broke whatever they'd been caught in, turning away from her and yanking his tie fully off before shrugging out of his suit coat.

Making her way to Luka, she took the pile of clothing he held out to her before she turned, gathering her hair over her shoulder. "I need you to unzip me," she said.

She could swear Luka's eyes flashed to vertical pupils, but maybe she'd imagined it. He wouldn't look at her as he quickly and efficiently pulled the zipper down the length of her spine. She didn't bother hiding anything. Both of these males had seen her naked. If anyone was bothered here, it was Theon. Or maybe Luka? Because that was definitely a bolt of lust slipping down the bond. She ignored it all, sliding on the usual athletic leggings and tank she always wore for these markings.

Luka was already handing her a hair tie when she went to search through the bag. The third Mark went on the back of her neck at the base of her skull. She quickly knotted her hair in a messy knot atop her head. She turned to say something, but whatever she'd been about to say slipped her mind when she found two sets of heated eyes on her. There was no mistaking the emotions filtering down the bond now.

Hot want and dark desire.

A mixture that had her thinking back to that morning and how she'd let herself pretend. She'd entertained a lot of what ifs in those quiet morning moments before Luka had started to stir. He always woke first, and he never groggily came out of sleep either. It was instant, and the moment he opened his eyes, he scanned the room. Then he turned to them. Theon first, naturally, and then her.

This morning, she'd felt his jolt of surprise at finding her eyes open and returning his gaze. The palm that was splayed across her belly moved, rough fingertips trailing along her hip. There was the barest touch as the pad of a finger brushed against bare skin where Theon's shirt had bunched up during her sleep.

And that was it.

That was all he'd done before he'd slid from the bed, once again completely naked, and went to the bathroom. But she'd let herself pretend a little longer after that. Pretended his hand had gone lower. Pretended he'd warned her to be quiet or there would be consequences, but she couldn't. Pretended Theon had woken to her muffled cries, been his usual possessive self until his darkness had—

*Godsdammit.*

Tessa quickly turned away from them, feeling her face heat as that unacceptable fantasy replayed in her mind at a very inopportune time. She couldn't believe she was actually grateful for the knock that sounded, signaling the arrival of the priestess.

The same priestess as before entered. She seemed more skittish this time. Tessa wasn't entirely sure why.

"Are you ready to proceed, my Lord?" she asked, standing several feet away.

"We are," Theon said.

"She will need the bands on," the priestess said.

The light wound around her wrists sparked, small bolts of energy emanating from it and charging the air around her. Tessa slid her gaze to Luka. "Did you not fill him in on what I told you?"

Theon looked at Luka, and Tessa could feel a mixture of pride and frustration coming from the dragon. The annoyance she was picking up on was all Theon.

"Tessa informed me last night after the Augury attack that if anyone tried to put those bands on her again, she would kill them," Luka said. "It is a threat I would take seriously."

"With all due respect, my Lord, there was little control when she had one band on with the previous Marking. I am uncomfortable staying in the room if she will not be wearing them for this Marking," the priestess said.

"Then do not stay," Theon said brusquely. "Give the Mark and wait outside. We will summon you when it is done."

"I am supposed to stay—"

"And witness?" Theon interrupted.

"Yes," she said, a slight quaver in her voice.

"You may stay," Theon said with a shrug. "But I cannot guarantee your safety this time. Luka's attention will be focused on helping me. Protecting you will be a secondary worry."

"But I…"

"You are grateful I am giving you a choice in the matter?" Theon asked pointedly.

"Yes, of course, my Lord," the priestess said, bowing her head.

"Let's get on with this then," Theon snapped, moving to Tessa. Lowering his voice so only she could hear, he said, "Are you sure about this, beautiful? The Marking will likely be easier with a band on."

She gave him a too sweet smile. "Please test that assumption. You'll have plenty of time to ponder the results during your time in the After."

Everything about him darkened at her words. "You are becoming rather bold, clever tempest."

"Someone they fear as much as they fear you," she replied.

Tessa stepped away from him, moving to the sofa. Frowning, she said, "How should I sit for this one?"

"You lie on your stomach," the priestess said.

She wasn't keen on that idea. She felt too vulnerable that way. Too many ways to trap her hands. But she lowered to her stomach, folding her arms along the armrest and resting her chin atop them. She felt Theon lower to his knees beside her, but she was focused on Luka, who had crouched before her. He didn't say anything, but something in her chest eased at being able to see him.

"Proceed," Theon said.

Tessa focused on her breathing as the priestess drew the Mark.

There was a growled "get out" before the scent of blood filled her senses. A moment later, she felt the sting of the dagger across her nape. Her power was already flaring, light and energy spilling out.

"You won't be able to do it, Theon," Luka warned.

"I can try," Theon retorted, but Tessa saw him pass the dagger to Luka out of the corner of her eye. She tensed as Theon leaned closer, his breath soft in her ear. "You have to let me win, Tessa. It's the only way."

"I can't," she whispered.

"I know."

And then she was burying her face in her arms as dark power poured into her. Theon's hand was clamped firmly to the back of her neck. He'd done it differently this time. Instead of giving her a minute to prepare, he'd more or less attacked, clearly hoping to catch her magic by surprise.

That was his mistake.

Her light sank into his darkness, crackling through it. Gold mist and violet sparks battled against inky pools of midnight.

"Tessa, look at me," Luka was urging, trying to tip her head back up. "Look at me, little one."

She sucked in a gasping breath as Theon's power attacked again and again, barely managing to lift her head.

"That's my girl," Luka said gruffly, his large palm cupping her cheek. "It's not going to work, is it?"

She knew what he was asking, and Tessa shook her head. "I need—" But she just shook her head again, unable to think around the pain.

Theon was grunting with effort as her power wrapped tighter around his darkness. He would lose. There was no doubt about it. Even if she'd wanted to submit to him and his power, she couldn't. Her magic wouldn't let her.

Until black flames were flaring around his darkness, drawing her light to it. Her magic didn't know which way to go, who to follow, who to attack. It had been like this with the last Mark when Luka's power had suddenly appeared. Her magic had been startled then; now it almost seemed enraptured.

Golden threads wound around both their powers, drawing it together. She could feel both of them, their determination strong down the bond, but she could also—

*Come on, Tessa. Give in.*

That was Theon's voice in her head.

Her entire body shuddered at the sensation, her power doing the same.

*Let go, little one. You don't have to fight back here.*

Luka's deep rumble sounded, his glowing eyes still on hers.

More darkness.

More flames.

Her light delighted in it all.

*Let us fight for you,* came Luka's growl again.

Her entire being faltered at those words, her gasping breath getting caught in her throat. Theon and Luka took advantage, both of their power barreling down on her in unison. The black, gold, and silvery-blue cords flared, illuminating the low-lit room. She felt them settle into her soul like the others.

The males both sat back, breathing heavily, and she already knew she'd be vomiting within minutes.

*A bowl.*

"I'll get it," Luka said, pushing to his feet.

*Fuck.*

*Her shields.*

*They could—*

"Take a minute before you shut us out," Theon said, running a hand up and down her back. She was still lying on her stomach, and his touch was soothing.

To the bond.

Not her.

Definitely not to her.

That was what she tried to tell herself as he helped her sit up. Her legs were draped over his lap, her brow to his shoulder. He murmured soft praises to her, but the nausea was there. Her blood was rushing in her ears. She was starting to panic, but the basin appeared, and then she felt the sofa dip behind her. A cool rag was pressed to her neck, and she could feel the heat emanating off of Luka as he leaned into her.

They let her get the first round of vomiting out of the way before they called for the priestess. She commented again about the Mark looking a little different, and now Tessa understood why. She'd been in too much pain and there'd been too many emotions bombarding her to understand the last time.

"You know she's going to report this back to the Lords and Ladies," Luka said, reclaiming his place beside her.

She let out a little sigh when he replaced the cool rag, and Theon brushed his lips along her brow.

"You did wonderfully, little storm," he murmured.

*If he only knew.*

"Only knew what?" Theon asked, sitting back to try to see her face.

"Nothing," she muttered, managing to get a thin mental shield in place.

"Don't waste energy on that right now, Tessa," Theon said, moving the bowl back in place.

"I'll just pretend," she murmured, her stomach clenching.

After another round of vomiting, she settled back against Luka. One of her hands was in Theon's. His other hand was dragging his fingers up and down her thigh. Luka had an arm behind her, ready to catch her if she moved too quickly.

Two people here.

Two people tending to her.

Two people who actually *cared*.

That's what she let herself pretend.

"You were supposed to be mine," she whispered, hardly able to keep her eyes open. "Not his. And he…"

"He what, Tessa?" Luka asked, running a hand along her brow and smoothing back her hair.

She didn't have it in her to speak any more. She just wanted to pretend.

So she let them hear her thoughts instead.

*He and I were always meant to destroy one another.*

*She couldn't breathe.*

*Not as Theon stood over her, a black dagger in his hand.*

*She couldn't get air down to even speak.*

*"Breathe, little one," Luka soothed. "We'll figure this out."*

*The dragon was near her head, a large palm cupping her cheek and keeping her gaze fixed on him. Always where she could see him.*

*But Axel wasn't here.*

*He was always here.*

*She choked down a sob, gasping as tears slid down her face. "Please, Luka. It doesn't have to be like this."*

*Luka's brow pinched, his gaze darting to Theon. "You know she's right, Theon. There's always a loophole. There's always—"*

*"We don't have a choice," Theon said, still standing over her, his hair stirring in the breeze.*

*A light rain was falling, thunder rumbling in the distance.*

*"I still think there is another way to interpret this."*

*Tessa's head snapped to the side to find a tall male. He looked familiar. Sapphire eyes. The cut of his features. But Tessa was sure she'd never met him. He had a sword strapped down his back, as did the female standing next to him. Her red-gold hair was braided over her shoulder, and flames flickered in her eyes. Standing next to them was Tristyn and Katya, a strange Mark stark against the back of the Fae's hand.*

*"Life must give, and death must take," Theon said flatly. "There is no other way to interpret that. Not if we wish to save this world."*

*For so long, Tessa had wished for death, and now, in this moment, she didn't want it. She'd finally found something to fight for, and gods, she was going to fight for it.*

*"You're wrong," Tristyn said, his features taut and his hands clenching and unclenching at his sides. "Have you learned nothing over these past months? Everything you thought you knew has been wrong. This is no different."*

*"It is all different. All that questioning has led me here. To understanding why we were drawn to each other," Theon said, his grip on the dagger tightening. "I tried to change it. I did everything I could, but destiny beckons and sacrifice demands."*

*"Theon, don't!" Tessa cried. "It's more than a bond! I know that now."*

*Emerald eyes cut to her. "You're right, and now that I understand what that means, I'm the only one who can do this."*

*She would fight, but she'd never win. Not with the ring on her finger keeping her separated from her gifts.*

*Luka pulled her into him, his hand smoothing down her hair.*

*"Luka," she sobbed, the sound defeated and broken.*

*"He won't do it, Tessa," he whispered. "He can't harm you. The bond—"*

*"This is wrong," the female with fire was saying to the other male. "This will alter everything."*

*"It will correct the balance," Theon said.*

*"It will tip it beyond repair!" Katya cried. "Theon, there's another way. We've spent hours together researching. We can find another way."*

*"We're out of time," Theon said. Then, in a barely audible murmur, he added, "Once again, I'm out of time."*

*"We cannot interfere," the familiar-looking male said, reaching for the female with fire when she took a step towards Tessa. "It will upset the—"*

*"Fuck the balance," the female seethed, shoving his hands away. "She sent us to help. This is the exact opposite of that!"*

*Howling nearby had Theon tensing.*

*"Theon, stop," Luka said, his hand never ceasing its movement along her hair as he clutched her tightly to him. "We will find another way."*

*"She can get here," the female was saying, panic in her voice. "She can stop this."*

*"Not even she will be fast enough," Theon answered.*

*"She is a World Walker and a queen among the realms. She—"*

*"And even she has been ordered not to interfere with this," Theon cut in, dropping to Tessa's side. "She is already tempting fate by sending you."*

*"She will not care," the female spat.*

*"She will be too late," Theon said again. Lowering to a crouch beside her, he*

slid his fingers along Tessa's jaw. "You will forever be mine, Tessa. Whether in this life or in the After."

"Please don't send me to the dark alone," she whispered, her body trembling in Luka's arms.

The male and female were arguing with Tristyn, but Tessa couldn't hear them. Not as she got lost in dark emerald eyes and black hair. In a small dimple and lips she'd kissed more times than she could count.

"I'm sorry I failed you, little storm," Theon said, sorrow flashing in his eyes. "I tried. I tried to save you."

"I understand," she whispered on another broken sob. "I'm sorry I loved you too late. But I'm yours. Every piece of me."

Theon didn't say another word.

In a sudden burst of power, his darkness yanked her from Luka's arms. She screamed, and Luka bellowed a roar that she felt in her soul. Black flames flared, but it was Auryon who appeared, blocking Theon's dagger with one of her own as Roan and Niylah prowled around them, brushing up against Tessa's legs. Midnight hair flowed around the female, her bare feet planted as she stared up at Theon, a dark grin on her face.

Her voice was a predatory purr as she said, "You may have stolen her Guardian from her, but that only means you must now deal with me."

"You know this has to happen, Auryon," Theon said, desperation entering his tone.

"I know a great number of things," the female replied, stepping to Tessa's side. "I know she was meant to be a tempest of wrath and vengeance in this world."

She never took her eyes off Theon as she reached for Tessa's hand.

And slid the ring from her finger.

# 40

## AXEL

K at shot to her feet when Axel came through the door of their room. He'd been across the hall in Luka's room. Tessa still slept, her body adjusting to the new Mark. Theon was awake, but looked exhausted. He was clearly still drained from the Marking. Luka had seemed just as tired. He likely hadn't slept while Theon and Tessa did, too paranoid to leave them in such a vulnerable state. Not that he didn't have a reason to be paranoid. Paranoia was just part of being raised in Arius House. Or maybe Arius Kingdom? Devram in general?

"What did he think about everything?" Kat asked, wringing her hands together. She'd offered to go with him, but she'd needed to get ready for this meeting with his father this morning.

Axel swiped a hand down his face. "They are going to spend the entire day researching everything. Maybe it will help Theon tomorrow."

"When we get back, we can help," she said, smoothing her hands down her dress.

It was a simple yet classy thing. Long-sleeves. Shallow v-neck. Material that clung subtly to her curves. His father would approve. It was why Axel picked it out for her to wear.

"Right," he said, flashing her a weak smile.

She wasn't an optimist. Kat was a realist. This was a show she was putting on for him.

But they'd both been in denial these past few weeks. There wasn't any other way to put it. Going about their days, coming back here at the end of them, and acting like this could ever be normal for them. What he would give for such a dull life of monotony if it meant he could spend his days and nights with her.

Kat cleared her throat before she said, "It hasn't felt this awkward since the first night you stayed in here."

He huffed a bark of laughter despite the circumstances. There was the bluntness he knew.

"Are you going to say anything?" she finally asked when Axel just leaned against the door. "It does not lessen the awkwardness when you stare at me like that."

"We've established multiple times I am a rude fuck," Axel said, but she was right. He was staring at her, trying to memorize this moment. Trying to memorize *her*. Like this. Whole. Happy. Safe.

The moment they left for the meeting she would no longer be the last one on that list. He doubted by the end of the meeting she would be any of those things.

This was his fault. He didn't get to sit here and memorize this and wish for something they could never have. He'd been selfish, and now she was going to suffer for it.

Pushing off the doorframe, he brushed past her and made his way to the closet. Having left the top two buttons of his shirt undone, he finished buttoning them now before grabbing a tie from the tie rack. Dark red.

Blood red.

Just in case.

He looped it around his neck, quickly knotting it before grabbing his black suit jacket.

When he came back out, Katya hadn't moved. She still stood in the same spot, hands clasped before her and waiting. But her eyes... Fuck, those godsdamn amber eyes were fixed on him, seeing straight to his soul like she always did.

Still he said nothing, moving around the room and gathering his things. A messenger bag with a laptop he rarely took out once he got home for the evening. Several files. A phone charger. Who knew how long he'd be gone, and if she didn't come back with him...

Well, he wouldn't want to stay in this room. It was why he was collecting all his essentials now.

Checking his watch, he found they had fifteen minutes until their ride would be here.

Yep, their ride. They were being godsdamn collected. That alone told him how this meeting was going to go. His father wanted him monitored and unable to leave on his own.

"Axel—" Katya finally started.

"Don't, Katya," he snapped. "Not now. Not… Just don't."

But of course she didn't stop. "I understand that you're anxious about this meeting."

Anxious.

That was one word for it.

"I need you to tell me what is happening here," she went on.

"You know what's happening here," he replied. "The Arius Lord has summoned us."

"Yes, but—"

"And outside these walls, the illusion we've built for ourselves here is nonexistent."

"An illusion?" she repeated, taking a small step back from him.

"What did you think we were doing here, Katya?"

"Katya," she whispered. Then, a little louder, she said, "That's the second time you've said my full name in a matter of minutes."

Axel brought his hands up, wanting to rake them through his hair, but he stopped himself. He didn't have time to fix it yet again. "I never should have—" He snapped his mouth shut. He couldn't be doing this.

"Never should have what?" she challenged, that agitation creeping into her tone.

"You can't do this," he retorted. "Whatever freedoms you think you've gained in this room, you haven't. If anything, I have only made things so much worse for you."

"Axel—"

"No," he interrupted sharply, advancing on her before he realized what he was doing. He had to give her credit. She didn't move until he was nearly on top of her. Only then did she stumble back a few steps. Instinctively, his hand shot out to catch her, gripping her arm.

That one touch had him gritting his teeth and sucking in a breath.

Which only caused him to be assaulted with jasmine and citrus and spices.

"You're hurting me, Axel," she whispered, and his gaze darted to where he still grasped her, his hold tight, directly over the scar she'd forever bare.

"You have no idea just how true that statement is," he replied, releasing her and stepping back.

"I need you to tell me what to be prepared for. I need you to..."

She trailed off, rubbing at her arm before bringing her eyes back to his. There was a renewed determination in them, and if he wasn't convinced he was about to watch her be brutally tortured, he'd have kissed her.

"I need you, Axel," she finally said, her voice full of that quiet fierceness he'd loved drawing out of her from the first moment he'd spoken to her.

"You don't need me," he retorted. "You shouldn't need me. You *can't* need me."

"But I—"

"Enough, Katya."

"No," she snapped, her hands landing on his chest and shoving hard.

He had to hold in his gasp at how *hot* her hands had been. When he looked down, he half-expected his shirt to be singed.

"Stop interrupting me, and let me speak, Axel St. Orcas," she demanded.

"This is what should have never happened," he shot back. "As much as we wish it were otherwise, we are still Fae and Legacy." He saw the wince, let himself feel it in his soul. "And because I was careless, selfish, and short-sighted, I let this happen."

"What, exactly, is *this*?"

"You think that—" He shook his head, trying to get his thoughts in order "No. You know what? You want to know what to be prepared for? Any manner of torture, Katya. That's what you should be prepared for. Be prepared for him to offer you to others. Be prepared for him to watch while it happens. Be prepared for him to conduct business with others while you are screaming. Or maybe he'll take another route. Maybe he'll force me to torture you. Draw blood. Taste it. Drink it. Maybe he'll use you to finally get what he's always wanted. Or maybe he'll simply kill you. Correction. He never gets his hands dirty. He'll make *me* kill you, and that, in turn, will kill me. But he won't let that happen either. He'll make sure I stay alive to relive that moment over and over."

"Axel," she breathed, and then her arms were around him, and he was clutching her tightly to his chest.

"I can't have this, Kat," he whispered into her hair. "And because I tried, you will suffer for it."

"I agreed to this, Axel. I—"

"You didn't know what you were agreeing to," he interrupted yet again. "You didn't know. You didn't—"

"I didn't know how cruel Legacy could be to Fae?" she said, cutting him off this time. Her voice had a sardonic edge he'd never heard from her before. "You forget where I grew up. You forget that before I came here, that's all I was: just another Fae. No different from Tessa or Lange or Corbin. There to serve, no matter what that looked like. I *asked* for this. I *wanted*. Do not belittle what I desired into something you think you somehow dragged me into."

Before he could question it, his mouth was on hers. This kiss was pure desperation and need, tongues swiping and teeth clashing. Her fingers curled into his shirt where her hands still rested against his chest. He clutched her hips, pulling her into him as though if he could keep her close, he could somehow protect her.

Then he felt the wards shudder as they were crossed.

He pulled back abruptly, both of them breathing hard.

"We have to go," he rasped.

Kat said nothing as she stepped away from him, smoothing her hands down her dress once more. He didn't say anything either, picking up the messenger bag he'd dropped to the floor at some point before crossing to the door and guiding her out.

Theon met them at the bottom of the stairs, tense and rigid.

"Do you know who is collecting you?" Theon asked, his voice low.

"I just assumed it was one of Father's personal guards," Axel replied.

"Pavil and Metias."

"You can't be serious."

Theon nodded grimly. "Be careful, Axel." His green eyes cut to Kat. "Thank you for everything you've done. Your help has been invaluable."

A goodbye.

Or the closest Theon would ever come to saying one.

Katya nodded, and Axel saw her throat bob. Maybe she was finally understanding how serious this was. He wasn't stupid. His father wouldn't kill a fire Fae, the only one in service to their kingdom at that, but she wouldn't be returning to the townhouse with him. They all knew that.

He probably should have packed some things for her now that he thought about it. Not that it would really matter.

"Let's go," Axel muttered.

"I'll check on you later," Theon called after him.

He just offered a wave over his shoulder.

"Axel, pleasure to see you, as always," Metias greeted, his voice as greasy as his slicked back black hair. Dark, beady eyes skipped to Kat, and the smile that curled on the male's lips could only be described as slimy.

"Metias. Pavil," Axel said, striding through the foyer but making sure he stayed between them and Katya. "Let's go."

"Of course. We certainly do not wish to be late," Metias said as Pavil pulled open the front door.

It was Kat who opened the back door of the car that was parked out front, falling into the role of submissive Fae as naturally as breathing. He suddenly found he didn't give a fuck what they were supposed to be portraying to the world. If this was going to be his last moments with her, they wouldn't be spent like this.

His hand falling to her lower back, he bent and whispered, "Get in."

She stiffened, but did as she was told, climbing into the backseat. He followed, pulling the door shut behind him. Pavil slid into the driver's seat, and Metias the passenger one. Wisely, the pair didn't say anything, and the drive to the manor was quiet.

Axel had never truly thought it would come to this. He'd always believed Theon would figure something out. Yes, he gave his brother endless shit about his asinine theories and obsessive reading, but he also knew it was those things that gave them the edge over their father.

Or at least he'd always hoped it would.

Theon had always figured things out, but not this time. And maybe it was his own fault for depending on him so godsdamn much.

The drive was somehow over in the blink of an eye, and he was reaching for the door handle. Pavil and Metias had already exited the vehicle, and before he pushed the door open, he turned to her.

Bright amber eyes.

Black curls framing her stunning face.

Jasmine, citrus, and spices.

Healthy and whole.

"I'm sorry, Kat. For everything that is about to happen. For what it's worth, I'm sorry," he said, hearing the defeated tone in his voice.

He saw the tears welling, but he didn't wait. He couldn't. He pushed open the door and stepped out, waiting while she did the same, before they followed Pavil and Metias up the stairs and into the manor.

They went straight through the foyer and down the hall to his father's study. The manor was outfitted so similar to Arius House, Axel felt like he was in the Ozul Mountains with the dark walls and general lack of light despite a bright winter day outside. Eviana watched them all file in from her chair near his father's desk. The dramatics of bowing and kneeling were done, and then he was sitting before his father. Pavil and Metias were on either side of him. Katya had been ordered to stand next to Eviana.

"I was surprised you didn't want to reschedule," Axel said, unable to stand the silence.

"Why would I do that?" his father asked, setting his pen down and leaning back in his chair.

Axel shrugged, settling his ankle over his knee. "Don't you have meetings regarding the recent attacks in a few hours?"

"Two hours, to be exact," Valter replied. "But the hearing tomorrow is why this meeting is happening."

His brows rose as he held his father's stare. "What do I have to do with the Tribunal hearing?"

"That blasted hearing shouldn't even be happening," his father said, shadows seeping into his irises. "It is all posturing and delaying the inevitable at this point."

"Making sure proper procedures are followed doesn't seem like posturing."

"I wouldn't expect you to understand. You were not raised to hold such a position, were you?"

At the pointed silence, Axel knew he was waiting for an answer. "No, that is not my role," he said tightly.

"Exactly. However, it *is* your brother's role. He was supposed to have come up with a solution and has failed." Gesturing in Kat's direction, he continued. "He was supposed to be bonded to a new Source by this point. This godsdamn hearing shouldn't even be happening."

"He did everything he could. We all did. We researched for hours, and—"

"I do not need excuses for his failures, Axel," his father cut in. "Nor do I need excuses for yours."

"Mine?" Axel repeated. "How, exactly, have I disappointed you this time?"

He winced at the flicker of power that washed over him, his shadows bristling beneath his skin. Of course ration day wasn't for another two days. He had no doubt his father had planned this meeting to coincide with that.

Then he was wincing for an entirely different reason when his father's hazel eyes flicked over to Katya. It was the only answer his father was going to give to his question, and it was the only answer he needed.

Axel's foot dropped to the floor, and he sat up straighter as his father started speaking once more. "As I said, this hearing shouldn't even be occurring. Because the other rulers are still holding this ridiculous affair, it leads me to believe they are attempting to alter prior agreements. I do not trust them."

"None of you trust the other," Axel said, trying to figure out how this was going to involve him and Kat.

"That's a fair statement," his father agreed. "But the nobles in our kingdom trust them even less. They are growing increasingly worried with Theon's failure to maintain control over the narratives and rumors that are circulating about her."

Axel's brow furrowed. "You mean Tessa?"

Valter nodded, his fingers drumming on his desk. "Your claim of a fire Fae certainly helped our cause, and the other two we claimed after Theon's recommendation are also promising."

"But?" Axel pressed, his palms beginning to sweat where he was gripping the arms of his chair.

"But we all agree a show of good faith would go a long way," his father said.

"Who is 'we?'"

"The nobles and my advisors."

Axel saw the subtle glance to his right where Metias sat, and he couldn't stop the next words that came from his mouth. "These fuckers?"

Valter's lips thinned as he rolled his eyes. "Always fucking theatrics from you."

"When did these two join your godsdamn advisors?" Axel demanded, ignoring the insult. "And why, for that matter?"

"Not that you have any right to question anything I do, but Metias and Pavil are not my advisors, Axel," his father said, his tone telling Axel just how close his father was to snapping entirely. "They are here on behalf of Julius and Mansel."

Axel felt the blood drain from his face. He knew those nobles well. They *were* his father's top advisors with tempers and tastes as vile as his father's. The things he'd been forced to witness—to *participate* in—because of them.

His father stood, buttoning his suit coat. "The nobles would like to spend some time with the fire Fae. They believe seeing her power in person will help quell rising concerns. I'm in agreement."

"How in the fuck will that help anything?" Axel asked, scrambling to his own feet.

His father sent him a look that told Axel exactly how stupid he found his second son to be. "Observing how powerful Theon's replacement Source will be will certainly placate them." He rounded his desk, Eviana standing as he approached, but he bypassed his Source, coming to a stop in front of Katya.

Her chin was dipped, eyes down, hands clasped in front of her.

It took every ounce of self-control Axel had to stay where he stood when his father reached out and brought her chin up with the tip of his finger.

"You are a pretty thing, aren't you?" Looking over his shoulder at Axel, he added, "I will admit I can see the appeal, Son."

Axel bit the inside of his cheek so hard he tasted blood.

Valter turned back to Kat, twining a curl around his finger. "But I do believe once our allies see how much more…obedient she is compared to Theon's current choice, any remaining concerns will no longer be an issue. Wouldn't you agree?"

Scrambling to think of *something* to stop this, Axel said, "I think Theon will be most upset if he learns his future Source was provided as entertainment to Julius and Mansel."

"Then perhaps he will remember the cost of failure," his father answered.

"You were already upset she was marred," Axel argued further. "You know she will come back worse than that."

"They were given strict orders of what is and is not acceptable," his father answered dismissively.

"You cannot be serious," Axel said, his voice rising, and that had his father turning to face him fully.

Darkness swarmed Axel, forcing him to his knees and lower. The pain of feeling his father's power seep into his veins and strangle his own shadows, had him curling in on himself. When the darkness cleared, his father was crouched over him, rage lining his features. The dagger he was twirling in his hand had blood dripping from the end, and it was only then that Axel registered the pain in his shoulder.

His father's voice was low and steely as he said, "You assured me there would not be any of your godsdamn tantrums when it came to her, yet here we are. If it weren't for your mother insisting we all be there for the fucking Solstice holiday celebrations this week, you would go with her to witness exactly what your unfavorable choices have wrought."

His father stood, his power keeping Axel on the floor as if it were a boot planted on his chest. "I know you were waiting for your brother to *fix* this for you. To be honest, a part of me was hoping you would attempt to change this outcome on your own. Instead, all you've done is once again affirm why you are the spare heir I hope to never have to use. How disappointing."

Turning to Pavil and Metias, he said, "A portal has been approved. Take her straight there." Jerking his chin to Axel, he added, "Take him with you. He can figure out his own way home from there."

"Of course, my Lord," Metias said, already on his feet.

"Come, Eviana," Valter said, striding for the door. "We mustn't be late for the meeting."

He left the door open when he exited, and Axel finally let himself look at Kat. She was so still, eyes wide as she stared at him on the floor. He could practically feel her debating if she dared come to him or if she should stay put.

Shaking his head at her, he rolled to his hands and knees, spitting out a curse as the wound near his shoulder flared in agony. He'd managed to get his feet under him when he saw Metias making his way over to Katya.

With a snarl, a whip of shadows snapped out and wrapped around the male's throat, yanking him backwards. "Do not fucking touch her," Axel growled.

"We have orders. What do you expect us to do?" Pavil demanded, but the male looked nervous.

He should be.

Axel knew what would happen if either of them touched her. The fuckers had gifts of fear and panic from the Gracil bloodline. They would amplify her greatest fears. Axel suddenly realized he didn't know what her greatest fear was, but he wasn't finding out this way.

"If you lay a single finger on her, what Theon did at Arius House will be nothing compared to what I will do," Axel warned, standing as straight as he could and making his way to Kat.

"We have to escort her—" Metias started.

"Do you think I am deaf?" Axel demanded, taking Kat's hand and threading his fingers with hers.

"What?" Metias asked, clearly confused.

"I asked if you thought I was deaf. Was I not here for that entire conversation?"

"Yes, but—"

"So either you think I am deaf and did not hear everything that was said, or you think you have some status in this room that makes you above me?" Axel said, his voice low and dangerous, because fuck. He was in pain and that just had him even more on edge.

"I don't believe either of those things, but with all due respect, Axel—"

"Heir St. Orcas," he interrupted.

Metias gave him a tight-lipped smile. "Heir St. Orcas. I do have to follow the *Arius Lord's* demands over yours."

"Touch her, Metias. I dare you. Then tell me whose demands you find it most prudent to follow in this moment," Axel said, a dark croon to his voice that had Kat pressing into his side.

Pavil shifted nearby, his phone in his hand. "My apologizes, Heir St. Orcas, but we were told to contact the Lord if you gave us any troubles."

"The only order I have given is to not touch her. Have I said anything about interfering with taking her to the portal?"

"No, but—"

Her hand still gripped in his, he pulled Katya behind him as he led the way out of the manor and back out to the car. He moved quickly, knowing she had to run to keep up with him, but he needed the few seconds this would give them to speak alone.

Pulling open the car door for her, he said in a low voice, "When the moment is right, call Tristyn. Tell him what is happening and ask him to help."

"Tristyn?" she repeated, rightfully confused.

"His number is in my contacts. You know how to unlock it," he said, sliding into the car behind her. "Hide that," he added, nodding at the phone.

She quickly slid it beneath her thigh as Pavil and Metias got into the vehicle.

He'd put Tristyn Blackheart's number in his phone after the male had given them his card when they'd run into him. Having the direct contact number for the head of Lilura Inquest was never a bad thing, and right now, he was thanking every god he could that he had it. He was also praying to those same gods Tristyn would be willing to help anytime like he'd offered, especially if it was Katya calling.

The trip to the portal station was tense and silent, and Axel used the time to get his mind wrapped around the pain in his shoulder. Theon and Luka would help him with it when he got back. Hopefully he could make it there.

He peeled off his suit coat, hissing at the movement of his shoulder. Kat eyed him worriedly, but she didn't reach for him. It took more effort than it should have, but he managed to roll back his sleeves and remove his tie before unbuttoning his top buttons.

Adrenaline was flooding his veins as Pavil drove around to the back of the terminal. Of course the Arius portal was shoved to the back of the building. His father always griped about it. Just another way Arius Kingdom was disrespected. Axel had never really given a fuck. His father rarely let them travel by portal anyway, but in this moment, he found himself grateful.

Fewer chances of witnesses.

Pavil and Metias glanced back at him nervously as Metias said, "We're here."

"You must assume I'm blind too," Axel drawled.

"No," Pavil said quickly. "Do you…want to come in with us or…?"

"Get the fuck out of the car," Axel said tightly, reaching for the door handle. He waited until they were out before he turned to Kat and said, "Call him. Ask him to meet us somewhere discreet."

Before she could reply, he was out of the car, and his shadows were swirling around him.

"Now, *Heir St. Orcas*," Metias said snidely, his phone raised and thumb hovering over the call button. "It only takes one press of my finger."

Axel smiled, walking towards him.

"Axel," Metias snapped.

"We're following orders," Pavil said.

Gods, was that the only thing he knew how to say?

He saw Metias's thumb twitch, but he was too late. There was a burst of shadows next to him, and Axel was there, reaching into the depths of that darkness and pulling out a nightstone dagger. One move had the dagger slicing clean through Metias's wrist, the hand holding the phone dropping to the pavement with a satisfying thud.

The male started to scream, but Axel already had his shadows winding down his throat. Crushing the phone beneath his shoe, he sank the nightstone dagger into Metias's chest, twisting it sharply before withdrawing it and slicing it across his throat from ear to ear.

See? The blood red tie would have been a good choice if he'd still been wearing it.

That was what he thought as he stood to face Pavil.

And then he went preternaturally still when he found him with Katya, a hand clamped over her mouth.

"I haven't done anything yet, but I will," the Legacy warned.

"Here I thought you were just a pathetic lackey," Axel said, taking in every single part of Pavil that was touching her. "But I did warn you not to touch her."

The male's eyes went wide as Axel's shadows struck. With brutal force, they pried him away from her, and she darted away.

He didn't have the ability to shatter bone with his shadows like Theon could. He couldn't send his shadows in to retrieve organs like Theon's darkness could either. But that only made him more hands on, and today? He didn't mind that so much.

Not as his shadows held Pavil down, ropes of nothing but dark mist holding him to the ground and silencing his wails as he methodically cut off fingers and sliced off flesh. Any part of him that had touched her landed in a pile beside the male's bleeding and mutilated body. He had to work quickly, which annoyed him. He would have liked to take his time with this. This was one of those times he'd told Kat about when he *enjoyed* the killing.

It wasn't until he was satisfied that any part of the male that had touched her had been cut from his body that he sank the dagger into his heart and finally ended his pitiful existence.

Standing, he ran his arm along his sweaty brow, lowering it to find it smeared in red. The pain of his shoulder slammed back into him in full force, and he sent the dagger away with his magic before turning back to Kat.

Gods, he needed blood.

"Did you call him?" he asked.

Wide golden eyes bounced from him to the dead Legacy.

With a few long strides, he was in front of her. Cupping her jaw, he forced her to look at him. "Did you call Blackheart, Kat?"

She nodded mutely, lifting a shaky hand. He glanced at the phone she held, the screen showing a call in progress. Taking the phone, he said to her, "Burn it all, kitten," before bringing the phone to his ear. "Blackheart?"

"Axel," Tristyn said. "What do you need?"

And it wasn't said sarcastically, but there was sincere concern in his voice.

"I need someplace to hide her. I don't know how long. She needs to be safe, and—"

"Bring her to Lilura Inquest. Go to the north side of the building. I'll meet you there."

"Thank you," Axel nearly choked out, ending the call and turning to find ashes flitting away in the winter wind.

"That will have to do, Kat," he said. "Get in the car. We need to go."

"But the evidence—"

"There isn't time. Get in the car," he said again.

His father would figure out what happened soon enough anyway.

"Where are we going?" she asked as Axel raced from the parking lot and headed to the business district of the Acropolis.

"Tristyn has a place to hide you."

"Axel, I can't— I can't run from my kingdom. It's a death sentence," she said. He could hear the frantic fear in her voice. He was hoping the male hadn't been lying, but his power had clearly touched her, amplifying her greatest fears to some degree.

"I will make sure you're not found," he said, hating that they didn't have time for him to properly comfort her.

"And what about you?"

"I'll be fine," he answered, speeding through a red light.

"I don't see how that's possible," she argued.

"As long as you are safe, it doesn't matter what happens to me," he answered.

Happy, safe, and whole.

That was what he needed her to be.

She might not be happy with this arrangement, but she'd be safe and whole. He'd settle for that.

"It matters to me," she said, her voice getting higher as she started to panic again.

"But you are more important."

"That makes little sense," she said as he brought the car to a screeching halt on the north side of the building, where he spotted Tristyn waiting for them. "You are an Arius Heir. I am just a Fae. You are far more important. Saying I'm more important isn't logical."

He turned in the driver's seat, reaching across the center console and clasping her face in his hands. "Nothing has been logical from the moment I laid eyes on you, Katya. Claiming you wasn't logical. Letting you have my room wasn't logical. Arguing with you, sleeping beside you, kissing you. None of it is logical. And it sure as fuck isn't logical that you consume me just by godsdamn existing, but you do, Katya. I cannot explain why. I've stopped trying. I'm a disappointment to many people on so many levels, but *please*, Kat. Please let me do this. Please let me keep you safe because it is the only mercy I can offer you in this godsforsaken realm."

There were tears tracking down her face, and he swiped at them with his thumbs, faint red streaks left in their wake from the blood on his hands.

"Promise me you'll come back for me," she whispered.

"I can't, kitten," he said. "I can only promise that you will be safe."

A tap on the window had him turning to find Tristyn opening the car door.

"I'm sorry to interrupt, but if we're doing this, we need to go. Now," the male said.

Axel nodded, he and Katya climbing from the car. They both rounded it, and he pulled her into him.

"I'll try," he whispered. "I promise I'll try to come back for you, but only if you promise me you'll try to be happy."

She didn't promise. She only clung to him tighter.

Lifting his gaze over her head to Tristyn, Axel said, "Swear to me she will be safe."

"I swear it, Axel."

"And you'll tell no one where she is? Not even me?"

An unreadable expression crossed the male's face. "I know what it means to sacrifice for love. You have my word this sacrifice will not be wasted."

Tilting her face up, he brushed his lips across hers one final time. "Remember that living isn't just logic and knowledge but feeling too, kitten," he murmured onto her lips.

"Remember that you are a *good* person, Axel St. Orcas," she whispered back. Some of that fiery determination was back in her eyes as the effects of Pavil's power started to wane.

Then Tristyn was whisking her away through a glamoured door into the building, and Axel was left standing in an alley with jasmine, citrus, and spices in the winter air.

# 41

## THEON

The knock on the door had him stirring. The bed shifted, and he opened his eyes to find Luka stalking across the room, stopping to pull on some undergarments. He hadn't been lying to Tessa all those weeks ago when he said he only slept naked.

Glancing at the clock on the bedside table, he found it wasn't even dawn yet. Who the fuck was at the door at this hour?

Tessa sighed in her sleep, drawing his attention. She'd been out since they returned from the third Marking. Sleeping for two to three days seemed to be what she needed afterwards, so it wasn't a surprise. What was a surprise were the random thoughts that drifted down the bond at times.

*You will be the beginning of endings.*

*More than a bond.*

*In all things, there must be balance.*

*The balance.*

Those thoughts were accompanied by mixed emotions of…resignation? Determination? Fury? Acceptance? They were so muddled, he couldn't decipher them all.

The door shut, and Luka made his way back, tossing an envelope at Theon before carefully settling onto the mattress once more.

"You know, if you had an actual bed, it would be easier to get in and out of," Theon grumbled, turning the envelope over. He was still pissed at the male for the years of secrets he'd kept from him. He didn't trust easily and godsdamn Traveling? That was a big secret. Not to mention his feelings for Tessa and how he'd been drawn to her all along.

"A bigger mattress would have the same results," Luka retorted, stilling when Tessa edged closer to him.

Theon ground his molars, but he couldn't say anything. Not as he felt her entire being calm when she settled into Luka's side. He knew what the bond did, what it required, and the fact that Luka'd had to help with the third Mark only made their connection stronger. Theon hated it, but he'd let it go for now if it was what she needed. If Axel and Kat were right and the first three Marks weren't Source Marks at all, maybe there was a way to sever whatever bond *was* there. They just needed to figure out where the three Marks were derived from.

His brother hadn't said much when he got back to the townhouse stabbed and covered in blood yesterday. They'd given him extra rations, and when he was cleaned up and behind the closed door of Luka's room, he filled them in with the barest details. Their father's demand. The stabbing. Killing Pavil and Metias to keep Kat from Julius and Mansel. Tristyn fucking Blackheart helping him. Not knowing where she was hidden.

He'd let her go to keep her safe knowing the cost of that action was going to be horrific.

If their father knew, he hadn't let on yet. He'd been in meetings all day yesterday regarding the citizens' concerns with the recent attacks, and later this morning was Theon's hearing.

Which was apparently what this envelope was regarding if the Devram seal on the back meant anything.

Sliding his finger beneath the seal, he opened it, withdrawing a piece of paper. He scanned it quickly, his pulse picking up with every word. "They can't be fucking serious."

Luka was on high alert now, propping himself up on his elbows. "What?"

"It's a formal summons for the hearing today," Theon snarled, reading it again.

"Did they think you wouldn't show? What is the purpose of it?" Luka said, lowering back down.

"It's not for me," Theon said, tossing the thing aside. "It's for Tessa."

"Are you fucking with me? She's not even conscious right now."

"I'm aware."

She must have sensed his irritation because she shifted again, arm reaching for him as she stayed snuggled next to Luka. He shifted closer, letting her fingers curl around his thigh.

*Always meant to destroy one another.*

Those cryptic words drifted down the bond again, and he reached over, smoothing the hair off her brow.

"Do you know what that means?" Luka asked, maneuvering onto his side so they could speak over her. It'd been like this since they got back here. One of them was always with her, always touching her, but she slept the most soundly when they were both within reach.

"I have ideas," Theon muttered, propping an arm behind his head and letting his eyes fall closed. He never needed as much time to recover after the Markings, but this time he'd been restless, worried about this hearing and trying to come up with anything that might save his ass or make a difference.

"Are you sharing them?" Luka growled in annoyance.

Theon sighed. "She's not supposed to be here."

"Are you — Are you saying you think the *Augury* is right?" Luka demanded, and Theon could tell he wanted to sit up, move, throw a punch, do *something*.

"What if they are?" Theon said. "What if they are right, and her being here is going to bring about some war we were never supposed to be a part of?"

"After all of this, that's what you're going with? What are you even fighting for then? What has been the godsdamn point?"

Luka's words were laced with anger, and Theon could see the smoke from his exhales even in the faint light of the room.

"It's a theory," Theon shot back. "It could all be bullshit. You asked if I had ideas. That was one of them. Do *you* have any ideas by what she meant when she said 'you were supposed to be mine, not his?' Or any of the other odd things we've heard down the bond, for that matter?"

"It could mean anything," Luka said. "Just like the whole 'we were always meant to destroy one another' could mean anything. You know what Cienna always says: trying to figure out fate is wasted time because fate is always changing."

Theon fell silent after that. Normally, he and Luka could discuss fate, theories, and whatever else came to mind for hours, but not with the betrayal of everything he'd kept hidden still so fresh.

He waited as long as he could before waking Tessa. They took turns getting ready so one of them was always with her. Luka had just come out of the bathroom, hair pulled up in a knot on his head, navy suit pants, and black tie. He was rolling back the sleeves of his light blue shirt. He wouldn't bother with a suit coat.

Tessa was nestled beside Theon, her head in his lap. He'd been scrolling through emails, and now he clicked his phone off, setting it aside. He felt like a complete jackass for having to do this.

Gently sliding the blankets off her, he shook her a little bit. "Tessa? Tessa, I need you to wake up."

Her brow furrowed, and she snuggled deeper against him, curling in on herself.

Yeah, this was going to go great.

Shifting her, he eased her away from him, severing any physical connection. There was a muffled whimper, and he felt her dismay down the bond.

"Tessa, you need to wake up," he said, jostling her again.

It took another moment, but bleary eyes blinked open, staring up at him. They flicked to Luka, who was standing over them, before coming back to Theon.

"What is happening?" she asked in a sleepy slur.

"We have the hearing today," Theon said. Her eyes started to flutter closed again, and he reached over, cupping her chin. "No, beautiful. Stay awake. You have to come with us."

"Why?" she mumbled, her eyes remaining closed.

"You were summoned by the Lords and Ladies. Failure to comply is not an option."

When she didn't answer, and a soft, even breath came from her, he swore. She'd fallen back asleep.

"This is going to be a godsdamn nightmare," Theon muttered.

"Just get her up," Luka said.

"I'm not just going to—"

But Luka reached over him, scooping Tessa into his arms and lifting her from the bed. "Let's go, little one. Go shower. It'll help wake you up," he said, lowering her to her feet when her eyes fluttered open again.

She blinked, leaning into Luka as she tried to wake fully. Her fingers curled into his shirt, and she frowned a little when his tie got in the way. He leaned down, tilting her chin up, trying to get her to focus.

"Tessa, you need to—"

And to Theon's absolute horror, she kissed him.

He watched as if it were happening in slow motion. Her gaze dropping to his lips. Luka's brow furrowing. Her pitching forward. The surprise that crossed Luka's features.

Her lips landing on his.

It lasted seconds, but it was hours, days, years to Theon before Luka was gently pushing her back. His face was carefully blank, but Theon could feel every godsdamn thing his friend was feeling because of this fucking bond.

The stunned shock.

The pleasant euphoria.

The desire to taste her mouth again.

"Tessa," Luka said, his voice raspy as he held her shoulders. "You need to get ready."

Her head tilted, as if she didn't understand what he was saying.

"It's okay," Luka said. "You're disoriented. A shower will help."

"I'm too tired to shower," she murmured, turning to the bed like she was going to crawl back onto it.

"Theon, help her shower," Luka hissed, but Theon still hadn't moved. He was still staring at the two of them, could still see her kissing him. "Theon!" Luka snapped. "She needs you."

That had him moving, scrambling to his feet. She immediately latched onto him, resting her head against his chest.

"Please let me sleep, Theon," she murmured.

"I can't, Tessa," he said, guiding her to the bathroom.

Luka said something about going to find her clothing, but Theon didn't acknowledge him, kicking the door shut behind him. He needed a minute, or a few hours, to process what had just happened.

"*In all things, there must be balance,*" she murmured as he helped her undress. "The fucking balance."

"What does that mean, Tessa?" he asked softly, reaching into the shower to turn it on and adjust the water temperature.

"I saw a dragon," she answered instead.

*You kissed a fucking dragon*, he thought bitterly to himself.

"I didn't kiss the dragon," Tessa said around a yawn. "But she rode it."

Right. The bond.

This fucking bond that was the cause of every godsdamn problem in his life right now.

"Who rode the dragon?" Theon asked tightly, reaching for her hand and guiding her to the shower.

She shrugged as she stepped inside, seeming to wake up more and more with each passing minute. "I don't know. There was a female underwater too."

Her visions.

She was telling him about her visions.

"What else, little storm?" he pressed as she let water cascade over her hair and bare skin.

"You killing me," she answered.

"Tessa, I—"

"But not last time. It changed," she said, reaching for shampoo.

"Changed how?"

"It always changes." She went quiet for a few moments, then asked, "Where is Luka?"

*It's just the bond.*

That was what he told himself.

It was just the bond making her need him, seek him out, ask for him.

The problem was, if he believed that, it meant everything he shared with her was just a byproduct of the bond too.

Just like she'd always said it was.

And he didn't know if he could face that.

He glanced over his shoulder to where Tessa sat beside Luka on the same bench she'd sat on a few months ago during the Tribunal hearing. She was pale. So godsdamn pale. Even her lips were bloodless. Leaning against Luka, his arm was wrapped loosely around her. Theon knew it was so she didn't slide off the bench, but it still made him grip the arms of his chair a little tighter as he pictured her lips on his for the hundredth time in the last hour.

Axel shifted beside him just as a door to the right opened, the Lords and Ladies filing through while the rest of them stood and bowed. The crowd was the same as before. Heirs and Sources. Some of the more elite Legacy. Even the Keeper was lurking in the eaves above.

"Rise and sit," Lord Jove said, his tone somehow sounding bored and severe at the same time.

Theon took his seat, staring up at the Lords and Ladies on the raised dais. His father gave nothing away. The Anala Lady's lips were pressed into a thin line that suggested she wasn't happy, while the Celeste Lady had a small smirk playing on her mouth. That didn't bode well for him.

"It's been a long couple of days, so let's get right to the point," Lord Jove said. "Theon St. Orcas, you were given until the Winter Solstice to uncover the lineage of Tessalyn Ausra. You were also instructed to report any such discoveries to us immediately. Since we have not heard from you, we can assume you were unsuccessful. Is that an accurate assumption?"

His fingers curled inward where his hand now rested on the table. "While I made headway on her heritage, I did not learn her entire lineage."

"Then you were unsuccessful," the Achaz Lord repeated.

"If we are looking at the matter as a simple success or failure, then yes," Theon answered. "But I think there is more to consider here."

"There is nothing else to consider," the Celeste Lady cut in. "You were given a task. You did not complete it. She will not remain yours."

"I am afraid Lady Candra is correct," Lord Jove said, steepling his finger along his temple. "She cannot remain yours. The bond will need to be severed."

"So your solution to this is to kill an Arius descendant?" Theon demanded.

"If the choice is between an Arius descendant or an Achaz one, there is no choice," Lady Candra said.

"And if a death is not required to sever the bond?" he countered.

"The Source bond can only be severed by death," the Falein Lady chimed in.

"But what if the Source bond isn't actually instilled until the final Mark?" Theon said.

The Lords and Ladies all exchanged looks before Lord Jove said, "Care to expound on that?"

"In our research we have found evidence that suggests the Source bond isn't truly initiated until the final Marking," Theon said, and he felt Tessa's confusion and surprise down the bond. She'd been sleeping when Axel had told him about what he and Kat had found. There hadn't been time to fill her in. "There is a book suggesting the Source Mark used to be one Mark, not four," he continued, watching the Lords and Ladies. "As we just found this information on Solstice Day, I haven't had time to research it more to investigate where the other three Marks come from, but… You all know this already," he said, sitting back in his seat, somewhat dumbfounded.

None of them seemed even remotely surprised by this revelation. If anything, they almost seemed uncomfortable that he'd uncovered this knowledge. In fact, within moments, the entire hearing room had been cleared save for the Lords and Ladies, their Sources, Theon, Axel, Luka, and Tessa.

"Where did you say you came across this supposed information?" Lady Farhan asked. Of course the Falein Lady would be the most interested in such knowledge.

"In a book," Theon returned tightly.

"Even if such a *theory* were true," the Serafina Lady cut in. "Your task was not to learn such things. Your task was to uncover the female's heritage. You did not."

"Forgive me if I am mistaken," Theon said, "but I do believe Lord Jove's words were 'should you learn she is indeed a Legacy and the Source bond cannot be severed another way, it is not an Achaz Legacy whose life will pay that price.' I have learned she is not a Legacy, at least not fully, and if the Source bond is not actually in place until the final Marking, there is nothing to sever at this point in time."

The Lords and Ladies sat in silence as Theon stared back at them. His father seemed almost pleased at the technicality Theon had found. Theon knew that small, cruel twitch of his mouth and the way he subtly relaxed back into his seat.

"One would think you studied at the academies of the Falein Kingdom with such knowledge and cleverness," the Anala Lady said, golden eyes studying him thoughtfully.

"Such knowledge is only found in the Falein Kingdom. It appears your few hours spent in my archives were indeed fruitful," Lady Farhan said tightly. "Even more concerning is the fact that you were not in the area of the archives that contained such knowledge. Which begs the question, how did you discover such a book? Or is it simply you were not monitored well enough?"

"The knowledge was not learned in a book found there," Theon replied. "There is no need to punish anyone."

"Then where?" she demanded sharply.

"A book of mine," Axel said. "It is an old book of mine."

"I would like to see this book."

"That book is not the subject of this hearing," Theon cut in, finally pushing to his feet. "You all set me an impossible task, left out valuable information, and now you seek to punish me for failure."

"What about your task was so impossible?" Lord Jove asked. "You said you learned some of her heritage. I imagine you would have eventually completed the task. You simply ran out of time. It is no fault of ours that you were unable to work within your time constraints."

"But, for the sake of curiosity, what lineage was learned?" the Serafina Lady asked, her silver hair pulled over her shoulder and reaching nearly to her waist.

"It seems that since I did not complete my task fully, such knowledge is not important," Theon countered.

Lady Isleen's eyes narrowed. "Careful, Child."

He'd known this hearing wouldn't go in his favor, but to learn he'd basically been set up for failure? He'd been prepared to argue his case, to present logic and facts. How fucking naïve he'd been. How godsdamn foolish to think they *didn't know* about the Markings. He knew how the realm worked. The deals made behind closed doors. The alliances that turned into back-stabbing. Muddled truths and half-secrets.

"You are truly not going to share what you've learned?" the Celeste Lady demanded.

"I am going to assume you already know her heritage at this point," Theon retorted, buttoning his suit coat. "In fact, I am going to assume I was assigned a pointless task to keep me busy and looking elsewhere. For what purpose? I do not know yet, but I will discover it."

"Theon," his father snarled, "remember your place."

"No, no, Valter. He has a right to speak. This is, after all, his hearing," Lord Jove said, getting to his own feet. Theon didn't particularly like the look on the Lord's face as he descended the few steps from the dais. "His denial of a request will not change the outcome of this."

"The fuck it won't," Theon snapped.

"It truly will not," the Lord replied with a sharp smile. "Even had you completed your task, she still would not have gone home with you today."

"Repeat that?"

"Yesterday's meetings brought us to the conclusion that all these attacks have been centered around Tessalyn. She will be housed at the Pantheon until things can be dealt with accordingly, and we can assure the safety of Devram," Lord Jove said, moving to step around Theon, but he wouldn't have it as he blocked his path.

"No," Theon said.

That was it. It was all he could think to say. This couldn't be it. After all he had done, all he'd discovered, all he'd learned. After everything he'd put her through. It couldn't be for nothing. He wouldn't stand for it.

"Lady Candra did not misspeak, Heir St. Orcas," the Achaz Lord said, light swirling in his eyes. "She is no longer yours."

"Those Marks on her say otherwise," Theon countered. "It might not be a Source bond, but there is a bond. Make no mistake about that. If you take her from me, it will cause harm."

"To you?" the Achaz Lord asked with an arched brow.

"To *her*," he all but yelled. "This has always been about her. Everyone here knows it."

Something on the Lord's features flickered, and Theon didn't know what to make of it. But he felt the jolt of surprise down the bond from Tessa.

"At the last hearing, her opinion was asked because this directly affects her. Should the same not be done here?" Theon asked, turning to where she was watching everything unfold with wary eyes.

She wasn't leaning against Luka anymore, but he was close, muscles tense and coiled. Her bands of light were wrapped around her wrists, and while she still looked pale and exhausted, her power certainly wasn't. He could feel it. His darkness could feel it.

Theon glanced at Luka, wondering if he'd picked up on anything from her, but the dragon only shook his head subtly. The agreement from a few months ago still stood. If they tried to take her, they were prepared to fight their way out.

Axel stood, coming to Theon's side, the two of them blocking access to her now, but to his utter shock, she spoke.

"Maybe they are right, Theon."

Violet-grey eyes held his, and he could truly feel her now. A bone-weary resignation that this was it for her.

"No, Tessa," he said on a breath as he took a step towards her. "No, they are wrong."

"Are they? You yourself say the attacks are to get to me," she said. "People are being endangered because I simply exist."

"Tessa, that's not—"

"It is a fact," Lord Jove said, using the distraction to step around him.

A low growl came from Luka, but Tessa held up her hand. When the Lord extended a hand to her, she took it. Theon could only watch as he guided her forward, too many emotions flooding through him. Horror. Shock. Anger. Betrayal. But more than any of that, confusion as to what was happening here.

"She understands the matter at hand quite well," the Achaz Lord said, motioning for his Source, Dysani, to step forward and help her.

"And what matter is that?" Theon demanded, his entire body trembling as he watched someone else help her, guide her, *touch* her.

"That she is not safe with you."

Darkness exploded from him at the words, but Luka and Axel were there. Their hands clamped on his shoulders, pulling him back. Shadows and black flames shielded them as other powers flared in the room.

And when the darkness and magic cleared, she was gone. So was the Lord's Source. Before Theon could say or do anything, he was on his knees, forced there by coils of light that made his darkness hiss and strain. This was nothing like Tessa's light.

"Do not move, Luka. Theon more than deserves this for his display here today," Valter snarled, and Theon knew his Guardian was fighting a shift at this moment.

The Achaz Lord stood over him, his features somehow pleasant as he spoke down to Theon. "She understands what is at risk here. It is not just you and a bond, but the realm. And I think deep down, you know that too."

"What have you said to her?" Theon demanded. "What have you told her?"

The Achaz Lord only smiled as he said, "Everything you have kept from her."

# 42

## LUKA

It took him longer than he thought it would to figure out where in the Pantheon Tessa was being kept. Theon always made it seem so easy. Like he just knew where she was all the damn time. He never faltered, going straight to her. This tracking Mark took some time to understand the subtle pulls and tells that he was on the right track. Not to mention the fact that he had to do this secretly, Traveling between corridors and levels. If Auryon had bothered to show up, she could probably help, but they hadn't seen her since the battle.

Luka was pretty sure he'd figured out where she was. There were sentinels outside the door. Six of them to be exact, so he was going to have to Travel directly into the room.

Hopefully she was alone.

With a steadying breath, he took a step as if moving through a rip in the air. The familiar pull at his navel was hardly noticeable after all these years. He shifted his eyes to adjust to the low lighting of the room. It was nearly identical to the Marking room they used. The main area was lit by a few sconces. There was a sofa, and a table with two chairs. Some fruit, cheese, and crackers were on the table. At least she'd eaten something.

Off to the right was a room, the door half closed, and he took silent steps towards it. Then he breathed out a sigh of relief to see her lying on her back, hands stacked on her stomach and bands of light glowing softly around her wrists. Her golden hair was down, fanning around her atop the white comforter. She'd changed since the hearing. Instead of the form-fitting dress, she wore pants that cuffed at her ankles and a top that stopped midway down her torso, leaving a couple inches of her stomach bare. Her legs were hanging over the edge of the bed, her bare feet swinging.

"You're not supposed to be here," she called out.

"I'm aware," Luka answered, leaning a shoulder against the doorjamb and crossing his arms.

She propped herself up on her elbows. "How did you get in?"

"Traveled."

"The wards?"

He shrugged a shoulder. "My best guess is they weren't expecting someone to Travel in, so the wards don't detect it."

She considered that for a moment before saying, "That makes sense." Then she fell back on the bed.

"You seem…better."

"I took a nap."

"Ah. A nap does tend to help unruly children," he replied.

She turned her head, sending him an unimpressed glare. "If you're just here to remind me you're an ass, good job. Consider it a success and kindly fuck off."

He fought the smirk trying to curl on his lips. "We were worried."

"I don't know why. I returned from Faven fed, bathed, and unharmed," she said, returning her gaze to the ceiling.

"This is very different from Faven, Tessa."

She sighed. "I know."

Pushing off the doorjamb, Luka crossed the few feet to the bed, sitting down beside her. Her mental shields were up, keeping him locked out. That was fine if that was what she felt she needed to do right now.

"This room is small," she said suddenly.

"You don't have to stay in here. The sitting room is larger," he replied, lowering onto his back beside her.

"Still no windows, though."

"At least you can make your own light."

Tessa lifted a hand, letting a glowing orb grow in her palm. "There is that."

They sat in silence for several minutes, and he watched her out of the corner of his eye. Watched her lips move as she murmured words he couldn't hear. Watched her fingers tap in a random rhythm along her stomach. Watched the steady rise and fall of her chest.

"I was thinking," she said.

"About?" Luka asked. He wanted to turn and prop himself on an elbow so he could actually look at her, but he was pretty sure any sudden movement would have her shutting down again.

"How you can Travel," she answered.

Luka swiped a hand over his mouth because *that's* what she was sitting here thinking about? "All right then. Let's hear it."

She turned her head to the side. "Really?"

"Do you want to talk about something else?"

"No," she said quickly.

"Then Traveling it is, I guess."

It took her another minute, but then she cleared her throat. "I think you can Travel because you're not from Devram. You weren't born here. Scarlett and Sorin could Travel, but they also weren't from here. Theon said the ability was taken from the Legacy when they were sequestered here, but maybe, since you weren't born here, it doesn't affect you."

"That seems like a pretty good theory," Luka said.

She rolled over to her stomach so she could see him, kicking her feet up behind her. "Do you wish you knew where you were born? Where you're from?"

Luka shrugged. "It doesn't really matter in the end, does it?"

Her gaze fell away from him as she said, "No. I guess not."

"But that doesn't mean I don't think about it," he added.

Violet-grey eyes lifted back to his. "Yeah?"

He nodded, fighting the urge to reach over and tuck her hair behind her ear. "It's okay to want to know, Tessa."

She swallowed, looking away again. "What if… What if there was a cost to know? Do you think it would be worth it?"

"I suppose it depends on the cost."

"I guess," she murmured. After a few more beats of silence, she asked, "Why did you really come here tonight, Luka?"

He'd told her the truth. He'd come because they were worried. Theon was downright frantic. But he'd come for her too. Knowing she was likely feeling all sorts of things she couldn't or wouldn't sort through. She knew he wasn't here to try and take her from this place. He'd be a fool to attempt it.

"A couple of reasons," he finally answered. "One is to explain why I never told you about the bond."

"It doesn't matter," she said, pushing up and sliding from the bed, but Luka sat up too, grabbing her arm.

"It does matter, Tessa."

Her eyes hardened as they slid from where he gripped her arm up to his face. "It really doesn't, Luka, but if it will ease your conscience some, then, by all means, continue."

The dragon under his skin bristled at her dismissal, but he let her go because she was right. How many times had Theon given her excuses for keeping information from her? He had done nothing different. She was under no obligation to hear him out, and if she told him an explanation wouldn't matter, who was he to push it?

His lack of immediate response apparently told her the subject was dropped because she disappeared from the small bedroom back out to the main room.

And he followed. Because like he told Theon, they were all moths to her flame. Or in this case, her light. Or just *her*.

He found her wandering around the space, dragging her fingers along the wall as she moved.

"You know you're only here because I'm allowing it, right?" she asked.

Leaning against the doorjamb once more, he said, "I'm aware they've given you some semblance of control as a show of good faith. But make no mistake, Tessa, you are still locked in a windowless room. It's just a little bigger than a wine cellar is all."

Her head whipped to him, violet eyes flashing with sparks of energy. "You have no idea what is happening here, Luka Mors."

"No?" he asked, cocking his head to the side. Brushing back hair that fell in his face with the movement, he pushed off the doorjamb. "You don't think you're being used here?"

"It isn't like that."

"Then tell me how it is, little one. Tell me how you've got this whole fucked up realm figured out in mere months, when we haven't been able to figure it out in decades," Luka said, stopping a few feet from her.

Her hands were in her hair, tugging at the ends as she started to pace. She was muttering low under her breath, and even with his enhanced hearing, he couldn't make out a word she was saying.

Suddenly, she spun to him again. The power around her wrists flared brighter, winding up her arms like golden thread. "What are you doing here, Luka?"

"I already told you. We were worried," he answered, watching her carefully and trying to find any crack in her mental shields. It was there. A flicker of longing. He wasn't quite sure what it meant, so he waited.

Theon was too impatient for this part of her, and to be fair, sometimes she needed that. Sometimes she *did* need someone to take care of her. Sometimes she needed to not think, to be out of her head and simply told what to do. No decisions to agonize over. But she also needed someone to simply trust she could do things on her own. Someone to believe she could make the right choices and figure things out. The thing was, she didn't know what to do with herself when given that space and confidence.

"What else?" she asked. "You said there were a few reasons you came here tonight. Is it night?" She pulled at her long strands again as she asked it, gaze darting around the windowless room.

It had him stepping forward, unable to watch her inflict harm on herself anymore. He slowly reached for her hands, and she stilled the moment he touched her. His dragon was pacing in his soul, wings shifting beneath his skin.

Gently unwinding her fingers from her hair, he said, "I came to bring you something."

Her eyes narrowed, and she cleared her throat as her hands dropped to her sides. "What is it?"

From a swirl of black flames, Luka pulled the gift Lord Jove had brought for her. It was still perfectly wrapped, and she blinked in surprise.

Reaching for it, she peered up at him from beneath her lashes. "You didn't open it?"

"Does it look like I opened it?"

"No, but you're talented enough. I'm sure you could re-wrap a gift," she retorted, fiddling with the gold bow atop the white wrapping.

"Theon has Solstice gifts for you," Luka said. "We have them at Arius House because we thought—"

"I don't want anything from him," she interrupted, moving to the sofa and sitting.

"And the ones from me and Axel?"

"How is Axel?"

Now it was Luka blinking in surprise. Rubbing at his jaw, he said, "He's worried. About a lot of things."

"Do you think my visions are real?"

How they'd gone from Axel to her visions was beyond him, but he said, "It seems that way, but visions are just that. They can change."

"Theon said the same thing," she muttered.

"Cienna is a Seer," Luka replied, taking a seat on the other end of the sofa. "We have some experience in the area."

"He was going to take me to her. I guess we ran out of time," she said, setting the gift aside. She pulled her knees to her chest, wrapping her arms around them. "There is one vision I have more than others."

He kept his face carefully blank and his emotions in check, but inside, he was more than a little surprised she was talking about this. He was afraid if he breathed wrong, she would shut down. So he propped his elbow on the arm of the sofa, resting his temple against his fist, and waited.

"Kat wasn't always in it. Or Tristyn. But they are now. And last time…" She trailed off, and he watched her curl and uncurl her toes into the sofa cushion.

"Last time, what, Tessa?" Luka finally asked.

She turned her head, her cheek resting against her knee. "Last time Axel wasn't there."

"What do you think that means?"

"I… I don't know. I don't understand the visions. I don't…"

Then she was on her feet again, pacing a few steps back and forth.

"I don't understand them until they pass, and others keep changing. Some are underwater. Some are in the sky. There are Fae and angels and a dragon—"

"A dragon?" Luka cut in, sitting up straighter.

"The land in the sky," she muttered, waving him off.

"Tessa."

"The cages and the collars."

"Tessa."

"Beginning and endings. Light and dark. Chaos and death and—"

"Tessa, stop," he said sternly.

She did. She always listened when he used that commanding tone, but the look on her face when she met his gaze had him moving to her in a few long strides.

"I don't know what any of it means," she said, a note of anguish to her voice.

Luka pulled her into his chest and her brow fell against it as he smoothed a hand over her hair. "We'll figure it out, Tessa."

She shook her head against him. "We don't. We don't figure it out. It's too late, and the visions..." She tipped her head back, and the look in her eyes had him sliding a hand along her jaw as she whispered. "I think I'm going mad."

"You're not, Tessa. You just came into your power a few months ago. No one is expecting you to have it mastered in such a short amount of time."

"Theon does."

"He doesn't," Luka argued. "Think about who has pushed for you to learn your craft. Who insisted on the private lessons? It wasn't him, Tessa."

She went quiet for a few seconds before she stiffened, stepping back from him. "Of course you side with him. That is where your loyalty will forever lie."

Luka didn't say anything because she wasn't wrong. He was Theon's Guardian. The Sargon line was forever bound to the Arius line. Sure she was Arius blood too, but she was just as much something else. Theon and Axel had been bred solely to strengthen the Arius bloodline, even with Cressida's Nith heritage.

Tessa stepped around him, moving to the table and swiping up a cracker, chewing on it thoughtfully. "Have you seen Auryon since the Augury attack?"

"No," he answered tightly, and it bothered him to no end. She'd known he could Travel, and he was very curious as to how she'd obtained that information.

She nodded, grabbing another cracker. "Is there anything else?"

"What?"

"Any other reason you are here?"

"Not particularly," Luka said, holding her gaze.

"I'm sure Theon is waiting for your report," she said casually.

"He likely is."

"Then you better get back to him," she said with a mocking smile.

A smile Luka could see right through.

Crossing his arms, he said, "I have time yet."

"Time for what?"

"For you."

An incredulous bark of laughter fell from her lips. "You don't need to do me any favors, Luka Mors. I don't need your pity."

His brows pulled together. "It isn't pity, Tessa."

"No? You giving me your extra minutes isn't because you feel sorry for me? Because there is no need," she snapped.

"I know that," he said calmly. "You don't need anyone to feel sorry for you. I've been training you. I know how strong you are."

She faltered, the sneer on her lips fading a little at his words. "You need to leave."

"Why?"

"Because I want you to."

He took a single step towards her, and he watched her throat bob. Felt the sliver of curiosity and want slip through her shields. Heard her curse herself in her thoughts.

"I'll leave if that's what you really want," he said after a moment.

"It is," she snapped.

"All right. Do you need anything before I go?"

"Do I— No," she said in a rush. "Thank you for bringing the gift. It is important to me."

"I thought you said you didn't know what it was," Luka said.

"I meant it is important to me so I don't upset Rordan," she answered, swiping up another cracker.

"I see."

Violet-grey eyes stared back at him, and he held her gaze, both of them acknowledging she was lying in that stare.

"You can reach us down the bond," Luka said, getting ready to Travel. "I can't promise we can come right away, or when I can even come again. But we can feel you, hear you." She said nothing. "Keep fighting, little one," he finally said before picturing where he wanted to go.

"Would it have been like this?" she blurted, halting him a heartbeat before he stepped through a rip in the air.

"What?" Luka asked.

She wouldn't look at him now. She lifted herself onto the table, her feet swinging as she sat, breaking her cracker in half and crushing the crumbs beneath her fingers. "I was to be your Match. Would it have been like this?"

"You need to be more specific, Tessa," Luka said. "Been like what?"

"You. Me. This. Like tonight. If it is still night. I know you didn't want it, but…" She shrugged as she trailed off.

In three long strides he was directly in front of her. He moved fast, and she lurched back in her surprise. Grapes rolled to the floor and dishes rattled, but he was stepping between her legs and taking her chin in his thumb and forefinger. A gasp escaped from her lips as her eyes snapped to his.

"Luka, what—"

"If you were my Match, I wouldn't call you such a thing," he said and her eyes darted to the side. Until he said, "I would call you my wife, my partner, my light. Anything but my Match." He heard her breath catch as she held his stare now, her face giving nothing away. "But you asked what it would have been like. What a casual night in would be like if you were those things to me."

"I did," she agreed on a breath, a slight tremor to her voice.

"Our nights wouldn't be spent like this," he answered, and he watched her face fall a little at the words. "Our nights would be spent on balconies under the stars talking or on sofas before fires watching a Chaosphere game. Our nights would be more than fucking fruit, cheese, and crackers. Our nights would be soft words instead of barbed ones to deflect and protect. Our nights would be intimate touches rather than frantic ones of uncertainty. Our nights would be *my* hands in your hair instead of your fingers pulling on the strands. Our nights would be anything *but* whatever the fuck this is. Our nights wouldn't involve mental shields blocking each other out, and if you tried, I'd call you out on that bullshit. But I can't do that right now, can I?"

She swallowed again, shaking her head in his grasp.

"Our nights would be dark, but you'd love it there because you'd realize we need your light as much as you crave the dark."

"I hate the dark," she challenged.

His lips curled in a knowing smirk. "You fear the dark *because* you crave it, Tessa. You hate it because you think you are alone there, but your nights would never be spent alone. Never again. That's what it would have been like."

"And Theon?" she asked with a shaky breath.

"Would have been there too," he said. "Because I think you know deep down it's more than a bond. Always has been. It's just that neither of you knows what to do with it. Neither of you understand it. None of us understand any of it."

"It's too late anyway," she whispered, her voice hardening with the words. "Villains and monsters don't get happy endings."

"Oh, little one, is that what you believe?"

She gave a sharp jerk of her chin, and he released her.

"Then you're not a monster at all, are you?"

Her nostrils flared in annoyance. "And why is that?"

"Because monsters don't settle, Tessa. They take their happy endings, even if they leave a blood trail in their wake," Luka said.

"And what about you, Luka Mors?" she sneered. "Where do you fall?"

"Don't you know?" he asked, leaning down and whispering in her ear. "Dragons eat the monsters."

Then he backed away from her, watching her struggle as her eyes flared and she pressed her thighs together. He felt the want and the confusion and the annoyance as her mental shields buckled before she scrambled to get them back in place.

He turned his back on her. If he watched her a moment longer, he wouldn't leave. Or worse, he'd step back between her thighs and *show* her what their nights would look like.

But she was right.

It was too late for any of that.

"Luka?"

He paused at her voice, turning to face her fully, and waited.

"It would have been nice," she said, a sad note edging into her voice. "If things could have been different."

"I know, little one."

Then he stepped through the air.

# 43
## AXEL

"She's fine," Luka said the moment he appeared in Theon's room at the townhouse.

Theon had been pacing the length of the room for the last three hours. Axel had quickly been brought up to speed on the whole Luka-being-able-to-Travel thing when he disappeared into thin air. That explained Theon's mood and the tension between the two lately. But Axel was more upset about being left in the dark about the gods-damn three-way bond the three of them apparently had now.

"Of course she's fine," Axel said, his elbows braced on his knees and hands in his hair. "What do you think they're going to do to her? More than that, you'd feel her if they were hurting her."

Tessa may be blocking their bond, much to Theon's chagrin, but if something was happening to her, they would definitely know.

Unlike him.

Who had no idea if Kat was all right. He'd received a single message from Tristyn. Or at least he assumed it was Tristyn. It came from an unknown number, and all it said was, 'The kitten is safe.'

"What did she say? Where is she? Is she by herself?" Theon asked, still pacing.

He was barefoot, something his brother never did, but he'd slowly undressed more and more as they waited for Luka to return. The suit coat and tie were haphazardly tossed over a chair. His shirt was untucked and unbuttoned, hanging open, but for whatever reason, he'd still rolled his sleeves up to his elbows rather than just taking the thing off completely.

Luka was pouring himself a drink as he answered, "She's at the Pantheon, just like they said. In a room just like the Marking rooms, only a floor up. And yes, she's by herself. There are half a dozen sentinels outside her room. She had food. Looked like she'd eaten some of it. She was lying on the bed when I got there. Apparently, she took a nap earlier today."

Axel had to give it to the dragon for knowing Theon well enough to give him a complete rundown of what he saw while he was there.

"What did she say?" Theon repeated, still pacing.

"Theon, get a drink, brother," Axel said, sitting back and crossing his ankle over his knee.

"I don't want a drink."

"Then get me one. Do something other than wear a hole in the floor."

Theon glared at him but made his way over to the drink cart anyway. It gave him something to do with his hands at least. He watched as Theon poured a drink, knocking the entire thing back before pouring another one and bringing it over to him. Then his brother turned to Luka expectantly.

Luka had already drained his own drink, toying with the empty tumbler as he said, "She's confused. Talked about her visions a little. But she seemed…settled, maybe? Like she knew to expect this."

"Knew to expect this?" Theon repeated. "Like it was planned? Like Lord Jove had told her things? And she'd kept them from us?"

"Obviously he told her things," Axel drawled. "He said he told her all the things you didn't. Does she know about the three-way bond?"

"Yes," Theon snapped.

"So I was the only one who didn't know. Got it."

"Don't act like that," Theon said, resuming his pacing. "We kept it from you to protect you. Just like her."

"Because that's worked out so well."

Theon rounded on him, his hands clenching at his sides and causing Luka to stand, stepping between them.

"Everyone just take a breath," Luka said. "We're all tense. We all have things on our mind, and we do need to discuss a few things she said."

"Like what?" Theon asked from between clenched teeth.

"Her visions. She doesn't understand them, and to be honest, they're driving her a little mad," Luka said. "But she kept talking about one she has repeatedly."

Theon went still. "What did she say about it?"

"That she has the same vision, but the details change." Luka turned, his gaze settling on Axel. "She said the last time she had it, Kat was there, but you weren't. She said it was strange because you're always there."

Axel leaned forward at her name. "But Kat was there? She was whole and healthy? Safe?"

"I guess I didn't ask," Luka said. "I was more worried about the you-being-absent part."

Something in his chest loosened at hearing that Kat was in that vision. He didn't really care that he wasn't as long as Katya was alive in it.

"Did she say anything else about the vision?" Theon asked.

"Only that when she first had it, Tristyn and Kat weren't in it, but they have been in the recent versions," Luka answered.

"Blackheart?" Theon said in dismay. "Again?"

"He's not all bad," Axel cut in.

"He's helpful when he wants to be," Theon muttered. "When it benefits him in some way. I'm sure you will owe some type of debt to him for his help with Kat."

Oh, yes. Axel had gotten a delightful lecture from his older brother about that. It didn't seem to matter that no oaths or vows were exchanged. Theon was convinced Axel was now indebted to the Legacy, but Axel gave him the same response he gave him now.

"If that's the case, whatever the cost is, I'll pay it."

Theon pulled his phone from his pocket and glanced at the screen as if Tessa might call as he said, "If Tessa's vision is any indication, you might not get the chance to pay that debt. The fact that father still hasn't confronted you about not delivering Katya is unsettling."

Didn't Axel know it.

He knew the call was coming. Knew that he was on borrowed time.

"So how are we going to stop it?" Luka asked.

Theon swiped a hand down his face. "You know how visions are, Luka. Sometimes trying to stop them is exactly what causes them to come to fruition. It's why Cienna and the Witches are so careful about trying to intervene with fate."

At the Witch's name, Axel pulled the mirror from his pocket. She hadn't made contact since their last trip to the Underground, but he'd sent her a message that Theon wanted to bring Tessa to visit. Cienna likely knew how the hearing would turn out and didn't bother trying to make time for them. Of course, Axel could have tracked her down himself, but he wasn't about to abuse the knowledge she'd entrusted him with.

"Was there anything else?" Theon asked

Luka seemed to debate his answer for a moment before he said, "Not really."

"Not really?" Theon repeated. He was like a godsdamn parrot tonight. "Anything she said could be useful."

"Nothing she said was useful," Luka said, smoke furling from his mouth as some anger Axel didn't understand took over. "You're so gods-damn worried about who's with her when you should be worried about the fact that they're leaving her alone."

That got Theon to stop pacing. "What do you mean by that?"

"That Fae isn't even with her," Luka said.

"Dex?" Theon clarified. "Good."

"No, not good Theon. They kept her isolated her entire life," Luka said. "She hates being alone. It keeps her in her head."

A scoff slipped from Axel at his last words at Theon not under-standing this. Axel understood being stuck in his head. Consumed by something you had no control over. Luka was right. Keeping Tessa isolated wasn't a mercy to her. It was a strategic move.

"It lets her sit and stew in emotions she's never learned to process. She just continually shoves them down until they break her. Leaving her alone lets her get lost to a power she doesn't understand," Luka said. Glowing eyes lifted to Theon as he said, "We failed her, Theon. You get that, right?"

But Theon was already shaking this head. "No," he said vehemently. "We can still fix this. I'll figure out—"

"For fuck's sake, Theon," Axel snapped, getting to his feet. "Admit it. We lost. We never had a chance. We're the delusional ones for thinking we ever did. You could have let her go. You didn't. You get to live with that."

"Axel, wait—"

But he was already striding from the room and down the stairs. For someone so book smart, his brother was an idiot. He'd had weeks to figure out how to get Tessa somewhere safe. Where she could be happy and whole. Instead, he spent the time trying to figure out a way to achieve his end goals. Okay, sure. He was doing it to better the lives of those in the Arius Kingdom, along with potentially being able to have an influence in Devram as a whole, but at what cost?

*Sometimes it requires choosing between two unwanted outcomes, but in the end, I think you will find your own costs just as steep.*

Scarlett's words filtered through his mind. She'd been here mere weeks ago, but so much had happened since then, it felt like years. Somehow, he felt like he was decades older than he was, had more experience than someone with only twenty-four years of life should have. But that experience is what had him pushing through the door and into his room.

Lange and Corbin froze on the sofa. Lange's arm was slung around Corbin's shoulders as they watched the Chaosphere game on the television. Everflames versus Whirlwinds. Normally he would care.

The Fae were scrambling to their feet. They were being shuffled around, and Axel felt a little bad about it. They'd been staying upstairs because Tessa refused to sleep in that room. Then they were kicked out when Theon got back today, so they came to Axel's room. He wasn't staying in here anyway.

"You guys can relax," Axel said, shutting the door behind him. "I'm just grabbing a few things."

"Can we help?" Corbin asked, his hands shoved deep into his pockets.

"Not unless you know how to stop the inevitable," Axel muttered.

"I mean, I'm sure I could find a book on it, or Corbin could hack his way into something," Lange said with a small chuckle followed by an *oomph* as Corbin elbowed him in the stomach.

That had Axel drawing up short. "What did you just say?"

"Godsdammit, Lange," Corbin said, his voice muffled as he swiped a hand over his mouth.

"Remind me again which estates you two came from," Axel said, quickly adding, "*Before* Celeste."

Lange was rubbing at the back of his neck before suddenly straightening, as if remembering they'd been trained not to fidget. "Corbin was at Anala, and I was at Falein."

"With Kat?" Axel said, stepping closer to them.

"Yeah, I guess," Lange answered. "I didn't see her much. She was usually assigned to the archives. There were a few scholars who... preferred her company."

"But you knew her?"

"The estates are large. I knew of her, but I'd never spoken to her until she came to the Celeste Estate."

Axel turned to Corbin. "And you? The Anala Estate?"

"Yes," he answered.

"How did that work? Without the fire magic thing," Axel asked, moving to his bedside table and grabbing an extra set of earbuds. He'd left his usual pair upstairs, and there was no way he was going back up there tonight.

"There are other Fae there besides fire Fae," Corbin said, his tone somber and respectful.

"Obviously," Axel said. "Is that where you learned all your technology skills?" When there wasn't an immediate answer, Axel turned to face him. "Who, exactly, taught you that anyway?"

"I'm mostly self-taught."

"Mostly," Axel deadpanned. When Corbin only stared back at him, he had to respect the Fae. Sure, he could force the issue, but the truth was, Axel didn't really care at this point. Turning his attention to Lange, he said, "Kat knew—*knows*—how to translate several languages. Can you do that?"

"It was part of our academics there," Lange answered.

"So if I need your assistance in the coming days with something...?"

"I'd be happy to help."

Axel huffed a humorless laugh as he muttered, "I'm sure you would."

No Fae was *happy* to help the Legacy.

"Enjoy the game," he added over his shoulder as he left the room and crossed into Luka's. He kicked the door shut behind him, stripping down to nothing but his undergarments before he threw himself down on the sofa. There was no way he was sleeping in the bed. He heard enough bitching from Luka last time about messing with his nest of blankets and pillows. The fucker could Travel. Why didn't he just go to his cave every night?

Probably too far from Theon and their super special Guardian bond.

Sighing, he slipped his earbuds in and started a playlist before fiddling with the small mirror.

An entire day without her.

It was terrible.

But she was safe and whole.

He pulled out his phone and pulled up the text thread with Tristyn, trying to decide if he was going to reach out. Then he tossed the mirror and the phone aside. He couldn't risk it. Not until his father reacted to losing Katya. The less he knew about her right now, the better.

With a flare of power, he pulled the book Cienna had given to Kat from a pocket realm. He should have given it to her before Tristyn had whisked her away, but there was too much happening and too much adrenaline. He was fucking useless with the thing, but if Lange could help him decipher it...

But he didn't know what he was looking for anymore. Information on the Source Marks? What was the point now? Everything they'd been researching for nearly three months was utterly pointless now.

Nevertheless, he opened the book, slowly flipping pages. It was the only thing keeping him company, along with classical music and bloodlust.

And the book was a little piece of her.

It wasn't until the earbuds were being pulled from his ears that he realized he'd fallen asleep. It took longer than it should have to realize a ring was being shoved onto his finger as his magic thrashed in resistance. His eyes flew open, taking too long to adjust to the dark room.

"You motherfu—"

But that was all he got out before the air was forcefully pulled from his lungs.

Then the world went dark.

# 44
## AXEL

The smell of Fae blood is what pulled him into consciousness, the bloodlust gnawing at him.

He blinked, finding himself on the floor of a stone chamber still in just his underwear. He shivered against the cold, sucking in a sharp breath as the memory of what had happened came flooding back. Trying to sit up, he found his hands bound behind him, not in chains but thick vines.

Fuck.

That was all he could think as he scanned the room, looking for Eviana. He found her standing nearby, turquoise eyes focused on him. Which could only mean—

"Finally awake," his father drawled.

Axel twisted as much as he could, the stone scraping against his bare skin. His father sat in a chair, looking bored and impatient.

"I figured the Fae blood would do it. Thank you for that, Eviana," his father added.

Axel glanced back at the Fae, finding her sleeve pulled up and blood dripping to the floor. Not sure how he'd missed that the first time.

Axel knew where he was. His father had a room in the basement of Arius House. Several rooms, actually, that held all manner of things, but this room? Axel was well acquainted with this room. His body was already starting to quake as he began to mentally prepare himself, his shadows churning and preparing to defend him.

Not that it would do any good.

He twisted, getting his legs underneath himself so he could at least push up onto his knees. The ring was gone. He couldn't feel the cool metal on his flesh. After all, he couldn't be wearing it if his father needed to drain his power.

His father stood once Axel had managed to get propped up on his knees, and he tipped his head back as the Arius Lord came to a stop inches from him. His father's power appeared, a whip of thick shadows that wrapped around his throat, yanking him forward but also keeping him upright.

"I assume you know why you are here," his father said, and it wasn't a question.

Axel said nothing. He only continued to hold his father's stare.

"Tell me why Julius and Mansel are upset right now," his father went on, so much darkness bleeding into his eyes, they appeared black.

"I suppose you should ask them," Axel answered. He'd learned a long time ago not to give up information if his father hadn't confirmed the knowledge yet.

The cold smile that appeared had Axel on full alert. His father had expected that answer, had planned for this. Just like he'd planned for that Ford fucker to incapacitate him. He had no doubt the Fae had delivered him to his father, who had then shadow-walked them here.

"What an excellent idea," the Arius Lord said, releasing Axel from the grasp of his magic before he casually made his way to the door on the far side of the room. A moment later, Julius and Mansel themselves came through, and it took all of him to control the panic. His heart was beating so fast he could hear the blood pounding in his ears.

Julius was the taller of the two advisors. Blonde hair that fell to his shoulders was tied back. Tall and thin, his pale blue eyes landed on Axel with interest. He was a Reselda Legacy, but while he was descended from the goddess of healing, he used his magic to do the exact opposite. His power could keep a wound from healing. Mansel, on the other hand, was more solid. He didn't have a warrior's build, but there were muscles beneath that three-piece suit. His auburn hair was cropped short, and mossy green eyes slid around the room, landing on Eviana before sliding back to him. He was a distant cousin of Axel's mother and was a Nith Legacy. He preferred to use the creativity gifted from his bloodline to come up with new and unconventional ways of inflicting pain.

His father made his way back to the chair he'd been sitting in, relaxing into it. His legs fell wide as he rested his temple on his fist. "Go ahead, Son. Ask them yourself."

Glaring at his father, he kept his mouth shut.

Until thorns burst from the vines binding his hands.

"Fuck," Axel hissed, feeling his blood stream down his arms. There had to be thorns on every surface of the things.

Of course, those wounds went deeper and were ripped wider by Julius. The male had his hands in pockets, and he rocked back on his heels, the sadistic curl of his lips telling Axel they were just getting started here.

"My father informed me you are upset," Axel gritted out, his power already fighting against Julius's magic, trying to keep him from doing more damage.

Already draining his reserves.

"Quite," Julius agreed.

"Why is that?"

"We are rather…concerned," Julius replied. "This whole debacle with Theon is rather worrisome."

"I don't see why," Axel replied. "He has a powerful being tied to him. Better our kingdom than another."

"Yet at this very moment, she is being housed away from him. We'd been assured this would be handled, but our confidence is understandably shaken," Julius said with faux trepidation.

"One bright spot in all of this, however, had been the acquisition of a fire Fae," Mansel cut in. "The Anala Kingdom has always been so greedy with their demands to not share them, but Lady Aithne, in particular, is a real bitch about it. We were rather delighted when you stole one from right under her nose. She has been raging about it ever since."

"She didn't seem all that upset at the Tribunal hearings," Axel said.

"Yes, but while you have been enjoying the Selection Year at the Acropolis, the rest of us have been continuing on as normal," Mansel said. "Your brother's shortcomings are becoming more worrisome, which is why we were so interested in meeting the fire Fae who was to become his new Source. Yet she never made it to us."

"It is my understanding Pavil and Metias were supposed to deliver her to you. Not me," Axel said, feeling the blood start to pool around his knees. "I am upset that I am just now learning she never made it to you. I have spent the last months guarding her, and they lost her in a matter of minutes?"

His father's dark huff of laughter echoed in the room. "You always were a terrible liar. Theon can convince anyone of a farce, but you? You've never been able to hide anything, have you?"

"I don't know what you're talking about," Axel gritted out.

His father sighed. "I had a feeling you would be difficult about this. You always are. The problem is, I cannot sacrifice my power right now, nor that of my Source. I will need to get you to the Underground when this is over, and I have what I expect to be a trying engagement after this."

Mansel was making his way to Eviana, where his fingers trailed along her hip as he moved behind her. His hand splayed across her stomach when he tugged her back against him, and he rested his chin on her shoulder. "You know we got to meet this one before she became our Lord's new Source as well. Still just as pretty, just as obedient, just as docile as she was that day."

*His new Source?*

Axel didn't know his father had ever had another Source. He assumed it had always been Eviana. They'd never been told any differently. Did Theon know?

"But your brother chose not to let us meet his current Source," Julius cut in. He still hadn't moved from where he stood. "And clearly, that has gone poorly. We all agreed it might be better if we met his soon-to-be-Source prior this time."

"What do I have to do with any of this?" Axel demanded. "Again, Pavil and Metias were supposed to deliver her to you. Not me."

"Yes, but you have been the one *guarding* her," Mansel said, drawing Axel's attention back to him. Eviana had created a wooden stake, the end a deadly point, and the Legacy took it from her as she yanked the vines on his wrists tighter again.

His shadows appeared as Mansel took a step towards him. Axel couldn't hold them back. They would draw this out. Force him to drain his reserves. That was the entire purpose of this.

"The guarding has led to fucking, which is understandable," his father cut in. "She is quite easy on the eyes, and I'm sure her cunt is just as enticing."

Axel stiffened, anger crashing through him at his father's words, and a low growl rumbled from his chest. His shadows thickened, swirling around him.

His father's lip curled up in disgust. "I warned you not to do this, but in true fashion, you had to be dramatic about it all."

"Be dramatic? Because I didn't want these sick fucks to touch someone who didn't deserve this?" Axel snapped, too consumed with anger and hatred to hold back.

Is this what Tessa felt like every time she lost control? No fucks to give because what was coming was inevitable anyway?

The kick to his side had him sprawling to the ground, his face crashing against the stone. The pain was immediately intensified by Julius, who'd finally moved now, circling him as Mansel twirled the stake in his hand. Apparently they'd be doing his father's dirty work today.

Axel rolled to his back, turning his head to the side and spitting blood just as the wooden stake pierced his thigh. He let out a string of curse words as Julius amplified the pain, making him feel everything tenfold before the stake was twisted and yanked out. He could feel the splinters left in the wound as if they were shards of glass burrowing deeper.

Whatever control he'd been clinging to was gone, and his shadows converged, rising up to defend him. He heard the grunt from Mansel as he was thrown back, but Julius was there, making the pain so unbearable that Axel couldn't focus. There must have been a wound on his head because there was suddenly blood dripping into his eyes as he was rolled to his front with a foot. Then a knee was digging into his back, and something sliced along his spine. It wasn't a wooden stake. This was a blade.

A blade of stone that was draining his magic faster.

He wasn't sure who was thrashing more, him or his shadows, as the pain all started to blend together. Pain from wounds. Pain from his power being pulled from him. Pain from empty power wells. Pain from a craving that was increasing by the second.

Then there was a hand in his hair, yanking his head back to see his father standing over him, adjusting the cuffs of his shirt. "Where is she, Axel?"

"I don't know," he rasped, feeling blood dripping down his chin, and he thanked the gods he'd been smart enough not to contact Tristyn.

His father scoffed as Mansel yanked harder, the knee pressing to his back shifted, centering on his forearm.

"Where is she, Axel?" his father repeated.

"I don't know," he spat again. "I made sure I didn't know."

His father straightened. "But you know how to find her."

Axel shook his head, drops of blood splattering with the movement.

"Then you are telling me you lost our fire Fae. Am I understanding that correctly?"

"I didn't lose anything," he sneered, his shadows beginning to stutter as they battled against Julius's power and tried to pry Mansel off his back at the same time. "I saved her. From this. From you. From—"

That was when his bone snapped beneath Mansel's knee, and he bellowed as Julius made it feel like every bone in his body was doing the same. Black spots danced in his vision, and bile rose in his throat, mixing with the coppery taste of blood.

His father gripped his face, his power batting away Axel's shadows as if they were nothing. They were at this point. Nothing but wisps of dark mist feebly trying to save him.

There was no saving him.

Not anymore.

The pain eased just enough to keep him conscious. He could see Julius still circling, but he held chains in his hands now.

Chains that would keep his power from replenishing.

"One last time, Axel. Where is the fire Fae?" the Arius Lord asked, his voice as dark as his soul.

And Axel laughed as a smile filled his face because in this one thing, he'd won. He'd finally beaten his father at something, and if his prize was unending agony, he'd suffer through it for her.

"You find this funny?" his father demanded, his rage clearly rising as Axel only laughed more.

"He's lost his mind," Mansel said, his hold loosening some.

"Not yet," his father said. "But he will. Eviana, come here."

The Fae appeared, lowering to her knees beside where her Master was crouched. Without a word, she held out her arm. In the next blink, his father sliced a blade across her arm from wrist to elbow. Blood immediately welled, and Axel went utterly still as the scent of it hit him.

With a snarl, he lurched forward, every part of him honed in on the one thing that could restore him, protect him, save him.

His father smiled. "You think you've won something here today, don't you?"

Axel hardly heard him. Not until his face was wrenched back to his father's did he process what had been said.

"I don't see her here. I don't see her broken at your feet, so yes, I've won," Axel rasped.

His father motioned to Julius, who stepped forward with the chains.

"Make no mistake, Axel, I am going to find her. But until I do, you can be *saved* the same way you saved her. Hidden away where no one can find you."

A manacle was clamped on his wrist, and Axel bellowed another cry of pain as his broken arm was jostled. A few light slaps to his cheek had him breathing through his teeth as he focused on the Arius Lord once more.

"And when I find her," his father continued, "I will bring her to you." Axel was already shaking his head, and his father's smile was growing. "She'll be bleeding from so many places, you'll be able to take your pick."

"I'll kill myself before I touch her," Axel snarled as the other manacle was secured to his wrist. Another set was fastened to his ankles, and then he was jerked to his feet. He stumbled, his knees buckling slightly due to the stab wound in his thigh that Julius was continually making worse.

"The only person you'll be killing is her," his father sneered, darkness starting to swarm around them as his father prepared to shadow-walk them all, presumably to the Underground. "Then you can tell me how you won with her blood on your hands and in your veins."

"You'll never find her," he gasped out.

The darkness thickened until he could see nothing, but he heard his father's words.

"Then no one will ever find you. Soon enough, there will no longer be a need for a spare heir, and you can finally fulfill your true purpose."

# 45

## TESSA

She was lying on the bed again, waiting and flipping through the book Rordan had given her for Solstice.

The book he'd held on to for her, then returned when she sent him a message asking for it. Everyone had assumed that message had gone to Auryon after the Augury attack.

It hadn't.

There was nothing else to do in this room. No television. No music. Just her and her thoughts, these godsdamn visions she didn't understand, and this book.

Tessa lifted a hand, watching the light pool and crackle like a miniature storm in her palm. She had her magic, she supposed. Everyone warned her not to fall prey to its calling, that it would control her, but she didn't think that was true. Her power offered her freedom. In the light, she didn't have to think. She could simply exist. She didn't have to worry about feeling or bonds or dragons or emerald eyes. She didn't have to worry about any of it.

A part of her was hoping Luka would appear in the room again. It was too quiet here. It was too easy to dwell on things that no longer mattered. Music playlists and doughnuts. Running and warm coffee. Waking up between two warm bodies and a mouth and fingers that knew exactly how to give her what she didn't even know she needed.

She could feel him on the other side of her mental shields, constantly searching for a crack. Constantly knocking, asking for entry. Keeping the shields in place was second nature now. Mastering them had consumed her, and now she could keep them out of her head and away from her emotions with little effort. There was nothing she could do about the physical presence, though. She could maybe block Theon and the bond, but not the fucking Tracking Mark that they all had. She didn't know how to render it obsolete.

Soon it wouldn't matter anyway.

But gods. It was too fucking quiet being alone. She hadn't spoken to or seen anyone since Luka left, and while she understood this was to be her life now, she couldn't help but let a crack form as she felt him pacing on the other side.

*What's it like?* she asked down the bond.

She felt the ripple of shock from both of them, but it was Theon's voice that echoed in her mind.

*Tessa? Fuck. Are you all right?*

*Why wouldn't I be all right?*

*I just— I don't know. I can't see you, feel you, hear you.*

*I'm fine,* she replied. *There are plenty of thoughts to get lost in and keep me occupied.*

*Tessa...*

*What's it like?* she repeated. *To never be alone? To know that you'll always have someone?*

*You're not alone, Tessa,* came Luka's voice.

*What do you need, little storm?* Theon asked.

*Nothing you can give me.*

The distant sound of a commotion had her sitting up and sliding off the bed, the book falling to the wayside. The floor was cool against her bare feet. She'd rolled up the rugs, stacking them in the corner earlier that day. She didn't like the feel of them. They reminded her too much of socks.

Her fingers connected to the wall as she pulled them along, her thin black gown swishing at her ankles. It was loose and flowing with an open back. Probably too cold for winter, but she didn't feel the chill.

She didn't feel much of anything anymore. Wouldn't let herself.

*I'm working on this, Tessa,* came Theon's voice. *I swear to you I'm going to fix this and then I'll prove—*

*I don't need anyone to fix anything for me,* she snarled down the bond.

*You're right. You don't. That came out wrong. I didn't mean—*

*I have to go. They're here.*

*Who is there? Tessa, wait. Don't shut us out again. Please, Tessa.*

She smiled to herself as she heard the cries and din of the fight on the other side of the door. She suddenly understood his obsession with hearing her beg. To hear him say *please*. To have that control.

*Who is there, Tessa?* came Luka's command for an answer.

*Who or what? It does not matter. This is the beginning of endings.*

There was a long silence down the bond, and when she started to put her mental shields back up, she felt the panic from both of them.

*What are you doing, Tessa?* Theon asked.

*Exactly as you asked of me,* she answered. *Someone they fear as much as they fear you.*

Then she shut them out as the door to the room was flung open, banging loudly off the wall. A handful of figures stood in the doorway, robes and masks in place. Her power flared as she stared back at them. One pulled bands from the pocket of their robes.

"Putting these on will make this…easier," came a gruff voice from beneath the hood. Even without hearing him, Tessa would have guessed he was male. Tall and broad, the fabric of his robes was pulled tight across his chest, and the ice forming around his feet told her he was an Anahita Legacy.

"Easier for who?" Tessa asked, her head tilting to the side as she clasped her hands in front of her to stop them from trembling.

"Just put them on," the male insisted, taking a cautious step into the room.

"Whoever puts those on me will die," she replied simply, her magic tense and buzzing, energy crackling in the air the same way it did right before a lightning strike.

"So you're going to resist?"

"I didn't say that," she said with a sharp smile, lifting her wrists in offering. Golden thread swirled around her arms, charged energy crackling at her fingertips.

"Just get on with it," snapped another figure, also male.

"You fucking do it then," the first retorted.

Another figure pushed his way through the door, the suddenly thin air telling Tessa he was a Sefarina Legacy. He stalked forward, snatching the bands from the first male. Holding them out to her, he said, "You can put them on yourself."

"Why would I do that?" Tessa asked.

"It's that, or we put them on you when you're unconscious. Your choice," he sneered, a tug on the air in her lungs a threat.

She extended a hand, her power hissing at the first touch of the metal. "Just so we're clear, you will be the one to die for this."

"You shouldn't even be speaking to us," he snarled, gripping her elbow hard enough to bruise once she had the bands on.

The Pantheon was quiet as she was led through the halls. She couldn't help but wonder where the numerous sentinels were. Probably paid off to look the other way while she was taken down several flights of stairs, past the main floor, then lower still. This was more steps than she'd descended going to the Pantheon archives. She should probably be worried about where they were taking her, but that required the whole *feeling* thing again.

Instead her fingertips glided across stone as she hummed to herself, wondering how exactly they were going to attempt to kill her this time.

She was tugged through a stone chamber, the broad figure stepping to her other side so she was sandwiched between them. This chamber was reminiscent of the large room the Emerging Ceremony had taken place in. No balconies overlooking the space, but it was circular, with a stage in the center.

Not a stage, she realized, but an altar.

They crossed to the other side where she was shoved through another door, and then her feet dug into the ground as she was plunged into darkness.

"Where are we going?" she demanded.

She couldn't see anything, but she could feel the moist dirt beneath her feet and smell the musty air. A tunnel of some sort. Beneath the ground.

*No, no, no.*

*Tessa? What's happening?* demanded Theon, his voice frantic in her head.

Fuck. Her shields.

And she couldn't breathe.

"Keep moving," said the gruff voice with a vicious yank on her arm, causing her to stumble forward.

*It's too dark here.*

*Use your magic, little storm.*

*I can't. The bands.*

She felt Theon's anger as Luka's voice filtered through. *One step in front of the other, Tessa. Can you do that for us? Close your eyes. Don't think, and just keep moving.*

One step in front of the other. She could do that.

*I am going to kill every one of these people.*

That was what she thought as she focused on the next step and then the next.

*That's our girl,* Luka coaxed, clearly feeling something down the bond.

She couldn't be that.

Not anymore.

Not now.

*Tessa, what do you mean 'not anymore?'* asked Theon.

This godsdamn bond.

She tried to lift her arms, wanting to drag her hands through her hair, but the hands clamped around her biceps tightened.

Right.

Underground.

In the dark.

Helpless and alone and being led to slaughter.

Except the ground was sloping upwards, and a few minutes later, she was breathing in fresh air and blinking against a setting sun. She'd had no idea what time of the day it was. Apparently early evening.

She halted as she looked around, the two males releasing her and stepping away to join the rest of the robed Augury members here.

They stood in some type of outdoor amphitheater, rows of seating ascending half the space. Looking over her shoulder, she found the door they'd emerged from set into the side of a hill. She could hear the sound of rushing water in the distance, likely the Wynfell River. The cloudy sky was sprinkling the ground with big, fluffy snowflakes that melted the moment they touched the ground. She curled her toes against the damp earth, feeling the soft snow turn to water against her bare flesh.

A surge of swirling midnight had her stumbling back several steps, her eyes wide as a male stepped from their depths, followed by a female. He wore robes like the rest of them, but no mask, his Source a step behind him.

The masked members made no move to bow or drop to a knee. For once the male before her didn't seem to care as hazel eyes locked on hers.

The Arius Lord.

"I do hope I didn't keep you waiting too long," Valter said, adjusting the sleeves of his robe the same way he always adjusted the sleeves of his suit jackets. "My last engagement took a little longer than expected."

Tessa blinked, not sure what to say. She hadn't expected him to be here. This hadn't been in the vision that had prepared her for this night.

Panic bubbled up. She'd put these bands on. She'd made herself defenseless. She'd created another fucking mess, and she didn't—

"We had to work around those little glimpses of the future you have," Valter said, drawing her focus back to him. She didn't know he'd known about them, about her Witch heritage. Theon hadn't divulged the information at the hearing, but of course he'd told his father. He must have told him in a report. Valter had probably known long before she did.

"Things weren't supposed to happen this way," he continued, his hands clasped behind his back as he rocked back on his heels, an action she'd seen both of his sons do numerous times.

"Then what way were they supposed to happen?" Tessa asked, lifting her chin as she held his gaze.

"For one, you were never supposed to be bonded to my heir," he sneered. "But I'd been told we'd lost track of you when that was clearly never the case. At least, not entirely."

"What?" Tessa asked, her head tipping to the side at this new information. She'd been told many things from Theon, from Mother Cordelia, from Rordan, but never about this. "What does that mean?"

A cruel smile tilted on his lips. "So innocent to trust so foolishly."

"I trust no one," she snapped. "Not you. Not Lord Jove. And certainly not your godsdamn son."

That smile faded as he sneered, "This would have gone so differently if he could have brought you to heel, but he couldn't even do that right, could he?"

It was her turn to smile. "Turns out I don't like collars," she retorted.

He was in front of her in the next blink, moving as fast as Theon sometimes did. His hand was at her throat, and this wasn't a firm grip of warning like Theon often gave her. Valter's fingers squeezed, digging into her flesh and restricting her air.

"The plans I had for you," he said, his tone low and vicious. "If he could have simply driven the wildness from you. Imagine having Achaz blood bound to the Arius Kingdom."

Her eyes widened at his admission as her hands clawed at his wrist, trying to get him to loosen his grip.

"Theon didn't tell you, did he?" Valter said, his eyes searching hers. He leaned in even closer, his words a whispered breath that made her entire body shudder in disgust. "He figured out your maternal lineage, Tessa. He figured it all out weeks ago."

"No," she gasped out, hardly feeling the sting of yet another betrayal from him.

"Oh, yes," he said, leaning back to see her better once more, his grip loosening enough to let her choke down a gulp of air before tightening again. "I suspect he's figured out your paternal line too. He may be weak in so many areas, but cleverness is not one of them. Of course, my idiot son hasn't told a single soul your full lineage. Not me. Not his Guardian. Clearly not you. Always so protective of the information he gathers. He hoards secrets." Valter shrugged. "Can't say that I blame him. We all do. It's how we get ahead in this world. Secrets and betrayals. I would say I taught him well if it weren't for the fact that he is withholding this information because he has grown attached to you rather than keeping it for personal gain."

The snow was starting to come down harder now, and it wasn't gently falling flakes. These were sharp, pelting frozen bits of rain shattering as they hit the ground. Valter didn't even seem fazed as he pulled her close to him, her chest pressing to his front.

"Everything would have been fine if he'd have just let me handle this, but he insisted on fighting for you," Valter went on. "Refused to back down. And how could I convince him without revealing secrets of my own?"

He forced her to turn her head then, letting her suck in another sharp breath as she scanned the black-robed figures around them. She'd been so startled by Valter's appearance, she'd forgotten they weren't alone. Theon had never let her be in his presence without him. Not once.

His lips were at her ear again as he spoke softly. "How was I supposed to explain that I'd had to keep him busy the night of your emerging when we realized who you were? That I had to give Rordan time to verify everything? Or at least, that's what I'd thought."

Her legs were trembling at his admission. He'd been working with Lord Jove this entire time. She shook her head, trying to get him to loosen his grip on her throat again. To her surprise, his fingers slackened the smallest amount.

"For centuries we'd been waiting for you to come and fulfill the prophecies of the Revelation Decree. We felt it, you know. The day you entered this world. The entire realm trembled the moment you appeared here. We all did."

"Who is all?" she asked.

"All of us. The ruling families. The Augury. Even the common Legacy and Fae. They simply didn't realize what it meant."

"And what did it mean?"

She felt him smile against her ear. "That Chaos was here. Chaos always comes when the balance tips."

He released her then, shoving her away, and she stumbled, nearly slipping on the slick ground.

"Of course, I couldn't look for you myself, sequestered in the corner of the realm. Others would become suspicious. But Rordan assured me he would find you. Imagine my surprise when Theon Selected you," Valter said, slowly circling around her. "I'm not a fool. I knew Rordan had his own plans. After all, he left the Augury five years ago. I knew then he'd found you and kept it from me, but he was so godsdamn careful. Never visiting you. Never letting on where you were."

"What do you mean he found me?" Tessa asked, her hair starting to become matted to her face.

"That is what you ask me about?" Valter asked, his steps pausing. "I tell you he left the Augury and you ask me about *that*?"

"I know all about that," she retorted, rubbing at her wrists as the bands grew colder and colder against her skin. "I know all about how you two formed this little organization together. I know all about how he left, and I know all about how *you* have been trying to kill me since the first Tribunal hearing."

She could see the shock ripple across Valter's features. The way his mouth dropped open. The way he lurched back a step. The way he stared at her.

And she smiled back at him.

"He did this," Valter said, color draining from his face. "That bastard knew what the cost of this would be, and still he brings war to the realm. He still brings destruction here."

Her head tilted. "He does not bring war here. I am here to end the war."

Clearly there was no further explanation needed as Valter drew two dark blades from a burst of swirling black. How stupid she'd been to put these bands on. Her visions had failed her. This wasn't supposed to happen yet. She'd seen this in her dreams last night. Had known they would come. The Arius Lord had somehow worked around them, and now she was in another mess of her own creation.

Reckless.

Impulsive.

Too much of a hassle.

She couldn't be those things. Not now. She had a purpose, and gods, if she fucked this up, she was only proving that Mother Cordelia had been right all along.

But the Augury was converging on her. Some held dark blades, others with ordinary daggers and swords. Vines were snaking around her as Eviana started to subdue her, keeping her in place.

"Wait!" Tessa cried, panic settling in. "You don't understand. You—"

Howling ripped through the air, and Valter cursed at the sound.

"Quickly, Eviana," he ordered, and Tessa was yanked so forcefully to the ground that the back of her head hit with a smack that made her ears ring and her vision fuzzy. She could feel the snow and mud sticking to her bare back, and she could do nothing, once again helpless when she swore she would never be so again.

Vines held her in place, her limbs stretched out. She couldn't fight back as Valter stood over her, looking so much like Theon. Dark hair. Same build and jawline. If it weren't for the hazel eyes filled with loathing, she'd swear it *was* Theon as he lifted the dagger.

She thought about saying goodbye to them. Lowering those shields just enough to pretend she'd be missed, but in the end, she left her shields in place. She squeezed her eyes shut, tears of fury leaking from the corners as thunder rumbled and the shards of rain fell harder, slicing into her skin. She screamed. A sound of broken rage and defiance to the skies and the stars and the realms.

That was when she realized the ground was shaking beneath her.

There were confused cries and shouts of surprise, and she opened her eyes to find the Augury members scattering back from her. A flare of light had her jerking her head to the side where a fissure was forming. Turning to the other side, she found another.

"Eviana, stop!" Valter snarled, but his Source was shoving him back from Tessa, pushing him away.

Trying to protect him, Tessa realized.

"We need to leave, my Lord," she begged, clinging to his arm.

"Not until we finish this," he snapped, shoving her off of him.

But her desperation to keep her Master safe had caused her focus to split, and Tessa was able to break free of the vines holding her arms in place. She sat up, reaching to tear at the binds on her ankles, until she realized what was happening.

There was a crevice forming around her in a perfect circle. Light flared up from the crack, and more of the Augury members were backing away. But some were stuck on this side of the crevice that was widening by the second, gold mist glinting in the setting sun.

There was fear, but not the panic that she'd experienced the last time she'd watched nearly translucent figures crawl up and out of the earth. They glided more than crawled, one after another. Far more than had appeared in the gardens. They floated a couple of inches off the ground, all identical. Pale skin. Tall and lean, with sharp, angular features. Short hair as white as the falling snow.

The three in the front tipped their heads back in unison, seeming to smell the air. One turned to the Arius Lord, while two spun to face her. One stepped forward, and it wasn't until he pulled the gold sword from nothing and raised it above his head as he made his way to her that Tessa reacted, a cry of terror ripping from her as he brought the sword arcing down.

Only to slash through the vines at her ankle.

In stunned shock, she watched him do the same to the other side before stepping back and bowing his head to her as the other stepped forward.

"Blood of death, yet blood of life," he said, his voice unearthly. It was raspy and icy and a whisper that latched onto her bones as if trying to burrow in like an entrancing. "We serve at his bequest, and thus at yours."

# 46

## TESSA

"At my what?" Tessa asked, still sitting on the godsdamn ground.

"You called, we answered," he replied, drawing closer. He lifted a hand, and Tessa flinched away as icy fingers didn't exactly touch her, yet somehow came away with her blood on them. She reached up, running her fingers over her hair to find them stained red too. She'd assumed she was wet from the snow and mud, but she must have hit her head hard enough to draw blood.

The being glided around her, coming closer as he spoke into her ear. "Daughter of Fury and Blood of Beginnings, you were threatened. You summoned us in answer to that threat."

No one was moving, as though the Augury members were frozen in place, watching and waiting. Even Valter was still, Eviana in front of him.

White, translucent figures on one side. Black-robed people on the other.

White and black.

Light and dark.

"We come to defend you. To defend him," the being continued, her hair fluttering as she felt him draw his fingers through her hair once more. "At your command, we will do so."

"Will do what?" she asked, her voice breathy and uneven.

He glided in front of her, reaching out and dragging a single finger along the Mark over her heart. She stared into white eyes that glowed. They had no pupils, just a faint light.

The same light she commanded.

"Defend you. Protect you. Fight for you," he said.

Then there was another at her back. She could feel its icy aura against her bare skin. "They seek to lock you, cage you, use you. They seek to destroy you and all you are. We cannot allow that. May we serve?"

They were…asking permission? Of her?

They were here to protect her. Fight for her. She had called, and they had answered.

And they were right.

They had forced her to put these bands on. They had locked her in the dark over and over. They wanted to kill her, use her as a message. Take her power. Force her to heel.

Shove her under tables.

Lock her in wine cellars.

Constantly lie to her and keep things from her.

Train her just enough to defend herself, but still keep her dependent on them.

Isn't that what tonight had proven? She still wanted them. Still wanted him. Still thought of them moments before death came for her once more.

*Theon is death.*

Endings that had upset the balance.

The one she was always meant to destroy.

And if she was going to answer the call of destiny, she couldn't think about them. She had to embrace what she was always meant to be.

Too impulsive.

Too reckless.

Too wild.

The beings beside her seemed to sense her shift, wicked smiles pulling at their perfect mouths.

There was nothing said. She gave no command, and the beings didn't say a word to each other. But they descended as one. All of them pulled swords from the air as they glided forward, converging on the Augury members.

The same way the Augury had come for her. Trapping her. Bringing her to her knees.

And they screamed.

There was no fighting against the beings. The weapons of the Augury went straight through them as if they were nothing but wisps of fog. The golden blades of the beings, however, were very, very real. Blood mixed with the falling frozen rain, turning everything red.

Tessa had never felt more free as she moved among the death swallowing up everything around her. No one touched her. No one came for her, too busy trying to stay alive.

And she smiled.

A voice she recognized had her turning her head as the Augury member tripped over his robes and fell to the ground. A being glided over to him, blade raised.

"Wait!" Tessa called.

The being immediately stilled, his head turning to her while he still held the blade aloft.

"My grace?"

*My grace?*

That made her pause. She'd never been addressed as such a thing.

Quickly gathering herself, she used her foot to kick the mask from the Legacy's face. She felt his power swirl around in the wind, but he must have used an abundance of it because it scarcely touched her. Or maybe that was the being beside her? She didn't really care as the male's eyes landed on her, something akin to relief flashing through them.

"Thank the gods," he said, a hand swiping down his face and leaving a smear of dirt and blood.

"Why do you thank gods that do not care for this world?" Tessa asked in curiosity. "They will not save you."

"I... I don't—" He stuttered, the panic reappearing.

Tessa held up her wrists. "You were the one who forced me to put these on, yes?"

Now his eyes were wide as he frantically tried to push away from her, crawling backwards.

"I did make it clear you would be the one to die for this," she said with a mocking sigh.

She held out her hand to the being, not even sure if it would work, but he placed the golden blade in her hand. Her fingers curled around the hilt. She'd never held a sword. Luka had never trained her to use such a thing. But she was pretty sure as long as the sharp end went through skin and tissue and muscle, it would accomplish its task, and she could certainly shove it into a chest.

"Just to make sure there is no misunderstanding on your end," she said, stepping closer, the being moving with her. "I am still going to kill you, and I do not need my power to do so. Although it would likely be more satisfying, I suppose a blade will do."

"No! Wait! I didn't mean to—"

She clicked her tongue. "Hush now. Don't be a liar as you cross to the After. You would have shown me no mercy, and to be frank, the Legacy deserve none."

And before he could reply, she plunged the golden sword into his throat before dragging down. She didn't know what kind of blade this was, but it was sharp enough to slice with ease as she slid it to his heart and plunged deeper.

Howls sounded again moments before Roan and Niylah appeared, jumping into the fray and taking down Augury members who were managing to escape the beings she'd summoned.

Hers.

That's what Auryon had said.

The wolves were hers.

They'd come to fight for her, protect her, avenge her.

Turning back to the being, she extended the sword back to him. "I need the Arius Lord and his Source left alive. The rest can die."

"As you wish, your grace," he answered.

Her magic was prowling in her soul, angered by the bands. The sky was flashing with lightning that was striking nearby. Something in her winced as life was taken before her eyes, some part of her knowing she was the cause of this. They were going to kill her, but did that warrant *this*?

This was what they were trying to stop and—

She went still as Auryon appeared. Not from a swirl of smoke and ashes, but stepping from the very air with Tristyn Blackheart.

"I told you she could summon them," Tristyn snarled as Auryon drew her bow and immediately nocked three arrows, letting them fly.

Tessa watched as they hit their target. The being hissed, whirling on Auryon, but then his mouth fell open, a wail of rage ringing as white wisps poured out of it before the entire being faded away.

"What are you doing?" Tessa cried, racing towards them. "Stop! They are helping me!"

"No, Tessa. They aren't," Tristyn said, as Auryon disappeared among her ashes this time. More wailing filled the air mixing with the cries of the Augury.

"What do you mean they aren't? I summoned them. They came to—"

"They are Hunters," he snapped. "They are not here to protect you. They are here to hunt down and kill any descendant of Arius."

"No," she said, shaking her head. "That can't be right because I—" She snapped her mouth shut before she said it aloud.

But she didn't need to.

"Because you are a descendant of Arius?" Tristyn asked, and gods. He sounded furious.

"You... What?"

Everything around her faded until it was muted and muffled.

*Tessa?*

Theon's voice echoed in her head.

And as she stared at Tristyn—yet *another* person who had betrayed her, kept things from her, *used* her—the sound of Theon's voice echoing in her mind is what broke her.

The one who had started all of this.

The one who wanted her to use her.

The one who whispered pretty words and dressed collars up with diamonds.

The one who left her in the dark.

The one always meant to destroy her.

"You know," Tessa said to Tristyn. "How long have you known?"

Tristyn wasn't even focused on her as his gaze bounced around the amphitheater before he reached for her, slipping the bands from her wrists. "These fucking things," he muttered. Then louder, he added, "I need to get you out of here."

She lurched back. "I'm not going anywhere with you."

Suddenly seeming to remember the persona he'd always had around her, he turned to face her fully. "I know you have questions. I can answer some of them, but—"

"No," she snapped, backing away another step. "You have had so many opportunities to answer my questions."

"You never asked them," he said, and there was an agonized plea in his voice. "You never asked the right questions, Tessa. I'm sorry I couldn't—"

"I'm asking now!"

"In the middle of a bloodbath," he replied. "It's not safe for you."

"I've never felt safer," she retorted as Niylah slunk to her side, baring her teeth at Tristyn.

The Legacy's fists curled at his sides. "This isn't how it's supposed to go. It can't go this way," he said. He extended his hand again. "Come back to Lilura Inquest with me. I'll—"

"Lilura?" Tessa repeated. "How do you know that name?"

"It is the name of my company. You know this."

"Your company," Tessa said, as more and more betrayal sank into her being. "How did you come up with it?"

She saw his throat work and watched as he formed the lie right in front of her. "It is just a name," he said hoarsely.

"So if I tell you Lilura lives, that will mean nothing to you?"

She could swear his knees almost buckled at the words, and he lurched towards her. "You've seen her?"

"Who is she?" Tessa said, her voice low and cold and detached.

"A Witch."

"Who is important to you?"

He swallowed again, russet eyes holding hers. "Who is everything to me."

"Everything," Tessa echoed. "Someone you would do anything for."

"Yes," he said. "But it's not what you're thinking."

"You know nothing about what I'm thinking," she hissed, Niylah growling at her side again and coming between her and Tristyn.

"They serve you because of whose you are," Tristyn said, glancing at the wolf.

"I am no one's," Tessa sneered.

"I meant the blood in your veins."

"You mean the blood you've known about this entire fucking time? The reason you sought me out to begin with?"

Regret filled his features, and if she wasn't so used to being lied to and manipulated at this point, she'd almost believe it was real.

As it happened, he only confirmed everything she already knew.

Ashes swirled, and Auryon appeared. "We need to go," she said, breathing heavily. "There are too many. I cannot kill them all."

"You don't need to kill them," Tessa said, Roan appearing from the fray along with one of the beings. A Hunter if Tristyn was to be believed.

"My grace, we have him," he said in that eerie rasp. "We await your orders."

"You can control them?" Auryon demanded.

The Hunter spun towards her, hissing like a mountain cat at her presence. "You cannot stop this, Huntress."

Auryon smiled, smoke swirling and leaving a dark dagger in her hand. "I can end you. That will leave me satisfied for now."

"We will come for your maker in time, Huntress," the Hunter said. "Tell Temural his time will come."

"Temural," Tessa said, feeling the blood drain from her face. "You know of Temural?"

There was no regret on her features like there had been on Tristyn's. No, there was nothing but an indifference that only added to the hurt as Auryon said, "No one else can send a Huntress to his daughter. We only answer to him."

With a broken laugh, she said, "It is best you leave now."

"Tessa, wait," Tristyn said. "Come with me. Please. I'll explain as much as I can."

"No," was all she said before she turned to face the ongoing destruction.

Auryon had done damage to the Hunters. There were a fraction of them left and a handful of Augury members along with the Hunters surrounding the Arius Lord and Eviana. Her wolves moved with her, and as she passed the still breathing Legacy in robes, energy and light emanated from her, taking life from them.

It only seemed to strengthen her own gifts as her magic feasted.

She turned just in time to see Tristyn disappear into the air, Auryon already gone.

Of course Tristyn could Travel. Just another secret she'd collected.

Turning back, the Hunters parted, letting her pass between them to where Valter was kneeling, two golden blades at his throat. He glared up at her, nothing but malice in his eyes as he said, "You will be the downfall of this realm."

She lifted a hand, drawing in the air with her magic before the message flared and disappeared.

"No," she said simply. "I will be the downfall of the Legacy in this realm. I will be the downfall of the imbalance that has plagued this world. But above all, I will be the downfall of your entire bloodline, and I will let you witness it all before I take your life from you."

# 47
## THEON

He jolted to his feet as he felt the bond snap to attention in excitement.

He'd been sitting in his bedroom at Arius House, a glass of liquor in hand as he'd stared at the fireplace. The flames flickered, too wild and reckless to be allowed outside of the safety of the glass. The bond had been muted, too far from Tessa, and she'd blocked him out completely once again.

That hadn't kept him from contemplating her words for the last hours.

*I couldn't be that.*

*Not anymore.*

*Not now.*

Those words had filtered down the bond as they were coaxing her through the dark. It was all they'd been able to do. They could have tried to go to her, but she was so heavily guarded and there was so much tension between him and the other kingdoms right now. Showing up could have made things worse. Showing up could have been a trap. The ruling Lords and Ladies had made it more than clear he wasn't to interfere anymore. Not that he'd be submitting to that, but he didn't have a plan yet, and not having a plan only put her in more danger.

But there'd been nothing from her since. Nothing but flashes of panic followed by flickers of surprise and then...

Wrath.

Rage.

Hurt.

So much fury.

He'd gone back to Arius House this morning mainly because he'd had no choice. His father wasn't here yet, and Axel had left early yesterday, not telling anyone. His brother had been holed up in his room since. Theon was giving him until tonight, and then he was breaking into his room. He'd sit and watch fucking Chaosphere with him if that was what needed to be done.

But if Tessa was here? That might change everything.

His phone buzzed in his pocket as he made his way out to the main room, half expecting her to be waiting for him.

**Luka:** *Is she there?*
**Theon:** *No. Do you have her?*
**Luka:** *No. Do you want me there?*

And wasn't that the question, because no. He didn't want him anywhere fucking near her right now. Not until they figured out a way to sever this bond, but she'd need Luka just as much as she'd need him.

He yanked the door open, looking up and down the hall, but she was nowhere to be seen. She was close, though. There was no fooling the bond.

Going back into the suite and shutting the door, he sent a message off to Luka. They didn't want to communicate down the bond because there was no way to block one person. It was all or nothing from what they could tell.

And it was weird as fuck to communicate with Luka down the thing.

**Theon:** *I'm not sure what to expect from her. Just wait. Let me see how she is...*

Luka didn't reply. Theon was sure he'd hear about it later. In the meantime, all there was to do was wait.

Feeling too jittery, he went back to his bedroom to retrieve his tumbler, hoping another glass of liquor would help, but he went still when he stepped into the room.

The double doors of the balcony were open, the winter air seeping into the room, and she stood just inside. She wore a thin floor-length skirt of navy blue that was so dark it was nearly black. The color reminded him of Luka's scales. It was lightweight and sheer, and her top was the same. It tied at her nape, dipping low in front and leaving her back exposed, a sliver of her stomach bare. Her bands of light glowed faintly around her wrists, and he could swear streaks of lightning flashed in her violet eyes. Her golden hair was loose, peppered with the lightly falling snow, and her feet were bare because she wouldn't have it any other way.

"Tessa," he breathed, unable to move. Unsure of what was happening. "How did you get here?"

"A portal," she answered, and he swallowed thickly because her voice had that eerie ring to it.

"There are no portals to Arius House," he countered.

"It's my own," she answered simply.

He didn't know what that meant.

"You should come in and shut the door. It's cold outside," he said, daring to take another step towards her.

She didn't move, her hands clasped in front of her. Theon shoved down every instinct to go to her and drag her away from the balcony.

Instead, he shoved his hands in his pockets, rocking back on his heels. Her head canted to the side at the movement. He wasn't sure why. Clearing his throat, he said, "Do you want to talk about what's happened the past few days?"

She smiled at that. A dark, wicked thing that sent a chill up his spine, which was saying something considering the things he'd done in his past.

"You want me to tell you about my time away from you?" she asked.

"If you need to talk about it, yes."

"It's a little late to worry about what I need, don't you think?"

He bristled inside at that, but kept himself under control. "Then what are you here for, Tessa?"

"To say goodbye."

It was his turn to smile. "Beautiful, there's no saying goodbye between you and me. You will forever be mine."

"I'm not here to say goodbye to *you*," she retorted. "I'm here to say goodbye to what could have been. Just one more..." She cleared her throat, lifting her chin. "No. I didn't come to say goodbye. I came to tell you a story."

His brows arched. "A story?"

She nodded, finally moving into the bedroom. He kept space between them as he made his way over to close the balcony doors. Once they were shut tight, he turned back, finding her staring at the same fire he'd been fixated on for the last few hours.

"Tell me this story, little storm," he said.

She peered over her shoulder at him. "It is a story of beginnings and endings."

"And where did you hear this story?" he asked cautiously.

"In my dreams."

"In a vision?"

She shrugged, reaching out as if she was going to touch the glass of the fireplace but stopped just short. "There was an agreement between beginnings and endings."

"Achaz and Arius," Theon clarified, trying to figure out where she was going with this.

"They were the perfect balance, and they were entrusted to keep that balance. They failed. Or rather, endings failed."

She wasn't looking at him, but rather had her attention fixed on the fire.

"He betrayed them all," she said.

"Arius?"

She nodded. "He betrayed all the gods, all the beings born of Chaos, when he took what did not belong to him." She looked over her shoulder again, violet-grey eyes connecting with his. "A sin his bloodline continues to commit."

"Then what does that make you, Tessa?" Theon countered.

"Hush," she snapped. "I'm not done with my story."

"My apologies. Please continue," he drawled.

She rolled her eyes, and something in his soul settled at seeing some of her snark peek through whatever this was.

"As if you know how to apologize for anything," she retorted. "If I recall, you don't show remorse."

He stepped towards her, heat flooding through him as he watched her breath hitch the smallest amount. This is where they thrived. The push and pull. The constant battle of wills.

"I'll never regret anything that led to this, beautiful."

Her eyes narrowed. "Can I continue my story now?"

"By all means," Theon said, edging closer still, smiling to himself when she didn't step away from him.

"Arius took what did not belong to him, and because of that, a war that was meant to end continued."

That had him pausing. "The Everlasting War?"

"They upset the balance. They could have ended one war, and instead started another. And now they must pay the price to right it."

"Who are they?"

"Arius and Serafina."

"Then what does that make you?" he asked again.

She smiled again, the smallest tilt of her lips. "Shh, Theon. I'm not done." When he only nodded, she went on. "They created life together, something forbidden for the Firsts. They kept their sins a secret. So many secrets locked away. But secrets still have consequences. They tipped the balance too far, and because of that, destinies were changed."

Theon waited for her to go on, and when she didn't, he asked, "Is that it?"

"Mhmm."

"Beautiful, that was a terrible story."

She finally turned to face him fully, stepping up to him. Her palm slid up his chest to his shoulder, and fuck. Her touch. It'd been far too long.

"Would you like to tell me a better one?"

"I'm not a very good storyteller," he replied, his voice dropping an octave as her other hand came up, fingers brushing along his belt.

"But there's one you know I would really love to hear," she purred, pushing onto her toes as her hand slid to the back of his neck. A slight tug had him appeasing her, bending so she could speak into his ear. "I want to hear the story of how you learned my lineage and kept it from me."

He snapped upright, his eyes going wide. How could she possibly know that?

"Tessa, I—"

She reached up, placing a finger at his lips. "I do not want lies or excuses. I simply want the story."

He held her gaze for a long moment before he said, "I figured it out while you were in Faven. It took me a little time to piece all the information together, so I can't say I was confident in my conclusions until a few weeks after."

"But you knew enough when I'd returned. You knew enough you could have told me. You knew enough that you could have proven them all wrong," she retorted, taking a step back from him and dragging her fingers through her hair where she tugged at the ends.

"Proven who wrong?"

"They told me," she murmured. "They warned me you would do this, but I... Gods, I was naïve, and then I found her there, in your room."

"*Our* room," he corrected, not sure why he thought now was a good time to make the clarification.

A bark of humorless laughter came from her. "It stopped being our room the moment I found her in there, Theon. Then again, it was never truly *our* room, was it? It was always to be a room you shared with her or some other female."

"Tessa, we talked about this. You know that was a set-up. You know I'm trying to figure it all out."

"But you did figure it all out, and you kept it from me."

"All of it was to keep you safe."

"I've never been yours to protect," she retorted.

He moved fast, his arm looping around her waist and hauling her into him. "You will forever be mine, Tessa. Whether in this life or in the After."

Something he didn't understand shuddered in her eyes at the words. "We were always meant to destroy each other," she said flatly, looking away from him.

He took her chin with his other hand, forcing her gaze back to his. "I crave destruction at your hands, clever tempest. If that's what it takes to keep you, then so be it."

"Such pretty words to get what you want," she murmured.

"You think I am lying to you?"

"I know you are."

His hand slid into her hair, tilting her head back. "And what about you, beautiful? Still lying to me?"

"I never stopped."

"Good," he said, then brought his lips to hers.

She opened immediately, sliding her tongue against his, and he deepened the kiss. Her hands slid to his shirt, deftly undoing the buttons as he kept her in place, refusing to let her go. When his shirt was hanging open, her palms landed on his chest, pushing him backwards. He let her, dragging her with him as he stumbled back to the armchair. He bumped the end table as he sat, the liquor glass falling to the floor and shattering.

Neither of them cared as she climbed onto his lap, and he groaned as she settled over him.

His hands slid to her ass, squeezing as she leaned back, her lips sliding along his jaw, down his throat.

"Tessa," he rasped.

"How much will you let me take, Theon?" she murmured, her words vibrating against his skin.

"Whatever you want. All of it," he answered, bunching the fabric of her skirt in his hands and dragging it up.

"All of it?" she repeated, her nails skimming down his abdomen, where she dragged them along the waist of his pants.

"Fuck, yes," he gasped, his mouth moving along her shoulder, her collarbone, down the valley of her breasts. "All of it."

She unbuckled his belt, unbuttoning his pants, and pulled out his cock. Her touch had him jerking beneath her, already seeking her warm heat. Her head tilted as she met his gaze again, her tongue peeking out to wet her lips. For a fleeting second, he thought she was going to take him in her mouth. She'd yet to do that, and he had no idea what would make her suddenly do it now.

But she didn't slide to her knees. She leaned back more, dragging a single finger up the underside of his cock, making his thighs tense and darkness burst free, swirling lightly around her. Her eyes fluttered closed for the briefest of moments, some of her light reaching out to tangle with his magic.

Theon's fingers dug into her hips as he tried to lift her, but she pressed her knees into the cushion beside his thighs, keeping herself in place.

"Tessa," he growled. Then he let out another hiss as her palm rolled over the head of his cock.

She leaned forward, the fabric of her top brushing against his chest. One of his hands left her hip, reaching to tug at the neckline.

"Did you know the Source Marks work both ways?" she asked casually, her hand sliding down his length now until she gripped the base.

His head snapped up as he tried to process that through the lust in his veins and the heat of her touch. "What?"

"Scarlett told me before she returned to her own world," Tessa went on, her fingers closing around him now and pumping up and down.

Up and down.

She paused on her next pass, a smirk filling her face before there was a sharp tug on his magic, his darkness going to her willingly, more entranced by her than ever.

"Tessa..." He started to push out of the chair, but a bolt of lightning had him dropping back into the seat, a hissed curse coming from his lips.

She was lifting on her own now, hovering over him before she dragged her wet cunt along his dick that was so hard it was painful.

No undergarments.

*Fuck. Me.*

"For the love of the gods, sit on it already," he snarled, again trying to move her where he wanted her.

Where he could feel her surrounding him.

Where she would be at his mercy.

Where he would have control.

Instead, he found his magic pushing him back into his chair with a hard shove.

*His* magic.

His darkness pressing against his shoulders, keeping him in place.

What the fuck?

"It's terrible, isn't it?" she sighed dramatically, dragging herself along his length again, sucking in a sharp breath as she ground her clit against him.

"What's terrible?" he asked, his eyes dropping to watch where she was moving against him. His hands shoved at her skirt, pushing it out of the way.

But then she was taking his chin between her thumb and forefinger, her nails digging in as she yanked his face up. "Eyes on me," she said with faux sweetness. "This is for me, not you. Now focus."

But how the fuck was he supposed to focus when she ground against him again, her fingers toying with the hair at the back of his neck, while her other hand smoothed along his jaw?

"Tessa, please," he rasped.

She sighed dramatically. "I do understand the allure of the begging, Theon," she said, leaning forward and pressing her lips to one corner of his and then the other. He turned his head, chasing her mouth as she leaned away from him again. "It's terrible trying to figure something out when something else is constantly demanding your attention." She gripped the hair at his nape, yanking hard and making him curse. "Like a bond you never wanted." She slid against him again, grinding harder. "Or a cunt you crave but can't have."

"I'm going to have it, Tessa," he snarled, reaching for her again.

Until bands of dark and light yanked his arms back and away from her, forcing his hands to the armrests.

"Time to tell me what the fuck is going on," he demanded as she smiled at him again.

"Like you told me how you figured out my bloodline?"

Fuck.

That was all he could think as he watched her.

"Or do you want to tell me how you believe everything the Augury is trying to do?"

"What? Tessa, no. You don't understand— *Fuck!*"

The curse came as she finally seated herself fully, and he couldn't think around feeling her surrounding him again. He couldn't breathe as she rocked against him, swiveling her hips in a way that clearly worked for her as she tipped her head back and let out a sound that had him thrusting up into her.

"Let me touch you, beautiful," he demanded, straining against his own magic that she was somehow controlling.

She shook her head, rocking against him again in a way that he knew made him drag against her clit. "You always take and take and take from me," she said, breathless as she continued to move. "I'm taking this time, Theon."

And take she did as she ground against him, her hands coming up and playing with her breasts. He watched as she rolled and tugged at her nipples through her thin top, the material providing friction that he was dying to provide with his mouth. Instinctively, he thrust up again, and she let out a small gasp at the movement.

"Even when you don't let me touch you, I know what you need," he growled. "Let me make it even better, Tessa. You know I can. You know it can be so much more than this."

"That's just it, Theon," she said, her hand sliding down her torso, over her belly, between her legs. She rubbed her clit, her fingers brushing against his cock with the movements. "We can never be more than this. Destiny beckons. Sacrifice demands, but Fate requires more."

He felt her start to clench around him, her thighs tensing as her head fell back.

"We'll always be more. You'll always need more. It'll never be enough, little storm," he said as her fingers moved faster, her hips grinding harder. "At the end of the day, you're still mine. All of you. From your fury to your pleasure."

"No," she gasped, her magic clawing at him as she teetered on the edge.

"Always, Tessa," he swore. "Now come. Give me what's mine."

She shuddered around him, her back arching and hands landing on his chest as she fell into her pleasure. Her light buzzed against his flesh like tiny shocks, and all of it was enough to have him driving up into her again and again.

Until she started lifting off of him.

With a startled gasp, he choked out, "What are you doing?"

Her legs were still trembling as she stood. He could see her knees shaking.

"I took what I wanted, Theon," she said, her voice still hoarse and breathy.

"You can't be serious," he demanded in disbelief as she reached for his dick, tucking him back into his pants.

"I have another story to tell you."

"I don't want another fucking story, Tessa," he spat in outrage.

"But it's a good one," she said, readjusting her skirt.

Theon tried to get up, but there was another yank on his magic that held him in place. "Tessa, stop," he said, struggling a little more. "How are you doing this?"

"I told you. The Source Marks work both ways."

"But they're not true Source Marks," he argued.

Her head tilted. "This is the second time you have said such a thing."

"I never got a chance to tell you," he said. He shifted in the chair, then winced as his pants brushed against the sensitive head of his cock, his balls already aching from the release she was denying him. "Kat and Axel found some information that strongly suggests the first three Marks aren't Source Marks at all."

"Then what are they?"

"I don't know."

The look she gave him told Theon she didn't believe that one bit.

"I swear, Tessa," he said. "I haven't had time to research it much. Axel told me the morning of the hearing."

"But there is a bond."

"I know."

"Is it not a Source bond?"

"I don't know. I don't have all the answers. Gods, I wish I did," he said, tipping his head back against the chair and pushing out a harsh breath.

"Would you like to hear my story now?"

Sighing again, his eyes fell closed. "Sure, Tessa. Tell me your story."

"There once was a daughter of wild and fury, unwanted and tossed away in a forgotten realm."

Theon slowly lifted his head, eyes connecting with hers. With each word she spoke, her features hardened, and anger flashed in her violet irises.

"She was hidden away, believed to be unworthy and told she was too wild, too impulsive, too reckless. She was told she was nothing, so she became nothing."

"Tessa—"

"Do not interrupt the story," she snarled, energy skittering across the floor in a flash of light. "She was lost to those who needed her and found by those who wanted to use her."

He opened his mouth to argue again, but she shot forward, moving so godsdamn fast. Her hand slammed over his mouth, her other hand bracing herself atop his arm still secured to the armrest.

"She was taken into the dark where she was forced to give and serve, bow and obey," she went on. "She begged to be seen, tried to do what was asked of her, but it was never enough. She gave everything and still they wanted more. Until the night she was set free. Until someone fought for her." Her hand slid along his jaw, her thumb brushing across his lips. "And for the briefest of moments, she thought maybe, just maybe, there could be more. For a breath, time seemed to still and wait, as if even Fate was waiting to see what would happen. She didn't know she needed to be saved."

Her hand had drifted again, her thumb making small strokes against his cheek now. She was still looking at him, but she was seeing through him, lost in her memories and thoughts. Her features had softened, and he could swear there was longing in her last words.

"What happened next?" he asked quietly.

She snapped back into herself, all that softness gone. "Instead of saving her, he broke her."

She straightened, and another vicious yank on his power had him grimacing. How was she doing that? Even if the Source Mark worked both ways, she didn't have the actual Source Mark.

But she was a direct descendant of Arius.

The realization flooded through him as if ice water had been dumped over him. All this time his power had been drawn to her, seeking her out, curious about her. She was as much darkness as she was light, even though she hated it. His darkness tried to call to her the same way she called to it. His magic wanted her to love it as much as she loved the light.

*He* wanted her to love the dark as much as she loved the light.

"She was told he would lie to her, hurt her, break her, but she didn't believe them. He had told her she knew what he knew. He'd sworn to her it was all to keep her safe, but she was still hunted, still hurt, still wanted only for what she could give. She realized they were right."

"*Who* were right, Tessa?"

"She accepted the truth that she'd been trying to deny for so long, no matter how many times the dreams came to her. So she accepted her destiny and embraced who she was always meant to be." She lifted a hand, a swirl of golden mist forming at her fingertips. When it faded, she held a scion and a dagger.

"Tessa, what are you doing?"

"We were always meant to destroy one another," she replied, placing the dagger on the side table. "But you already know that, don't you?" He didn't answer, and she smiled knowingly as she began to draw on the back of her right hand with the scion.

"What are you doing, little storm?" he asked again, trying to keep his voice calm and even. He could do nothing. She was stronger than him. That had been proven with the second and third Marks.

"Taking everything from you, just like you took everything from me," she answered as she continued to work. After a moment, she dropped the scion to her feet, holding her hand out to examine it before turning the back of her hand to show him.

The final Source Mark.

"Where did you learn to do that?"

She smiled. "It was in a book. I've been practicing."

"Marks have to be drawn precisely. If you don't—"

"I just said I've been practicing," she interrupted, swiping up the dagger. Her head tilted to the side. "Isn't this what you wanted? To keep me? Stay bound to me? Forever inseparable?"

"Yes, but—"

"So I made that happen. That was our Bargain after all."

"Our Bargain was that you would convince everyone you had embraced the bond," he said, panic building as she twirled the dagger.

"And I did," she answered. "I *asked* to stay with you. Told them there was a bond. I agreed to the Second Mark, and I continued my classes. I even convinced *you* I was accepting the bond."

He shook his head in denial, and her malicious smile only grew.

"Why do you think your timeline was pushed back? I *requested* to be given the third Mark, Theon."

"Bullshit," he spat, and she laughed.

Tipped her head back and *laughed* at him.

"Do you think you are the only one with plans? Do you think you were the only one researching these last months?" A mocking pout formed on her lips as she reached out and lightly slapped his cheek a few times. "Oh, Theon, you will learn soon enough that being the most cunning and wicked is the only way to survive in a realm of villains."

Then the dagger was slicing across his palm before she was dragging it across the back of her hand.

"I won't do it, Tessa," he said, trying to come up with any idea to stop this. "I won't overpower you. I *can't*."

"Weren't you listening, Theon? The Source Mark works both ways," she said, tossing the dagger aside. It skittered across the floor. "Which means I only need to overpower *you*."

Forcing his palm to the back of her hand, he clamped down on the cry of agony that formed in his throat as her power flooded into him. Bright and glaring and fierce, it eclipsed his darkness. His magic shrank back, trying to wrap itself around him as if it could shield him from her, but she was a storm as her power poured into him, taking and never wavering. It claimed what it wanted, and while he tried to fight back because this could certainly not end well for him, her power sank its teeth into his and didn't let up until he yielded.

"Tessa, stop!" he cried as his power started to wane, submission so close.

"Just give in, Theon," she crooned mockingly, parroting words he'd spoken to her when he'd given her the very first Mark.

"Little storm," he pleaded. "I was trying to save you. I've always been trying to save you."

With another vicious smile, she said, "You failed. I suppose you're used to such a thing by now, though."

He couldn't swallow down the bellow of pain as her power lashed out at him again, tearing into his magic with claws and fangs. The familiar cords of obsidian black and purest gold floated up, twining around each other until he couldn't tell where one ended and the other began, before it settled back into them, sinking into his soul.

Theon sat back in his chair, chest heaving and gulping down air. It took him a moment to realize there was a searing pain on his left hand. He looked down to find Tessa with the scion once more, this time drawing a Mark on his left hand. He tried to yank it back, but he was drained, and she clearly wasn't as her power held him in place.

"Tessa…" he rasped, his stomach churning.

"The nausea will come and go for the next several hours," she said conversationally. "I suggest being near a bathroom soon. It is rather exhausting."

She tossed the scion aside this time, the stick rolling under the bed across the room. He felt her power release him, and he lifted his hand to find three interconnecting triangles marked there. Not inverted like hers were.

The Achaz symbol.

Marked on the Arius Heir.

"I thought it only fitting that if I had to bear your Mark, you should bear mine," she said, slowly backing away from him. "I know you'll never be mine, not fully, but at least your power will be."

"Do you have any idea what you've done?" Theon demanded, too exhausted to even lift from the chair. Tessa had always slumped to the floor after a Mark. Now he understood why.

"I know exactly what I've done," she replied. "I've fulfilled my end of the bargain."

"In case you've forgotten, that only happens when I am ruling Arius Kingdom," Theon rasped, leaning forward and bracing his forearms on his knees as another wave of nausea hit him.

"Consider it done, *my Lord*," she said, and he raised his head to find she'd lifted her shirt, exposing her torso.

Her bare torso.

The Bargain Mark gone from her skin.

He glanced down at his own abdomen, finding the sun and stars along the side of his torso still there. She'd fulfilled her end of the Bargain, freeing herself from it, but he still had to fulfill his side.

"He's not dead," she said simply. "Not yet anyway. I still need him for a bit, so your other...contracts still stand. As for me..." She stepped forward, a single finger pressing under his chin and tilting his head up. "I claim my side of the bargain to decide if and when and how I see you. I will decide if you ever get access to my power, but your power? It's now mine, isn't it? And let's not forget that Guardian mark that's incorporated, requiring you to now protect me. I will fulfill my purpose of correcting the balance in this realm."

"Tessa, if you leave here, if you do this, you are doing exactly what the Augury feared. There will be a war," he said, feeling cold sweat trickle down his neck.

"Once again, I am doing exactly what you wanted," she said. "A constant battle between us, but I warned you, eventually someone has to lose. At the end, the question will finally be answered."

"What question?"

"Who will be left standing when Chaos comes to reign?" she replied, backing away from him again.

"Tessa, wait," he gasped, trying to stand but instantly slumping to his knees, too weakened by the Source Mark. "We can figure this out. I can't do this without you. I need—"

Her head tilted. "What do you need, Theon? My power? You can't have it. The bond? It's still there. My cunt? You just had it. My loyalty? You never had it. My help? You never let me actually do so. My trust? You were close, but you lost it."

His head was pounding, and he couldn't think around the pain and the nausea as the dregs of his power reached for her. "Your love," he blurted, unable to stop himself. "Will it matter if I say I love you, little storm?"

She went still for a long moment before she closed the distance between them once more. Reaching out, her hand slid along his jaw and under his chin, tilting his face up to hers. "Oh, Theon," she simpered mockingly. "You don't know how to love. You only know how to own and possess and control. You only know how to break someone, not love them." She bent then, leaning in to speak into his ear. "Remember this moment, *Master*. When you come to destroy me, when the final battle ensues, remember this moment. Remember how you tried to once again persuade me with pretty words."

Then she was backing away, turning and striding through the balcony doors. He never saw a portal. Only a flash of light.

It hadn't been a lie. He hadn't said the words in some last ditch effort to keep her at his side. He'd meant them with every ounce of his being.

And once again, she hadn't cared.

She'd left him on his knees in the dark.

# 48
## LUKA

This was fucking great.

That was all Luka could think as he stared at Theon curled over the toilet in his suite at Arius House.

He'd felt the two of them down the bond, but more than that, he'd felt Theon struggling. It had been a bitch fighting against the Guardian bond and the need to go defend him, but Theon had said to wait. Luka didn't know what state Tessa was in, and she was so impulsive and reckless. His sudden presence could have very well made everything worse, so he'd stayed away. But that wasn't the only reason.

The other reason had been the phone call he'd received that had him sitting at Lilura Inquest for the last hour.

It wasn't until he felt his friend's utter heartbreak and ruin that he'd Traveled to Arius House and found him.

"How long have you been on the bathroom floor?" Luka asked, taking a seat on the vanity stool just as he'd done when he'd watched Tessa in this same position.

"Since she left," Theon rasped, heaving himself up so he was leaning against the wall. "Had to fucking crawl to get in here."

"Did she stay to watch that? I imagine it is something she would have enjoyed."

Theon said nothing. Only lifted his middle finger, tipping his head back against the wall.

Luka leaned forward, resting his elbows on his knees as he clasped his hands in front of him. "What happened?"

Theon didn't speak for a long time, and Luka knew him well enough to know he was collecting his thoughts. Funny he never figured out Tessa needed the same courtesy.

"You were right all along," Theon finally said.

"Right about what?"

"She wasn't the one for this, and because I tried to force her to be, I've brought about the very thing we were trying to prevent."

"What are you talking about?" Luka asked, sitting up straighter.

Emerald eyes met his, fractured and broken. "We thought if we overthrew my father, things would be better. We didn't want Devram like he did. We just wanted our kingdom and the Underground. That's all we ever wanted, but it's always been about so much more."

"Theon…"

"My father isn't the only one who wants the realm. The Augury has been right all along."

"The Augury is a bunch of eccentric zealots," Luka said.

Theon shook his head, but then winced, his eyes darting to the toilet as if he was debating whether or not he was going to vomit again. "They're extremists, yes, but their beliefs about the Revelation Decree and what it truly means are not. I've always said it's a prophecy or omen of some kind." He lifted his gaze to Luka's again. "It's always been about her. It's always been part of something bigger, and she's a major player without realizing it."

"How can you possibly figure that?" Luka demanded as Theon struggled to articulate his thoughts.

"Because she is the granddaughter of Arius, yes, but she is also a direct descendant of Achaz. She's both. Light and dark. Beginnings and endings."

"But the Witch heritage," Luka argued.

"I translated some old texts. If it is correct, Achaz had a child with one of Zinta's daughters."

"And you think Tessa is this daughter?" Luka shook his head. "I'm dying to hear how you made that leap."

"I don't know if she's that daughter, but Tessa has to be a descendant. Arius and Serafina. Achaz and Zinta. All four," Theon said flatly, face pale and eyes rimmed in red. "She's not a Legacy. She's too powerful. Cienna said she may as well be a god. All power comes from Chaos; she has more than anyone in Devram. Tessa may as well be Chaos, and she now sides with Achaz."

"Did she say that?" Luka snapped, getting to his feet. To do what? He wasn't sure, so he started pacing in the small space.

Theon shook his head again. "No, but it all fits. The Decree was a prophecy given to ensure Devram didn't fall. The first ruling Lords and Ladies decided the Decree was meant to govern the realm. It became what it is today over time, but that was never the original intention of the Decree."

How many times had Luka listened to Theon go on and on about this theory? Too many times to count. So many times, Luka and Axel eventually started turning up the Chaosphere games they'd be watching to drown him out. Eventually, he'd stopped talking to them about it. He recognized this had played a minor role in Theon's need to have things figured out and sorted before filling everyone else in, but fuck. This was still so ludicrous, and yet after talking with Tristyn, it wasn't as far-fetched as he'd once believed.

"None of this explains why you think it's connected to Tessa," Luka said.

"She's bringing war to Devram," Theon replied. "There are too many coincidences for her not to be connected to it all. I don't know how. I'm still working on it, but she'll play a role. And I..." His throat bobbed as he swallowed, wincing at the action. "I just lost her."

Luka slid his phone from his pocket. "Have you heard from Axel?"

Theon shook his head. "Not since he stormed out of my room at the townhouse."

Luka's brows furrowed. "He's not here? When did he leave the townhouse?"

"I assumed yesterday, needing some time to mourn his choices with Kat," Theon answered. "I left this morning. Brought Lange and Corbin to your rooms for now. I assumed you'd be spending most of your holiday at your cave."

That *had* been the plan, especially if Tessa wasn't going to be here anyway.

"Can you get up? Function? I need to tell you some things, and Axel should be here for it," Luka said.

The mere act of answering seemed to pain Theon, but he said, "Help me up. I'll rinse off and change. Give me an hour."

Reaching out a hand, Luka pulled Theon to his feet. The male had to lean against the wall just to move. He'd be lucky if it only took an hour to shower and change. At least when Tessa had been recovering from the Marks, Theon had stayed by her side, allowing the bond to comfort her. She'd truly left him with nothing.

Well, not nothing.

Luka had felt the lust down their bond. He'd felt more than that, so he didn't feel quite as terrible as he probably should have for Theon. At least he got to satisfy that part of the bond.

She'd also left him with a Mark on his hand. He'd bring that up later.

He left Theon to try to shower while he made his way through Arius House. Axel's rooms were on the opposite side in another wing. He didn't run into Cressida as he traversed the halls, pounding a fist on Axel's door when he finally stood outside his rooms.

"Axel? We have some shit to discuss. Open up," Luka called, pounding on the door again. When there was still no answer, he sighed. He was used to the St. Orcas brothers throwing tantrums, but this was more than that. "I'm coming in, Axel," he called out before placing his palm on the door and using his magical signature to enter. They all had access to each other's rooms, and Luka pushed through the door.

Axel's sitting area was empty. In fact, it looked like nothing had been touched. There was no music playing. No shoes at the door. No dishes. Nothing was out of place.

"Axel?"

Luka moved deeper into the space, crossing to the bedroom. The bed was perfectly made. One look in the bathroom found no towels on the towel rack or toiletries out.

Axel hadn't been here at all.

But if he'd left the townhouse and hadn't come here, where was he?

Pulling his phone from his pocket, he tried calling Axel as he made his way back across Arius House, but it went straight to his voicemail. His phone was either off or dead. Neither of those options eased the growing dread in Luka's gut.

Stopping at his own rooms, he knocked quickly to warn the Fae on the other side before he opened the door. He wanted to see when they'd last seen Axel since they'd been staying in his room at the townhouse. Corbin and Lange were at the table, some crackers and peanut butter between them.

"What are you two doing?" Luka asked, coming to an abrupt halt.

The Fae both shot to their feet, Lange edging in front of Corbin a little. "We weren't given any instruction on food, and it was all we could find," Lange said, speaking quickly.

Luka blinked. "That's all you've eaten since you got here this morning?"

Lange winced. "Since last night, actually."

Of course his rooms hadn't been fully stocked yet. He'd notified the staff he'd be returning tomorrow afternoon sometime.

"Come with me," Luka said, jerking his head to the door.

They followed, their footsteps tentative, but a few minutes later they were entering Theon's rooms. Theon wasn't out here yet, but his kitchen pantry was fully stocked.

"Help yourself to whatever you want," he said, gesturing to the kitchen.

Neither of the Fae moved.

By the gods, he knew the Fae were taught to be submissive, but the outright terror that came from these Fae was unexpected. The Fae he'd grown up around had all been assigned to the Arius Kingdom, used to their roles and comfortable with their space. The Fae fresh from the estates didn't have any of that yet. Luka couldn't exactly blame the nerves, but they'd seen Tessa and Kat around them.

"You're fine here," Luka sighed. "Either go help yourselves, or I'm going to attempt to make food. It likely won't be edible."

"You can't cook for us," Corbin said immediately.

"You're right. I can't cook," Luka said. "Which is why I'm strongly advising you to get your own food."

"Whose rooms are these?" Corbin asked, both of the males shifting.

"Theon's," he answered. "But it's fine. I swear nothing will happen. You've seen us with Kat."

"Yeah, but Kat was Axel's—" Lange started, but Corbin elbowed him in the ribs. "Fuck. Ow," Lange hissed.

"Kat was Axel's what?" Luka asked, taking a seat on the sofa.

"His... Just *his*," Lange said.

"Have you seen Axel lately?"

"No," Corbin answered. "Last time we saw him was two nights ago."

When he'd left Theon's room in anger.

They'd all been waiting for the consequences of Axel's decision to hide Kat away rather than deliver her to Julius and Mansel. The dread in his stomach grew as he realized Axel's absence was more than him needing time to mourn Katya. It wasn't unusual for Axel to disappear for days at a time, especially if he was in the Underground, but he usually gave them somewhat of an idea as to where he was going to be.

"Seriously, eat some food," Luka said, getting back to his feet to go check on Theon.

He found him in the giant dressing room, leaning against the island dresser. He was still pale as death with sweat beading his brow, but he'd managed to get loose pants on somehow.

"She did this three times," Theon said, dragging a hand through his still wet hair.

"She had someone taking care of her every time, and she could sleep for three days afterwards," Luka said. "It's different."

Theon didn't reply.

"I know you probably want to just fall into bed, but we have some things to talk about. Lange and Corbin are out there. You good if we talk in front of them?"

"Why would we do that?" Theon asked, looking like he was preparing himself for the simple act of standing on his own.

"One, because they've known Tessa longer than we have. Two, because they were the last people to see Axel," Luka answered.

The mention of his brother like that had Theon on high alert. "What does that mean?"

"Let's talk about it where you can sit down," Luka said. "Do you need help or—"

"I can fucking walk," Theon muttered, but Luka stayed close anyway as he shuffled out to the living space and practically collapsed onto the sofa.

Corbin and Lange were in the kitchen, all the fixings out for a sandwich, but they momentarily paused at Theon's appearance.

"It goes without saying you don't repeat a word of what you hear or see here," Luka said with a growl.

"Of course," Corbin said quickly, going back to the sandwich he was making.

"Did Axel say anything to you when you saw him last?" Luka asked.

Lange shrugged. "Not really. He asked about which estates we were at before we were moved to Celeste, and then he asked if I'd be able to help him translate some things."

"You are from the Falein Estate?" Theon asked, trying to prop himself up on some pillows.

"I am," Lange said with a nod.

"Nothing else?" Luka asked.

"Not that I can recall," Lange answered.

Luka turned back to Theon. "We can't reach him. I think Valter has him. Punishment for Kat."

"Fuck," Theon cursed, trying to sit up again and failing.

"Is Valter at Arius House yet?" Luka asked.

"No," Theon answered. "And he's not going to be."

"What the fuck does that mean?"

Theon let out a pained grunt as he forced himself into a sitting position. "Tessa has him."

"*What?*" Luka nearly yelled.

Gesturing to his torso, he said, "Tessa has him. Said she fulfilled her side of the Bargain."

"How does that fulfill the Bargain?"

"The Bargain was she would aid me in overtaking my father and once I ruled Arius Kingdom—"

"But you don't rule Arius Kingdom. If he still lives, he is the Arius Lord," Luka argued.

"But if she indeed has him, I am now ruling in his stead," Theon answered. "It was clearly enough for her end of the Bargain to be fulfilled."

"She found a loophole," Luka said in disbelief.

"She's clever. More so than I ever gave her credit for," Theon said. "I don't know where we go from here."

Luka swiped a hand down his face because what he had to tell him was only going to make things worse.

"I spoke to Blackheart today," he said.

Theon tipped his head back against the sofa. "And?"

"He was trying to get a hold of you," he continued. "When you weren't answering your phone, he called me."

"I was with Tessa."

"I'm aware, but Theon…" Luka rubbed at the back of his neck. "Tessa is…"

"I know," Theon said when Luka didn't continue. "I already said we've lost her."

"When we felt her panicking, she was being taken to an ambush. There were dozens of Augury members there, and she summoned things Tristyn called the Hunters."

"The Hunters?"

"According to Tristyn, they are beings created by Achaz to hunt down the Arius bloodline."

"How did they get here?"

"Tessa can summon them."

"Because of her Achaz bloodline," Theon said in understanding.

Luka nodded. "I didn't want anything you said earlier to be true, but yeah. I think that's why. They have golden blades."

"Like the ones found in the gardens," Theon said immediately. "She summoned them the day Pavil and Metias attacked her."

"It gets worse. In answer to the Hunters, Temural and Anala came together and created Huntresses." Luka paused before adding, "Beings who can move through smoke and ash and create weapons from nothing."

"Auryon."

"Apparently Temural sent her to aid Tessa."

There was utter silence in the room. Even Corbin and Lange had set down their food.

"Well?" Luka asked.

"Well, what?" Theon returned.

"What do you have to say about it?"

"Nothing."

Luka sank into a chair. "You? You have nothing to say about this?"

"My brother is missing. I was just tricked into becoming a Source. I am suddenly in charge of an entire kingdom, and I can't stand for more than a few seconds without falling to my knees. She walked away from me, and now I learn she can summon an army of beings whose sole purpose is to hunt down and kill my bloodline. No, Luka, I have nothing to say," Theon retorted, slightly out of breath after he finished his rant.

"Theon, we have to react to this threat. It's the Arius Kingdom. There are hundreds of thousands with Arius blood. From what Blackheart said, they don't discriminate. A drop of Arius blood will be enough to be their death," Luka said.

"What does that mean for Tessa, then?" Lange asked, picking his sandwich back up. "Isn't she half Arius blood?"

"I don't know," Theon answered. "I don't know what to do with any of this. Once again, everything I thought we knew was just overturned."

"It sounds like this is part of a bigger war," Lange offered.

"What?" Theon said, turning to look at the Fae.

"If Achaz created the Hunters to hunt down Arius blood, it doesn't sound like they were created specifically for Devram," Lange continued.

"It's part of the Everlasting War," Theon said, trying to sit up again, and Luka recognized the excited undertone despite his exhaustion.

"The biggest question is why was Tessa sent to Devram in the first place?" Corbin cut in. He still hadn't resumed eating, but Luka found he was the more cautious of the two.

"And what has Lord Jove told her?" Theon said. "She kept saying this was her destiny, that we were always meant to destroy one another. If this is all true, then she's right. She believes only one of us will survive. The Augury has been right this entire time. It was why they've been trying to kill her."

"Why didn't you just tell her what you learned?" Luka asked.

"I was trying to protect her," Theon said. "You know that. It's what I've always done. And now I've lost her and Axel."

"You were trying to protect her because you needed her power," Luka said. Theon opened his mouth to argue, but Luka stopped him. "Don't deny it, Theon. Your entire plan to overthrow your father hinged on your Source."

That muscle feathered in Theon's jaw before he said, "Initially, yes, but it became more, and then I was more terrified of losing her. I thought if she didn't know, they wouldn't try to get the information from her. We were all trying to understand. I was trying to get a plan in place to keep her safe from all of this…" He trailed off for a moment before he sighed. "In the end, we've all just been pawns."

"The Lords and Ladies all have secrets," Corbin said, drawing their attention back to the Fae. "They are constantly betraying one another."

"I know that," Theon said.

"Do you?" Corbin asked. "Because Arius Kingdom is very cut off from the rest of the realm."

"We were forced to be," Theon said. "It is why my father wanted to overtake the realm. I just wanted to forge new relations with the other kingdoms for the betterment of our people. He was set on vengeance. It was them against us."

"That is not entirely true," Corbin replied. "I think you will find allies in unexpected places if you choose to fight back."

"Fight back," Theon repeated.

"Against Tessa and the Achaz Kingdom."

"The Achaz Kingdom?" Luka asked.

"You think the Lord hasn't orchestrated all of this?" Corbin asked.

"How do you know all this?" Theon demanded. "You are just— You are a Fae."

"From the Anala Kingdom," Corbin replied. "A kingdom with secrets of its own. A kingdom that refuses to let others have fire Fae. Haven't you ever wondered why that is?"

"It was part of the early accords," Theon answered.

"Yes, but *why*?" Corbin said.

"To be honest, I just always assumed it was a power move," Theon said.

"It absolutely is, but there is always motive driving those power moves. Lady Aithne keeps them close because she is waiting for the Achaz Kingdom to make their move."

"Again, how do you know all this?" Luka cut in.

"I was close with Gatlan, the Anala Heir's Source," Corbin said. "More than that, the Anala Estate is not as rigid as the others, and the kingdom itself allows the Fae more freedoms. We are not treated as... We have more freedoms there."

"Why are you telling us any of this?" Theon asked.

"Because we are friends of Tessa's," Lange said. "And she doesn't deserve to be used in the way any of you want to use her."

"No, she doesn't," Theon said quietly.

And Luka felt something he didn't know what to do with down the bond. He usually felt this sense of resignation and acceptance from Tessa. Never from Theon. He'd never known the male to accept something he didn't want. He fought back, never settling, and took what he wanted, even if it meant leaving blood and death in his wake. Always for Arius Kingdom. Always for the people he was trying to protect.

Theon's eyes bounced between Lange and Corbin. "If I asked for your help, would you give it?"

"We are bound to the Arius Kingdom," Lange said, a hint of sarcasm creeping into his voice. "We don't have a choice."

"Valid point," Theon said. "But will you be difficult about it?"

"If it's for Tessa, no," Lange answered. Then he winced, glaring at Corbin. "Stop doing that."

"Stop letting your mouth run in front of the Arius Heir," Corbin snapped.

"You are the one telling Anala secrets," Lange groused.

"This is what we're going to do," Theon said, and Luka settled back in his chair because this is where Theon excelled. He was all about the action and the next move to bring him closer to his end goals. It's why he struggled so much with Tessa, because she hindered those moves around every corner, and his plans weren't progressing as quickly as he wanted. Luka had tried and tried to tell him it would end that way, but he was set, and there was never changing his course once that happened.

Which is why the feelings of resignation and acceptance from earlier were so foreign coming from him.

"I need to sleep for the next day," Theon said. "Then we're going to figure out where Axel is."

"How do you plan on doing that?" Luka asked, a brow arching.

"I'm going to contact Blackheart. Since I am the acting ruler of the Arius Kingdom right now, I can rescind the order of having Kat delivered to Julius and Mansel. We will get Katya back, and then we will figure out where Axel is."

"If Tessa has your father, wouldn't it be easier to ask him?" Luka asked.

"Yes, which is why you're going to Tessa," Theon answered.

Luka sat up straighter, shock rippling through him. "Say that again?"

"You're going to Tessa, Luka," he repeated. "She wants nothing to do with me. More than that, our Bargain states she gets to decide when she sees me now."

"It sounds like she wants revenge," Lange said around a bite of sandwich. Then he jumped back, avoiding another jab. "Seriously, Corbin. Knock it the fuck off."

"You've always known how to speak to her, Luka, and she talks to you," Theon said, his voice lowering again. "So you will go to her."

"You think she's going to trust me, Theon? You cannot be serious," Luka argued.

"If anyone can bring her back, it will be you, Luka, not me. Tell me nothing. I want to know nothing she tells you. She needs to know—" He paused, his gaze darting to the side as his throat bobbed.

"You're giving up on her?" Luka demanded. "You're walking away? You're letting her go? Why put her through all that if you're content to suddenly step aside?"

"I'll never let her go. What I said still stands. I will forever fight for her," Theon retorted, a faint trace of darkness forming before drifting away to nothing. "But she needs to know someone chose her for her. That it's not about her power but *her*, and she will always assume that is my underlying motive. I've never given her a reason to believe otherwise."

"So you are sending me away?" Luka clarified.

"I am. It's not an option. It's an order from your acting Lord," Theon said, sounding and looking utterly pathetic as he slumped lower on the sofa. "You will get Tessa; I will get Axel."

"And what about the Guardian bond?" Luka said. "What the fuck am I supposed to do with that?"

"We've been apart before."

"For short periods of time, you idiot," he growled. "You truly think I'll be able to sit and listen to her plan to kill you when I am sworn to defend you at the expense of my own life? We need a better plan than this."

"I've been told the plans are pointless, and we're already fucked," Theon replied.

Luka muttered another curse under his breath. "And after you find Axel?"

Theon tipped his head back against the sofa, his eyes falling closed. "It sounds like we're preparing for war."

# 49
## TESSA

Her bare feet padded softly on the cool, white marble steps as she descended them, her fingers dragging along the wall made of the same. There were sconces every few feet. Orbs of golden light filled them. The same golden light that crackled at her fingertips as she reached the bottom of the stairs.

Her breath hitched. Even with the ceiling so high above her and the space vast and open, she was still underground. Even with her light around her wrists where bands had once caged, she could still feel the remnants of them. She took a moment, willing her racing heart to calm. It wasn't that she couldn't be down here. She could go anywhere in the Faven palace she chose. There were no rules. No orders. No demands made of her. Not here. It was the one place people had never lied to her. It was the one place her questions were always answered when asked.

Yet still…

She sighed.

Dex was going to be upset that she had wandered off. He'd said something about going into the city later. Oralia had been assigned as her personal aide, which was…great. Something about making sure she was comfortable with familiar faces and friends, but there was nothing comforting about her high-pitched voice waking her up in the mornings to start her day.

A cold nose nudged her hand, and she peered down at the wolf beside her. She didn't know if she'd ever get used to how massive he was. As large as *his* hounds were. She'd always called them wolves. Her fingers glided through silky fur such a light shade of grey it appeared silver in the lighting. The wolf nudged her hand again, a low whine coming from him.

Taking another deep breath, she moved forward, following a wide hall. Thick panes of glass lined the passageway, allowing her to see into the rooms on either side. A few were occupied; most were vacant. Cells to hold any manner of being.

She sang softly to herself as she moved. Lines from a decree that wasn't a decree at all.

"In all things there must be balance. Beginnings and Endings. Light and Dark. Fire and Shadows. The sky, the sea, the realms. But when the scales tip, and Chaos rains, who will fight? And who will fall?"

Her long gown swished as she moved, the silky fabric cool against her skin. The white dress dipped low between her breasts, reaching nearly to her navel and revealing just as much skin down her back. The material tied at her shoulders, and a deep slit up the side let her move freely. Threads of black and gold and pale blue were woven into the garment.

The colors both grounded her and drove her mad.

"Life must give, and Death must take. But Fate requires more." She came to a stop before one of the glass cells. "Destiny beckons, and sacrifice demands." The glass sparked, imbued with the same magic in her veins to contain the male within.

Valter stared back at her, sitting against the wall. He'd been stripped of his suit, looking utterly ridiculous in loose linen pants and a short-sleeved tee shirt. His black hair was a mess, and she could see the scruff on his face from where she stood.

She smiled as she sang, "Who will be left standing when Chaos comes to reign?"

"Where is Eviana?" Valter demanded, as if he had the authority to demand anything of her anymore.

"Your bond is there," Tessa replied. "I know you can still speak with her the same way I could speak with Theon if I wanted to."

Valter pushed to his feet before coming right up to the glass, careful not to touch it. "You were reckless to leave his side."

Tessa released a harsh laugh. "Do not worry, Valter." She smiled wider when he stiffened at being addressed by his first name. "Your son and I are still tied together," she added, lifting her right hand to show him the final Source Mark in place on her skin. "I told you I would let you witness the downfall of your bloodline before I ended it."

Valter laughed, a cruel and dark thing. "You think you are better off here, under an Achaz roof, than you were with my son?"

"They do not try to chain me and use me here," she snapped.

"So foolish," Valter scoffed. "They've made you believe captivity is freedom."

"Yet I am not the one locked up."

"Only because you are aiding them at the moment. Invisible shackles are still chains."

"And if I had aided you and your son in your desires to overtake the realm, then you wouldn't have tried so hard to have me— How did you phrase it? Come to heel?" Tessa retorted. "You wouldn't have been so adamant about my bond with Theon being broken?"

"You were never meant to be bonded to Theon," Valter sneered. "Rordan and the ruling Ladies were never going to let that stand. Even if Theon had managed to complete his task, they would have found another reason to deny his request. I was at least going to give you some semblance of freedom *and* protection by Matching you with Luka."

"To breed me for my power," she scoffed.

"Everything is about power," Valter snapped in irritation. "The sooner you accept that, the sooner you will realize Rordan is attempting the same thing you accuse me of."

"Are you trying to tell me you do not wish to rule Devram?"

"Of course I do," he retorted. "My people deserve the freedom to move about the realm. The Arius Kingdom has been shunned for centuries. We have paid our penance, but it has never been enough."

"So you desire vengeance," she clarified.

"As do you," he countered.

She shrugged because he wasn't wrong. She knew all about giving everything you had, and it not being enough.

"And you are under the illusion that Rordan will help you have it, but this is much bigger than you and Theon and the politics of Devram. If you don't believe me, ask the one who brought you to the realm in the first place."

Tessa went preternaturally still. "What did you just say?"

Valter smiled wider. "You heard me, Tessalyn. You want answers? There is one at the end of this passage."

"You lie," she hissed, her fingers curling into Roan's fur.

"I do not. Rordan, however? He might not lie to you, but that does not mean he hasn't kept secrets, Tessalyn."

Tessa pressed her hand to the glass. Energy crackled at the touch, but she absorbed it. "You're wrong," she said simply. "I know how Arius tipped the balance. I know what must be done to correct it. I know my destiny."

"Your only destiny is sacrifice," Valter sneered.

Tessa stepped back, her hand dropping to her side. "I am aware."

"Go see who else is kept in these cells," he said, turning his back on her and retreating to the back of the space. He slid back down to a seated position. "He's had him for over two decades, and still never gotten what he wanted."

She knew the Arius Lord spoke in lies and deception. Everyone did in Devram. She'd learned to do the same. But she'd also learned that those lies were often lined with twisted truths.

Tessa ignored Valter's smug curl of his lips as she turned and took steps farther down the passage. Anxiety prickled, and she ignored the feeling she was doing something she shouldn't. If there were indeed secrets here, they were ones Rordan didn't mind if she discovered. Otherwise he wouldn't have let her have full access to the palace, right?

But as she moved deeper down the passage, this all began to feel familiar, and she suddenly knew exactly what she was going to find when she reached the end. Taking a deep breath, she turned and faced the cell to her left.

A male sat on the floor. His brown hair was long, reaching well past his shoulders. It was a tangled mess of knots and needed to be washed and trimmed. Based on the state of his hair, she would have expected his facial hair to be more unkempt. He had a beard that was trimmed close, as if it had been more recently tended to. A large onyx ring that matched *his* sat on his finger, but she was more interested in the manacle at his throat. A thick band of pure white stone, it contained flecks of gold.

Flecks of light and energy.

A chain attached to the manacle was anchored to the wall, allowing for such little movement, she was unsure how the male could even eat or take care of his needs. He wore loose linen pants, the same that had been provided to Valter, but this male's torso was bare, allowing her the perfect view of the Marks that ran the length of his left arm.

Roan whined beside her, lowering to his belly as Tessa stepped forward, resting a hand on the glass. The male lifted his head, bright sapphire eyes connecting with hers, and she sucked in a sharp breath.

Dragging a fingertip along the glass in a slow arc, she asked, "Who are you?"

The male didn't answer. He just held her with his piercing gaze, unmoving.

Roan whined again, and the male's eyes dropped to the wolf.

Tessa's brows rose. "You know him," she said, dropping to a crouch and scratching behind Roan's ears. "Do you know who I am then?"

He spoke then, his voice hoarse and gruff, and Tessa wondered when the last time was that he'd uttered a single word.

"Do *you* know who you are?" he asked.

She sent him a knowing smile. "A daughter of wild and fury." He held her gaze, and she forced herself not to shift under his scrutiny. After a long moment, she couldn't stand the silence anymore. "You look like someone I know."

She saw the flicker of interest that was quickly gone.

"You are not supposed to be here," he finally said.

"I can go wherever I please."

"I mean here. In this palace."

"Are you supposed to be here?" she countered, lifting her chin.

To her surprise, he huffed a gruff laugh. "You are stubborn and combative like her."

"Like who?"

He shifted again, stretching his legs out in front of him and crossing his ankles. "You said you knew who you were."

She settled onto the floor with a scowl, Roan shifting closer and placing his head on her lap. "You are aggravating like him." His lips twitched in a familiar way that made her want to punch something. "Why are you locked in here?"

"Why do you keep the Arius Lord in here?"

Tessa leaned back on her hands. "There are various reasons."

"I am certain some of those reasons are the same reason I have been here for decades."

"Are you always this evasive?"

"When I do not trust someone and suspect this is yet another attempt to gain information from me, yes."

She smiled. "I don't even know who you are. I don't think I was supposed to find you."

"Achaz does nothing without intention."

"You mean Rordan?"

"I did not misspeak," the male answered.

"You speak as if you know him personally," Tessa scoffed.

The male said nothing.

Tessa sat forward. "Where are you from?"

"Where are *you* from?"

"Answering my questions with a question is annoying," she grumbled.

After several minutes of silence, she sighed and got to her feet. This was pointless.

But as she took her first step away from him, he spoke again. "You are not supposed to be here."

"You already said that," she said, glancing back over her shoulder.

He shook his head, the chain connecting his collar to the wall clanking. "No, Tessalyn. You are not supposed to be *here*. She thought she could hide you here, but he always knows."

Tessa turned back to face him again, her palms pressing to the glass. "Enough with the cryptic innuendos," she snapped, light flaring and energy crackling, bleeding into the magic of the glass. "Who are you?"

"That's her fury too," he said, and Tessa could swear there was a fondness in his voice.

"That does not answer the question," she retorted. "You know my name. It is only right that I should know yours."

"I cannot tell you," he said with a mocking look she knew all too well.

"Cannot or will not?"

He shrugged. "The latter, I suppose."

She huffed in annoyance.

"But know this, daughter of wild and fury," he said, holding her gaze. "They will use you if you let them."

"You think I do not know that?"

"You believe your destiny is set, but you do not realize you stand at a crossroads," he went on. "Salvation or destruction, the choice is yours."

"How do you know that saying?" she asked, her voice softer than she intended.

"The path you are on is destruction," was his answer.

"And the path to salvation?" she countered harshly.

He shifted again, settling back and seeming to get comfortable once more. "The path to salvation has always been death."

# IN THE MOST DESPERATE HOUR

Tristyn Blackheart moved quickly through the tunnels of the Underground. He hadn't dared enter this place in years, but his Bargain made with Theon allowed him a free pass, no questions asked.

A few more turns had him stepping into an expansive cavern. There were four other passageways leading off the room. Shelves lined one wall, and there was a hearth dug into the stone wall. Several tables littered the space, a tall female with mahogany hair bent over one.

"What have you done?" she demanded harshly, not even bothering to look at him.

"I am not in the mood for your attitude of superiority, dear sister," Tristyn replied, snatching up a vial and holding it up to the light.

"I am not in the mood to listen to you moan and whine, yet I know I am about to endure just that," she retorted.

"Charming as always," he replied, setting the vial down. "Is Katya well?"

"She is."

"Where is she?"

"Reading."

"Are we really doing this, Cienna?" Tristyn sighed.

Finally, his sister lifted her gaze, violet eyes meeting his. "Yes," she snapped. "We are doing this. You have jeopardized everything. She has sided with Achaz, and if he takes this realm, the balance will never recover."

"What would you have me do?" Tristyn demanded. "We can only guide and push and hint so much before we are crossing a line, and if I cross it, I am not the only one who will pay the price."

"Maybe she has already paid it," Cienna said, moving to another table and aggressively pulling apart dried herbs.

"She hasn't," he retorted, stepping to her side and grabbing a handful of dried plants. "Tessa saw her."

Cienna paused, looking up at him. "She saw Lilura?"

Tristyn nodded. "She said 'Lilura lives.' She doesn't know what it means, but when she learned it meant something to me… It was just another betrayal to her. I spent these last months building trust, as much as I could, and now…"

"You're fucked," Cienna finished for him.

"Always so eloquent," he deadpanned.

"Truth is rarely pleasant."

Didn't he know it.

"But now you are here to see if I have seen anything that will help us," Cienna continued, gathering the chopped herbs and placing them into a pouch.

"I cannot fail, Cienna," he answered. "I refuse. I have sacrificed much and will sacrifice more."

"I am aware," Cienna muttered. "It is why we are here in the first place. Lucky for you, help is coming."

There was a swirl of smoke and ashes, Auryon stepping from them a breath later. Her bow was looped over her back, and she held an apple in hand.

"Is it done?" Cienna asked.

"It is," the Huntress replied. "Gia is collecting them."

"Collecting who? What was done?" Tristyn asked in confusion.

"The High Queen of the World Walkers is apparently incredibly adept at finding loopholes when it comes to oaths and fate," Cienna said.

"Scarlett?" Tristyn asked in surprise. "She is back?"

"Not Scarlett," Cienna replied. "But she left Auryon with a way to summon help should we become desperate. Losing her to the Achaz Kingdom seemed like a desperate hour."

He didn't miss the accusation in his sister's tone.

"She left me a vial to crush, and when I did, shadows and white embers swirled," Auryon said, taking a bite of her apple.

"Then what?" Tristyn asked.

She shrugged. "Now we wait."

"For what?"

"To see who answers," Cienna said.

"You don't even know who to expect? You just sent a random call into the stars? What if someone else answers it?" Tristyn demanded, knowing just how easily a message between realms could be intercepted.

"Do you think I would have Gia go collect them if I had the smallest doubt of who would answer?" Cienna asked coldly.

That was a good point, but still.

"Make yourself useful while we wait," Cienna ordered, shoving more dried plants at him.

He sighed, getting to work. It had been a long time since he'd worked beside his sister like this. They'd been in Devram for far too long, waiting for the one who could free them.

And now they'd lost her.

It was nearly an hour later when he heard the footfalls. He finished stirring the elixir Cienna had told him to mix up. He was surprised she trusted him with such a thing. Elixirs and potions were her strong area. He was stronger with spellwork and glamours.

A few moments later, Gia stepped from one of the branching passageways, and two others emerged behind her. The male was taller with brown hair and an expression that said he was already bored. There were no visible weapons on his person, but Tristyn instinctively knew he didn't need them. The female had red-gold hair that was braided down her back, grey eyes taking in the space. She wore pants and a tunic, some type of leather armor atop her clothing. There were several Marks visible on her, including one atop her heart. The female did have a sword strapped down her back, but he somehow knew she didn't really need it either.

"Any trouble?" Cienna asked.

"No," Gia said. "The sleeping drafts were effective."

"And you made sure nothing was disturbed?"

"Of course," Gia answered.

"Scarlett sent you?" Tristyn asked, taking in the newcomers. She was Fae, but the male? He was a Legacy, and when sapphire eyes met his, he knew exactly which god he descended from.

Clever of the silver-haired queen to send him.

"Who are you?" the female asked, and there was no cowering like the Fae did here. This one was fierce and demanding. Tristyn was fairly certain if anyone tried to give her an order, she might stab them.

"Tristyn Blackheart," he said, watching them carefully. "And you?"

"Razik Greybane," the male answered, a hand falling to the female's back possessively. "This is Eliza."

"You know Scarlett?" Tristyn repeated.

"Unfortunately," Razik muttered.

The female rolled her eyes. "Can you try to be a little pleasant?"

"Why?"

"By Anala," she muttered, turning back to Tristyn. "Yes, we know Scarlett. I serve in her Court. We were sent to aid you."

"But in true fashion, she told us nothing of her plans. Just told us to find you," Razik said, a growl lacing his words.

"What do you know of Devram?" Tristyn asked.

His sister was silent. Typical. She gave him shit about keeping information from Tessa, yet she was more close-lipped than he was.

"Not enough," Eliza said, her hands landing on her hips. A black Mark was on the back of her right hand, the Mark extending down some of her fingers. A quick glance at Razik found the same Mark on his hand.

"I do not know why she sent you. Neither of you will be welcome here," Tristyn said, leaning against the table.

"Well, we're what you got," Eliza snapped, that fire flickering in her eyes once more. "Things must be dire if you called for help from another realm."

"She has a cousin," Tristyn said.

Eliza's brows knitted. "Who does?"

"Scarlett."

"For fuck's sake. *Another* blood relation? Cethin and Scarlett aren't enough chaos?" Razik griped.

"Stop speaking," Eliza snapped.

"As you wish, milady," he replied with a smirk.

Tristyn thought she might punch the male, but her attention settled back on him as she asked, "Who and how?"

"A daughter of Temural. His only blooded child, actually."

"And her mother?"

"The daughter of Achaz."

"Impossible," Razik cut in. "That would make her beginnings and endings. The balance forbids it."

He was well read, this one.

"Then you understand the problem," Tristyn said.

Eliza looked up at Razik in confusion. "I don't understand."

"In all things, there must be balance," Razik replied, his voice tight. "And if the balance is not corrected, more than the Fates intervene."

"By the gods, speak plainly, Raz," she snapped in frustration.

"She shouldn't be here."

"In Devram?"

"She was never meant to *exist*," Razik clarified. "She will only bring destruction. If the balance is not corrected, it is not only this world that will fall, but all realms. If the balance is not corrected, Chaos will reign."

# BONUS CHAPTER

Need more Luka? Who doesn't?
Don't miss out on a special bonus chapter from the last dragon!

You can find it on my website at https://www.melissakroehrich.com
under Book Extras.

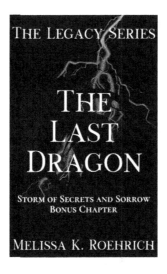

# A NOTE FROM MELISSA

Can you believe we're at the end of another book?

Where do we start with this Legacy crew? Let's just say they've had their own way of doing things from the beginning. They once again took my plans, said no, and gave us this masterpiece instead. We dove deep into why they are the way they are, and we're not done. We have two more books to go, and maybe some trauma is just starting...

Life is messy and complicated, and we all see our world through our own set of glasses based on what we've been told and what we've observed. Devram is no different, and learning that nothing is as it seems and how to navigate that is hard. Healing is hard work. Trusting again after betrayal is scary. Admitting you've been wrong is humbling. Our crew has some work to do.

Speaking of humbling, you guys humble me every single day. Every day I wake up and wonder how we got here. Please know I never take any of it for granted. On the hard days, your excitement and love pushes me through. You make the drafting process so fun, and our Cave Chats and Zoom Chats are some of my favorite things ever. Thank you is never enough, but know you make a difference just by reading a book.

Until next time, remember that you are worth fighting for-

XO- Melissa

# ACKNOWLEDGMENTS

I always have to start these with **you, the reader**. Without you reading the words that make it to the page, this is all for naught. Thank you for sticking with me. Thank you for trusting the process. Thank you for getting excited over snippets and drinking wine with me on Lives. From the depths of my being, thank you.

To my Book Slut Besties: **Brit Irvin, Sara Abel, and Tracey Goodson**, thank you for still being here. I literally could not do this without you. You pick me up on the hard days, and your loyalty knows no bounds. I will forever be grateful that book spoilers brought us together. To keep this from getting too sappy, I fucking love you.

To **Sarah Mori** and **The Realm Studios**, you saved me when I was drowning these past few months. For every single damn thing you do, thank you.

To my beta readers, **Ashley Nolan and Rachel Betancourt**, your reactions and love while you read makes me smile so hard. To my editor, **Megan Visger**, you make every book better, and I'd be lost without you. Don't ever leave me. To **Covers by Jules**, I'm still obsessed with everything you do. To my audiobook narrators, **Laura Horowitz and Christian Leatherman**, I will never not be amazed at how you bring this world and these characters to life. To my agent, **Katie Shea Boutillier** and the Donald Maass Literary Agency, I am so grateful for all your guidance and knowledge as I've navigated new things in my author world this last year.

To my **ARC/Street Team**, you guys never cease to amaze me, and I am so honored you choose to stay with me time after time. Thank you for cheering me on, for shouting from the rooftops, and for loving on these books so dang hard.

To **my boys**— You're a little older now. You're starting to see that dreams take hard work and passion, but the payoff is worth all the blood, sweat, and tears. Know your worth, my loves, and always fight for yourself.

To **my husband**— Thank you for continually falling into utter madness with me.

# ABOUT THE AUTHOR

Melissa K. Roehrich is a dark romantic fantasy author living her best life in the Middle-of-Nowhere, North Dakota. She resides on a hobby farm where she homeschools her three boys with her husband. They have four dogs, several barn cats, and chickens. When she's not writing or reading, she's probably watching reruns of *How I Met Your Mother* or *Gilmore Girls* while trying to convince her husband they need to add goats to the farm. She loves coffee and traveling and dreams of owning a dragon someday.

Scan the QR code links to social media and other ways to stay connected!

Printed in Great Britain
by Amazon

49326402R00371